CURSE OF THE MISTWRAITH

Janny Wurts

CURSE
OF THE
MISTWRAITH

VOLUME I

The Wars of Light and Shadow

RoC

A ROC BOOK

ROC
Published by the Penguin Group
Penguin Books USA Inc., 375 Hudson Street,
New York, New York 10014, U.S.A.
Penguin Books Ltd, 27 Wrights Lane,
London W8 5TZ, England
Penguin Books Australia Ltd, Ringwood,
Victoria, Australia
Penguin Books Canada Ltd, 10 Alcorn Avenue,
Toronto, Ontario, Canada M4V 3B2
Penguin Books (N.Z.) Ltd, 182-190 Wairau Road,
Auckland 10, New Zealand

Penguin Books Ltd, Registered Offices:
Harmondsworth, Middlesex, England

Published by Roc, an imprint of Dutton Signet, a division of Penguin Books USA Inc.
Previously published in Great Britain by HarperCollins Publishers.

First ROC Printing, February, 1994
10 9 8 7 6 5 4 3 2 1

 REGISTERED TRADEMARK—MARCA REGISTRADA

LIBRARY OF CONGRESS CATALOGING IN PUBLICATION DATA: 93-084966

Printed in the United States of America
Set in Trump Medieval

*For Gladden Schrock,
guiding light for dreams
and closet albatrosses—
here is one that flew.*

Acknowledgments

Curse of the Mistwraith kicks off a massive project whose inception has been smoothed by guidance and expertise and generous gifts of time. Thanks to the following friends, whose professions and hobbies and suggestions added touches of reality between the magic.

Jane Johnson, editor extraordinaire; David E. Bell, Mike Floerkey, Mickey Zucker Reichert, Suzanne Parnell, Raymond E. Feist, Rosemary Prince, and of course, Don Maitz, my husband, without whom the sheer weight and scope of the project probably would have flattened me.

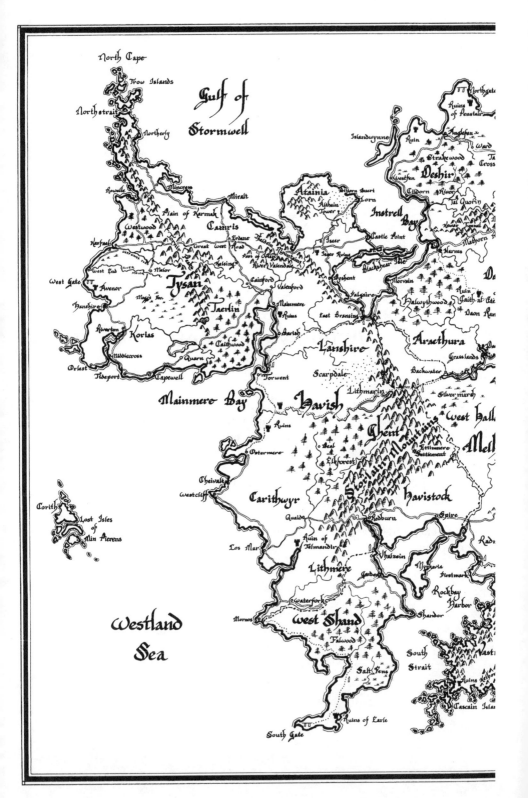

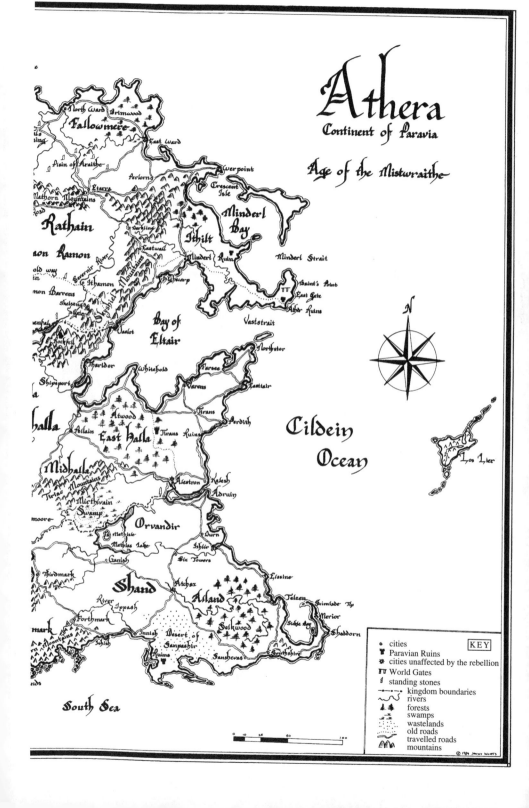

Contents

Prologue

The Wars of Light and Shadow were fought during the Third Age of Athera, the most troubled and strife-filled era recorded in all of history. At that time Arithon, called Master of Shadows, battled the Lord of Light through five centuries of bloody and bitter conflict. If the canons of the religion founded during that period are reliable, the Lord of Light was divinity incarnate, and the Master of Shadow a servant of evil, spinner of dark powers. Temple archives attest with grandiloquent force to be the sole arbiters of truth.

Yet contrary evidence supports a claim that the Master was unjustly aligned with evil. Fragments of manuscript survive which expose the entire religion of Light as fraud and award Arithon the attributes of saint and mystic instead.

Because the factual account lay hopelessly entangled between legend and theology, sages in the Seventh Age meditated upon the ancient past, and recalled through visions the events as they happened. Contrary to all expectation, the conflict did not begin on the council stair of Etarra, or even on the soil of Athera itself; instead the visions started upon the wide oceans of the splinter world, Dascen Elur.

This is the chronicle the sages recovered. Let each who reads determine the good and the evil for himself.

All for the waste of Karthan's lands
the Leopard sailed the main.
s'Ilessid King then cursed s'Ffalenn,
who robbed him, gold and grain.

—stanza from a ballad of Dascen Elur

I. Captive

The longboat cleaved waters stained blood red by sunset, far beyond sight of any shore. A league distant from her parent ship, at the limit of her designated patrol, she rose on the crest of a swell. The bosun in command shouted hoarsely from the stern. "Hold stroke!"

Beaten with exhaustion and the aftermath of battle, his crewmen responded. Four sets of oars lifted, dripping above waters fouled by oil and the steaming timbers of burned warships.

"Survivors to starboard." The bosun pointed toward two figures who clung to a snarl of drifting spars. "Quick, take a bearing."

A man shipped his looms to grab a hand compass. As the longboat dipped into the following trough, the remaining sailors bent to resume stroke. Oar shafts bit raggedly into the sea as they swung the heavy bow against the wind.

The bosun drew breath to reprimand their sloppy timing, then held his tongue. The men were tired as he was; though well seasoned to war through the feud which ran deadly and deep between Amroth and Karthan's pirates, this had been no ordinary skirmish. Seven fully rigged warships in a fleet of seventeen had fallen before a single brigantine under the hated leopard banner. The bosun swore. He resisted a morbid urge to brood over losses; lucky, they were, to have the victory at all. The defeated brigantine's captain had been none other than Arithon s'Ffalenn, called sorcerer and Master of Shadow.

The next swell rolled beneath the keel. Heaved and lifted on its crest, the longboat's peaked prow momentarily eclipsed the castaways who struggled in the water. Afraid to lose sight of them, the bosun set the compass man as observer in the bow. Then he called encouragement while his oarsmen picked an erratic course through the splintered clots of planking and cordage which wallowed, treacherous as reefs upon the sea. The crew labored in dead-faced silence. Not even the scraping bump of the corpse which passed beneath the keel caused them to alter their stroke. Horror had numbed every man left alive after the nightmare of fire, sorcery, and darkness that Arithon had unleashed before the end.

The boat drew abreast of the survivors. Overtaken by a drift of wind-borne smoke, the bosun squinted through burning eyes. Only one victim looked to be conscious. He clung with whitened fingers to the nearer end of the spar, while at his back, another sailor lay lashed against the heaving pull of the waves. The knots at this one's waist were half loosened, as if, seeing help on the way, his companion had clumsily tried to free him.

"Ship oars!" Gruffly the bosun addressed the man in the water. "Is your friend wounded?"

The wreck victim raised listless, glassy eyes, but said nothing. Quite likely cold water had dulled the fellow's wits. Weary of senseless ruin and the rescue of ravaged men, the bosun snapped impatiently, "Bring him in. We'll get the other second, if he still breathes."

A crewman hooked the spar with his oar shaft to steady the boat. Others leaned over the thwart to lift the half-drowned sailhand aboard.

The victim reacted with vengeful speed and doused his rescuers with seawater.

Stung nearly blind by the salt, the nearer oarsman yelled and lunged. His hand closed over a drenched mat of hair. The man in the water twisted against the restraint. He kicked clear of the spar, ducked, and resurfaced, a flash of bare steel in one fist. The oarsman recoiled from him with a scream of pain and surprise, his wrist opened stark to the bone.

"Ath, he's Karthan's," someone shouted.

The longboat's crew erupted in confusion. Portside, those seamen within reach raised oars like clubs and retaliated. One blow, then another struck the enemy sailor's head. Blood spilled from his nose and mouth. Chopped viciously on the shoulder, he floundered. His grasp loosened and the dagger dropped winking into the depths. Without even a curse of malediction, the Karthish sailor thrashed under, battered and finally drowned by the murderous hatred of enemies.

"Man the oars!" The bosun's bellow restored order to the wildly rocking longboat. Men sank down at their benches, muttering epithets, while seawater lapped tendrils of scarlet from the blades of the portside looms. Too tired even to curse, the officer tossed a scarf to his wounded oarsman. Then he pointed at the unconscious survivor who drifted still lashed to the spar. By now the smoke had cleared enough to see the Karthish dog still breathed. "Fetch that one aboard. The king will want him for questioning, so mind you handle him wisely."

Sailors sworn to the pirate king's service seldom permitted themselves to be taken alive. With one casualty wrapping his wrist in the stern, no man rushed the task. Amroth's seamen recovered the last crewman of Karthan's brigantine from the sea with wary caution and dumped him face down on the floorboards. The bosun regarded his prize with distaste. Barefoot, slightly built, and clad in a sailhand's patched tunic, the man seemed no one important. Only the silver ring on his left hand occasioned any notice at all; after hours of thankless labor, the oarsmen deserved reward for their efforts.

"Beer booty," invited the bosun. He bent, caught the captive's wrist, and tugged to pry the ring from a finger still swollen from the sea.

"Cut 'er free," suggested the crewman who nursed his slashed forearm.

Feud left no space for niceties. The bosun drew his rigging knife. He braced the captive's hand palm upward against the stern seat, and lifted his blade to cut. At that moment the longboat rocked. Dying sunlight caught and splintered in the depths of an emerald setting.

The bosun gasped. He snatched back his knife as if burned, for the ring he would steal was not silver but white gold. The gem was carved with a leopard device, hatefully familiar.

"Fate witness, he's s'Ffalenn!" Shocked and uncertain, the bosun straightened up. He had watched the enemy brigantine burn, her captain sprawled dead on her quarterdeck; but a glance at the black hair which dripped ignominiously in the bilge now belied that observation. Suddenly hand and ring were tugged from his grasp as an oarsman reached out and jerked the captive onto his back.

Bared to the fading light, the steeply angled feature and upswept brow line of s'Ffalenn stood clear as struck bronze. There could be no mistake. Amroth's seamen had taken, alive, the Master of Shadow himself.

The sailors fell back in fear. Several made signs against evil, and someone near the fore drew a dagger.

"Hold!" The bosun turned to logic to ease his own frayed nerves. "The sorcerer's harmless, just now, or we'd already be dead. Alive, don't forget, he'll bring a bounty."

The men made no response. Tense, uneasy, they shifted their feet. Someone uttered a charm against demons, and a second knife sang from its sheath.

The bosun grabbed an oar and slammed it across the thwarts between sailors and captive. "Fools! Would you spit on good fortune? Kill him, and our liege won't give us a copper."

That reached them. Arithon s'Ffalenn was the illegitimate son of Amroth's own queen, who in years past had spurned the kingdom's honor for adultery with her husband's most infamous enemy. The pirate king's bastard carried a price on his head that would ransom an earl, and a dukedom awaited the man who could deliver him to Port Royal in chains. Won over by greed, the sailors put up their knives.

The bosun stepped back and rapped orders, and men jumped to obey. Before the s'Ffalenn bastard regained his wits, his captors bound his wrists and legs with cord cut from the painter. Then, trussed like a calf for slaughter, Arithon, Master of Shadow and heir apparent of Karthan, was rowed back to the warship *Briane*. Hauled aboard by the boisterous crew of the longboat, he was dumped in a dripping sprawl on the quarterdeck, at the feet of the officer in command.

A man barely past his teens, the first officer had come to his post through wealth and royal connections rather than merit or experience. But with the captain unconscious from an arrow wound and the ranking brass of *Briane's* fighting company dead, none remained to dispute the chain of command. The first officer coped, though shouldered with responsibility for three hundred and forty-two men left living, and a warship too crippled to carry sail. The bosun's agitated words took a moment to pierce through tired and overburdened thoughts.

The name finally mustered attention.

"Arithon s'Ffalenn!" Shocked to disbelief, the first officer stared at the parcel of flesh on his deck. This man was small, sea-tanned, and dark; nothing like the half-brother in line for Amroth's crown. A drenched spill of hair plastered an angular forehead. Spare, unremarkable limbs were clothed in rough, much mended linen that was belted with a plain twist of rope. But his sailhand's appearance was deceptive. The jewel in the signet bore the leopard of s'Ffalenn, undeniable symbol of royal heirship.

"It's him, I say," said the bosun excitedly.

The crew from the longboat and every deckhand within earshot edged closer.

Jostled by raffish, excitable men, the first officer recalled his position. "Back to your duties," he snapped. "And have that longboat winched back on board. Lively!"

"Aye, sir." The bosun departed, contrite. The sailhands dispersed more slowly, clearing the quarterdeck with many a backward glance.

Left alone to determine the fate of Amroth's bitterest enemy, the first officer shifted his weight in distress. How should he confine a man who could bind illusion of shadow with the ease of thought, and whose capture had been achieved at a cost of seven ships? In Amroth, the king would certainly hold Arithon's imprisonment worth such devastating losses. But aboard the warship *Briane*, upon decks still laced with dead and debris, men wanted vengeance for murdered crewmen. The sailhands would never forget: Arithon was a sorcerer, and safest of all as a corpse.

The solution seemed simple as a sword thrust, but the first officer knew differently. He repressed his first, wild impulse to kill, and instead prodded the captive's shoulder with his boot. Black hair spilled away from a profile as keen as a knife. A tracery of scarlet flowed across temple and cheek from a hidden scalp wound; bruises mottled the skin of throat and chin. Sorcerer though he was, Arithon was human enough to require the services of a healer. The first officer cursed misfortune that this bastard had not also been mortal enough to die. The king of Amroth knew neither temperance nor reason on the subject of his wife's betrayal. No matter that men might get killed or maimed in the course of the long passage home; on pain of court-martial, *Briane*'s crewmen must deliver the Master of Shadows alive.

"What's to be done with him, sir?" The man promoted to fill the dead mate's berth stopped at his senior's side, his uniform almost unrecognizable beneath the soot and stains of battle.

The first officer swallowed, his throat dry with nerves. "Lock him up in the chart room."

The mate narrowed faded eyes and spat. "That's a damned fool place to stow a such a dangerous prisoner! D'ye want us all broken? He's clever enough to escape."

"Silence!" The first officer clenched his teeth, sensitive to the eyes that watched from every quarter of the ship. The mate's complaint was just, but no officer could long maintain command if he backed down before the entire crew. The order would have to stand.

"The prisoner needs a healer," the first officer justified firmly. "I'll have him moved and set in irons at the earliest opportunity."

The mate grunted, bent, and easily lifted the Shadow Master from the deck. "What a slight little dog, for all his killer's reputation," he commented. Then, cocky to conceal his apprehension, he sauntered the length of the quarterdeck with the captive slung like a duffel across his shoulder.

The pair vanished down the companionway, Arithon's knuckles haplessly banging each rung of the ladder-steep stair. The first officer shut his eyes. The harbor at Port Royal lay over seventeen days' sail on the best winds and fair weather. Every jack tar of *Briane's* company would be a rich man, if any of them survived to make port. Impatient, inexperienced, and sorely worried, the first officer shouted to the carpenter to hurry his work on the mainmast.

Night fell before *Briane* was repaired enough to carry canvas. Clouds had obscured the stars by the time the first officer ordered the ship under way. The bosun relayed his commands, since the mate was too hoarse to make himself heard over the pounding of hammers under the forecastle. Bone weary, the crew swung themselves aloft with appalling lack of agility. Unbrailed canvas billowed from the yards; on deck, sailhands stumbled to man the braces. Sail slammed taut with a crash and a rattle of blocks, and the bow shouldered east through the swell. Staid as a weathered carving, the quartermaster laid *Briane* on course for Amroth. If the wind held, the ship would reach home only slightly behind the main fleet.

Relieved to be back under sail, the first officer excused all but six hands under the bosun on watch. Then he called for running lamps to be lit. The cabin boy made rounds with flint and striker. *Briane's* routine passed uninterrupted until the flame in the aft lantern flicked out, soundlessly, as if touched by the breath of Dharkaron. Inside the space of a heartbeat, the entire ship became locked in darkness as bleak as the void before creation. The rhythm of the joiners' hammers wavered and died, replaced abruptly by shouting.

The first officer leaped for the companionway. His boots barely grazed the steps. Half sliding down the rail, he heard the shrill crash of glass as the panes in the stern window burst. The instant his feet slapped deck, he rammed shoulder first into the chart room door. Teak panels exploded into slivers. The first officer carried forward into blackness dense as calligrapher's ink. Sounds of a furious struggle issued from the direction of the broken window.

"Stop him!" The first officer's shout became a grunt as his ribs bashed the edge of the chart table. He blundered past. A body tripped him. He stumbled, slammed painfully against someone's elbow, then shoved forward into a battering press of bodies. The hiss of the wake beneath the counter sounded near enough to touch. Spattered by needle-fine droplets of spray, the first officer realized in distress that Arithon might already be half over the sill. Once overboard, the sorcerer could bind illusion, shape shadow, and blend invisibly with the waves. No search would find him.

The first officer dived to intervene, hit a locked mass of men, and felt himself dashed brutally aside. Someone cursed. A whirl of unseen motion cut through the drafts from the window. Struck across the chest by a hard, contorted body, the first officer groped blindly and two-handedly hooked cloth still damp from the sea. Aware of whom he held, he locked his arms and clung obstinately. His prisoner twisted, wrenching every tendon in his wrists. Flung sideward into a bulkhead, the first officer gasped. He felt as if he handled a careening maelstrom of fury. A thigh sledge-hammered one wrist, breaking his grasp. Then someone crashed like an axed oak across his chest. Torn loose from the captive, the first officer went down, flattened to the deck under a mass of sweaty flesh.

The battle raged on over his head, marked in darkness by the grunt of drawn breaths and the smack of knuckles, elbows, and knees battering into muscle. Nearby, a seaman retched, felled by a kick in the belly. The first officer struggled against the crush to rise. Any blow that connected in that ensorcelled dark had to be ruled by luck. If Arithon's hands remained bound, force and numbers must ultimately prevail as his guardsmen found grips he could not break.

"Bastard!" somebody said. Boots scuffled and a fist smacked flesh. Arithon's resistance abated slightly.

The first officer regained his feet when a low, clear voice cut through the strife.

"Let go. Or your fingers will burn to the bone."

"Don't listen!" The first officer pushed forward. "The threat's an illusion."

A man screamed in agony, counterpointed by splintering wood. Desperate, the first officer shot a blow in the approximate direction of the speaker. His knuckles cracked into bone. As if cued by the impact, the sorcerer's web of darkness wavered and lifted.

Light from the aft running lamp spilled through the ruptured stern window, touching gilt edges to a litter of glass and smashed furnishings. Arithon hung limp in the arms of three deckhands. Their faces were white and their chests heaved like runners just finished with a marathon. Another man groaned by the chart locker, hands clenched around a dripping shin; while against the starboard bulkhead, the mate stood scowling, his color high and the pulse angry and fast behind his ripped collar. The first officer avoided the accusation in the older seaman's eyes. If it was unnatural that a prisoner so recently injured and unconscious should prove capable of such fight, to make an issue of the fact invited trouble.

Anxious to take charge before the crew recovered enough to talk, the first officer snapped to the moaning crewman, "Fetch a light."

The man quieted, scuffled to his feet, and hastily limped off to find a lantern. As a rustle of returned movement stirred through the beleaguered crew in the chart room, the first officer pointed to a clear space between the glitter of slivered glass. "Set the s'Ffalenn there. And you, find a set of shackles to bind his feet."

Seamen jumped to comply. The man returned with the lantern as they lowered Arithon to the deck. Flame light shot copper reflections across the blood which streaked his cheek and shoulder; dark patches had already soaked into the torn shirt beneath.

"Sir, I warned you. Chart room's not secure." The mate insisted, low-voiced, "Have the sorcerer moved to a safer place."

The first officer bristled. "When I wish your advice, I'll ask. You'll stand guard here until the healer comes. That should not be much longer."

But the ship's healer labored yet with the task of removing the broad head of an enemy arrow from the captain's lower abdomen. Since he was bound to be occupied for some time yet to come, the mate clamped his jaw and did not belabor the obvious: that Arithon's presence endangered the ship in far more ways than one. Fear of his sorceries could drive even the staunchest crew to mutiny.

That moment one of the seaman exclaimed and flung back. The first officer swung in time to see the captive stir and awaken. Eyes the color of new spring grass opened and fixed on the men who crowded the chart room. The steep s'Ffalenn features showed no expression, though surely pain alone prevented a second assault with shadow. *Briane's* first officer searched his enemy's face for a sign of human emotion and found no trace.

"You were unwise to try that," he said, at a loss for other opening. That the same mother had borne this creature and Amroth's well-beloved crown prince defied all reasonable credibility.

Where his grace, Lysaer, might have won his captors' sympathy with glib and entertaining satire, Arithon of Karthan refused answer. His gaze never wavered, and his manner stayed stark as a carving. The creak of timber and rigging filled an unpleasant silence. Crewmen shifted uneasily until a clink of steel beyond the companionway heralded the entrance of the crewman sent to bring shackles.

"Secure his ankles." The first officer turned toward the door. "And by Dharkaron's vengeance, stay on guard. The king wants this captive kept alive."

He departed after that, shouting for the carpenter to send hands to repair the stern window. Barely had the workmen gathered their tools when *Briane* plunged again into unnatural and featureless dark. A thudding crash astern set the first officer running once more for the chart room.

This time the shadow disintegrated like spark-singed silk before he collided with the chart table. He reached the stern cabin to find Arithon pinned beneath the breathless bulk of his guards. Gradually the men sorted themselves out, eyes darting nervously. Though standing in the presence of a senior officer, they showed no proper deference. More than a few whispered sullenly behind their hands.

"Silence!" Crisply the first officer inclined his head to hear the report.

"Glass," explained the mate. "Tried to slash his wrists, Dharkaron break his bastard skin."

Blood smeared the deck beneath the Master. His fine fingers glistened red, and closer examination revealed that the cord which lashed his hands was nearly severed.

"Bind his fingers with wire, then." Provoked beyond pity, the first officer detailed a man to fetch a spool from the hold.

Arithon recovered awareness shortly afterward. Dragged upright between the stout arms of his captors, he took a minute longer to orient himself. As green eyes lifted in recognition, the first officer fought a sharp urge to step back. Only once had he seen such a look on a man's face, and that time he had witnessed a felon hanged for the rape of his own daughter.

"You should have died in battle," he said softly.

Arithon gave no answer. Flame light glistened across features implacably barred against reason, and his hands dripped blood on the deck. The first officer looked away, cold with nerves and uneasiness. He had little experience with captives, and no knowledge whatever of sorcery. The Master of Shadow himself offered no inspiration, his manner icy and unfathomable as the sea itself.

"Show him the king's justice," the first officer commanded, in the hope a turn at violence might ease the strain on his crew.

The seamen wrestled Arithon off his feet and pinioned him across the chart table. His body handled like a toy in their broad hands. Still the Master fought them. In anger and dread the seamen returned the bruises lately inflicted upon their own skins. They stripped the cord from the captive's wrists and followed with all clothing that might conceal slivers of glass. But for his grunts of resistance, Arithon endured their abuse in silence.

The first officer hid his distaste. The Master's defiance served no gain, but only provoked the men to greater cruelty. Had the bastard cried out, even once reacted to pain as an ordinary mortal, the deckhands would have been satisfied. Yet the struggle continued until the victim was stripped of tunic and shirt and the sailhands backed off to study their prize. Arithon's chest heaved with fast, shallow breaths. Stomach muscles quivered beneath skin that wept sweat, proof enough that his body at least had not been impervious to rough handling.

"Bastard's runt-sized, for a sorcerer." The most daring of the crewmen raised a fist over the splayed arch of Arithon's rib cage. "A thump in the slats might slow him down some."

"That's enough!" snapped the first officer. Immediately sure the sailhand would ignore his command, he moved to intervene. But a newcomer in a stained white smock entered from behind and jostled him briskly aside.

Fresh from the captain's sickbed, the ship's healer pushed on between sailor and pinioned prisoner. "Leave be, lad! Today I've set and splinted altogether too many bones. The thought of another could drive me to drink before sunrise."

The crewman subsided, muttering. As the healer set gently to work with salve and bandages, the s'Ffalenn sorcerer drew breath and finally spoke.

"I curse your hands. May the next wound you treat turn putrid with maggots. Any child you deliver will sicken and die in your arms, and the mother will bleed beyond remedy. Meddle further with me, and I'll show you horrors."

The healer made a gesture against evil. He had heard hurt men rave, but never like this. Shaking, he resumed his work, while under his fingers, the muscles of his patient flinched taut in protest.

"Have you ever known despair?" Arithon said. "I'll teach you. The eyes of your firstborn son will rot and flies suck at the sockets."

The seamen tightened their restraint, starting and cursing among themselves.

"Hold steady!" snapped the healer. He continued binding Arithon's cuts with stiff-lipped determination. Such a threat might make him quail, but he had only daughters. Otherwise he might have broken his oath and caused an injured man needless pain.

"By your leave," he said to the first officer when he finished. "I've done all I can."

Excused, the healer departed, and the deckhands set to work with the wire. As the first loop creased the prisoner's flesh, Arithon turned his invective against the first officer. After the healer's exemplary conduct, the young man dared not break. He endured with his hands locked behind his back while mother, wife, and mistress were separately profaned. The insults after that turned personal. In time the first officer could not contain the anger which arose in response to the vicious phrases.

"You waste yourself!" After the cold calm of the Master's words, the ugliness in his own voice jarred like a woman's hysteria. He curbed his temper. "Cursing me and my relations will hardly change your lot. Why make things difficult? Your behavior makes civilized treatment impossible."

"Go force your little sister," Arithon said.

The first officer flushed scarlet. Not trusting himself to answer, he called orders to his seamen. "Bind the bastard's mouth with a rag. When you have him well secured, lock him under guard in the sail hold."

The seamen saw the order through with a roughness born of desperation. Watching, the first officer worried. He was a tired man with a terrified crew, balanced squarely on the prongs of dilemma. The least provocation would land him with a mutiny, and a sorcerer who could also bind shadow threatened trouble tantamount to ruin. No measure of prevention could be too drastic to justify. The first officer rubbed bloodshot, stinging eyes. A final review of resources left him hopeless and without alternative except to turn the problem of Arithon s'Ffalenn back to *Briane*'s healer.

The first officer burst into the surgery without troubling to knock. "Can you mix a posset that will render a man senseless?"

Interrupted while tending yet another wound, the healer answered with irritable reluctance. "I have only the herb I brew to ease pain. A heavy dose will dull the mind, but not with safety. The drug has addictive side effects."

The first officer never hesitated. "Use it on the prisoner, and swiftly."

The healer straightened, shadows from the gimballed lantern sharp on his distressed face.

The officer permitted no protest. "Never mind your oath of compassion. Call the blame mine, if you must, but I'll not sail into a mutiny for the skin of any s'Ffalenn bastard. Deliver Arithon alive to the king's dungeons, and no man can dispute we've done our duty."

Daunted by the raw look of fright on the first officer's face, the healer called his assistant to finish bandaging his patient. Then, too wise to be hurried, he rummaged among his shelf of remedies. "Who will answer if the young man's mind is damaged?"

The first officer drew a ragged breath. "Dharkaron, angel of vengeance! We'll all be executed, even to the cabin steward, if our sailors

get panicked and slit the bastard's throat. He's crazed enough to provoke them. How in the name of the king can I be on hand every minute to stop disaster?"

Jars rattled under the older man's hand. He selected one, adjusted
his spectacles to read the label, then said, "We're twenty days' sail
from Port Royal, given weather and luck. No man can be drugged
into a coma that long without serious risk of insanity. I've read texts
which claim that mages possess training to transmute certain poisons. To make sure of your Shadow Master would call for a dose of
dangerous potency."

"We'll land at South Island harbor, then." Saved by sudden inspiration, the first officer blotted his flushed and sweating brow. "The
crown prince is there for the summer, to court the earl's daughter.
That's only five days' sail, given just middling wind. Drug Arithon
only until then, and let His Grace shoulder the task of getting his
mother's bastard presented to the king."

The healer sighed and reached for his satchel, forced to accede to
the plan. Five days of strong possets would cause discomfort but no
permanent harm; and Prince Lysaer's custody was perhaps the wisest
alternative for the pirate heir of Karthan. His Grace's inborn gift of
light was a match for sorcery and shadows, and his judgment, even in
matters of blood feud, was dependably, exactly fair.

Crown Prince

The tap and clang of swordplay rang from the sun-washed sand of the earl's practice yard. The courier sent up from the harbor heard the sound and slowed his pace to a walk. Lysaer, Crown Prince of Amroth, had guested at South Isle often enough that even the servants knew: a man did not interrupt His Grace at sparring if the weapon of choice was steel. Accordingly, the messenger paused in the shaded archway of the portico. He waited, though the news he carried was urgent enough that delay might earn him ill favor.

The prince noticed the man's arrival immediately. Sword engaged in a parry, he flung back coin-bright hair, then winked in friendly acknowledgment. He did not seem distracted. Yet on the next lunge, his opponent executed an entirely predictable disengage that, somehow, managed to disarm him. The royal sword drove a glittering arc in the sunlight and landed, scattering sand.

Laughing, generous, handsome enough to make maidens weep, the prince flung up his hands. He turned the dagger he yet held en gauche and flung it, point first, into the soil beside the sword. "There's silver won for your lady, my lord. Ath bless the heir she carries."

Unexpectedly presented the victory, the dark-haired nobleman straightened on the field in astonishment. "Highness, the Fatemaster himself doesn't know so much of my affairs. Who told you?"

The prince laughed again. "About which, the bet or the baby?" He reached up to tidy his shirt laces, then started for the courier in the portico.

The nobleman suspiciously regarded the sword and the still quivering dagger. "You cheated to give me the honor, curse me if you didn't."

Lysaer, first son of the king of Amroth, stopped dead between strides. He widened surprised blue eyes. "Did I? Well then, I'll buy your lady a pearl, and we'll fight on the morrow to decide who pays for the setting." Then, the smile still on his face, the prince acknowledged the courier. "You bring news?"

The runner in the earl's livery bowed and pointedly glanced at the servant who attended the prince from the sidelines. "For your ears, only, Your Grace."

The prince sent the servant to retrieve his discarded weapons, then stepped into the shadow of the arch, his manner immediately sober. "My pathetic cripple of an auntie hasn't fallen from her bed and died, now has she?"

The jest was too graceless to amuse, but the prince had gauged the effect to a nicety. The courier visibly relaxed. "That lady is well, Your Grace. The first officer of his majesty's warship, *Briane*, sends compliments instead. I'm advised to tell you that he has in his custody the pirate king's bastard, Arithon s'Ffalenn."

Lysaer stopped as if struck. The flush of recent exertion drained from his face and his hands clenched white at his sides. "Alive," he said softly.

Seven generations of bloodshed between Amroth and Karthan's pirates had never seen a moment to match this. Lysaer suppressed a primal surge of triumph. The vendetta had threaded discord and grief through his earliest memories; an altercation before his birth had killed the realm's first queen and a daughter no one near the king dared to mention. All Lysaer's life, the court had lived in dread of his father's rages, and always they were caused by s'Ffalenn. Still, the prince fought the irrational hatred the name reflexively inspired. The prisoner in *Briane's* hold was his half-brother. Whether he was also a criminal deserving of the cruelty and death that the royal obsession for vengeance would demand was a distinction no man of honor dared ignore.

Trapped in an awkward silence, the courier held his breath; as if his discomfort were a catalyst, the prince tossed off dark thoughts. He touched the fellow's shoulder to reassure. "You need not worry. The fate of my mother's bastard is a problem too weighty for any but the king's justice. The commander of *Briane*'s company was quite right to entrust his custody to me."

The courier bowed with evident relief.

"The kitchen staff will give you refreshment," the prince insisted. "A page from my retinue can run down to *Briane* to inform that I wish to see the prisoner."

Excused with more grace than a man with difficult news might expect, the courier bowed again and departed. The prince lingered briefly in the corridor. His blue eyes stayed deep and intense, even as his sparring partner stepped to his side in curiosity.

"Your Grace? What has passed?"

The crown prince of Amroth started as if from a trance. "Trouble," he said briefly. His frown changed to chagrin as he recalled his dusty, sweat-damp clothes.

Anxious to please, the nobleman snapped his fingers at the servant who waited with the swords. "Send for the prince's valet."

"And the captain of the earl's guard," Lysaer added quickly. "Admit him to my private chambers. If he curses the rush, tell him directly that I'll pour him another beer."

The key turned stiffly in the lock. Greeted from within by the acid-sharp consonants of a curse, the first officer pushed wide the wooden door. He hung his lantern from a spike in the beam overhead, then gestured for his prince to pass ahead of him.

Briane's sail hold was stifling in the noon heat. The air reeked of mildew and damp; though the ship rode at anchor, the hatch overhead was battened down as if for a gale. The lantern threw long, starred shadows which swung with each roll of the swell.

Nervous to the point of jumpiness, the first officer pointed to the darkest corner of the room. "There, Your Grace. And be careful, he's roused from the drug, and dangerous."

Resplendent in gold silk and brocade, glittering with the sapphires of royal rank, Lysaer of Amroth stepped forward. "Leave us," he said gently to the officer. Then, as the door creaked shut at his heels, he forced back a tangle of emotional turmoil and waited for his eyes to adjust.

Dead still in the uncertain light, Arithon s'Ffalenn sat propped against a towering pile of spare sail. Biscuit and water lay untouched by his elbow. A livid swelling on the side of his jaw accentuated rather than blurred the angled arrogance of features which decidedly favored his father. His eyes were open, focused, and bright with malice.

The look chilled Lysaer to the heart. Hampered and unsettled by the dimness, he lifted the lantern down. The light shifted, mercilessly exposed details that up until now had stayed hidden. The queen's bastard was small, the prince saw with a shock of surprise. But that slight stature was muscled like a cat, and endowed with a temper to match; the flesh at wrists and ankles had been repeatedly torn on the fetters, leaving bruises congested with scabs. The hands were wrapped with wire and sorrowfully crusted with blood. The prince felt a surge of pity. He had heard the first officer's report; the fright of the sailors was understandable, yet after fetters and chain, the added restraint of the wire seemed a needless cruelty.

Embarrassed, Lysaer replaced the lantern to its hook. He drew breath to call for the bosun, a sailhand, any ship's officer who could bring cutters and ease the prisoner's discomfort.

But Arithon spoke first. "We are well met, *brother.*"

The crown prince ignored the sarcasm. A blood feud could continue only as long as both sides were sworn to antipathy. "Kinship cannot pardon the charges against you, if it's true that you summoned shadow and sorcery, then blinded and attacked and murdered the companies of seven vessels. No rational purpose can justify the slaughter of hapless sailors."

"They happened to be crewing royal warships." Arithon straightened with a jangle of chain. His clear, expressive voice lifted above the echoes. "Show me a man who's harmless, and I'll show you one stone dead."

Lysaer stepped back, set his shoulders against the closed door to mask a shiver of dismay. The first officer had not exaggerated to justify the severity of his actions. In silence the crown prince regarded a face whose humanity lay sealed behind ungoverned viciousness.

" '*Kill thou me, and I shall helpless be.*' " Arithon capped his quote with a taunting smile. "Or perhaps you're too squeamish to try?"

The crown prince clamped his jaw, unsettled by the depths of antagonism such simple words could provoke.

Arithon pressured like gall on a sore spot, his accent a flawless rendition of high court style. "By the rotted bones of our mother, what a dazzle of jewels and lace. Impressive, surely. And the sword. Do you wear that for vanity also?"

"You'll gain nothing by baiting me." Determined to learn what inspired the prisoner's unprincipled attacks, Lysaer held his temper. "Except, perhaps, a wretched death I'd be ashamed to give a dog."

"But you offer a dog's life," Arithon shot back. He twisted suddenly, and wire-bound fingers knocked over the water bowl. Cheap crockery rattled across the boards, and a trail of puddles spilled and widened with the motion of the ship. "I chose not to lap like an animal from a dish. And bait you? Innocent, I haven't begun."

Arithon's eyes sharpened. A sudden sting of sorcery pierced the prince's awareness. Too late, he recoiled. In one unguarded instant the Master of Shadow smashed through his defenses. A probe like hot wire flashed through the prince's mind, sorting, gathering, discarding in an instant all the fine intentions that acted for fairness and compassion. The s'Ffalenn bastard repudiated honor. He ransacked his brother's past to barb his insatiable malice, and into his grasp like a weapon fell the recall of a childhood memory far better left forgotten. . . .

The young prince was much too lively to sleep. Overindulged with sweets, and stirred to nervous excitement by the festivities in celebration of his birthday, he ran on short legs and tumbled, laughing, on the carpet. "Want to see Mama!" he shouted to the chamberlain, who steadily looked more rumpled and weary. A day spent managing an over-exuberant three-year-old had taxed his dignity sorely.

The royal nursemaid lifted the child from the floor. Deft as she was with little ones, still, the boy managed to twist in her arms and tangle his nightshirt around his neck. "Here," she scolded. "Want to choke yourself to death?"

The prince crowed with laughter. "Want to see Mama."

Exasperated, the nursemaid set his mussed clothing to rights. "If I say yes, and you stay only long enough for a kiss, will you close your eyes and lie still until you fall asleep?"

The boy smiled in the way that never failed to melt the hearts of his attendants. "I promise."

"Now, a prince never breaks his word," warned the nurse.

Young Lysaer returned a solemn nod.

"Well, see that you don't, young man." The nurse ruffled his gold hair, then returned him to the long-suffering arms of the chamberlain. "Take him down, sir. He's a good boy, usually, and on his birthday the queen won't mind."

The prince chattered all the way down three flights of stairs. Though an elderly man, the chamberlain's hearing was excellent. His ears rang by the time he reached the royal apartments, and with the prince squirming in energetic anticipation against his neck, he missed the warning gesture of the guard.

Beyond the embroidered hanging, the Lady Talera's anteroom lay ominously deserted; chests and jeweled tapestries glittered in candle-light abnormally dim for the hour. The chamberlain hesitated.

Warned of something amiss, he set the prince down; and the child, too young to notice nuance, tugged his hand free and ran ahead.

The moment Lysaer crossed the threshold to his mother's chambers, he sensed something wrong. His father sat with the queen, and both of them were angry.

"You'll use no child of mine as an axe in your feud with s'Ffalenn," said his mother in a tone Lysaer had never heard before. His bare feet made no sound as he shrank in the shadows, uncertain. Trapped helplessly in the foyer, the chamberlain dared not risk the king's temper. He knotted his hands in white hair, and prayed the young prince had sense enough to withdraw.

But Lysaer was frightened, and too small to understand arguments. He stayed still as a rabbit in the corner, while the queen spoke again. The lilt of her Rauven dialect lent her words a raw quality of force. *"Our son's gift is no weapon.* Dare you abuse him? By Ath, I swear if you try, you'll get no second child from me."

Lysaer frowned, tried to sort meaning from the adult words. He knew they spoke of him, and the sparkling lights he could make in the air whenever he wished, or dreamed of the sun.

The king rose abruptly from his chair. His shadow swooped in the candlelight as he bent and seized the queen's wrists. "Woman, defy me, and I'll make you wretched with childbearing. Blame your father. He should have made your dowry more accessible. Sorcery and babies made a misfortunate mix."

Bracelets clashed as the queen wrenched free. Her elbow struck a side table and a crystal bowl toppled, scattering the carpet with glass and sugared nuts. Lysaer whimpered, unnoticed by the doorway. He wanted to run, but the chamberlain was nowhere in sight.

The king jerked the queen to her feet. "You've been indisposed long enough, you royal witch. I'll bed you now, and every night afterward until you conceive the master of shadows I was promised."

Gems sparkled on the king's sleeves as he locked his arms around his consort. She fought him. He crushed her roughly against his doublet. Silk tore like the scream of a small animal between his hands, baring her slim back in the firelight.

The king laughed. "The s'Ffalenn will curse your lovely, gifted children from the bottom of the sea."

The queen struggled. Blond hair tumbled from diamond pins and snagged on the man's rough fingers. From the doorway, Lysaer saw tears in his mother's eyes, but her voice stayed ringingly steady. "Force me, and by the stones of Rauven Tower, I'll even the stakes. The s'Ffalenn pirates will share my bride gift to s'Ilessid, and grief and sorrow will come of it."

"Curse me, will you? Dharkaron witness, you'll regret this." The king struck her. Flung off balance, the queen crashed backward across a table. Linen rumpled under her weight, and a carafe toppled, flooding wine like blood across the cloth.

Traumatized by the violence, Lysaer at last cried out. "Father! Don't hurt her anymore!"

The king started, spun, and saw his son in the entry. His face contorted like a stranger's. *"Get out of here."*

"No!" The queen pushed herself erect and extended a trembling hand. "Lysaer?"

The frightened, hysterical child ran to his mother and buried his face in her warmth. He felt her shaking as she held him. Muffled by the cloth of her gown, the prince heard the king say something. Then the door slammed. The queen lifted Lysaer and stroked hair as bright and fair as her own.

She kissed his cheek. "It's all over, little one."

But Lysaer knew she lied. That very night she left Amroth, never again to return. . . .

With a crack like a split in crystal, the sail hold spun back into focus. Lysaer shuddered in shock at the change. Tears wet his face. Whipped into fury by the pain of childhood betrayal, he forgot two decades of maturity. Into that breech, that long-forgotten maelstrom of suffering, Arithon s'Ffalenn cast shadow.

An image pooled on the deck before the prince. Sanded wood transformed to a drift of silken sheets, upon which two figures twined, naked. Lysaer felt the breath tear like fire in his throat. The man was dark-haired and sword-scarred, unmistakably Avar s'Ffalenn; beneath him, couched in a glory of gold hair, lay Talera, Queen of Amroth. Her face was radiant with joy.

Abruptly, Arithon withdrew from the prince's mind. He smirked toward the couple on the floor. "Shall I show you the rest of the collection?"

Lysaer's hand closed hard on his sword. His mother and her illicit lover blinked out like blown candles, and left, like an afterimage, the face of the bastard's shameless scorn. Seared by rage like white fire, Lysaer saw nothing in the son but the fornicating features of the father. The lantern swung, echoed his motion in a frenzy of shadows as he drew and struck a blow to the side of the prisoner's head.

The impact slammed Arithon over backward. Wired wrists screeched across sail hanks as he toppled and crashed to the deck. Loose as an unstrung puppet, he lay on his side, while blood twined in ribbons across his jaw.

"What a superb effort, for the flat of the blade," he managed between whistling breaths. "Why not try the edge?" But Arithon's voice
missed his usual vicious note entirely.

Jarred back to reason, and burned by a shame that left him soiled,
Lysaer strove for control. In all of his life he had never struck a helpless man; the novelty left him aching. Breathing hard, the lifted edge
of the sword poised over his enemy, he said, "You *want* me to kill
you!" Sickened to discover his hand shaking, he flung away his
weapon. "By Ath, I deny you that satisfaction. Your father's lust for
vengeance will fall on some other head than mine."

The blade struck crosswise against the door. As the clamor of
echoes dwindled, Arithon stirred and shut his eyes. A shudder swept
him. That brief instant his control slipped, to reveal tearing grief and
a shocking depth of desperation. Then, his mask of indifference restored, he said, "I sailed as first officer on board the *Saeriat*. The brigantine was my father's command."

The crown prince of Amroth drew breath, wrung by terrible
understanding. *Briane*'s original log entry had been correct; *Saeriat*'s
captain had burned with his brigantine. The pirate king of Karthan
was dead. Here, helplessly fettered and pleading to die, was his sole
heir, the last s'Ffalenn left living.

Arithon did not miss the change in his half-brother's manner. He
raised himself on one elbow, head flung back. "Loan me your knife.
As one prince to another, I promise, the feud between s'Ffalenn and
s'Ilessid will end here without any more cause for bloodshed."

"I cannot." Lysaer stared down at the mauled face of the captive
and qualified with sympathy that cut. "Your death would ruin every
man on this vessel, by my father's decree."

Arithon responded with damning sarcasm. "How admirable. Don't
neglect to mention the gold which rewards the virtue of such loyalty." Green eyes flicked up, pinned by lamplit highlights. "You preserve me solely for the king of Amroth. In his hands, I become a
puppet for him to torment, a target for the hatred inspired by our
mother, my father, and seven generations of captains who practiced
piracy before me."

Arithon lowered his gaze. "I beg not to be forced to that role. Let
me take my life. That will spare me and your family further shame."

The bare simplicity of the appeal caught the crown prince like a
blow. Left no breath to speak, he avoided answer by retrieving his
fallen sword. He rammed the blade into the scabbard with a violence
born of raw nerves. The original purpose of his visit seemed tawdry,
a meaningless, arrogant charade that unmasked a hypocrite player.
Unable to trust his reactions, he backed out of his half-brother's pres-

ence and shot the bolt on the door. A few short minutes of madness had nearly brought him to murder, to sacrifice the lives of loyal sailors to end the misery of a criminal. Shaking, driven almost to nausea by the intensity of his sympathy, the crown prince of Amroth gripped the companionway rail. "Fatemaster's judgment, you deserve what you get," he murmured to the closed door behind him.

"Your Grace? Are you all right?" *Briane's* first officer had remained on guard in the passage, but with the lantern left in the sail hold, darkness had hidden his presence.

Lysaer started in surprise. He had thought he was alone, and the sudden discovery of company embarrassed him. "I'm all right," he said quickly.

The first officer was too much a courtier to offer comment. Instead he fetched the light from the sail hold, then reset both bar and lock with studied concentration.

Lysaer pushed away from the bulkhead, self-conscious in his sweat-damp silk. The sting of s'Ffalenn manipulation seemed still to pry at his thoughts. Uncertainty weakened the tenets of honor. Worse yet, he still felt pity. Arithon's plight at the hands of the king would be unpleasant and prolonged. For the first time in his life, Lysaer fully understood his father's deranged hatred of s'Ffalenn; to the last son left living, they were a breed of fiends.

Aware of the first officer quietly awaiting instruction, the prince raked a hand through his hair. "I'm all right," he repeated. At least his voice had stopped shaking. "Send down the healer, and be sharp about it. I want the prisoner drugged unconscious, and this ship under sail for Port Royal before the turn of the tide."

The first officer raised frightened eyes to his prince. "Your Grace, that's not wise. Prolonged overdose of the herb is sure to cause madness."

Lysaer raised eyes gone hard as the cut sapphires at his collar. "Ath's grief, man, I know that! But insanity will surely be a mercy beside the judgment and sentence our prisoner will receive as s'Ffalenn. Let this pass beneath the Wheel be an easy one for him, for in truth, he is the last."

The first officer looked up in surprise. "The pirate king died also?"

Lysaer nodded. "That should please my father well enough. If the healer fears royal retribution, tell him and every man of *Briane's* crew that I'll sail along with them to intercede."

Tracer

Daybreak glimmered through the arches of Rauven Tower and outlined the concerned face of the high mage in silver and deepest shadows. He had stopped pacing the floor. His tired eyes studied the
listener who sat at his feet, but the tranced man's form showed no
stir of returning consciousness. The farseer's features remained remote; fragile hands stayed folded and limp in the lap of his bordered
robe as they had since sundown the day before.

The high mage wrestled extreme impatience. No sign hinted
whether the images gathered by the listener's delicate talent were terrible or benign.

"What has happened to my grandson?" The words escaped before
the high mage realized he had spoken aloud, but worry allowed no
chink for regret. The gaunt old sorcerer waited in stillness with the
breath stopped in his throat.

The listener opened distant eyes. By the outburst and the expression on his master's face, he became one of the few to discover how
deeply the high mage loved his daughter's s'Ffalenn bastard. He
phrased his answer with extreme tact.

"I see a place in constant motion, but lightless. It smells of canvas, mold, and damp." But the listener mentioned nothing of the
pain, hunger, and thirst also encountered in that place. Why grieve a

lonely man's heart when for hours Arithon's condition had not altered, except for a brief visit by a prince who wore the gold on blue of Amroth?

The listener closed his eyes once more. *What words could tell an aging man that his beloved grandson had tried to provoke his own death? Did phrases exist that could soften the despair behind such an act; that a king's blind hatred for a wife's transgressions might fall upon the hapless flesh of her son?*

The listener misliked delivering ill news without a promise of hope. He slipped back into trance, braced to endure Arithon's misery until he gleaned some small fact to lighten the grandfather's distress. Far off, beyond the shudder of ship's planking and the foaming splash of seawater, the high mage's restless steps resumed.

Sunrise shone livid red through the tower windows. Gaunt as a crow in his dark robe, the high mage stopped with his heart chilled by foreboding.

The listener stiffened. Brown eyes sprang open in a face blanched like fine linen. "Dharkaron have mercy."

"The news is bad," said the high mage. "Tell me quickly."

The listener drew a shaking breath and looked up. His hands knotted helplessly. "Arithon is imprisoned aboard a warship of Amroth. He tried with all his will to avoid surrender to the king's justice alive. His effort failed. His captors have drugged him senseless. They intend to keep him passive until their ship can deliver him to Port Royal."

The features of the high mage hardened like a carving blasted by wind. Behind blank, stunned eyes, his mind locked on the memory of a black-haired boy at the moment he mastered his first lesson of illusionary magic.

"But it works like music!" Alight with the wonder of discovery, a grandson's trusting joy had absolved in an instant all the anguish of a daughter's youthful death.

The high mage clung to the rough stone of the sill. "Arithon is the most gifted apprentice I have ever trained." The listener's hand settled lightly on the elder man's shoulder in comfort. The touch was shrugged off in irritation. *"Do you know what that boy renounced when he left to accept his father's inheritance?"*

The high mage directed his words through the window, as if the breakers which crashed on the rocks beneath could hear and respond to his pain. Harshly he continued, "If Arithon suffers harm, Amroth's king will wish Fate's Wheel could turn backward, and past actions be revoked. I will repay every cruelty, *in kind,* on the mind and body of his first born."

"Who is also your grandson!" cried the listener, frantic to avert the anger behind the high mage's threat. But the entreaty fell upon ears deaf to all but the sigh of the breeze off the sea.

Fragments

Summoned by the officer on sea watch, Amroth's senior admiral counts sails as his returning war fleet breasts the horizon beyond Port Royal; and when the tally reaches nine, he curses s'Ffalenn for eight more delayed, destroyed, or captured. . . .

Aboard the warship *Briane,* a healer sucks greedily at a rum flask in a vain attempt to dull the screams as drug-induced nightmares torment the man held captive in the sail hold. . . .

Under misty skies, in another place, a world awaits with a prophecy five centuries old, and not even its most wise yet know that a Prince and a Prisoner hold all hope for deliverance between them. . . .

II. Sentence

Twenty days out of South Isle, the last unaccounted warship breasted the horizon off Port Royal; *Briane* backed sail and dropped anchor in the harbor of Amroth's capital. Word of her s'Ffalenn captive overturned propriety in the decorous court of the king. Wildly shouting, the nobles presiding in the council hall abandoned themselves to celebration. *Briane*'s first officer emerged from his audience with a dukedom; the king's own collar of state circled his neck, and the fingers of both hands, including thumbs, were encrusted with rings bestowed by exuberant royal advisers. When word reached the streets, angry crowds gathered; the s'Ffalenn name was anathema in Amroth. Guardsmen in ceremonial regalia set about closing the stalls on Harbor Street, and the royal honor guard marched out under the crown prince's direct command to transfer the Master of Shadows from *Briane*'s hold to the security of the south keep's dungeons.

"The bastard sorcerer is mine to break," said the king.

The announcement brought a frown to the face of the realm's high chancellor. His liege's obsession for vengeance had caused events to transpire with unnatural speed. Although the facts of the prisoner's condition were listed in the crown prince's report, at present that document lay scattered on the carpet under the feet of a congratulatory crowd of favorites. The prince himself had been summarily dismissed to muster guardsmen; that others who were equally informed did not dare broach the subject was predictable. Over matters concerning the s'Ffalenn, too often the king's ire had broken the heads of the innocent.

Within the city of Port Royal, one man alone remained oblivious to the commotion. Arithon s'Ffalenn never knew the men at arms who carried him through cordoned streets to the south keep of Amroth castle. Still drugged, he heard none of the obscenities shouted by the roisterous mob which choked the alleys beneath the wall. The more zealous chanted still, while a smith replaced the wire which bound his hands with riveted cuffs and steel chain, without locks that might be manipulated by magecraft. When the guardsman dragged him roughly from the forge, the rabble's screams of spite passed unnoticed; the cell which finally imprisoned the Master of Shadows was carved deep beneath the headland which sheltered Port Royal from the sea. No sound reached there but the rustle of rats. Shut in darkness behind a barred grille, the last s'Ffalenn lay on stone salted like frost with the residue of countless floods. Hours passed. The drug which had held Arithon passive for over two fortnights gradually weakened, and the first spark of consciousness returned.

He ached. His mouth burned with thirst and his eyelids seemed cast in lead. Aware, finally, of the chill which nagged at his flesh, Arithon tried to roll over. Movement touched off an explosion of pain in his head. He gasped. Overwhelmed by dizziness, he reached inward to restore his shattered self-command.

His intent escaped his will like dropped thread. Despite a master's training under the sorcerers of Rauven, his thoughts frayed and drifted in disorder.

Something was seriously amiss.

Arithon forced himself to stillness. He started over, tried again to engage the analytical detachment necessary to engage basic magecraft. Even small tricks of illusion required perfect integration of body and mind; a sorcerer only held influence over forces of lesser self-awareness.

But his skills answered with supreme reluctance. Distressed, Arithon fought to dampen the pain which raged like flame across his forehead. Had he misjudged his balance of power? A mage who attempted to manipulate a superior force would incur backlash upon himself at the closing moment of contact. Arithon felt a small stir of fear. A mis-cast of this magnitude could not be careless error, but an act which bordered upon suicide. *Why?* He drew a shuddering breath.

The air smelled stale, damp, salt-sour as flats at ebb tide. His eyes showed him vistas of blank darkness. Unable to pair either circumstance with logic, Arithon emptied his mind, compelled himself to solve his inner turmoil first. Step by step like a novice, he cut himself adrift from physical sensation. Discomfort made concentration difficult. After an interval he managed to align his mental awareness; though the exercise took an appalling amount of effort, at last he summoned mastery enough to pursue the reason.

With balanced precision, Arithon probed his physical self and compared what naturally should exist to any detail imposed from without. A cold something encircled his wrists and ankles. The pattern matched that of metal; steel. No botched enchantment had snared him here; *somebody had set irons on him.* Firmly Arithon turned the implications of that discovery aside. He probed deeper, dropped below the surface sensations of chill, ache, and muscle cramp. The damage he found internally made him recoil in shock. Control broke before an overwhelming tide of horror, and memory returned of the driven desperation that had ruled his every action since capture. He had sought the clean stroke of the sword because he had not wanted to reach Amroth alive. But now, oh now, *the s'Ilessid who had taken him had no right!*

Arithon expelled a whistling breath, enraged by the nausea which cramped his gut. Instead of granting death, his captors had poisoned him, drugged him with an herb that ruined body and mind just to salve their king's demand for vengeance.

Arithon stilled his anger, amazed that so simple an exercise sapped his whole will to complete. Enemies had forced him to live. He dared not allow them liberty to unravel his mind with drug madness. As a mage and a master, his responsibilities were uncompromising: the dangerous chance that his powers might be turned toward destruction must never for an instant be left to risk. Rauven's training provided knowledge of what steps he must complete, even as the self-possession that remained to him continued irretrievably to unravel. Already the air against his skin seared his nerves to agony. His stomach clenched with nausea, and his lips stung, salty with sweat. The stress to his physical senses had him pressed already to the wretched edge of tolerance; experienced as he was with the narcotics and simples used to augment prescience, for this onslaught he had no space at all to prepare.

Slowly, carefully, Arithon eased himself onto his back. Movement made him retch miserably. Tears spilled down his temples and his breath came in jerks. The attack subsided slowly, left his head whirling like an oil compass teased by a magnet. *Steady,* he thought, then willed himself to belief. Unless he maintained strict mental isolation from the bodily torment of drug withdrawal, he could neither track nor transmute the poison's dissolution. Should he once lose his grip on self-discipline, he would drown in reasonless, animal suffering, perhaps never to recover.

Arithon shut his eyes. Raggedly he strove to isolate his spirit from the chaos which ravaged his flesh. Dizziness ruined his concentration. His muscles tightened until he gasped aloud for air. An attempt to force will over a wheeling rush of faintness caused him to black out.

He woke to torment beyond his power to subdue. Doubled with cramps and shivering violently, Arithon reached for some personal scrap of self to hook back his plummeting control. The effort yielded no haven, but opened the floodgates of despair.

"No!" Arithon's whisper of anguish flurried into echoes and died. His thoughts unraveled into delirium as the past rose and engulfed him, vivid, inescapable, and threaded through with the cutting edges of broken dreams.

Five years vanished as mist. Arithon found himself poised once again in a moment when a decision had faced him, and he had chosen without thought for bitter consequences. Called in from a snow battle with the other apprentices at Rauven, he sat on the embroidered hassock in his grandfather's study. Ice thawed from his boots and steamed on the stone before the hearth; the smells of ink and chalk and aged parchment enfolded him in a quiet he had appreciated too little at the time.

"I've heard from your father," the high mage opened.

Arithon looked up, unable to suppress a flush of willful excitement. At long last, Avar, King of Karthan, had chosen to acknowledge the existence of the son raised by sorcerers at Rauven. But Arithon held himself silent. He dared not be rude before the high mage.

The sorcerer regarded the boy at his feet with dark, passionless eyes. "Your father has no heir. He asks my leave to name you his successor." The high mage held up a hand and smiled, forestalling Arithon's rush to reply. "I've already answered. You will have two years to decide for yourself."

Arithon forgot courtesy. "But I know now!" Often he had dreamed of inheriting his father's crown. "I'll go to Karthan, use magecraft to free the waters beneath the sand, and help the land become green again. With grain growing in the fields, the need for piracy and bloodshed will be ended. Then s'Ffalenn and s'Ilessid can stop their feuding."

"My boy, that is a worthy ambition." The high mage's voice remained reserved. "But you must not be hasty. Your talents are music and sorcery. Consider these, for you have great potential. A king has no time for such arts. As a man who holds judgment over others, his life belongs wholly to his subjects."

The high mage's warning rolled like thunder through Arithon's dreaming mind. *Fool!* he raged at his younger self, *you'll go only to fail.* But the drug vision broke like storm surf, battering protest asunder. The boy felt himself whirled ahead to another time, as he entered the selfsame chamber. Then his interval of decision had passed and he knelt before the high mage to renounce the home he had known and loved for twenty years.

"How can I stay?" Arithon found himself saying, for the mastery he had earned had left him wiser. "How can I remain at Rauven studying music and books when my father's people, and mine, must send husbands and sons to kill for bare sustenance? How dare I ignore such need? I might bring Karthan hope of lasting peace."

Arithon looked up at the high mage's face and there read terrible understanding. *Heed your heart,* his present, drug-tortured awareness pleaded. Forget kingship. Abjure your father's inheritance. Karthan might be made fertile from shore to shore, but Amroth will never be weaned from hatred. *Would you suffer s'Ilessid vengeance for your mother's broken marriage vows?*

Yet time rippled out of focus once again. Arithon heard himself utter an oath of acceptance, the strong, callused hands of his father resting on his dark head. He rose to his feet aflame with pride and purpose, and before the weather-creased eyes of Karthan's captains, accepted Avar's sword as token of his heirship.

The weapon was rarely beautiful. Memory of smoke-dark steel chilled Arithon's palms, and the chased silver inscription which twined the length of the blade made the breath catch in his throat. Legend held that his father's sword had been fashioned by hands more skilled than man's; that moment, Arithon believed the tale. His decision became difficult to complete.

He knelt at once before the high mage. The emerald in the sword hilt glimmered green fire as he laid the weapon flat at the sorcerer's feet. "Let this blade remain at Rauven to seal my pledge. I go to restore peace in Karthan."

Arithon stood carefully, afraid to look upon his father's face— afraid of the anger he might find there. But Karthan's captains raised a great cheer, and Avar smiled upon his heir with something more than approval. At the time Arithon had barely heard the parting words of the sorcerer who had raised him. Now, they resounded like the horn call of Dharkaron, mocking ruined hopes and racking him through with the knowledge of present circumstance.

"My grandson, you chose responsibility above your inner talents.

That is a difficult turning. Win or lose, you give yourself in service to others. Although men might be inspired by a bard or enchanter, they cannot be led by one. The master's mysteries you have learned at Rauven must never be used for political expedience, however pressing the temptation. You must guide your kingdom to the same harmonic balance you once would have striven to find in those gifts you now renounce. The ballad you write, the craft you cast, must henceforth be sought in the land and the hearts of Karthan. Ath bless your efforts."

Torn from the vision of his grandfather's final embrace, Arithon strove to stem the forward rush of time. But the reins of delirium ripped fate from his grasp. Again he sailed, and again he endured Karthan's wretched poverty. He wept to relive the silent anguish of the widows when the casualty lists were read, and tears spilled silver down cheeks too proud to hide the face of grief.

Arithon shouted, tormented by the image of a fleet under the leopard banner of s'Ffalenn. "Stop them! Somebody stop them!" Vast, unreasoning rage lent him a giant's proportions. He reached out with hands the size of mountains and tried to fence the brigantines in the harbor. There were sons, fathers, and brothers on board who would never return. But wind swelled the dirt-red sails; the vessels slipped free of fingers robbed of strength.

Transformation of Karthan's spoiled farm lands had proceeded too slowly to bring rain; one last voyage had been undertaken to beg Rauven for the aid of another mage. Tortured by cruel remorse, Arithon smelled blood and murder on his flesh. He screamed aloud within the confines of his cell, while the battle that had claimed his father's life and his own freedom opened like a wound in his mind. Sucked into a vortex of violence, cut by a guilt that seared him blind, Arithon screamed again. "I used sorcery, as Ath is my witness. But never directly to murder. Not even to spare my liege lord."

His cries brought guards. The cell door crashed back, rending the darkness with echoes. The captain of the king's halberdiers peered down at the prisoner's contorted, quivering frame. "Dharkaron's vengeance, he's raving."

Arithon's eyes flicked open, lightlessly black under the lantern. Men bent over him. Mail and gold braid hung a star field of reflections above his head. His whole sight filled with weapons forged for killing; strapped to shoulder, wrist, and belt, they shone fiery as the gates of the damned. Hands in scale gauntlets reached out, touched his sweating skin.

Arithon flinched. Chain wailed across stone as he flung an arm over his face.

"He's fevered," someone said.

Arithon knew the statement for a lie. He was chilled, frosted by the winter grip of the steel which collared the wrist against his cheek. His blood seemed to shrink from the cold and slowly congeal in his veins.

"Fetch the king's healer." The voice lifted urgently. "Hurry!"

Mailed fingers grasped Arithon's arms. The drug-born demon in his head screamed refusal. *No man born would save him as sport for Amroth's courtiers.* Arithon thrashed, and the unhinged fury of his strength caught the guardsmen unprepared. Jerked half free of restraint, he lashed out at the nearest pair of legs. Chain whipped, impacted with a jangle of bruising force.

"Damn you to Sithaer!" The injured guardsman aimed a kick in vindication. His boot struck Arithon's head, and the ceiling fell, crushing torches, men, and voices into dark.

The banquet to commemorate the demise of the last s'Ffalenn was an extravagant affair, though arrangements had been completed on short notice. The king presided at the feast. Sumptuous in indigo brocade, his red hair only slightly thinned with gray, he gestured expansively and urged his guests to share his enjoyment of good fortune. Crowded on trestles before his dais were bottles of rare vintage wines, one for each s'Ilessid who had died at the hands of a s'Ffalenn. Since second and third cousins had been included in the count, as well as prominent citizens, the tally after seven generations was imposing. Dispatch ships had sailed claret at speed from the cellars of the neighboring duchy, since the king's own stock proved insufficient.

Gathered in the great hall to feast and drink until the last bottle had been drained to the lees were Amroth's courtiers, dressed in their finest plumage. Spirits were rarely higher. By dessert, not a few lords were snoring under tables, and even the prudent had grown spirited in an atmosphere of wild celebration. At midnight came the smock-clad figure of the royal healer. Drab as blight in a flower stall, he made his way between benches and tables, and stopped with a bow at the feet of his sovereign lord.

"Your Grace, I beg leave to speak concerning the health of your prisoner." The healer stood, uncomfortably aware of the courtiers who fell silent around him. He hated to interrupt the festivity with such news, but a brutal, exhausting hour spent in south keep had stripped the last shred of his patience. "The s'Ffalenn suffers severe drug addiction from his passage aboard the *Briane.*"

The king silenced the musicians with a gesture. Between the

costly glitter of wax candles and gold cutlery, conversation, dancing, and laughter in the vast hall faltered, then settled to an ominous hush.

"How bad is he?" demanded the king. His voice was much too soft.

Warned to danger, the healer weighed his wording. Six soldiers had been needed to hold Arithon pinioned while he performed his examination. The brilliant, close warmth of the hall made the experience seem distant as nightmare by comparison. With a shudder, the healer chose bluntness. "Your captive's life is gravely in jeopardy. The herb that was used to hold him passive is ruinously addictive, and an overdose such as he has endured quite often proves irreversible. Withdrawal can cause madness without remedy."

The king's knuckles tightened on the handle of his bread knife, and the blade glanced in reflection like lightning before a cloudburst. "Arithon s'Ffalenn is a prisoner of the crown of Amroth. I'll have the head of the man who dared to meddle with his fate."

The banquet hall went painfully silent; musicians fidgeted uneasily over muted instruments, and the advisers nearest to the dais all but stopped breathing. Into that stunned silence arose the voice of the prince.

"*Briane*'s healer acted under protest, my liege. I thought my report made that clear." Eyes turned, settled on the trim person of Lysaer as he stepped briskly from the dance floor. The prince paused only to see his pretty partner to a chair. Then, the fair-headed image of his father, he left her and strode straight to the dais. "My orders alone kept the s'Ffalenn under influence of the herb."

"Your orders!" The king of Amroth regarded his son in narrow-eyed fury. "You insolent puppy! How dare you presume to cosset an enemy whose birth is a slight to the kingdom's honor?"

Stillness deepened over the hall and Lysaer turned tautly pale. He had seen his father angry, but never before had the king made mention of his queen's indiscretion in public hearing. Cautioned by the precedence, the crown prince bowed in respectful ceremony. "Your Grace, I acted to ensure the prisoner's safety. His shadow mastery and his training by the Rauven mages make him dangerous. No warship on the face of the ocean offers security enough to confine such a man. The drug was the only expedient."

A whispered murmur of agreement swept the chamber, while more than one royal adviser regarded the prince with admiration.

But as if the prince were not present, the sovereign of Amroth set down his knife. Eyes as gray as sleet turned and narrowed and fixed on the countenance of the healer. "If the s'Ffalenn bastard is to be salvaged, what must be done?"

Wearily the healer shook his head. "Your Grace, the prognosis is not good. If the drug continues, the body will waste and die. If the drug is stopped, the shock will cause agony that by now may be more than the mind can support."

On the dais, the royal favorites waited in wary stillness, but the king only threaded ringed knuckles through his beard. "Will Arithon be aware that he suffers?"

Grimly the healer understood the price of his honesty. "Most certainly, my liege."

"Excellent." The king signaled his page, who immediately went running for a scribe. By the time the stooped old man arrived with his inks and parchments, the frown had smoothed from the royal brow. If the smile that replaced the expression eased the courtiers' restraint, it boded ill for the prisoner.

Again the hall stilled. Slouched back with his feet on the table, the king passed judgment on the healer. "Arithon is to be brought before my council in a fortnight's time, cured of addiction to the drug. You are commanded to use every skill you possess to preserve his mind intact. Success will reward you with one hundred coin weight in gold." The king plucked a grape from the bowl by his elbow and thoroughly mashed it with his teeth. "But if Arithon dies or loses sanity, your life, and the life of *Briane*'s healer, shall be forfeit."

The healer bowed, afraid but far too wise to protest. Only Lysaer dared intercede. Justly angry that his personal honor had been repudiated, he stepped to the edge of the dais and slammed his fists on the table.

For the first time in living memory, the king spurned his firstborn son. "Let this be a lesson to a prince who oversteps his appointed authority."

The scribe flipped open his lap desk. Too cowed to reveal any feelings, he scratched his quill across new vellum, inking in official words of state the terms of Arithon's survival, bound now to the lives of two healers. Warm wax congealed beneath the royal seal, setting the document into law.

The king grabbed his flagon and boisterously raised it high. "To the ruin of s'Ffalenn," he toasted.

A wild cheer rose from the onlookers; but frozen in fury before his father's chair, the crown prince did not drink.

Forced to forgo supper for south keep and the Master of Shadow, the royal healer of Amroth barred his heart against mercy. The king's orders were final; Arithon s'Ffalenn must at all costs be weaned from the drug. Troubled by the ache of arthritic knees, the healer knelt on cold stone and cursed. A raw apprentice could see the task required a miracle. Time increased the body's demand, and the doses given Arithon in the course of *Briane's* passage had far exceeded safe limits. To stop the drug would cause anguish; if the man's mind did not break, physical shock might kill him.

The healer lifted his hands from stressed, quivering muscle and gestured to the men at arms. "Let him go."

The guardsmen released their grip. Beyond voluntary control, Arithon curled his knees against his chest and moaned in the throes of delirium.

Very little could be done to ease a withdrawal severe as this one. The healer called for a straw pallet and blankets, and covered Arithon's cold flesh. He ordered his staff to bind their boots with flannel to keep noise and echo to a minimum. They restrained the patient when he thrashed. When his struggles grew too frenzied, they prepared carefully measured possets. Arithon received enough drug to calm, but never enough to satiate; when bodily control failed him entirely, they changed his fouled sheets.

Morning brought slight improvement. The healer sent for sandbags to immobilize the prisoner's head while they forced him to swallow herb tea. At midday came His Grace, the king of Amroth.

He arrived unattended. Resplendently clad in a velvet doublet trimmed with silk, he showed no trace of the drunken revelry instigated at the banquet the night before. Guards and assistants melted clear as his majesty crossed the cell. His unmuffled step scattered loud echoes across the stone. The healer bowed.

Careless of the courtesy, the king stopped beside the pallet and hungrily drank in details. The bastard was not what he had expected. For a man born to the sword, the hands which lay limp on the coverlet seemed much too narrow and fine.

"Your Grace?" The healer shifted uneasily, his old fingers cramped in his jacket. "Your presence does no good here."

The king looked up, blue eyes steeped with hostility. "You say?" He grasped the blankets in his jeweled fist and whipped them back, exposing his enemy in plain view. "Do you suppose the bastard appreciates your solicitude? *You speak of a criminal.*"

When the healer did not answer, the king glanced down and smiled to meet green eyes that were open and aware.

Arithon drew a careful breath. Then he smiled also and said, "The horns my mother left are galling, I'm told. Have you come down to gore or to gloat?"

The king struck him. The report of knuckles meeting helpless flesh startled even the guards in the corridor.

Shocked past restraint, the healer grasped the royal sleeve. "The prisoner is too ill to command his actions, Your Grace. Be merciful."

The king shook off the touch. "He is s'Ffalenn. And you are insolent."

But the sovereign lord of Amroth did not torment the prisoner further; as if Arithon had spent his strength on his opening line, the drug soon defeated his resistance. The king watched his enemy thrash, the flushed print of his fist stark against bloodless skin. Tendons sprang into relief beneath the Master's wrists. The slim fingers which had woven shadow with such devastating cleverness now crumpled into fists. Green eyes lost their distance, became widened and harsh with suffering.

Avid as a jealous lover, the king watched the tremors begin. He lingered until Arithon drew a rattling breath and cried out in the extremity of agony. But his words were spoken in the old tongue, forgotten except at Rauven. Cheated of satisfaction, the king released the blanket. Wool slithered into a heap and veiled his enemy's mindless wretchedness.

"You needn't worry," said his majesty as the healer reached to tidy the coverlet. "My court won't have Arithon broken until he can be made to remember who he is."

The instant the king departed, the healer called an attendant to mix a fresh posset. The remedy was much ahead of schedule, but the prisoner's symptoms left no option.

"I can manage without, I think." The words came ragged from Arithon's throat, but his eyes showed a sudden, acid clarity.

The healer started, astonished. "Was that an act?"

A spark of hilarity crossed the prisoner's face before his bruised lids slid closed. "I gave his grace a line from a very bad play" came the faint but sardonic reply. For a long while afterward, Arithon lay as if asleep.

The royal healer guessed otherwise; he called for a chair and prepared for an unpleasant vigil. He had treated officers who came to endure the secondary agony of dependence after painful injuries that required extended relief from the drug. They were men accustomed to adversity, physically fit, self-contained, and tough; and like Arithon they began by fighting the restless complaint of nerve and mind with total stillness. An enchanter's trained handling of poisons might stall the drug's dissolution; but as hallucinations burned away reason, the end result must defeat even the sternest self-discipline. The breath came quick and fast. First one, then another muscle would flinch, until the entire body jerked in spasm. Hands cramped and knotted to rigidity, and the head thrashed. Then, as awareness became unstrung by pain, and the mind came unraveled into nightmare, the spirit at last sought voice for its agony.

Prepared, when the pinched line of Arithon's mouth broke and air shuddered into lungs bereft of control, the healer muffled the hoarse, pealing screams under a twist of bed linen with the gentleness he might have shown a son. An assistant rushed to fetch a posset. In the interval before Arithon blacked out, his eyes showed profound and ragged gratitude.

The healer smoothed the damp, rutched linens and kneaded his patient's contorted muscles until their quivering eased off into stillness. Then, bone weary, he pushed his stiff frame erect. Informed by his assistant that the sun had long since set, he exclaimed aloud, "Ath's merciful grace! That man has a will like steel wire."

By morning, the drug was no longer necessary. Through the final hours of withdrawal, Arithon remained in full command of his wits. Although such raw, determined courage won him the healer's devoted admiration, no strength of character could lessen the toll on his health. Bereft of strength, and depleted to the point where bone, muscle, and vein stood in relief beneath bloodless skin, Arithon seemed a man more dead than alive.

When he woke following his first period of natural sleep, the healer consulted him. "The king shall not be told of your recovery until absolutely necessary. You need as much time as possible for convalescence."

The prisoner reacted unexpectedly. Weary distaste touched the face of a man too spent to curb emotion. "That's a costly risk. The king would execute you for daring such sentiment. And I will suffer precisely as long as mind and body remain whole enough to react." Arithon turned his head toward the wall, too fraught to frame his deepest fear: that grief and despair had unbalanced him. That his fragile grip on self-restraint might snap under further provocation and tempt him to an unprincipled attack through magecraft. "If I'm to be scapegoat before the court of Amroth, let me not last an hour. Free of the drug, I believe I can achieve that." He ended on a wounding note of irony. "If you wish to be merciful, tell the king at once."

The healer rose sharply. Unable to speak, he touched Arithon's thin shoulder in sorry sympathy. Then he left to seek audience with the king. All along he had expected to regret his dealings with the Master of Shadow, but never until the end had he guessed he might suffer out of pity.

* * *

Resplendent in silks, fine furs, and jewels, officials and courtiers alike packed the marble-pillared council hall on the day appointed for Arithon s'Ffalenn to stand trial before the king of Amroth. The crown prince was present despite the incident at the victory feast that had set him out of favor with his father. Although the ignominy stung, that his chair as the kingdom's heir apparent would stand empty on the dais, his ingrained sense of duty prevailed. Seated in the gallery normally reserved for royal guests, Lysaer leaned anxiously forward as the bossed doors swung open. Halberdiers in royal livery entered. The prisoner walked in their midst, bracketed by the steely flash of weapons. A sigh of movement swept across the chamber as highborn heads turned to stare.

Lysaer studied the Master of Shadows with rapt attention and a turmoil of mixed emotions. The drug had left Arithon with a deceptive air of fragility. The peasant's tunic which replaced his torn cotton draped loosely over gaunt shoulders. Whittled down to its framework of bone, his face bore a withdrawn expression, as if the chains which dragged at wrists and ankles were no inconvenience. His graceless stride betrayed otherwise; but the hissed insults from the galleries failed to raise any response. As prisoner and escort reached the foot of the dais, Lysaer was struck by an infuriating oddity. After all this s'Ffalenn sorcerer had done to avoid his present predicament, he showed no flicker of apprehension.

Dazzled by the tiered banks of candles after long weeks of confinement, Arithon stood blinking before the jeweled presence of the court. Stillness claimed the crowded galleries as his sea-cold gaze steadied, passed over banners and richly dyed tapestries, swept the array of dignitaries on the dais, then fixed at last on the king.

"You will kneel," said the sovereign lord of Amroth. He had yearned thirty years for this moment.

At the center of the cut marble flooring, Arithon stood motionless. His eyes remained distant as a dreamer's, as if no spoken word could reach him. A rustle of uneasiness swept the packed rows of courtiers. Only Lysaer frowned, troubled again by incongruity. The cold-handed manipulation he had escaped in *Briane*'s sail hold had certainly been no coincidence. If a clever, controlled man who possessed a sorcerer's talents chose a senseless act of bravado, the reason could not be trite. But the king's gesture to the halberdiers arrested the prince's thought.

The ceremonial grandeur of the chamber left abundant space for free movement; banners and trappings rippled in the disturbed air as nine feet of studded beech lifted and turned in a guardsman's fists.

Steel flashed and descended, the weapon's metal shod butt aimed squarely at the s'Ffalenn back. Yet with uncanny timing and a grace that maddened the eye, Arithon dropped to his knees. The blow intended to take him between the shoulder blades ripped harmlessly over his head.

The halberdier overbalanced. The step he took to save himself caught, sliding, on links of chain. He went down with a jangle of mail in full public view of the court. Somebody laughed. The guardsman twisted, his face gone beefy with outrage, but the lunge he began in retaliation was forestalled by Arithon's rejoinder.

"The wisest of sages have said that a man will choose violence out of fear." The Master's words were expressive but cold, and directed toward the king. "Is your stature so mean that you dare not face me without fetters?"

A flurry of affront disturbed the council. The king responded without anger, a slow smile on his lips. The courtiers stilled to hear his reply. "Guardsman, you have been personally shamed. Leave is given to avenge yourself."

The halberdier recovered his feet and his weapon with the haste of a bad-tempered bear. The stroke he landed to restore his dignity threw Arithon forward on his face. Hampered by chain, the prisoner could not use his hands to save himself. His cheek struck the marble edge of the stair, and blood ran bright over pale skin. With the breath stopped in their throats, Amroth's finest noted the royal gesture of dismissal. The halberdier stepped back, his eyes still fixed on his victim.

Lysaer searched the sharp planes of the s'Ffalenn face, but found no change in expression. Arithon stirred upon the floor. Subject to a thousand inimical stares, he rose to his feet, movements underscored by the dissonant drag of steel.

The king's hand dropped to the sceptre in his lap. Candlelight splintered over gemstones and gold as his fingers tightened around the grip. "You exist this moment because I wish to see you suffer."

Arithon's reply came fast as a whip crack. "That's a lie! I exist because your wife refused you leave to use mastery of shadow as a weapon against s'Ffalenn."

"Her scruple was well betrayed then, when you left Rauven." The king leaned forward. "You sold your talents well for the massacre of s'Ilessid seamen. Your reason will interest us all, since Lysaer never sailed with a war fleet. He never wielded his gift of light against Karthan."

Lysaer clamped his fists against the balustrade, stung to private anger by the remark. No scruple of the king's had kept him ashore, but Rauven's steadfast refusal to grant the training that would allow him to focus and augment his inborn talent.

If Arithon knew that truth, he did not speak. Blood ran down the steep line of his cheek and splashed the stone red at his feet. Calm, assured, and steady, he did not chafe at his helplessness; neither did he act like a man distressed for lack of options. Bothered by that cold poise, and by the courtiers' avid eagerness, Lysaer wrestled apprehension. Had he sat at his father's side, he could at least have counseled caution.

"Well?" Gems flashed as the king raised his sceptre. "Have you nothing to say?"

Silence; the court stirred, softly as rainfall on snow. Lysaer swallowed and found his throat cramped. Arithon might have engaged sorcery or shadow; the fact he did neither made no sense, and the unbroken tranquillity reflected in his stance failed to match the earlier profile of his character. Annoyed by the incongruity, Lysaer pursued the reason with the tenacity of a ferret burrowing after rats.

The king shifted impatiently. "Would you speak for your freedom?"

Poised between guardsmen, unmercifully lit by the massive bronze candelabra, Arithon remained unresponsive. Not an eyelash moved, even as the royal fingers clenched and slowly whitened.

"Jog his memory," said the king. Sapphires sparked blue in the candleflame as he let the sceptre fall.

This time the captive tried no last-minute trick of evasion. The halberdiers bashed him headlong onto his side. Arithon struck the floor rolling and managed to avoid the step. But after that he might have been a puppet mauled by dogs, so little effort did he make to spare himself. The guardsmens' blows tumbled his unresisting flesh over and over before the dais, raising a counter-strophe of protest from the chain. Not yet ready to see his enemy ruined by chance injury, the king put a stop to the abuse.

Arithon lay on his back adjacent to the carpeted aisle that led back through the crowd to the antechamber. His undyed cotton tunic hid any marks of the halberdiers' ministrations. The guards had been careful to avoid crippling damage, which perhaps was a mistake, Lysaer thought. The bastard's insufferably remote expression remained unchanged.

Except to glance at the king, Arithon spoke without altering position. "The same sages also wrote that violence is the habit of the weak, the impotent, and the fool." His final word became torn short as a guardsman kicked his ribs.

The king laughed. "Then why did you leave Rauven, *bastard?* To become impotent, weak, and foolish? Or did you blind and burn seven ships and their crews for sheer sport?"

Again Arithon said nothing. Lysaer restrained an urge to curse. Something about the prisoner's defiance rang false, as if, somehow, he sought to tune the king's emotions to some unguessed-at, deliberate purpose.

"Speak!" The king's bearded features flushed in warning. "Shall I call the healer? Perhaps a second course of drugs would improve your manners."

Arithon spread his hands in a gesture that might have suppressed impatience. But Lysaer's spurious hope that the prisoner's control might be weakened died out as Arithon dragged himself back to his feet. His upturned face sticky with blood, he confronted the king with acid apology. "I could talk the fish from the sea, your royal grace. You would hear nothing but the reflection of your own spite." Forced to lift his voice over swelling anger from the galleries, Arithon finished. "*Still, you would remain impotent, weak, and a fool.*"

The king succumbed to fury. He shouted to the guardsmen, and mailed fists smashed Arithon to the knees. More blood spattered the tiles, while Amroth's aristocracy vented its approval with cheers.

Lysaer sat frozen through the uproar. Unsettled by the turn of events, his thoughts churned like a millrace. A halberd spun. Arithon's head snapped with the impact. Black hair fanned over the toe of a guardsman's boot. The man at arms laughed and pinned it beneath his heel. The next blow fell full on the prisoner's exposed face, while onlookers howled their approval.

Sickened by the violence, Lysaer became arrested by the sight of the prisoner's outflung arm. The fine fingers were limp, *relaxed*. Memory of that same hand all splayed and stiffened with agony rose in the prince's mind. Revelation followed. The odd calm which had puzzled Lysaer throughout was nothing else but indifference. Quite likely, Rauven's training enabled Arithon to divorce his mind from his body; *certainly now he felt no pain at all.*

The conclusion followed that the halberdiers might kill him. If death was the goal Arithon had striven with such cunning to achieve, this time no man could be blamed but the king. The feud would be ended in a messy, honorless tangle of animal savagery. Shamed to find himself alone with the decency for regret, the crown prince of Amroth rose sharply to leave. Yet before he could duck through a side door, a deafening crackle of sorcery exploded over the dais steps.

A shadow appeared in the empty air. The blot darkened, then resolved into the image of a woman robed in the deep purple and gray worn by the Rauven sorcerers. With a horrible twist, Lysaer made out the fair features of his mother under the cowled hood. If Arithon chose to repeat his tactics from the sail hold in full public view of the court, his malice had passed beyond limit. Alarmed for the integrity of the king, and this time in command enough to remember that his gift of light could banish such shadows, the crown prince reversed his retreat and shoved through the press of stupefied courtiers. Yet his dash for the throne was obstructed.

Around him, the council members shook off surprise. A yammering cry erupted from the galleries. The king drove to his feet. The sceptre hurtled from his hand, passed clean through the apparition's breast, and struck tile with a ringing scream of sound. The halberdiers abandoned Arithon; with leveled weapons, they converged at a run to surround the ghostly image of the queen.

"She's only a sorcerer's sending!" From his pose of prostration on the floor, Arithon pitched his voice cleanly through the clamor. "An illusion threatens no one with harm. Neither can it be dispelled by armed force."

Lysaer was blocked by a well-meaning guard; slowly the panic subsided. Silence blanketed the chamber. The bastard rolled and pushed himself upright, while the king glared at the image of his wife, his face stamped with alarming and dangerous animosity.

Arithon reached his feet. No guard restrained him as he moved against the drag of his chains to the base of the dais. Before the spectre of the queen, he stopped and spoke a phrase in the ancient language used still on Rauven. When the woman did not respond, Arithon tried again, his tone fiercely commanding.

The image remained immobile. Taut with uncertainty, Lysaer watched as Arithon shifted his regard to the king. Wearily the Master said, "The spell's binding is keyed to another. I cannot unlock its message."

The king sat down abruptly. With an irritable word he dispatched a page to retrieve his sceptre; and the sound of the royal voice brought the apparition to life.

The queen tossed back her gray-bordered hood and spoke words that carried to the farthest recesses of the galleries. "To his grace of Amroth, I bring word from Rauven. Flesh, bone, blood, and mind, you are warned to treat my two sons as one."

The king stopped breathing. His florid features paled against the gold-stitched hangings at his back, and his ringed hands tightened into fists. He ignored the sceptre offered by the page as if the subjects who crowded his hall had suddenly ceased to exist. At length, his chest heaved and he replied. "What does Rauven threaten if I refuse?"

The queen returned the quiet, secretive smile which even now haunted her husband's dreams at night. "You should learn regret, my liege. Kill Arithon, and you murder Lysaer. Maim him, and you cripple your own heir likewise."

Chilled by apprehension, the crown prince ducked past the guard. He leaped the dais stair in a rush and knelt by his father's knee. "This sorcery might be no threat from Rauven, but a ruse designed by the bastard."

His words went unregarded. The king acknowledged no advice, but answered only his past wife in words that smoldered with hatred. "And if your accursed offspring remains unblemished?"

"Then the crown prince of Amroth will prosper also." Like a shadow excised by clean sunlight, the queen's image vanished.

The king's brows knotted into a scowl. He snatched his sceptre from the page with unwarranted force, while an ominous mutter of anger rose from the assembled courtiers. Lysaer stood stunned through the uproar, his attention arrested by the sight of Arithon s'Ffalenn with all subterfuge gone from him. Surprise and an emotion Lysaer could not place showed briefly on the prisoner's battered face. Then a halberdier seized the Master's bruised shoulder. Arithon started, rudely recalled to his circumstance.

"Turn and hear your sentence, bastard," the guard said unpleasantly.

Now frantic, Lysaer had no choice but to stand down. No adviser cared to question whether the sending was a wile of the Master's or a genuine ultimatum from Rauven; most showed deep disappointment that a vendetta which had raged through seven generations could be abandoned in a few short seconds.

The king leaned forward to speak. "Arithon s'Ffalenn, for the crime of piracy, in reprisal for seven ships and the lives of the men who crewed them, you will suffer exile through the Gate on the isle of Worldsend." The king clapped his hands, lips drawn taut with rage. "Return the bastard to confinement until escort and a ship can be arranged. Let me not set eyes on him again."

Halberdiers closed in, eclipsing Arithon's dark head. Weapons held at the ready, they hurried the prisoner away through the tense, resentful stillness of a crowd whose hungers remained unsatisfied. Lysaer stood torn with uneasiness. Reprieve of any sort had seemed inconceivable just a scant moment before. Afraid, suddenly, that events had turned precisely to the whim of the Master, the prince braced his composure and touched his father's sleeve.

"Was that wise?" His blue eyes searched the face of the king, as he begged to be heard without prejudice. Whatever passed the Worldsend Gate's luminescent portal never returned; not even the sorcerers could answer the enigma, and Rauven's power was great. "What if Arithon's exile becomes my own as well?"

The king turned venomous eyes toward his eldest, fair-haired son, who right now bore unbearable resemblance to the traitorous sorceress who had borne him. "But I thought this sending was a ploy, engineered by the cunning of s'Ffalenn?"

The prince stepped back in dismay. His warning had been heard; yet the moment was past, the sentence read. Little gain would result if he qualified what had already been ignored. In silence the prince bowed and took his leave.

The king's bitter words echoed after him. "You worry for nothing, my prince. Rauven's terms will be held to the letter. The s'Ffalenn bastard will go free without harm."

Ocean world Dascen Elur
Left unwatched for five score years
Shall shape from High Kings of Men
Untried arts in unborn hands.
These shall bring the Mistwraith's bane,
Free Athera's sun again.

—Dakar's prophecy of West Gate
Third Age 5061

Prelude

On a high, windswept terrace at Rauven, a robed man stirred from trance and opened troubled eyes.

"The king of Amroth has chosen to banish Arithon through the Worldsend Gate," the listener announced to the high mage. Neither knew his words were overheard by a second mind incomprehensibly distant. . . .

In a world of fog-bound skies, another sorcerer in maroon robes paused between dusty tiers of books. Misty, distracted eyes turned sharp and immediate as a falcon's. Sethvir of the Fellowship had kept records at Althain Tower since the Mistwraith had overturned all order and banished sunlight five centuries earlier. Events sifted past his isolation like snowflakes beyond glass; as the fancy struck him, he penned them into manuscript and catalogued them for the archives. Although the listener's phrase was one of thousands which intruded upon his thoughts hourly, the sorcerer focused his attention instantly to probe its origin.

Power great enough to shatter mountains answered Sethvir's will. Faultlessly directed, it bridged the unimaginable gulf between worlds and retrieved the vision of the starlit embrasure where a mage sat with a sword of unearthly beauty clenched between his hands. The blade bore patterns of silver inlay, and a spindle of green light blazed

in a gem set at the hilt. The mage regarded the weapon with a raw expression of grief, while the clairvoyant tried vainly to comfort him.

Sethvir recognized that blade. Memories of past events aligned
like compass needles, pairing fact with circumstance whose significance shattered a calm that was legendary. Sethvir of the Fellowship
whooped like a boy. In the time before the Mistwraith's curse, that
same weapon had been carried by an Atherian prince through the
Worldsend Gates to the west. Three other royal heirs had fled with
him, seeking sanctuary from a rebellion which threatened their lives.
Then the Mistwraith's conquest banished all sunlight; the Gates were
directionally sealed on the promise of a mad man's prophecy, and the
princes' exile became permanent. Yet if the royal heirs had been
abandoned to their fate, they had not been forgotten. At last Sethvir
beheld the first sign that the princes' betrayal had not been in vain.

The sorcerer released the image. Blue-green eyes softened with a
reverie that masked keen thought. The mage who held the sword had
also seemed no stranger; Sethvir himself had trained the man's ancestor in the foundational arts of power. Only one possible interpretation fitted such coincidence: the sorcerer witnessed the birth pangs of
the great West Gate prophecy, the one which forecast the defeat of
the Mistwraith and the return of Athera's banished sunlight.

Sethvir's exuberance drove him to run from the library. Disturbed
air raised dust from the shelves as he banged through the door and
raced up the stairwell beyond; but his thought moved faster still,
spanning a distance of leagues to deliver the news to his colleagues
in the Fellowship of Seven.

Interlude

In another place, amid the weedy tangle of a fog-shrouded field, water dripped sullenly down the stems of last summer's bracken.

"I bring news of Dascen Elur," said an intrusive, familiar voice.

Dakar the Mad Prophet started in surprise where he sat, drunk and soaked to the skin. A sigh escaped his bearded lips. Luck was a witch, to have abandoned him with the ale jug barely emptied. Dakar rolled sour, cinnamon eyes toward the Sorcerer who approached. He tried to forestall the inevitable. "The prince who returns will be s'Ilessid, or I drink only water for the next five years," he announced with slurred finality.

The Sorcerer, who was Asandir of the Fellowship of Seven, stopped still in his gray tunic and blue cloak. Wind ruffled silver hair over features that split with amusement. "You speak of the West Gate prophecy?" His tone was deceptively polite.

Dakar felt his stomach heave and silently cursed. Either he was too sober to handle fear of the reprimand he knew must come, or he was too drunk to master the urge to be sick. Asandir was seldom lenient with his apprentices. Nevertheless, Dakar managed a sloppy grin. " '*Ocean world Dascen Elur/Left unwatched for five score years . . .*' " he recited, obligingly quoting himself.

Crisply, Asandir stole the following lines. " '*Shall shape from High Kings of Men/Untried arts in unborn hands.*' " Hands capable of restoring order to a world that had known barbarous dissolution, decadence, and blighted, misty weather for half an age. Asandir smiled, tolerant still. "But the foreordained hands are unborn no longer, my prophet. The time of deliverance is at hand."

The reference took a muddled moment to sink in. When Dakar caught on, he whooped and flopped backward into a milkweed thicket. Pods exploded, winnowing a flurry of seeds. These were not fluffy white with clean health, but musted with the mildews the sunless damp endlessly fostered. "Where?" demanded Dakar, and followed immediately with: "Who? s'Ahelas, s'Ellestrion, s'Ffalenn, or better, because I've a whopping wager, s'Ilessid?"

But Asandir's lapse into levity ended. "Up with you. We leave for West Gate at once."

Dakar inhaled milkweed seeds and sneezed. "*Who?* I've a right to know. It's my prophecy," and he grunted as Asandir's boot prodded his ribs.

"Come with me and see, my sotted seer. I just heard from Sethvir. The Worldsend Gate out of Dascen Elur was breached only this morning. If your s'Ilessid *is* on his way, he currently suffers the ninety and nine discomforts of the Red Desert. Assuming he survives, that leaves us five days to reach West Gate."

Dakar moaned. "No liquor, no ladies, and a long, nasty ride with a headache." He scrambled awkwardly to his feet, a short, plump man with a clever face and seed down snagged like feathers in his stiff red beard.

Asandir appraised him with a stare that raised sweat on cheek and temple. "No s'Ilessid, and you're pledged to five years' sobriety."

"Next time remind me to swallow my tongue with my ale," murmured Dakar. But the phrase held no rancor. Behind heavy lids, his cinnamon eyes gleamed with excitement. At last the wait would end. Through West Gate would come a descendant of Athera's royal houses, and with him, wild, unknown talents. " '*These shall bring the Mistwraith's bane/Free Athera's sun again.*' " Grapes would sweeten again under a cleared sky, and the vintner's vats would no longer turn spoiled and sour. . . . Dakar chuckled and hastened toward the dripping eaves of the tavern stables.

Agelessly sure, Asandir fell into step beside him. The austere fall of his cloak and bordered tunic offered sharp contrast to the stained russet which swathed Dakar's rotund bulk.

"Prudence, my prophet," the Sorcerer rebuked. "The results of prophecies often resolve through strangely twisted circumstance." But if Asandir was yet aware that the promised talents were split between princes who were enemies with blood debts of seven generations, he said nothing.

Three Worlds

At Amroth Castle, a king celebrates the exile of his most bitterly hated enemy, but fails to notice the absence of his own heir until too late. . . .

In a dusty hollow between dunes of rust-colored sand, twisted trees shade the ivy-choked basin of a fountain from the heat of a scarlet sun. . . .

A world away from fountain and wasteland, an enchantress observes an image of a Sorcerer and a Prophet who ride in haste through fog, and droplets fly from the bracken crushed beneath galloping hooves. . . .

Who drinks this water
Shall cease to age five hundred years
Yet suffer lengthened youth with tears
Through grief, death's daughter.

—inscription, Five Centuries Fountain
Davien, Third Age 3140

III. Exile

The crown prince of Amroth awoke to a nightmare of buffeting surf. Muddled, disoriented, and unaccountably dizzy, he discovered that he lay facedown on the floorboards of an open boat. The fact distressed him; he retained no memory of boarding such a craft. Through an interval of preoccupied thought, he failed to uncover a reason for an ocean voyage of any kind.

Lysaer licked his lips, tasted the bitter tang of salt. He felt wretched. His muscles ached and shivered, and his memories seemed wrapped in fog. The bilge which sloshed beneath his shoulder stank of fish; constellations tilted crazily overhead as the boat careened shoreward on the fist of a wave.

The prince shut his teeth against nausea. Frustrated by the realization that something had gone amiss, he tried to push himself upright. A look over the thwart might at least identify his location. But movement of any kind proved surprisingly difficult; after two attempts he managed to catch hold of the gunwale. The boat lurched under him. A stranger's muscled arm bashed his fingers from the wood, and he tumbled backward into darkness. . . .

The prince roused again as the boat grounded. Gravel grated against planking, and voices called in the night. The craft slewed, caught by the drag of a breaker. Lysaer banged his head on the sharp edge of a rib. Shouts punched through the roar of the waves. Wet hands caught the boat, dragged her through the shallows and over firm sand to the tidemark. The bearded features of a fisherman eclipsed the stars. Then, callously impatient, two hands reached down and clamped the royal wrists in a grip that bruised. Limp as a netted fish, Lysaer felt himself hauled upright.

"D'ye think the Rauven mage would care if we kept the jewels on 'im?" said a coarse, male voice.

The prince made a sound in protest. His head whirled unpleasantly, and his stomach cramped, obscuring an unseen accomplice's reply. The grip on him shifted, then tightened, crushing the breath from his lungs. Lysaer blacked out once more as his captors dragged him from the boat.

His next lucid impression was an inverted view of cliffs silhouetted against the sea. Breakers and sky gleamed leaden with dawn. Slung like a sack across a back clad in oilskins, Lysaer shut his eyes. He tried desperately to think. Facts slipped his grasp like spilled beads, and his train of thought drifted; yet one fragment of memory emerged and yielded a reason for his confusion. Whatever drug his abductors had used to subdue him had not entirely worn off. Although the effects were not crippling, the prince felt inept as a newborn.

His captor slipped. A bony shoulder jarred Lysaer's stomach. Consciousness wavered like water-drowned light. Shale rattled down a weedy slope as the man recovered his footing. Then his accomplice gripped the prince, and the sky spun right side up with a sickening wrench. Hefted like baled cargo, Lysaer felt himself bundled into a cloak of rancid, oiled wool. He twisted, managed to keep his face uncovered. But clear sight afforded no advantage. High overhead rose the chipped arch of an ancient stone portal; between the span swirled a silvery film, opaque as hot oil spilled on glass. The proximity of unnatural forces raised goose flesh on Lysaer's skin. Shocked to fear and dread, the prince recognized the Worldsend Gate.

He struggled violently. Too late he grasped the need to escape. His enemies raised him with merciless force, cast him headlong into mother of pearl whose touch was ice and agony. Lysaer screamed. Then the shock of the Gate's forces ripped his mind to fragments. He plunged into fathomless dark.

The crown prince of Amroth roused to the sting of unbearable heat. Bitter dust dried the tissues of his nostrils at each breath, and strange fingers searched his person, quick and furtive as rat's feet.

Lysaer stirred. The invading hands paused, then retreated as the prince opened his eyes.

Light stabbed his pupils. He blinked, squinted, and through a spike of cruel reflection, made out the blade of his own dagger. Above, the eyes of Arithon s'Ffalenn appraised him from a face outlined in glare.

"We're better matched this time, brother." The bastard's voice was rough, as though with disuse. Face, hands, and the shoulder underneath his torn shirt showed flesh frayed with scabs, and congested still with the purpled marks of abuse.

Sharply aroused from his lethargy, Lysaer scrambled upright. "What are you waiting for? Or did you hope to see me beg before you cut my throat?"

The blade remained still in Arithon's hand. "Would you have me draw a brother's blood? That's unlucky."

The words themselves were a mockery. A wasteland of dunes extended to an empty horizon. Devoid of landmark or dwelling, red, flinty sands buckled under shimmering curtains of heat. No living scrub or cactus relieved the unrelenting fall of white sunlight. The Gate's legacy looked bleak enough to kill. Stabbed by grief, that his royal father's passion for vengeance had eclipsed any care for his firstborn, Lysaer clung wretchedly to dignity. Shaken to think that Amroth, his betrothed, every friend, and all of the royal honor that bound his pride and ambition might be forever reft from him, he drew breath in icy denial. "Brother? *I* don't spring from pirate stock."

The dagger jumped. Blistering sunlight glanced off the blade, but Arithon's tone stayed inhumanly detached. "The differences in our parentage make small difference now. Neither of us can return to Dascen Elur."

"That's a lie!" Rejecting the concept that his exile might be permanent, Lysaer gave way to hostility. "The Rauven sorcerers would never permit a favored grandson to wither in a desert. They'll reverse the Gate."

"No. Look again." Arithon jerked his head at the iron portal which arched behind. No curtain of living force shimmered there; the flaking, pitted posts framed only desert. Certainty wavered. This gate might truly be dead, sealed ages past against a forgotten threat, and beyond any power of the Rauven mages to restore. Lysaer battled shattering panic. The only living human who remained to take the blame was the s'Ffalenn bastard who crouched behind a knife in studied wariness.

"You don't convince me. Rauven spared you from execution." He paused, struck cold by another thought. "Or did you weave your shadows to shape that sending of the queen as a plot to invoke Rauven's vengeance?"

The blade hung like a mirror in the grip of dirty fingers; inflectionless, Arithon said, "The appearance of the lady and your presence here were not of my making." He shrugged to throw off wry bitterness. "Your drug and your chains left small room for personal scores."

But the baiting of the king had been too bloodlessly thorough to inspire s'Ilessid trust. "I dare not believe you."

"We're both the victims of bloodfeud," Arithon said. "What's past can't be changed. But if we set aside differences, we have a chance to escape from this wasteland."

As crown prince, Lysaer was unaccustomed to orders or bluntness; from a s'Ffalenn whose wretched misfortune might have been arranged to deprive a kingdom of its rightful heir, the prospect of further manipulation became too vicious to bear. Methods existed to disarm a man with a dagger. Sand warmed the prince's boot soles as he dug a foothold in the ground. "I don't have to accept your company."

"You will." Arithon managed a thin smile. "I hold the knife."

Lysaer sprang. Never for an instant off his guard, Arithon fended clear. He ducked the fingers which raked to twist his collar into a garrot. Lysaer changed tack, closed his fist in black hair, and delivered a well-placed kick. The Master twisted with the blow and spun the dagger. He struck the prince's wrist bone with the jeweled pommel. Numbed to the elbow by a shooting flare of pain, Lysaer lost his grip. Cat quick in his footwork, Arithon melted clear.

"I could easily kill you," said the hated s'Ffalenn voice from behind. "Next time remember that I didn't."

Lysaer whirled, consumed by a blind drive to murder. Arithon evaded his lunge with chill poise. Leary of the restraint which had undone Amroth's council, the prince at once curbed his aggression. Despite his light build, the bastard was well trained and fast; his guileful cleverness was not going to be bested tactlessly.

"Lysaer, a gate to another world exists in this desert," the Master insisted with bold authority. "Rauven's archives held a record. But neither of us will survive if we waste ourselves on quarreling."

Caught short by irony, the prince struck back with honesty. "Seven generations of unforgiven atrocities stand between us. Why should I trust you?"

Arithon glanced down. "You'll have to risk. Have you any other alternative?"

Alien sunlight blazed down on dark head and fair through a wary interval of silence. Then a sudden disturbance pelted sand against the back of Lysaer's knees. He whirled, startled, while a brown cloth sack bounced to rest scarcely an arm's reach from him. The purple wax that sealed the tie strings had been fixed with the sigil of Rauven.

"Don't touch that," Arithon said quickly.

Lysaer ignored him. If the sorcerers had sent supplies through the Gate, he intended to claim them himself. He bent and hooked up the sack's drawstring. A flash of sorcery met his touch. Staggered by blinding pain, the prince recoiled.

Enemy hands caught and steadied him. "I warned you, didn't I?" said Arithon briskly. "Those knots are warded by sorcery."

Riled by intense discomfort, the prince shoved to break free.

"Stay still!" Arithon's hold tightened. "Movement will just prolong your misery."

But dizzied, humiliated, and agonized by losses far more cutting than the burns inflicted by the ward, Lysaer rejected sympathy. He stamped his heel full force on Arithon's bare instep. A gasped curse rewarded him. The offending hands retreated.

Lysaer crouched, cradling his arm while the needling pains subsided. Envy galled him, for the arcane knowledge he had been denied as his enemy loosened the knots with impunity. The sack contained provisions. Acutely conscious of the oven-dry air against his skin, the prince counted five bundles of food and four water flasks. Last, Arithon withdrew a beautifully crafted longsword. Sunlight caught in the depths of an emerald pommel, flicking green highlights over features arrested in a moment of unguarded grief.

Resentfully, Lysaer interrupted. "Let me take my share of the rations now. Then our chances stand equal."

Arithon's expression hardened as he looked up. "Do they?" His glance drifted over his half-brother's court clothing, embroidered velvets and fine lawn cuffs sadly marred with grit and sweat. "What do you know of hardship?"

The prince straightened, furious in his own self-defense. "What right have you to rule my fate?"

"No right." Arithon tossed the inventoried supplies back into the sack and lifted his sword. "But I once survived the effects of heat and thirst on a ship's company when the water casks broke in a storm. The experience wasn't very noble."

Despising the diabolical sincerity of this latest of s'Ffalenn wiles, Lysaer showed bitterness despite his effort to match the Master's control. "I'd rather take my chances than live on an enemy's sufferance."

"No, brother." With unhurried calm Arithon slung the sack across his shoulders. He buckled on the sword which once had been his father's and said, "You'll have to trust me. Let this prove my good faith." He neatly reversed the knife and tossed it at the prince's feet.

The jeweled handle struck earth, pattering sand over gold-stitched boots.

Lysaer bent. He retrieved his weapon. Impelled by antagonism too powerful to deny, he straightened with a flick of his wrist and flung the blade back at his enemy.

Arithon dropped beneath the dagger's glittering arc. He landed rolling, shed the cumbersome sack, and was halfway back to his feet again at the moment Lysaer crashed into him. Black hair whipped under the impact of the prince's ringed fist.

Arithon retaliated with his knee and returned a breathless plea. "Desist. My word is good."

Lysaer cursed and struck again. Blood ran, spattering droplets over the sand. His enemy's sword hilt jabbed his ribs as he grappled. Harried in close quarters, he snatched, but could not clear the weapon from the sheath. Hatred burned through him like lust as he gouged s'Ffalenn flesh with his fingers. Shortly the Master of Shadow would trouble no man further, Lysaer vowed; he tightened his hold for the kill.

An explosion of movement flung him back. Knuckles cracked the prince's jaw, followed by the chop of a hand in his groin. He doubled over, gasping, as Arithon wrested clear. Lysaer clawed for a counter hold. Met by fierce resistance and a grip he could not break, he felt the tendons of his wrist twist with unbearable force. He lashed with his boot, felt the blow connect. The Master's grasp fell away.

Lysaer lunged to seize the sword. Arithon kicked loose sand, and a shower of grit stung the prince's eyes. Blinded, shocked to involuntary hesitation by dirty tactics, Lysaer felt his enemy's hand lock over both of his forearms. Then a terrific wrench threw him down. Before he could recover, a hail of blows tumbled him across the ground.

Through a dizzy haze of pain, Lysaer discovered that he lay on his back. Sweat dripped down his temples. Through a nasty, unspeakable interval, he could do nothing at all but lie back in misery and pant. He looked up at last, forced to squint against the light which jumped along the sword held poised above his heart.

Blood snaked streaks through the sand on Arithon's cheek. His expression flat with anger, he said, "Get up. Try another move like that, and I'll truss you like a pig."

"Do it now," the prince said viciously. "I hate the air you breathe."

The blade quivered. Lysaer waited, braced for death. But the sword only flickered and stilled in the air. Seconds passed, oppressive with heat and desert silence.

"Get up," the Master repeated finally. "Move now, *or by Ath, I'll drive you to your feet with sorcery.*" He stepped back. Steel rang dissonant as a fallen harp as he rammed the sword into his scabbard. "I intend to see you out of this wasteland alive. After that, you need never set eyes on me again."

Blue eyes met green with a flash of open antagonism. Then, with irritating abandon, Arithon laughed. "Proud as a prize bull. You *are* your father's son, to the last insufferable detail." The Master's mirth turned brittle. Soon afterward the sand began to prickle, then unpleasantly to burn the prince's prone body.

Accepting the risk that the sensation was born of illusion, Lysaer resisted the urge to rise. The air in his nostrils seared like a blast from a furnace, and his hair and clothing clung with sticky sweat. Wrung by the heat and the unaccustomed throes of raw pain, the prince shut his eyes. Arithon left him to retrieve the thrown dagger. He gathered the fisherman's cloak which had muffled Lysaer through his passage of the Gate, and stowed that along with the provisions. Then the Master walked back. He discovered the prince still supine on the sand and the last of his patience snapped.

Lysaer felt his mind clamped by remorseless force. Overcome by the brilliant, needle-point focus in the touch which pinned him, he lost his chance to resist. The blow which followed struck only his mind, but a scream of agony ripped from his throat.

"Get up!" Sweat plowed furrows through the dirt on Arithon's face. He attacked again without compunction. The prince knew pain that seared away reason; left nothing beyond an animal's instinct to survive, he screamed again. Peal after peal of anguish curdled the desert silence before the punishment ended. Lysaer lay curled in the sand, shaking, gasping, and angered beyond all forgiveness.

"Get up."

Balked to speechless frustration, Lysaer complied. But wedged like a knot in his heart was a vow to end the life of the sorcerer who had forced his inner will.

The half-brothers from Dascen Elur traveled east. Red as the embers of a blacksmith's forge, the sun swung overhead, heating sand to temperatures that seared exposed flesh. Arithon bound his naked feet with strips torn from his shirt and urged the prince on through hills which shimmered and swam in the still air. By midday, the dunes near at hand shattered under a wavering screen of mirage. The Master tapped his gift and wove shadow to provide shade. Lysaer expressed no gratitude. Poisoned through by distrust, he alternated between silence and insults until the desert sapped his fresh energy.

Arithon drove on without comment. The prince grew to hate beyond reason the tireless step at his heel. In time the Master's assumption that he was his father's son became only partially true; the rage which consumed Lysaer's thoughts burned patient and cold as his mother's.

The heat of day peaked and waned, and the sun dipped like a demon's lamp toward an empty horizon. Tried by the day-long trek more than dignity would admit, Lysaer hiked through a haze of exhaustion. His mouth was bitter with dust. The flinty chafe of grit in his boots made each step a separate burden. Yet Arithon permitted no rest until the desert lay darkened under a purple mantle of twilight. The prince sat at once on a wind-scoured rock and removed his boots. Blood throbbed painfully through heels scraped raw with blisters. Yet Lysaer preferred discomfort to the prospect of appealing to the mercy of his enemy. If he could not walk, the Master could damned well carry him.

"Put your hands behind your back," Arithon said sharply.

Lysaer glanced up. The Master stood with his sword unsheathed in one hand and an opened water flask in the other. His expression remained unreadable beneath clinging dust and dried blood. "You won't like the outcome if I have to repeat myself."

Distrustfully the prince complied. Steel moved with a fitful gleam in the Master's hand. Lysaer recoiled.

"Stay still!" Arithon's command jarred like a blow. "I'm not planning to kill you."

Angered enough to throttle the words in his enemy's throat, Lysaer forced himself to wait while smoke-dark steel rose and rested like a thin line of ice against his neck.

Arithon raised the flask to Lysaer's lips. "Take three swallows, no more."

The prince considered refusing. But the wet against his mouth aggravated his craving past bearing; reason argued that only the s'Ffalenn bastard would benefit from water refused out of pride. Lysaer drank. The liquid ran bitter across his tongue. Parched as he was, the sword made each swallow seem an act of animal greed. Although Arithon rationed himself equally, the prince found neither comfort nor forbearance in the fact.

Moved by the hatred in the eyes which tracked his smallest move, Arithon made his first unnecessary statement since morning. "The virtues of s'Ilessid have been justice and loyalty since time before memory. Reflect your father's strengths, Your Grace. Don't cling to his faults."

With a slice of his sword, the Master parted the twine which bound a wrapped package of food. His weapon moved again, dividing the contents into halves before his battered scabbard extinguished the dull gleam of the blade. Arithon looked askance, his face shadowed in failing light. "Show me a rational mind, Prince of Amroth. Then I'll grant you the respect due your birthright."

Lysaer hardened his heart against truce; s'Ffalenn guile had seduced s'Ilessid trust too often to admit any pardon. With nothing of royal birthright left beyond integrity, self-respect demanded he endure his plight without shaming the family honor. Lysaer accepted cheese and journey biscuit from Arithon's hand in silence, his mind bent on thoughts of revenge in the moment his enemy chose to sleep.

But the Master's intentions included no rest. The moment their meager meal was finished, he ordered the prince to his feet.

Lysaer wasted no resentment over what he could not immediately hope to change. Driven outside impulsive passion, he well understood that opportunity would happen soonest if Arithon could be lulled to relax his guard. With feigned resignation the prince reached for his boots only to find his way blocked by a fence of drawn steel.

Sword in hand, Arithon spoke. "Leave the boots. They'll make your feet worse. Blame your vanity for the loss. You should have spoken before you got blistered."

Lysaer bit back his impulse to retort and stood up. Arithon seemed edgy as a fox boxed in a wolf's den; perhaps his sorcerer's self-discipline was finally wearing thin. Sapping heat and exertion would exact cruel toll on the heels of a brutal confinement. Possibly Arithon was weak and unsure of himself, Lysaer realized. The thought roused a predator's inward smile. The roles of hunter and hunted might soon be reversed. His enemy had been foolish to keep him alive.

At nightfall, the sky above the Red Desert became a thief's hoard of diamonds strewn across black velvet; but like a beauty bewitched, such magnificence proved short-lived. The mild breeze of twilight sharpened after dusk, swelling into gusts which ripped the dry crests of the dunes. Chased sand hissed into herringbone patterns, and the alien constellations smoldered through halos of airborne dust.

Lysaer and Arithon walked half bent with their faces swathed in rags. Wind-whipped particles drove through the gaps at sleeve and collar, stinging bare flesh to rawness. Isolated by hatred and exhaustion, Lysaer endured with his mouth clamped against curses. His eyes wept gritty tears. Every hour his misery grew, until the shriek of sand and wind seemed the only sound he had ever known. Memories of court life in Amroth receded, lost and distant and insubstantial as the movements of ghosts. The sweet beauty of his lady left at South Isle seemed a pleasure invented by delirium as reality became defined and limited by the agony of each single step.

No thought remained for emotion. The enemy at Lysaer's side seemed form without meaning, a shadowy figure in windblown rags who walked half obscured by sifted drifts of sand. Whether Arithon was responsible for cause or cure of the present ordeal no longer mattered. Suffering stripped Lysaer of the capacity to care. Survival forced him to set one sore foot ahead of the other, hour after weary hour. Finally, when the ache of muscle and bone became too much to support, the prince collapsed to his knees.

Arithon stopped. He made no move to draw his sword, but stood with his shoulders hunched against the wind and waited.

The sand blew more densely at ground level. Abrasive as sharpened needles, stony particles scoured flesh until sensitized nerves rebelled in pain. Lysaer stumbled back to his feet. If his first steps were steadied by the hands of an enemy, he had no strength left to protest.

Daybreak veiled the stars in gray and the winds stilled. The dust settled gradually and the horizon spread a bleak silhouette against an orange sunrise. Arithon at last paused for rest. Oblivious to hunger and thirst, Lysaer dropped prone in the chilly purple shadow of a dune. He slept almost instantly, and did not stir until long after daylight, when mirage shimmered and danced across the trackless inferno of sand.

Silence pressed like a weight upon the breezeless air. Lysaer opened swollen eyelids and found Arithon had propped the hem of the fisherman's cloak with rocks, then enlarged the patch of shade with his inborn mastery of shadow. The fact that his makeshift shelter also protected his half-brother won him no gratitude. Though Lysaer suffered dreadful thirst, and his muscles ached as if mauled by an armorer's mallet, he had recovered equilibrium enough to hate.

The subject of his passion sat cross-legged with a naked sword propped across his knees. Hair, clothing, and skin were monochromatic with dust. Veiled beneath crusted lashes, green eyes flicked open as Lysaer moved. Arithon regarded his half-brother, uncannily alert for a man who had spent the night on his feet.

"You never slept," the prince accused. He sat up. Dry sand slithered from his hair and trickled down the damp collar of his tunic. "Do you subsist on sorcery, or plain bloody-minded mistrust?"

A faint smile cracked Arithon's lips. He caught the water flask by his elbow with scabbed fingers and offered refreshment to the prince. "Three swallows, Your Grace." Only his voice missed his customary smoothness. "Last night was the first of many to come. Accept that, and I'll answer."

Lysaer refused the challenge. The time would come when even Rauven's advantages must yield before bodily weakness. Conserving his strength for that moment, the prince accepted his ration of water. Under the watchful gaze of his enemy, he settled and slept once again.

The three days which followed passed without variation, their dwindling supplies the only tangible measure of time. The half-brothers spent nights on the move, fighting sand-laden winds which permitted no rest. Dawn found them sharing enmity beneath the stifling wool of the fisherman's cloak. The air smelled unrelentingly like baked flint, and the landscape showed no change until the fourth morning, when the hump of a dormant volcano notched the horizon to the east.

Lysaer gave the landmark scant notice. Hardship had taught him to hoard his resources. His hatred of Arithon s'Ffalenn assumed the stillness of a constrictor's coils. Walking, eating, and dreaming within a limbo of limitless patience, the prince marked the progressive signs of his enemy's fatigue.

Arithon had been thin before exile. Now thirst and privation pressed his bones sharply against blistered skin. His pulse beat visibly through the veins at neck and temple, and weariness stilled his quick hands. The abuse of sun and wind gouged creases around reddened, sunken eyes. Ragged and gaunt himself, Lysaer observed that the sorcerer's discipline which fueled Arithon's uncanny alertness was burning him out from within. His vigilance could not last forever. Yet waking time and again to the fevered intensity of his enemy's eyes, the prince became obsessed with murder. Rauven and Karthan between them had created an inhuman combination of sorcery and malice best delivered to the Fatemaster's judgment.

On the fifth day since exile, Lysaer roused to the cruel blaze of noon. The leg and one arm which lay outside the shade of the cloak stung, angry scarlet with burn. Lysaer licked split lips. For once Arithon had failed to enlarge the cloth's inadequate shelter with shadow. Paired with discomfort, the prince knew a thrill of anticipation as he withdrew his scorched limbs from the sun. A suspicious glance showed the bastard's hands lying curled and slack on the sword hilt; finally, fatally, Arithon had succumbed to exhaustion.

Lysaer rose with predatory quiet, his eyes fixed on his enemy. Arithon failed to stir. The prince stood and savored a moment of wild exultation. Nothing would prevent his satisfaction this time. With the restraint the Master himself had taught him, Lysaer bent and laid a stealthy hand on the sword. His touch went unresisted. Arithon slept, oblivious to all sensation. Neither did he waken as Lysaer snatched the weapon from his lap.

Desert silence broke before the prince's cracked laugh. "Bastard!" Steel glanced, bright as flame as he lifted the sword. Arithon did not rouse. Lysaer lashed out with his foot. Hated flesh yielded beneath the blow; the Master toppled into a graceless sprawl upon the sand. His head lolled back. Exposed like a sacrifice, the cords of his neck invited a swift, clean end.

Irony froze Lysaer's arm mid-swing. Instead of a mercy stroke, the sight of his enemy's total helplessness touched off an irrational burst of temper. Lysaer's thrust rent the fisherman's cloak from collar to hem. Sunlight stabbed down, struck the s'Ffalenn profile like a coin face. The prince smiled in quivering triumph. Almost, he had acted without the satisfaction of seeing his enemy suffer before the end.

"*Tired*, bastard?" Lysaer shoved the loose-limbed body onto its back. He shook one shoulder roughly, felt sinews exposed like taut wires by deprivation. Even after the abuses of Amroth's dungeon, Arithon had been scrupulously fair in dividing the rations. Lysaer found the reminder maddening. He switched to the flat of his sword.

Steel cracked across Arithon's chest. A thin line of red seeped through parted cloth, and the Master stirred. One hand closed in the dust. Before his enemy could rise, Lysaer kicked him in the ribs. Bone snapped audibly above a gasp of expelled breath. Arithon jerked. Driven by mindless reflex, he rolled into the iron-white glare of noon.

Lysaer followed, intent upon his victim. Arithon's eyes opened, conscious at last. His arrogant mouth stretched with agony, and sweat glistened on features at last stripped of duplicity.

The prince gloated at his brutal, overwhelming victory. "Would you sleep again, bastard?" He watched as Arithon doubled, choking and starved for breath. "Well?" Lysaer placed the sword point against his enemy's wracked throat.

Gasping like a stranded fish, Arithon squeezed his eyes shut. The steel teased a trickle of scarlet from his skin as he gathered scattered reserves and forced speech. "I had hoped for a better end between us."

Lysaer exerted pressure on the sword and watched the stain widen on Arithon's collar. "Bastard, you're going to die, but not as the martyred victim you'd have me think. Sithaer will claim you as a sorcerer who stayed awake one day too many, plotting vengeance over a bare sword."

"I had another reason." Arithon grimaced and subdued a shuddering cough. "If I failed to inspire your trust, I could at least depend upon my own. I wanted no killing."

The next spasm broke through his control. Deaf to his brother's laughter, Arithon buried his face in his hands. The seizure left him bloodied to the wrists, yet he summoned breath and spoke again. "Restrain yourself and listen. According to Rauven's records, the ancestors who founded our royal lines came to Dascen Elur through the Worldsend Gate."

"History doesn't interest me." Lysaer leaned on the sword. "Make your peace with Ath, bastard, while you still have time for prayer."

Arithon ignored the bite of steel at his throat. "Four princes entered this wasteland by another gate, one the records claim may be active still. Look east for a ruined city . . . Mearth. Beyond lies the gate. Beware of Mearth. The records mention a curse . . . overwhelmed the inhabitants. Something evil may remain . . ." Arithon's words unraveled into a bubbling cough. Blood darkened the sand beneath his cheek. His forearm pressed hard to his side, he resumed at a dogged whisper. "You've a chance at life. Don't waste it."

Though armored to resist any plea for the life under his sword, the prince prickled with sudden chills. *What if, all along, he had misjudged? What if, unlike every s'Ffalenn before him, this bastard's intentions were genuine?* Lysaer's hand hesitated on the sword while his thoughts sank and tangled in a morass of unwanted complications. One question begged outright for answer: *Why had Arithon not knifed him straightaway as he emerged, drugged and helpless, from the Gate?*

"You used sorcery against me," Lysaer accused, and started at the sound of his own voice. The aftershock of fury left him dizzied, ill, and he had not intended to speak aloud.

The Master's features crumpled with the remorse of a man pressured beyond pride. Lysaer averted his face. But Arithon's answer pursued and pierced his heart.

"Would anything else have stiffened your will enough to endure that first night of hardship? *You gave me nothing to work with but hatred.*"

The statement held brutal truth. Lysaer lightened his pressure on the sword. "Why risk yourself to spare me? I despise you beyond life."

The prince waited for answer. Smoke-dark steel shimmered in his hand, distorted like smelter's scrap through the heat waves. If another of Arithon's whims prompted the silence, he would die for his insolence. Nettled, Lysaer bent, only to find his victim unconscious. Trapped in a maze of tortuous complexity, the prince studied the sword. Let the blade fall, and s'Ffalenn wiles would bait him no further. Yet the weapon itself balked at an execution's simplicity; exquisitely balanced, the tempered edges designed to end life instead offered testimony in Arithon's behalf.

The armorers of Dascen Elur had never forged the sword's equal, though many tried. Legend claimed the blade carried by the s'Ffalenn heirs had been brought from another world. Confronted by perfection, and by an inhuman harmony of function and design, for the first time Lysaer admitted the possibility the ancestors of s'Ffalenn and s'Ilessid might have originated beyond Worldsend. Arithon might have told the truth.

He might equally have lied. Lysaer could never forget the Master's performance before Amroth's council, his own life the gambit for whatever deeper purpose he had inveigled to arrange. The same tactic might be used again; yet logic faltered, gutted by uncertainty. Torn between hatred of s'Ffalenn and distrust of his own motives, Lysaer realized that Arithon's actions would never be fathomed through guesswork. Honor did not act on ambiguity. Piqued by a flat flare of anger, he flung the sword away.

Steel flashed in a spinning arc and impaled with a thump the fisherman's cloak. Lysaer glowered down at the limp form of his half-brother. "Let the desert be your judge," he said harshly. Aroused by the blistering fall of sunlight on his head, he left to collect half of the supplies.

Yet beneath the ruined cloak, irony waited with one final blow; the sword had sliced through the last of the water flasks. Sand had swiftly absorbed the contents. Barely a damp spot remained. Lysaer struck earth with his knuckles. Horror knotted his belly, and Arithon's words returned to mock him: *"What do you know of hardship?"* And, more recently, *"You've a chance at life. Don't waste it . . . "* The sword pointed like a finger of accusation. Lysaer blocked the sight with his hands, but his mind betrayed and countered with the vision of a half-brother lying sprawled in pitiless sunlight, the marks of injustice on his throat.

Guilt drove Lysaer to his feet. Shadow mimed his steps like a drunk as he fled toward empty hills, and tears of sweat streaked his face. The sun scourged his body and his vision blurred in shimmering vistas of mirage.

"The wasteland will avenge you, bastard," said Lysaer, unaware the heat had driven him at last to delirium.

Arithon woke to the silence of empty desert. Blood pooled in his mouth, and the effort of each breath roused a tearing stab of agony in his chest. A short distance away, the heaped folds of the cloak covered the remains of the camp he had shared with his half-brother. Lysaer had gone.

Arithon closed his eyes. Relief settled over his weary, pain-wracked mind. Taxed to the edge of strength, he knew he could not walk. His sorcerer's awareness revealed one lung collapsed and drowned in fluid. But at least in his misery he no longer bore the burden of responsibility for his half-brother's life. Lysaer would survive to find the second gate; there was one small victory amid a host of failures.

The Master swallowed, felt the unpleasant tug of the scab which crusted his throat. He held no resentment at the end. Ath only knew how close he had come to butchering a kinsman's flesh with the same blade that symbolized his sworn oath of peace. Cautiously, Arithon rolled onto his stomach. Movement roused a flame of torment as broken bones sawed into flesh. His breath bubbled through clotted passages, threatened by a fresh rush of bleeding. The Master felt his consciousness waver and dim. A violent cough broke from his chest, and awareness reeled before an onslaught of fragmenting pain.

Slowly, patiently, Arithon recovered control. Before long the Wheel would turn, bringing an end to all suffering. Yet he did not intend that fate should overtake him in the open. Death would not claim him without the grace of a final struggle. Backing his resolve with a sorcerer's self-will, Arithon dragged himself across the sand toward the fisherman's cloak.

Blood ran freely from nose and mouth by the time he arrived at his goal. He reached out with blistered fingers, caught the edge of the wool, and pulled to cover his sunburned limbs. As the cloak slid aside, his eyes caught on a smoky ribbon of steel. Cloth slipped from nerveless fingers; Arithon saw his own sword cast point first through the slashed leather of the water flask.

A gasp ripped through the fluid in his chest. Angry tears dashed the sword's brilliance to fragments as he faced the ugly conclusion that Lysaer had rejected survival. *Why?* The Master rested his cheek on dusty sand. *Had guilt induced such an act?* He would probably never know.

But the result rendered futile everything he had ever done. Arithon rebelled against the finality of defeat. Tormented by memory of the lyranthe abandoned at Rauven, he could not escape the picture of fourteen silver-wound strings all tarnished and cobwebbed with disuse. His hopes had gone silent as his music. There stood the true measure of his worth, wasted now, for failure and death under an alien sun.

Arithon closed his eyes, shutting out the desert's raw light. His control slipped. Images ran wild in his mind, vivid, direct, and mercilessly accusing. The high mage appeared first. Statue straight in his hooded robe of judgment, the patriarch of Rauven held Avar's sword on the palms of his upraised hands. The blade dripped red.

"The blood is my own," Arithon replied, his voice a pleading echo in the halls of his delirium.

The high mage said nothing. His cowl framed an expression sad with reproach as he glanced downward. At his feet lay a corpse clad in the tattered blue and gold of Amroth.

Arithon cried out in anguished protest. "I didn't kill him!"

"You failed to save him." Grave and implacably damning, the vision altered. The face of the high mage flowed and reshaped into the features of Dharkaron, Ath's avenging angel, backed by a war-littered ship's deck. By his boots sprawled another corpse, this one a father, shot down by an arrow and licked in a rising rush of flame.

As the sword in the Avenger's grip darkened and lengthened into the ebony-shafted Spear of Destiny, Arithon cried out again. "Ath show me mercy! *How could I twist the deep mysteries?* Was I wrong not to fabricate wholesale murder for the sake of just one life?"

Gauntleted hands leveled the spear point at Arithon's breast—and now the surrounding ocean teemed and sparkled with Amroth's fleet of warships. These had been spared the coils of grand conjury, to be indirectly dazed blind through use of woven shadow, their rush to attack turned and tricked by warped accoustics to ram and set fire to each other until seven of their number lay destroyed.

Dharkaron pronounced in subdued sorrow, "You have been judged guilty."

"No!" Arithon struggled. But hard hands caught his shoulders and shook him. His chest exploded with insupportable agony. A whistling scream escaped his throat, blocked by a gritty palm.

"Damn you to Sithaer, *hold still!*"

Arithon opened glazed eyes and beheld the face of his s'Ilessid half-brother. Blood smeared the hand which released his lips. Shocked back to reason, the Master dragged breath into ruined lungs and whispered. "Stalemate." Pain dragged at his words. "Did Ath's grace or pity bring you back?"

"Neither." With clinical efficiency Lysaer began to work the fisherman's cloak into a sling. "There had better be a gate."

Arithon stared up into eyes of cold blue. "Leave me. I didn't ask the attentions of your conscience."

Lysaer ignored the plea. "I've found water." He pulled the sword from the ruined flask and restored it to the scabbard at Arithon's belt. "Your life is your own affair, but I refuse responsibility for your death."

Arithon cursed faintly. The prince knotted the corners of the cloak, rose, and set off, dragging his half-brother northward over the sand. Mercifully, the Master lost consciousness at once.

Shaded by twisted limbs, the well lay like a jewel within a grove of ancient trees. The first time Lysaer had stumbled across the site by accident. Anxious to return with his burden before the night winds scattered the sands and obscured his trail, he hurried, half sliding down the loose faces of the dunes, then straining to top the crests ahead. His breath came in gasps. Dry air stung the membranes of his throat. At last, aching and tired, the prince tugged the Master into the shadow of the trees, and silence.

Lysaer knew the grove was the work of a sorcerer. Untouched by desert breezes, the grass which grew between the bent knuckles of the tree roots never rustled; the foliage overhead hung waxy and still. Here quiet reigned, bound by laws which made the dunes beyond seem eerily transient by comparison. Earlier, need had stilled the prince's mistrust of enchantment. Now Arithon's condition would wait for no doubt. The well's healing properties might restore him.

At the end of his strength when he drank, Lysaer had discovered that a single swallow from the marble fountain instantly banished the fatigue, thirst, and bodily suffering engendered by five days of desert exposure. When the midday heat had subsided, and the thick quiver of mirage receded to reveal the profile of a ruined tower on the horizon, the prince beheld proof that Mearth existed. Though from the first the Master's protection had been unwanted and resented, s'Ilessid justice would not permit Lysaer to abandon him to die.

The prince knelt and turned back the cloak. A congested whisper of air established that Arithon still breathed. His skin was dry and chill to the touch, his body frighteningly still. Blood flowed in scalding drops from his nose and mouth as Lysaer propped his emaciated shoulders against the ivy-clad marble of the well.

Silver and still as polished metal, water filled the basin to the edge of a gilt-trimmed rim. Lysaer cupped his palms, slivering the surface of the pool with ripples. He lifted his hand. A droplet splashed the

Master's dusty cheek; then water streamed from the prince's fingers and trickled between parted lips.

Arithon roused instantly. His muscles tensed like bowstrings under Lysaer's arm, and his eyes opened, dark and hard as tourmaline. He gasped. Then a paroxym of trembling shook his frame. Deaf to the prince's cry of alarm, he twisted aside and laced his slender, musician's fingers over his face.

Lysaer caught his half-brother's shoulder. "Arithon!"

The Master's shielding hands fell away. He straightened, his face gone deathly pale. Without pause to acknowledge his half-brother's distress, he rolled over and stared at the well. Settled and still, the water within shone unnatural as mirror glass between the notched foliage of the ivy.

Arithon drew breath, the congestion in his lungs vanished as if he had never know injury. "There is sorcery here more powerful than the Gate."

Lysaer withdrew his touch as if burned. "It healed you, didn't it?"

The Master looked up in wry exasperation. "If that were all, I'd be grateful. But something else happened. A change more profound than surface healing."

Arithon rose. Brisk with concentration, he studied every tree in the grove, then moved on to the well in the center. The prince watched, alarmed by his thoroughness, as Arithon rustled through the ivy which clung to the rim of the basin. His search ended with a barely audible blasphemy.

Lysaer glimpsed an inscription laid bare beneath ancient tendrils of vine, but the characters were carved in the old tongue, maddeningly incomprehensible to a man with no schooling in magecraft. In a conscious effort to keep his manners, Lysaer curbed his frustration. "What does it say?"

Arithon looked up. Bemused by the irony, he said, "If these words spell truth, Daelion Fatemaster's going to get a fair headache over the records before the Wheel turns on us. We appear to have been granted a five-hundred-year lifespan by a sorcerer named Davien." The Master paused, swore in earnest, and ruefully sat on the grass. "Brother, I don't know whether to thank you for life, or curse you for the death I've been denied."

Lysaer said nothing. Taught a hard lesson in tolerance after five days in the desert, he regarded his mother's bastard without hatred and found he had little inclination to examine the fountain's gift. With Dascen Elur and his heirship and family in Amroth all lost to him, the prospect of five centuries of lengthened life stretched ahead like a joyless burden.

Transgression

Lirenda, First Enchantress to the Prime, glared wrathfully at the junior initiate who sat across the worktable, her hands clenched and idle amid bundled herbs, glass jars, and the mortar and pestle set out for the mixing of simples. In a quiet faintly broken by the distant shouts of boys who raced to capture chickens for the butcher, the senior's face slowly reddened beneath netted coils of black hair. "What misbegotten folly do you suggest now, miss?"

Elaira, whose bronze locks perpetually escaped even the stiffest of pins, stared stubbornly aside through rain-washed glass, though fog had marred the view since centuries before her birth.

Her senior ranted on. "Asandir rides the west road in haste. Every Sorcerer in the Fellowship is alerted, and you tell me, *'the second lane requires no watch duty.'* A toad has better perception."

Elaira transferred her gaze from the window to Lirenda's livid face. "Sithaer take the second-lane watch!" She pushed impatiently at the half-made charm between her hands, this one a shepherd's ward to guard young stock from the lung sickness that stunted newborn lambs. "That's not what I meant." She need not elaborate, that Asandir on the road with Dakar in tow could well indicate the resolution of the great West Gate prophecy. If sunshine was restored, the diseases she mixed talismans to prevent would be banished along with the fog that had fostered them. Yet Koriani enchantresses had no oracle but guesswork derived from images. Recklessly rebellious, Elaira restated in bluntness beyond any tact to forgive, "Why shouldn't we ask Sethvir to locate the lost Waystone? If we recovered the great crystal, the Prime Enchantress would *know* what was afoot without this tedious idiocy of nitpicking details."

Lirenda gasped and her smooth, porcelain face drained of color. Elaira restrained a heady urge to laugh. Though she found the sight of her senior's distress rare enough to be funny, she had already defied protocol by broaching the two most unmentionable subjects known to the Prime Circle.

Misplaced since the chaos of the Mistwraith's conquest, the spherical crystal known as the Waystone could encompass the powers of one hundred and eighty Koriani enchantresses and bind them into a single force. Probably Sethvir knew the gem's location, but the sisterhood by tradition regarded the Fellowship of Seven with deep and bitter resentment. Elaira despised her seniors' silly pride, which forbade a request for assistance, but never until now had she been brash enough to say so. Through the hush while the First Enchantress recovered her poise, Elaira wished her impulsive words unsaid.

"You'll learn prudence." Lirenda tilted her head with the grace of a cat stalking prey. "Since you daydream through the task of making hearth-cures, and disparage your order's means of tracking news, you will stand eighteen hours of second-lane watch, without relief. If I hear any complaint from the senior in charge, I'll take the matter before the Prime."

Lirenda whirled and left the workroom, silk skirts rustling above the hammering fall of rain against the casement. Left alone with the fusty smells of herbs and old dust, Elaira cursed in frustration. Eighteen hours, and there would have to be a storm, she thought miserably—a pity her talents did not encompass all four of the elements, or she might have performed her task in flame, warm and dry. But water minded her meager skills best. Angrily leaving the candle alight, and the jars on the table untidied, Elaira yanked her cloak from its peg, kicked open the planked outer postern, and stamped down worn steps into the chilly afternoon.

The slate of the old earl's courtyard gleamed like steel underfoot, marred across with moss-choked cracks. Low walls that once bordered flowerbeds now leaned under hedges of burdock and a rank explosion of briars burned brown by early frost. The sunless fogs clipped short the seasons, to the waste of the earth's rightful harvest. The hardened black stalks of spoiled berries rattled wizened fists in the wind. A crow stretched dark wings over the dripping lip of a fish pool, then took flight at Elaira's approach. Resigned, the enchantress perched herself in the space the bird had vacated. She gazed down into brackish, leaf-lined depths.

With trained resolution she blocked the surface sensations of rain and chill and annoyance from her mind. The details of her surroundings receded, replaced by the poised stillness of perfect inner balance. Presently a thin, pulsating whine struck across her mind; Elaira recognized the siren song of the second lane, one of twelve channels of magnetic force which arrayed Athera's world. She tuned her consciousness into harmony, then blended, ranging north pole to south, sustained by the current of the lane's narrow band.

Droplets beaded her hair and trickled icily down her collar. Elaira shivered, unaware. With the finesse of practiced control she linked the deflections in the second lane's resonance to a net between mind and water. A shadow appeared on the pool's rain-pocked surface. The form sharpened, spindled, and resolved into an image: a silver-haired Sorcerer and a fat Prophet reined lathered mounts before the lichen-splotched arch of a World Gate. Elaira dutifully recorded their presence and moved on. . . .

Curse of Mearth

Tumbled past semblance of design, the ruins of Mearth thrust walls like jagged teeth through dunes of rust-colored sand. Lysaer walked into the shadows cast by lowering sunlight and wondered what manner of folk would build a city in a wasteland. Arithon remained largely silent, except to say that heat probably posed less danger than Mearth in the hours after dark. Accordingly, the half-brothers had left the grove under the full glare of noon, and exchanged scant conversation since.

Arithon broke the silence. "Lysaer, what do you know of your gift?"

Braced for mockery, the prince glanced at his half-brother. But the Master's gaze rested uninformatively on a gap in the crumbled brick rubble which once had been Mearth's west postern. "How well can you focus light? I ask because we may be needing a weapon."

Though Lysaer preferred to leave the question unanswered, the perils ahead forced honesty. "I had none of your training. Except for the practice of healing, the king banned the elder lore from court after his marriage failed. I experimented. Eventually I learned to discharge an energy similar to a lightning bolt. The force would kill, surely."

Years of solitary practice lay behind the prince's statement. Control of his inborn gift had come only through an agony of frustration.

That Arithon should absorb the result without comment roused resentment.

Lysaer considered the man who walked at his side. Delicate as his hands appeared, they bore the calluses of a master mariner. Wherever ships sailed, Arithon could earn a place of respect. Lacking that, his quick mind and enchanter's discipline could be turned to any purpose he chose. If a new world waited beyond the Red Desert's gate, the Master would never lack employ.

Lysaer compared his own attributes. His entire upbringing had centered upon a crown he would never inherit. As exiled prince, he would be a man with a commander's skills but no following, and neither birthright nor loyalty to bind one. In peace, he might seek a servant's position as fencing tutor or guard captain; and in war, the honorless calling of mercenary. Hedged by the justice demanded by fair rule and sound statesmanship, Lysaer shrank in distaste at the thought of killing for a cause outside his beliefs. Anguished by a gnawing sense of worthlessness, the prince brooded, studied and silent.

The sun lowered and Mearth loomed nearer. Centuries of wind had chiseled the defenses left behind, until bulwark, wall, and archway lay like tumbled skeletons, half choked with sand. The citadel was not large, but the size of the fallen blocks from the gate towers suggested builders mightier than man.

Arithon crested the final rise. "According to record, Mearth's folk were gem cutters, unequaled in their craft. The fall of a sorcerer is blamed for the curse that destroyed the inhabitants. Beggar, tradesman, and lord, all perished. But Rauven's archives kept no particulars." He glanced with fleeting concern at Lysaer. "I don't know what we'll find."

Lysaer waded down the steep face of the dune. "The place seems empty enough."

Remarked only by the voice of the wind, the half-brothers reached the tumbled gap that once had framed the outer gateway. A broad avenue stretched beyond, bordered by a row of columns vaulted over by empty sky. Nothing moved. The air smelled harsh from hot stone. Their shadows flowed stilt-legged ahead of them as they entered the city; breezes sighed across a thousand deserted hearth stones.

Arithon skirted the torso of a fallen idol. "Empty, perhaps," he said finally. "But not dead. We had best move quickly."

Lacking a sorcerer's awareness, Lysaer could only wonder what inspired the precaution. He walked at his half-brother's side through a chain of cracked courtyards, past defaced statuary, and fallen porticoes. Stillness seemed to smother his ears, and the whisper of his steps between crumbled foundations became a harsh and alien intrusion.

Suddenly the Master's fingers gripped his elbow. Startled, Lysaer looked up. Broken spires thrust against a purple sky, rinsed like blood by fading light. Beyond rose the scrolled silhouette of a World Gate; a silvery web of force shimmered between its portal, unmistakable even from a distance.

"Daelion Fatemaster, you were right!" Elated, Lysaer grinned at his companion. "Surely we'll be free of the Red Desert by sundown."

Arithon failed to respond. Nettled, Lysaer tugged to free his arm. But his half-brother's grip tightened in warning. After a moment Lysaer saw what the Master had noticed ahead of him.

A blot of living darkness slipped across the sand, uncannily detached from the natural shade cast by a fallen corbel. Even as the prince watched, the thing moved, shadow-like, along the crumbling curve of a cistern; the phenomenon was partnered by no visible object.

Arithon drew a sharp breath. "The curse of Mearth. We'd better keep going." He hastened forward. The shadow changed direction and drifted abreast of him.

Chilled by apprehension, Lysaer touched his half-brother's arm. "Will the thing not answer your gift?"

"No." Arithon's attention stayed fixed on the dark patch. "At least not directly. What you see is no true shadow, but an absorption of light."

Lysaer did not question how his half-brother divined the nature of the darkness which traced their steps. His own gift could distinguish reflected light from a direct source, flame light from sunlight, and many another nuance. No doubt Rauven's training expanded Arithon's perception further.

The shadow changed course without warning. Like ink spilled on an incline, it curled across the sand and stretched greedily toward the first living men to walk Mearth's streets in five centuries.

Arithon stopped and spoke a word in the old tongue. Lysaer recognized an oath. Then the Master extended his hand and bunched slim fingers into a fist. The shadow convulsed, boiling like liquid contained in glass.

"I've pinned it." Arithon's voice grated with effort. Sweat glistened in streaks at his temples. "Lysaer, try your light. Strike quickly, and powerfully as you can manage."

The prince raised clasped hands and opened his awareness to a second, inner perception which had permeated his being since birth. He *felt* the reddened sunlight lap against his back, tireless as tidal force, and volatile as oil-soaked tinder to the spark his mind could supply. But Lysaer chose not to redirect the path of existing light. Against the shadow of Mearth, he created his own.

Power rose like current to his will. From an inner wellspring beyond his understanding, the force coursed outward, its passage marked by a thin tingle. Aware of deficiencies in his method but unsure how to correct them, Lysaer grappled the energy with studied concentration, then opened his hands. A snap answered his motion. Light arced, brilliant, blinding, and struck sand with a gusty backlash of heat. When flash-marked vision cleared, no trace of the shadow remained.

Arithon released a pent-up breath. The face he turned toward his half-brother showed open admiration. "You did well. That shadow contained a sorcerer's geas, compulsion-bound by enchantment. Contact would have forced our minds to possession by whatever pattern its creator laid upon it. Dharkaron witness, that one meant us harm. There's not much left of Mearth."

Warmed by the praise, Lysaer moved ahead with more confidence. "What makes the spell susceptible to light?"

Arithon lengthened stride at the prince's side. "Overload. The geas appears as shadow because it absorbs energy to maintain itself. But the balance which binds its existence isn't indestructible. A sharp influx of force can sometimes burn one out."

Lysaer had no chance to ask what might have resulted had his handling of his gift failed them in defense. A pool of darkness twin to the first seeped from beneath a jumbled heap of masonry. After a moment the thing was joined by a second.

Arithon aligned mastery with will and raised a barrier against them. Green eyes intent, he watched the blots of blackness weave against his ward. Even as he strengthened his defenses, another trio stole around an overturned pedestal.

"Ath's grace, the place is riddled with them." Lysaer glanced nervously to either side, fighting to hold the calm necessary to focus his gift. Arithon said nothing. Although the Gate lay no more than a stone's throw away, the distance between seemed unreachable. Pressed by necessity, the prince plumbed the source of his talent and struck.

Light cracked outward. Unexpectedly blinded by a flat sheet of radiance, Arithon cried out. Sand, barrier, and shadows roared up in a holocaust of sparks. Wind clapped the surrounding ruins like a fist as hot air speared skyward in updraft. Stunned for the span of a second, Lysaer swayed on his feet.

Hard hands caught his shoulder. *"Keep moving."* Arithon pushed him forward.

Lysaer managed a stumbling step. When his senses cleared from the explosion, his eyes beheld a vista of nightmare. Arithon's ward extended like a bubble overhead; shadows battered the border, licking and wheeling and insatiably hungry to pry through to the victims inside. The prince glanced at his half-brother. Tense, sweat-streaked features flickered as shadows crossed the afterglow of sunset. Arithon looked whitely strained. If he became pressured past his limit, Lysaer feared they might never live to reach the Gate. Second by second, the shadows thickened. At each step his half-brother's defenses became ever more taxing to maintain.

Lysaer gathered strength and lashed out. Light flared, blistering white, and seared the horde of shadows to oblivion. The prince trod over ground like heated metal. Determined to escape Mearth's sorcerous threat, he ran, narrowing the distance which separated him from the world portal. At his side, Arithon erected a fresh barrier. For still the shadows came. From cracks in stone and masonry, from chinks in the sand itself, the scraps of darkness poured forth. Forced back to a walk, the half-brothers moved within a vortex of flitting shapes.

Breath rasped in Lysaer's throat. "I think the light energy draws them."

"Without it we're finished." Stripped to bleakness by fatigue, Arithon missed stride and almost stumbled. As if his loss of balance signaled weakness, the shadows closed and battered against his barrier with inexhaustible persistence.

Lysaer caught his brother's wrist. He gathered himself, pressed forward, smashed back. Mearth shook with the blast. Stonework tumbled, glazed with slag. Desperation drove the prince to tap greater depths. Light hammered outward. Sand fused into glass. Winds raised by the backlash gusted, howled, and flung Arithon like a puppet against his half-brother's shoulder. Their next step was completed locked in mutual embrace.

"Sithaer, will they never relent?" Lysaer's cry burst from him in an agony of exhausted hope. Though the Gate lay a scant pace ahead, his eyes discerned nothing beyond a horrible, flittering darkness. Pressed on by the awful conviction that his banishment rendered him powerless, Lysaer took a reckless step and channeled the whole of his awareness through his gift.

Arithon caught his half-brother at the moment of release. "Easy, Lysaer." He tempered the wild attack with shadow, but not fast enough to deflect its vicious backlash.

Light speared skyward with a report like thunder. Sand churned in the fists of a whirlwind and scoured the surrounding landscape with a shriek of tormented energy. Lysaer's knees buckled. Arithon caught him as he fell. Barriers abandoned, he locked both arms around his half-brother and threw himself at the bright, mercurial shimmer of the Gate.

Darkness closed like a curtain between. Conscious still, Arithon felt icy chills pierce his flesh. Then the geas snared his mind. A shrill scream left his lips, clipped short as the white-hot blaze of the Gate's transfer wrenched him into oblivion.

Predators

A man traverses a misted maze of bogland; slime pools ripple into motion as he passes, and footfalls pad at his heels, yet he pays no heed, prodding the hummocks as he steps with a staff of plain gray ash. . . .

Clad in leather and fur, a band of armed men lie in ambush beside a bearded captain, while a pack train laden with silk and crystal emerges from a valley banked in fog. . . .

A black, winged beast narrows scarlet eyes and dives off a ledge into cloud, and a long, wailing whistle summons others into formation behind its scale-clad tail. . . .

IV. Mistwraith's Bane

The slivery sheen of West Gate rippled, broke, and spilled two bodies into the foggy wilds of Athera. Blond hair gleamed like lost gold through the cross-thatched fronds of wet bracken.

"S'Ilessid!" Dakar's exuberance shook raindrops from the pine boughs overhead as he swooped like an ungainly brown vulture to claim his prize.

The Sorcerer Asandir followed with more dignity but no less enthusiasm. "Careful. They might be hurt." He stopped at Dakar's side and bent an intent gaze upon the arrivals from Dascen Elur.

Dirty, thin, and marked by cruel hardship, two young men lay sprawled on the ground, unconscious. One fair-skinned profile revealed s'Ilessid descent. Though the other face was blurred by tangled hair and a dark stubble of beard, Asandir saw enough to guess the eyes, when they opened, would be green.

When neither traveler stirred with returning life, Asandir frowned in concern. He bent and cupped long, capable fingers over the nearest sunburned forehead. Misted forest and Dakar's chatter receded as he projected awareness into the mind of the man under his hands. Contact revealed immediate peril.

The Sorcerer straightened. Questions died on Dakar's lips beneath the sheared steel of his glance. "They've been touched by the shadows of Mearth. We must move them to shelter at once."

Dakar hesitated, his tongue stilled before a thorny snarl of implications. The shadows' geas bound the mind to madness; already Athera's hope of renewed sunlight might be ruined. Sharp words prodded the Mad Prophet back to awareness.

"Attend the prince, or your wager's lost." Quickly Asandir unpinned his cloak and wrapped the dark-haired man in its midnight and silver folds.

A pale, uncharacteristically sober Dakar did likewise for the s'Ilessid. Then he forced his fat body to run and fetch the horses from their tethers.

Asandir had requisitioned use of a woodcutter's cottage the day before. But since the Mistwraith's conquest of sky and sunlight, men shunned the old places of power. West Gate proved no exception; the woodcutter's dwelling lay five leagues from the site, seven hours' ride on mounts doubly laden, and night fell early over the fog-shrouded forest.

Dakar cursed the dark. Branches clawed him, wrist and knee, as his horse shouldered through trackless wilds. Rain splashed down his collar. Though chilled to the marrow, the Mad Prophet refrained from complaint, even though his cloak had been lent to another. The five-hundred-year hope of all Athera rested with the unconscious man in his arms. The s'Ilessid prince he sheltered was heir to the throne of Tysan, yet not so much as a hearth fire would welcome his arrival to the kingdom he should rule. The woodcutter was away to West End for the autumn fair; his dwelling lay vacant and dark.

Night gave way to dawn, cut by misty reefs of pine trees. Sorcerer and Prophet at last drew rein inside the gabled posts of the dooryard. The cottage inside was dry and functional, two rooms nestled beneath a steep, beamed roof. Asandir placed the refugees from the Red Desert on blankets before the hearth. When he had a fire lit and water set heating in an iron kettle over the flames, he knelt and began stripping sodden clothing from the nearest body.

The door banged. Finished with bedding the horses in the shed, Dakar entered, his arms weighted down with a dripping load of tack. "Why didn't you start with the Prince of Tysan?"

Asandir did not look up. "I chose according to need." Tattered cloth parted under his hands, revealing a chest marred across by an ugly scab. Older weals glistened by flame light, and scarred wrists showed evidence of recent and brutal captivity.

"Ath's mercy!" Bits jingled against stirrups as Dakar dumped his burden on the settle. "Why? Is he outcast, or criminal, to have been punished like that?"

"Neither." The Sorcerer's brisk tone discouraged questions.

Concerned, Dakar bent over the s'Ilessid. To his immediate relief, the prince had suffered nothing worse than desert exposure. With a feverish efficiency quite outside his usual manner, Dakar saw his charge bathed and moved to the comfort of a pallet in the next room. When he returned to the hearth, he found Asandir still preoccupied.

Dakar pitched his bulk into the nearest chair and grimaced at the twinge of stiffened muscles. Chilled, damp, and wearied through, he failed to appreciate why Asandir wasted time with a servant when the West Gate prophecy in all probability stood completed by the s'Ilessid heir in the other room. After a brief struggle, impatience triumphed over prudence; Dakar interrupted. "Is he truly worth such pains?"

The Sorcerer's glance returned warning like ice water. Apt to be maddeningly oblique, he said, "Did you notice the blade he carries?"

Dakar extended a foot and prodded the discarded heap of clothing by Asandir's elbow. Frayed cloth tumbled to expose the smoky gleam of a sword hilt. Above the graceful curve of quillon and guard, an emerald glimmered in a setting too fine to be mistaken for anything crafted by man. Dakar frowned, more puzzled than enlightened. Why would a peasant carry a blade wrought by Paravian hands?

"Why indeed, my Prophet?" Asandir said aloud.

Dakar swore in exasperation. His mind was clumsy from lack of sleep. All three Paravian races, unicorns, centaurs, and sunchildren, had vanished since the Mistwraith's foggy conquest. The sword was an impossible paradox. With a sizeable wager and his most coveted prediction as yet uncertainly resolved, the Mad Prophet succumbed to annoyance. "Dharkaron take you, I'm tired of being baited." And flinching in anticipation of well-deserved rebuke he added, "Can't you tell me straight just once in a century?"

Yet, incredibly, his outburst drew only silence. Cautiously, Dakar looked up and saw his master's head still bent over the renegade from Dascen Elur. Firelight bronzed both figures like statuary. Shown all the signs of a long wait, Dakar settled back with a sigh and stretched aching feet toward the hearth. Practicality yielded better reward than prophecy, anytime, and since Asandir had chosen quarters of reasonable comfort for a change, Dakar refused to waste time fretting. With hedonistic simplicity he nodded in his chair and slept.

When the first reedy snore escaped the Mad Prophet's lips, Asandir's forbidding manner softened. His fingers smoothed black hair from a profile all too familiar, and his smile widened with amusement. "So, our Prophet thinks you a servant, does he?"

Sadness weighted the Sorcerer's phrase, even through his humor. *How had a royal son of s'Ffalenn come by the abuse so cruelly marked into youthful flesh?* The sight was an offense. Dascen Elur must have changed drastically in the years since the Fellowship sealed the Worldsend Gate for the cause of Athera's drowned sunlight.

Asandir studied burned, peeling features and silently asked forgiveness for the past. Then he shut his eyes and focused his awareness to know the mind beneath. Swift, direct, and deft as a surgeon's cut, his probe should have pierced the surface layers of memory undetected by the will within. But against all expectation, the s'Ffalenn cried out. His body twisted against the Sorcerer's hold and his eyes opened blindly.

Asandir withdrew, startled. "Peace," he said in the old tongue. The word closed like a snare, blanketing all sensation of roused awareness. Intent as a falcon, the Sorcerer waited until eyes as green as the promise of a sword's emerald misted over and closed.

Calculation framed Asandir's thoughts. Somewhere this prince had received training in the arts of power; his mind was barriered, and his strength considerable if his defenses extended beyond waking perception. Gently the Sorcerer straightened the scarred limbs. He had no choice but to break through, and not only to heal the damage wrought by the curse of Mearth. Upon this man, and the s'Ilessid heir with him, rested the hope of an age.

Asandir steadied himself and began again. He blended shallowly with the mind beneath his hands, as water might soak dry felt. Despite his subtlety, the s'Ffalenn scion noticed. Uneasiness transmitted across the link, and the Sorcerer felt the skin under his touch roughen with gooseflesh.

"Easy." Asandir kept his contact fluid, melting away whenever the mind he explored tried to grapple his hold. He did not possess but waited, patient as stone. Eventually the man raised his own identity against intrusion of the unknown. *Arithon:* the word brought Asandir to sharp attention. Whoever had named this prince had known what they were about, for the Paravian root of meaning was "forger," not of metals, but destiny.

The Sorcerer's surprise roused opposition. Asandir dodged his charge's challenge, shaped his will as a mirror, and deflected Arithon's defense back upon itself. The Master countered. Before the Sorcerer could lose his awareness in a maze of reflected self-hood, he let up, yielded to apparent passivity. But across his wary mind lay a will whetted keen as a knife. Against him, Asandir released a word tuned entirely to compassion. *"Arithon."*

Nothing happened. Taken aback, Asandir paused. This prince could *not* be other than mortal. Logic paralleled his initial surmise. Suffering could alter a mind, Ath knew, and Arithon had known more than any man's share. With abrupt decision the Sorcerer pitched his second attempt with the force he would have accorded a near equal.

Resistance broke this time, but not as Asandir expected. The Master drove across his own barriers from within, as if recognition of his opponent's strength inspired a desperate appeal for help. Through the breach stormed images poisonously barbed with s'Ffalenn conscience, and also, *incredibly, s'Ahelas foresight, which linked cause to consequence!* Yet the revelation's enormity barely registered.

Bound into sympathy with Arithon's mind, the Sorcerer knew a quarterdeck littered with corpses. Through a sheen of tears, he watched a father's streaked fingers worry an arrow lodged between neck and heart. The labored words of the dying man were nearly lost in the din of battle. "Son, you must fire the brigantine. Let Dharkaron take me. I should never have asked you to leave Rauven."

Fire flared, crackling over the scene, but its presence seemed ice beside the cataclysmic rebuttal in the mind which guided the torch. "*Fate witness, you were right to call me!*" But Arithon's cry jarred against a canker of self-doubt. Had he avoided the constraints of Karthan's heirship, he need never have faced the anguished choice: to withhold from misuse of master conjury, and to count that scruple's cost in lives his unrestricted powers could have spared. Sparks flurried against his father's bloodied skin, extinguished without trace like Karthan's slaughtered countrymen.

"*Fire her, boy.* Before it's too late . . . let me die free."

"No!" Arithon's protest rang through a starless, unnatural night. "Ath have mercy, my hand has sealed your fate already." But rough, seaman's hands reached from behind and wrenched the torch from his grasp. Flame spattered across the curves of spanker and topsail. Canvas exploded into a blazing wall of inferno, parted by a sudden gust. Debris pinwheeled, fell, then quenched against wet decking with a hiss of steam; but the mizzen burned still, a cross of fire streaming acrid smoke.

"Move, lad," said the seaman. "Halyard's burned near through. Ye'll get crushed by the gaff."

But instead Arithon dropped to his knees beside his father. He strove in abject denial to stanch the bleeding loosed by that one chance-shot shaft. But the same hands which had snatched the torch jerked him away.

"Your father's lost, lad. Without you, Karthan's kingless." Weeping outright, the brigantine's quartermaster hurled him headlong over the rail into the sea.

There followed no respite. Guided by pitiless force, the scene began to repeat itself. Yet by then Asandir had gained control enough to recognize the pattern of Mearth's curse. Originally created to protect the Five Centuries Fountain from meddlers, Davien's geas bent the mind into endless circles around a man's most painful memories. The effect drove a victim to insanity or, if he was rarely tenacious, to amnesia, since the only possible defense was to renounce recall of all but innocuous past experience.

Asandir snapped the cycle with a delicacy born of perfectly schooled power. Released, the mind of Arithon s'Ffalenn lay open to his touch. With gentleness tempered by compassion, the Sorcerer sorted through his charge's memories. He began with earliest childhood and progressed systematically to the present. The result wrung his heart.

Arithon was a man of multiple gifts, a mage-trained spirit tailored by grief to abjure all desire for ruling power. Scarred by his severe s'Ffalenn conscience, and haunted past healing by his mother's s'Ahelas foresight, Arithon would never again risk the anguish of having to choose between the binding restraints of arcane knowledge and the responsibilities of true sovereignty. Asandir caught his breath in raw and terrible sympathy. Kingship was the one role Athera's need could not spare this prince.

Descended of royal lines older than Dascen Elur's archives, Arithon was the last living heir to the High Kingship of Rathain, a land divided in strife since the Mistwraith had drowned the sky. Although Arithon's case begged mercy, Asandir had known the separate sorrows of generations whose hopes had endured for the day their liege lord would return through West Gate. That the s'Ffalenn prince who arrived might find his crown intolerable proved tragedy beyond imagining.

Asandir dissolved rapport and wearily settled on his heels. Years and wisdom lay heavy on his heart as he studied the dark head in the firelight. Arithon's freedom must inevitably be sacrificed for the sake of the balance of an age. Direct experience warned the Sorcerer of the depths of rebuttal a second crown would engender. He also understood, too well, how mastery of shadow, coupled with an enchanter's discipline, granted Arithon potential means to reject the constraints of his birthright. Athera could ill afford the consequence if the Mistwraith that afflicted the world was ever to yield its hold on sunlight.

Asandir stifled the pity aroused by slim, musician's fingers whose promise begged for expression, even in stillness. Arithon's fetter marks no longer moved him, awakened as he now was to the inconsolable grief of spirit engendered by a sand spit called Karthan. Asandir sighed. If he could not release this prince from kingship, he might at least grant peace of mind and a chance for enlightened acceptance.

"Ath's mercy guide you, my prince," he murmured, and with the restraint of a man dealing a mercy stroke, he re-established contact with Arithon's mind. Swiftly the Sorcerer touched the links of association which made kingship incompatible with magecraft and set those memories under block. His work was thorough but temporary. The law of the Major Balance which founded his power set high cost on direct interference with mortal lives. Asandir controlled only recognition, that Arithon be spared full awareness of a fate he would find untenable until he could be offered the guidance to manage his gifts by the Fellowship of Seven.

Afternoon leaked gray light around the shutters by the time the Sorcerer finished. The fire had aged to ash-bearded coals, and Dakar at some point had abandoned his chair for a blanket spread on the floor. His snores mingled in rough counterpoint with the drip of water from the eaves.

Asandir rose without stiffness. He lifted Arithon and carried him to the next room, where an empty cot waited. Sleep would heal the exhaustion left by the geas of Mearth. But Asandir himself was not yet free to rest. Directed through the gloom by a coin-bright gleam of gold, he knelt at the side of a s'Ilessid prince whose destiny was equally foreordained.

Dakar woke to darkness. Hungry and cold, he shivered and noticed that Asandir had allowed the fire to die out. "Sorcerers!" muttered the Mad Prophet, and followed with an epithet. He rose and bruised his shins against unfamiliar furnishings until he located flint, striker, and kindling. Nursing annoyance, Dakar knelt on the empty blanket and set to work. Sparks blossomed beneath his hands, seeding a thin thread of orange against the wood.

With bearish haste the Mad Prophet moved on to the woodcutter's root cellar. He emerged laden like a farm wife with provisions, but the whistle on his lips died before any melody emerged. New firelight flickered across imperious features and the folds of a bordered tunic; Asandir stood braced against the mantel, imposing as chiseled granite.

"Well?" Dakar dumped cheese, smoked sausage, and a snarl of wrinkled vegetables onto the woodcutter's trestle table, then winced over the words uttered in bad temper only moments before. "How long have you been waiting?"

"Not long." The Sorcerer's voice revealed nothing.

Dakar disguised a shiver by rattling through the contents of a cupboard. He knew better than to expect Asandir would forgive his latest slip of tongue. With obstinate concentration the Mad Prophet selected a knife and began slicing parsnips. A second later, he yowled and pressed a cut finger to his mouth.

Asandir seemed not to notice. "Daelion's Wheel, what a tangle your prophecy has spun!"

Dakar lowered his hand, startled. No hidden veil of meaning emerged to chastise his impudence. Complex and awesomely powerful as a Sorcerer of the Fellowship was, Asandir seemed wholly preoccupied. Too lazy to bother with amazement, Dakar dived in with a question. "*Now* will you explain why a serf carries a Paravian blade?"

Asandir's brows rose in sharp surprise. "Is that all you saw? Best look again."

Hunger forgotten, Dakar abandoned the vegetables. The sword still lay on the floor beside the hearth, the glitter of its jewel like ice against the rags. Earlier, the Mad Prophet had not noticed the rune cut into the face of the emerald. Now the sight made his fat face crease into a frown. Absently blotting his bloodied thumb on his tunic, he moved closer. *No,* he thought, *impossible.* Anxious for reassurance, Dakar closed sweaty hands over chill metal and pulled.

The weapon slipped free of its scabbard with the dissonant ring of perfect temper. Flame light sparked across the silver interlace which traced the blade, but the steel itself glimmered dark as smoked glass.

Dakar's cheeks went white. "No!" Outrage, then disbelief crumbled as he read the characters engraved on the cross guard. Confronted by undeniable proof, he spun and faced Asandir. "Ath! That's Alithiel, one of the twelve swords forged at Isaer from the cinder of a fallen star."

Asandir stirred. "That should not surprise you. Arithon is Teir's'Ffalenn."

Stunned by the translation, which meant successor and heir, Dakar said, "*What!*" He watched accusingly as the Sorcerer pushed tangled bridles aside and seated himself on the settle.

"You might at least have told me. If my prophecy's disproved, I'd like to know."

"The prophecy of West Gate is valid." Asandir loosed a long breath. "*Blessed Ath, quite more than valid.*" This time Dakar managed restraint enough to stay silent.

"You predicted the Mistwraith's bane, surely enough, but only

through an aberration of every law designated by the Major Balance."
Asandir looked up, bleak as spring frost. "Our princes are half-
brothers through s'Ahelas on the distaff side. The affinity for power
Sethvir once nurtured in that line has evolved unselectively on
Dascen Elur, to the point where direct elemental mastery was
granted to unborn children, *all for a bride's dowry.*"

Dakar swallowed and found his mouth gone dry. Sworn spellbinder to Asandir, he had trained for half a century before learning
even the basic craft of illusion. Elemental mastery lay beyond him
still, for such power was limited only by the breadth of a wielder's
imagination. "Which elements?"

"Light," said Asandir, "and shadow, granted intact upon concep-
tion. That's enough to destroy the Mistwraith, but only if the half-
brothers work jointly. I'll add that our princes are opposites with a
heritage of blood feud between them."

Sensitized to the cold, deadly burden of the weapon in his lap,
Dakar shivered. "Do the princes understand their gifts?"

"One does." A log fell. Sparks flurried across an acid silence. Then
Asandir reached down and tested the sword's cruel edge with his finger. "Athera's sunlight might be perilously bought."

Suddenly stifled by the uneasy, hollow feeling that often preceded
prophecy, Dakar surged to his feet. Steel flashed, fell, struck stone
with a belling clamor which shattered the very air with discord.
Dakar turned widened eyes toward the Sorcerer, beseeching reassurance. "Have we any other choice?"

"No." Asandir lifted the sword. Emerald light spiked his knuckles
as he restored the blade to the sheath. "Man's meddling created the
Mistwraith. By the tenets of the Major Balance, mortal hands must
achieve its defeat." The Sorcerer set Alithiel aside, his bearing suddenly gentled. "The risk is not without counterbalance. The royal
lines retain their founding virtues, despite five centuries of exile on
Dascen Elur."

Dakar managed a wry grin. "*Teir's'Ffalenn!* I must have been
stone blind."

"Hasty," Asandir corrected. "Some days I fear Dharkaron's own
vengeance couldn't make you notice what's in front of you."

Arithon returned to awareness in the confines of an unfamiliar
room. Burned low in an iron bracket, a tallow candle lit a shelf jumbled with whittled animals; a badger's muzzle threw leering shadows
across walls of rudely dressed timber. Rain tapped against shingles,
and the earthy smell of a packed dirt floor carried a sickly tang of
mildew.

The Master stirred. A wool coverlet unpleasantly pricked his naked, half-healed flesh. Lysaer lay on an adjacent cot. Cleansed of dirt and dust, blond hair fell like flax across a sun-darkened cheekbone. Arithon shivered, but not from chill. He threw off his blanket and arose.

Someone had laid out clothing on a chest in one corner. Arithon fingered linen cloth and frowned; such generosity seemed at odds with the poverty evidenced by the cabin's rude furnishings. As a penniless exile, Arithon wondered what price might be demanded in exchange. The thought raised recollection of Mearth and nightmare— and the fearfully focused mastery in the hands which had restored his troubled mind. Recognition of power greater than any he had ever known stirred the hair at Arithon's nape. He dressed swiftly in breeches and shirt too large for his thin frame.

Lysaer stirred while he fussed the laces tight. The prince opened blue eyes, gasped, and rolled over. Startled by his surroundings, he drew a quick breath.

Arithon dropped his half-tied points and stopped the prince's outcry with his hands. "Speak softly," he warned in a whisper.

Past his initial shock, Lysaer ducked his half-brother's hold. "Why?"

"Whoever gave us shelter does so for more than kindness' sake." Arithon dumped the second set of clothes on his half-brother's chest.

Lysaer shot upright. He snatched with both hands as neatly folded linen toppled. "How do you know?"

Arithon shook his head. He stared unseeing at the wan flicker of the candleflame. "Our benefactor is a sorcerer more powerful than any on Dascen Elur." *One strong enough to found a World Gate, or bind added lifespan arcanely into water;* but Arithon shied from voicing the thought.

Alarmed nevertheless, Lysaer shoved out of bed, disturbing an avalanche of cloth. Arithon stopped his brother's rush with forceful hands. "Bide your time! Power on that scale never moves without purpose. We have no choice but to act carefully."

Naked unless he accepted the clothing at his feet, Lysaer battled his pride. Suspicious of sorcerers, and bereft of kingdom and inheritance, he disliked the thought he must rely on charity and a former enemy's judgment. "What do you suggest?"

Arithon considered his half-brother's dilemma and tried through his own uncertainty to ease the damage tactless handling had created. "Power without wisdom eventually destroys itself. This sorcerer is old beyond estimate. At present, I think we might trust him."

Lysaer retrieved the fallen shirt. In silence he rammed taut fists into sleeves plainer than those he had known as crown prince.

Arithon watched, mildly exasperated. "Since neither of us has suffered any harm, I advise caution. Maintain your manners at least until our host reveals a motive."

Lysaer paused, half clad. "I hear you." The glare he turned upon his half-brother all but made the s'Ffalenn flinch, so clearly did the look recall the unpleasantness of Amroth's council chamber. A moment passed, charged with tension. Then the prince swore softly and some of the anger left him. "By the Wheel, I'm tired of being shoved in beyond my depth!"

"Your judgment isn't lacking." But Arithon averted his face lest his expression betray the truth: Lysaer's ignorance was insignificant, and all of Rauven's learning a fevered dream before the presence which resonated against his awareness. Hounded to restlessness, Arithon paced to the door.

Orange light gleamed between crudely joined panels. The Master pressed his cheek to the gap and peered into the room beyond. Stacked logs cast drifts of shadow against mud-chinked walls. Herbs hung drying from the peaked beams of the ceiling, their fragrance mingled with woodsmoke. Before the hearth, on a stool of axe-hewn fir, a short man stirred the contents of a kettle; a rumpled tunic swathed his bulging gut, and his hair was a nest of elflocks.

Arithon shifted, his hands gone damp with apprehension. On the settle sat a second man, so still his presence had nearly been overlooked. Silver hair gleamed against the curve of a grind-stone wheel. A log settled in the fire; light flared, broken into angles against the man's face. Arithon glimpsed dark, jutting brows, and an expression of unbreakable patience. Though lean and stamped by time, the stranger himself defied age. Touched again by the impression of power, Arithon felt his breath catch.

"What do you see?" Lysaer leaned over his shoulder, expectant.

Unready to share his suspicions, Arithon stepped back from the door. Nothing could be gained if he allowed his mage-schooled perception to overwhelm his wits with awe. He shrugged to dispel his uneasiness. "The plump fellow will probably do the talking. *But watch the other.*"

Yet quietly as the Master raised the door latch, the bearded man noticed at once. He looked around with the alertness of a fox, and his plump hands paused on the spoon handle. "Asandir?"

The older man lifted his head. Eyes light as mirror glass turned upon the two young men in the doorway. "Be welcome. Your arrival is the blessing of Athera."

He phrased his words in Paravian, known to Dascen Elur as the old tongue. Lysaer frowned, unable to understand. But at his side, Arithon gasped as if shocked by cold. The Sorcerer's scrutiny caught him with his own awareness unshielded, and what self-possession he had left became rocked by a thundering presence of leashed force. Control failed him. Firelight and solid walls dissolved as his perception imploded, pinpointed to insignificance by the blinding presence of the infinite.

Lamely the Master struggled to speak. Lysaer's hand supported his elbow. Steadied by the touch, Arithon forced back vertigo to respond. "Lord, we thank you for shelter."

"The cottage does not belong to me," Asandir rebuked, but his expression reflected amusement as he rose from his place at the settle. "I hold no land, neither do I bear title."

Dizzied to faintness, Arithon responded the only way he could manage. "I know. I beg forgiveness." He knelt abruptly and his following line struck through a stunned and sudden silence. "I had not intended to slight you."

"Arithon!" Lysaer's exclamation was followed by the clatter of a wooden spoon upon the hearth. Unable to contain himself, the fat man capped the uproar with an astonished yell. "Dharkaron!" Then he clamped both palms to his mouth and blanched like a split almond.

Asandir gave way to laughter. "Have you all gone mad?" In a stride he reached Arithon's side and firmly raised him to his feet. "You must forgive Dakar. Your arrival has fulfilled his most important prophecy. Though he's wagered enough gold on the outcome to founder a pack mule, I've forbidden any questions until after you've had a chance to eat."

The Sorcerer paused, embarrassed by Lysaer's blank stare. He shifted language without accent. "Come, be welcome and sit. We'll have time enough for talk later. If our greeting lacks courtesy, I hope our hospitality will remedy the lapse."

Relieved not to be excluded from conversation, Lysaer relaxed and accepted the Sorcerer's invitation. He pulled out the nearest bench and seated himself at the trestle. But beside him, the Master hesitated.

Dakar swung the pot from the fire and began to ladle stew into crockery bowls. From tousled crown to boots of crumpled leather, he looked more like a village tavern keeper than a gifted seer. Yet the curiosity which simmered beneath his unkempt appearance whetted Arithon to fresh wariness. He took his place next to his half-brother with carefully hidden foreboding.

Dakar's interest suggested higher stakes than gold at risk on a wager. Unsettled by evidence that supported his initial concern, Arithon responded with firm inward denial. Karthan had taught him a bitter lesson; his magecraft and his music would not be sacrificed to the constraints of duty a second time. Though Sorcerer and Prophet held every advantage, Arithon intended to keep the initiative, if only to cover his intent with distraction. With the food yet untouched in his bowl, he caught the Sorcerer's attention and asked the first question that sprang to mind. "Who is Davien?"

Dakar gasped. He froze with the ladle poised over air, and broth dripped unnoticed on the clay brick of the hearth. Lysaer looked on, stiff with uncertainty, as tension mounted round his half-brother like a storm front.

Asandir alone showed no reaction. But his answer was sharp as a rapier at guard point. "Why do you ask?"

Arithon clenched his jaw. Luck had provided him opening; he had not guessed his query would rouse such a disturbed response. Though he had urged Lysaer to avoid confrontation, he recklessly snatched his chance to provoke. "I think you already know why I ask."

The stew pot clanged onto the boards. "Daelion's Wheel!"

Asandir silenced Dakar's outburst with a glance and turned impervious features upon Arithon. "Davien was once a Sorcerer of Athera's Fellowship of Seven, as I am. Contrary to the rest of us, he judged mortal man unfit to reign in dynastic succession. Five and a half centuries ago, Davien stirred the five kingdoms to strife, and the order of the high kings was overthrown. There has been no true peace since. By his own choice, Davien was exiled. Does that answer you?"

"Partly." Arithon strove to keep his voice level. Though he knew all pretense was wasted on Asandir, Dakar observed also, rapt as a merchant among thieves. The Master spread his hands on the table to still their shaking. Prophecies rarely centered upon individuals with small destinies. Arithon gripped that fear, voiced it outright as a weapon to unbalance his opposition. "Are Lysaer and I promised to restore the prosperity Davien destroyed?"

This time Dakar was shocked speechless. Lysaer's expression masked a statesman's dismay, and for a prolonged moment the curl of steam rising from the stew pot became the only motion in the room.

Throughout, Asandir showed no surprise. But his economy of movement as he sat forward warned of ebbing tolerance. "A Mistwraith covered all Athera soon after the fall of the high kings. Its withering blight has sickened this world, and no clear sky has shone for five hundred years." The fire's sibilant snap dominated a short pause. "A prophecy as old tells of princes from Dascen Elur who will bring means to restore sunlight to heal the land. You and your half-brother are that promise made real. *Does that answer you?"*

Arithon caught his breath. "Not directly. No."

Amazingly, it was Lysaer who slammed his fist on the table with such force that stew splattered from the bowls. "Ath's grace, man, did you learn nothing of diplomacy as heir of Karthan?"

Arithon turned upon his half-brother. "The lesson Karthan taught me—"

But the sentence died incomplete; a gap widened in the Master's mind as Asandir's block took him by surprise. Memory of Karthan's conflict dissolved into oblivion. Puzzled by quenched emotions, Arithon pursued the reason with full possession of his enchanter's reflexes.

Haziness barriered his inner mind. The Master drove deeper, only to find his self-command stolen from him. The anger which exploded in response was reft away also, numbed and wrapped against escape like an insect poisoned by a spider. Arithon lashed back. The void swallowed his struggle. Brief as the flare of a meteor, his conscious will flickered into dark.

Arithon woke, disoriented. He opened his eyes, aware that Lysaer supported his shoulders from behind.

" . . . probably an aftereffect from the geas of Mearth," Dakar was saying. Yet Arithon caught a look of calculation on the prophet's clownish features. The platitude masked an outright lie.

Lysaer looked anxiously down. "Are you all right?"

Arithon straightened with an absent nod; confusion ruled his thoughts. He recalled Mearth's geas well. But strive as he might, he found nothing, not the slightest detail of what had caused his momentary lapse in consciousness.

"You had a memory gap," said Asandir quietly.

Arithon started and glanced up. The Sorcerer stood by the fire, his expression all lines and fathomless shadows. "You need not concern yourself. The condition isn't permanent. I promise you full explanation when our Fellowship convenes at Althain Tower."

That much at least was truth. Arithon regarded the Sorcerer, braced for disappointment. "Have I any other choice?"

Asandir stirred with what might have been impatience. "Althain Tower lies two hundred and fifty leagues overland from here. I ask only that you accompany Dakar and myself on the journey. Firsthand experience will show you the ruin caused by the Mistwraith which oppresses us. Then the destiny we hope you've come to shoulder may not seem such a burden."

Arithon buried a reply too vicious for expression; the room itself had become too oppressive for him to bear. Stifled by dread of the Sorcerer's purpose, the Master rose and bolted through the door. Stout planking banged shut on his heels, wafting the scent of wet autumn earth. Lysaer stood, visibly torn.

"Go to him if you wish," said Asandir with sympathy.

Shortly a second bowl of stew cooled, abandoned on the table. When the Mad Prophet also moved to follow, the Sorcerer forbade him. "Let the princes reach acceptance on their own."

Dakar sat back against the boards, his restriction against questions forgotten. "You placed the s'Ffalenn under mind block, or I'm a grandmother," he accused in the old tongue.

Asandir's eyes hardened like cut glass. "I did so with excellent reason!"

His bleakness made the Mad Prophet start with such force that he bruised his spine against the planking. Unaware of the anguish behind his master's statement, Dakar misinterpreted, and attributed Asandir's sharpness to mistrust of Arithon's character.

The Sorcerer startled him by adding, "He didn't like it much, did he? I've seldom seen a man fight a block to unconsciousness."

But with his dearest expectations thrown into chaos by intemperate royalty, Dakar was disgruntled too much for reflection. He seized an iron poker from its peg and jabbed sourly at the fire. "They'll come to odds, half-brothers or not."

Asandir's response cut through a spitting shower of sparks. *"Is that prophecy?"*

"Maybe." Dakar laid the poker aside, propped his chin on plump knuckles, and sighed. "I'm not certain. Earlier, when I held the sword, I had a strong premonition. But I couldn't bear to see five centuries of hope destroyed on the day of fulfillment."

The Sorcerer's manner turned exasperated. "So you dropped Alithiel to distract yourself."

"Dharkaron break me for it, yes!" Dakar straightened, mulish in his own defense. "If they *are* going to fight, let me be the very last to find out!"

Overview

In a cleft overlooking a mountain pass, Grithen, fourteenth heir of a
deposed earl, huddled closer to the ledge which concealed his position from the trade route below. Wind whipped down from the snow
line, ruffling bronze hair against his cheek as he stared down the
misty defile where the caravan would cross. Though his body ached
with cold, he remained still as the stone which sheltered him.
Hedged by storm and starvation, survival in the wilds of Camris
came dear. But unlike the mayor who now ruled the earl's castle in
Erdane, Grithen had not forgotten his origins; he kept clan etiquette
despite the leggings and jerkin of laced wolf hide which differentiated
him from the courtly elegance of his ancestors.

A metallic clink and a creak of harness sounded faintly down the
trail. Grithen's knuckles tightened on his javelin. The jingle of weaponry always roused memories, few of them pleasant. As a boy,
Grithen had learned of the uprising which had swept Erdane in the
wake of the High King's fall. . . .

A tambourine had clashed in the minstrel's hands, even as mail,
swords, and bridles did now. The ballad began with the slaughter of
the earl in his bed. In clear minor tones, the singer described a castle
bailey splattered red by torchlight, as the mob claimed the lives of
council and family retainers. Atrocity had not ended there. With

dusky emotion the bard sang on, of refugees who struggled for survival in the wilds, hounded through winter storms by the head hunter's horn.

When Grithen was three, the ballad recounting the fall of the
house of Erdane had scalded his eyes with tears. At seven, the murder
of his two brothers on the stag spears of the mayor's hunting party
stamped hatred in his heart for any man born within town walls.
While most clansmen served scout duty in the passes by lot, Grithen
stayed on by choice. No comfort in the lowland camps sweetened his
mood like vengeance.

The caravan's advance guard rounded the outcrop, featureless as
ivory chess pieces in the close grip of the mist. The men at arms
marched two abreast, weapons clasped with joyless vigilance. Five
centuries past, such men might have served Grithen as retainers.
Now they rode as his prey. Product of his violent heritage, the young
scout had marked this caravan for raid.

Iron-rimmed wheels grated over stone as the carts rounded the
bend. A teamster cursed a laggard mule in coastal accents. Forgetful
of the chill, Grithen studied wares well lashed under cord; his eyes
missed no detail. Bundles wrapped in oiled canvas would contain
tempered steel, if the caravan traveled from seaside. A brand on a
cask confirmed.

Eight wagons passed beneath the ledge. Grithen smiled with predatory glee, yet made no other move. Caution meant survival. Town
officials still paid bounties, and a scout discovered by guardsmen was
unlikely to die cleanly. The caravan passed well beyond earshot before Grithen rose. Preoccupied, he withdrew from his cranny and beat
his arms and legs to restore circulation. A movement on the cliff
above startled him motionless, until he identified the source.

An elderly clansman descended from the heights. Wind tumbled
the pelt of his fox fur hat, and his weathered features were pulled into
a squint by a scar.

Grithen bent his head in deference. "Lord Tashan."

Silent through a lifetime of habit, the elder gestured at the road,
empty now except for mist. "There can be no raid." A smile touched
his lips as, quietly, he explained. "A bard rides with the baggage. He's
friend to the clan, protected by guest oath."

Chilled, stiff, and disgruntled, Grithen scowled. "But he plays for
townsmen now, and I saw tempered steel on this haul."

Tashan spat. *"Earl Grithen!* You speak like a mayor's get, born
lawless and bereft of courtesy! Next you'll be forgetting how to greet
your liege lord."

Color drained from Grithen's cheeks at the insult. Although the scout placed little faith in the prophecy which claimed the return of a s'Ilessid high king, he would defend clan honor with his life. There lay the true measure of his birthright. "As you will, Lord Tashan."

The elder nodded with curt satisfaction. But Grithen followed him from the ledge with rebellious resolve. The next townsmen to cross the pass of Orlan would be expertly plundered, and neither bards, nor elders, nor force of arms would preserve them.

Preview

With an expression abstract as a poet's, Sethvir of the Fellowship sat amid opened piles of books and penned perfect script onto parchment. Suddenly he straightened. The quill trailed forgotten from his hand, and his cuff smeared the ink of his interrupted sentence.

I send word of the Mistwraith's bane. Asandir's message bridged the leagues which separated Althain Tower from the forests in Korias near West Gate.

"Words alone?" Sethvir chuckled, rearranged the contact, and drew forth an image of the clearing where Asandir stood, heavily cloaked against the damp. Dakar waited close by along with two others of unmistakably royal descent.

The blond prince raised one arm. Light cracked from his hand, sharp-edged as lightning. As the mist overhead billowed into confusion, a black-haired companion raised darkness like a scythe and cut skyward. Fog curdled in the shadow's deadly cold. Flurried snow danced on the breeze.

The Mistwraith recoiled. Murky drifts of fog tore asunder and revealed a morning sky streaked with cirrus. Sunlight lit the upturned faces of Sorcerer, Prophet, and princes, and for an instant the drenched ferns under their feet blazed, bejeweled.

Then the Mistwraith boiled back across the gap. Light died, pinched off by miserly fingers of fog.

Sethvir released the image and absently noticed the remains of his quill buckled between his fists. "Have you mentioned anything of the heritage due s'Ffalenn and s'Ilessid?"

No. Reservation hedged Asandir's reply. Dakar had a premonition. The princes derive from a background of strife which may lead to trouble with the succession.

"Well, that tangle can't be sorted in the field." Pressured already by other troubles this further complication would not speed, Sethvir buried ink-stained knuckles in his beard. "You'll be coming to Althain, then?"

Yes. Asandir's touch turned tenuous as he prepared to break rapport. We'll travel across Camris by way of Erdane. The perils of an overland journey will give the princes a powerful understanding of the problems they must inherit before sovereignty clouds their judgment.

Sethvir drew the contact back into focus with a thought. "Then you think the heirs are worthy of kingship?"

Asandir returned unmitigated reproof. *That's a broad assumption, even for you.* Gravely serious, he added, *Difficulties have arisen that will need tender handling. But yes, if their past history can be reconciled, these princes might mend the rift between townsman and barbarian.*

Concerned lest any former rivalry imperil the suppression of Athera's Mistwraith, Sethvir absorbed the spate of fact and speculation sent by his colleague across the link. Behind eyes of soft, unfocused turquoise, his thoughts widened to embrace multiple sets of ramifications. "Mind the risks."

The words faded into distance as Asandir's contact dissolved.

Envoys

The Prime Enchantress of the Koriathain calls a messenger north to Erdane, and since late autumn promises unpleasant traveling, Lirenda suggests Elaira in hopes the journey might blunt the edge of her insolence. . . .

A raven released from Althain Tower flies southeast over the waters of Instrell Bay, and each wingbeat intensifies the geas which guides its directive. . . .

In the deeps of the night, an icy draft curls through the cottage where Asandir sits watchful and awake; and the disturbance heralds the presence of a bodiless Fellowship colleague, arrived to deliver a warning: "Since you mean to cross Tornir Peaks by road, know that Khadrim are flying and restless. The old wards that confine them have weakened. I go to repair the breach, but one pack has already escaped. . . ."

V. Ride from West End

The overland journey promised by Asandir began the following morning, but not in the manner two exiles from Dascen Elur might have anticipated. Roused from bed before daybreak and given plain tunics, hose, and boots by Asandir, Lysaer and Arithon hastened through the motions of dressing. This clothing fit better than the garments borrowed from the woodcutter; lined woolen cloaks with clasps of polished shell were suited for travel through cold and inclement weather. The half-brothers were given no explanation of where such items had been procured; in short order, they found themselves hiking in the company of their benefactors through wet and trackless wilds. In the fading cover of night, Asandir conducted them to a mist-bound, woodland glen at the edge of the forest, and baldly commanded them to wait. Then he and the Mad Prophet mounted and rode on to the town of West End, Dakar to visit the fair to purchase additional horses, and Asandir to complete an unspecified errand of his own.

Dawn brought a gray morning that dragged into tedium. Arithon settled with his back against the whorled trunk of an oak. Whether he was simply napping or engrossed in a mage's meditation, Lysaer was unwilling to ask. Left to his own devices, the prince paced and studied his surroundings. The wood was timelessly old, dense enough to discourage undergrowth, and twistedly stunted by lack of sunlight.

Gnarled, overhanging trees trailed hoary mantles of fungus. Root beds floored in dank moss rose and fell, cleft in the hollows by rock-torn gullies. Strange birds flitted through the branches, brown and white feathers contrasted by the bright red crests of the males.

Unsettled by the taints of mold and damp-rotted bark, and by the whispered drip of moisture from leaves yellow-edged with ill health, Lysaer slapped irritably as another mosquito sampled the nape of his neck. "What under Daelion's dominion keeps Dakar? Even allowing for the drag of his gut, he should have returned by now." The prince scratched the welts which already marred his fair skin, then cursed as his fingers drew blood.

Arithon roused and regarded his half-brother with studied calm. "A visit to the autumn fair would answer your question, I think."

Though the smothering density of the mists deadened the edge from the words, Lysaer glanced up, astonished. Asandir had specifically instructed them to await the Mad Prophet's return before going on to make rendezvous by the Melor River bridge when the town bells sounded carillons at noon.

Arithon said in distaste, "Would you stay and feed insects? I'm going in any case."

Suddenly uneasy, Lysaer regretted his complaint. "Surely Asandir had reasons for keeping us here."

Arithon's mouth twisted in a manner that caused his half-brother a pang of alarm. "Well I know it." A madcap grin followed. "I want to know why. Thanks to Dakar's tardy hide, we've gained a perfect excuse to find out. Will you come?"

Uncertainty forgotten, Lysaer laughed aloud. After the restraint imposed by arcane training, he found the unexpected prankster in his half-brother infectious. "Starve the mosquitoes. What will you tell the Sorcerer?"

Arithon pushed away from the tree trunk. "Asandir?" He hooked his knuckles in his sword belt. "I'll tell him the truth. Silver to bread crusts we find our prophet facedown in a gutter, besotted."

"That's a gift, not a wager." Lysaer shouldered through the thicket which bounded the edge of the woodland, his mood improved to the point where he tolerated the shower of water that rained down the neck of his tunic. "I'd rather bet how long it takes Dakar to get his fat carcass sober."

"Then we'd both eat bread crumbs," Arithon said cuttingly. "Neither of us have silver enough to wait on the streets that long." Enviably quick, he ducked the branch his brother released in his face and pressed ahead into the meadow.

Fog hung leaden and dank over the land, but an eddy of breeze unveiled a slope that fell away to a shoreline of rock and cream-flat sands. An inlet jagged inward, flanked by the jaws of a moss-grown jetty. Set hard against the sands of the seacoast, the buttressed walls of West End resembled a pile of child's blocks abandoned to the incoming tide. Looking down from the crest, the half-brothers saw little beyond buildings of ungainly gray stone, their roof lines motley with gables, turrets, and high, railed balconies. The defenses were crumbled and ancient, except for a span of recently renovated embrasures which faced the landward side.

"Ath," murmured Lysaer. "What a wretched collection of rock. If folk here are dour as their town, no wonder Dakar took to drink."

But where the exiled prince saw vistas of cheerless granite, Arithon observed with the eyes of a sailor and beheld a seaport gone into decline. Since the Mistwraith had repressed navigational arts, the great ships no longer made port. The merchants' mansions were inhabited now by fishermen, and the wharfs held a clutter of bait barrels and cod nets.

The mist lowered, reducing the town to an outline, then a memory. Lysaer shivered, his spurt of enthusiasm dampened. "Did you happen to notice where the gate lets in?"

"West. There was a road." Arithon stepped forward, pensive; as if his timing was prearranged, bells tolled below, sounding the carillon at noon. "Our prophet is late indeed. Are you coming?"

Lysaer nodded, scuffed caked mud from his heel with his instep, and strode off hastily to keep up. "Asandir's going to be vexed."

"Decidedly." Arithon's brows rose in disingenuous innocence. "But hurry, or we might miss the fun."

A cross-country trek through sheep fields and hedgerows saw the brothers to the road beneath the gates. There, instead of easier going, Lysaer received an unpleasant reminder of his reduced station. Accustomed to traveling mounted, he dodged the muck and splatter thrown up by rolling wagons with a diligence not shared by other footbound travelers. Ingrained to an enchanter's preference for remaining unobtrusive, Arithon noted with unspoken relief that the clothing given them to wear seemed unremarkably common. Amid the wayfarers bound for West End, he and his half-brother passed the guards who lounged beside the lichen-crusted gate without drawing challenge or notice.

The streets beyond were cobbled, uneven with neglect, and scattered with dank-smelling puddles. Houses pressed closely on either side, hung with dripping eaves and canting balconies, and cornices spattered with gull guano. Tarnished tin talismans whose purpose was unknown jangled in the shadows of the doorways. Confused as the avenue narrowed to a three-way convergence of alleys, Lysaer dodged a pail of refuse water tossed from a window overhead. "Cheerless place," he muttered. "You can't want to stop and admire the view here?"

Arithon left off contemplation of their surroundings and said, "Does that mean you want the task of asking directions through this maze?"

Lysaer pushed back his hood and listened as a pair of matrons strode by chattering. Their speech was gently slurred, some of the vowels flattened, the harder consonants rolled to a lazy burr. "The dialect isn't impossible. On a good night of drinking, I expect we could blend right in."

The crisper edges to his phrasing caused one of the women to turn. The expression half glimpsed beneath her shawl was startled, and her exclamation, openly rude as she caught her companion's elbow and hastened past into a courtyard. Rebuffed by the clank of a gate bar, Arithon grinned at the prince's dismay. "Try being a touch less flamboyant," he suggested.

Lysaer shut his mouth and looked offended. More practiced with ladies who fawned on him, he stepped smartly past a puddle and approached a ramshackle stall that sold sausages. Sheltered under a lean-to of sewn hide, and attended by a chubby old man with wispy hair and a strikingly pretty young daughter, the fare that smoked over a dented coal brazier seemed smelly enough to scare off customers. At Lysaer's approach, the proprietor brightened and began a singsong patter that to foreign ears sounded like nonsense.

Caught at a loss as a laden sausage fork was waved beneath his nose, the prince tore his glance from the girl and offered an engaging smile. "I'm not hungry, but in need of directions. Could your charming young daughter, or yourself, perhaps oblige?"

The man crashed his fist on the counter, upsetting a wooden bowl of broth. Hot liquid cascaded in all directions. The fork jabbed out like a striking snake, and saved only by swordsman's reflexes, Lysaer sprang back, stupefied.

"By Ath, I'll skewer ye where ye stand!" howled the sausage seller. "Ha dare ye, sly-faced drifter scum, ha dare ye stalk these streets like ye own 'em?"

The girl reached out, caught her father's pumping forearm with chapped hands, and flushed in matching rage. "Get back to the horse fair, drifter! Hurry on, before ye draw notice from the constable!"

Lysaer stiffened to deliver a civil retort, but Arithon, light as a cutpurse, interjected his person between. He caught the sausage seller's waving fork and flashed a hard glance at the girl. "No offense meant, but we happen to be lost."

The vendor tugged his utensil and lost grip on the handle. Arithon stabbed the greasy tines upright in the ramshackle counter, and despite penetrating stares from half a dozen passersby, folded arms unnaturally tan for the sunless climate and waited.

The girl softened first. "Go right, through the weavers' lane, and damn ye both for bad liars."

Lysaer drew breath for rejoinder, cut off as Arithon jostled him forcibly away in the indicated direction. Whitely angry, the prince exploded in frustration. "Ath's grace, what sort of place is this, where a man can't compliment a girl without suffering insult out of hand!"

"Must be your manners," the Master said.

"Manners!" Lysaer stopped dead and glared. "Do I act like a churl?"

"Not to me." Arithon pointedly kept on walking, and reminded by the odd, carven doorways and curious regard of strangers that he was no longer heir to any kingdom, Lysaer swallowed pride and continued.

"What did they mean by 'drifters'?" he wondered aloud as they skirted a stinking bait monger's cart and turned down a lane marked by a guild stamp painted on a shuttlecock.

Arithon did not answer. He had paused to prod what looked to be a beggar asleep and snoring in the gutter. The fellow sprawled on his back, one elbow crooked over his face. The rest of him was scattered with odd bits of garbage and potato peels, as though the leavings from the scullery had been tossed out with him as an afterthought.

Mollified enough to be observant, Lysaer did an incredulous double-take. "Dakar?"

"None else." Arithon glanced back, a wild light in his eyes. "Oh, luck of the sinful, we've been blessed."

"I fail to see why." Lysaer edged nervously closer, mostly to hide the fact that his half-brother had crouched among the refuse and was methodically searching the untidy folds of Dakar's clothing. "You'll have yourself in irons and branded for stealing."

Arithon ignored him. With recklessness that almost seemed to taunt, he thrust a hand up under the tunic hem and groped at Dakar's well-padded middle. The Mad Prophet remained comatose. After the briefest interval, the Master exclaimed on a clear note of triumph and stood, a weighty sack of coins in his fist.

"Oh, you thieving pirate." Lysaer smiled, enticed at last to collusion. "Where do we go to celebrate?"

"The horse fair, I think." Arithon tossed the silver to his companion. "Or was that someone else I heard cursing the mud on the road below the gatehouse?"

Lysaer let the comment pass. Thoughtful as he fingered the unfamiliar coinage inside the purse, he said, "This must be a well-patrolled town, or else a very honest one, if a man can lie about in a stupor and not be troubled by theft."

Arithon skirted the sagging boards of a door stoop and said, "But our prophet didn't leave anything unguarded."

Lysaer's fingers clenched over the coins, which all of a sudden felt cold. "Spells?"

"Just one." The Master showed no smugness. "From the careless way the bindings were set, Dakar must have a reputation."

"For being a mage's apprentice?" Lysaer tucked the pouch in his doublet as they passed the front of a weaver's shop. Samples of woolens and plaids were nailed in streamers to the signpost, but the door was tightly closed and customers nowhere in evidence.

"More likely for scalding the hide off the hands of any fool desperate enough to rob him." Arithon tucked his pointedly unblemished set of fingers under his cloak as if the topic under discussion was blandly ordinary.

They arrived at the end of the alley, Lysaer wondering whether he could ever feel easy with the secretive manner of mages. A glance into the square beyond the lane revealed why activity on the gateside quarter of town had seemed unnaturally subdued; West End's autumn horse fair became the centerpiece for a festival, and the stalls that normally housed the fish market were hung with banners and ribbon. Picket lines stretched between, and haltered in every conceivable space were horses of all sizes and description. Urchins in fishermen's smocks raced in play through whatever crannies remained, scolded by matrons, and encouraged by a toothless old fiddler who capered about playing notes that in West End passed for a jig. To Arithon's ear, his instrument needed tuning very badly.

Wary since the incident with the sausage seller, the half-brothers spent a moment in observation. Except for a pair of dwarf jugglers tossing balls for coins, the folk of the town seemed an ordinary mix of fishermen, craftsmen, and farm wives perched upon laden wagons. The customers who haggled to buy were not richly clothed; most were clean, and the off-duty soldiers clad in baldrics and leather brigandines seemed more inclined to share drink and talk by the wine seller's stall than to make suspicious inquiries of strangers. Still, as the brothers ventured forward into the press, Arithon kept one arm beneath his cloak, his hand in prudent contact with his sword hilt.

A confectioner's child accosted them the moment they entered the fair. Though the half-brothers had eaten nothing since dawn, neither wished to tarry for sugared figs, even ones offered by a girl with smiling charm. Lysaer dodged past with a shake of his head, and in wordless accord Arithon followed past a butcher's stall and an ox wagon haphazardly piled with potted herbs. Beyond these sat a crone surrounded by crates of bottled preserves. Tied to a post by her chair stood a glossy string of horses.

Lysaer and Arithon poised to one side to examine the stock. Nearby, ankle deep in straw that smelled suspiciously like yesterday's herring catch, and surrounded by a weaving flock of gulls, a farmer in a sheepskin vest haggled loudly with a hawk-nosed fellow who wore threadbare linen and a brilliantly dyed leather tunic.

"Seventy ra'el?" The farmer scratched his ear, spat, and argued vigorously. "Fer just a hack? That's greedy overpriced, ye crafty drifter. If our mayor hears, mark my guess, he's sure to bar yer clan from trading next year."

The hag amid the jam boxes raised her chin and mumbled an obscenity, while the colorfully dressed horse dealer ran lean hands over the crest of the bay in question. "The price stands," he finished in a clear, incisive speech only lightly touched by the local burr. "Seventy royals, or the mare stays where she is. Just a hack she might be, but she's young and soundly bred."

"Ath, he's hardly got an accent," Lysaer murmured in Arithon's ear.

The Master nodded fractionally. "Explains a great deal about the way we were received." All the while his eyes roved across the animals offered for sale. His half-brother watched, amused, as his interest caught and lingered over a broad-chested, blaze-faced gelding tied slightly apart from the rest.

"I like that chestnut, too," Lysaer admitted. "Nice legs, and he's built for endurance."

The old woman twisted her head. She stared at the half-brothers, intent as a hawk and unnoticed as the farmer departed, cursing. Before another bidder could come forward, Arithon stepped into the gap and said, "What price do you ask for the chestnut?"

The horse trader half spun, his features wide with astonishment. His glance encompassed the bystanders, confused, and only after a second sweep settled on Arithon, who, except for Lysaer, now stood isolated as the farmers on either side backed away. The drifter answered back in offense. "Daelion's hells! What clan are you from, brother, and is this some jest, you here bidding like a townsman?"

Arithon ignored both questions and instead repeated his query. "How much?"

"He isn't for sale," snapped the trader. "You blind to the tassels on his halter or what?"

That moment the crone began to shout shrilly.

Unnerved as much as his brother had been at finding himself the target of unwarranted hostility, Arithon cast about for a way to ease the drifter's temper.

Before he could speak, a smooth voice interjected. "The tassels of ownership are obvious." Townsmen on either side heard, and started, and hastily disappeared about their business; and the grandmother by the jam bottles stopped yelling as the Sorcerer, Asandir, touched her shawl and strode briskly in from behind. To the man he added, "But the finer horses in the fair are sold already, and my companions need reliable mounts. Will you consider an offer of three hundred royals?"

The drifter met this development with raised eyebrows and a startled intake of breath. He took in the weathered features, steel gray eyes, and implacable demeanor of the Sorcerer with evident recognition. "To you I'll sell, but not for bribe price. Two hundred royals is fair."

Asandir turned a glance quite stripped of tolerance upon the princes who had disobeyed his command. "Go," he said. "Untie the chestnut, and for your life's sake, keep your mouths shut while I settle this." To the drifter the Sorcerer added, "The horse is your personal mount. Take the extra hundred to ease the inconvenience while your next foal grows to maturity."

The drifter looked uncomfortable, as if he might argue the Sorcerer's generosity as charity. But the grandmother forestalled him with a curt jerk of her head; Asandir produced the coin swiftly. Before the culprits who had precipitated the transaction could attract any closer scrutiny, he cut the tassels of ownership from the gelding's halter and led his purchase away. Lysaer and Arithon were swept along without ceremony.

The Sorcerer hustled them back across the square. Fishermen turned heads to glare as chickens flapped squawking from under his fast-striding boots; they passed a butcher's stall, crammed with bawling livestock and strangely silent customers. The chestnut shied and jibbed against the rein, until a word laced with spell-craft quieted it. Dreading the moment when such knife-edged tones might be directed his way in rebuke, Lysaer maintained silence.

Arithon perversely rejected tact. "You found Dakar?"

The Sorcerer flicked a look of focused displeasure over one blue-cloaked shoulder. "Yes. He's been dealt with already." Asandir changed course without hesitation down the darker of two branching alleys. Over the ring of the chestnut's shod hooves, he added, "You've already left an impression with the drifters. Don't cause more talk in West End, am I clear?"

He stopped very suddenly and tossed the chestnut's leading rein to Lysaer. "Stay here, speak to no one, and simply wait. I'll return with another horse and a decent saddle. Should you feel the urge to wander again, let me add that in this place, people associated with sorcerers very often wind up roasting in chains on a pile of oiled faggots."

The Sorcerer spun and left them. Watching his departure with wide and unmollified eyes, Arithon mused, "I wonder what fate befell Dakar?"

That subject was one that his half-brother preferred not to contemplate. Suddenly inimical to the Master's provocations, Lysaer turned his back and made his acquaintance with the chestnut.

Asandir returned after the briefest delay, leading a metal-colored dun with an odd splash of white on her neck. His own mount trailed behind, a black with one ghost eye that disconcertingly appeared to stare a man through to the soul. Piled across its withers was an extra saddle allotted for Lysaer's gelding.

"You brought no bridle," the former prince observed as he undertook a groom's work with sheep fleece pads and girth.

Asandir gave the oversight short shrift. "The drifters of Pasyvier are the best horse trainers in Athera, and that gelding was a clan lord's personal mount. It won't require a bit. If you're careless enough to fall, that animal would likely sidestep to stay underneath you." His say finished, the Sorcerer tossed the dun's reins to Arithon. "She's not a cull, only green. Don't trust her so much you fall asleep."

The company of three departed the instant the half-brothers gained the saddle. Asandir led, and did not add that his choice in horses had been guided by intent; he wanted Arithon kept preoccupied. From an urchin by the gates, the Sorcerer collected a pony laden with blankets and leather-wrapped packs of supplies. Attached to its load by a rope length was the paint mare belonging to Dakar. The Mad Prophet himself lay trussed and draped across her saddle bow. Someone had dumped a bucket of water over his tousled head, and the damp seeped rings into clothing that still reeked faintly of garbage. The wetting had done as little for the snores. Dakar rasped on unbated as Asandir drove the cavalcade at a trot through West End's east-facing gate.

Once the farm lands surrounding the town fell behind, the road proved sparsely traveled. The surface had once been paved with slate, built firm and dry on a causeway that sliced a straight course through the boglands that flanked the coast. Centuries of passing wagons had cracked the thick stone in places; the crisscrossed muck in the wheel ruts grew rooster tails of weed. The mists pressed down on a landscape relentlessly flat, and silver with the sheen of tidal waterways edged by blighted stands of reed. The air hung sour with the smell of decomposed vegetation. The chink of bits and stirrups, and the isolated clink as horseshoes scraped rock offered lonely counterpoint to the whirring wingbeats of waterfowl explosively startled into flight.

Reassured that the Sorcerer had yet to denounce anyone for the illicit visit to the West End market, Lysaer spurred his horse abreast and dared a question. "Who are the drifters, and why do the people dislike them?"

Asandir glanced significantly at Arithon, who fought with every shred of his attention to keep his mare from crabbing sideways. "Since the rebellion which threw down the High Kings, the drifters have been nomads. They breed horses in the grasslands of Pasyvier, and mostly keep to themselves. The townsmen are wary of them because their ancestors once ruled in West End."

The party crossed the moss-crusted spans of the Melor River bridge, while the mare bounced and clattered and shied to a barrage of playful snorts. Arithon maligned her as the drag of the reins tore his scabs, but his curses betrayed an admiration born of sympathy for her wayward spirit. Masked by the antics of the dun, Asandir added, "There are deep antipathies remaining from times past, and much prejudice. Your accents, as you noticed, allied you with unpopular factions. My purpose in asking you to wait in the wood was to spare you from dangerous misunderstanding."

Lysaer drew breath to inquire further, but the Sorcerer forestalled him. "Teir's'Ilessid," he said, using an old-language term that the prince lacked the knowledge to translate. "There are better times for questions, and I promise, you shall be given all the answers you need. Right now I'm anxious to set distance between the town and ourselves before dark. The drifters are not fools, and the folk who saw you will talk. The result might brew up a curiosity far better left to bide until later."

Lysaer considered this, his hands twisting and twisting in the chestnut's silken mane. Less than sure of himself since the loss of his heirship, he regarded the dismal, alien landscape and tried not to smile as his half-brother battled the flighty, scatter-minded dun through one disobedient rumpus after another.

The incessant clatter of her footfalls at first overshadowed Dakar's moans of returned consciousness. These soon progressed to obscenities, also ignored, until a full-throated yowl of outrage brought the company to a precipitous halt.

A look back showed that the Mad Prophet's distress was not solely caused by his hangover.

Tied still to the paint's saddle bow, the Mad Prophet kicked in a red-faced, fish-flop struggle that stemmed from the fact that his cloak had somehow coiled itself around his neck and more peculiarly appeared to be strangling him.

"Iyats," Asandir said shortly, then qualified as his mouth turned upward in unmistakable amusement. "What folk here most aptly name fiends."

Dakar swiveled his head and eyes, and with the aggrieved determination of a bound man whose face dangled upside-down, gagged out, "You planned this." Possessed by an energy sprite native to Athera, the cloak slithered inexorably tighter around his throat. The fullness of the Mad Prophet's cheeks deepened from red to purple. "Tortures of Sithaer, are you just going to watch while I choke?"

Asandir urged his black forward and drew rein with ineffable calmness. "I've warned you time and again to restrain your emotions when dealing with iyats. Your distress just goads them on to greater mischief."

Dakar spluttered and gasped through a tightening twist of fabric. "That's fine advice. You aren't the one under attack."

As if his sarcasm sparked suggestion, the cloak very suddenly went limp. The whoop as Dakar sucked in a starved breath quite wickedly transformed into laughter as a puddle peeled itself away from the ground and floated upward, precariously suspended in mid-air.

While Lysaer and Arithon stared in stupefied astonishment, Asandir calmly regarded the churning, muddy liquid that threatened to douse his silver head. Without any change in expression he raised his hand, closed his fingers, then lowered his fist to his knee. As if dragged by invisible force, the iyat-borne puddle sloshed after—until the Sorcerer snapped his fist open, and the mass lost cohesion and exploded in a spatter of grit-laden droplets.

Well drenched by the run-off, Dakar uttered a bitten obscenity. "That's unfair," he continued on a strained note that stemmed from the fact he was overweight, and sprawled face downward over a saddle that for some while had been galling his belly. "You've a reputation for quenching fiends, and they know it. They don't go for you in earnest."

Asandir raised one eyebrow. "You make a fine mark for them. You won't leash your temper. And they know it."

Dakar squirmed and failed to settle his bulk into a more accommodating position. "Are you going to cut me free?"

"Are you sober enough to stay mounted?" The Sorcerer fixed impervious, silver-gray eyes on his errant apprentice and shook his head. He said gently, "I think it would be appropriate if you spent the next hour contemplating the result of your untimely little binge. I found our two guests at large in the horse fair at West End."

Dakar's eyes widened like a hurt spaniel's. "Damn, but you're heartless. Can I be blamed because a pair of newcomers can't follow direct instructions?"

Asandir gathered the black's reins. Silent, he slapped the paint's haunches and passed ahead without turning as the animal lurched into a trot that threatened to explode Dakar's skull with the aftereffects of strong drink. Deaf to the moans from his apprentice, Asandir answered Lysaer's avid question, and assured that the iyat would not be returning to plague them.

"They feed upon natural energies—fire, falling water, temperature change—and that one we left behind is presently quite drained. Unless it finds a thunderstorm, it won't recover enough charge to cause trouble for several weeks to come."

The riders continued westward through a damp, gray afternoon. Although they stopped once for a meal of bread and sausage from the supply pack, Dakar was given no reprieve until dusk, when the horses were unsaddled and the small hide tents were unfurled from their lashings to make camp. By then exhausted by hours of pleas and imprecations, he settled in a sulk by the camp fire and immediately fell asleep. Tired themselves, and worn sore by unaccustomed hours in the saddle, Arithon and Lysaer retired after supper. They crawled into blankets and listened to the calls of an unfamiliar night bird echo across the marsh.

Despite the long and wearing day, Lysaer lay wide-eyed and wakeful in the dark. Clued by the stillness that Arithon was not sleeping, but seated on his bedding with his back to the tent pole, the prince rolled onto his stomach. "You think the Sorcerer has something more in mind for us than conquest of the Mistwraith, Desh-thiere."

Arithon turned his head, his expression unseen in the gloom. "I'm sure of it."

Lysaer settled his chin in his fists. The unaccustomed prick of beard stubble made him irritable; tiredly, resignedly, he put aside wishing for his valet and considered the problems of the moment. "You sound quite convinced that the fate in question won't be pleasant."

Silence. Arithon shifted position; perhaps he shrugged.

Reflexively touched by a spasm of mistrust, Lysaer extended a hand and called on his gift. A star of light gleamed from his palm and brightened the confines of the tent.

Caught by surprise, a stripped expression of longing on his face, Arithon spun away.

Lysaer pushed upright. "Ath, what are you thinking about? You've noticed the sickly taint the fog has left on this land. In any honor and decency, could you turn away from these people's need?"

"No." Arithon returned, much too softly. "That's precisely what Asandir is counting on."

Struck by a haunted confusion not entirely concealed behind Arithon's words, Lysaer forgot his anger. There must be friends, even family, that the Shadow Master missed beyond the World Gate. Contritely the prince asked, "If you could go anywhere, be anything, do anything you wanted, what would you choose?"

"Not to go back to Karthan," Arithon said obliquely, and discouraged from personal inquiry, Lysaer let the light die.

"You know," the prince said to the darkness, "Dakar thinks you're some sort of criminal, twisted by illicit magic, and sworn to corruption of the innocent."

Arithon laughed, softly as a whisper in the night. "You might fare better if you believed him."

"Why? Wasn't one trial on charges of piracy enough for you?" That moment Lysaer wished his small fleck of light still burned. "You're not thinking of defying Asandir, are you?"

Silence and stillness answered. Lysaer swore. Too weary to unravel the contrary conscience that gave rise to Arithon's moodiness, his half-brother settled back in his blankets and tried not to think of home, or the beloved lady at South Isle who now must seek another suitor. Instead the former prince concentrated on the need in this world, and the Mistwraith his new fate bound him to destroy. Eventually he fell asleep.

The following days passed alike, except that Dakar rode astride instead of roped like a bundled roll of cloth goods. The dun mare steadied somewhat as the leagues passed; her bucks and crab steps and shies arose more in spirited play than from any reaction to fear. But if Arithon had earned a reprieve from her taxing demands on his horsemanship, the reserve that had cloaked him since West End did not thaw to the point of speech. Dakar's scowling distrust toward his presence did not ease, which left the former Prince of Amroth the recipient of unending loquacious questions. Hoarse both from laughter and too much talk, Lysaer regarded his more taciturn half-brother, and wondered which of them suffered more: Arithon in his solitude, or himself, subjected to the demands of Dakar's incessant curiosity.

The road crooked inland and the marsh pools dried up, replaced by meadows of withered wildflowers. Black birds with white-tipped feathers flashed into flight at their passing, and partridge called in the thickets. When the party crossed a deep river ford and bypassed the fork that led to the port city of Karfael, Dakar took the opportunity to bemoan the lack of beer as they paused to refill their emptied water jars.

Asandir dried dripping hands and killed the complaint with mention that a merchant caravan fared ahead.

"Which way is it bound?" Dakar bounded upright to a gurgle and splash of jounced flasks.

"Toward Camris, as we are," Asandir said. "We shall overtake them."

The Mad Prophet cheerfully forgot to curse his dampened clothing. But although he badgered through the afternoon and half of the night, the Sorcerer refused to elaborate.

On the fourth day the roadway swung due east and entered the forest of Westwood. Here the trees rose ancient with years, once majestic as patriarchs, but bearded and bent now under mantling snags of pallid moss. Their crowns were smothered in mist, and their boles grown gnarled with vine until five men with joined hands could not have spanned their circumference. Daylight was reduced to a thick, murky twilight alive with the whispered drip of water. Oppressed by a sense of decay on the land and the unremitting gray of misty weather, no one was inclined toward talk. Even Dakar's chatter subsided to silence.

"This wood was a merry place once, when sunlight still shone," Asandir mused, as if his mage's perception showed him something that touched off maudlin thoughts.

They passed standing stones with carvings worn away until only beaded whorls of lichens held their patterns. Aware that Arithon studied these with intent curiosity, Asandir volunteered an explanation. "In times past, creatures who were not human tended these forests. Attuned to the deepest pulses that bind land and soil to Ath's harmony, they left stones such as these to show which ground and which trees could be taken for man's use, and which must stay whole to renew the mysteries. Once the protection of sacred ground was the province of the high king's justice. Pastures and fields were cut only where the earth could gracefully support them. But now such knowledge is scarce. The name for the guardians who dwelled here meant giants in the old tongue." But the huge, gentle beings Asandir described were more clearly a breed of centaurs.

When Lysaer inquired what had become of them, the Sorcerer sorrowfully shook his head. "The last of the Ilitharis Paravians passed from the land when Desh-thiere swallowed sunlight. Not even Sethvir at Althain Tower knows where they have gone. Athera is the poorer for their loss. The last hope of redeeming their fate lies in the Mistwraith's defeat."

Dakar glanced aside and caught Lysaer's attention with a wink. "Small wonder the old races left these parts. No taverns, no beer, and wet trees make lousy company."

Fed up with rain, and nights of smoking fires, and bedding down on dampened ground, the former prince could almost sympathize. He joined Dakar in questioning the existence of Asandir's caravan, and was almost caught off guard when they overtook a fugitive by the wayside.

The man wore brilliant scarlet, which spoiled his attempt to escape notice by the approaching riders. The hem of his garment was sewn with tassels. One of these caught on a briar and flagged the attention of Asandir, who reined up short in the roadway and called immediate reassurance. "We're fellow travelers, not bandits. Why not share our fire if you're alone?"

"On that, I had no choice" came the chagrined reply. The man spoke rapidly in dialect, his accents less burred than the prevailing variety in West End. Rangy, tall, and carrying what looked like a grossly misshapen pack, he stepped out from behind the moss-shagged bole of an oak. "A supposedly honest caravan master already relieved me of my mount, so luck has forsaken me anyway." He approached at a pained gait that revealed that his boots were causing blisters, and the hand left white-knuckled on his sword hilt betrayed distrust behind his amiable manner.

"You may share the road also, if you can keep up," Asandir offered back.

Dakar assessed the oddly bulky pack for the possible presence of spirits, and was first to announce the stranger's trade. "You're a minstrel," he burst out in surprise. "By the Wheel, man, why are you starving in the wilderness when you could be singing comfortably in a tavern?"

The man did not reply. Close enough now to make out details and faces, he was engrossed in staring at Asandir. "I know you," he murmured, half awed. He pushed back his hood, and a shock of wavy hair spilled over his collar. The revealed face showed a mapwork of laugh lines and a stubble of half-grown beard. The hazel eyes were merry despite the swollen purple weals that marred him, forehead and cheek.

Asandir's sharpness cut the forest silence like a whiplash. "Ath in his mercy, we are come on ill times. Who in this land has dared to abuse a free singer?"

The minstrel touched his battered skin, embarrassed. "I sang the wrong ballad. After being stoned from an inn on the coast, I should have learned better. Tales of old kingdoms are not appreciated where mayors rule." He sighed in stoic dismissal. "This last one cost me my horse and left me stranded in the bargain."

Asandir cast a glance toward Arithon; if argument existed in favor of shouldering responsibility for restoring this world to sun and harmony, here walked misfortune that a fellow musician must understand. Before the Sorcerer could emphasize his point, the minstrel raised his trained voice in a mix of diffidence and amazement.

"*Fiend-quencher, matched by none; white-head, gray-eyed one. Change-bringer, storm-breaker; Asandir, Kingmaker.*

"You," the minstrel added, and his theatrical gesture encompassed Dakar. "You must be the Mad Prophet."

Aware of a sudden guardedness behind Arithon's stillness, Asandir responded carefully. "I won't deny your powers of observation, Felirin the Scarlet. But I would urge that you use more caution before speaking your thoughts aloud. There were innocents burned in Karfael last harvest upon suspicion they had harbored a sorcerer."

"So I heard." the bard shrugged. "But I learned my repertory from barbarians, and something of their wildness stayed with me." He looked up, his swollen face bright with interest. "There must be good reason for a Fellowship Sorcerer to take to the open roads." And his gaze shifted to the half-brothers who traveled in Asandir's company.

Dakar opened his mouth, quickly silenced by a look from the Sorcerer, who interjected, "This is no time to be starting rumors in the taverns. And should I be aware of another way into Camris beyond the road through Tornir Peaks?"

Felirin understood a warning when he heard one. He shifted his bundle, prepared to fall into step as the Sorcerer's black started forward, but Arithon abruptly dismounted and offered the reins of the dun.

"You have blisters," he observed, "and I have sores from the saddle that an afternoon on foot might improve."

The excuse was a lie, Dakar knew. He watched the Master's face and saw the buried edge of something determined, but the shadowed green eyes held their secrets.

Peaks of Tornir

The caravan that had stranded Felirin the bard stayed elusively ahead through the coming days of travel. Dakar diverted his frustration each evening by badgering incessantly for drinking songs. As a result, the camp fires through the eastern quarter of Westwood became rowdy as a dockside tavern, and many a nocturnal predator went hungry due to the din. When Dakar became too hoarse to frame an intelligent request, the bard would delve into his store of ancient ballads that told of times before the Mistwraith. When pressed, he admitted he did not believe in the sun as the woodland barbarians did; but lore and legend fascinated him and he collected old tales as a curiosity. None could deny that the melodies set to such fancy were lyrically complex, a dance on fret and string that a musician could challenge a lifetime of skill to perform.

As the hills steepened, and the winds of increased altitude caused the company to huddle closer to the fire for warmth, more than once Felirin caught Arithon studying his hands as he played. After days of cleverly rebuffed questions, and despite Lysaer's genial charm in conversation, Arithon's fixation with the lyranthe was the only opening the bard had managed to discern. Inspired by a fractional movement of the dark-haired man's fingers as a fallen log fanned up the flames, Felirin silenced his strings in mid-stanza and rubbed his knuckles on his jerkin. "Damn the weather," he said. "The hands are cold and stumbling over grace notes."

Dakar predictably complained. "You aren't quitting, Felirin, not so soon. Better we freeze to a misplayed tune than abide our sobriety in silence."

The bard feigned a yawn to hide his smile. "Arithon plays," he said in sly suggestion. "Why not ask him for a song?"

"Arithon?" Dakar puffed up his cheeks. "Play music?" He darted a glance to either side; with Asandir off to check the picket lines, he dared a whisper in conspiracy. "I'll bet you silver he doesn't."

Watching through peripheral vision, Felirin saw Arithon turn utterly still. Lysaer sat up and took interest. "How much would you stake me?" asked the bard.

The Mad Prophet laced his hands across his paunch. "Ten royals. Double as much if I'm wrong."

Felirin chuckled and, still smiling, extended his instrument toward the cloaked figure to his left. "Indulge me. Give us a tune."

Arithon returned a dry chuckle. "I'll establish your mastery by contrast," he threatened. But Felirin had plotted to a nicety; after days of unmerited provocation, Arithon took his chance to humble Dakar.

His movements as he lifted the soundboard to his shoulder were recognizably reverent. Arithon poised tentative fingers, sounded a shower of practiced harmonics, and found an interval off. He corrected the pitch, neatly and precisely. When he looked up, his eyes were laughing.

Dakar muttered something stinging concerning close-mouthed brigands who betrayed a comrade to wasted silver. Lysaer politely held back comment, and Felirin silently congratulated his powers of intuitive perception. Then all three of them lost track of surface thoughts as Arithon started to play.

The first chords rang across the firelit dell with a power of sheer captivation. Arithon tested and quickly found the instrument's mettle; at once he broke his opening into an intricate theme that threaded, major to minor, in haunting sweeps across keys. By then no one remembered this magic had been instigated by an interchange of grudges and a bet.

Startled into rapt concentration, Felirin realized he had discovered a treasure. Whoever Arithon was, whatever his origins and his purpose in accompanying a Sorcerer, he had been born with the natural gift to render song. There were rough patches in his fingering and fretwork that could be smoothed over with schooling; skilled guidance could ease some awkwardness in his phrasing. His voice lacked experience and tempering. But even through such flaws the bard could appreciate his raw brilliance. With Lysaer and Dakar, his heart became transported from the discomforts of a drafty camp and led on a soaring flight of emotion as a tale of two lovers unfolded like a jewel in the firelight.

Arithon stilled the strings at the end, and the spell unequivocally shattered.

"Young man," the bard demanded. "Play again."

Arithon shook his head. "Collect your winnings from Dakar." If he had regrets, they stayed invisible as he slipped the instrument back into the lap of its owner. "Your lyranthe is very fine. She plays herself."

"That's foolishness!" Felirin reached out more demandingly than he intended, and caught hold of Arithon's sleeve. The wrist beneath his touch was trembling. To ease what he took for self-consciousness, the bard added, "You're gifted enough to apprentice."

Arithon shook his head and moved to disengage, but Felirin's grip tightened angrily. "How dare you waste such rare talent? Can't you accept your true calling?"

Green eyes flashed up, and almost—only Lysaer could recognize it—Arithon drew breath for rebuttal in the same vicious style he had used at his trial by Amroth's council. Then confusion seemed to flicker behind his eyes. The Master looked away. He worked gently free of the bard's fingers. "Daelion turns the Wheel. One cannot always have the choice."

He arose, quietly determined to retire, and managed to avoid Asandir, returned from his check on the horses.

The bard turned his puzzlement on the Sorcerer. "What did the lad mean by that?"

Asandir sat on the log that the Master had just left vacant and settled his dark cloak around his knees. "That these are troubled times for all of us, my friend. Arithon has the gift, none can doubt. But music cannot be his first calling."

Dakar suggested hopefully that spirits could ease the most wretched of life's disappointments. His quip was ignored. No one inclined toward lightheartedness. Felirin abandoned the fireside to pack away his lyranthe, followed by the crestfallen prophet. Only Lysaer lingered. Aware of the steel beneath Asandir's stillness, and unwarmed by the wind-fanned embers by his feet, the s'Ilessid recalled his half-brother's reaction to a past, insensitive query. *"Never to go back to Karthan,"* Arithon had said in unresponsive wish to kill the subject. Lent fresh perspective by tonight's discovery, his half-brother shared insight into a misery that no heroic calling could assuage.

Some men had no use for the responsibilities of power and renown. The coming quest to suppress the Mistwraith that restored meaning to Lysaer's life became a curse and a care for Arithon, whose gifted love for music must be sidelined.

Morning came. Hunched against a wind that whined through tossing branches, the party passed into the foothills of Tornir Peaks. The great trees of Westwood thinned in concert with the soil, and the road wound between stripped, rock-crowned promontories sliced by stony gullies. Sleet had fallen during the night, and the slate paving was icy in patches, treacherous even at a walk. Arithon led his flighty dun by the bridle. Lysaer flanked him on foot, while Felirin took a turn in the chestnut's saddle.

The cold and the cheerless landscape buoyed no one's spirits, but Dakar's irrepressible tongue stayed unaffected. "Damn you for a thief, Felirin, I swear you conspired against me to win that bet last night."

The bard twisted back and checked the ties which secured his lyranthe to the saddle for the third time since he had mounted. Balked yet by Arithon's reticence, his reply came back clipped. "Forget the bet. Just buy me an ale when we get to Erdane."

"Now, there speaks a guilty man," the Mad Prophet pronounced. He kicked his paint forward and set the dun dancing as he drew alongside the Master. "Did the two of you plan to split the take?"

Jerked half off his feet as his mare skittered sideways, Arithon returned a quick laugh. "Why bother? As I remember, I needed no rigged wagers to part the silver from your belt."

Reminded of his mishap in the alley in West End, Dakar turned purple. He bent over his saddle bow and spoke so Felirin could not hear. "You'll pay for that."

"You say?" Arithon brought the dun under control by rubbing her ear to distract her. When she settled, he slapped her fondly and added a barbed remark to the Mad Prophet concerning slipshod spells.

Dakar deflated in moody silence.

"You've made a clam of him," Lysaer observed with a smile. "Thank Ath. My ears were tired."

But the friendliness in the comment did not warm. Apart from the others, and keenly wishing an hour of solitude to sort through troubled thoughts, Arithon strode at the dun's shoulder while a round of banter designed to bait Dakar developed between Felirin and Lysaer.

The party rounded a bend where the road snaked beneath an overhang, and the talk suddenly died. A driving clang of hoofbeats echoed down from the rise ahead. A horse approached through the mist at a headlong gallop that begged for a fatal fall. The bridleless chestnut flung up its nose and neighed.

"Hold here," called Asandir.

The next instant, a riderless gray stallion thundered into view through the fog. He clattered downslope in lathered, wild-eyed terror, his reins flying, broken, from the bit rings. The smoke-dark mane was fouled and dripping blood. Dakar's paint caught the scent first. It spun and tried to bolt.

Arithon cursed with eloquent force and fought his shying dun; Lysaer stepped hurriedly to aid him.

Astride the quivering but obedient chestnut, Felirin recognized the martial style of the runaway animal's tack. "Hey, that's one of the horses from the caravan guard!"

Only the black that bore Asandir seemed immune to alarm. Under the Sorcerer's guidance it advanced in spell-wrought, nerveless calm, swung across the road, and blocked the way. The riderless animal checked in a sliding scrabble of hooves, then stood with lifted tail, blowing hard and rolling white-rimmed eyes. Asandir dismounted slowly. He held out his hand and spoke a word, and the frightened horse appeared to settle. Then, his own black left unattended, the Sorcerer advanced and with perfect lack of ceremony captured the stallion's bridle.

"Maybe he should have a turn at Arithon's dun," Lysaer suggested. But no one appeared to be listening.

Dakar had lost his impertinence, and Felirin showed open alarm. As Asandir approached, leading both the black and the stallion, all could see a shallow, ragged gash in the animal's neck. Deeper marks clawed through the seat of the saddle, and bloodstains marred the leather that had not been left by the horse.

"Daelion Fatemaster," Lysaer swore. "What sort of predator caused that?"

"You don't want to hear," said Felirin. He raised his voice and called to Asandir. "There are Khadrim in the pass, yes?"

"I fear so." The Sorcerer halted the horses. With quick fingers he unbuckled the reins from the black's bridle and hitched them to the caught stallion's bit. Then he cut off the ends of the broken pair and offered the animal to the bard. "I want everyone mounted."

The remark included Arithon, who looped his reins over the dun's ears, while Felirin slid off Lysaer's chestnut and accepted possession of the gray. The bard asked and received permission to leave his lyranthe where it was; no sense in trusting a strange horse with an awkward and unaccustomed burden. "This was the guard captain's mount," the bard added, rueful as he adjusted the leathers for his much longer legs. "This fellow is probably trained handily for war, but damn, his saddle was made for a man with narrow buttocks. What little stuffing the Khadrim might have left has blown away on the wind."

"Sit down too hard on the armor studs and you'll find yourself singing soprano," Dakar retorted smugly.

The bard shot him a dark look, and dabbed at drying bloodstains before he set foot in the stirrup and mounted. "At the end of this day's ride, I'll be thankful to count only bruises." He settled his reins and addressed Asandir. "I presume we're going to be crazy and continue on, not turn back?"

The Sorcerer nodded. His gaze fixed on the half-brothers through a brief, measuring moment. "There could be danger, but the risk will stay manageable if nobody loses their head. Keep together, whatever happens. Arithon, when I tell you, and only when, draw your blade."

The Mad Prophet slapped his forehead. "Ath, that's right!"

Asandir's eyes went wide with incredulity. "Dakar! You scatterbrain, don't tell me you'd forgotten the sword?"

"I did." The Mad Prophet returned a pouting scowl. "Small wonder, with the rest of you conspiring to rig my bets."

The Sorcerer disgustedly turned and remounted his black. "Remind me never, ever to rely on your memory in a pinch." He noticed and answered Arithon's look without pause to turn his head. "Boy, your sword was forged ten and a half thousand years past, expressly for war against the Khadrim."

"War," interjected Lysaer. "Then the creatures are intelligent?"

Arithon barely heard Asandir's affirmative reply; he ignored Felirin's curious query and regarded the hilt which protruded from the scabbard at his hip with absolute, icy detachment. Whatever curiosity he might once have held for his inherited weapon, he had never owned an inkling that the blade might be so ancient. That he carried spell-wrought steel was undeniable, though the nature of its powers had escaped the wisdom of Dascen Elur's mages. The chance the sword might bind him further to a duty he wanted no part of became just another weight upon his heart.

Having lost his royal inheritance, Lysaer would treasure the chance to bear a great talisman; Arithon caught the suppressed flash of envy in his brother's blue eyes. Yet before the Master could offer his last true possession as a gift, Asandir came back with rebuttal.

"You can never relinquish that blade, except to your own blood heir."

Arithon knew an inward surge of protest, a fleeting, angry impression that he had cause to take exception to the Sorcerer's words. Yet as had happened before when Felirin had pressured him over music, the Master could not quite frame the concept. As he tried, his thoughts went vague, and his perceptions scattered, disoriented. By now he had learned that if he stopped fighting back, the confusion would quickly pass; the unreliable dun distracted him sufficiently in any case. Yet each successive incident left Arithon less satisfied with Asandir's explanation in the woodcutter's cottage. The gaps in his memory were not natural; that Dakar watched him with predatory speculation each time he recovered lent evidence to justify suspicion. Arithon guessed some telling fact had been withheld from him. Before he could be cornered in a position he could not escape, he determined to find out what and why.

Beyond the draw where they captured the runaway horse, the road steepened sharply. The crags on either side reared up to ever more jagged promontories, their lofty, looming summits lost in mist. Patches of early snow mottled the northern faces, cut by rockfalls and boulder-choked ravines where vegetation clawed desperate footholds. Here the slate paving showed the abuse of harsh winters, split and heaved crooked by frosts. The horses picked carefully over uneven footing, and the air took on the reek of cinders. When they rounded a switchback they saw why.

The stud balked, snorting with alarm. Ahead, between the smoking wreckage that remained of two dozen wagons, the drovers of the caravan that had ousted Felirin lay strewn across the way like dirtied rags. Man and mount and cart mule, there were no survivors. Corpses littered the ledge. Charred clothing clung to exposed bones, and whatever flesh remained had been mauled to ribbons by something disinterested in hunting for the sake of sustenance. Lysaer cupped a hand to his mouth, sickened by the sight of an eviscerated woman, and a horse with half its hindquarters seared to stinking, blackened meat. Something with monstrous jaws had snapped the head off the neck.

Stung into memories of strife and battle by the bodies of so many slain, Arithon looked quickly beyond. What drained the blood from his face was something black and scaled that lurked half glimpsed in the mist: a creature straight out of legend, with silvery leathered wings that extended an impossible sixteen spans from the ridge of the armored breastbone to each outstretched, claw-spurred tip.

"Stay close," commanded Asandir. He reached across one-handed and calmed Felirin's sidling gray with a touch, then scanned the sky with worried eyes.

"There are more of them, and not far off," Dakar said with an odd and unusual briskness.

That moment a shrill whistle split the mist overhead. The sound was eerie, rich and complex with harmonics that seemed to tantalize the edge of understanding. Other whistles answered, echoing from a gallery of unseen cliffs. A huge, shadowy form shot above the roadway, and the acrid breeze of its passage set every horse in the company trembling outright in fear.

"Now, Arithon," Asandir said quietly. "Give yourself space and draw your steel."

The dun mare surged forward the instant her rider gave rein. Arithon set his back against her and curbed her hot impulse to bolt, but the mare was too wild to settle. She skittered sideways, carved an angry pirouette by the overturned hulk of a wagon, and bucked. One rebellious hind hoof banged against the wreck, and a welter of cloth goods spilled loose from the torn canvas cover. The edges of the bolts were singed and horribly spattered with blood. The sudden movement and the smells of death and burned silks caused the mare to rip into a rear.

"Arithon!" shouted Asandir. "The sword!"

His cry was cut by a screeling bellow from the mist directly above. The sound reverberated with stinging, incalculable fury that wounded the ears with subsonics. The dun mare arched higher, striking the air with her forelegs. There she swayed, ears flattened and tail clamped to her croup in taut panic. Arithon pressed into her neck and soothed with hands and voice to coax her down.

That moment while horse and rider struggled vulnerably to regain balance, the Khadrim stooped to the attack.

It descended in a rush of furled wings, a bolt of killing black streamlined from the dagger claws of fang and talon. It arched down as a spear might fall, red-eyed and fork-tailed, and purely bent on murder. Arithon glanced up. Through the mare's streaming mane, he saw the nightmare in its earthward rush to take him.

"The sword!" screamed Asandir. Violet light flashed as he raised his hands to shape wizardry.

The Khadrim saw the spell, snapped out wings broad as sails, and sliced into a bank. Before the Sorcerer could strike it from the sky its neck curved back, blackly scaled and sinuous as a venomous snake. For an instant the monster's red eyes turned unwinking on the man and the horse standing separate. Then the armored jaws opened and a torrent of fire spat forth.

Flame roared in a crackling whirlwind and entirely engulfed the dun mare. Her rider became an indistinct silhouette, then a shadow lost utterly in the heart of the conflagration.

The Khadrim clashed closed its jaws. Hot, seared air dispersed in a coil of oily black smoke, fanned away under the wingbeat of the terrible creature as it swooped and shot back aloft.

On the roadway, within a seared circle of carbon, Arithon sat his quivering, mane-singed mare, untouched and cursing in annoyance.

Felirin screamed out a stupefied blasphemy.

The Khadrim doubled back in midair and roared in frustrated rage; while Arithon freed a fist from the reins and finally set hand to his sword.

The dark blade slipped from the scabbard with a sweet, cold ring. From the instant the tip cleared the guard loop, Arithon was touched by a haunting sensation, like song, like loss, like a peal of perfect harmony set vibrating upon the air. His ears rang to a timbre so pure his heart flinched; and the sword in his hands came alive. Light ripped along the silvered lines of inlay, blindingly intense, a shimmer like harmony distilled to an exultation of universal creation.

The Khadrim shrieked in pain. Like some great, broken child's kite tossed in the grip of a gale, it flung sideways and crashed with a threshing flurry of wings against the mountainside. The forked tail lashed up rocks, hurled stunted bits of vegetation downslope in a rattling fall of flung gravel. Then its struggles ceased, and it wilted to final stillness, a black-scaled, hideous monstrosity couched in a bed of bloodied snow.

For a moment longer, the sword in Arithon's hand flashed through a silver glare of spells. Then the phenomenon faded to a glimmer and died away. The Master of Shadows stared at plain black steel chased with patterns that no longer appeared familiar. There were tears in his eyes, dripping unheeded down his cheeks.

None of the wisdom at Rauven had approached the likes of this. Arithon had been awed by the nearly cataclysmic forces held in check within Asandir; for all the Sorcerer's perfectly schooled strength, his powers seemed a brute statement compared with the energies laid down in perfect stillness in a span of tempered steel. Arithon had known magework, but never, ever had he touched a force that left him feeling bereft, as if the world where he stood had grown coarser, more drab, somehow clumsy and tearingly *lacking* in a manner that defeated reason. Arithon stared at the blade in his hand and felt lacerated for no reason under sky he could name.

"The Khadrim have gone," Asandir called, and the wounding stillness was broken. "You may sheath your weapon."

"Dharkaron, Avenging Angel," Felirin swore in falsetto. "Who is that man, to pass unscathed through living flame, and what in Sithaer made that sword?"

Asandir turned bland eyes upon the much shaken minstrel. "He is

Arithon, Master of Shadows, and if you'll help raise a cairn over the unfortunate dead from your caravan, I'll give you explanation for the sword."

Past the stupefied bard, Dakar the Mad Prophet raised a hand and touched the shoulder of Arithon's utterly crestfallen half-brother. In a voice of conspiratorial conciliation he said, "Lysaer, don't feel slighted. Your moment will come in due time."

Alithiel's Story

The five riders bound for Camris suffered no second attack by Khadrim, though for safety's sake through several of the narrower defiles, Asandir asked Arithon to ride with his sword unsheathed in his hand. The blade evinced no glow of warning, and then the pass fell behind. The pitch of the road became less rugged, and the jagged crags rounded to hills. At twilight, the company made camp in a cave on the far slopes of Tornir Peaks.

The shelter was often used by summer caravans, and passing generations of wagoners had built in some comforts over time. Benches of split logs surrounded a rock-lined fire pit, and a crude stand of fencing had been erected beneath the underhang of a natural outcrop. In places, moss-grown remnants of stone walls showed where sheds and an earlier inn had been leveled in some forgotten past conflict. Once the horses were unsaddled and Dakar sent off to gather wood, Asandir crouched down with kindling and chips and began clearing away the ashes left by last season's travelers. He gestured through the failing light as Lysaer knelt to help. "If the mist were to lift off the valley, you could see lights from here, wayside inns on the plain of Karmak. The roads of north Korias might have gone wild, but the trade routes from Atainia cross Camris. The lands are better traveled there, and on the east shore, ships still ply the bay."

Lysaer stared out into gathering darkness, but his eyes saw only mist. Descended from an island culture, he could not imagine the vast spread of continent the Sorcerer's words described. "It must have been hard, seeing your civilization shrink to a shadow of its former greatness."

Asandir paused, his hands settled on his knees. His eyes turned, piercing into distance. "Harder than you know, young s'Ilessid. But the sun will shine over us again."

Felirin and Arithon entered, adding the smells of healing herbs and wet leaves to the dusky scent of dry charcoal. The wound on the gray stallion's neck had been washed and cared for. The bard carried a handsome, silver-bossed saddle, his own, recovered that day from the corpse of his former palfrey. Asandir had retained a replacement set of reins, but the rest of the wagons and goods they had burned, lest unwitting passersby linger for salvage and tempt the Khadrim to further massacre.

Outside the cave, the wind picked up, moaning through a stand of stunted pines. "Winter's coming early," Felirin observed. "Seems to move in a little sooner every year."

Unaware that such shifts in the seasons were the ongoing effects of Desh-thiere, he dumped his saddle over a log bench and sat, the skirt flap a welcome backrest after exhausting hours astride. As Asandir's efforts graced the cave with a curl of pale flame, the bard inspected his hands and cursed. The fingernails he needed to pluck his strings were split to the quick from shifting rocks. Arithon's were no whit better, and made bold by shared commiseration, Felirin gathered nerve and made inquiry.

"I don't recall any stanzas that mention a Master of Shadows."

Asandir settled back, his face washed gold by flame light. "That song has yet to be written." Gently, as an afterthought, he added, "Felirin, it would not do to speak of this yet in the taverns. But you could see stars and sun within your lifetime."

The bard gaped in astonishment, his glibness at a loss for reply. Asandir allowed the import of his words a moment to sink in. Then he said, "Lysaer and Arithon are the potential of a restored sky made real, the Mistwraith's bane promised five centuries ago by Dakar's prophecy of West Gate."

Caught dumbfounded, Felirin struggled to recover something resembling equanimity. He swore once, hoarsely. Then, left only his performer's dignity, he said, "How many of the old ballads are not myth but true history?"

"Most of them." Asandir waited, his look gravely steady, as this became assimilated through another shaken interval of silence. "You are one of a chosen few know."

Dakar picked that moment to return, puffing under an armload of damp faggots. He had not bothered to shear off the dead branches, and his laziness had torn his better shirt. The ordinary intensity of his irritation became an anchor upon which Felirin hung sanity. Informed that his whole world stood poised on the brink of upheaval and change, the bard caught a shivering breath. "For the sake of one commonplace mortal, save the rest until after we've had supper. I'm hungry enough to hallucinate, and hearing the impossible doesn't help."

Later, warmed by leek stew and the coals of a generous bonfire, the Sorcerer gave the history of Arithon's sword. The tale was lengthy, beginning ten and a half thousand years in the past, when twelve blades were forged at Isaer by the Paravian armorer, Ffereton s'Darian, from the cinder of a fallen star.

"Ffereton was Ilitharis, a centaur," Asandir began. "The Isaervian swords were his finest, most famed creation, wrought at need to battle the vast packs of Khadrim that were the scourge of the Second Age. The histories that survive claim each blade took five years' labor, a full decade if one were to count the sorceries that went into the sharpening. When Ffereton finished, the steel held an edge that time or battle could never blunt."

Here, the Sorcerer paused and asked Arithon to bare his blade from the scabbard. "You'll see there are no nicks, no flaws from hard usage. Yet Alithiel has known the blows of two ages of strife." Asandir turned the quillons between his hands, and firelight flashed on the inlay which twined the dark length of the blade.

"The swords were given over to the fair folk, called sunchildren, for finishing. It was they who made the hilts and chased the channels for the inlay, no two patterns the same. But perhaps the greatest wonder is the metal set into the runes themselves." Asandir ran a finger over the inscriptions, and an answering flare of silver traced his touch. As if the light somehow gentled him, his manner softened into reverence. "Riathan, the unicorns, sang the great spells of defense. Masters of the lost art of name-binding, they infused the alloy with harmonics tuned to the primal chord of vibration used by Ath Creator to kindle the first stars with light. Legend holds that twenty-one masters took a decade to endow Alithiel alone."

Asandir slipped the sword back into the scabbard. "The enchantment was balanced to peak in defense of the sword's true bearer, dazzling the eyes of his enemy, but only if the engagement was just. Very few causes that drive a man to kill are righteous ones. Probably Arithon's father never knew the nature of the weapon he left to his son."

Arithon confirmed this with a nod, but did not speak. Haunted by his encounter with the sword's arcane powers, he feared to betray the dread that partnered such mystery: that some role waited to be asked of him to match such a grand weight of history. Determined to control his own fate, the Shadow Master sat with locked hands while, with the skilled resonance of a storyteller, Asandir continued:

"The Isaervian blades were crafted for the hands of six great Lords of the Ilitharis, and the six exalted lines of the sunchildren. Alithiel was the oddity. She was forged for Ffereton's son, Durmaenir, who was a centaur born undersized. The blade was tailored to match his proportions, from the length to the balance of the grip. In the wars that followed, thousands of Khadrim died, their last memory the flaring brilliance of an Isaervian sword's enchantment. Sadly, Durmaenir was one of the fallen. His grieving father passed Alithiel to the king's heir."

Arithon heard this and restrained a forcible wish to stop his ears, walk away, even shout nonsense—any reaction to halt this brilliant, weighty tapestry of names and sorrows far more comfortably left to the ghosts of forgotten heroes. Yet the stilled powers in the sword by their nature commanded his respect; he could not bring himself to interrupt.

If Asandir noticed Arithon's distress, he held back nothing. "The prince at that time was a sunchild, and true to type for his kind, he stood just one span in height. The sword's length reached nearly to his chin. He had a shoulder scabbard fashioned for ceremonial appearances, and took up the traditional king's blade upon accession at his predecessor's death. Alithiel was given over to the line of Perhedral. They too were sunchildren, ill suited to the weight of a large weapon. When King Enastir died childless, the Teir's'Perhedral claimed the kingship. Since another sword accompanied the crown, Alithiel remained in the treasury until another rise of Khadrim threatened peace. A centaur lord wielded her through the war that followed, but the blade handled like a toy in his huge grip. Afterward the sword Alithiel changed owners again, this time becoming the property of the high king's cousin by marriage. It passed through his heirs to Cianor, who earned the honorific of Sunlord."

This drew a gasp from Felirin, who knew at least a dozen ballads made in praise of the Sunlord's long reign.

Asandir smiled at his reaction. "May the memory of those days never fade. Yet Cianor Sunlord did little but possess the sword. He assumed the Paravian crown in Second Age 2545, and as others before him, took up the king's blade out of preference. By then Alithiel carried a second name, Dael-Farenn, or Kingmaker, because three of her bearers had succeeded the end of a royal line.

"But if the sword brought kingship to her wielder, she never became a cherished possession. Awkward size made her handling a burden, and though the Isaervian blades that survived the mishaps of time were coveted, no Paravian lord cared to claim one that carried a tragic reputation.

"Cianor eventually awarded Alithiel to a man, for valor in defense of his sister, Princess Taliennse. Her grace was rescued from assault by Khadrim in the very pass we just crossed." Here Asandir nodded in deference to Arithon. "The emerald in your sword was cut by a sunchild's spells. The initial in the leopard crest changes with the name of the bearer, and since the blade fits the hand of a man to perfection, each heir in your family has carried her since."

Asandir folded long hands. "Arithon, yours is the only Isaervian blade to pass from Paravian possession. To my knowledge, she is the last of her kind on the continent."

Lysaer regarded the polished quillons with rueful appreciation. "Small wonder the armorers of Dascen Elur were impressed. They held that sword to be the bane of their craft, because no man could hope to forge its equal."

Asandir rose and stretched like a cat. "The centaur Ffereton himself could not repeat the labor. If, in truth, he still lives."

Felirin raised dubious eyebrows. "Did I hear right? Could a centaur be *expected* to survive for ten and a half thousand years?"

The Sorcerer fixed the bard with a bright and imperious sadness. "The old races were not mortal, not as a man might define. The loss of the sun touched them sorely, and even my colleagues in the Fellowship can't say whether they can ever be brought to return. The tragedy in that cannot be measured."

A stillness descended by the fireside, broken by Asandir's suggestion that all of them turn into their blankets. The weather was shortly going to turn, and he wished an early start on the morrow. Arithon alone remained seated, the sword handed down by his ancestors braced in its sheath across his knees. The flames flickered and burned low, and subsided at last to red embers. Hours later, when the others seemed settled into sleep, he put the blade aside and slipped out.

Mist clung in heavy, dank layers beneath the evergreens, and the darkness beyond the cave was total. Yet Arithon was Master of Shadow; from him the night held no secrets. He walked over rocks and roots with a cat-sure step and paused by the rails that penned the horses.

"Tishealdi," he called softly in the old tongue. "Splash."

The name fell quiet as a whisper, but movement answered. An irregular patch of white moved closer, and a muzzle nosed at his hand: the dun, come begging for grain. Arithon reached out and traced the odd marking on the mare's neck. Her damp coat warmed his cold hands, and the uncomplicated animal nearness of her helped quiet the turmoil in his mind. "We can't leave, you and I, not just yet. But I have a feeling we should, all the same."

For he had noticed a thing throughout Asandir's recitation: while in the presence of the bard, the Sorcerer took care to avoid any mention of his or Lysaer's surname.

The mare shook her head, dusting his face with wet mane. Arithon pushed her off with a playful phrase that died at the snap of a stick. He spun, reflexively prepared for retreat. If Dakar or the Sorcerer had followed him, he wanted no part of their inquiries.

But the accents that maligned the roots and the dark in breathless fragments of verse were the bard's. A bump and another snapped stick ended the loftier language. "Daelion's judgment, man! You've a miserable and perverse nature, to bring me thrashing about after you, and never a thought to carry a brand."

Arithon loosened taut muscles with an effort concealed by the night. "I don't recall asking for company."

Felirin tripped and stumbled the last few yards down the trail and fetched against the fence with a thud that made the boards rattle. The dun shied back into the snorting mill of geldings, and the gray, confined separately, nickered after her.

The bard looked askance at the much too still shadow that was Arithon. "You're almost as secretive as the Sorcerer."

Which was the nature of a spirit trained to power, not to volunteer the unnecessary; but Arithon would not say so. "Why did you come out?"

Felirin returned a dry chuckle. "Don't change the subject. You can't hide your angst behind questions."

Arithon said nothing for an interval. Then, with clear and deliberate sting, he said, "Why not? You know the ballads. Show me a hero, and I'll show you a man enslaved by his competence."

The bard took a long, slow breath. A difficult man to annoy, he had neatly and nearly been goaded to forget that Arithon's mettlesome nature defended a frustrated talent.

"Listen to me," Felirin said quickly, and an honest desperation in his entreaty made Arithon ease off and give him space. "Promise me something for my foolishness. There's a singer, a Masterbard, named

Halliron. If you meet him, I beg you to play for him. Should he offer you an apprenticeship, I ask for your oath you'll accept."

Silence; then footfalls as curious horses advanced from the far side of the corral. Then a chilly gust of air rattled through the trees. Arithon pushed off from the fence boards and cursed in an unfamiliar language through his teeth. "Like sharks, you all want a part of me." His voice shook, not with fury but with longing.

Felirin smiled, his relief mixed with guilt-tinged triumph. "Your oath," he pressured gently. "Let me hear it."

"Damn you," said Arithon. In a shattering change of mood, he was laughing. "You have it. But what's my word against the grandiloquent predictions of a maudlin and drunken prophet?"

"Maybe everything," Felirin finished gently. "You're too young to live without dreams."

"I wasn't aware that I didn't." Lightly firm in his irony, Arithon added, "Right now, I wish to go to bed." He walked away, left the bard to thwarted curiosity and the crowding attentions of the horses.

Back Trail

On the downs of Pasyvier, by the flames of a drifter's fire, a seer speaks sharply to a grand dame returned from the autumn horse fair. "Say again, you saw a Sorcerer? And with him a blond-haired stranger who spoke the speech of the true-born? I tell you, if you did, there will be war. . . ."

In the hall of judgment in West End, seated on his chair of carved oak and carnelian, a town mayor listens, sweating, to a similar description from the half-wit who played fiddle in the square. . . .

Under mist in the Peaks of Tornir, a wild, screeling wail calls Khadrim in retreat back to spell-warded sanctuary, and the harmonics ring of death by spell-cursed steel not seen for a thousand years. . . .

VI. Erdane

The walls of Erdane had been raised at the crossroads two ages before the uprising which threw down the high kings had bloodied its maze of narrow streets. Now, five centuries later, the city wore change like a tattered, overdressed prostitute. Guild flags and a mayor's blazon fluttered over the Grand West Gate, built by Paravian hands of seamless, rose-veined quartz. The stone at street level was left pitted and scarred by siege weapons, and grayed by the passage of uncounted generations of inhabitants. Had the sentries in the mayor's guard been as vigilant as their counterparts in times past, they would have challenged the woman in the shepherd's cloak who passed the gatehouse, hooded. Boots of sewn sealhide showed beneath her ankle-length skirts, but their soles were not made for walking. Her hands were callused from the bridle rein, and her eyes a clear and disturbing gray.

But the captain of the watch barely glanced up from his dice game, and the teenage soldier who lounged on his javelin stayed absorbed by a whore, who paraded her bedizened attractions for the eyes of a loud-voiced drover.

Elaira, Koriani enchantress and message bearer for the Prime, entered Erdane unremarked between a wagon bearing three sows and the rumbling wheels of an ale seller's dray. She was the first of her kind to pass the city gates for close to four hundred years, and the only one to try without any sanction from her seniors. Had she been recognized for what she was, she would have been stripped and publicly burned after barely a pretense of a trial.

Other women had suffered that sentence inside the past half decade. If the mayor of Erdane suspected the charges against those accused were false, his conscience never bothered his sleep. What troubled his guild masters and council to cold sweats was the fear that powers from the past might arise out of legend and claim vengeance. For unlike the commoners and the craftsmen, the Lord Elect of Erdane had access to archives that detailed a history of conspiracy and murder. To him, to his council, and his general of armies, the sun was no myth, but a harbinger of sorcery and certain doom.

Elaira was cognizant of the risks. She kept her knot-worked hood pulled over her forehead and took care not to pass between the flirtatious whore and her sources of male attention. When the ale dray pulled up precipitously to avoid a running urchin, the enchantress ducked out of the main thoroughfare. She hastened down streets of marble-fronted guild halls, threaded across the artisans' district, then turned through a moss-dark arch.

The alley beyond was barely wider than a footpath. Fallen slates and rat-chewed ends of bone clogged the gutters. Seepage dripped in mournful counterpoint from the moss-crusted planks of half-rotted, open-air stairways, and from spell-charmed strips of tin nailed up to ward off iyats. Unlike many such talismans, these held true power to guard. Elaira could sense the faint resonance of their protection as she wound her way past ill-smelling puddles and locked shutters.

This slum by the edicts of town law should never have managed to survive.

It had no wine shops or pot traders on the lower levels. Dirty children did not play in the gutters, and drunks did not snore off binges; whores sought no customers here, nor did headhunters with old campaign scars loiter between assignments to boast of kills. This was a street whose inhabitants Erdane's mayor sorely wished to eradicate—except that in the teeming maze of the wall district, its location was most difficult to know. Wayfarers came seeking the archway and found themselves inexplicably sidetracked. They might blink and miss the entry, or be distracted by a noise or a thought, and before they had grasped they had missed something, they would have passed on by.

For anyone untrained in spell-craft, to pause here, even for a second, was to become lost in a mage-worked tangle of deception.

Elaira found the stairwell with carved gryphons on the newels. This was the house—here. She had all but sold her jewel for directions. For the Koriani matron who had received the scrolls from the Prime had been garrulous enough to repeat rumor. If she was right, the mayor's most persistent nightmare was already halfway realized: a Fellowship Sorcerer and two old-blood princes were temporarily in residence within Erdane.

Elaira mounted the alarmingly shaky stairway and paused on the landing at the top. With a shiver of sinful anticipation, she knocked and asked for entry. "Is this the home of Enithen Tuer?"

A muffled clang, then the ring of a bar being drawn back; the door cracked, and a white-lashed milk-pale eye peered through. "Ath's Avenger, it's a witch," rasped a reedy, aged voice. "Girl, you're very brave or just stupid."

Elaira tightened her grip on her cloak laces. "Probably stupid." She held back a nervous laugh. "Are you going to let me in?"

The eye blinked. "I will. You may be sorry."

"I will be sorry." Elaira threw an unsettled glance over her shoulder; the alley remained empty, dimming rapidly in the falling dusk. Nobody watched from the rows of shuttered windows. Still, her proscribed visit would be noticed very fast if she tarried too long in the open. As the door creaked wider, Elaira stepped through in a rush that betrayed apprehension.

A tiny hunchbacked crone bounced backward out of her path. "Yeesh. Came here without sanction, did you?"

Elaira pushed back her hood. The room did not match the alley's rundown squalor, but was snug and comfortably furnished. Candles lit the enchantress's face like a cameo against the purple-black silk of a second cloak, concealed underneath the rougher wool. Inside, somewhat mussed by the muffling layers, coiled a braided knot of bronze hair. "Maybe I just want my fortune told."

The crone grunted. "Not you. And anyway, you don't need a seer to tell your future's just branched into darkness."

"Sithaer." Elaira sucked an unsteady breath. "So soon?" She fumbled at the ties of her wraps and caught sight of two young men who watched her, interested, over a half-completed game of chess.

Elaira's eyes widened. They were here! And unmistakably royal, the blood lines perpetuated over many generations still apparent as the nearer one rose to meet her. Light from the sconces edged pale s'Ilessid hair in shining gold. The prince possessed an elegance that went beyond his handsome face. His eyes were jewel blue. He carried his well-knit frame with the dignity of a man schooled perfectly to listen, and a pride unself-conscious as breathing.

"Lady, may I?" he asked in courtly courtesy, and hands tanned dark by alien suns reached out and slipped the shepherd's cloak from her shoulders.

Elaira thanked him with a haste that sprang from embarrassment. Unused to male solicitude, she blushed and evaded his smile, and found her sight drawn to the other prince, whose black hair at first glance had caused him to blend into shadow.

This one regarded her with eyes of s'Ffalenn green, but also something else: the still, small shock of an awareness that recognized power. Elaira repressed stark surprise, while the s'Ilessid prince said something polite that her mind interpreted as background noise.

Before she could recover the poise to apply her trained skills to draw intuitive deductions through observation, the seer, Enithen Tuer, caught her elbow. Crabbed hands spun her toward a doorway, which opened to reveal the Fellowship Sorcerer she had defied her order's strictures to visit.

Asandir proved taller than Elaira had expected from images garnered through lane-watch. Lean as toughened leather, he wore plain clothing with a bearing she had always before thought imperious. In person, she revised that to a stillness that brooked no wasted motion. His hands were still also, the straight, tapered fingers clean as bleached bone on the latch. The face beneath the trimmed silver hair was carved by years and experience to a fierce mapwork of lines. The eyes in their deep-set sockets regarded her with a serenity that unnerved and exposed.

"What brought you here, Elaira of the Koriathain?" said Asandir of the Fellowship of Seven.

"She wasn't sent," the seer interjected. A palsied nudge sent the enchantress toward the imposing figure in the doorway.

"I see that." As if aware that the leashed force in him intimidated, Asandir caught Elaira's elbow and steered her toward a chair. His touch was light as a ghost's, gone the instant it was noticed as he stepped back and away and closed the door.

Elaira sat, for lack of the nerve to do otherwise. Feeling nakedly foolish, she buried unease in a study of her surroundings. The room was crowded with shelves, a workplace that smelled of herbs and waxed wood and oiled wool; a basket of carded fleece was in one corner, beside the worn frame of a spinning wheel. The woven rug underfoot had faded with age to a muddle of earth tones and grays, and the walls were piled high with crates of yarn and old junk.

"What brought you here, lady?" the Sorcerer asked again.

He bent with a servant's unobtrusiveness and began to build up the fire. Flame brightened as the birch logs caught and lined his hard profile in light.

Elaira stared down at her boots, and the muddied hem of her skirts which now gave off faint curls of steam. All the excuses, every elaborate and reasonable-sounding word she had rehearsed through the afternoon fled in the rush of her fast-beating heart. She was out of her depth. She knew it; before she could think, she spoke honestly. "I was curious."

Asandir straightened up. Stern but not unkindly, he looked at her, from her splashed skirts to her open, angular face. His eyes were penetrating, yet utterly without shadow. The awful strength behind his presence spoke of purpose rather than force. He reached out, hooked a stool from beneath the spindle, and sat with his back to the lintel by the grate. Then, hands folded on his knees, he waited.

A hot rush of blood touched Elaira's cheeks. With utmost tact and patience, he expected her to compose herself and qualify on her own. Oddly released from her awe, she unlaced shaking fingers. She slipped the violet cloak of her order over the chair back and tried to assimilate the particular that, unlike a Koriani senior, this Sorcerer would pass no judgment upon her; no debt would be set on her demands.

She gathered her nerve and blurted, "I wanted to see, to know. If the prophecy of West Gate was filled, and whether Desh-thiere's bane has come at last to Athera."

Asandir regarded her, unblinking. "You passed its substance on the way in."

He would elaborate on nothing unless she pressed him. Her betters insisted as much, endlessly: Fellowship Sorcerers gave up nothing freely. Eager to test that platitude for herself, Elaira dared a question. "I observed that the Teir's'Ffalenn has been initiated to the disciplines of power. Is this what gives him ability to dominate the Mistwraith?"

Asandir straightened, sharpened to sudden attention. "That took both initiative and courage, neither one a praiseworthy attribute in the entrenched opinion of your sisterhood." He smiled in gentle humor. "I intend to give you answer, Elaira, but in the expectation you will treat the information with a foresight your superiors might hold in contempt."

Elaira suppressed astonishment, that a Fellowship Sorcerer in his multiple depths of power might share frustration with her colleagues' preoccupation with the present.

But her interest was cut short as Asandir said, "In the times of the rebellion, when four of the high kings' heirs were sent to safety through West Gate, the Fellowship granted foundational training to the Teir's'Ahelas to increase her line's chances of survival. Her descendents on Dascen Elur continued her tradition, but forgot certain of the guidelines. In the course of five centuries of isolation, the mages there achieved what the Seven could not."

"Is that possible?" Elaira interjected.

Asandir's silvered brows tipped up. "What is possible does not always coincide with what is wise."

Instantly Elaira felt stupid.

And yet, perversely, instead of rebuke for her thoughtless words, Asandir chose to explain the bride gift which granted two men an inborn command of elemental mastery. "Together our princes can vanquish Desh-thiere. Separately, you must know, their gifts might potentially inflict greater harm than the wraith their powers must defeat."

Arrogance did not admit fallibility and reticence did not offer explanation; about the Fellowship, the Koriani Senior Circle was emphatically mistaken. Just accorded the insight of a colleague or an equal, Elaira sat stunned and still.

"You have noticed in the Teir's'Ffalenn a familiarity with the inner disciplines," Asandir continued, his eyes turned down toward his hands. "He spent his boyhood with the s'Ahelas mages, and their teaching was not wasted on him. One can hope that the sensitivity inherent in his lineage will keep his eyes opened to responsibility. In that, he will have all the support the Fellowship can offer."

Floundering through a quicksand of overturned beliefs, Elaira said, "Then the success of Dakar's prophecy is not assured?"

"Could it be?" Asandir arose from the stool, an understated strength inherent in even his simplest movement. "Men created Desh-thiere. The hands of men must bring it down. Exchanges of power on that scale are never bought without peril. Athera must endure the price. And your question has been answered now, I think."

In response to his note of finality, Elaira arose from her chair. She gathered her violet cloak, her normally impertinent nature repressed behind a frown.

As if attuned to her thoughts about him, Asandir said, "Your order has ever been dedicated to intolerance."

Elaira steeled herself and looked up into those terrifying, unruffled eyes. "My seniors hate to admit to incompetence."

"Lesser strength does not add up to uselessness." The Sorcerer crossed the room.

The enchantress followed, reluctant. "Our First Enchantress to the Prime, Lirenda, would disagree."

Asandir regarded her as he lifted the door latch. "But you are different."

He warned her. Elaira understood as much as he guided her

through the door with the same feather touch that had admitted her, as if his hands innately knew their capacity to unleash cataclysm, and in wariness adhered to gentle opposite. She would do well to apply the same principle and curb her outspoken brashness.

"You have a clear eye for truth," the Sorcerer said. "Don't replace one mistaken set of principles for others as narrow-minded."

Elaira quailed before the thought that Asandir had credited her with far too balanced a mind. She was not impartial where her seniors were concerned, and yet that seemed what this Sorcerer expected her to become. She crossed the outer room, where the chess board had been set to rights and two chairs now stood empty. The seer Enithen Tuer sat in her rocker, blinking clouded eyes through the smoke of an aromatic pipe. If the crone saw past a dark and tangled future, she offered no advice as the younger enchantress gathered up her shepherd's cloak and quietly let herself out.

Night had fallen, dense in the absence of any lamps. Elaira's progress down the moss-caked stair became careful and slow with uncertainty. She had taken on more than she bargained for. As she applied the nuances of her training to analyze the interview in retrospect, she realized how easily Asandir had tuned her expectations, lulled her sense of caution with a touch of human fragility and an air of attentive solicitude. Now aware in the chill of the alley how subtly she had been pushed to think beyond her limits, the enchantress shivered outright. The Sorcerer had not used her. But he could have, deftly as a potter turning unformed clay on a wheel.

The Prime Circle's obstinate fears were not in the least bit unfounded.

Elaira roused herself, mechanically continued until she reached the base of the stair. Asandir had warned of consequences. Through queasy, unsettled nerves, the enchantress who had dared the unthinkable sorted out the single thread that mattered. A Fellowship Sorcerer had trusted her. Why remained a mystery, but were she to reveal what she had learned—that the Mistwraith's bane rested solely in the hands of two men bred to rule, and that the Fellowship itself could not directly limit the result—the Koriani Prime Circle would be roused to bitterest anger, or worse, outright obstruction.

Elaira kicked a loose piece of slate; her boots sloshed through puddles with only minimal awareness of the wet. She could not escape a reprimand; if under questioning by her seniors she were to conceal that her knowledge of the two princes had derived from a confidence shared by Asandir, some other escapade must replace it. Before the enchantress on watch duty touched her presence, she must contrive another circumstance to match the surface facts. Or else the larger truths that she had most unwisely asked to know could not possibly be kept hidden.

"Daelion, master of the Wheel," she swore to the ink-dark night. "What in Dharkaron's conscience can I do that's more outrageous than meeting with a Sorcerer of the Fellowship?" She paused a second, her breath clouding in the close and misty dark.

Struck by sudden inspiration, Elaira spun around. She left the alley by way of another arch and asked after the Inn of Four Ravens. There, if rumor and luck held good, she would find Dakar the Mad Prophet drowning his miseries in mead—for word went that the taskmaster Asandir had hurried his charges across the breadth of Karmak, and not spent one night in a tavern.

The Four Ravens

After Erdane's gates closed at dusk, the taproom at the Inn of Four Ravens was a rough and ill-considered place for a woman to linger by herself. Located in the disreputable wall district, the tavern was the nightly hangout of headhunters, coarse-voiced laborers, and a hard-bitten, boastful contingent of off-duty garrison soldiers. The air reeked of overheated humanity and spilled beer and unscrubbed layers of cooking grease. The hearth smoked. By the quantity of large-busted barmaids and the sleek look of the innkeeper, the upstairs rooms were obviously rented for activities other than lodging.

The Ravens' gathering of ruffians were habitually too deep in their cups to discriminate between those girls who were goods and others who might be paying customers. Wedged between a drover who smelled like his mules and a bone-skinny journeyman cobbler, Elaira jerked her braid out of the indigo fingers of a dyer who leaned across three dicers to proposition her. She looked into the moist brown eyes of Dakar and said, "You've lost. Again."

She turned the last battered cards in her hand face up on the sticky trestle.

Dakar blinked, stirred from his stupor, and glared intently at painted suits and royalty. "Damn t'Sithaer."

A stir erupted to Elaira's left as her blue-handed admirer tried to shoulder through the press to crowd closer. As if he did not exist, the enchantress leaned across the table toward the Mad Prophet. "Your forfeit. Answer my question. Tell the name of the dark-haired man who shares your travels with Asandir."

Dakar shoved straight. "I'm drunk," he announced with injured cunning. "Can't remember." More to the point, he knew that Asandir would disapprove.

Elaira said nothing, but waited in persistent determination. She dared not reach for her focusing jewel. Even a fool would not try spell-work in this place—not to bring clarity to Dakar's muddled mind, or to drive off unwanted male advances. Erdane's citizens had aversions that ran to violence when confronted by any form of witchery; a disproportionate mix of the most zealous seemed to patronize the taproom at the Ravens. Dakar was crazy to come here at all, except that his sorrowfully rumpled appearance did not equate with his station as apprentice to a Fellowship Sorcerer.

Artlessly innocuous, he huddled like a lump on his bench, his cheeks crumpled up under eyes like dreamy half-moons. He leaned on stump-fingered fists and sucked on his lower lip until Elaira wanted desperately to shake him. "Arithon," Dakar said at last, in snarling, petulant concession.

Elaira bit back triumph. A neatly timed thrust of her elbow interrupted the dyer's amorous swoop. Gouged in a place that made him grunt, he backed off and was fortuitously rescued by a bar wench. Laughter arose, and a smattering of ribald comment, as the pair plowed a path toward the stairway.

Sweating, tired, and faintly queasy from nerves and smoke, Elaira raked the cards in a pile. What relief she might have felt was cancelled twice over by aggravation. The junior enchantress assigned lane-watch was lazy; she should have disclosed the location of her errant colleague hours since and dutifully reported to her senior. Until the gambling match needed for an alibi became substantiated, Elaira of necessity could not depart.

The minstrel in the corner stopped playing and laid aside his lyranthe. One of the listeners who arose from his circle would doubtless come pawing for favors, this man more drunken and lecherous than the last. Trapped, Elaira shuffled the dog-eared pack and began to deal another hand.

Dakar reached out and hooked her sleeve before the first card hit the trestle. "Tankard's dry."

Elaira looked for herself, and resignedly signaled the barmaid.

"No ale, no bets." Dakar managed a beatific smile.

The tavern door opened. A chill wafted through stale air as the crowd jostled to admit a newcomer. Roused by the draft from outside, the Mad Prophet laced his fingers across his paunch. He swayed a moment, hiccuped, and suddenly slammed up straight. Something he saw over Elaira's shoulder caused his eyes to show round rings of white. Distinctly he said, "Like the tax collector, here comes trouble."

Then the excitement and the drink undid him all at once, and he slumped on his face and passed out.

Elaira cried a frustrated epithet. Left no partner for a stake ostensibly set up to explain what she knew from Asandir, she threw down her cards and shoved from her seat to kick the Mad Prophet from his stupor.

Yet something in the quality of the disturbance at her back made her pause. She turned full around and craned her neck over the jostling press of male bodies, and her eyes went wary as Dakar's.

Arithon, Teir's'Ffalenn and Prince of Rathain, had entered the Ravens unaccompanied.

He stood just three paces inside the doorway. His hood lay half turned back from his face, the knuckles of both hands clenched on the fabric as if he had frozen in mid-gesture. Elaira traced the direction of his gaze and realized at once what transfixed him. Nailed to the grease-darkened rafters above the bar was a banner all torn and faded with years, its blazon the gold on blue star that times past had been sigil of s'Ilessid, sovereign dynasty of Tysan. In Erdane, since the rebellion, the taproom's coarse-minded celebrants had used the standard for target practice. Two arrows, a tatty collection of darts, and more than one rusted throwing knife skewered the artifact dead center.

Arithon stared at the desecrated banner, a look of shocked confusion whitening the planes of his face. He took a step toward the bar, caught his weight on his hands as if dazed, and unwittingly jostled someone's elbow.

The bump slopped beer from a tankard, for which the owner snapped a furious obscenity.

Arithon apologized like a diplomat, and the edged clarity of his accent turned every head in the room.

Conversations died to blank silence. Arithon's chin jerked up. His confusion fled as he recognized his error and his danger, both disastrously too late.

A headhunter slammed back his chair and shouted. "Ath defend us, he's barbarian!"

Someone else threw a tankard, which missed; the wench behind the bar ducked for cover. Then the whole room surged into motion as every besotted patron in the Ravens leaped to lay hands on the intruder. They thought the man they chased was an old-blood clansman who had dared to come swaggering inside town walls.

A moment ago, Arithon might have been dizzy, as well as dangerously ignorant, but he was cat-fast to react under threat. He sidestepped the first swung fist. As his first aggressor overbalanced and stumbled against the rush of surging bodies, he dodged through a fast-closing gap and nipped behind the nearest trestle table. Plates, hot soup, and chicken bones flew airborne as he upended the plank into his attackers.

Curses and yells erupted as the foremost ranks were borne backward. Diners still seated on the bench made a grab at the wretch who had upset their meal.

Arithon was already gone, raised by his arms and half a kick into a somersault over the ceiling beams. He descended hard on a soldier, slammed the man's jaw against his breastplate, and sprang off as his victim went down.

"Hey!" an ugly voice responded. "Turd who was born through his mother's asshole! Yer gonna die here, an' not by the mayor's executioner."

Hotly pursued, Arithon jumped and caught hold of a wrought iron torch sconce. As hands grabbed for his heels, he hoisted himself up out of reach into the cross-braced timbers of the rafters. Nimble as a sailor, he footed the width of the taproom, target for a cross fire of crockery. He somehow shed his cloak between sallies. With the fabric he netted a plate and sundry items of cutlery before a toss accomplished on a followthrough mired two pursuers in the folds. The casualties tangled and crashed in a clatter of dropped knives and wool. Stripped to shirtsleeves and tunic, Arithon ran; and his enemies saw he was unarmed.

Elaira knew sudden, draining fear. The irreplaceable heir to a kingdom could be pulled down, beaten to his death by these roistering, ignorant townsmen. Dakar snored away in drunken oblivion, and the only soul in the taproom who had the decency to look concerned was the scarlet-clad singer by the fireside.

Arithon had no allies to call on for rescue. The Ravens' enraged riffraff swarmed onto trestles and benches, the most maddened and aggressive among them bearing down from two sides on the bracing beams. Arithon leaped across air to the adjacent span of rafters. Cornered against the far wall, he laughed at the mob and called challenge. Elaira fretted over the chance that he might resort to shadow mastery or magic, but better sense or maybe instinct restrained him. He crouched instead and seized a pot hook from the peg beside the chimney. Back on his feet in an eye blink, he spun his purloined implement like a quarterstaff and rapped the legs from under his closest pursuer. The man toppled into an arm-waving plunge that ripped down a swaying knot of combatants.

Arithon reversed stroke and jabbed. The next soldier in line nearly fell as he windmilled back out of range. Arithon moved to press his hard-won advantage. Then someone in the melee flung a dagger.

Warned by a silvered flash of steel, Arithon swung the pot hook. The blade clanged against iron and deflected point first in a plunge that grazed the forearm of a bystander. At the sight of his own running blood, the afflicted broke into shrill screams. The mood of the mob changed from ugly to instantly murderous. The headhunters pressed now for revenge instead of bounty, and the off-duty guardsmen drew swords. Everyone else abruptly seemed to acquire weapons, and all without exception converged on the prince poised vulnerably in the rafters. Aware he was exposed, Arithon dropped.

His pot hook blurred in a stroke that whistled the air and intimidated space on the floorboards. He landed and two men with long swords engaged him. The clang of thrust and parry rang dissonant over the shouting. Elaira saw Arithon sidestep and swing to position a wall at his back. Wholly engaged in self-defense, he appeared not to notice that his stand had been made against a doorway.

"Merciful Ath," cried the minstrel from the fireside. "Someone in the scullery's going to sally from the pantry and skewer him."

Elaira spun in her tracks and fastened in desperation on the bard. "That entrance connects to the kitchens, back there?" Answered by a nakedly worried nod, she made a ward sign against misplaced trust and begged a favor of a total stranger. "Make me a diversion."

The scarlet-clad minstrel rose to the occasion with a floor-shaking shout of discovery. "Ath perserve us, there are clansmen outside the windows!"

A dozen attackers abandoned Arithon and rushed to assess this new threat; in the moment while the fracas stood diverted, one frightened witless enchantress centered her mind in her focusing jewel. She cobbled together a glamour of concealment and disappeared.

Elaira did not physically vanish, but assumed an aura of sameness, one that mirrored the grain of worn pine and dented pewter and sanded floorboards. Had anyone amid the Ravens' tumult paused and actually searched for her, she would have instantly been spotted. As it was, the press of the brawl directed Arithon's aggressors everywhere else but toward her. The enchantress slipped rapidly across the taproom, unnoticed as she skirted upset trestles, and bands of fist-waving craftsmen, and barmaids who scuttled on hands and knees in a frantic attempt to rescue crockery.

Elaira reached the side door undetected. The lamp there had gone out; screened by convenient shadows, she fumbled at her collar and pulled out the white crystal she wore tethered to her neck by a silver chain. She cupped the jewel in her palm and murmured litanies to refocus her innermind. Her hand shook. So did her voice. She ignored impending panic and prayed instead that the junior initiate on lanewatch would not choose this moment to expose her; far from an afterthought, she added her plea that no swordsman had attention to spare beyond Arithon's fast-moving pot hook. Acting with unconscionable recklessness, Elaira closed her gathered energies into a hard rune of binding.

Tiny, violet sparks snapped across the hinge pins at Arithon's back; the doorway stood secured. By then Elaira was sprinting in a breathless charge that carried her headlong through the scullery. Cooks and pot boys scattered from her path. She dodged the swing of the knife-waving drudge by the spit, slipped someone else's grasping hands, then tripped over a pastry rack and stumbled through a rain of falling scones to snatch up the rolling pin that lay in a bowl of dough beyond. Before the befuddled kitchen staff could catch her, Elaira darted into the pantry closet, trailing a dusting of flour. The scrambles at her back became more frantic. All but within reach of her goal, she gasped, "Ath, stand back! There's a riot out there, can't you hear?"

Then she elbowed through a hanging string of onions and reached the narrow doorway to the taproom. A barrage of threats and thuds issued from the opposite side. Elaira recovered her wind, reassured. The s'Ffalenn prince still fought vociferously for his life. The wood under her palms bounced and vibrated to the rasping clash of swordplay, then the thump of a body fallen, and somebody's bitten-off oath. Elaira tripped the latch, readied her stolen bludgeon, then snapped the spell-bindings on the hinges with a shuddering whimper of fright.

The door crashed open, shoved her staggering as Arithon's shoulder bashed the panel inward under force of a narrowly missed parry. A sword blade whined through string; onions bounced helter-skelter as five men harried the prince backward. Their eagerness hampered their weapons, which ironically worked to help spare him; the pot hook had long since fatigued under punishment, and Arithon defended with only the stub of the sheared-off handle. Elaira caught her balance and retreated as the fight erupted wholesale into the pantry. Bruised against corners of shelving, she received an impression of furious faces, a battering circle of steel, and the tense, hard-driving brilliance of Arithon's close-pressed defense. Then she caught her enchantress's jewel in a grip that gouged her palm, and struck the pastry roller on the crown of the prince's dark head.

He folded at the knees, eyes widened in a moment of shocked surprise. His look became what might have been prelude to laughter before the charm Elaira wrought to fell him blanked his mind. He collapsed on the floor at the enchantress's feet. She jumped past, committed beyond heed for further risks. Her crystal burned against her skin as once again she raised power. Her hastily wrought net of spells caught and strained to stay the mob, who now surged to butcher an unconscious victim.

"Stop!" Elaira shouted clearly. "This one's mine. I claim his life as spoils."

The front-rank aggressors rocked to a stupefied stop, hostility stamped on every red and sweating face; the swords flashed at angles still eager for slaughter. Trembling before that hedge of raised weapons, Elaira held her ground. Should even one man control hatred enough to see reason, the whole crowd would discover she was not the painted doxie her glamour made her over to appear.

Yet grudges in Erdane ran obsessively deep.

Startled by female intervention, and emotionally charged from adrenaline, the furious ones were easiest to deflect. Elaira's mazework of confusion hooked their anger and carved out a foothold for change; in something like sheepish embarrassment men glanced at the prince behind her knees. Their minds recalled no barbarian imposter, but instead saw a wine-raddled street rat who had carelessly offended someone else.

The few who had sustained injuries were far less easily diverted. Some of these shoved forward, waving bludgeons of snapped-off chair legs; not a few still wielded knives, and the fellow who had tumbled from the rafters was howling in self-righteous indignation. Sweating, Elaira strove to extend her spell of influence. But her fragile fabric of illusion only thinned and shuddered near to breaking; she had no more resource left to spare.

Beyond hope, past all recourse, she faced defeat. Erdane's ongoing feud with the past was going to end her life and that of the prince she had rashly tried to rescue.

Then like a miracle, the voice of the minstrel offered surcease. "Let the doxie have him, and be done! Dharkaron knows, he's filthy enough to disgust a hog. Probably going to leave her with the Avenger's own pox to remember him by."

The slur raised a wave of scattered laughter.

"Sithaer, now," Elaira added, somehow through terror and an unstable grip on two spells finding a note that approximated disgust. "It wasn't my bed I'd be offering him!"

A weatherbeaten captain toward the fore loosed a bellowing guffaw. "Leave him to her!" he said. "She'll probably scald his ears well enough." He shrugged to unlock a battered shoulder, then sheathed his steel; around him, other off-duty companions backed off smiling. The most rabid of the headhunters wavered, and in that instant of reprieve Elaira hooked the door adjoining pantry and common room and slammed the panel closed. For the benefit of the kitchen staff who gawked in the path of her retreat, she jabbed her fallen prize in the ribs, then launched into spiteful imprecations.

"Daelion mark ye in the hereafter for stinking bad habits! Ye wasted lump of a lout, ye dare te be stealin' my hard-earned coin fer spendin' on tankards at the tap!"

The cook stepped into the breach and shook Elaira's arm. "Wench, if you're minded to scold, spare us some peace and do it elsewhere."

The enchantress whirled in crazed fury. "How will I, with himself sprawled there with the onions and limp as dead dog meat in the bargain?"

She waved the fist with the pastry roller and set a row of canisters tottering. The cook snatched the implement away from her, jerked his greasy bangs toward his staff, then barked a command to lift the unconscious object of this madwoman's scorn and forcibly heave him out.

The pot boys grinned and lent their efforts to the cause. Arithon was hefted under the armpits, dragged through dustings of spilled flour and the grease-scummed runoff from the dish tubs, and ejected through an exit that led to the rear of the tavern.

Elaira followed, crying curses. She swore with redoubled vehemence upon discovery they had pitched her hard-won royalty headlong into the midden.

She shrilled at the fast-slamming door. "Dharkaron break ye for rogues, now I've got te wash his blighted clothing!"

The panel banged shut and a bar dropped in place with a final, sour clank.

Elaira subsided, shaking.

The alley behind the Four Ravens was dark and damply cold. Feeling the chill to her bones, the enchantress sucked a breath past her teeth that came shudderingly near to a choke as she gagged on the rank stench of garbage. "Sithaer and Dharkaron's Five Horses," she muttered to the form at her feet. "What in this life am I to do with you?"

The prince, sprawled limply in a nest of wilted carrots, returned an involuntary groan; then, from the shadow to one side, a sane voice proffered reply. "Where do you think he would be safe?"

Startled, Elaira spun and released a hissing gasp. The speaker proved to be the singer, leaning against the alley wall with the prince's salvaged cloak draped on his wrist. He smiled in quick reassurance. "You probably saved Arithon's life back there. He'd better thank you properly for the risks you undertook. If he doesn't, make sure to break all his fingers, then tell him I gave you permission."

Weak in the knees with relief, Elaira slumped against the midden door. "You know this man?"

"We're acquainted." The bard picked his way through the compost and crouched to check the victim's prone body; satisfied to find no lasting damage, he clicked his tongue. "Now, where are you wanting to hide him? Or do you trust him so much you'd have him wake up alone and maybe blunder into further mischief?"

Elaira thought quickly. "The hayloft, please." Since the gates closed at sundown, no mounted travelers could be expected to arrive or depart from the tavern until daylight; the grooms would be carousing, and the horse boy predictably asleep.

"All right, then," the bard said agreeably. "Help me lift him before some churl inside sits up and notices I didn't duck out to use the privy."

The loft above the Ravens' innyard was dusty with the meadowsweet scent of hay, and warm from the couriers' mounts and coach horses stabled in stalls down below. Couched in a cranny between haystacks and the high, windowless north wall with Arithon sprawled by her knees, Elaira bent over a bucket and wrung out a strip of linen torn at need from the lining of her shepherd's cloak. Lit by a glimmer from her crystal, the enchantress dabbed caked dirt and sweat from the unmistakably s'Ffalenn features of the prince. Belatedly she discovered blood in his hair. His scalp had been split by the pastry roller.

She bit her lip, chagrined. She had surely not struck him so hard; his current unconscious condition was more due to her stay-spell than to the head blow staged to disguise her blatantly foolish use of magic.

Why then was she reluctant to free him?

Elaira regarded Arithon's still face, its severe planes and angles unsoftened by her jewel's faint radiance. Under her hands she felt the corded tautness of him, the light-boned, lean sort of strength that was easiest of all to underestimate. His handling of attackers and pot hook had proved him no stranger to violence, and the raw new scars that encircled his wrists hammered home the recognition that only his bloodline was familiar. The man himself had a past, and a personality unknowably separate. He had not even been raised on Athera.

The intuitive deduction that marked Koriani origins shot Elaira's uneasiness into focus. She had been mistaken to bring this prince here, alone. Even incapacitated, his person bespoke a man wayward in judgment, and decisively quick to take action. The association that had set him off balance when he entered the Four Ravens must run deeper than a defaced kingdom banner; he had not expected to be attacked. When he woke, Arithon, High Prince of Rathain, was bound to be mettlesomely, royally enraged.

Elaira blotted flour off a miraculously ungrazed set of knuckles; the fingers seemed too finely made for the offensive delivered by the pot hook. She tossed aside her rag as if it burned her. The remiss young junior on lane-watch *still* had not touched her presence; worse yet, Elaira had no clue how she should handle the man, or herself, when the moment came to wake him up.

Arithon stirred on his own in that wretchedest moment of uncertainty. Elaira had time to panic and jackknifed clear as the heir apparent to a high kingship gathered his wits and sat up.

An immediate grimace twisted his face. He reached up, touched the swollen cut in his scalp, and looked at her. "Which wheel from the afterlife did you spare me from, Daelion Fatemaster's, or those of Dharkaron's Chariot? I feel like I've been milled under by something punishing from the Almighty."

"How could you be so utterly, unbelievably stupid!" Elaira burst out. Damn him, he was laughing! "They could have killed you in there, and to what purpose?"

Arithon lowered his fingers, saw blood, and thoughtfully hooked the rag she had discarded. He folded the frayed edges neatly over on themselves and pressed the compress to his wound. "Now, that's a question you might answer for me."

"Dharkaron, Ath's avenger!" Elaira was fast becoming exasperated. "You're in *Erdane!* Your speech patterns are perfectly barbarian. And the Ravens is a headhunters' haunt."

Very still, Arithon said, "Whose heads are the hunted?"

His curiosity was in no wise rooted in insolence. Filled by creeping disbelief, Elaira said, "Asandir never told you? They pay body weight in gold for the fugitive heirs of the earls. Half weight for clan blood, and probably every jewel off the mayor's chubby daughters for anything related to a prince."

Arithon lazed back on one elbow in the hay, his face tipped unreadably forward as he knotted the cloth around his head. "And what do you know of any princes?"

Elaira felt her heart bang hard against her ribs. "Do you mean to tell me, *that you don't know who you are!*"

His response came back mocking. "I thought I did. Has something changed?"

"No." Elaira gripped both hands in front of her shins; two could play his game. "Your Grace, you are Teir's'Ffalenn, prince and heir apparent of the crown of Rathain. All that pompous rhetoric means true-born son of an old-blood high king. Every able man in this city, as well as the surrounding countryside, would give his eldest child to be first to draw and quarter you."

A sound between a choke and a gasp cut her short.

Elaira glanced up to find Arithon's hand fallen away and his head thrown back. The face beneath the black hair was helplessly stripped by confusion.

He had not been baiting her; he had plainly not been told. That was not all; around Arithon's person Elaira sensed a gathering corona of power, invisibly triggered and unmistakably Asandir's. She had a split second to note that the forces that rang in opposition to Arithon's will were in fact an ingeniously laid restraint; then the gist of what she had said lent an impetus that provided him opening. He reacted with a practiced unbinding, and the fabric of the ward sheared asunder.

A snap like a spark whipped the air.

Then Arithon did get angry, a charged, blind-sided rage that left him wound like a spring and staring inward.

"*Teir's'Ffalenn,*" he said flatly. His Paravian was accentless and fluent, and the repeated term translated to mean "successor to power." In the glow of the jewel, the ratty twist of rag around his head lent the shadowed illusion of a crown. "Tell me about Rathain."

His command allowed no loophole for refusal; afraid to provoke an explosion, Elaira chose not to try. "The five northwestern principalities on this continent were territories in vassalage to Rathain, whose liege lord once ruled at Ithamon." She shrugged wretchedly. "Since sovereignty of Athera passed from Paravians to men, the high king crowned there by the Fellowship has always, without exception, been s'Ffalenn."

Arithon moved, not fast enough to mask a flinch. He ripped the rag from his head as though it were metal, and heavy, and an anguish he could not bury needled his reply to sarcasm. "Don't tell me. The people of Rathain are subject to misery and strife, and Ithamon is a ruin in a wasteland."

In point of fact, he was correct, but even rattled to shaking, Elaira was not fool enough to say so. There had to be a reason why Asandir had kept knowledge of this prince's inheritance a close secret.

Arithon arose from the hay. He paced in agitated strides across the loft, and barely a board creaked to his passing. At length he spun about, his desperation sharp as unsheathed steel. "What about Lysaer?"

Elaira tried for humor. "Oh, well, there's a kingdom waiting for him, too. In fact, we're sitting in the middle of it."

"Ah." Arithon's brows tipped up. "The banner in the Ravens. And perhaps such unloving royal subjects were the reason for Asandir's reticence?"

Careful to suppress other, more volatile suppositions, the enchantress nodded placating agreement. She watched the s'Ffalenn prince absorb this, and wondered what enormity she had caused, what balance had shifted while Arithon went from tense to perceptively crafty.

"I can keep this fiasco from Asandir," he said in answer to the very thought that had made her bite her lip.

Elaira widened her eyes. "You?" Merciful Ath, had he failed to perceive the awful strength in the ward she had accidentally lent him leverage to unbind? "How? Are you crazy?"

Arithon inclined his head in the precise direction of the Ravens, though the barn wall before him had no window. "Lady, how did you get across the taproom?"

Elaira reached up and smothered the light of her jewel in time to hide her expression. In the taproom, diverted by fighting, he could *not* have seen through her glamour.

A breath of air brushed her face out of darkness; Arithon was moving again, restless, and his words came turbulently fast. "Asandir won't have expected me to break through a block of that magnitude." Hay rustled as he gestured, perhaps with remembered impatience. "Sithaer's furies, I'd been trying to achieve its release for long enough. Trouble was, if I pushed too hard, I went unconscious."

Elaira turned white as she connected that the banner in the taproom had initiated Arithon's compulsive moment of unsteadiness. "I wonder why the Sorcerer didn't tell you."

Hands caught her wrists; deceptively and dangerously gentle, they pulled her fingers away from the jewel. Light sprang back and revealed Arithon on one knee before her, his expression determinedly furious. "Because I happen not to wish the burdens that go with a throne!"

He let her go, shoved away as though he sensed her Koriani perceptions might draw advantage from his stillness. "Kings all too often get their hands tied. And for what? To keep food in the mouths of the hungry? Hardly that, because the starving will feed themselves if left alone. No. A bad king revels in his importance. A good one hates his office. He spends himself into infirmity quashing deadly little plots to make power the tool of the greedy."

Elaira looked up into green eyes, frightened by the depth of their vehemence. She argued anyway. "Your friend Lysaer would say that satisfaction can be found in true justice."

Arithon stood up and made a gesture of wounding appeal. "Platitudes offer no succor, my lady. There's a very little beauty in satisfaction, and justice rewards nobody with joy." He lowered his hands and his voice dropped almost to a whisper. "As Felirin the Scarlet would tell you."

He referred to the minstrel in the Ravens who had abetted his narrow escape. Not the least bit taken in by his show of surface excuses, Elaira drew her own conclusion. Arithon had slipped his Sorcerer chaperon and ventured abroad in Erdane looking expressly to provoke. He might not have known the townsmen's pitch of antagonism; or he might have simply not cared. His wildness made him contorted as knot-work to decipher.

In a typically rapid shift of mood, he managed a civilized recovery. "I owe you, lady enchantress. You spared me some rather unpleasant handling, and for that you have my thanks. Someday I hope to show my gratitude."

Which was prettily done and sincere, but hardly near the point. "I saved your life," Elaira said in a bald effort to shake his complacency.

He just looked at her, his clothing mussed over and his face a bit worn, and his reticence underhandedly reproachful. He had *not* been defenseless. The pot hook was only a diversion, since he had both training and shadow mastery carefully held in reserve. Touched by revelation, Elaira saw that indeed, he had not been backed against the passage to the pantry by any accident but design.

Beginning to appreciate his obstinacy, Elaira choked back a snort of laughter. "You were on course for the midden in any case?"

Arithon smiled. "As the possibility presented itself, yes. Have you lodgings? I'd like to see you back safely."

"Oh, that's priceless," Elaira gasped. Her eyes were watering. She hoped it was only the dust. "You're a damned liability in this town."

"In any town." The Shadow Master paid her tribute with a bow. "You shouldn't worry over things that I'm too lazy to bother with."

"That's the problem exactly." Elaira allowed him to take her hand and draw her to her feet. His strength was indeed deceptive, and he seemed to release her fingers with reluctance. She said, "I can find my way just fine. The question is, can you?"

She did not refer to the wards that concealed the location of the seeress's house where he lodged.

Her deliberately oblique reference did not escape him. "Asandir knows I went out for air." Arithon made a rueful face at the odiferous stains on his clothing. "There are several suitably smelly puddles in the alley near Enithen Tuer's. And dozens of hazardous obstacles. A man prone to odd fits of dizziness might be quite likely to trip."

He reached out and began with light hands to pluck the loose hay from her hair. That moment, when all care for pretense was abandoned, the junior initiate on lane-watch stumbled clumsily across Elaira's presence.

The enchantress stiffened as the energies of her distant colleague passed across her, identified her, and responded with a jab of self-righteous indignation. The backlash hurt. "Sithaer's furies, not now!" Elaira capped her dismay with a fittingly filthy word.

Taken aback, Arithon stepped away. "I beg your pardon?"

"You did nothing," Elaira assured, her mind only half on apology. Apparently there were worse offenses than visiting Sorcerers of the Fellowship, or even engaging in card games with disreputable apprentice prophets; by the repercussions sensed in the background, Elaira understood that speaking with princes in haylofts after midnight was undeniably one of them. Yet to explain the particulars of her crisis would take by far too much time. "I have a scrape of my own to work out of—my personal version of Asandir."

Arithon grinned and melted unobtrusively into the shadows. "Then I commend you to subterfuge and a fast soft landing in a midden."

She heard his soft step reach the ladder.

"Farewell, lady enchantress." Then he was gone, leaving her alone with a larger dilemma than the one she had found in the room at Enithen Tuer's.

Guardian of Mirthlvain

Cupped like a witch's cauldron between the jagged peaks of the Tiriacs and the north shore of Methlas Lake, Mirthlvain Swamp was not a place where even the boldest cared to tread. Submerged under vaporous mists, the pools with their hummocks of spear-tipped reeds spawned horrors in their muddy depths that the efforts of two civilizations had failed to secure behind walls. Yet a man did dare the dangers and walk here, on the crumbling stone causeway that remained of an ancient and long overrun bulwark. Grievously shorthanded as the Fellowship Sorcerers had been through the years since the Mistwraith's conquest, never for an instant was Mirthlvain Swamp left unwatched.

The master spellbinder Verrain crouched on a precarious span of stonework with his elbows braced on his knees. A rust-colored cloak lay furled at his feet, and untrimmed blond hair fringed his collar with beads of accumulated damp. He had poised for a very long time, motionless, his large, capable hands with their puncture scars from old bite wounds curled over an equally battered staff.

Wavelets flurried fitfully against the decayed wall, disturbed by something that lurked unseen in the depths; then the waters subsided to oily stagnation. A line creased Verrain's brows and one ivory knuckle twitched. Black eyes regarded blacker water, both invisibly troubled.

The misted sky reflected in the pool shivered faintly, as if bubbles sprang from the muck underneath and rose in a sequin shimmer— except that no trapped air broke the surface. Verrain pursed lips that a very long time in the past had been the delight of Daenfal's barmaids. He loosed a hand from his staff and slowly, carefully, extended his arm above the pool.

He spoke in accents as antiquated as the doxies, who were all six centuries dead. "Show yourself, spawn of the *methuri.*"

Then he closed his fingers. The ribbon of power he held leashed in readiness uncoiled through lightless fathoms.

Ripples bloomed to a curl of froth as a whip-thin tail sliced the surface, splashed, and vanished.

"Ah," said Verrain thoughtfully. "I am not so easily evaded." He murmured a word that unbound a restraint; a force like an arrow speared through the murk in pursuit of a creature that zigzagged in patterns of wild flight.

Muck flurried up from the depths. Then the peaty waters moiled and burst into spray as a serpentine shape slashed through. The snake was narrow, its head the distinctive wedge of a viper. The eyes it pinned on its tormentor were scarlet as jewels, and malevolent.

The spellbinder forced himself not to recoil. Though aware the sculling serpent was fully capable of a strike, he traced a symbol upon the air. A shimmer remained where his finger passed.

The snake stayed trained upon the ward glyph as, crouched on the heels of worn boots, and bare of any artifice or talisman, Verrain transformed thought into power. His palms began faintly to glow. He handled raw energy as though it were solid and twisted it into a strand. The serpent hissed, fighting the ward that held it bound; its tail flicked a silver fin of water into the tangled banks of reed.

Verrain's forehead ran with sweat. Faster now, his fingers wove spell-thread into a snare which he cast over the creature that knifed the water.

The pool exploded into spray. Unnaturally vocal for its kind, the creature screamed like a rabbit as the ward clamped over its coils.

The hair prickled on Verrain's neck as it twisted. He blocked its attempt to dive. The snake screamed again. The spellbinder's nostrils flared against the vapors thrown off by churning water. Grim with concentration and braced as if for a blow, he released the rest of the energies he had pooled throughout motionless hours of waiting.

Light pulsed across his fine-knitted spells. The mesh unraveled in a flash, and the serpent's cry ceased as if pinched. A last reflexive surge shot it full length from the marsh before it fell back, limp.

Verrain snatched up his staff. Fast as a swordsman, he hooked one flaccid coil before it could sink beyond sight. A practiced snap of his wrist flipped the serpent clear of the pool. Its dripping four-foot length spilled with a slither on the moss-rotten stone of the wall.

Exposed to full view, it gleamed sleekly black. A row of barbs ridged the length of its spine. Verrain prodded the head into profile. The red eyes were slitted like a cat's. An ivory diamond patterned the throat; the rest of the underbelly was dark. Verrain pried open the mouth and extended the fangs from their membrane sheaths. Venom seeped out, odorless and diamond clear, but the drop that splashed the rock left a caustic, smoking stain.

Verrain scrambled back beyond reach of the fumes. His wide, expressive mouth lost all trace of the fact he had ever smiled. He had expected this serpent might be a fresh variation; the creatures bent into mutation in past ages to serve as hosts for *methuri,* or hate-wraiths, interbred with persistent success. Although the Fellowship of Seven had exterminated the last of these iyat-related parasites five thousand years back, Mirthlvain Swamp continued relentlessly to brew up leftover crossbreeds.

Diamond-throated meth-snakes cropped up in many forms, ranging from harmless to virulently poisonous. This one Verrain had snared as a formality, never suspecting its bite might carry a cierl-ankeshed toxin. He shuddered to think of the risk he had taken, to name-trance the creature bare-handed. Weak in the knees and finely shaking, he leaned on his staff and thanked Ath Creator he was unharmed and still standing upright.

Even skin contact with that deadliest of poisons caused a wasting of the nerves, a screaming firestorm of agony that resulted in twitching paralysis. His body might have lain on this wall and suppurated for days before the life finally left it.

Aware through Sethvir that the Fellowship was taxed thin by an outbreak of Khadrim and the development of the West Gate prophecy, Verrain frowned. His discovery was not going to please; cierl-ankeshed was a threat that his masters securely believed had been eradicated.

Suddenly drained by his weariness, the spellbinder who was Guardian of Mirthlvain straightened. He shook out his rust brown cloak, raised up his staff, and nudged the dead snake from the wall. The corpse fell with a splash but did not sink. Even as Verrain moved away, his footsteps cautious on the unstable stone of the wall, the ink black waters behind him boiled up in a froth as scavengers converged in a frenzy to devour the meth-snake's remains.

Observations

In the city of Castle Point, a raven drops out of misty sky and alights on the shoulder of a Sorcerer who wears black, and whose dark, sad eyes are shadowed further by a broad-brimmed hat with a patterned silver band. . . .

Southward, beneath the shattered spires of the old earl's court, the enchantress of the watch bears report to the Prime that Elaira has culminated an illicit visit to Erdane with clandestine meetings with a prince in a tavern hayloft. . . .

Sethvir, Sorcerer and archivist at Althain Tower to Asandir, in residence at the home of Enithen Tuer: *"Cross Camris promptly. Trouble pending; migrant strain of meth-snakes with cierl-ankeshed venom confirmed in Mirthlvain Swamp. . . ."*

VII. PASS OF ORLAN

T he morning following Arithon's escapade at the Four Ravens, Asandir recalled the horses from the smithy where they had been reshod, then rousted a hungover Dakar from the brothel that had sheltered him through the night. Whether the Mad Prophet had been sober enough to enjoy the doxie whose bed had warmed him appeared dubious; he sat in the paint's saddle with a pronounced list. Yet the malaise that unstrung his balance seemed not to dampen his complaints.

"When I pass beneath the Wheel, Dharkaron Avenger's going to seem like an angel of mercy." He crooked his reins in one elbow, cradled his head, and managed with well-practiced grumpiness to direct his injury toward Asandir. "You *said* we'd be in Erdane for two more days."

The Sorcerer replied too softly to overhear, but the effect upon Dakar was profound.

His cheeks went white as new snow. Suddenly straight in his saddle, he swung the paint's head and promptly spurred down the lane toward the gates. No further protest escaped him, even when the party clattered out of Erdane and turned eastward at a pace guaranteed to inflame his hangover.

Lysaer for once forbore from teasing. Aware that his half-brother had stolen out last night by himself, and disappointed not to have been asked along, he gained no chance for tactful inquiry; Arithon's nighttime outing remained unexplained. No mention was made of the tunic which a peculiarly wakeful Enithen Tuer had snatched off to wash before dawn. Asandir's mood seemed preoccupied and brisk, and had been so since daybreak. Had Dakar felt inclined to be talkative, he might have offered a fellow miscreant fair warning: with a Fellowship Sorcerer, silence on any topic boded trouble.

Yet Arithon was disinclined to worry in any case. With the mystery behind his mind block resolved, the cutting edge eased from his reserve. Left less wary than watchful now that he understood the stakes involved a kingship, he trusted time and circumstance would show him an opening to overset Asandir's prerogatives. Until then he rode at his half-brother's side, and not even his restive mare diverted him from rapid-fire conversation. Lysaer welcomed the entertainment. Since too much quiet let him brood over the undermining losses of his banishment, he fielded Arithon's quips in a spirited enthusiasm that outlasted interruptions by fast-riding couriers, and packed farm drays, and once, a dusty band of cattle whose herd boys yipped and goaded their charges to market.

Then, as with West End, the farmlands thinned and ended. One hard day's travel beyond Erdane, the way became wild and untenanted. The brush-clothed scrub lands of Karmak gave rise to forested downs laced with streamlets. The mist seemed alive with the rush of running water, and the air keen and brittle with coming snow. More than once the party startled deer from the thickets. If the bucks were royally antlered, their incoming winter coats were flat and lacking gloss; even after summer's forage, the does were sadly thin.

The mist's blighted legacy afflicted more than creatures in the wild.

After nightfall, perhaps due to the chill, Asandir relented and engaged a room at a rundown wayside tavern that in better times had been a hospice tended by Ath's initiates.

"What became of them?" Lysaer asked.

"What happens to any order of belief when its connection to the mysteries becomes sullied?" Asandir chose not to entrust his tall stallion to the ill-kempt groom, but attended to his saddle girths himself. "Desh-thiere's darkness disrupted more than sunlight on this world. The link that preserved was lost along with the Riathan Paravians."

The pent-back sorrow in his statement did not invite further inquiry; and if the carved gates at the innyard were still intact, the beautiful, patterned sigils of ward had lost any power to guard. The tavern's musty attic proved to be riddled with iyats, which perhaps explained the dearth of clientele.

By the time the Sorcerer banished the pests, the hour had grown late; the common room with its great blackened beams stood lamentably empty. While here the accents of outland strangers did not provoke hostilities, still the stooped old innkeeper took care not to turn his back. He served his odd guests in silence, while his wife stayed hidden in the kitchen.

The fare was bland and too greasy; Lysaer left his plate barely touched. Arithon had seen worse on a ship's deck. After sighs and a martyred show of eye rolling, Dakar righteously forwent ale for mulled cider and a bowl of the inn's insipid stew. The bread had no weevils that he could see, so he ate it, and Lysaer's portion, too. Then he stalked from his emptied bowls to a bed that he swore would have lice and mildew in the blankets.

This failed to secure him permission to retire in the hayloft. Perhaps as a precaution, Asandir sat the night through in the hallway, his back against the door panel.

"Unforgiving as a reformed priest," Dakar commiserated to Arithon; yet whether the Sorcerer stood vigil to curb the excesses of his apprentice, or to curtail further outings by the Master of Shadows, or whether he simply wished space for clear thought, the Mad Prophet was too wise to ask. He flopped crosswise on a mattress of dusty ticking, and his chain reaction of sneezes changed into snores that would have done credit to a hibernating bear.

Busy scooping ice from the enameled ewer of wash water, and striving to rise above low spirits, Lysaer regarded the sleeping prophet with a mix of laughter and distaste. "If he weren't apprenticed to a Sorcerer, he would have made a splendid royal fool."

"What a curse to lay on a king," Arithon observed from the corner, where, stripped down to his hose, he spread out his blankets on bare floor. A cockroach scurried up from a crack near his foot; he reacted fast enough to crush it, changed his mind, and let it race to safety under the baseboard. "Not mentioning that every princess within reach would have her bottom pinched to bruises."

Lysaer splashed frigid water on his face, gasped, and groped for his shirt, that being the nearest cloth at hand; the innkeeper was too stingy to provide towels. The prince chafed his half-brother, "I'd say that upbringing by mages left you cynical."

By now half muffled under bedclothes, Arithon said in startled seriousness, "Of course not."

Lysaer rested his chin on his fists and his damply crumpled shirt. Statesman enough to guess that the meat of the matter sprang from

Arithon's ill-starred heirship of Karthan, and not eased that the thrust of s'Ffalenn wiles were now bent toward contention with Asandir, he gently shifted the subject. "Well, the loss of your roots doesn't bother you much."

One corner of Arithon's mouth twitched. After a moment the expression resolved to a smile. "If it takes sharing confidences to prove that you're wrong, there was one young maid. I was never betrothed, as you were. Sithaer, I barely so much as kissed her. I think she was as frightened of my shadows as I was of telling her my feelings."

"Perhaps you'll find your way back to her." The wind whined mournfully through the cracks in the shutters and a draft stole through the small room; touched by the chill, Lysaer shrugged. "At least we could ask Asandir to return us to Dascen Elur once we've defeated the Mistwraith."

"No." Arithon rolled over, his face turned unreadably to the wall. "Depend on the fact that he won't."

"You found out something in Edrane, didn't you," Lysaer said. But his accusation dangled unanswered. Rebuffed and alone with his thoughts, and hating the fate that left him closeted at the whim of a Sorcerer in the fusty lodgings of a second-rate roadside tavern, he shook out his damp shirt and blew out the candle for the night.

Two days later, the riders in Asandir's party reached Standing Gate, a rock formation that spanned the road in a lopsided natural arch. Centaurs in past ages had carved the flanking columns into likenesses of the twins who had founded their royal dynasty. Since before the memory of man the granite had resisted erosion; the kings Halmein and Adon reared yet over the highway, their massive, majestic forelegs upraised in the mist and their beards and maned backs stained the verdigris of old bronze with blooms of lichen.

Mortal riders could not pass beneath their shadow without experiencing a chill of profound awe. Here the footfalls of the horses seemed to resound with the echoes of another age, when the earth was fresh with splendor and Paravians nurtured the mysteries. Standing Gate marked the upward ascent to the high valley pass of Orlan, sole access through the Thaldein mountains to Atainia and lands to the east.

But even under the frosts of coming winter, in the years since the fall of the high kings, travelers who fared through Standing Gate never passed unobserved.

Asandir's party proved no exception, as Arithon discovered in a pause to water his mare on the bank of a fast-flowing creek. Muffled against the stiff breeze, he sat his saddle with both stirrups dropped and his reins slipped loosely through his fingers. Suddenly the dun flung her head up. Her rider did not see what spooked her; the woolen hood of his cloak masked his peripheral vision as she snapped sideways and wheeled. Stalled from bolting by an expert play on the reins, the mare crab-stepped, stopped, and blew noisily. Her sable-edged ears pricked toward a stand of scrub pine that rattled and tossed in the gusts.

Nothing moved that did not appear to belong there.

Yet when Arithon urged the mare on, she stamped and rigidly resisted. Warned by her keener senses, he recovered his stirrups and stroked her neck in pretense of coaxing her away; at the same time he centered his mind and cast an enchanter's awareness over the thicket.

A man crouched there, motionless, clad in jerkin and leggings of sewn wolf skin. Weather had roughened his face beyond his years, and his ruddy hair was tangled from the wind. The consciousness Arithon touched held a predator's leashed aggression paired with tempered steel: a matched set of long knives and a javelin with a braided leather grip.

Although to face away from the thicket as if no armed man watched his back was a most unwelcome exercise, Arithon pressed his mare forward in earnest. The instant the rocky footing allowed a faster pace, he trotted his horse and caught up with the others.

Dakar regarded him slantwise as the dun overtook his paint. "How was the assignation? Or did you dawdle to swim?"

"Neither." Arithon returned a grin of purest malice. "Remind me to recommend you as chaperon for some jealous pervert's catamite."

He ignored the Mad Prophet's thunderous scowl and disturbed Asandir's preoccupied silence. "We're being watched."

The Sorcerer's gaze stayed trained ahead, as if he saw beyond the misty road which wound upward between steepening rocky outcrops. "That's not surprising."

Wise to the subtleties of mages, Arithon withheld unwelcome questions; presently the Sorcerer's steely eyes turned from whatever inward landscape he had been contemplating. "This is the townsmen's most dreaded stretch of highway. The clans that ruled Camris before the rebellion make their stand here. If we were a caravan bearing metals or cloth goods, we would require an armed escort. Not being town-born, our party has little to fear."

"The Camris clans were subject to the high king of Tysan?" Arithon asked.

Asandir returned an absent glance. "The old earls of Erdane swore fealty. Their descendants will not have forgotten."

Unfooled by the Sorcerer's apparent inattention, Arithon reined in his mare. As she curvetted and recovered stride by the shoulder of Lysaer's chestnut, the green eyes of her rider showed a glint of veiled speculation. Covered by the clang of hooves on cleared rock, he said, "We're going to see action in the pass."

Lysaer rubbed a nose nipped scarlet by the chill, his expression turned gravely merry. "Then someone better tell Dakar to tighten his saddle girth. Or the first quick move his paint makes will tumble him over on the rocks."

"I heard that," interjected the Mad Prophet. He flapped his elbows, his reins, and his heels, and contrived to overtake the half-brothers without mishap. To Lysaer he said, "Let's be sporting and wager. I say my saddle stays put with no help from buckles, and you'll kiss the dirt before I do." Brown eyes slid craftily to the Shadow Master. "And one thing further—there won't be any trouble in the pass."

"Don't answer," said Arithon to his half-brother. "Not unless you fancy pulling cockle burrs from your saddle fleeces."

"That's unfair," Dakar retorted, injured. "I only cheat when the odds are hard against me."

"My point precisely." Arithon ducked the swing the Mad Prophet pitched in his direction, then sidled his mount safely clear as the paint's saddle slid around her barrel and disgorged her fat rider in an ignominious heap on the trail.

By the time the commotion settled and Dakar had righted the paint's maladjusted tack, flurries eddied around the rocks. The snowfall thickened rapidly. Within minutes all but the nearest landmarks became buried in whirlwinds of white. The storm that had threatened through the past day and a half closed over the mountains, whipped in by a dismal north wind.

The riders continued over ever more steepening terrain. Bothered by Arithon's mention of trouble, Lysaer urged his horse past a stand of boulders to find opening to speak with Asandir.

"When we reach the next town, might I sell my jewels to buy a sword?"

The Sorcerer returned a look like blank glass, his cragged brow sprinkled with settled snow. "We'll cross no more towns before arrival at Althain Tower."

More forthright than his half-brother, Lysaer persevered. "Perhaps we could find a tavern keeper with a spare blade available for purchase, then."

Asandir's vagueness crystallized to piercing irritation. "When you have need of a weapon, you shall be given one."

The Sorcerer urged his mount on with speed. Concerned lest the road become mired too deeply for travel, he allowed no stop until dusk, and then only for the barest necessities. The riders fed their horses and swallowed a hasty meal. Sent out to assess conditions, Lysaer returned to report that, even should the blizzard slacken, the gusts had increased; drifting might render the mountains impassable by daybreak.

"We'll be through the pass before then," Asandir stated flatly. Despite outspoken resentment from Dakar, the Sorcerer quenched the fire and ordered the horses resaddled.

The riders pressed eastward through a long and miserable night. All but blind in the blizzard, they made torturous headway through the dark. The road narrowed to a trail hedged by knife-edged promontories and sheer drops, each dip and ditch and gully smoothed innocently over by drifts. Horses floundered through heavy footing or clattered perilously across ice-sheened rock. The winds buffeted all the while with relentless ferocity. Manes and cloaks became mantled in ice. The driving sting of snow crystals needled any exposed patch of flesh, and hands and feet ached from the penetrating cold.

The horses forded the icy current of the Valendale and emerged, dusted with hoarfrost from spume thrown off by the waterfalls. In times before the Mistwraith, the cascades could be seen falling like ribbons of liquid starlight as the feed springs of hundreds of freshets tumbled over clefts into the gorge.

Daybreak saw the riders deep into the pass of Orlan. By then the snowfall had eased, but Desh-thiere's mists sheathed the saw-toothed ridges and the wind still cut like a sword. The riders traversed the high notches submerged in whipping snow devils as gusts stripped the black rock of the Thaldeins and harried across a desertscape of drifts.

At times visibility closed until only the mage-trained could maintain sure sense of direction. Asandir and Arithon broke trail by turns, relieved on occasion by Dakar; yet despite the cold and the rough, floundering gait of his horse through the snow, the Mad Prophet unreliably tended to fall asleep in his saddle. Since a rider who blundered over a precipice was unlikely to be found before the thaws, and Asandir stayed wrapped in his silences, the chance to take fate by the horns became too tempting for Arithon to resist.

He chose his moment to volunteer, then pressed his dun to the fore. Throughout the next hour he drew gradually ahead, until a lead of fifty paces separated him from the others.

Here, at the storm-choked heart of the pass, the road dropped sheer on the north side, cliffs of trackless granite fallen away into a gulf of impenetrable mist; south, escarpments towered upward to summits buried in storm. The drifts lay chest-deep and packed into layers by the gusts. Curtained in wind-whirled snow, Arithon spoke gently to his mare as she shouldered tiredly ahead. His deadened hands gave rein as she stumbled; he balanced her, coaxed her forward with the promise of shelter and bran as she clawed toward a scoured expanse of rock. Stung by a gust that watered his eyes, Arithon ducked his face behind his hood just as the mare struck out off packed footing. Her legs skated wildly. Pitched against her neck as she scrambled, Arithon kicked free of the stirrups and dismounted. He flung his cloak over her steaming back and freed his dagger. When the mare steadied he lifted a foreleg and chipped out the ice ball that had compacted in the hollow of her hoof. The relentless snows had long since scoured away the preventive smear of grease applied on the banks of the ford.

When a glance backward showed the others halted to tend their own mounts similarly, Arithon straightened. Hopeful the barbarians were still watching, he hooked the dun's reins and led her off without troubling to dust the accumulated snow from his shoulders. His jerkin had soaked through in any case, with his cloak left draped across the flanks of his mount. The mare was dangerously weary and chilled, and if her reserves became spent, the pass offered no shelter.

Arithon crossed the cleared patch, battered by blasts of driven ice. Beyond, where the gale's direct force was cut by an overhanging rock spur, the drifts lay piled and deep. The mare sank to her brisket and floundered to an uncertain halt.

While the weather continued to howl outside this one pocket of stillness, a voice called challenge from above.

"Don't move." The accents were crisp, commanding, and by town standards, purely barbarian. "Make one sound and you'll gain a dead horse."

The dun snorted in hotheaded alarm. Grasping for advantage in mired footing, Arithon dug his knuckles in her ribs. As she shied face about toward the cliff, he snatched the cloak from her flank, cracked the cloth to fan her alarm, then let the force of her spin fling him sideways. The mare was a fast-moving target when the barbarian made good his threat. An arrow shot from a niche overhead nicked a gash across her shoulder, then buried with a hiss in rucked snow.

The sound and the sting undid the dun. She bolted in panic, her gallop striking sparks from exposed stone as herd instinct impelled her to backtrack. She hit the last expanse of drifts in a white explosion of snow clods, then disappeared completely as a gust roared like smoke across the trail.

Sheltered under cover of the eddies, Arithon dropped his cloak, drew Alithiel, and flattened his back against the underhang. The wind lulled. Tumbling snow winnowed and settled to unveil chaos as the mare charged through the oncoming riders. Her loose reins looped the nose of the chestnut and spun him plunging in a spraddle-legged stagger. Lysaer kept his seat through skilled horsemanship, but could not avoid collision with Asandir's black. Both mounts floundered sideways. Nose to tail just behind, the paint and the pack pony rocketed back on their hocks. Pans clanged and a poorly tied tent flapped loose. The pony ripped off a buck that scared the paint, and caught sound asleep in the scramble, Dakar toppled headfirst into a snowdrift. He flopped back upright shouting epithets referring to bitch-bred donkeys; while bearing their food stores and necessities, the pack pony joined the paint and the dun in headlong stampede down the trail.

Arithon seized the moment while the others were delayed and took swift stock of his surroundings. In a cranny above his sheltered hollow, he caught his first glimpse of his attacker: a gloved hand, a sleeve trimmed in wolf fur, and the dangerously leveled tip of a deer arrow, the broad, four-bladed sort designed to rip and kill by internal bleeding. Arithon repressed a shiver through a moment of furious re-assessment. Chance had favored him; his horse had escaped without worse damage than a scratch. But if his spurious ploy was not to bring disaster, he would have to do something about Lysaer. Like the spirited dun, the prince had too much character to meet any threat with complacency.

The drawn broadhead abruptly changed angle; Arithon jammed himself tight to the rock as the archer's torso momentarily reared against the sky.

The man wore leather and undyed wolf pelts. Hair spiked with frost fringed the rim of his brindled cap, and an impressive breadth of shoulders matched the recurve bow held poised at the rim of the abutment. Motionless, afraid to exhale lest the plume of his breath disclose his position, Arithon grinned outright as his adversary took painstaking aim down the defile.

"Move away from the rocks," the archer called. "I have you covered." The moan of a rising gust drove him to urgency. "Move out! Now!"

The wind peaked. Snow sheeted in a blanketing shower and the barbarian fired blind. As the shaft slashed through his discarded cloak, Arithon scaled the rock face. Sobered by discovery that clansmen balked at killing not at all, he kicked through a cleft and sought the lair of the bowman before his reckless ploy had time to backfire.

The gust passed and the air cleared. As the archer leaned out to account for his hit, the Master stalked, his footfalls silenced by snow.

The archer discovered his error, cursed, and whirled to cover his back. He caught his erstwhile quarry in the act of a counter ambush. Unfazed by surprise and fast for his bulk, he nocked another arrow. Arithon's thrown dagger sliced his bowstring in mid-draw. The bow cracked straight in backlash. Snapped around by a severed end of cordage, the arrow raked the clansman's wrist.

"Fiends!" the scout cursed. He disentangled his arm from his disabled recurve, not quite soon enough. Arithon closed his final stride and poised Alithiel for a fatal thrust through the throat.

Brown eyes met green through a tigerish instant of assessment. Though larger by a head and doubly muscled, the barbarian chose not to risk a grab for his dagger; the blade at his neck was by far too nervelessly steady.

"Try not to be foolish," Arithon said. He looked up at his bulkier adversary with an expression implacably shuttered. "By the love of the mother who bore you, I urge you to *think*. Ask why I would do a thing, then forfeit all I had gained." Slowly, deliberately, he turned his blade and dropped it point downward between the cross-laced boots of his captive.

Steel sliced through snow and stood quivering, the dark metal with its striking silver tracery the dangerous invitation to a riddle. The clansman bridled his fury with an effort. A moment passed, filled by the howl of wind and the wet swirl of snow, and the slow drip of blood from the fingers of a weapon-callused hand. The smoke-dark steel in the drift stayed untouched amid gathering spatters of scarlet. Then, as if nothing untoward had just happened, the barbarian's lips twisted into a vexed and humorless smile. "Move and you die," he told Arithon. "Behind you stand six of my companions, every one of them armed."

Arithon felt a prick at his lower spine. At bay on the point of a javelin, his complacency remained unshaken. "I'm required to surrender twice?"

His unforced clarity of speech caused a stir through the band that had trapped him.

The bowman alone stayed unmoved. "Take the upstart," he snapped.

"Grithen, you're wrong," somebody protested—the voice sounded female. "This catch is certainly no townsman."

"You say?" The redheaded ringleader swore. "Do you see clan identification anywhere on this bastard? Accents can be faked. If this man were clan born, but in league with the mayors, he'd know better than to leave town walls."

Arithon looked at Grithen, calm through an uncomfortable blast of wind. "And if I am neither?" His indecipherable expression stayed with him. "What then?"

"Well, whoever values your foolhardy hide will pay us a bountiful ransom." Grithen signaled left-handedly, and this time his henchmen responded.

Arithon found himself pitched forward into the snow. Hands searched his person for weapons, found none, and pinioned with a thoroughness that hurt. Arithon twisted his head sideways. "Furies of Sithaer!" he exclaimed in derisive and blistering consternation. "Had I wanted a fight, don't you think I'd have knifed something more than a bowstring?"

"Then why trouble with decoy and ambush in the first place?" Wolfishly contentious, Grithen exacted payment for the shame of his earlier misjudgment. "Bind him."

Jerked to his feet, Arithon watched with a sailor's appreciation as the scouts cut their rawhide laces and expertly tied up his wrists. Then he averted his gaze, spat blood from a cut lip, and endured an ignominious interval while more cords were looped tightly around his ankles. "The heart of the dilemma," he conceded to Grithen in a final, acid afterthought. "Did I act out of purpose or folly? You'd better figure out which, and quickly."

Down the trail, Asandir's party had successfully recovered their strays; they were starting back up the pass with obvious urgency and concern, and though no one appeared to watch them, their progress was covertly marked.

"Suppose I had a companion too prideful to submit to a threat." Arithon looked keenly at his captor, who was frowning and flicking blood from his leathers. "Say my friend had no fear of danger, and he forced you to harm him to make your capture. That might be a pity. His skin is pricelessly valuable."

Grithen whistled and shot a triumphant glance at his henchmen, one of whom was indeed a scarred and grim-faced woman. Then his leonine beard parted in a grin of forthright appreciation. "Which one is he? I assure, we'll handle him as delicately as a flower."

Arithon raised his brows. "Flower he isn't, but don't worry. If he doesn't cooperate and surrender, *my life will surely be forfeit.*"

Grithen caught up the hilt of Arithon's relinquished blade and tested the balance, his smile turned suddenly corrosive. "You're a boy lover," he concluded in disgust. "That's why you gave yourself up. To protect your beloved."

"By Dharkaron," Arithon murmured, "how you'll wish that was true." He showed no rancor at the insult, and at long last his barbarian captor saw past his hostage's wooden expression. The wretch he ordered manhandled and tied and dragged toward the edge of the outcrop was desperately struggling not to laugh.

"Mad," Krithen concluded under his breath. He traced the sword's edge with a fingertip and flinched as the steel nicked flesh. Uneasy, but too rabidly committed for retreat, he whistled the call of the mountain hawk and alerted the band still in hiding to initiate the next stage of his ambush.

The dun mare shied back, snorting over the jingle of bit rings and gear as the riders approached the promontory where their companion had lately come to grief.

"Whoa," Lysaer soothed gently. Astride his disgruntled chestnut and leading his half-brother's mount by the bridle, he slacked rein as the mare jibbed backward. "Whoa now." The patience in his voice overlaid a worry that burned his thoughts to white rage. Obstinate the Master of Shadows might be, and most times maddeningly reticent, yet as Lysaer combed through wind-whipped snow for a man perhaps fallen and injured, he did not dwell on past crimes or piracy. However cross-grained, no matter how secretive or odd a childhood among mages had made him, Arithon's motives before exile had likely not been founded in malice.

He was kin, and the only other in this mist-cursed world who recalled that Lysaer had been born a prince.

The mare shied again, hauling the chestnut a half pace sideward. Fixed and diligent in his search, Lysaer kept his seat out of reflex. He swept the gray rocks and the trampled spread of drifts and finally sighted the cloak, crumpled in a shallow depression and pinned by the black shaft of an arrow. His breath locked in his throat. The dun had not come by the gash on her shoulder through mishap, and now he had proof.

Tautly controlled as a clock spring, Lysaer looped the dun's lead through a ring on his saddle and crisply addressed Asandir. "Arithon suspected trouble in these mountains. *Why?*"

Before the Sorcerer gave answer, shouts cut the misty pass. The abutments came alive with archers.

"Halt!" called a bearded ruffian from the cliff top. "Dismount and throw down your arms!"

Lysaer spun in his stirrups, his bearing of command unthinking and wrath like torchflame in his eyes. "What have you done with my half-brother?"

"Shot a hole in his cloak, as you see." Accustomed to arrogance from the mercenaries hired to guard caravans, the barbarian dared an insolent grin. "If you're minded to protest, I can add to that."

He rapped orders to someone in position over his head. There followed a flurry of activity, and a bundle appeared, suspended over the cliff face by a swinging length of rope. As the wind lulled and the snow settled to clear the view, Lysaer recognized Arithon, bound hand and foot, and suspended face first over a drop that vanished straight down into mist. The brutes had gagged his mouth.

Provoked to instinctive reaction, Lysaer forgot he no longer held royal authority. Very pale but with unassailable dignity, he accosted the raiders on the ridge. "Lend me a blade. For the sake of the life you threaten, I'll set honor above cowardly extortion and offer trial by single combat as settlement."

"How very touching!" The barbarian ringleader raised up a dark-bladed weapon, unmistakably Arithon's Alithiel, and set the sharpened edge against the hanging cord. One ply gave way, loud as a slap in the silence. "You mistake us for our ancestors, who perhaps once affected such scruples. But as long as mayors rule, there are no fair fights in this pass. Who will hit ground first, you?" The ruffian dismissed Lysaer and dipped the sword toward the hostage who dangled without struggle over the abyss. "Or this one, who provoked us by drawing first blood?"

"Would that Arithon had done worse," Lysaer cried back in indignation. "Unprincipled mongrel pack of thieves! Had I an honor guard with me, I'd see the last of you put to the sword!"

A hand restrained his arm, Asandir's, restoring Lysaer to shattering recollection that his inheritance was forever lost; in cold fact he owned nothing but a poignard to manage even token self-defense.

"Dismount as they wish, and quickly." The Sorcerer did so himself, while more barbarians armed with javelins closed in a ring from the cliff.

Stiff with wounded pride, galled enough to murder for the brutality which had befallen his half-brother, Lysaer watched in seething compliance as Asandir threw the reins of his black to his apprentice and confronted the cordon of weapon points.

"Who leads this party?" the Sorcerer demanded.

"I'll ask the questions, graybeard," said the red-bearded young spokesman who descended in a leap from the outcrop. Cocksure, even ruthless with contempt, he strode through the circle of his companions.

"Ask then," Asandir invited in a silken politeness that caused

Dakar to wince outright. "But take care, young man. You might gain other than you bargain for."

"You overstep your value, I think," the barbarian said, while the wind parted the furs of his jerkin and cap and spun the fox-tail trappings on his belt. "The advice of old men is widespread as the mist and as easily ignored." He gestured a bloodied fist at the hostage strung over the mountainside. "For his life, and yours, some grandchild or relative had better come up with a ransom."

"It's not gold you want." Asandir surveyed the barbarian from his red-splashed boots to the crown of his wolf-pelt cap. "For your sake, you should have heeded the wisdom of your elders! Vengefulness has lured you into folly."

The raid leader drew a fast breath. He found no words. The Sorcerer pinned him in a regard like deathless frost, then killed off refutation with a command. "Lysaer, come forward and remove your hood."

The barbarian gave way to blind outrage. "The next man who speaks or moves will wind up butchered on my signal!"

"Not so easily," rebutted the one who stepped forth, a figure muffled in ordinary wool, whose fingers bore neither ring nor ornament as he slipped off his gloves and raised his hands; but a man so unconsciously sure of his position that every clansman present paused to stare.

Dark cloth slipped back to reveal honey gold hair, blue eyes still glacial with fury, and features that reflected a bloodline not seen in Camris for centuries, but recognizable to every clan along the Valendale.

"S'Ilessid!" exclaimed the scar-faced woman at the fore. "By Ath, he's royal, and who else could be his spokesman but the Kingmaker himself, Asandir?"

Jolted as if he had been struck, Lysaer saw the Sorcerer return the barest nod. "At least one among you recalls tradition. I bring you Prince Lysaer, Teir's'Ilessid, scion of the high kings of Tysan, and by unbroken line of descent, your liege lord."

The snow seemed suddenly too white, the air too painfully thin and cold to breathe; stunned by the impact of astonishment, Lysaer stood as if paralyzed.

The raid leader went from ruddy to waxen pale. First to react, he stepped back, undermined by horrified, weak-kneed humility. "Merciful Ath, how was I to know?" He set Arithon's sword point down in the snow at Lysaer's feet and dropped to his knees. "My liege," he said in strangled apology. "I place myself and my companions at your mercy."

"At last you recall the manners of your forefathers, Grithen, son of Tane." Asandir's cool regard passed over the barbarian to encompass the shocked ragged circle of aggressors as bows and javelins were lowered, then let fall with a clatter onto the trail; more movement followed. All the scouts in the company prostrated themselves before their prince until only the Sorcerer, Dakar, and a stunned, speechless Lysaer remained standing.

For a half-dozen heartbeats, nothing stirred on the exposed spine of the ridge but swirls of gale-whipped snow. The revealed heir to Tysan's high kingship kept his feet and his bearing only through unbending royal pride.

Then, encouraged by a smile from Asandir, the reflex of command reasserted; the prince raised a voice of stinging authority. "Restore my half-brother to firm ground and set him free."

A pair of scouts scrambled to their feet, sped by the mention that the captive they had manhandled was royal also. Lysaer showed their consternation little mercy, but swept up Arithon's sword. "You," he said coldly. He touched the naked blade against the nape of Grithen's neck. "Mayors might rule in Erdane, but honor shall not be forgotten. Remain on your knees until my half-brother is returned safely to my side. Then, since anger might bias my fair opinion, I leave your fate in the hands of Asandir."

"That won't be necessary," the Sorcerer interjected. "The Fellowship of Seven passes no judgment upon men, but Maenalle, Steward of Tysan, will properly perform this office. She is qualified, having dispensed the king's justice in the absence of her liege most ably through the last two decades."

Chilled through his leggings by melted ice, and shamed by the steel which revoked his last vestige of dignity, Grithen submitted without a whimper; if the s'Ilessid prince was displeased by the rashness of his scouts, Maenalle was going to be mortified. Her verdict was certain to be ruinous, and no comfort could be gained from the fact that Lord Tashan, clan elder and Earl of Taerlin, had opposed the attack from the start. No doubt the old fox had recognized a true Sorcerer, Grithen thought in despair; word of Asandir's party had perhaps crossed the passes already.

Stilled with dread, acutely suffering from cramped muscles, Grithen silently cursed his sour luck. Given Maenalle's hard nature, he would not be the least bit surprised if he became disbarred from his inheritance as a result of this one ill-favored raid.

An Arrival

Despite Asandir's insistence that Grithen not send ahead with the news of Prince Lysaer's arrival, his party with its escort of clan scouts was greeted at the head of the valley by no less than Maenalle herself, companioned by a ceremonial guard of outriders.

With the storm past and the cloud cover thinned, the mists of Desh-thiere prevailed still; the vale beyond the passes lay enshrouded in featureless gloom. Warned by the clear call of a horn, then by the dimmed flash of gold trappings, Grithen groaned in pained apprehension. Lord Tashan had indeed roused the camp, for no less than a Fellowship Sorcerer could get Maenalle, Steward of Tysan, out of hunting leathers and into anything resembling formal dress.

A companion jeered in commiseration. "Who would have guessed the old earl could still skip on his shanks like a lizard?"

The young lord responsible for the disaster in the pass was not the only one taken aback. At the head of the column, beside Asandir, the freshly pronounced heir to the throne of Tysan hid confusion behind princely decorum as he confronted the glittering guard from the outpost.

"The woman who wears the circlet and the tabard with your colors is Maenalle," Asandir said quickly. "She is Steward of the Realm, last heir to a very ancient title. She and her forebears have safeguarded Tysan's heritage in the absence of the king through the years since the rebellion. Let me speak to her first. Then you shall greet her with due respect, for all that she rules she has held in your name."

The travel-worn arrivals drew rein before the ranks of clan outriders. This company wore no furs, but livery of royal blue velvet and sword belts beaded with gold. The bridles of their matched bay coursers were gilt also, and polished to smart perfection. The woman at the fore was boyishly slim, mounted side-saddle and fidgeting with impatience. Her habit was sable, her fur-trimmed shoulders and slender waist engulfed by a tabard bearing the gold star blazon of Tysan. In her hand, she carried a sprig of briar, and her graying, short-cropped hair was tucked back under a silver fillet. She rode to meet Asandir, drew rein as he dismounted, then laughed a merry welcome as he raised his hands and swung her down.

A servant took her horse and the Sorcerer's, as she raised tawny eyes and offered greeting. "Welcome to Camris, Asandir of the Fellowship." Her voice was clear as a sprite's and younger than her face, which wore the years well on prominent cheekbones. "You do us high honor, but thank Ath, not often enough for me to grow accustomed to wearing skirts!"

From her hands Asandir accepted the thorn branch that symbolized the centuries of bitter exile. A smile touched his eyes. Smoothly as a drawn breath he engaged his arts. Green suffused the stem between his fingers. A burst of new leaves unfurled from the barren sprig, followed by a bud, then the wine-deep flush of a flawless summer rose.

While the company looked on in awed silence, the Sorcerer stripped the thorns and tucked the bloom into the steward's fading hair. "Lady Maenalle," he said gravely, "after this I dare say you'll need skirts for better occasions." He turned her gently, raised her hand toward the rider on the chestnut who sat in his saddle like a man born to rule. "I give you Prince Lysaer s'Ilessid, scion of Halduin the First, and by blood descent your liege lord."

Lysaer looked down at the steward his kingship would supplant, a woman who radiated command in her own right through every unconscious movement; unsure of his newfound status, he anticipated a reaction of enmity, resentment, even shock. But Maenalle's hawk-bright eyes only looked stunned for a second before they filled with tears. Then she cried aloud for sheer joy, curtsied without thought for slushy ground, and gave up her hand for his kiss.

"My royal lord," she murmured, looking suddenly fragile beneath the mantling weight of state finery.

Feeling dirty, reminded the instant he smelled her perfume that he reeked of woodsmoke and sweat, the prince set his lips against a palm welted with callus like a swordsman's. He mastered surprise at the steward's mannish incongruities, overcame embarrassment, and belatedly applied himself to courtesy.

"Your arrival is the light of our hope made real." Maenalle smiled brightly, turned, and shouted back to her escort of men at arms. "Did you hear? A s'Ilessid! A blood descendent of Halduin himself! Lysaer, Teir's'Ilessid, has returned to reclaim the throne of Tysan!"

A mighty shout met her words. Protocol was abandoned. Men leaped from the backs of their horses and closed in ecstatic excitement around the steward and their acknowledged prince.

"You must forgive any disrespect, Your Grace," Maenalle shouted over the tumult as Lysaer was swept from his saddle, embraced, and pummeled roundly on the back by dozens of welcoming hands. "Five centuries was a very long time to wait for your coming, and the times in between have been harsh."

Too breathless to manage even banal reply, Lysaer struggled to recover equilibrium. Accustomed to royal propriety, and formal even with friends, the rough-cut comraderie of Maenalle's discipline bruised his dignity. Thrust unwarned into inheritance of a kingdom unknowably vast, he coped with no knowledge of precedence to lend him grace.

The wholehearted abandonment of decorum permitted no opening for questions, not about the prince's return from Dascen Elur, or concerning the demeaning, mishandled raid in the pass of Orlan. Tactfully reminded by the Sorcerer that the storm had kept his party traveling through two nights with scanty sleep, Maenalle called her escort back to order. Quickly, efficiently, her outriders formed up into columns and set off to hustle their prince and all his company to the comforts of the clan lords' west outpost.

While the needs of royal guests were attended, and tired horses led off to stables, the crude plank door of the camp cabin appointed as the steward's privy chamber clicked gently shut behind Maenalle. She had shed the magnificence of circlet and tabard. Shadowy in the fall of her black habit, her feathered hair pale as a halo around her face, she regarded the Sorcerer who warmed himself by the hearth across a cramped expanse of bare floor. Although the room functioned as an office, it held neither pens nor parchments, nor any furnishing resembling a desk. A dry wine tun in one corner was stuffed with rolled parchment maps. Past an unsanded split-plank table, the only hanging to cut the drafts through ill-fitted board walls was a wolf pelt pegged up and stretched with rawhide.

"You wished to speak to me," Asandir prodded gently. Startled to discover she had been holding her breath, Maenalle clasped her hands by her hip where her sword hilt normally rested. "You can tell me now what you wouldn't say in public."

She had always had blistering courage; warmed by air that smelled of cedar and oiled leather, Asandir peeled back damp cuffs and chafed his wrists to restore circulation. When he faced her next, he was unsmiling. "If your people wish to celebrate, the festivities to honor their prince's return must be brief. An outbreak of virulently poisonous meth-snakes has arisen in Mirthlvain. They derive from migrant stock, and if they spread in widespread numbers, our departure could be urgently swift."

Still sharp from her interview with Grithen, Maenalle said, "Dakar already told me: you planned to travel on to Althain Tower in any case." She pushed away from the door panel, pulled a hide hassock from the fireside, and perched with an irritable kick at the skirts that mired her ankles. "Distant troubles in Mirthlvain don't explain your cagey choice of language."

"You're asking to know if you can shed your office along with your tabard?" Asandir's sternness loosened into a smile. "The Seven have not yet formally sanctioned Lysaer's accession to Tysan's crown, that's true. But not because the prince is unworthy."

"Well, thank Ath for that." Maenalle arose and walked the floorboards. Though she wore hard-soled boots for riding, her footfalls out of habit made no sound. "If I told the camp they couldn't celebrate, I'd probably face an armed uprising."

Moved by her leashed note of hope, Asandir spoke honestly and fast. "If Lysaer and his half-brother can successfully defeat the Mistwraith, you shall have your coronation as swiftly as injustices can be put right."

"Are the old records true?" Maenalle seemed suddenly hard as sheathed steel as she propped her back against the chimney nook. "Was your colleague who barred South Gate against the mist's first invasion left broken and lame by his act?"

"Yes." Seeing the tension quiver through her, Asandir arose, touched her elbow, and gently urged her to take his chair. In contrast with her staunch strength, her bones felt fragile as a bird's. "I'll not give you platitudes. Desh-thiere is an unknown and dangerous adversary. Dakar's prophecy promises its bane, clearly enough. But no guarantee can be given that the half-brothers who shoulder the burden of its defeat will emerge from their trial unscathed. Lysaer's official sanction for royal succession must be withheld until after full sunlight is restored."

Outside the nailed flap of hide that shuttered the window, boisterous calls and laughter set a dog yapping over the everyday screel of steel being ground on a sharpening wheel. Maenalle took a moment to recover the steadiness to trust her voice. "What will become of my clansmen if our s'Ilessid heir is left maimed or dead?"

Now reluctant to meet her brave scrutiny, Asandir faced toward the fireside. "If Lysaer is impaired, he will have heirs. If he is killed, we know for certain there are other s'Ilessid kinsmen alive beyond the Gates in Dascen Elur." To show to what extent he shared her worry, he added, "The kingdom of Rathain is not so lucky. Since the Teir's'Ffalenn now with us is the last of his line, rest assured, Lady Maenalle. The Seven will guard the safety of both princes to the limit of our power and diligence."

A Return

The journey south from Erdane to the old earl's summer palace in the foothills ordinarily took three days for a rider traveling light. Though the return dispatches Elaira carried for the Prime were not urgent, she crossed the distance in less. A sudden freeze and the late season's sloppy mud discouraged caravans at a time when the trade guilds had stockpiled their raw materials for the winter. Left the latitude to order her priorities, the enchantress used her travel allowance for extra post horses instead of lodging. She hoped that a late-night arrival would allow her the chance for a hot bath and a rest before she faced reckoning for the Ravens.

Weather conspired to foil her. In the dark, through driving rain, landmarks became invisible, and the lane leading westward from Kelsing had fallen into decay since the Mistwraith. Only a ghostly trace of wheel ruts crossed the barren hilltops; the sheltered soil in the valleys encouraged brush and thickets, and oak groves choked the washes under obliterating drifts of rotted leaves. Since the mare collected from the last livery stable was her own beloved bay, Elaira could hardly drive at speed through scrub lands riddled with gullies and badger setts that could snap a horse's legs on a misstep.

Daybreak was well past when, skin wet and sore, and made cross by storm and delay, she reined in the little mare before a disused postern that let into the ruined palace gardens.

A novice initiate awaited her. Miserable in the heavy fall of rain, she announced with clipped asperity that the incoming message rider was expected to report at once to the main hall.

Elaira dismounted with a dispirited sigh. If word of her doings concerned the Prime Council, she would have been met on arrival however inconvenient the hour. Rain hammered in sheets across the flags, rinsing rivulets through the arches overhead. Elaira draped her reins on the mare's steaming neck and started to loosen girth buckles.

"You should call a groom for that." The novice was shivering, as thoroughly drenched as Elaira, except that her vigil had been performed after breakfast and a warm night's sleep. "The Prime Enchantress is displeased, and delay will just worsen your case."

Elaira felt the cold go through to her marrow. "*Morriel* wants me?" She tried and failed to hide her distress. "But I thought—"

"That today was the time appointed to review the orphan wards," the novice interrupted, prim to the point of cattiness. "It should be. Your doings in Erdane caused the roster to be rearranged."

A tingle of blood suffused Elaira's face. Already her disgrace had seeded gossip. Had she not been the daughter of a street thief before the Koriani claimed her for training, shame might have hampered the wits that allowed her to rally. "I'd best not wait for a page, then. If their evaluation has been put off, the boys will have time on their hands. You'll only need a minute to find one to see my mount cooled and stabled."

The pages were all eating dinner at this hour, and it would serve one junior novice right, Elaira thought as she fumbled with icy fingers to unbuckle the satchel of dispatches from the saddle rings. If the Prime herself was displeased, that made for worries enough without every new snip in the order troubling to point up the fact. Before the flummoxed girl could utter protest, Elaira surrendered her reins, shouldered her burden of papers, and pushed on through flowerbeds choked with bracken and hedgerows run together into moss-green tunnels snarled with creepers and thorn.

The wing to the ladies' chambers nested amid the overgrowth like a pile of moss-rotten stone. The beams that roofed the porticos had caved, spilling slate like shattered pewter over what once had been marble mosaic. Elaira kicked down a daunting stand of weeds to reach the doorway. The original portal of cedar and filigree had long since rotted away. Bronze hinges cast in a tracery of rose leaves now hung rough-hewn planks nailed together with a strip of boiled cowhide. Wet leaves jammed the sill. Elaira wasted minutes in prying the panel open; she persisted rather than go around the front way, and would endure obstacles far worse before she traipsed in her dripping, bedraggled state past the eyes of her curious peers.

That prideful scruple cost her skinned knuckles and added sweat to her smell of wet horse. Militant despite Asandir's counsel of temperance, Elaira hastened through a chain of moldering bedchambers; if the Prime Enchantress saw fit to demand audience after an all-night ride with no bath, she deserved to endure the result.

In better, idle moments, the carved wainscoting and decaying bas-reliefs that ornamented the cornices and ceilings invited daydreams of the original inhabitants. But on a morning made gloomy by cascades of falling rain, the rooms of dead earls' ladies seemed musty with sorrowful memories. Elaira let herself out into a brick and flag-stone inner corridor and proceeded through shadowed archways and around puddles let in by leaks to the anteroom where the enormous halfwit who served as Morriel's door guard granted her instant admittance.

The gentle man was not smiling, a distressing sign.

Left alone beneath the cavernous vaults of the great hall while the panels boomed shut on her heels, Elaira stopped short. The chairs before the frieze-work dais stood empty, and no fire burned in the grate. The Prime Council's review had not just been deferred, but cancelled for today altogether. No disdainful circle of seniors awaited; only two cowed-looking pageboys, scarcely twelve years of age and identically blond, bearing the paired standards and crested crane device that symbolized Morriel's authority.

The Prime herself held audience. Aged and thin as a whip, she sat her seat of power looking faded in official purple robes and skin as translucent as antique porcelain. Yet her shoulders were not bowed; her hand on her order was unyielding as north-facing granite, hard as the diamonds that netted her bone-white hair and flashed on her blue-veined wrists. Couched amid calculating wrinkles, her eyes gleamed black as a carrion crow's.

Clumsy at the worst of moments, Elaira tripped on the hem of her traveling cloak.

Morriel looked up at the sound, sharp cheekbones and hawk nose enhancing her bird-like rapacity. She waved her hand. The bundle of cloth by her elbow stirred upright and turned around with an unmistakably feline grace. Elaira caught her breath in true fear as she identified First Enchantress Lirenda, present all the while, and whispering in the matriarch's ear. Clad in judiciary black, veiled in muslin, she stood in attendance as Ceremonial Inquisitor.

For her late transgressions in Erdane, Elaira was not to suffer enquiry but the formal, closed trial reserved for enchantresses who broke their vows of obedience.

Frowning, scared, and chilled from more than damp clothing, Elaira reviewed her mistakes: she had spoken with a Sorcerer, but not to betray her orders' secrets; she had gambled with a drunken prophet, but except for flouting an unwritten code of manners, she had committed no indecency. If Erdane's officials had caught her at spell-craft, she might have burned, but no others in the sisterhood had shared her risk. Last and surely least, her talk with the s'Ffalenn heir in the hayloft had passed in absolute innocence.

Why should she be called in for judgment as if she had plotted a grand offense?

Rumpled and travel-stained before her seniors' immaculate presence, Elaira lowered the message satchel. She slipped the strap from fingers gone nerveless and threw off her muddied cloak. Her knees shook through her curtsy, a detail made obvious by her riding leathers. Somehow she managed a level voice. "I stand before my betters to serve."

Prime Enchantress Morriel inclined her head, the shimmer of her diamonds and lace netting pricked with light like new tears. She did not speak; since by custom the Prime addressed no outsiders, oath breakers fell under the same stigma.

First Enchantress Lirenda spoke in Morriel's stead, her enunciation as ominous as the cross of swords behind her veil. "Junior initiate Elaira, you were sent north with routine dispatches for the house matron outside of Erdane. Instructions did not mention taverns, or brothels, or card gambling with drunken prophets who consort with Sorcerers of the Fellowship."

Left light-headed by the pound of her fast-beating heart, Elaira returned the only excuse she could plead. "I was told to be observant, to bring back the news of the road." Dakar had told more in five minutes than lane-watchers had gleaned through a month of tedious observation; yet that truth would but incense the Prime further. Elaira stared at the floor. "Mistakenly, I thought facts were of greater importance than the methods used to seek them."

Morriel twitched a finger at Lirenda, her nail a yellowed claw against thin-skinned fairness. "Ethics do not matter?"

The First to the Prime elaborated upon the matriarch's dry statement. "Dakar sober would hardly reveal his master's purposes. Drunken, he is incapable of separating fact from fancy. Not in collective memory has our order stooped to scouring brothels and taprooms for knowledge of events. To your shame, you're the first initiate who has tried."

The Prime rapped her knuckles against the ebony arm of her chair. Done with lecturing, Lirenda stepped to a side table. She fetched back a steel-bound coffer secured by a mesh of interlaced wardspells that shed a resonance to wring dread from even the least talented perception. The pageboys behind Morriel's chair shifted in wide-eyed discomfort as the First Enchantress laid the box on the silk-covered lap of the Prime.

The Koriani matriarch released the wards one at a time. As protective enchantments gave way with snaps like overwound harp strings, Elaira fixed desperately on the young pages. Though their sex disbarred them from training, the children had spent their early lives surrounded by arcane mysteries. Whatever they had witnessed concerning that coffer's contents made them quake to the soles of their feet.

Lirenda accepted the unsealed box from the Prime and raised the lid. Inside, the focus jewel of Skyron glittered cold blue as an ice shard. Although this crystal could not channel anywhere near the same degree of power as the amethyst Great Waystone, lost since the rebellion, any enquiry directed through its matrix would be impossible for Elaira to defy.

Only the thinnest tissue of secondary circumstances masked her forbidden interview with Asandir. One straight fact, one opening to invite a direct question concerning her doings in the earlier evening, and her paper-thin weaving of subterfuge at the Ravens would collapse.

"Begin," Morriel commanded, her eyes fixed darkly on her Inquisitor.

"Look into the crystal, Elaira," Lirenda instructed. "Surrender your will absolutely."

The accused must show immediate compliance, or else condemn herself outright by refusing a direct command. Consumed with anxiety, aware that if she was judged guilty, the self-awareness that defined her individuality would forever become forfeit, Elaira bent her mind into the crystal's twilight depths. She locked her teeth against protest and lowered her inner barriers.

Arcane restraints blazed over her mind like the slamming jaws of a trap. Her senses swam through a moment of vertigo; then the gloomy expanse of the hall became seared away by an indigo force that smothered her will to quiescence. Elaira drifted. Dissociated wholly from her surroundings, she did not hear Lirenda's voice asking questions, nor did she frame verbal replies. Instead, like some tired, played-over script, past scenes were pried out of her memory and picked through in embarrassing detail.

She saw the face of Arithon s'Ffalenn, framed by a cloak hood wrung in the grip of white knuckles; again and again until she ached, she braved the smoky taproom of the Ravens and waited while Dakar spoke a name. Time froze, looped back, paused again while the moment was analyzed, her tiniest reflections jabbed out and examined. Somewhere in a locked-off corner of her mind she was screaming in frustration and fear, but the inquest continued inexorably.

The past became present. Again she wrought spells to stem the mob of headhunters, and again she made her stand amid the cluttered shelves of the Ravens' pantry. Since the enchantress on lane-watch had discovered her in the hayloft, her business at Enithen Tuer's and her interview with Asandir were mercifully left overlooked, but the particulars of her encounter with Arithon were exhaustively tracked and studied, until the brief moment he had touched her hand, and the brush of his fingers removing straw from her hair sawed at her nerves like pain.

Every word he had spoken, every line she had replied, was replayed, dissected to underlying nuance, and then cross-checked against her later reflections in the course of her return journey south.

By the time her tormentors released her will from the shadowed blue confines of the focus jewel, Elaira was no longer merely tired but physically hurting from exhaustion. Emotionally ragged, all but reduced to tears, she recovered self-awareness in fragments. Hearing returned first and gave her Lirenda's voice emphatically expounding a point.

" . . . for this I remain unconvinced. She's possibly hiding something. I strongly advise a deeper probe."

The Prime's reedy voice interjected, while Elaira struggled to overcome draining dizziness. Aware of a hard chair beneath her, of ice-cold feet cased in tight-laced, sodden boots, she dragged a breath against the sensation of weight that bound her chest. Even through confusion she realized she had not betrayed Asandir's trust, because her inquisitors had combed only those events where her overriding concern for Arithon s'Ffalenn had eclipsed any thought of her interview. Left in dread of a possible second inquest, Elaira knew that chance could not possibly spare her twice.

Lacerated in nerve and mind, she was driven at last to rebellion. "What earthly purpose can another interrogation prove?" Her eyesight came and went, rent by patches of darkness. "I'm aching with weariness, and so stiff it's a trial just to sit here. If I'm disgraced, name my punishment and be done, for nothing else prompted my doings in Erdane beyond an ill-advised quest after knowledge."

"Tell her to be silent!" Morriel's immutable eyes fixed on the space above Elaira's head. "The initiate has no cause for imperti- nence. Plainly she had inclinations toward a personal entanglement with the Teir's'Ffalenn, but she is so emotionally disorganized she seems unaware of her lapse. Let me remind that as Koriani she is pledge to avoid involvement with any man, no matter how exalted his bloodline."

Elaira bowed her head. A Sorcerer of the Fellowship had entrusted her to be wise; trapped by his steel-clad expectation, she stifled an impetuous retort and overlaid defiance with submission.

The hush in the chamber grew prolonged.

Lirenda seemed faintly disappointed. After an interval, Morriel said, "I withhold judgment. Inform the accused."

The First Enchantress removed her veils, her manner stiff with thwarted vindication. "You are warned, Elaira. Dissociate yourself from the prince of Rathain. Cleanse your thoughts of his memory and dedicate your heart to obedience. You are charged to be mindful. Your actions henceforward shall be weighed until the Prime sees fit to is- sue verdict."

Morriel inclined her head.

Frostily, Lirenda interpreted. "You are declared on probation and hereby excused from this audience."

Elaira pushed upright and curtsied before the dais. Measured by the carrion-bird scrutiny of the Prime, watched enviously by the duty-bound pageboys, she beat a quick retreat from the hall. Relief left her weak in the knees. Lirenda might cling to suspicions, but Morriel seemed satisfied that a card game had prompted her sojourn into Erdane; there would be no more enquiries, no deeper truth search by crystal, not unless she incited further cause.

Adroit enough to dodge her communal quarters and the ques- tioning curiosity of her peers, Elaira slipped out to the stables to check on her travel-weary mare. Surrounded by horses, the near to mystical quiet of their presence scented by straw and oiled leather, she groomed the bay's damp-matted coat with unseeing, mechanical efficiency. In the yard outside, a boy ward whistled as he split kin- dling for the kitchens, but the ordinary peace of the moment failed to settle her composure.

By now recovered enough to think, Elaira reviewed the ramifica- tions of Morriel's suspended verdict. Her unease increased. In cold re- flection, the accusation concerning Arithon no longer seemed silly and far-fetched. The restraints of probation felt unpleasant to the point of suffocation, and the shadowed stillness of the stables offered no refuge at all.

Not when the smell of hay and warm horses reminded inescapably of the man.

Stung by a pitfall that should never, ever have entrapped her, Elaira threw aside brush and curry and let herself out of the stall. The mare shoved a friendly nose over the door, her nudge for attention unnoticed. Her young mistress saw nowhere but inward. With the ritual phrase, *"You stand warned,"* ringing in cold echoes through her mind, Elaira cursed for a long and breathless minute in the gutter dialect of her early childhood.

The words of Enithen Tuer returned to haunt her. *"You don't need a seer to tell your future's just branched into darkness."*

Shivering in her damp and crumpled leathers, Elaira fled into the misty afternoon. Four hours and an eternity ago, a warm bath and bed had been all the earthly comfort she had desired.

Portents

On the marshy banks of a sink pool, a serpent with blood-dark eyes pauses, flicks its tongue, then slithers purposefully through a crevice in a crumblingly ancient stone wall; it is followed a moment later by another and another, until soon a horde of its fellows seethe after, breaking eddies through murky waters and shivering pallid ranks of reeds. . . .

North and west, under a hide tent pitched in misty forest, a scar-faced barbarian chieftain tosses in sweat-soaked furs; yet before his lady can waken him from the grip of prescient dreams, he has seen the face of his king, and the blood of his own certain death. . . .

In a wild stretch of grasslands, on the crest of a wind-swept scarp, four tall towers loom above a ruined city, while rainfall gentle as tears rinses the shattered foundations of a fifth. . . .

VIII. Clans of Camris

L ysaer awoke at dusk to strangely carved walls, a warm fire, and blankets of softest angora that wrapped his sweating limbs in clinging, suffocating heat. He tossed away the coverlets, rose naked from the feather mattress, and paced across fine carpet to a casement paned with glass. Outside, clustered around a snow-trampled compound spread the tents, stone huts, and rough, log-timbered buildings that comprised the permanent mountain outpost maintained by the clans of Camris. Amid falling gloom the descendents of Tysan's aristocracy set about their evening chores as they had through five centuries of exile. They carried cressets, because lanterns were scarce. Most wore the leathers and furs of wilderness scouts. Grim in aspect as occupants of a war camp, or a settlement too long under siege, no one walked without arms, even those few who were women. If any of the tents housed families, Lysaer sighted no children, though he lingered unseen at the window to study his new subjects while they were yet unaware.

Shouts arose from two hunters who dragged in the carcass of a deer. A woman called back in derision, and laughter dissolved into banter that coarsely disallowed even token respect for her gender. Lysaer rested his coin-bright head on his wrists. He did not feel refreshed. Nightmares had dogged his sleep and the expensive scents of sandalwood oil and rare spices upon his skin left him faintly queasy.

The beautifully appointed furnishings at his back gave no comfort; gold-embossed chests and patterned carpets were far too much an anomaly in this bleakest of mountain settings.

"We give you the King's Chamber," Maenalle had said matter-of-factly as she opened a door to a room that held the atmosphere of a lovingly maintained shrine. The manservant who brought water for the royal bath had explained that every clan encampment in Tysan kept similar quarters, perpetually held in readiness for the day of their sovereign's return.

Deferentially left to his privacy, unused to being worshiped as a legend come to life, Lysaer needed badly to speak with Asandir.

But the Sorcerer had gone off with the clan chiefs while he, as acknowledged royal heir, had been spirited off for food and rest. Where Arithon might be was difficult to guess; presumably, Dakar would have found oblivion in some ale barrel by now. Lysaer scrubbed clammy palms across his face, distressed to be left at a loss in a land where civilized merchants would slit the royal throat and barbarians who preyed on the trade roads welcomed their prince with open arms.

"Your Grace?" said a youthful voice by the doorway.

Lysaer started, spun, and only then noticed the pageboy who hovered past the edge of the candlelight.

"I'm Maenalle's grandson, Maenol s'Gannley, Your Grace." Barely eleven, his livery too large over breeches of cross-gartered hide, the boy bowed with a confidence that any senior courtier might have envied. "I've been sent to assist with your dressing."

Unable to foist his bleak thoughts on a child, Lysaer returned the charm that had endeared him to other foot pages back in Amroth. "What have you brought, Master Maenol?"

The boy grinned, showing a broken front tooth. "People call me Maien, which means 'mouse' in the old tongue, Your Grace." His grin widened and his small, tabarded shoulders straightened with pride. "What else would I bring but your hose, surcoat, and arms?"

The boy stepped toward a stool and chest where an array of courtly clothing had been laid out. The sword in its sapphire scabbard was gilded steel, adorned by blue silk tassels, and in its way as venerable as Alithiel.

"Daeltiri," Maien said in response to his prince's admiring glance. "The blade of the kings of Tysan. When the city of Avenor was desecrated, one part of the royal regalia was entrusted to each clan lord for safekeeping. Until today the earls of Camris have faithfully held your sword." The boy crossed the chamber, impatience reflected in the toss of his ash brown hair. "But hurry, Your Grace. The banquet in the main hall cannot begin until you're ready."

Lysaer slipped into the silken hose, lawn shirt, and finely embroidered tabard with a relief that bordered on shame. He had not appreciated the comforts of rich clothing until he had been made to do without. Humbled by the honest recognition that he desired the throne these clansmen offered at least as desperately as their disunited realm needed sound rule, he laced gold-tipped points and fastened mother-of-pearl buttons and tried to dismiss his suspicion such luxuries might have been dishonestly procured. As Maien buckled the sword Daeltiri at his side and handed him the matching chased dagger, Lysaer, Prince of Tysan, felt whole for the first time since exile through Worldsend.

He quieted his creeping doubts over the lifestyle of the realm's subjects until he could know them better. Under fair consideration, he might find the differences between Athera's wild clansmen and Amroth's more sophisticated courtiers were just reflections of profoundly changed perception. He was no longer the pampered prince who had been haplessly tossed through the Worldsend Gate. In a rakingly perverse turn of conscience, he wondered which promised the sounder reign: the cosseted and idealistic royal heir he had been before banishment, or the more self-sufficient man who needed a crown to feel complete.

Outside, the temperature had fallen severely. Chilled through his fine velvets, Lysaer followed Maien's lead across the compound and through the midst of brisk activity as a company muffled in furs and armed with bows and javelins prepared to depart on patrol. Faces seamed by weather and scars lit at the sight of their prince. The men and two women offered him brisk salute while they checked laces and shouldered weapons, then slipped quietly away into the gathering mountain dusk.

"Where are they going?" Lysaer asked.

Maien regarded his prince slantwise. "Out to the pass on night watch, Your Grace."

"To raid caravans?" Almost, Lysaer let slip the contempt he held for such thievery.

"Partly," said the grandson of Tysan's steward, brazenly unabashed. "They guard the camp as well."

The pair skirted the blood-spattered snow where the deer carcass had lately been butchered. The prince received a smile and a wave from another sword-bearing woman who carried yoke buckets toward the horse pickets. Past the tied-back flap of a tent, a man whistled over the scrape of a blade on a whetstone. Maien turned down a much trampled path that led through a final stand of cabins, threaded into a steep-sided defile, and dead-ended before the shadowed double arch of a gateway cut into the mountain. The doors were armored. Stonework barbicans built against the rocks on either side lent the impregnability of a fortress. If the place had ever seen battle, any scars had been painstakingly repaired; four fur-clad sentries stood duty, the leather-wound grips of their javelins worn shiny from hard use. They dressed weapons in smart salute at the approach of their liege.

Maien spoke a password at a niche. Lysaer heard the clank of a windlass and a dismal rattle of chain; then the great portals ground on their hinges and cracked open.

Asandir strode from the gap. "Good, you've arrived." He dismissed the prince's young escort with a smile. Maien darted ahead to alert the herald as the Sorcerer ushered Lysaer from the cold, into the torchlit vault of an outer hall. Walls and floor of rough-hewn stone sheared his voice into echoes as he said, "Maenalle awaits you."

Above the din as the defense works were laboriously cranked closed, Lysaer said, "You might have given me warning."

"I might have done the same for Grithen's clansmen," Asandir returned. "I chose not to."

Stonewalled, and for no apparent cause, Lysaer reined back annoyance. "Is this a kingdom that encourages lawlessness?"

Asandir regarded the prince with eyes like unmarked slate. "This is a land afflicted by mismanagement, greed, and vicious misunderstanding. The clans rob caravans to ease a harsh existence, and the mayors pay headhunters to exterminate as a means to ease their terror. Your task is not to judge but to set right. Your royal Grace, justice must be tempered by sympathy if the unity of the realm is to be restored. So I did not explain, because words cannot substitute for experience."

The heavy doors boomed shut, leaving a ponderous quiet.

Asandir gestured toward the light and warmth that spilled through a second set of arches. "Go in," he urged while ahead, in cultured accents, Maenalle's appointed herald announced the royal presence. "For these people you are the living embodiment of hope. Listen to their woes and understand what they've sacrificed to preserve their lives and heritage."

Lysaer squared his shoulders under his exquisitely embroidered tabard. What Asandir expected of him was a great deal more than tolerance; he could return no less than his best.

"You are favored with the gifts of your ancestors," Asandir reassured as they walked side by side into a chamber transformed since afternoon. "If the Seven believed you incapable, you would never have stood before these clans as a candidate fit to rule."

The drab rock walls beyond the threshold were covered over by tapestries, masterful weaving and bright dyes depicting a kingly procession that celebrated the first greening of spring. Lysaer stared in delight. For an instant he seemed to view through a window into a prior age, when Paravian habitation had graced hills unsullied by Desh-thiere's mists. Here in shining glory lay the centaurs' fire-maned majesty, spritely dancers wreathed in flowers who were the fair-formed sunchildren, and mystical as moonlight on water, the snowy grace of unicorns. Entranced, caught into thrall by emotion, Lysaer blinked—and the spell snapped. The weaving on the wall became just a fabric of ordinary thread, worked with extraordinary artistry. Left dazed by split-second bewilderment, Lysaer shook off gooseflesh and continued after Asandir and Maien, over patterned carpets imported from far-off Narms. Torches were replaced by tiers of wax candles, and glittering in their smokeless light were the clan born of the west outpost, descendants of Camris's aristocracy.

They looked the part, Lysaer thought in astonishment. Divested of furs and weapons, reclothed in velvets, dyed suedes, and jeweled brocades, one could almost forget that most of the women carried sword scars, or that the wrists of young and old alike were lean as braided sinew from the hunt.

Maenalle waited at the head of a delegation of clan lords. Regally gowned in black and adorned with silver interlace, she wore only a badge of rank to denote her office. "Colors are never worn in the royal presence," she explained in response to Lysaer's compliment that a brighter wardrobe would become her. "By tradition, the Steward of the Realm wears sable, since the true power of governance lies in the crown. Before the rebellion, my office was sometimes called *caithdein*, or shadow behind the throne." She regarded the prince at her side, her tawny eyes fierce in a face too weathered from outdoor living. "Liege, I am proud to become so once again."

There was no envy in her, Lysaer observed, while she steered him through introductions to the officers and elders of her council currently in residence at the outpost. As the self-contained, able woman guided him past a bowing honor guard and rows of candlelit, damask-covered trestles toward the dais at the head of the hall, he watched with a ruler's perception. Maenalle did not resent yielding leadership to a younger, unknown man; in steady, unquestioned, and understated confidence she placed absolute faith in the s'Ilessid name.

Prepared for the eventual trial of winning loyalty from these fierce and independent clansmen, of proving his fitness to rule, Lysaer found the gift of her trust unnerving.

He was shown to the seat of honor at the center of a trestle covered by fine linen and set with an earl's ransom in crested silver and crystal. Asandir was placed on his right, Arithon and Dakar to the left, while Maenalle and the elder clan chiefs assumed the places opposite, between their prince and the lower hall as surety for their hospitality. Since potential threat must first pass through their ranks, any retainer who sought harm to a guest must first commit public treason and strike his sworn lord in the back. Visitors' rights had not been forgotten in the wildest reaches of Camris, although in the towns, old ways had been replaced by the fashion of placing important persons at the head of the boards.

"Insult as well as folly," Maenalle admitted sadly. "A guest seated there is isolated, a target for foul play should a turncoat defile the lord's house. What respect can a host claim who would expose another in place of himself?"

Hiding discomfort, Lysaer watched Maien pour the wine. Amroth's court had kept no such elaborate custom, and rather than risk insult out of ignorance, the prince forebore to comment.

A touch on his forearm recalled his thoughts: Asandir, with reminder that the hall expected a guest oath. That ritual at least was familiar. Lysaer rose to his feet. The glittering array of gathered clansfolk stilled deferently before him as he raised his goblet in fingers too proud to tremble.

"To this house, its lady, and her sworn companions, I pledge friendship. Ath's blessing upon family and kin, strength to your heirs, and honor to the name of s'Gannley. Beneath this roof and before Ath, I share fortune and sorrow as your brother, my service as steadfast as blood kin."

Maenalle arose, smiling, to complete the ancient reply. "Your presence is our grace." She raised her callused hands, took the prince's goblet, and drank a half portion of the wine.

Lysaer accepted the cup back from her, drained it, and laid it rim downward on the table between. "Dharkaron witness," he finished clearly.

Maenalle faced around toward her following. "Honor and welcome to s'Ilessid!"

As prince and steward took their seats to thunderous cheers from the clan scouts, the banquet began in earnest. Accustomed to court fare as Lysaer was, he could not help being impressed. Surrounded by all but barren rock, caught at impossibly short notice, the Camris barbarians proved as warmly hospitable as any grand fete held in

Amroth. But although in manner and bearing these people seemed flawlessly refined, their high-table conversation better reflected the temper of the culture underneath.

"The arrogance of the townsmen swells beyond belief," the eldest chief, Lord Tashan, confided over his soup. "We confiscated a wagon recently. Among the goods were paper documents dividing land into portions and alotting coin value to each." The spry old lord laughed hugely. He set aside his spoon and fingered his goblet without drinking, concern threaded through his amusement. "Next they'll be trying to tax the air a man breathes, do you guess?"

"Mortals have been known to presume far worse," Asandir interjected. A sharp glance warned Lysaer to silence as he added, "What was done with those papers?"

"We burned them," Lord Tashan said in disgust. Now he did take a swallow, a deep one. "Without ceremony, as tinder to kindle a watch fire. It's an affront against Ath's creation to number a mountain among one's possessions. Thrice damned to Sithaer, and Dharkaron's curse on the mayor who started the infamy. If he dares to cross Orlan, we'll speed the Wheel's turning for him, and send the blooded arrow to his heirs."

Asandir locked eyes with the older noble. "The matter is beyond your jurisdiction, and the mayor's life subject to the king's justice."

The chieftain bowed to the rebuke, but his outrage smoldered hot as the candle-caught glint of his rubies as he turned in appeal to Lysaer. "I ask pardon, my prince. Avenor has been five centuries in ruins, and as many years have passed since a royal heir has graced our land. Survival has forced a harsh code of law, and from habit, I forgot my place. Judgment remains the king's right. But I'm confident you'll resolve the matter firmly on the day your high council reconvenes."

Lysaer hid unsettled thoughts by toying with the meat on his plate. Land owning, an inalienable tradition on Dascen Elur, appeared to be bloodletting violation in Tysan. The prince held the concept daunting and uncivilized, that he might one day be expected to punish a man for laying claim to the farmland he tilled. If Tysan's charter of governance denied the security of home and hearth rights, small wonder the townsmen had let sedition from a spiteful sorcerer incite them to bloody rebellion. Anxious to change the subject, if not the injustice of such laws, Lysaer admired the exceptional beauty of the tapestries.

Lord Tashan chuckled with relish. "They were the unwilling donation of the first mayor of Erdane, damn his memory."

"Stolen?" Lysaer prompted.

The old chief's smile faded. "Not precisely, my liege. The weaving was originally done by the masters at Cildorn, before the old races vanished from the world. The clan chiefs of Taerlin paid fair price for the art, though the records that prove this burned when their holdings were stripped in the uprising. The more valuable spoils were sent north, catalogued as tribute. As a protest, my kinsmen in Caithwood saw fit to lighten the mayor's wagons. The bloodstains washed out well enough. But the forest caves turned dismal with mildew since the mists, so the Paravian tapestries were brought here for preservation."

Lysaer measured the cavernous grotto surrounding him with new eyes: ruffians who lived by the sword would have small use for grand celebrations. The chamber where these barbarians feasted had not originated as a guest hall; more likely it had been fashioned as a storehouse, a vault carved into mountain rock to safeguard generations of plunder.

Maenalle's eldest son, and Maien's father, went on to describe the particulars of that historical first raid. Tashan's comment concerning bloodstains had been no understatement. Trapped in public scrutiny, Lysaer hid his disgust like a diplomat. Nobly born or not, these folk endorsed outright robbery. Filled by dismay, the prince who must one day rule them understood that the fine cloth, the jewels, even the plates and cutlery that graced the table, were no less than the spoils of generations of ambush and murder. Upright trade did not exist among these clansmen—only knowledge of arms and tracking, and a predatory penchant for raiding. Alarmed to find his hands shaking, Lysaer set down his fork. His adroit attempt to change the subject became foiled by his half-brother, whose forthright laughter encouraged further tales of thievery from their hosts.

Unpleasantly reminded of the past, Lysaer lost interest in the food. Arithon had sailed with Karthish pirates; naturally it followed that he had no sensibilities to offend. That he showed no rancor for the rough handling inflicted upon his person in the pass seemed a perverse and unlikely reaction for a man whose intense preference for privacy seemed the cornerstone for an unforgiving character. Objective, self-honest in his standards, Lysaer unflinchingly pursued his conclusion.

The musician who had played Felirin's lyranthe by the fireside possessed the skills of a consummate actor, for such depths of sensitivity could surely not sanction tonight's callous enjoyment of violence. Left heartsick and isolated by the temper of Tysan's clansmen, Lysaer strove without success to rally his equanimity; he had seen the hardworking merchants in Amroth suffer the butt of s'Ffalenn effrontery too many times for complaisance. The blight on s'Ilessid justice remained, and the bitter taste of outrage was transferred to any brigand who presumed to rob for gain.

Lysaer endured the meal; guest courtesy forbade him to do otherwise. Distant, even majestically polite, he listened to the rounds of wild stories until the boards were drawn for the revels. Then, without compunction, he sought council from Asandir.

"How can I rule these clansmen?" he demanded. "The townsfolk are no less Tysan's subjects than they. In all fairness, is it right to set brigands and thieves as overlords above the very same craftsmen they have victimized?"

Asandir broke off contemplation of something in the chamber's far corner, and weighed the prince's distress with silver, imperious eyes. "Have tolerance, Your Grace, at least until you've sat at a mayor's table and listened to the boasts of his headhunters. For where a townsman has lost riches, the clans have paid with the blood of kinsmen and heirs. These whom the townborn name barbarians have seen their children slaughtered like game deer, their wives, sisters, and daughters mercilessly raped and murdered. They inhabit the wastes and the wilds because everywhere else they are persecuted."

Hands clenched hard in his lap, Lysaer drew breath to temporize. The Sorcerer cut him off. "Do not presume that I justify the lifestyles of clansman or townborn. I only point out the dissent that has plagued this land through the centuries since Davien's rebellion. When sunlight is restored, we must all strive for peace. You'll have time to study the problems before then, and no end of encouragement and counsel at the time you finally assume your crown."

Further discussion was curtailed by the evening's entertainment, a superlative demonstration of knife throwing, followed by sword dancers who performed an intricate display to no other accompaniment than the rhythmic chime of crossed steel. Lysaer applauded their performance in admiration, for although he had watched similar gymnastics in Amroth, the dancers had never been female. The steps exhibited for his pleasure in Camris had been dangerously more demanding, and performed at frightening speed.

Warmed by the prince's enjoyment, Maenalle apologized for lack of the gentler arts. "We don't risk our bards in the mountains. Masters of the lyranthe remain in the foothills with our families, that our children learn grace before hardship."

Lysaer's surprise must have showed.

"I forget you weren't raised among us," Maenalle apologized. "We're not entirely the barbarians the townsmen name us. Our women serve with the scouts until marriage, and after that only by choice. The experience at arms is necessity, for in the event of attack, some of the mothers must defend while the households are taken to safety."

Left self-conscious by his steward's perception, Lysaer did his best to return her direct courtesy. "Your hall need not go tuneless this night. My half-brother is accomplished on the lyranthe."

"But I have no instrument," Arithon protested, as if all the while his ear had been tuned to the exchange. Having somehow evaded the ceremony due the half-brother of a prince, he wore his plain tunic and much worn scabbard still. Though conspicuous in his lack of finery, his preferences had been humored without offense until Maenalle saw fit to correct matters.

"You shall have your pick of instruments," she announced, and waved over one of her captains. "Escort the prince's half-brother to the vaults and let him choose a lyranthe that suits him."

Servants rolled one of the smaller tapestries aside, and a key was brought that fitted the grilled doorway behind. Arithon and the leather-clad captain took candles and disappeared within, while Lysaer, who had not missed proof that his surmise concerning treasure stores was accurate, involved himself praising the knife dancers.

An interval later, Arithon returned. Rested in the curve of his arm was a lyranthe so battered and plain it almost looked fit to be discarded. The tuning pegs were chipped and not one string remained intact.

"He would have none of the jeweled ones," the officer who escorted him explained hastily.

Maenalle's gaze turned stormy. "Do you mock us?" At her tone the knife dancers melted away; nearby clansmen broke off conversations and went very suddenly still.

Arithon looked up from the instrument on his arm. "I chose the best," he said, bemused beyond thought for deceit. "Listen, lady." He whistled very softly over the sound board just ahead of the bridge. The wood in his hands caught the tone and responded in a resonance of absolute, dusky purity.

The sound caused Asandir, involved in discourse with Lord Tashan, to turn full around and stare. "Ath in his mercy," the Sorcerer exclaimed. "Allow me to examine that lyranthe."

Clansmen stepped aside as the Sorcerer approached and lifted the worn old instrument from Arithon's hands. Asandir ran his fingers down the wood, scraped grime off one tarnished fret, then turned the neck in his hands to view the back. There, begrimed under layers of yellowed lacquer lay a single Paravian rune, inlaid in abalone that somehow through the years had not chipped.

"Well, here we are," the Sorcerer murmured. He scraped the inlay with a fingernail and bared a rainbow glimmer of fine pearl. "There was truth to the tale that a second lyranthe crafted by Elshian remained behind on the continent." He returned the instrument to Arithon with reverence. "One is held in trust by Athera's Masterbard, Halliron. The other now belongs to you, by courtesy of Camris generosity. Guard her well. The sunchild Elshian was the most gifted bard known to history, and an instrument made by her hands sings more beautifully than all others."

Maenalle laughed in flushed triumph at Arithon's evident dismay. "Return us the gift of your playing," she said, then dispatched Maien to the tents to fetch wire.

But Asandir raised a hand in restraint. "Wait, lady. Brass strings will break on that instrument." He considered a moment, then added, "If you provide a few ounces of silver, I can refit her as the maker intended."

Without hesitation Maenalle removed her left bracelet.

"Any bent spoon would do as well," Asandir said gently.

Maenalle's eyes flashed. "Mine the honor, Kingmaker."

The Sorcerer inclined his head, accepted the heavy, interlaced band, and cupped it between his palms. The clansmen crowded closer to watch as, unmindful of his audience, Asandir bowed his head. No other move did he make, but a power sang upon the air. The bracelet in his hands shimmered, then flashed incandescently white. The watchers nearest to Arithon felt a sear of heat on their faces. Yet the Sorcerer's flesh did not burn. His hands moved, and the light grew blinding, and the ones who dared the dazzle saw the metal in his grip glow red. As if he handled nothing in the least beyond the ordinary, the Sorcerer twisted the ore between his fingers and drew out a glowing filament.

The task took scarcely a minute; then light and magic faded and the Sorcerer opened unmarked fists. He held half an arc of silver knotwork and a shiningly perfect length of wire. As if the ruined symmetry of Maenalle's bracelet prompted him to further inspiration, he gave a mischievous glance to the lady steward, then murmured, "Indeed, it is not meet that so great a gift should keep such mean appearance." And spell-light rinsed his hands once again as he reached out and cupped the fragment of interlace to the unadorned fretboard of the lyranthe.

A snap like a shock whipped the air. When the Sorcerer released the old wood, the silver knotwork remained, its pattern transmuted into the ebony as though stamped there from the day of creation. Arithon ran his fingertip over the result. He felt not a single raised edge; the inlay had fused with the surface beyond any hint of a flaw.

When the lyranthe was restrung with the Sorcerer's spell-tempered wire, the virtue of Elshian's craftwork became apparent from the instant Arithon struck the first note for tuning. The scratched wood in his hands came alive with a tone that touched the farthest recesses of even that cavernous stone hall. Harmonics seemed to shiver and melt upon the air, and every conversation faltered to a hush. Speakers forgot their next words, and listeners heard nothing beyond the dance of Arithon's fingers, and the languid, gliding sweetness of the strings as he turned each peg to true the pitch. When his work was done and the first full chord rang out under his hands, he stopped breathing, bowed his head, then damped the magnificent sound to silence.

"Lady Maenalle," he said, in his voice a jar like heartbreak, "this lyranthe is too fine for me. Let me play this one night and return her for your master bards in the lowlands."

But the Steward of Tysan dismissed his conscience with an imperious lift of her chin. "I don't begrudge you my bracelet," she called across the quiet. "And our bards, every one of them, passed over that instrument for another of prettier appearance. Since they chose by their eyes and not their ears, I call their claim forfeit."

Arithon's hand remained frozen against the glittering bands of new strings.

"If the word of a prince carries weight, I stand by Maenalle's judgment." Lysaer chose a seat and by example all in the chamber followed suit. "Brother," he said on a strange edge of exasperation, "will you have done with moping and play?"

Lacking the knowledge of Athera's lore, Arithon chose a sea ballad from Dascen Elur, a lively recap of a pirate raid in which a wily captain reduced three merchanters to ruin. Although the names of the vessels were changed in deference to his half-brother, Lysaer remembered the incident well; the merchanters had died badly, the seamen's widows and their families forced to beg charity to survive. Yet singer and lyranthe wove their spell deftly. The clan lords responded to the tale in raucous and wholehearted enjoyment. No one beyond the performer ever guessed how the laughter stung their prince's pride. In fairness, Lysaer could not blame Arithon; his duty was to please his hosts, and in a camp without wives or sweethearts, he had performed with a minstrel's true insight, his choice most apt for the setting. Yet the thievery that delighted these barbarians had roots in a past that reminded how terribly wide lay the gulf between subjects and sovereign.

Lysaer took his leave early, pleading weariness. He retired to the small chamber with all its comforts, but hours passed before he undressed and went to bed, and the peace of sound sleep did not visit him.

Confrontation

The hour grew late. Candles burned low in the hall by the time Arithon plucked the closing bars to his last dance jig of the evening. Although admiring listeners still surrounded him and the exultant flush remained high on his face, he silenced the rich tones of Elshian's instrument with something very near to relief.

"Another drinking song!" called a roisterer from the back.

Arithon shook his head and set the lyranthe gently down on the boards of an empty trestle. "My fingers are shot, my voice long gone, and I've a kink in my back from too much sitting."

"Have a beer, then," a younger woman invited.

"What, and spoil my head for clear thought?" Arithon rose, grinning with the abandon of a thief. "I've swallowed enough to ruin me already. Too much praise has done the rest. Have some mercy and let me retire while I still have the wits to find my bed."

"She'd likely show you to hers," somebody quipped from the sidelines.

But the admirers nearest at hand perceived the musician's weariness. Reluctantly they parted to give him passage between the bare trestles, the last few occupied chairs, and the boys who cleared away goblets and gathered up the linens from the feast. Though the clansmen of Camris had entertained lavishly, there were no drunks on the floors. The celebrants who lingered in the late hours were alert enough that an alarm from a messenger could see their finery exchanged for weapons at short notice. Quietly, unobtrusively, Arithon crossed the expanse before the arch. He disappeared into the gloom of the outer hallway without drawing Maenalle's notice; but slumped in a heap with one hand still curled around an ale mug, Dakar opened one eye. He saw Asandir break off his discourse with a clan chieftain and take purposeful strides toward the door.

"I thought so," the Mad Prophet mumbled through his knuckles. "Our Master of Shadow is going to catch an ungodly dressing-down." Dakar licked his lips and smiled before he slipped back into stupor; but his self-righteous prediction proved slightly premature.

Asandir did not follow Arithon immediately, but visited the quarters of Tysan's prince for a lengthy interval first. Afterward, as the winds sang cold off the heights and the mists of Desh-thiere obscured the early blush of coming dawn, the Sorcerer let himself out to find Arithon.

The Teir's'Ffalenn was alone at the horse pens, his back to the inside rails and his hands busy working tangles from the black forelock of the dun. Asandir approached without sound across the compound of trampled snow. For all his care, he was noticed. Arithon spoke as the Sorcerer paused behind his shoulder.

"Elshian's lyranthe should remain here." Pain threaded a voice worn rough by extended hours of performance. Too spent for nuance, Arithon added, "Better than I, you know how little she will be played."

Asandir folded his arms on the top rail of the fence. Cloakless and hoodless in the cold, the wind stirred his silver hair and the night-darkened fabric of his tunic. "Much can change in the course of five centuries."

Arithon at this moment preferred to forget the legacy left him by Davien's enchanted fountain; he shrugged. "Quite a lot has not changed at all in the course of five centuries."

At which point, directly confronted with the purpose of his visit, Asandir abandoned tolerance. "Did you believe me unaware of what happened in the loft of the Ravens' stableyard? Or that, the other day in the pass of Orlan, you baited Grithen and his scouts with intent to force my hand and expose your half-brother's inheritance?"

"Lysaer has what he longs for: a crown and the cause of truth and justice." The dun blew softly through her nostrils, stepped back, and left Arithon's hands empty. The cold made him wish he had his gloves.

Asandir seemed impervious to the wind's cruel bite. "Let me tell you a thing, Teir's'Ffalenn. You were left to your devices because the mindblock I set was never intended to bend your will."

"Was it not?" Arithon retaliated fast and hard as a blow. "Then why bother setting any ward at all?"

The Sorcerer did not rise to anger. Measured and wholly mild, he said, "Would you warm a man just tortured by fire before an open hearth? The memories of your failures in Karthan were all too hurtfully recent."

Arithon flinched. The Sorcerer pressed on, remorseless, though he never once sharpened his voice. "Maenalle was to receive the Prince of Tysan today. The Fellowship had already decided. She would have been informed of his lineage in private, that Lysaer not learn of his heritage until he had experienced the atrocity of the mayors firsthand. Except that your meddling with events caused your halfbrother an unpardonable shock, and Grithen has been sent in shame to the camps in the low country. He may be denied his inheritance."

Now Arithon went still as fire-hardened stone.

Asandir resumed, quietly precise as the tap a gem cutter might use to shear diamond. "Grithen is the last living heir to the late Earl of Erdane. Since his two siblings died on a headhunter's spears, yesterday's affray in the pass could disrupt a succession that has endured since the years before the uprising."

Arithon did not leap to claim the implied responsibility. Inflectionless as the windborne scrape of loose ice, he said, "You're telling me things that might all have been prevented."

"If the Fellowship were to use power to compromise a man's destiny, yes." Asandir regarded the knuckles left at rest on the midnight cloth of his sleeves while Arithon absorbed implications: that his fate was neither absolute nor proscribed. That he might cross the corral, saddle the dun mare and ride out, and not be pursued, except by townsmen who mistook him for a clan-born barbarian. Or he might take up the superlative lyranthe given him by Maenalle and study under her bards in the lowlands to the advanced senility of old age.

Arithon faced around and met the Sorcerer's eyes, which were clear as mirrors and as matchlessly serene. "You would let me go that simply?"

"I would." The Sorcerer added, "But let us be accurate. Would you let yourself?"

Struck on a nerve left raw since Dascen Elur, Arithon could no longer curb bitterness. "Dharkaron, Ath's Avenger might show more mercy."

"Who will speak for the clansfolk of Rathain?" Asandir said, a dark and terrible weight of sorrow behind his words. "For them, what mercy will there be when the sun returns, and the townsmen order killings caused by fear of a king who is not there?"

Arithon made a sound halfway between a sob and a curse. The biting sarcasm he used to deflect unwanted inquiries would not serve, but drive through Asandir's tranquillity like a spear cast through seawater: passion dispersed without trace by the infinite. The Sorcerer watched his struggle with neither cruelty nor challenge, but only an understanding as steady and deathless as sunlight.

Through a throat racked by tears he refused to acknowledge, Arithon said, "You give me Karthan all over again."

"The man would not stand here, who did not choose Karthan first."

"Oh, Ath." Arithon let go a twisted laugh. "The bitterest enemy is myself, then." For the open-handed freedom set before him was no choice at all: just the repeat of a fate poisoned through by an unasked-for burden of human suffering.

"I asked only that you to travel with me to Althain Tower," Asandir said. "Wherever else will you find the guidance to reconcile your powers as a mage with the responsibilities of your birthright?" The compassion in his tone was a terrible thing, a whip and a scourge upon a mind already mauled by the quandaries of duty. Arithon spun away, weeping regardless, and cursing the light hand of his tormentor. One threat, one compulsion, one word spoken with intent to bind, would have given him opening to escape.

But Asandir closed the net with a pity that shattered and crucified. "If you finish the journey, your case will be brought before the Fellowship. I can make no promise. But if a compromise can be found to release you from kingship, I will plead in your favor."

"The last nail in the coffin lid," Arithon managed. "Of course under protest, I accept." The air ached his lungs and his head hurt. His back to the Sorcerer, his eyes on the shifting shadows of the horses, he clung to the fence, mostly to keep his hands from violence.

Asandir looked at him and did not miss the murderous undertones of conflict. "For Desh-thiere, the Mistwraith, the Fellowship has no other choice."

"Ath," Arithon said. He managed a savage jab at humor. "Dakar would be crushed if we wrecked his precious prophecy. But against the Mistwraith, I do recall giving my word."

"Of the two, your kingdom is equally important." The Sorcerer might have departed then, his movements masked by a gust from the north.

Yet Arithon sensed his intent. Not yet ready for solitude, he whirled around, met the endlessly deep eyes, and planted a barb of his own. "Then we understand each other all too perfectly well."

Given clear warning that Arithon remained ambivalent concerning his inheritance, Asandir showed no annoyance. Rueful instead, he listened to the sigh of the wind across the compound as though it held answer to all suffering. "I'd like to know," he said at last to the prince who waited in jaggedly prideful silence, and who was far too wise to vent frustration through belief that the Fellowship Sorcerers were his enemies. "If our roles were reversed, what would you do?"

Arithon hesitated barely an instant. "Find the Paravians."

Asandir sighed. A sadness settled over him as oppressive as the mists on the mountains. "We tried," he said bleakly. "Ciladis of the Fellowship took on that quest, for he treasured the old races most of all." A minute stretched painfully through silence. "He never returned."

As if the night were suddenly too dark, or the cold off the peaks too penetrating, Asandir abandoned the subject. He strode back toward the lights of the outpost, leaving Arithon to the company of the horses and a moil of frustrated thoughts.

Traithe

Set on a knoll above the scrub-covered dunes that bordered the Bittern Desert, the spire of Althain Tower endured winds that never eased. Time and seasons might change, but in snowfall or sultry summer, drafts moaned through the shutters on the highest floor, riffling the corners of parchments caught between musty stacks of books. Unwashed tea mugs nested between the piles like abandoned eggshells in straw; walled around by clutter, surrounded by unstoppered ink wells and a row of meticulously sharpened quills, Sethvir of the Fellowship minded his cataloguing. While his awareness ranged far and wide beyond his tower eyrie, tracking events and portents that encompassed the grand movements of armies to the change of polliwogs into frogs, he penned neat script onto parchment and recalled candles only as an afterthought. Darkness came and went in its daily rhythms, unmarked by sleep or lighted sconces.

And yet amid the wail of a gust off the fells, when something flurried at the casement as slight as the scuffle of a mouse, Sethvir lifted his head. His poet's eyes lost their vagueness as he laid aside his quill pen.

"Traithe?" he said, on his feet in an instant. A six-day accumulation of dust billowed up from his robe as he shoved between chairs heaped with scrolls and opened the shutters on a predawn sky coiled with mist.

Rewarded the next moment by a downward rush of dark wings, the Sorcerer's pensive frown melted. "Welcome back, little brother," he greeted the raven that alighted on the knot-worked border of his cuff. The bird croaked. It cocked a pert head and blinked an eye intent with intelligence.

Sethvir shut the casement, a detail he intermittently neglected. "Did you bring your master, little one?"

The raven hopped to his shoulder and reproachfully preened its left primaries. When Sethvir responded by waiting, it shifted its feet and spoke again, sharply impatient. The Sorcerer chuckled. "All right, I'm on my way."

Forgetful that wet ink now hardened on his favorite nib, the Warden of Althain bore the bird from the copy chamber and down the bare spiral stairwell that accessed the tower's nine stories. Shadows of past ages lingered thickly here, but no place more than at ground level, where the mist-filtered gleam of first light etched the marble-carved statues of centaurs, sunchildren, and unicorns. Jeweled eyes and gilt trappings flashed at Sethvir's passage, wakened to glittering reflections as he brightened the torches by the tower's sole entry. At the foot of a shallow flight of steps, Sethvir caught a ring from a recessed socket and slid aside gold-chased panels of red cedar. The dusty smells of books and old tapestries gave way before the sharper tang of oiled steel, while new flame light threw grim highlights over a clockwork array of counterweights and chain. The raven unfurled its wings for balance as the Sorcerer set hands to the windlass. He cranked back the bars on two massive, metal-bound gates, which opened on a vaulted sally port cut through the base of the tower.

Here the drafts sang in dissonance through arrow loops and murder holes. Sethvir touched ink-stained knuckles to a secondary barrier of carved oak; the arcane bindings he released next collapsed in a blue-white sheet of clean fire, letting in the moist scents of grasses and mist and damp earth.

Sethvir paused, fleetingly touched by regret. That Althain Tower had ever needed its antiquated, Second-Age defense works was sorrowful enough, but that he should require wards, and that he should need to *unbind* such protections to admit another Sorcerer of the Fellowship went beyond tragedy.

The guard spells that Sethvir had dissolved on a thought, that he could have *stepped through* with little more difficulty than breathing, lay beyond the grasp of Traithe, who, at cost of the greater share of his powers, had single-handedly sealed the south Worldsend Gate in the hour of greatest peril. For the Mistwraith that afflicted Athera was but one splintered portion of a vaster whole; had Traithe not limited its access, Desh-thiere's rank coils would have strangled more than sun, and choked off all life on the planet.

The raven flapped irritably.

"All right, little brother." Harried back to duty, Sethvir unbarred the wooden doors.

Outside, beyond the battered barrier of a final portcullis, stood a Sorcerer, his deeply lined face and hooked nose shadowed under a wide-brimmed hat. A patterned silver band and straight-cut silver-white hair were the only bright aspects about him; the rest of his clothing including scuffed boots was fashioned of unadorned black. The raven did not wait for Sethvir, but bounded through the grille to light on its master's shoulder.

"Welcome," murmured the Warden of Althain, the usual misty distance restored to his blue-green gaze. "I trust your passage was swift?"

Traithe of the Fellowship shrugged, his iron-clad stoicism shaded ineffably toward disgust. "I was only in Castle Point."

The clang of the outer winch re-echoed through the arch while the portcullis ground ponderously upward. Traithe shouted over the din. "I searched for six days before I found a captain still willing to sail the coastline!"

The portcullis stopped. Sethvir ejected a rude word that rang isolated across fallen silence. Then he said, "That frustration won't last, my friend. Banish Desh-thiere, and you can restore the lost arts of navigation."

"But that would take—" Traithe's somber mien transformed before a smile of wounding hope. "The prophecy of West Gate? Is this why you called me? A prince has returned from Dascen Elur?"

"Princes," Sethvir said succinctly, "s'Ilessid and s'Ffalenn, on their way here with Asandir."

Traithe chuckled outright. "Even better! Ath, I was going to grumble about sore feet, and here you'll have me dancing on them instead." He reached down, lifted the saddle and bridle heaped by his boots as though he no longer felt the miles he had ridden through the night.

Determinedly bent to mind the winch, Sethvir took no brightness from his tidings. That Traithe, who had sacrificed more than any to avert the desecration of Desh-thiere, who was most vulnerable to harm if town factions should discover his identity, who through these late and troubled years was most resilient over his failures— that of the Seven, Traithe must wait weeks and travel miles to receive news that Asandir, Kharadmon, and Luhaine had all known on the wings of the moment itself was a grievous injustice.

Through the passage, Sethvir reset gates and defense wards with the motions of long habit, while Traithe regarded the statues commemorating old-race heroes of a past that now seemed febrile as a dream, though the jeweled settings were polished brightly and the caparisons on the centaurs hung rich as if fresh from the loom. "However the world comes to suffer, the sanctity of Althain remains unbreached. Your wardenship rests lightly here."

Mildly pleased, Sethvir returned a vague gesture. "The upstairs is a shambles. If you ask for tea, we'll need to scrounge for clean cups."

Traithe made his way in halting steps toward the stairwell. "Well, you do have more on your mind than all the rest of us put together."

"Sometimes." Pursued by echoes, forgetful of lamps, the Warden of Althain began the ascent. Through the pause as Traithe deposited his horse gear in the armory, he added, "Right now, just Mirthlvain."

Traithe tripped on a doorsill, and not because of his limp. For Mirthlvain Swamp to command his colleague's undivided attention meant trouble of fearful proportions. The raven resettled disturbed balance with an indignant ruffle of feathers while, worn from travel and oppressed by the mists, Traithe felt the frost go through to his bones. He fumbled at his belt, hooked the thong that hung his flint striker, and seeded a spark in the sconce by the storage level.

In the sulfurous flare of new lamplight, Sethvir's gaze glinted hard and immediate as chipped glass. "Forgive me," he said. "The tea must wait. Meth-snakes have bred with cierlan-ankeshed venom, and Verrain has just now sent word: there are many of them, and a mass migration is imminent."

Unsurprised that a disaster of such shattering proportions should be announced in the midst of banalities, Traithe said, "And the others?" Worry eclipsed his weariness. If these meth-snakes spread beyond Mirthlvain, country folk from Orvandir to Vastmark could be decimated in a matter of days.

"I've called them." Sethvir's voice seemed to echo beyond the confines of Althain's stairwell, to bridge the wide leagues that separated the far-scattered members of the Fellowship.

"Well, at least I'm at hand to be helpful," Traithe added, and this time his bitterness showed.

Still focused and fully attentive, Sethvir surveyed his companion from lined, dark eyes to scarred hands, to the limp and travel-stained cloak that the raven had torn threadbare at the shoulders. "There was never a time that you failed us, old friend."

Then, as if Desh-thiere's desecrations were trivial, and large-scale catastrophe from Mirthlvain did not threaten the kingdom of Shand, the Sorcerer clapped both hands to his temples in contrition. "Dear me. There must be a thousand or so books heaped in the upper library, and Ath's own jumble of inkwells lying about without caps. By nightfall we're going to be needing the table underneath."

"Well," said Traithe benignly. "Between you and the spawn of the *methuri*, we've got a dashed handful to tidy up."

"Mess?" Fixed on the underlying concept, Sethvir raised bristled eyebrows. "There's really no mess. Just not enough corks for the inkwells, *that's* what drives me to chaos." He whirled and rushed up the stairs.

Traithe followed. In the deliberate, sure-footed manner that masked the worst of his infirmities, he lit sconces the entire height of Althain Tower. Asandir might not need them, nor would Kharadmon and Luhaine; but the two princes arrived from Dascen Elur were bound not to welcome a mage's disregard of the dark.

Summons

Far off, where daybreak has long since brightened Desh-thiere's oil-thick murk, cold winds whip across the grass-gowned hills of Araethura, stirred by the essence of a Sorcerer who whirls his way south in grave haste. . . .

South and west, with the ease of an entity long discorporate, a second Sorcerer, once called the Defender, rides the force of the flooding tide in response to a distress call from Althain. . . .

Under gust-swept peaks in Camris, wrapped in dawn-lit mist, the Sorcerer Asandir pauses as if listening on the threshold of his quarters in the barbarian outpost; a moment passes, then he whirls at a run for the guard post to prepare for immediate departure. . . .

IX. Althain Tower

Accustomed to threats and fast action, Maenalle's scouts had horses saddled and provisions secured on the pack pony only minutes after the urgent summons from Althain Tower reached the west outpost and Asandir. Lysaer emerged from his quarters looking hollow-eyed. Secretly relieved to be quit of the company of subjects he found disturbing, he remained in flawless command of his manners, a trait young Maien admired as he held the stirrup for his prince to mount. Not all men would be so pleasant to serve after being rousted at dawn on the heels of a rowdy celebration.

Arithon sat his dun looking murderous. He had not rested. Neither had he been so far into his cups the evening before that indulgence should have spoiled his sleep. As Asandir swung into the black's saddle, the Master said, "I should have liked to ask for audience with Lady Maenalle."

The Sorcerer adjusted his reins without reply, and while the wind chased a cloak-snapping blast of cold off the heights, his reason for silence became apparent.

"If you wanted to speak for young Grithen, spare the trouble," announced Tysan's lady steward, present all the while as observer. Dressed like her scouts, her hair bundled under the hood of a sewn hide cloak, she had passed unnoticed in the bustle.

Grudging to show surprise beyond a fractional rise of one brow,

Arithon greeted her. As close to apology as Lysaer had ever seen him, he said, "Surely I have reason to plead the man's case."

Maenalle's features stayed hard. "Tysan's scouts do not act for personal vengeance. No matter what the provocation, they are forbidden to take hostages. We are not like Rathain's clans, to extort coin and cattle for human lives. For breaking honor, Grithen must answer. The fact he was invited into his temptation and that his action also threatened his liege bears very little on his punishment. The code that condemns him is one that upholds clan survival."

The dun sidled under Arithon's hand as he fielded the nuance in challenge. "You disapprove of your counterparts to the east?"

Maenalle's lips tightened. Though aware that the dun's combative crab steps reflected the mood of the rider, she responded with the bluntness that abashed the most brash of her scouts. "Unlike your subjects in Rathain, my following need not contend with the trade city of Etarra. Feud between clanborn and townsman is pitiless there. In the eastlands the governors' council can execute a man for the offense of singing the wrong ballad. Play your lyranthe in those halls with caution, young prince."

The Shadow Master said, "Spare the title, lady. I might never acknowledge any claim to the city you speak of."

Again Maenalle matched his offensive. "Would you risk the perception that inspires your talent by hardening your heart against need?"

And Arithon suddenly laughed, his anger absolved by admiration for her unflinching toughness. He bent in his saddle, raised Maenalle's hand, and kissed it sincerely in farewell. "Were you *caithdein* of Rathain, I might find myself sorely oppressed. Dare I suppose that Etarra's governors would also find their ways compromised?"

Strikingly free of vindictiveness, Maenalle said, "If you want my earnest opinion, there can be no remedy for Etarra except to raze it clean to the ground."

Piquant as her remark was, the chance was lost to pursue it as Dakar emerged from his cabin, stumbling in the grip of two scouts. They had needed to shepherd him into his clothes, for his voice arose in complaint that his britches were laced inside out, and both his boots on wrong feet. His keepers only smiled at his protests and hoisted him toward his waiting horse. Maenalle disengaged her hand from Arithon's grasp and took hurried leave of her sovereign. If Lysaer's response was cool with propriety, the reason became lost in the rush. The instant the Mad Prophet's bulk was stowed astride, Asandir wheeled his stallion and urged his party to the road.

"Ath's mercy," Dakar cried in vociferous injury. "What disaster brings this uncivilized change of plans? I *thought* I could nurse last night's hangover under dry blankets for a change."

Asandir answered between the snow-muffled thunder of hooves. The words *Mirthlvain* and *meth-snakes* carried forth with incisive clarity, and Dakar's recalcitrance withered.

Lysaer observed this. Despite an ambivalence resharpened by last night's ballads, he spurred abreast of the dun mare. If the unaccustomed rub of Maenalle's lyranthe left the creature wayward and spooked, the Master was seasoned to her tricks. Aware his half-brother would respond though his hands were full, the prince called over her rebellious snorts. "The page who wakened me said our Sorcerer had received emergency summons from Althain. What horror in this land do you suppose might be worse than Khadrim?"

The Master grinned back in speculation. "We do seem in a hurry to find out." He did not add that Maenalle's scouts had shown him maps; Althain Tower lay ninety leagues distant, a six-day journey over roads sparsely stationed with posts for adequate remounts. Yet Asandir spurred toward the foothills at a pace not intended to spare horseflesh.

After scrambling descent of a rock-strewn slope, the riders clattered onto a level stretch flanked by wind-stunted cedars. The footing softened to frost-crusted mud, safe for a prudent trot. Asandir shook his black to a canter, and conversation dwindled before the need to duck clods spattered up by its hooves.

The peaks lost altitude as the Sorcerer's party progressed. Under muted daylight, the heavy snows of the passes thinned to slush sluiced by ribbons of runoff. Lowland damp blunted the cold to a miserable ache, and the horses streamed lathered sweat. The dun abandoned her antics, her wind and energy consumed entirely by running, and still Asandir pressed on, the stride of his rangy black unflagging through league after passing league.

"By the Wheel," Lysaer called in distress. "Is he going to run our horses till they founder?"

Dakar roused from his misery, surprised. "Asandir? Never." Morosely he added, "One could wish the Sorcerer spared some pity for the aching head of his apprentice."

"Magecraft," Arithon explained as Lysaer questioned such unnatural display of endurance. "Touch your horse and you'll feel the energy."

Lysaer stroked his chestnut's steaming neck, and snatched back from the tingling warmth that surged in a wave from his fingertips.

Nettled to be alone in his ignorance, he glanced across whipping strands of mane. "Could you make such a spell?"

Arithon regarded his brother with eyes unnervingly thoughtful. "Not for so long, and not without harm. A balance must be maintained. If the horses don't suffer, the Sorcerer must stand as their proxy."

Curiosity overshadowed Lysaer's distrust. "Then Asandir depletes himself to replenish the strength of our mounts?"

"In effect, yes." As if reluctant to elaborate, Arithon faced forward into the wind as they thundered on into the lowlands.

Morning wore on toward noon.

The countryside steadily flattened, and the road improved to a span of stone paving scored white by the passage of cartwheels. Asandir pressed the horses to gallop through gentle hills and vine-tangled orchards, stopping only once at a wayside tavern to buy raisins, sausage, bread, and spirits for refreshment. While his companions ate and swallowed dry whiskey, horse boys toweled lather from the horses and checked their hooves for loose shoes. Within minutes, the company was back in their saddles, still cold, still sore, but none more haggard than the Sorcerer, who seemed a figure pinched out of clay as they clattered back onto the thoroughfare.

"How much longer can he keep this up?" Lysaer asked as his horse picked up a brisk trot. The pause at the tavern had not refreshed him. His muscles had stiffened, wet breeches had chafed his knees raw, and he owned no mage-trained detachment to set such discomforts out of mind.

Dakar glanced wistfully over the gates of a farmstead; smoke from the chimney carried an aroma of roast ham. Lighted cottage windows glimmered through bare trees and birch copses, their cheery shelter as useless as mirage to travelers harried by rain, and mounts hard-driven over slate gray and glistening with puddles. When Lysaer repeated his query, the Mad Prophet shrugged like a sodden crow. "Who can fathom the limits of a Fellowship Sorcerer? I've studied for centuries, and I daren't."

Lysaer was too spent to question whether magecraft or lying cussedness gave rise to the Mad Prophet's claim to unnatural longevity.

Cantering again, they crossed a blacksmith's yard. Blocked by a packed herd of sheep across the roadway, Asandir wheeled his black into the weed-choked ditch by the wayside. His party followed, raked by branches, while the ewes beaded up in alarm against the far bank and the abused shepherd's shouted invective faded behind.

The rain fell harder and farmsteads thinned away into wilderness before the Sorcerer at last drew rein. Engrossed in miserable discomfort, Lysaer jounced against the chestnut's crest as it clattered to a halt underneath him.

"We leave the road here," Asandir called while Dakar and Arithon pulled up. "Dismount and stay close. Every minute counts."

Saddle-galled and sore, Lysaer managed not to stagger as his numbed feet struck ground. He swiped back wet hair and surveyed a site that seemed unremittingly desolate. "Here?"

Asandir turned the black's bridle and shouldered without reply into holly and briars that hooked and snagged threads from his cloak. A stone's throw back from the verge, the brush subsided. Trees eaten hollow by age choked the light, and faint depressions and upthrust stone curbs revealed the ruin of an older road. Asandir pointed out a canted megalith traced over with weather-worn carving. "That stone marks the third lane, one of twelve channels of earthforce we will tap for swift travel to Althain. The soil itself sings with power here." As if the land's living pulse could also be drawn to sustain him, the Sorcerer quickened pace.

Forced to keep up, Lysaer and the others stumbled over lichen-capped stones and splashed through bogs, their road-weary mounts trailing droop-tailed and tired over hummocks browsed short by deer. The failing day dimmed the mist in louring veils, broken ahead by a wall that once had been dressed white marble. The eroded pillars of an arch yet stood where they had originally passed through. Beyond, patched with bracken and a crisscrossed stitchery of game trails, the land sloped into a bowl-shaped hollow too symmetrical to be natural, and ringed by oaks scabbed over with ancient blotches of lichen.

Footfalls silenced by wet leaves and moss, the party moved through the green-tinged twilight of the grove. In places of thinned vegetation, iron-shod hooves clanged across weathered black agate. Runes were inset in the half-bared slab, fashioned from a light-reflective mineral. Passing seasons had matted debris across the design, but the artistry in those fragments left visible roused an uncanny prickle across the skin.

Lysaer tugged his wet cloak around his shoulders, while Arithon scuffed away sticks and leaves to lay bare the ringed pattern of a cipher. "A power focus," he mused in an awed whisper.

Asandir stopped his horse. "Yes. We stand at the center of the Great Circle of Isaer, built in the First Age to channel earthforce to guard the halls of the earliest Paravian kings. Those defense works are long vanished, yet the Circle itself was maintained, at least until the conquest of Desh-thiere."

Arithon passed his reins to his half-brother and took an entranced step forward.

"Don't stray," Asandir cautioned. "In fact, you might wish to rest. This will be your last chance before we relocate to Althain Tower."

Arithon regretfully contained his curiosity. "Are there any Paravian cities left standing?"

Sorrowfully the Sorcerer shook his head. "Unlike mortal men, the old races seldom built, and then only through necessity. What hold-fasts remained from the First Age were laid waste in the course of the rebellion, except the towers of the citadel in Ithamon. Those stand protected by mighty wards, and the armies who came to desecrate could not enter."

But mention of the city ruled by s'Ffalenn ancestors withered Arithon's interest. He retrieved his horse and subsided into thought while Asandir fetched a flask from his saddle bag and offered a round of strong spirits.

Too late Arithon noticed Dakar's unusual abstinence. He ran his tongue over his lips, but detected no trace of an aftertaste, or any sweetness that might mask the suspect taint of drugs. His knees turned weak despite this. He had time to see Lysaer slump forward before his own senses whirled into vertigo. In the maddening space of a heartbeat, and despite his most desperate anger, he collapsed on wet stone in an oblivious heap beside his brother.

"That was a dirty trick," Dakar observed.

Asandir shoved the stopper in the flask of ensorcelled spirits, his eyes gone steely with urgency. "Necessary, my imprudent prophet." Through arcane manipulation of an earth lane, Arithon's inquisitive awareness and Lysaer's ignorance of grand conjury were complications best avoided to save delay. "Meth-snakes are stirring across Mirthlvain even as we speak, and I need you to quiet the horses."

Dakar caught the reins the Sorcerer threw him, then haltered the drifter-bred chestnut. Pale from more than his headache, he coaxed four lathered mounts into a huddle, then squeezed his eyes stoically closed while the paint rubbed her headstall against his chest, and the insolent dun lipped his cloak hood. "Keep doing that," he murmured, over and over like a litany. "Just keep on, and pay no mind to the wizardry."

The last time he had been told to steady horses through the topsy-turvy disorientation of a lane transfer, he had suffered a dislocated shoulder. Unless Sethvir had much changed his ways, there would be a dearth of hard spirits in Althain Tower's cupboards, even for medicinal emergency.

For Arithon, the spell-wrought sleep induced by Asandir did not last undisturbed. Brushed first by a passing energy current, then immersed in a burgeoning bloom of ward radiance, his enchanter's sensitivity reacted even through the veil of unconsciousness. Trained reflex took over and aligned his awareness to trace the source. The vibrations pursued by his innermind assumed hazy form, and he roved a landscape like dream but not.

Even asleep, a part of him recognized that the energy net which drew him into vision was not fancy, but a peril less forgiving than a sword's edge.

Arithon perceived a stand of reeds thrust through the inky, still waters of a marsh, no mere bog, but a vast expanse of wetlands crisscrossed with crumbled walls. Mist and night chilled air already dank with rotting vegetation; in the absence of moon or stars, ward glyphs glimmered above drifted fog, wraith-pale and sharp-edged as blades, their forces interlocked to form a boundary. Inside, under apparently calm pools, the swamp's depths moiled; serpents darted and dived, fanged, venomed, and guarded by a still figure in russet. Disturbed as if startled by footsteps in a place where no man dared tread, the watcher sharply looked up.

A soundless shock jarred the vision as the eyes of the guardian and the perception of the dreamer met; then the marshlands whirled away, replaced by a lofty tower chamber, walled with leather-bound books, and centered by an ebon table upon which a brazier burned like a star. Around this charged point of power, truesight identified the signature energies of Asandir, the Mad Prophet's muddled contradictions, and a third mage strangely shadowed and overhung by the spread wings of a raven. That moment Arithon felt his awareness gathered in by a touch of inexpressible gentleness. His vision narrowed to encompass the face of a fourth mage seated with the others.

Mildly snub-nosed, seamed like crumpled parchment, the Sorcerer's features expressed grandfatherly bemusement, lent a benign touch of frailty by a wooly shock of white hair and beard mussed for want of recent grooming. The impression of childlike senility proved deceptive. Half buried beneath bristled brows, eyes of diffuse greengray reflected all the breadth of Ath's Creation.

"Teir's'Ffalenn," pronounced a voice that rang through Arithon's mind like the sonorous stroke of a gong.

The Master of Shadow snapped awake. His eyes opened to a red-carpeted chamber warmed by a hearth of banked embers. A kettle dangled from an iron hook wrought into the serpentine loops of a dragon. Nearby stood a marble plinth, but in place of artwork or porcelain ornament, this one held a tea canister that somebody thoughtless had left open.

Arithon blinked. Utterly disoriented, he stirred, then recalled
Asandir's ensorcelled flask. If transfer from the power focus at Isaer
had been accomplished while he slept, this place would be located in
Althain Tower. He lay on a cot under blankets. His boots had been
removed; also his tunic, belt, and breeches. He still wore his shirt,
damp yet from rain. A heartbeat shy of a curse, Arithon spied his
missing clothes, slung over a chair alongside a bridle in need of
mending and a snarled-up twist of waxed thread. An awl jabbed irrev-
erently upright through a sumptuous velvet seat cushion. His sword,
drawn from its sodden sheath and oiled, rested against a table heaped
with books, some flopped face downward. Others were dog-eared at
the corners, or jammed with torn bits of vellum or frayed string
pressed into service as page markers. The dribbled remains of a tallow dip lay couched in an exquisite silver candle stand, and chipped
mugs, used teaspoons, and mismatched inkwells filled any cranny
not encroached on by clutter.

Nested amid oak-paneled walls and age-faded tapestries, the air of
friendly disorder offered the weary traveler a powerful incentive to relax and rest. But charged to disquiet by the tingling, subliminal ache
that partnered the proximity of thundering currents of power,
Arithon felt nettled as a cat in a drawstring bag. Although Lysaer lay
curled in contentment in a cot alongside, his half-brother tossed off
his blankets, arose, and pulled on his rain-damp clothing. Since his
boots were nowhere to be found, he crossed the thick carpet barefoot
and opened the chamber's single door, a studded oaken panel strapped
and barred with heavy iron. The sconce-lit stairwell beyond removed
any doubt that Althain Tower had been built primarily as a fortress.
Chilled by fierce drafts through the arrow slits, Arithon stepped out
and closed the latch softly behind him. A moment of considered
study revealed the power's source to be above him. He set foot upon
worn stone and climbed to the highest level, where he encountered
a narrow portal as starkly unornamented as the first. The latch and
bar were forged iron, frosty to his touch as he set hand to the grip and
cracked the panel.

Inside lay the round, book-lined room from his dream. The central
table was supported by ebon carvings of Khadrim, and seated there,
faced away from him, were Dakar, Asandir, and a black-clad stranger.
Opposite sat another, robed in maroon with sleeves banded in dark
interlace and rubbed thin at the cuffs. He was neither tall nor portly,
but his presence had a rootedness like the endurance of storm-
whipped oak, and his face and eyes matched that of the Sorcerer, who
had spoken his title and aroused him.

"Arithon of Rathain?" said Sethvir, Warden of Althain, in gentle inquiry. "Enter, and be welcome."

Dakar swiveled around in astonishment. "You should be asleep and beyond reach of dreaming," he accused as the Shadow Master stepped through the doorway.

"How could I?" Aware of all eyes upon him, not least the attention of the black-clad stranger, Arithon pulled out an empty chair and sat. He rested his hands on the table edge, careful not to look directly into the brazier. More like a spark than natural flame, its blue-white blaze carved the chamber into starred, knife-edged shadows, but radiated no heat, for its source was drawn directly from the third lane. To Dakar, Arithon retorted, "Could you lie abed, with such a grand spate of earthforce in flux just over your head?"

To Sethvir, he added, "I came to offer help, if you'll accept it."

Befuddled in appearance as any careworn old man, the Warden of Althain said, "We cannot deny we're short-handed. But you should be aware, there is peril." Though mild, the look that followed searched in a manner unnervingly subtle.

Read to his innermost depths, Arithon was touched by a contact so ephemeral, it raised no prickle of dread; and yet, the image conveyed to him harrowed. The swamp-dwelling serpent he had first seen in dream recurred now in migrating thousands, possessed of an intelligence that hungered, and envenomed with a poison more dire than anything brewed up by nature. Secure within Althain Tower, Arithon *felt* the restlessness that drove the meth-snakes in their hordes to seek the defenseless countryside beyond the marsh. Shown the villagers, children, and goodwives whose lives were endangered, he was given, intact, the knowledge of the forces currently at work to stay the migration; then, in blunt honesty, the daunting scope of energy needed to eradicate the threat.

"Now then," Sethvir finished aloud. "You would bear no shame if you wish to retire below and sleep. A wardspell might be set to isolate your awareness, if you desire."

Arithon measured the Warden, whose kindliness masked a razor-keen perception. After a slow breath he said, "*If* I were to retire, I'd be asking no protections where plainly none can be spared."

As he made no move to rise, Sethvir laced together fingers blue-veined as fine marble. "Very well, young master. Our Fellowship would be last to deny that against the meth-snakes of Mirthlvain, every resource is needful. You may stay, but these terms will apply." His regard pinned Arithon without quarter. "You will lend support to the spellbinder, Dakar, unconditionally, and from trance state. You will hold no awareness of the proceedings as they occur, and retain no memory afterward."

Severe strictures: Arithon understood that if the conjury went awry, his life would be wrung from his body as a man might twist moisture from a rag. He would have no warning, no control, no shred of will. Across the table, the Sorcerer in black watched him with feeling akin to sympathy; Asandir stayed firmly nonjudgmental. If heirship of Rathain seemed no hindrance to a perilous decision, expectations remained nonetheless. Whipped to resistance by that certainty, the Master moved on to Dakar, and there read fatuous contempt, for why should any trained master lend a brother's trust to an apprentice who binged on beer to evade discipline?

Moved to black and bitter humor, the Master looked back at Sethvir. "I accept." The words were charged with challenge: if limits existed to the free will Asandir had inferred he still possessed, he would risk his very life to expose them.

Sublimely untroubled by such byplay, the Warden of Althain rested misty, poet's eyes upon the Master. "As you choose. You may set your mind in readiness at once, for meth-snakes won't wait for second thoughts."

Arithon bowed his head, aware through closed eyes of Dakar's unadulterated dismay. The faintest smile curved the s'Ffalenn mouth, then faded as he engaged his self-discipline and submerged his consciousness into trance.

A great deal less gracefully, and with a martyred sigh the Master of Shadows was quite beyond hearing, Dakar gathered his own, more scattered resources.

Through the isolated interval of concentration, while the Mad Prophet assimilated the link offered by Arithon, Sethvir turned in piercing dismay toward Asandir.

"Difficulty with the succession was an understatement, my friend." The Warden of Althain waved an exasperated hand at Rathain's now unconscious prince. "You inferred a past history of blood feud, but this!"

At Traithe's blank look of inquiry, Sethvir hooked his knuckles through the tangled end of his beard. "Our Teir's'Ffalenn has the sensitivity imbued in his forefather's line, but none of the protections. His maternal inheritance of farsightedness lets him take no step without guilt, for he sees the consequences of his every act, *and equally keenly feels them.*"

"That doesn't explain his recklessness," Traithe said. "Nor such guarded resentment."

"No." Asandir answered his colleague levelly back. "A prior conflict between ruling power and trained awareness of the mysteries has already broken Arithon's peace of mind. An attempt on my part to ease his despair misfired and nearly earned his enmity."

Sethvir steepled his hands, thoughtful. "Set him free, then. Let him pursue his gift of music, marry, and let us seek Rathain's prince among his heirs. After the passage of five centuries, what is another generation, or even two?"

"I beg to differ," Traithe broke in, his quiet, grainy voice tinged to regret. "If Etarra's merchant factions are not curbed with the advent of clear sunlight, their intrigue could grow too entrenched to break."

Silence fell, harsh under the glare of the brazier. Each of three Fellowship Sorcerers pondered upon the trade city that commanded the heart of Rathain's trade routes. There the old hatreds ran deepest, and there misguided justice had brewed a morass of bloody politics and decadence. For Etarra there could be no tolerance. The prince who assumed Rathain's crown would be charged with dismantling that nest of corruption, and no chance offered better opportunity than the time of Desh-thiere's defeat, when governors and guilds would be plunged into disarray by the return of the open sky.

"The long-range effects bear careful study," Sethvir concluded. "We shall cast strands when this matter of meth-snakes is resolved." Then, since the task of quelling serpents was dire in itself, he took brisk stock of their resources.

Two other Fellowship Sorcerers rushed to the site of trouble had earlier raised a barrier ward to seal off the swamp. Their combined efforts were barely sufficient to stay the serpents' migration, which left Mirthlvain's guardian, the spellbinder Verrain, alone in the old watch keep at Meth Isle. Although the fortification had been augmented with a fifth-lane power focus to combat worse horrors in the past, an unaided apprentice could never man such defenses without becoming charred to a cinder.

"I see no alternative but to shape and direct the power from here." Sethvir sighed in naked regret. "What else can we try but to bend the third-lane current across the continent in a reduced vibration that Verrain can safely transfer to bolster the barrier ward?"

To hear such a note of uncertainty from the Warden of Althain was enough in itself to inspire fear. By now in firm rapport with the resources lent by Arithon, Dakar shot a glance around the table. Traithe was openly sweating, and Asandir sat with one fist braced in trepidation. In a stillness more eloquent than words, each Sorcerer faced the appalling truth: never in five thousand years of history had they been so critically understaffed. The circle they would close for the task of saving Shand would only be effective as its weakest link.

Miserably conscious of his shortcomings, Dakar knotted clammy hands and cursed Arithon s'Ffalenn for scheming arrogance. Never mind that the Master's magecraft held none of the shifty cunning his conscious mind affected; however he might disparage Dakar for slipshod ways, the trust he gave in trance was clear-edged and forthright as his music.

The paradox jabbed like insult, that a spirit so exactingly controlled should vengefully surrender all that he was into jeopardy.

For as Sethvir described the coming trial, Dakar would become the check-rein on that awesome flow of power to be channeled through Verrain thousands of leagues away. If the spellbinder at Meth Isle should misstep, and Dakar keep less than perfect vigilance, the influx sent from Althain would merge unchecked with the fifth lane. The overload would sear the heartlands of three kingdoms to waste, while the meth-snakes that compelled such unconscionable risk would themselves evade annihilation.

Riddled through by anxiety, Dakar started at a touch upon his shoulder. Sethvir stood beside him, his manner tempered with sympathy. "We ask a great deal more than is reasonable of you."

Dakar shook his head, struck mute. He had watched a man suffer death by cierlan-ankeshed venom; the memory still harrowed him in nightmares. Any stresses he might share through his link with Verrain must surely be less than the horrible invasion that threatened Shand.

"I'll cope," Dakar mumbled.

The Warden of Althain was never so easily deceived. "You will guard Verrain's well-being, and your own. Arithon's strength will back you, but his safety will be mine to secure. He need never know. But as the last living s'Ffalenn, his line is too precious to risk."

Sethvir gave Dakar a last pat in reassurance, then bent over Arithon's limp form and with a gesture wove a protective ward that stung the eyesight to witness.

Although relieved of a burden, the Mad Prophet felt galled to no end that the Master should pass unscathed through a direct challenge of the Fellowship's wishes. "It's not as if he gave a whistle for the land, or the people, or even a spit over principles," Dakar grumbled as he stuffed shaky fingers in his cuffs to wedge them still.

Already attuned to larger matters, Sethvir returned a vague murmur. "You misunderstand the man gravely."

But since the Mad Prophet had been engrossed beyond hearing through the Fellowship's recent discussion, Dakar believed only that Arithon's genius for duplicity had caused Sethvir himself to be misled. The Warden of Althain settled in his seat with a rustle of robes, and his misty-eyed regard touched his colleagues.

No spoken signal passed between the three, yet when the Fellowship Sorcerers at Althain commenced rapport, the air in their presence quickened at the call of some unseen current. Shadows swelled as the spark in the brazier condensed to a pinpoint, dim at first, then waxing as their touch bound the pulse of Athera's third lane ever more relentlessly into focus. The light flared to piercing brilliance. Forced to avert his eyes, the Mad Prophet was awed to find the Sorcerers unmoved by the dazzle. Rooted as stone, they twined the earthforces tighter still, until the chamber resonated with a palpable, mounting charge. A stinging bite of ozone eclipsed the book smell. The tower's granite walls lost aspect, became edgeless and transient before the vast tide of power which itself seemed to cancel time.

The atmosphere became stillness before storm, and out of pent silence Sethvir spoke a word.

Light arced from the brazier toward Traithe.

He received it unflinching, cast it around space and time in a manner that defeated reason. A snap sheared the air into wind as the ray honed out of earthforce bridged the wide distance to Meth Isle.

Dakar bit his lip. The salt taste of sweat seemed unreal on his tongue, as if the proximity of lane force estranged him from bodily sensation. Then the connection completed. His thoughts were slammed to incoherence as, across the breadth of the continent, the spellbinder who was Guardian of Mirthlvain recaptured the current sent from Althain. The focus pattern on the stone floor at Meth Isle keep flashed scarlet as power lapped against power, and the fifth lane's inherent energies surged in sympathetic resonance.

Barefoot, terrified, and stripped down to animal reflex, Verrain wrested the flux apart with a cry that echoed outward into the night beyond his walls. He rocked under a buffeting slap, shared by Dakar, as the awesome, fiery rush of power deflected through his body, and on into the deft control of the Sorcerers, who held the barrier along Mirthlvain's perimeter. Although stepped down to a finer resonance by the pair Asandir and Sethvir, the current's passage was a dry, lacerating wind of agony. Dakar drew gasping breaths and struggled. He must preserve self-identity against the burning assault of sensation experienced by Verrain, or risk himself and all who depended on him.

The powers whipped and raged. Dakar fought not to be swept from control, though he had no anchor. The chair beneath his body had no meaning, or the stone under his feet. He was a mote in a whirlpool, flexed, twisted, shoved, and driven until physical orientation seemed an illusion cast outside reality.

Sethvir sensed the Mad Prophet's distress, even through the shaping of the third lane's raw bands. "Sometimes it helps if you hold someone's hand," he said gently, and offered his own.

Dakar accepted with a gratitude compounded by desperation. Like a boulder in the thrash of a millrace, the touch steadied him. Distantly he was conscious of Sethvir's link with Asandir, and the incomprehensible strength they engaged to tame the wild pulse of the third lane. Dakar blinked tears, or maybe sweat, from his eyes. Confusion enveloped him, and a duality that dizzied. He endured, held to the body seated at Althain Tower, though a part of him also stood, barefoot, chilled, and blinded by the inflamed focus pattern that channeled the untapped fifth lane. Dakar suffered with Verrain as wave after wave of energies coursed through their twinned awareness, to be snatched and turned again, before they merged in ruinous concert with the native currents underfoot.

Beyond moss-streaked keep walls, and across the silvered waters of Methlas Lake, the mists of Desh-thiere muted a dance and flash of blue light, as the last two Sorcerers in the chain fused with the borrowed powers to stabilize their defense ward. The critical moment arrived, when the vast and intricate matrix had been strengthened enough to be passed into the control of one Sorcerer. Apprehension stirred through the circle gathered at Althain.

"Steady, hold steady," Asandir said aloud.

Traithe returned a sharp nod.

Dakar felt Sethvir's fingers tighten over his own. He had no chance to wonder if stress or reassurance prompted the gesture, for Verrain's recoil as the power flow shifted unbalanced him as well.

Through a terrible, precarious interval the Mad Prophet battled for cohesion, the will that held him to cognizance gone febrile as a spider's silk stretched against a gale. By the time the onslaught eased, Luhaine, once known as Defender, now contained the serpents' migration, bolstered by assistance from Althain Tower. With one mage less in the link, every risk lay redoubled. Dakar's mouth felt packed in ash. Should the energy flow from Althain to Meth Isle keep fail now, Luhaine's barrier would crumple, and meth-snakes in teeming thousands would descend like a plague upon the countryside.

Yet such perilous preparation had at last freed the other Sorcerer on site at Mirthlvain to act. Ruthless as Ath's avenging angel, Kharadmon brought his powers to bear upon the boglands. Stale pools lashed up into foam as a living torrent of serpents seethed, pursued out of cranny, mud pool, and reed bed by a corona of killing light. The serpents writhed in futile flight, turned at bay against Luhaine's ward. They struck at air, at wind-lashed hummocks, and in a madness of frustrated fury, at each other's struggling flesh, while the night passed and their hordes were pared back relentlessly by the efforts of the Fellowship's circle.

Then Verrain faltered at Meth Isle. The fifth-lane focus there crackled to a blaze that signaled cataclysm.

Caught without warning, Dakar felt his senses upend into vertigo. All his control unraveled. His teeth clenched and every muscle cramped, and his body twisted as if he tumbled in a fall from a great height.

Warned by Dakar's groaned shout, Sethvir sensed the disaster. As though he was not enmeshed in rapport with Asandir, the whole untamed force of the third lane whipped to submission between, he severed the power transfer. Snapped out of range of all pain, the Mad Prophet slammed back in his chair. His composure dissolved into ugly, racking sobs that were the best he could manage for breathing.

"Ath," he gasped, half unhinged. "I feel like every hangover I ever earned has joined force in triplicate to plague me."

Swept by giddy hysteria, Dakar jammed a fist in his mouth to stop his babbling tongue. His vision had gone patchy and his ears boomed to a surf-roll of sound. Somewhere in the echoing, hollow void where thought seemed to flurry and vanish, he re-encountered the current channeled in from the Master of Shadows, reduced now to an ember, but pitched with the same rock-steady vibration that had marked its presence from the start. Merciless in his need, Dakar seized upon that glimmer. He tapped Arithon's source to anchor failing senses and recover the strength to look up.

"Luhaine's ward!" he cried out, pierced by a raw blade of fear.

A stark silhouette against the blue-white glare of lane forces, and the pallid gray light beyond the casement, Asandir caught his shivering shoulders. The Sorcerer's fingers were not steady, but the grip they delivered bruised bone. "Bide still, Dakar, it's all right."

The supporting hands fell away, and the Mad Prophet slumped forward, his cheek cradled on crossed forearms. Beside him, a haggard Traithe had done likewise. Through ears muddied with bell tones of ringing sound, Dakar heard Sethvir's voice assure that before the defenses failed, the meth-snakes had been reduced to manageable numbers. Kharadmon could track down and eradicate the survivors with a fair chance of success.

Verrain's collapse had been due to exhaustion and overextension. Luhaine would tend him, and keep watch at Mirthlvain until the Guardian spellbinder's recovery.

Like a shell sucked clean of meat, Dakar allowed himself to be ushered to his feet. He was aware of jostling, of movement, as the

Sorcerers bore him up along with the limp form of Arithon s'Ffalenn. Perversely vindicated that at least such damnably arrogant self-discipline had just limits, Dakar inclined toward a rich laugh—except the crushing intensity of his headache permitted only breathless speech. "The prodigy overreached himself. Bothersome meddling mind of his will have no choice but to sleep off the reaction now."

"Indeed," Sethvir responded in remarkable pique. "Our Teir's'Ffalenn won't escape his bed for at least the next few days."

The Sorcerer said something more in the lilting cadence of the old tongue, but the words escaped comprehension. Poised at the head of the stairs, Dakar swayed precariously. His knees let go all at once. As a falling rush of darkness claimed him, he fuzzily concluded that drunken binges befuddled a body less than overindulgence of magecraft any day. Most urgently he needed to remember to clarify that point with Asandir.

Strands

Eventide saw the Fellowship Sorcerers, Asandir, Sethvir, and Traithe, gathered once more in Althain Tower's upper chamber. The blaze of the brazier lent crispness to profiles already hardened by the demands of the times. Conversation stayed light as they waited upon their colleagues Kharadmon and Luhaine, both of whom were discorporate spirits, able to cross the continent from Meth Isle at whim. Certain topics were avoided; as unflinchingly as any Fellowship Sorcerer still physically embodied had weathered the setbacks engendered by Desh-thiere and Davien's rebellion, none cared to count how many places would stand empty tonight. In better years, at other summons, the ebony table had seated the full Fellowship of Seven, five high kings, and a representative from the three Paravian races; apprentice spellbinders had not been required to shoulder responsibilities beyond their training to fill, and mist had not smothered the land to the harm of the fruitful earth.

Sethvir sought his usual solace, scrounging in his cupboards for tea, when Traithe's raven raised wings and flapped, disturbed by a draft that spilled through the east casement. The sudden inrush of wind carried a distinctive scent of grasslands spiked with frost.

Poised with his hands full of crockery, Sethvir addressed what seemed vacant air. "Kharadmon? You're not too spent to project an image? The Mad Prophet, I think, would be appreciative."

As the eddy swirled to stillness, the tower chamber rang with deep laughter. "Where is Dakar?" said a voice in resonant Paravian that issued from a point inside the shutter.

A shadow coalesced in the spot, resolving into the slender form of a Sorcerer in sable and green. A cloak lined in orange silk spilled from elegantly set shoulders; the face inside the hood was an elfin arrangement of angles, accented by a spade-shaped beard, a glib smile, and a hooked nose. The apparition raised tapered hands and pushed the cloth back, smoothing black-and-white-streaked hair. Freed from shadow, the eyes were pale green and direct as a cat's. The visual projection of the discorporate mage Kharadmon skimmed a glance over the assembled company and, in throughly changed inflections, repeated, "Where is Dakar?"

"On his way." Asandir gave a boyish grin. "Though I fear a bit the worse for drink. Sethvir had cider in his cupboard, and our prophet drank it dry to blunt the aches of exhaustion."

Kharadmon's smile widened to show foxy, even teeth, and features that had no substance in reality flashed a look of pure deviltry.

Two stories below Althain's topmost chamber, the Mad Prophet roused from dreamless stupor with a start that cracked his knee into Sethvir's chess table. Ivory and ebony counters cascaded to the floor, the clatter of their upset entangled with Dakar's peevish oath.

"Dharkaron's chariot!" He catapulted from the armchair that had supported his untimely nap, slammed into the table again, and slipped and skated across rolling pawns through several unbalanced steps. A spectacular trip landed him belly down across a footstool and a racked set of fire tongs.

"Blessed Ath," Dakar wheezed on the breath bashed out of his lungs. "I'm *coming!*"

Moments later, the Sorcerers upstairs were disrupted by the solid thud of a body against the iron-bound door to their chamber. The latch rattled sharply but did not unfasten; after an interval of fumbling and swear words, Dakar burst in from the stairwell, his face beet red under a tangled nest of hair.

"I came as fast as I could." The Mad Prophet licked a bruised knuckle, tugged at his rumpled tunic, and glowered at Asandir. "Your gift of a nightmare was bad enough without setting stay spells on the latch."

Sethvir clutched his tea mugs, innocuously intrigued, while the Sorcerer so addressed sat back in his seat, his smile gone and one silvered brow tipped upward. "How thoughtlessly quick you are with accusations."

Dakar yanked out a chair and dumped himself in a miffed heap. "Only Kharadmon would have—" Suspicion congested his round features.

"Greetings, Mad One," said the discorporate Sorcerer.

Dakar shot straight, wildly searching, but his gaze surveyed the room repeatedly without enlightenment. As the other Sorcerers gave way to amusement, his injury flattened to disgust.

He announced scathingly to no one, "If you're going to bait me, ghost, you might be sporting and show me a visible target."

The spirit returned unbridled laughter, and Dakar's eyes found focus at last as the illusion that marked the Sorcerer's presence became revealed to him. "You're beyond your depth, anyway, my prophet." Kharadmon pulled out a chair, carelessly sliding the seat through his thigh and a fold of green cloak. Since tormenting Dakar was a favorite diversion, he might have added more, but Sethvir broke in to ask after Luhaine.

Kharadmon's eyes went veiled. "On his way, this moment." Blandly he added, "I always best him at travel, argument, and cards."

As if whipped to instability by his words, the torches in the sconces by the doorway streamed and flickered, and though no breeze had arisen to partner the disturbance, one blinked out.

"I protest that statement," a bass voice said in reproof. A second discorporate materialized alongside the table, this one wizened and bald, a beard as broad as a waterfall fanned across his chest. His corpulent form was robed in blue-gray. Apple-round cheeks were capped by brows peaked in prim inquiry, and eyes sharp and black as an irascible scholar's were trained upon the elegantly seated image of Kharadmon. More than usually petulant, the newcomer announced, "Your claim is unfounded, unjust, and entirely unforgiven. We shall contest it later."

"Luhaine," Sethvir interrupted, "could we dispense with tired rivalries and get started?"

The second of the disembodied Sorcerers transferred his vexation to the Warden of Althain. "You asked to determine the impact of Desh-thiere's bane upon Athera. Might I know what's gone amiss?"

Belatedly, Sethvir recalled his clutch of crockery; he deposited the lot with a sigh on the last bit of uncluttered shelf, while Asandir leaned forward, his robe lit indigo by the brazier. In careful phrases, and as much for Dakar's sake, he described the backgrounds and personal attributes of the princes from Dascen Elur whose shared talents comprised the heart of the West Gate prophecy. His words were received in grim quiet, even Luhaine moved to silence as he summed up.

"The powers the half-brothers command are unquestionably direct, and evenly split. The risks are self-evident. Lysaer and Arithon are opposites in character and upbringing. Both inherit the gifts of two royal lines, which makes an uneasy legacy. Should their past heritage of feud become renewed, the consequences could be ruinous. Since Dakar has been troubled by precognizance to that effect, it seems wise to cast strands and seek a clear course for the future."

Luhaine's image blinked out and reappeared, seated with fingers laced on the tabletop across from Kharadmon. His assent followed, instantaneous and emphatic since elemental mastery of any sort was potentially limitless. Set at odds, Lysaer and Arithon between them could wreak havoc on a scale not seen since Davien the Betrayer roused the five kingdoms to rebellion.

Quiet as shadow, Traithe arose from his chair.

"Cupboard underneath the Lanshire histories, third shelf," Sethvir murmured distractedly. He dissipated the spark of lane force that burned in the brazier. Asandir removed the bronze tripod, while Kharadmon extinguished the other sconce. Unhindered by total darkness, Traithe found the place designated and retrieved a square of black velvet, which he shook out and spread across the table.

Luhaine's brow creased as the cloth passed unimpeded through his elbow. "Has Dakar mastered the effects of tienelle yet?"

The Mad Prophet rolled his eyes and groaned. "I'd feel better after a draught of deadly nightshade." Then, on a plaintive note to Asandir, "Is seersweed truly necessary? Last night was awful enough. Today I don't feel in the least like volunteering to ruin my health all over again."

The rare, high-altitude herb he wished to avoid at all costs. Valued for its mind-expanding properties, tienelle's narcotic was also a poison that caused cramps, headache, and a sudden onset of dehydration that could end in coma and death. Spellbinders were schooled to transmute its toxicity, for need occasionally arose for them to perceive complexities beyond their training to encompass.

Asandir measured his apprentice with a calm that disallowed pity. "Had you not dropped a sword, once, to disrupt your native gift of prescience, you would not be required to attend this session."

Dakar slammed his palms on the tabletop, his frustration damped to an unsatisfying thump by the heavy velvet covering. "Ath, you won't forget a detail, not even once in a century."

"Under the north window seat, in the coffer," Sethvir interjected in apparently idle afterthought.

The Mad Prophet was not fooled. If Asandir's memory forgave nothing, Sethvir knew the precise location of every unwanted item in Ath's creation. Since Traithe would not trouble to fetch and carry for an apprentice, and Kharadmon's whetted interest promised mischief, Dakar heaved to his feet. Too lazy, or too obstinate, to engage the self-discipline for mage-sight, he noisily smacked shins and knuckles in the dark and searched out the herb stores for himself. He clumped back to his chair clutching a stone pipe and a carved wooden canister, and busied himself with a martyred sigh. Most pointedly he ignored the Fellowship Sorcerers as they prepared for a ritual undertaken only at direst need.

Power gathered in the hands of Asandir. Above the dark velvet he spun a rod of energy, a glimmer like a line of veiled starlight. To this he added a second, then a third, each for the triad of mysteries that embodied Prime Power and underlay all Athera's teeming life. Next he added twoscore lesser lengths, to which Sethvir assigned Names in a Paravian ritual that summoned the essence of the ruler, place, or power, and stamped its quickened current on the spell. The strands assumed identity and altered, each according to assigned nature. The governors' council in Etarra manifested as hurtfully bright, a hedge of scintillant angles; the trio for the Paravian races interwove to the evocative beauty of lacework before fading to a near subliminal glimmer; the spark that captured the collective spirit of the clansfolk in their exile scribed an enduring sweep of arc. To cities, and human consciousness, and natural forces were added individuals; and after these, plants, animals, and natural elements, until a geometric lattice glimmered above the velvet backdrop, an entire world's interlinked complexity recorded in precise proportion and line.

The visionary mind of a Fellowship Sorcerer could interpret such at a glance. Where other methods of precognizance might sound only broad-scale highlights, the strands were superlatively sensitive. Each would react as its nature dictated, mapping even minute shifts of balance with pinpoint accuracy. The futures that might spring from alternate sets of events could be assessed instantaneously, even the least nuance made plain. To read the analog set down into pattern without laborious mathematical analysis, Dakar packed his pipe with the notched, silver-gray leaves of tienelle. The scent of the herb permeated the room, sharp, bitter, and edged as a winter wind.

The pattern over the tabletop reached completion, shedding radiance like summer moonlight over the faces of the surrounding Sorcerers. Dakar accepted a spark off the finger of a sardonically smiling Kharadmon to ignite his pipe.

"Commence," Sethvir said softly.

The Mad Prophet sucked hard on his pipe stem, filling his lungs with aromatic smoke. Vertigo spun his awareness, followed by a kick akin to adrenaline; his senses cartwheeled and slammed back into focus, enhanced to painful sensitivity. His ears recorded sound with unnatural nuance, and his vision assumed a razor-edged clarity. The strands that reflected the power balance of the living world lost their random shapes, became a comprehensible whole. Configurations of lines and angles spread out like tapestry, the fates of kingdoms intertwined with the births and deaths of field mice.

Yet across the rhythms of this grand design, disharmonies stood out like botched tangles in string. Here lay a twist that told of a mayor's prejudice, jealousy, and greed; there a warped line revealed a sapling stunted by the unending mists of Desh-thiere. Where the shining braid of Paravian presence had once enhanced the central axis of the prime vibration, Ath, a channel of emptiness remained, like notes lost from a bar of flawless counterpoint. Dakar wrestled to stem a flood of tears. Another pull from the pipe, and the tienelle honed sorrow into a blade that harrowed his heart. His time sense blurred. Over the shining lines of Athera's present, he sensed changes wrought over the ages, the strengthening of some aspects and the splitting, weakening, or dissolution of others. He suffered knowledge of all pasts and possible futures in their thousands, until awareness of Asandir's eyes upon him pierced through his strayed concentration. His mind might soar through a spiraling flight of enlightenment, but at a price. He must not neglect self-awareness. Even as the drug freed his thoughts, its poisons ravaged his body. Death could overtake him if he forgot to guard his physical health.

The moment when the Sorcerers raised power came as an icy chill that flowed the length of Dakar's spine. The strands became suffused with terrible light as the Fellowship sought futureward and called forth the events that might occur as a result of the works of two princes from Dascen Elur.

Desh-thiere's fall became manifest as an explosion of new lines of power. Forests, fields, and all of the natural landscape brightened to an ascendence of recovered vigor. The politics of the trade guilds whipped into kinks of recoil, and a new axis sheared through their sundered town councils: *Lysaer,* Dakar perceived in wide surprise. The s'Ilessid prince would one day unite the towns, make war to claim all the wildlands for the mayors, and subdue and finally eradicate the barbarian clans. Arithon's part appeared not in Rathain, but as a figure of self-contained elegance that flowed from place to place, dedicated wholly to music. Yet the art he created was framed by a backdrop of unprecedented persecution.

The Sorcerers' unadulterated dismay disrupted the flow of probability. Dakar stole the moment to regroup, then scrambled to keep up as, vehemently fast, the strands unreeled to a new sequence. The Fellowship traced out the only alternative at hand to thwart that turn toward disaster: let the Mistwraith's hold over sky and sun abide unbroken, while the powers that offered its sole downfall, two princes' inherited gifts of Light and Shadow, became sundered by their hand to preserve the peace.

Shocked through change by a rippling cascade of forecasts, the pattern hardened. The motif that represented the Paravians dimmed to invisibility, then vanished away into darkness.

The spell froze. Stunned shock passed between the Sorcerers; the impact of their collective dismay threatened to stop Dakar's breath.

The disappearance of the old races had been sorrow enough to endure; the potential for their irrevocable extinction became as a tear in the fabric of Ath's creation, an insupportable loss to any who had known their living presence. Although Dakar had been just a boy when the last of the creatures had vanished, childhood memories of one encounter had left him marked for life. Tears ran unchecked down his face.

That such shining beauty should pass beyond memory into legend could not be borne. Distinct from his own experience, Dakar shared poignant memories from the Sorcerers; and the one that cut deepest was that of unicorns dancing under starlight in the vale of Caith-al-Caen. The blighted patch of dark amid the strands, which had personified the penultimate grace, warned of a harm beyond healing.

"*So much for allowing events to run their course untouched,*" snapped a thought from Traithe across silence.

As one, the Fellowship Sorcerers rallied crushed hopes. Devastated by necessity, grimly wedded to purpose, they recast an alternative sequence they had earlier hoped to avoid. The strands flickered, interlaced, clean curves and sharp angles reformed to show a coronation at the trade city of Etarra. Charged by the Fellowship to accept Rathain's crown, Arithon's line bloomed into a jagged nexus of anguish that peaked and peaked repeatedly yet endured; *and still the axis of Lysaer's power roused the townborn to war.* A great schism tore the width of the continent, with strife predominant. Yet the cipher that reflected Paravian survival glimmered on wanly, preserved.

Sethvir's observation cut between. "*Desh-thiere. The Mistwraith itself lies at the root of this.*" He need not belabor his frustration that the entity inflicted upon Athera by the worlds beyond South Gate could not be directly tracked; as a thing un-Named and foreign in origin, it had no signature energy that could be set into the pattern. The strands could only reflect its effects. As the Sorcerers refocused their resolve, Traithe's face showed a drawn look of anguish.

Again the pattern flowed into change, with discord harrowing all order. Futures in their myriad thousands described a legacy of battle and bloodshed. Dakar stared at violence until his eyes burned, and Kharadmon's image became partially transparent with negligence. The strands flicked and interwove above the velvet, their motion unbroken but for the split second needed by the Fellowship to assess the impact of each destiny. And still the patterns forecast war. The room grew stale with pipe smoke. Beyond the window, night gave way to hazy dawn, while the Sorcerers pursued cascading trains of circumstance, unsatisfied. Their persistence unveiled no solution. The strands unraveled over and over into strife. Thwarted in their search for a peaceful expedient, the Fellowship sought answer in the far distant future. Despite the expanded awareness of the tienelle, Dakar was left hopelessly behind.

Midday washed the chamber in dull gray before the strands stilled, freezing to a last blazing pattern that faded away like afterimage. Sethvir raised eyes reddened from smoke haze. Kharadmon's coloring was dimmer, and Luhaine had lost detail. No face present escaped the impact of the quandry spelled out in the strands. Dakar tapped ash from his pipe into the lid of the tienelle canister, and as though roused by the sound, the Warden of Althain spoke.

"Never in memory have the patterns converged so strongly to a path of alternatives this narrow. We are forced to unpleasant choices."

The strands foretold, unequivocally, that Lysaer and Arithon would oppose, with full and bitter consequences. To strip them of their inborn powers as a deterrent in all cases yielded Desh-thiere's continued dominance. That in itself promised changes in the natural order, none of them to the good; but to deny the vanished Paravians a return to natural sunlight was to take the role of executioner. Men might engender war and suffering, but over the course of ages, even fanatical hatreds must fade. To act for immediate peace was to seal the extinction of a mystery beyond mortal means to restore.

"If we only knew where they had fled, we might shelter them," Traithe said on a clear note of anguish.

"Desh-thiere caused their disappearance from the continent," Luhaine pointed out. "If the old races allow themselves to be found at all, the Mistwraith's fall must come first."

The last avenue of debate became Arithon's royal inheritance. No longer able to follow nuance, Dakar hunched in a stupor in his chair.

His head was beginning to pound, and his stomach tightened with the first unpleasant symptoms of tienelle withdrawal. Through a haze of mounting discomfort, he gathered the Fellowship inclined toward freeing Arithon from obligation to Rathain's throne. If schism between the half-brothers must occur, best the powers of sovereignty were not involved. Dakar lost the thread of concentration. Words whirled in and out of his pain-laced thoughts, unheeded. Hounded by rising nausea and dripping poisoned sweat, he knew he should rise and find drinking water. His mouth was bitter with the burnt taste of tienelle; his awareness rolled like a ship on oily billows, jumbled and buffeted by after-visions. No mage in the chamber was more surprised than he when the name of the outcast Sorcerer whose works had engendered the rebellion fell through his thoughts like a stone.

Davien.

Dakar shoved straight as his gummy, clogged perception broke before a cold wave of prescience, and prophecy claimed his tongue. Though churning sickness tugged at his gut, his words fell in solemn clarity on a sudden, arrested silence.

"Davien the Betrayer shall hear no reason, nor bow to the Law of the Major Balance; neither shall the Fellowship be restored to Seven until the black rose grows wild in the vales of Daon Ramon."

"Black rose!" Sethvir shot upright, intent as a hunting falcon. "But none exists."

"There will be one," Dakar gasped, slammed by a second precognizance that blazed through him like lightning etched across darkness. "The briar will take root on the day that Arithon s'Ffalenn embraces kingship."

A dismayed round of glances crossed the table, for the strands had not deviated on one point: that if Arithon were left to free will, he would live and die as a bard. Only under duress would he accept the sovereignty of Rathain, and not even then with sincerity.

"Arithon's freedom must be sacrificed," Traithe said. "The choice is a foregone conclusion."

That moment, amid strained and unsettled apprehension shared between Fellowship Sorcerers, Dakar gave way to the sickness brought on by the tienelle. Doubled over with dry heaves, he all but tumbled from his chair. By the time his spasms eased, he retained no memory of the prophecy, and confronted by disappointment at every turn, he managed a dogged apology before illness rendered him speechless.

Unlikeliest of benefactors, it was Kharadmon who moved to the Mad Prophet's side and eased his suffering. As Asandir ushered his ailing apprentice downstairs to bed, the remaining Sorcerers grappled with the new prophecy like starving dogs thrown a marrowbone. The judgment and exile of Davien had been their most tragic expedient, and the disappearance of their seventh colleague, Ciladis, in his search for the Paravians had become their most mourned loss. The prophecy entangled with Dakar's black rose offered the first tangible hope that the reverses that had disrupted the Third Age might one day be righted.

Traithe, least likely advocate of individual sacrifice, had spoken rightly. Even without the fates of the two absent Sorcerers thrown into jeopardy, the loss of the old races could not be risked. By the time Asandir had returned from seeing Dakar safely settled, several distasteful resolutions had become final.

For the sake of Paravian survival the princes who held Desh-thiere's bane between them would use their gifts to restore sunlight, regardless of the wars to follow; and Arithon would be crowned High King of Rathain at the trade city of Etarra, to open the channel of probability that gave rise to Dakar's Black Rose prophecy.

There remained only the task of setting safeguards, where such could be done, to limit the scope of the damage. If Lysaer went on to claim sovereignty in Tysan, he would act without Fellowship sanction. The townsmen's loyalty he might win on his own, but that of the clans must be held in reserve, leaving Tysan's steward, Maenalle, free to safeguard her people as she could. And if the fabric of four realms was to be torn apart by conflict, the fifth must be granted firm leadership.

"The heir to Havish must be brought out of hiding," said Sethvir. "He will need to be educated, for the day he comes of age, we must see him securely on his throne." In one of the kingdoms, at least, town factions and barbarian clans would not be abandoned to disunity.

Little else was exchanged in speech after that, as the Sorcerers divided up the tasks at hand. Bleak as the future might become, the land would not be thrown wholesale to the bloodshed interlinked with Desh-thiere's defeat.

The Fellowship concluded their conference well past mid-afternoon. Kharadmon was first to depart, his wild laugh and ready smile fading through the casement as he swept south on the desert breeze. Luhaine's image dissolved in pursuit, a score left to settle concerning his colleague's cavalier boasts.

Traithe shoved to his feet. His limp turned pronounced by exhaustion, he descended the stairs to guard Dakar through tienelle withdrawal, and to offer Lysaer when he woke the hospitality due to a prince.

Left alone with Asandir, Sethvir stood by the opened casement, his eyes veiled in contemplation. The tea mugs he had belatedly arisen to recover stayed empty as he said, "We have an immediate problem. The crown jewels of Rathain."

Asandir sighed. "I'd not forgotten."

The gems included in the heritage of past high kings had been cut by the Paravian artisans of Imarn Adaer, each one a power focus tuned to respond to the descendants of their respective royal lines. But the master's training given Arithon by Dascen Elur's mages already enabled his finer perceptions; augmented by the crown jewels' attributes, his gifts could potentially become unmanageable.

The focusing properties of the stones would not be annulled by recutting; future generations would need them, even had the artisans of Imarn Adaer not been long dead, their knowledge gone to dust in the desecration brought by the Curse of Mearth. Sethvir and Asandir instead sought a ward to conceal the stones' arcane nature from the s'Ffalenn prince who must hold them for the duration of his reign.

The project took the remainder of the day.

Dripping sweat, tinged greenish by reflections thrown off an untidy hoard of cut emeralds, the two Sorcerers locked glances as they emerged from combined trance.

"Ath Creator," the Warden of Althain murmured in disgruntled vehemence. "You realize the Teir's'Ffalenn and his confoundedly sensitive perception has brought us one damnable fix?"

Asandir raked silver hair from his temples. "Today I don't need the reminder. I only hope we set our safeguards deep enough."

Sethvir arose and scooped the gems into a battered coffer. "Take no chances. Set a geas to avert scrutiny when Arithon first sets hand to the royal regalia. If I'm any judge, he'll notice the resonance of the wards."

"I had that hunch," Asandir confessed. "And I'm still concerned. The man has little vanity. Emeralds by themselves won't impress him, and would *you* want to try to convince him that his jewelry shouldn't be traded for something inherently more practical?"

Sethvir laughed. "I should have guessed, when we decided the latent s'Ahelas talents should be trained, that Princess Dari's descendents might cause us a fearful set of headaches. She argued the entire time I tutored her." The Warden of Althain planted the coffer with its irreplaceable contents amid a clutter of unshelved books, then revived the dropped thread of inquiry. "I'd much rather brew tea, and challenge you to chess, than persuade any s'Ffalenn prince against his natural inclinations."

Artifacts

Lysaer burrowed out of a comfortable muddle of bedclothes to find himself in a chamber lamplit against the gloom of falling dusk. The air smelled of sealing wax and parchment. Relieved to be free of open-air campsites and barbarian hospitality, he took in the scholarly clutter of books and pens, the scarlet carpet, and the mismatched array of fine furnishings, and decided the pallet where he lay must be inside Althain Tower. The room was not deserted.

By the settle sat a black-clad stranger, his hands busy with awl and waxed thread, mending a broken bridle. A raven perched on his shoulder swung its wedge-shaped head at Lysaer's movement, ruffled knife-edged feathers, and fixed the prince with a gaze of bead-bright intelligence. As though given warning by a sentry, the man stopped stitching and looked up.

Lysaer's breath caught.

The stranger's eyes might be soft brown and his clipped hair silvered with age, but the implacable stamp to his features and the profound stillness about his presence unmistakably marked him as a Fellowship Sorcerer. "You must be famished," he opened kindly. "My name is Traithe, and in Sethvir's stead I welcome you to Althain Tower."

Lysaer forced his fingers to release their cramped grip on the blankets. "How long have I been here?"

The raven cocked its head; Traithe knotted his last stitch like a farm wife and nipped off the thread with his teeth. "Since yesterday evening." At Lysaer's raised brows, he added blandly, "You were very tired."

Discomfited by more than his saddle sores, Lysaer surveyed the form of his half-brother, sprawled on the adjacent pallet in unprecedented and oblivious sleep. Struck that Arithon's pose seemed less than restful, and more a jumble of limbs folded like knucklebones in a quilt, Lysaer turned away. This once determined to keep the edge, and not feel pressured to keep pace with his half-brother's fast perceptions and trained awareness of mages, he slipped clear of the covers and hooked his breeches and shirt from a nearby chair. He dressed with princely unself-consciousness, inured to the lack of privacy imposed by the lifelong attentions of servants.

The Sorcerer in black was too tactful to seem curious in any case. He moved like a swordsman bothered by old injuries as he pushed aside his mending, shed his raven in an indignant flurry of wings onto the settle, and rose to build up the fire. As disturbed embers flared to sudden flame, Lysaer glimpsed palms and wrists ridged with scars that would have left a lesser man crippled.

Unable to picture the scope of a calamity that could harm a Fellowship Sorcerer, the prince averted his glance. Devoted to politeness, he set about lacing his sleeve cuffs. His awkwardness as always caused the ties to knot. Embarrassed that even so simple an act as dressing could still make him ache for the comforts lost with exile, he jerked at the snarl. Rather than succumb to expletives, he wondered if any place existed in this Ath-forsaken land where there was gaiety, laughter, and dancing in streets not guarded by sentries. He missed the gentle company of women, and his betrothed left beyond Worldsend most of all. Pride forbade the weakness of recriminations. Still, mastering self-pity took all the effort of a difficult sword form, or the thorniest problem of state ever assigned to his charge as royal heir.

When the contrary laces were set straight, the prince had recovered his poise. He looked up to find Traithe finished tending the fire. Still as shadow, limned in that indefinable mystery that clung to spirits of power, the Sorcerer regarded him intently. His features were less chiseled than marred by hard usage to wrinkles like cracks in fine crystal. Laugh lines remained, intertwined through others cut by sorrow. As if moved by caprice, Traithe said, "We're not all relentless taskmasters like Asandir, you know." He flipped the poker back on its hook with a playful flourish and smiled.

Startled to reckless impulse, Lysaer said, "Prove that."

"I should have expected you'd ask." Traithe turned back, shame-faced as a dog called down for misconduct. "The Sorcerer to answer should be Kharadmon. But he left this morning, feckless ghost that he is. As fool, I'd make a sorry replacement." Betrayed by a weariness that had not at first been apparent, Traithe settled back into his chair. A snap of his fingers invited the raven back to its accustomed perch on his shoulder, where, out of habit, he raised a crooked knuckle and stroked its breast. "We could mend bridles," he suggested hopefully. "Enough worn ones are strewn about, though Ath only knows where Sethvir collects them. Unless Asandir or I happen by, the stables here shelter only mice."

Amazed at how smoothly he had been set at ease, Lysaer gave back the smile he kept practiced for difficult ambassadors. "I'm a poor hand with a needle."

"Any man would be who'd eaten nearly nothing for a day and a half." Traithe pushed back to his feet. He had the build and the balance of a dancer, and the shuffling hesitation in his stride made harsh contrast as he crossed to the doorway. "Shall we see what Sethvir has bothered to stock in his pantry?" He pushed the panel open, and the raven launched off and flew ahead into the torchlit stairwell beyond.

Lysaer set aside the unbuttered sweet roll he had long since lost interest in eating. Across the narrow, cushioned cranny that Sethvir kept for a supper nook, Traithe elbowed his own crumb-littered plate aside.

"You feel bothered that Arithon should still be asleep," he surmised.

Unsettled enough without having the thoughts in his head voiced outright, Lysaer flinched. His bread knife clashed against the china, and startled the raven on the Sorcerer's shoulder to a flurried flap of wings. While Traithe reached up to soothe it, Lysaer looked down and away, anywhere but toward the whitened scars that crisscrossed the Sorcerer's knuckles. The nook might be cozy, and the cutlery rich enough for a king's boards, but the cruciform openings in the walls had originally been cut as arrow slits. The drafts through the openings were icy, the view beyond drab gray. Civilized, sunlit comforts heretofore taken for granted seemed unreachable as marvels in a child's tale in this world of unending mists and bleak minds schooled to mysteries.

"We've been here since nightfall yesterday." Princely manners showed a hint of acid as Lysaer challenged, "You don't find it strange that a man should still be abed after twenty-four hours of rest?" Particularly one like the Master, who tended to recoil out of nerves from his blankets at every two-point shift in the wind.

Traithe showed no break in affability as he hissed at the raven, which edged down his sleeve toward the table, its sideward-tipped eye greedily fixed on the butter. Careful to turn his disfigurements from the prince's angle of view, he shoved the candle stand between the bird and temptation. Through halos of disturbed flame light, he regarded the s'Ilessid half-brother. "Had Arithon been unwell, your concern would be shared by the Fellowship."

The black-clad Sorcerer volunteered nothing else—except his easy manner invited questions.

Lysaer gave rein to curiosity. "Would you mind telling me what happened?"

Traithe shrugged. "An outbreak of poisonous serpents in the kingdom of Shand took a forceful show of sorcery to eradicate."

The last was understatement, Lysaer determined, since the mage's expression went suddenly inscrutable as his raven's. Piqued to be left out when momentous matters were afoot, he said, "I might have liked to help."

"Your half-brother was used," Traithe stated baldly. "His power was channeled from him like wine from a vessel of sacrifice. When he recovers enough to reawaken, he'll retain no memory of the event." Mindful of this prince's staunch loyalty, the Sorcerer added, "Arithon volunteered at the outset."

The raven chose that moment to try a furtive sidle toward the butter. Traithe batted it aside without ceremony. Through its outraged croak and the breeze fanned up by its wing beats, he said, "Has no one ever thought to school you to understand your birth-given gift of light?"

Touched on a lifelong source of bitterness, Lysaer spoke fast to keep from hitting something. "No one considered it necessary."

The raven retreated to the top of the door jamb and alit on a gargoyle crown piece.

"Ah." Traithe set his chin on his fist. "For a prince in direct line for a crown, such judgment was probably sound. But you've been brought here to battle a Mistwraith. That alters the outlook somewhat."

But Lysaer worried at his hurt with the persistence of an embedded thorn. "Why did Asandir not suggest it?"

Traithe chuckled. "Did you think any one of us is omnipotent? Asandir has Dakar for an apprentice. Teaching that scatterbrain anything would frustrate the patience of bedrock." Then, to smooth the dismay that might spring from an unmentioned depth of commitment, the Sorcerer pushed out of the window seat. "I've an errand to complete in the storerooms. Perhaps you'd care to come along?"

Lysaer brightened and stood. "I'd welcome the chance."

He trailed Traithe through the pantry, while at their backs the raven swooped to the tabletop, folded wings like a furtive scholar, and hopped onto the plates to scavenge crumbs.

"Sethvir lets the butter go rancid in the larder, anyway," Traithe confided as he let himself into the stairwell. "He thinks eating a bother, but run out of tea and he's desolate."

Not eased to learn that mages seemed heir to human foibles, Lysaer followed his host into the tower's lower levels. Even without arcane perception, Althain's starkly plain construction and rough-cut granite bespoke haste and stop-gap desperation.

The air smelled of books, wet firewood, and the indefinable tang left over from spell-craft. Somewhere high above, the wind jostled a shutter against its pins. Lysaer found himself wondering whose feet had rubbed the edges from these stairs, and the hands of which crowned rulers had polished the axe-hewn oak rail. He had heard Asandir's reverence for the old races; yet in this place, under low, vaulted roof beams blackened by centuries of torch smoke, there lingered only a forlorn sense of ending. Any past enshrined within Althain seemed faded to desolation and a haunting resonance of perished hope.

The mist beyond the arrow slits concealed the view that might indicate the floor of the threshold where Traithe finally stopped. He unlatched a crude door and disappeared into total darkness. "Use your gift to light your way," he suggested to the prince, who hesitated at his heels. "Sethvir is haphazard about candles, always. I might need a moment to find one."

Self-conscious as he had not been while rising from bed stark naked, Lysaer engaged his powers. Not easily, and not without trepidation, he summoned a silvery spark; but if the Sorcerer thought his method crude, no comment was given on the matter.

The chamber revealed by the witch-light was larger than its doorway suggested. Timber racks lined walls that curved into shadow, crates piled in tiers picked out by the glint of hobnail-studded leather or brass hasps. The stores reeked of oil and old dust, yet when the Sorcerer touched flame to the torch in the wall sconce, the pitch-soaked rags caught and unveiled a clean-swept stone floor and shelving kept clear of cobwebs. The stores had been tended unstintingly, except for labels. Those bales and boxes that were catalogued bore crumbling tags marked in antique script that time had faded illegible.

Traithe paused in the center of the chamber, rapt in manner as his raven. "I doubt much has changed since the Paravians left."

Intrigued beyond awkwardness, Lysaer said, "What are we looking for?"

"Sethvir could have described *which* of the twenty odd coffers on the third shelf by the north wall, at least." Stirred from vexation, Traithe gave a rueful smile. "We're looking for rubies, and the circlet worn by the princes of Havish in ceremonial affirmation of their rights of succession."

"You have a surviving heir?" Lysaer inquired, starved for information on Athera's royal lines.

"Tucked away in the hut of a hermit who dyes wool, yes." Traithe sighed. "The boy's just twelve, and about to learn there's more to life than bartering for alum to color fleeces."

Lysaer fingered an intricate pattern of vine leaves tooled into what looked like a highborn lady's dower chest. "Where do we start?"

"Here, I think." The Sorcerer singled out two boxes and a crate stamped with a hawk sigil that might in years past have been red. "At least, I would expect to find the regalia of the kings of Havish in a chest with the royal seal."

Lysaer offered his assistance, and found himself handed the smaller crate. As his hands closed over ancient wood, he shivered in anticipation. His forebears had ruled a high kingdom; piqued by the thought that relics of his own heritage might be cached here with the antiquities, Lysaer unlatched heavy bronze catches that slid easily despite heavy dents from rough usage. The Warden of Althain had not been lax in his care, for the hinges also turned without a creak.

The odor of leather and parchment immediately identified the contents: document scrolls looped in musty ribbons, and books with illuminated bindings and titles inscribed in the old tongue. The covers were not jeweled or clasped with gold, but darkened and scuffed with age. Regretful the words between lay beyond his schooling, Lysaer fingered the pages in fascination.

"The packages we're looking for won't seem very interesting," Traithe said, his features eclipsed by the dome of the adjacent trunk. "You'd best check beneath those journals before you go any further."

Lysaer closed a rust-flocked cover. "What are these?"

"Ancestral records that trace the line of the kings of Havish, back to the founder, Bwin Evoc s'Lornmein." Yet if the Sorcerer meant to elucidate, a shuffling step and a carping voice interrupted from outside the doorway.

"Did you *have* to set that raven loose to rampage through the but-

ter?" Green-faced and suffering what looked to be a punishing hangover, the Mad Prophet traipsed into the storeroom.

Traithe barely spared him a glance. "I'm encouraged to see you've
recovered enough to have an appetite."

"I *woke up* because I was starving." Dakar fumbled with the strap
of his belt, which was buckled but not tucked in its keepers, and immediately resumed accusations. "Sethvir's too lazy to stock much beyond plain tea." The Mad Prophet winced, abandoned the particulars
of his clothing, and cradled his brow as the echoes of his own vehemence played havoc with his sore head. "And olives preserved in oil
sit poorly on a queasy stomach."

Busy unfurling an object swathed in linen, Traithe was cheerfully
unsympathetic. "That didn't keep you from eating them, I see."

Dakar clammed up rather than admit culpability. Neither did the
misery of his bellyache stop him from quartering the chamber, randomly fingering the varied contents of the shelves. "Sethvir chose
like a ragpicker when he decided what should be salvaged." A bored
gesture encompassed a lumpish bundle wrapped in leather tied with
twine.

"I wouldn't handle that," Traithe warned, already too late.

The Mad Prophet's meddlesome fingers triggered a burst of blue-
violet light. A crack shocked the air, capped by Dakar's yell of pain.
He recoiled, still howling, while the bundle he had disarranged rolled
precipitately off the shelf.

It struck the floor with a note like sheared glass, and another
blinding flash seared away the leather wrappings. Blinking through a
veil of afterimage and an acrid puff of ash, Lysaer saw a melon-sized
violet jewel bounce and roll across the flags. The facets blazed and
fountained sparks at each contact with the stone.

"Fiends plague it!" Dakar licked smarting knuckles and turned a
baleful glare upon Traithe. "That's the Waystone of the Koriathain!"

"Obviously so." Shadows swooped in the flame light as the Sorcerer pushed aside his opened chest, leaned down, and matter-of-
factly fielded the rolling crystal. The sparks died. No punitive sting
met his touch.

"Morriel would sell her virginity to know where that thing
went!" Mollified, Dakar added, "She and her pack of witches have
been searching for centuries, and Sethvir's kept her Waystone here,
hidden all this time!"

Traithe turned the huge amethyst in his hands, absorbed by the
captured light that spiked through its purple-black depths. "Since nobody asked your crude opinion, I shall tell you once: the Prime Enchantress had only to inquire after the Waystone's location." His eyes

flicked up, piercingly sharp. "Naught but Morriel's stubborn pride kept the jewel at Althain."

But nuance was wasted upon Dakar, who loosed a boyish whistle. "The bitches will be hot when they learn."

The prospect of a scandal none but a fool would precipitate spurred Traithe to reproach. "We would all be better served if you would go and ask Sethvir for scrap leather that would do for replacement wrappings."

Too wily to cross a Sorcerer who used that tone of voice, Dakar departed grumbling obscenities. Left in the company of an undesirably curious prince, Traithe made an end of the matter. "The Waystone was mislaid during the rebellion. As you observed, it is perilously warded. The Koriani Senior Circle was negligent to leave so powerful a talisman unguarded."

Traithe did not add that the loss of their great focus had also curtailed the order's propensity for interfering in affairs beyond their understanding. Sethvir was unlikely to volunteer the Waystone's location to the Prime Circle, which craved its recovery. The Warden of Althain could be guileful as Davien the Betrayer when he chose; never mind that he appeared as honest as a clear glass of water.

Traithe fixed Lysaer with a gaze impenetrable as ink. "If you'll finish unwrapping this bundle, I think you'll find what we came for." And he set aside the great Waystone and tossed across one of two items half-swaddled on the lid of the trunk.

Lysaer caught the packet and stripped off the final layers of linen to bare a thin gold circlet, unornamented beyond a thready, age-worn line of runes. The smaller item undone by Traithe proved to be a hexagonal tortoise shell box. Inside, nested in sheepskin, sparkled a matched collection of rubies.

At least a dozen in number, the set was cut to a perfection beyond reach of mortal artisans. The gems required no setting to impress; their depth of color glinted like live fire in the flare of the torch by the doorway. Lysaer gasped, dazzled by the legacy that awaited the dyer's lad soon to be unveiled as the crown prince of Havish.

"The regalia was melted down for bounty gold," Traithe remarked sadly. For an instant he seemed less than wizard and more a lame, very worn old sword captain lost in reminiscence of ill times. "The desecration was a great pity. But Telmandir was the first of the royal seats to be sacked and set to the torch. Only the jewels and the king's youngest child could be saved."

Lysaer noted the Sorcerer's regret, but only distantly. Starkly plain though the circlet in his hands might be, it was *old*; its nicks and dents bespoke modest origins. Diminished to realize how very ancient were the high kingdoms of Athera, and given sense of the wide span of generations the bloodlines handpicked by the Fellowship must have ruled, Lysaer was moved to awe.

The battered circlet of the princes of Havish, and the rubies torn at need from a regalia whose magnificence could only be imagined, implied a stability shattered wholesale; and sacrifice akin to the straits that had caused the Paravians to build Althain Tower in the bleak hills of a wilderness to safeguard an irreplaceable tradition. Lysaer felt humbled.

His inheritance as s'Ilessid on Athera was vast in comparison to the tiny island kingdom left behind on the world of his birth.

The pomp, the wealth, every ceremonial pageantry that had seemed part and parcel of kingship abruptly became rendered meaningless: he perceived how narrow was his experience, and how limited his vision. The presumption shamed him, that he had dared to set judgment on the lives of the Camris barbarians. Their plight must be better understood to be fairly handled—a stricture that must start with rebuilding trust with his half-brother. Brought to painful self-honesty, Lysaer realized that to do right by the kingdom of Tysan, he must embrace a new concept of justice. The tinker's workmanship in the old circlet and the uncanny loveliness of Havish's crown jewels compelled a cold and difficult review of his mortal strengths and talent.

Lysaer returned the artifact to Traithe, gentled by diffidence he had shown no one living. "I'm thankful for your offer to school my gift of light. But I see very clearly: a mage's training is not my course to pursue. My part in confronting the Mistwraith is but the prelude to healing the rift between townborn and clansman. The greater good of Tysan must demand my total dedication."

Struck by the depths of sincerity that prompted this prince's self-sacrifice, Traithe closed his hands, quenching the blood-fire of the rubies. His sorrows as Sorcerer were compounded with fierce foreboding for the future spelled out by the strands. Like the great Waystone the Koriani enchantresses ached to recover, the cache of sapphires that were the crown jewels of Tysan must remain in Sethvir's trust at Althain. That this gently reared descendent of Tysan's kings, whose shining talent was inspired rule, should one day through the Mistwraith's machination refute the fine intentions that now moved his mind and heart seemed an impossibly cruel twist of fate.

Harbingers

In the cold light of dawn, a dark horse with a black-clad rider canters south, for Ghent, in the kingdom of Havish; beneath the hunting bow and trap lines of a forester's trade, he bears a concealed set of rubies and a circlet, while a raven swoops on a following breeze over his silver-banded hat. . . .

High above land, outside even the coiling fogs of Desh-thiere, the discorporate Sorcerer Kharadmon arrows east on the winds of high altitude, his intent to measure and map the power base of the governors' council of Etarra. . . .

Too obdurately frugal to hurry, Luhaine drifts west into Camris, bearing tidings and grave portents for Maenalle, Steward of Tysan. . . .

X. Daon Ramon Barrens

For a confirmed hedonist and established late riser, Dakar climbed Althain Tower's central stair in suspiciously buoyant spirits. Enjoying the early hour without a hangover, he barged into the room where the half-brothers slept with a clang of the bar and a shove that swung the oaken door to a thunderous boom against the stops.

The racket rivaled the impact of a siege engine.

Accustomed to solicitude, courtly deference, and a chamber valet selected for quiet habits, Lysaer squinted through a hurtful flare of torch flame. He buried his face in his pillow, nettled enough to curse when rude hands grasped his shoulder and shook him.

The assault on his person ended with a raw hoot of laughter. Lysaer faced around. He endured the ache until his eyes adjusted to the sudden fullness of light and made out the form of his tormentor. Bent double and gripping his belly as if he hurt, Dakar wore a shirt that needed washing, a leather tunic ripped ragged at the hem, and a plaid sash so sun-faded the only recognizable color was gray. The glare of princely displeasure left his paroxysms unfazed.

Lysaer propped himself on one elbow. Made aware as he flicked back tangled hair that the view beyond the shutter was night black, he said, "I don't see any humor in being wakened before dawn by a maniac."

Dakar sat on the adjacent cot. The frame gave a squeal of leather and wood at the load, and the mattress canted. Its slumbering occupant slid like a dropped puppet in the direction gravity dictated. Blocked from tumbling to the floor by the planted bulk of Dakar, Arithon showed no sign of awakening.

"Well?" Lysaer fixed glacial eyes upon the Mad Prophet. "Are you going to share your joke?"

"Joke?" Dakar hiccupped and looked aggrieved. "I made none. But I'll bet you never used that many filthy words in one breath before."

"Meaning I forgot my manners." Recovered enough to find tolerance, Lysaer gave back a wicked grin. "My reputation's hardly spoiled. You don't look to me like a lady I need to impress." Before Dakar could throw back rejoinder, he added, "Try that last move on the Master, and see what sort of words *he* uses."

"Oh?" Dakar twisted, reached out, and pinched Arithon's cheek, but failed to raise any response. Arithon never twitched an eyelid. Prosaically the Mad Prophet said, "Won't be waking up this morning, not at all. Too used up still, and better so. Asandir wants him napping."

Warned by a hint of recalcitrance that purpose underlay Dakar's remark, Lysaer got up and reached for his breeches and shirt. "We're leaving Althain today?"

"Tonight. The sun's not up yet." All cow-eyed innocence, Dakar heaved off the cot. He regarded his knuckles, still nicked with scabs since his encounter with the door panel stuck shut by Kharadmon. Against all better sensibility, he could not resist adding more. "We go within the hour. But against any natural inclination, we won't be making passage across Instrell Bay by boat. The Sorcerers have decided we're in a rush."

Lysaer measured his shirt laces against each other to even them up for tying. "Why?"

Transparently reluctant to answer, Dakar crooked a finger in an end of his tangled beard and shrugged. "Daelion Fatemaster himself couldn't fathom ways of the Fellowship." Impelled to neglected duty, he abandoned his affectations and launched off toward a nearby chest, where he scooped up Arithon's clothing. Onto the heap he tossed boots, hose, cloak, and belatedly, the sword Alithiel, which still lay naked against the table. "Didn't this come with a scabbard?"

Lysaer unhooked the Master's baldric, which hung in plain sight from a chair back, and handed it over without comment.

Still grumbling, Dakar shed his armload of garments onto Arithon's chest. He then sheathed the blade, dumped that on top, and announced, "Right now I've got other problems, like lugging your bastard brother down five courses of stairs."

"Half-brother," Lysaer corrected. Regarding the Mad Prophet's ministrations askance, and grateful to be alert enough to attend himself, he retrieved his weapons and cloak from the armoire. "I'm not so fordone I don't recall we're only four flights above ground level."

Nonplussed, Dakar said, "I can count properly when I'm sober. We aren't leaving by the gate. Sethvir's got a third-lane focus pattern in his dungeon, and Asandir's of a mind to hurry."

By now acquainted with Athera's geography through Sethvir's collection of charts, Lysaer paused in the act of fastening his baldric; the distance inferred was well over two hundred leagues, with a span of open water in between. "We're traveling on to Daon Ramon Barrens by sorcery?"

Dakar smiled, mooncalf features all innocence. "You're going to witness wonders. That is, unless you get disoriented and lose your breakfast on the way. Personally, I find lane transfers across latitude nearly as lousy as sailing. But then my stomach tries to get seasick in a bathtub." A last, hasty inspection showed nothing indispensable had been forgotten from his collection of Arithon's things; the Mad Prophet in prosaic efficiency rolled both Shadow Master and belongings up in the blankets he slept on.

As Lysaer took up station at the foot of the cot to help lift the inert body, Dakar confided, "Our boy here's going to be mad as blazes when he finally does wake up." A pause ensued as prophet and prince hefted their load and shuffled out of step around Sethvir's clutter toward the doorway. Dakar elbowed the panel aside, backed through, and cheerfully began the descent. "Angry as a rock-bashed snake."

"Maybe that has something to do with Asandir's sudden haste?" Lysaer suggested, hoping to pry loose an explanation.

"All of that." Dakar grinned, perversely uninformative. "Your half-brother's going to be *furious.*"

Lysaer shifted his grip on the blankets, which were an impractical way to handle a comatose body down a stairwell. Since pressing the issue might make him the butt of Dakar's next prank, he maneuvered past the first landing. The draft swirled unpleasantly across his shoulders; somewhere a loosened shutter grated sullenly in the wind. The steepness of the risers stalled conversation until something Dakar saw as he rounded the bend doused his overweening mood of smugness.

Caught on the uphill end of a precarious and unwieldy load, Lysaer discovered in embarrassment that Sethvir stood on the landing, the voluminous cuffs of his sleeves for once shaken clean of dust.

Sight of the Teir's'Ffalenn trussed in his bedclothes caused the Warden of Althain to blink like an owl exposed to sunlight. "I asked you to bring him down," he murmured in vague reproof. "Did you have to bundle him up like stolen goods in a carpet?"

"Next time you carry him," the Mad Prophet retorted between wheezes.

Sethvir hurried ahead down the corridor, maroon robes flapping around feet tucked hoseless into ridiculously oversized fur buskins. His reply trailed back with all the daft overtones of a hermit caught talking to himself. "Teir's'Ffalenn are well able to right their own injustices, this one better than most. He's Torbrand's descendant, after all, every inch of him touchy. You're welcome to his revenge by yourself, fool prophet."

To this Dakar spoke phrases that cast biological doubt upon Arithon's already illegitimate ancestry. Sethvir gave back a blank glance and traipsed ahead into darkness. Their course meandered, stopped, backtracked, and circled between ranks of Paravian statuary faintly visible, as sparkles of gold weave and gemstones caught glancing torchlight from the stairwell. Lysaer lost count of how many times he stubbed toes, or whacked his elbows and shins; the muscles of his arms and shoulders ached unmercifully. That his discomforts might have been staged as a lesson did not dawn, until the Sorcerer paused and, without any fumbling, hooked an inset steel ring in the floor. A counterweighted trapdoor sprang open and raw light flooded upward to show features as blithe as a pixie's. Lysaer recalled with a snap of annoyance *that mages saw perfectly in the dark.*

Sethvir's blue-green eyes held a twinkle. "Go ahead. Asandir has the horses waiting below."

"Horses!" Lysaer eyed the narrow stairwell that spiraled downward toward a glow too steady to be lamplight. His skin crept, even as the nuance of his gift confirmed the play of unnatural energies. "How did he ever get them down here?"

Dismissing the question as irrelevant, Sethvir beckoned prince and prophet and the unconscious bundle carried between them on ahead. "Where you're going, you'll be glad not to walk." He closed the trapdoor after himself with barely a whisper of a creak.

The air radiated a tang like a blacksmith's forge intermixed with the charge of inbound storms. Lysaer checked, while behind him, Dakar snarled in annoyance that princely fainthearted hesitation was going to wind up tripping him.

Lysaer sucked a quick breath and pressed ahead into burgeoning light. Assured by now that the Fellowship's grand magics would not harm him, his reluctance stemmed as much from indignity. Accustomed to responsibility as a king's heir, he found the Sorcerer's secretive authority deeply irritating. Had he been apprised of their plans one step beyond the immediate, or been granted some insight to their motivations, he might have felt less unnerved. Traithe alone had addressed this need, but the black-garbed mage had ridden off to tutor the heir to Havish, and some event since arrival at Althain had turned Asandir bleak as chipped granite.

The stairs ended. Circular and doorless as a vault, the deepest chamber of Althain Tower was incised into seamless white marble. A floor of polished onyx held eight leering gargoyle sconces arrayed on pedestals at the compass points. No torches burned in their sockets; the light emanated from a webwork of lines scribed across a wide, bowl-shaped depression. The patterning shaped three concentric circles, edged in Paravian runes and centered by an intricate, looping interlace that hurt the eyes to follow. Asandir waited in the middle, on a starburst formed by the intersection of five axes, his shadow merged in the silhouette of a massive, high-wheeled mason's dray. Dakar's paint mare was harnessed between the shafts, and the other mounts tied to the tail boards stamped and blew in nervous snorts. The rap and clang of shod hooves raised no echoes in that windowless, enclosed space, and for all that hellish glare, the air retained no warmth. The draft that wafted off the pattern was charged with unnatural, arctic cold.

Touched to spine-tingling uneasiness and soaked in icy sweat, Lysaer shivered. He started at a touch on his shoulder and spun around to meet the myopic, inquiring eyes of Sethvir.

"You're looking at a power focus, charged and enabled with the natural forces that flow in lines across the earth," said the Warden of Althain in measured reassurance. "The energies gathered here will allow Asandir to effect a direct transfer to the ruins west of Daon Ramon Barrens."

Lysaer shut his eyes against patterns that glared and sparked like fireworks against enigmatic black stone. Through an odd and unpleasant ringing in his ears, he heard Dakar's petulant interruption. "Why not go straight to the focus at Ithamon?"

Sethvir replied, imperturbed. "For Arithon's sake you'll travel overland from the focus at Caith-al-Caen."

"The Vale of Shadows!" As if the translation shoved home a violation of something sacred, Dakar cried, "Why protect him?" As if the unconscious man in the blanket was a curse he felt driven to shed, he rounded in disgust on Sethvir. "Arithon showed you how lightly he regards your commitment to Rathain. After his insolence at the summons, do you think he gives a damn for your solicitude?"

"Suppose with all his heart that he wished he did not?" Sethvir interjected. To Lysaer, who listened in confusion from the lip of the bottom stair, the Sorcerer added, "The floor is solid, and certainly safe to step on."

The oblique shift in subject silenced Dakar. Since Arithon's dead weight had long since tired his arms and shoulders, Lysaer proceeded forward. For all his apprehension, the pattern's burning lines caused no sensation beyond a queer tingle as he stepped over and around them. Dakar of necessity straggled after, muttering mutinous curses that attributed Ath's angels to acts of scatological impossibility.

Still by the stair, Sethvir said nothing. Something in his quiet shamed Lysaer to recrimination. Dakar's outrageous attitudes notwithstanding, he had shown callousness unworthy of a prince when he had failed to defend his half-brother's dignity.

Asandir was less restrained when the pair with their burden slung between them crossed the last circle of the focus. Eyes bright and ruthless as sword steel flicked over blankets, belongings, and the head that dangled backward, black hair trailing within inches of the rune-scribed floor. "Lay the Teir's'Ffalenn behind the buckboard and see him comfortably arranged. No reason this side of the Wheel can excuse the extra care you should have taken to fix a litter."

"I'd sooner coddle a viper," the Mad Prophet unwisely retorted. "Why rush to stir up disaster?"

"Arithon gave his trust into your hands without terms the other night," Asandir snapped back. "Is that how you thank him?" Low-voiced, he added something else that made Dakar cringe like a kicked dog.

Then the Sorcerer's glance snapped to Lysaer, driving home a rebuke not solely directed elsewhere. Stung for his lapse into pettiness, Lysaer hefted Arithon into the dray. He attended his half-brother's needs with a servant's humility, while around him the vault became preternaturally quiet. The horses stopped sidling and stood glassy-eyed, their ears and tails hanging limp. The pattern in the floor began to sing in a tone just outside of hearing, and the air gained a charge that lifted the hairs on their backs.

"Get into the wagon and hold on," Asandir commanded.

Dakar leaped the buckboard and scrambled to snatch up the reins. Lysaer scrambled over the high sides behind the wheel, while the Sorcerer strode forward, grasped the paint's bridle, and positioned his feet precisely upon the nexus of the focus.

Sethvir called out in farewell, and the vault burst asunder in an explosion of unbearable blue light.

Darkness ripped down hard after, relentless as the void between the Veil. If Lysaer cried out, his ears recorded no sound. His senses overturned, as if he, the rough wood he sat on, even the horses tied by their bridle reins, overturned in a gut-twisting series of somersaults. Too late he recalled Dakar's flippant comment; but having no breakfast in him to lose, only bile burned the back of his throat.

Thrilled and frightened by the pull of forces beyond understanding, Lysaer clung to the fast-fraying shreds of self-control.

Then a jolt slammed the boards beneath his body. Wind was compressed from his lungs, and his stomach plummeted back into his middle in a wrench fit to tear a gut. The unsprung dray hit earth with a crash that jarred the supplies in back, Arithon's limp form, and everyone else's teeth with undivided viciousness. Pebbles spanged out from under the iron-rimmed wheels, and with an appalling creak, and a clatter of hooves from panicked horses, the vehicle lurched and rolled as natural order intended.

Winter wind slashed through Lysaer's hair. He recovered a ratcheting breath, discovered his eyes squeezed shut and his hands locked rigidly to the side boards. When he mastered the wits to risk a look, disbelief shocked him like ice water. Tower, vault, and pattern were wholly swept away. Through a dissolving haze of blue sparks and an after-stink of ozone, he beheld a changed landscape and mist silvered with new day. Under a brooding gray sky, gusts raked through feathered brown grass, stripped trees, and black, striated rock that gouged through soil and dead briar. Lysaer felt dizzied, sick, and disoriented. He was still battling to reconcile his shaken nerves when the impossible solidity of the land, the rutted dirt lane the dray thundered down, and the flying clods gouged up by the horses, who raced ahead in stark fear—everything preternaturally made *real* by the loosening coils of grand magic—tilted hard sideways and overturned.

"You're going to faint," Asandir said with incisive clarity from a point somewhere inside the wagon.

Vertigo swallowed Lysaer's sight. He sensed no pain as his gold-thatched head banged into a sack of iron cooking pots, but heard only the clang of impact melded with words made blurred through a distance of fading awareness. "Ath's mercy on you, Prophet, for I'll show none if the s'Ilessid heir falls out."

The Paravians called the place Caith-al-Caen, Vale of Shadow, by the dawn of the Second Age. Common usage corrupted the name of the ruin there to Castlecain, though from a vantage halfway up a mist-cloaked hillside, the reason seemed obscure. The site never held any fortress. All that remained of the clay and thatch croft where Cianor Sunlord had been born were hummocks where orchards had stood. Yet as Asandir wound his way over ground that once had held gardens of scented, flowering trees, his eyes saw beyond bleak mist and sere landscape. Did he look with his mage's vison, the shadows, the memories, that abiding resonance of mystery that lingered wherever the old races had cherished the earth skeined like starlit thread through the cross-laced, dead canes of briar.

Ballads held that a place beloved by unicorns never quite lost the aura of their presence. At Caith-al-Caen, the adage held true; while Asandir strode through weeds napped like velvet with dew, his peripheral vision and the limits just beyond hearing entangled him in echoes of the past. Here, when the splendors of the Second Age were yet young, the Riathan had gathered each solstice to renew the earthpowers and to rejoice in the turn of the seasons. The ecstacy in their music had marked the very soil, and now wind itself mourned the loss. Even after a thousand years, the land remained blessed with a grace that haunted. An energy coursed through the soil that glorified life; even under Desh-thiere's curse, the hills each spring put forth a knee-high carpet of flowers, and rowan still thrust through the bracken.

Now, under winter's frosts, only the spirits lingered, ethereal as shadings in silverpoint, their dance songless and silent. The Sorcerer walked, careful not to look too closely to either side. The memories of too many friends watched his back with pity and reproach. Sorrow had scribed too many creases around his eyes, and hope had eased too few.

"*Dael-Farenn, kingmaker!*" lisped the wind as it curled through his hair. "*What have you done with your hope, your dreams, your joy? The dance is not ended, not yet. For the song will renew with the sunlight.*" Could Asandir close his ears, he would have, but the hearing of a mage went beyond reliance on the flesh. The voices and the spirits dogged his innermind at each step; he would answer their pleas, but at a cost that harrowed him to contemplate.

He crested the rise. Beyond spread the hollow where the Ilitharis Paravians had first Named the winter stars. The place retained a serenity that would abide through ages still to come, however much strife marred the world. Informed of the Master's presence by a bright-edged spill of lyranthe notes, Asandir stopped dead. His hands and his throat tightened. As though touched by his sharp trepidation, the voices on the wind palled to murmurs and the spirits swirled away, brilliance dimmed; while through a perception that threatened to unman him, Asandir heard Arithon play Maenalle's gift with a touch unfettered by bitterness.

Arpeggios rippled and soared, linked by grace notes that revealed, like unfinished tapestry, the latent promise of the bard. Cut diamonds had less clarity. The s'Ffalenn heir already possessed a skill that could pierce the heart; offered freedom to pursue his desire and given the right master, his talent could be refined to a grace that held power to captivate.

Woodenly, Asandir pressed forward. His deerhide soles grated over stone, deliberate warning to the minstrel that solitude had been breeched. Arithon glanced over his shoulder, saw his visitor, and smiled. The reflexive, hair-trigger wariness that on prior occasions had hardened him never arose. As if his license to share the risks in quelling the meth-snakes had triggered catharsis, the music flowed from him unchecked. By the lyrical, ringing undertone, no Fellowship Sorcerer could mistake that this time the s'Ffalenn heir played to share unconditionally.

Asandir fought his wish to turn away, to retrace his path to the valley, and leave Caith-al-Caen to the spirits and the bard; instead he steeled his will and assimilated the hurtful whole: his mage's vision showed him the colors of Arithon's aura shot through with absolute trust.

The final steps toward the hollow became unbearably hard to complete. Asandir managed, though the wear left by centuries of service suddenly bore down on him, and the wind pried his hair and clothing like the tug of hostile hands. He reached the stone where Arithon sat, and regarded the mist and the shadows until the song reached its natural end. When the last note faded into stillness, he settled at the Master's side.

"Why?" he asked softly, though in depth he already knew.

Arithon settled the lyranthe into the crook of his elbow and answered the question's drift. "I finally had proof that your promise of free will was genuine." Green eyes turned, but Asandir could no longer meet them. Imperturbed, where in a more guarded moment he might justly have taken alarm, Arithon continued. "I challenged my right to self-destruction, and was shown an open door." He paused, looked down, and his hands opened. "You'll forgive my cantankerous behavior, I hope. I'm capable of better, as you'll see."

Asandir masked a flinch, for the words the Master had chosen had echoed those of another s'Ffalenn ancestor, caught in an equally untenable position. And in the moment when memory and pity stole speech, Asandir shared in fine-textured empathy the unshielded confidence of a friendship.

The offering itself was a rarity for a man unaccustomed to companionship: *a lonely boy, raised in the company of elderly mages who had all loved him at a distance. He had grown without a moth-*

er's affection, but hereditary compassion had turned him from resentment. He readily forgave what he did not understand, and defined his joy through his competence. Praise for his achievements kept him from discovering the depths of his isolation, the cost of that misapprehension still yet to be paid.

The true friend, the caring lover, could absolve all hurt from the growth that inevitably must be forced upon the grown man. The lesson might be learned through care and happiness, that the self-worth Arithon instinctively sought in music was a separate thing from accomplishment—had Desh-thiere and a crown not hung between.

Asandir hid bitterness. His own role disallowed mercy. Inwardly connected the Master might be, and strong as well, but along with his confidence came infinite power to wound. Asandir came close to recoil as another image touched his consciousness: *a young girl's face, with shy, smiling lips, eyes like aventurine, and ash brown hair caught up in braids. Arithon had wanted to kiss her, but women confused him; while walking in the hills to gather herbs, they had spoken of music and poetry, and then of things more personal. And trembling in his arms, she had admitted that his powers, the given gift of Shadow he had labored so long to master, frightened her. He had let her go, not knowing what to say.*

The girl's name had been Tennia, Asandir recalled from the clutter of past recollections he had probed after breaking the Curse of Mearth; the events themselves were not new, nor the regrets they had left marked in memory. The Sorcerer's gall and surprise stemmed instead from distinction that now his insight into Arithon's consciousness was openly given in trust.

Asandir watched the winds comb the dry, frost-brittle grasses with bleak eyes. This time, in keenest irony, inherited s'Ffalenn compassion had set the reins into his grasp; s'Ahelas farsight offered the whip. His mage's perception recognized Arithon's inner fiber, and its naked vulnerability stirred him to grief sharp as outrage: for he could, *he would, and he must,* manipulate this prince into voluntary betrayal of everything he held dear.

"This place," Arithon said, interrupting Asandir's inward turmoil. "It has a quality, a feeling, as if the rocks, the soil, even the wind, are something more than inanimate."

"Caith-al-Caen is aligned with an earth-lane," the Sorcerer replied in what seemed measured calm, but a shiver flawed his composure. *Mercy upon you,* he thought to the prince at his side, for Arithon had unwittingly invited the opening the Fellowship in its desperate need required. Over the whisper of wind, and through the multiple levels of his mage's awareness, Asandir chose his words. "Here, in the past, the old races danced at the turn of each season, to deflect the earth's forces into latitudinal channels to enrich the surrounding land. So were all of Athera's twelve lanes once interconnected into a lattice to nourish all life. The resonance that shaped the ward lingers still."

Self-control prevailed; a voice could be compelled to sound conversational though anguished self-revulsion stormed beneath, for the first strand of the snare would be spun, here and now, of the purest thing left to this world: the beauty and wild grace impressed upon Caith-al-Caen by the dance of the Riathan Paravians. "I can show you, if you like."

It did not help to know that the ultimate course of the world depended upon this deception, as Arithon straightened in surprise. His eyes lit with pleasure, and a longing that was entirely spontaneous tipped up the corners of his mouth. "I would be honored."

Somehow, Asandir unlocked numbed fingers. He reached down, picked up a lichened bit of stone, and said, "Give me your hands." And he offered his own, palm upward, the pebble cradled like the mythical seed of temptation in the left one.

Arithon laid his lyranthe aside. A gust fanned his hair and the coarse linen of his sleeves as he reached to engage his grip. Warm hands were given into the Sorcerer's cool ones. As if air itself were abrasive to his skin, Asandir accepted the touch.

He guided Arithon's fingers to cup the fragment of stone, then molded his own over top. "You were taught to clear and center your mind. Do that. But this time, include our bit of stone as if it were part of your flesh, and leave me an open channel."

Unaware of impending destiny, Arithon closed his eyes. Without looking, Asandir could sense the change as he underwent the necessary preparation, and the clamor of inward consciousness settled to listening stillness. As a shepherd might lead his best lamb to slaughter, the Sorcerer threaded his awareness into the fragment of stone, hooked the residual glimmer of Paravian magic, and set it free, to pour through Arithon's unshielded spirit and weave its undying line of melody.

The effect at first was subtle, little more than a sensation of warming from the stone, followed by a tingle of nerves akin to a rush of exuberance. Arithon underwent a moment of quivering, inward realignment, as if a chord had been struck in harmonic resonance with his being. Asandir felt the ripple of reaction course through the flesh under his grip; he removed his hands and watched, aggrieved and silent.

Arithon opened his eyes to the vision of unicorns dancing.

The statues of Riathan enshrined at Althain Tower might reflect an artist's proportion and line. But perfection carved in cold marble could never capture motion, or the lightness and flight of cloven hooves, or the lift of tails and manes more fine than spun silk; not the spiraled twist of horns that shimmered with an energy visible to mages, or the soaring, heart-searing sweetness of song that underlay the sigh of the wind. Caith-al-Caen rang with a purity of tone just beyond grasp of the mind.

Arithon dropped the bit of stone, helplessly overwhelmed. He sank to his knees before the cranny where he had sheltered. Assaulted by a rapture beyond hope, the half-glimpsed promise of limitless light, he laughed aloud, and then trembled. His eyes filled with tears and overflowed. "Blessed Ath," he managed finally, his words wrung to harshness by awe. "I never guessed. Yet the beauty in the sword should have warned me."

Asandir regarded the lyrical pavane of the spirit forms, mute. Their image held power to captivate, surely; but the palliative brought only hunger, akin to the cravings of delirium. These illusions were just poor, starved shadows, an imprint like an afterimage left by creatures whose existence transcended mortality. The reality made pearls seem as sand. For one who had beheld the wisdom in a unicorn's depthless eyes, for any who had once experienced the current of undefiled exultation that abided in their presence, the ghosts scribed here by trace resonance exposed only wretched emptiness. Asandir wept also, but for loss beyond words to encompass, and for a future set into motion that must not now be undone.

Cut by regret and infinite pity, he bent also and gathered Arithon's shivering shoulders into the embrace a parent might show to a child about to be orphaned. "You can block the visions at will by sealing off your inner sight."

Arithon twisted against the Sorcerer's hold, his face all puzzled delight. "Why ever should I want to?"

Asandir released his grip as though burned. Too choked up to breathe, far less speak, he whirled away and strode off. *Almighty Ath, the irony wounded, endlessly, and straight to the heart.* For Arithon would wish very shortly that he had never owned mage-sight, or been attuned to the resonance of Paravian mystery.

The spirits that haunted Caith-al-Caen were as pale glimmers, their measure a dance of celebration incanted and renewed through countless turns of seasons. Here the Paravian singers had transmuted only joy. The vibrations imbued within the ruins of the traditional s'Ffalenn seat of power, Ithamon, where the Fellowship proposed to see Desh-thiere's stranglehold over sky and sunlight broken, were not at all the same.

Amid foundations shattered by the uprising, and the bones of un-
buried dead, the four towers raised by the Paravians still stood, their
wards pristine and still radiant. The contrast between their enduring,
virginal harmony, and the tormented backlash of magics unleashed
by the fall of the King's Tower that coiled like a wraith through the
wreckage, was a thousand times more poignant than the haunting of
Caith-al-Caen, and stark with the blood and tragedy of displaced lives
and dreams.

Arithon might shut such clamor out, but at the cost of his bardic
inspiration; and the compassion that was permanently ingrained in
every scion of the s'Ffalenn line would disallow any such voluntary
deafness.

Irony within irony, Asandir knew, as his feet stumbled in unabashed haste and his clothing hooked on the briars. The king for
Rathain would be bought in false guilt, against every dedicated principle of the Fellowship, whose first task was to foster enlightenment.
For the prince now entranced by the unicorn spirits lacked the hardened self-wisdom to stand down Ithamon's past. He was too young,
too strong, and too much the puppet of pity to perceive that responsibilities were always self-imposed.

On fostering that lie Athera's need depended, and on a tender innocence paired like a curse with resilience enough not to flee.

The road across Daon Ramon Barrens was barely more than a dirt
track, half overgrown and winding between hills raked by winds that
never seemed to quiet. Tired of the whisper and rattle of dead
bracken, of the incessant tug and snap at his cloak hem, and hair perpetually whipped into tangles, Lysaer kept good spirits, buoyed by
certainty that the interval of being adrift without kingdom or purpose
would end after conquest of Desh-thiere.

Never mind that, league on league, the landscape was unremittingly deserted and bare, that winter rains soaked his clothing and
blankets, and Dakar's invective worsened since the morning he woke
up with iyats in his boots and Asandir once again had to rescue him
from the energy sprites' bedevilment. No other diversions arose
through weary days of travel, for their route took them far from even
the most isolated initiate's hostel; tinkers, traders, and caravans did
not travel the old road to Ithamon. As if the way itself, with its lichened markers and rolling, briar-grown hills, were haunted, not even
the ruins of farm hamlets or villages remained to remind of a prosperous past.

"That's because there were none," Asandir confided over the jingle of harness and the booming grind of the dray's wheels over bare

scarps of stone. The rain had stopped at midday, and water puddled silver in the hollows. "Daon Ramon in the old tongue means 'golden hills.' The place was the province of the Riathan Paravians, and unicorns require no dwellings."

Unwilling to let the Sorcerer lapse into the forbidding silence that had gripped him since Althain Tower, Lysaer gestured toward the hillsides with their cover of bracken and thorn. "It seems hard to picture this place as fertile and green."

"It was, and beautifully so." Asandir urged his mount over a gully where the road had washed out and the slates lay jammed like old bones in a spongy bed of moss. His silver-gray eyes seemed to pierce the mantle of mist and peer far into distance. "All that you see was a grassland, rich with herbs and wildflowers. Winters were short and mild. But that changed after the rebellion. Townsmen believed the magic of the Paravians could not abide in a land without water. They went to astonishing lengths to assuage their fears. The governors' council of Etarra funded a task force of mercenaries to dam the Severnir. A great canal was cut through the Skyshiel Mountains to divert the river at its source. The current flows east now and empties into Eltair Bay."

"That seems a mighty effort to base on a superstition," Lysaer commented.

Asandir rode on in troubled silence. Then he said, "So long as these hills remain a desert, no Paravian would return to dwell here. So you see, the townsmen's intent was suited after all."

The damp weather held, and night fell early. By then Asandir's party made camp in a grotto formed by a jutting outcrop of cracked boulders. The only bit that stayed dry was the nook where the fire burned, and Dakar crouched there, roasting rabbits that Arithon and Lysaer had snared before dusk. Asandir knew where to find herbs, and beside the odors of wet earth and damp horses, the air carried the savory smell of stew.

Lysaer huddled between the slow drip of a natural spring and a falling spray of runoff, shirtless, his cloak tossed across his shoulders. With a needle and thread borrowed from the supply pack, he was immersed in determined effort to mend a tear where a briar had torn his sleeve. Attendant on his progress was the Mad Prophet, in rare high humor at the prospect of a meal of fresh meat.

"You're making that thing into ruffles better suited to a tavern doxie," Dakar said in unasked-for criticism.

Embarrassed by his ineptness when he had been surrounded by women at their embroidery all his life, Lysaer managed a laugh. "If the ruffles keep out the cold, I don't care."

Dakar sampled the contents of his supper pot, licked the spoon, and resumed stirring. "Don't jerk the stitches so tight. Everybody knows you're irritated."

At a loss for subtle rejoinder, Lysaer welcomed the intrusion when Arithon stirred from the shadows and insinuated himself in the fray.

"Don't gloat," the Master advised the Mad Prophet. "Princes don't freely choose to keep their clothes until they rot in rags off their backs."

Laid open to insult by his threadbare and weather-faded plaid, Dakar subsided to a glower. To his half-brother, Arithon added, "If you don't mind wearing what looks like a sail maker's patch, there's a better way to fix that."

Relieved to be rescued from his ignorance, Lysaer surrendered needle and linen with a gratitude that unfailingly melted hearts. "These clothes would hardly impress anyone before they were torn." To Dakar, quietly, he added, "The s'Ffalenn bastard's made a fool of you again. You promised a scathing show of temper after Althain Tower. Now I'm left to wonder which of you is the more devious: Arithon, for an act that would fool a saint, or you, for a lying diversion to escape getting dressed down for rudeness."

Dakar's ebullience died. Rather than admit to his own bafflement at Arithon's contrary manner, he hunkered down by his cooking pot like a disgruntled broody hen. "Wait," he muttered morosely to the fair-haired and smiling prince. "Just wait until we get to Ithamon."

After five days' journey, the hills of Daon Ramon lost their rocky crowns and became clothed and gentled by heather. Valleys that until now had been channeled with dried gullies and stunted stands of scrub oak smoothed over into vales half hidden in fog. If the view had once been beautiful, Desh-thiere rendered everything bleak; the winds that never stilled gained the bitten edge of frost. For league upon league there seemed no living thing but gray-coated deer, rabbits furred in winter white, and the lonely, dissonant calls of hawks that sailed like shadows through the mist in search of prey.

The horses grew lean and tough, nourished more by the grain carried by wagon than on the rank brown grass. Lysaer wearied of venison, but was careful to keep the fact from his half-brother, who spent as many hours hunting as playing upon his lyranthe. As always fed up with abstinence, Dakar seized upon every opening to bemoan the dearth of beer.

Asandir kept his own counsel, forbidding as north-facing rock.

The closer the party drew to the heartland of Daon Ramon, the less the Sorcerer bothered to chastize his spellbinder for whining.

Well warned that such silence boded trouble, Lysaer noticed the moment when the Mad Prophet abandoned complaint. More sensitive than before to nuance, he watched for any circumstance that might find the Shadow Master discomfited.

But snow fell, and the days passed in anticlimax. Arithon did not oblige Dakar's expectations and grew darkly moody. He asked companionable questions of Asandir, and spent hours regarding ice-scabbed trees, stunted brush, and the white-clothed shoulders of the hills as though his mage-trained sight showed him wonders.

"The Riathan Paravians," Dakar whispered upon Lysaer's puzzled inquiry. "Unicorns ran in these hills and bore young in the meadows here. The mystery of their presence lingers even now."

Wide-eyed, skeptical, Lysaer peered through dripping bangs. An unseasonal thaw had softened the trail to muck, and slush seeped rivulets of wet down slopes like rucked old burlap. As far as the mist would allow, nothing met his gaze but bleak landscape that lacked the redeeming comfort of a single man-made structure.

Perched on the dray's hard buckboard, Dakar slapped the reins over the paint's steaming back and jogged her abreast of the chestnut gelding. Swaddled like a vegetable in wet cloaks, a derisive grin splitting his beard, he called over the rumble of rolling wheels. "Don't try to look with your eyes, but use your feelings."

"To find what?" Lysaer shrugged to vent frustration. "Every morning I wake up as though eyes are on my back, watching me, and each night I step away from the camp fire, I get chills that have nothing to do with the cold. This place is hauntingly, hurtfully deserted, as far as I can tell."

"That's the point." Dakar puffed up his cheeks and looked smug. "Asandir and Arithon might appreciate what's missing from this Ath-forsaken wasteland, but I suspect like me, you'd rather be in a crowded tavern knocking back mugs of spiced ale."

Although Lysaer did not precisely share Dakar's sentiment, he would have welcomed any human presence to allay the aching, hollow *something* that tugged at his nerves like pain. At each bend in the road, behind every storm-stunted bush, he seemed to see the lady he was to have married, her eyes liquid with tears, and her hands held out in entreaty. He remembered how her auburn hair had blown in the sea breeze off South Isle, and echoes of her lost laughter ached his heart. No noble dedication to purpose could ease his longing for home in this wilderness. His suffering stayed silent out of pride; and until the Mad Prophet had spoken, he had not guessed that his depression might arise from a source outside himself.

At noon riders and wagon paused for a cold meal beside a spring whose waters rose bubbling through a cleft in milky quartz rocks. Snow rendered the site gray on white, cross-stitched with the arched-over stems of dead briars.

Sent down to the pebbled edge of the pool to refill water flasks, Arithon returned whitely shaken. He looked as a man who fended off pleas from the spirits of murdered children, his lips pinched shut to stifle outcry. "You might have warned me," he lashed at Asandir in tones dragged flat by upset.

The Sorcerer did not answer, but accepted the dripping flasks to stow back into the wagon. Then, as if in response to a spoken word of address, he turned eyes as chilly as the weather upon the s'Ilessid prince who watched the exchange, and offered an unasked-for and edged explanation.

"A centaur was beset during the rebellion and pulled down here. Moss does not grow where his blood spilled. The sunchildren sang a lament to commemorate his passage, and the words and the melody still ring upon the wind, to any with sensitivity enough to listen."

Stung by what felt like rebuke, Lysaer straightened in affront, then doubled over with a gasp, robbed of his royal dignity by an elbow in the ribs from the Mad Prophet. Finished graining the horses, Dakar thrust himself headlong between Sorcerer and s'Ilessid with oat chaff bristling from his hood.

"What was that for?" Lysaer demanded, outraged.

"To quiet your foolish tongue, Prince." As Asandir turned away about his business, the Mad Prophet winked sidelong in conspiracy. "For a sorcerer, this place is hurtful to walk past, let alone stop and linger."

"That Fellowship mage has feelings?" Lysaer shot back, his eyes following Asandir's hands as they laced and jerked tight the lashings that secured the oiled canvas over the supplies in the wagon bed.

Dakar picked a seed head from his sleeve and looked thoughtful. "My ever so powerful master is doing his best at this moment to keep from weeping outright."

"You say." A billow of mist rolled past, rendering horses, men, and dray as featureless as silhouettes. Lysaer raised his eyebrows.

"Well," the Mad Prophet amended, "I've lived with Asandir for centuries, my friend. I know this place bothers him, and I'd wager one thing further. He stopped here on purpose, to use its effect as a weapon. If you think I'm lying, *look at your half-brother.*"

The prince forgot his pique and did so.

Still dead pale, his eyebrows snarled into a frown, Arithon had remounted his dun mare. He hunched against the wind as if he were wounded and bleeding, and tears traced silver down his face.

Embarrassed as if caught at eavesdropping, Lysaer spun back to face Dakar. "Why don't you feel anything? Why don't I?"

The Mad Prophet clawed back an untidy lock of hair. Cold had reddened the tip of his nose, and his eyes looked unwarrantedly bloodshot; yet a chilling and dignified majesty cloaked him all the same as he said, "Do you want to?"

The question hit hard. Driven to see into himself with uncanny depth and clarity, struck naked before his own judgment, Lysaer perceived that the confusion that had harried him since exile held a core of ugly truth. No longer did the glamor of noble purpose veil fact: that his brave resolve to Traithe in Althain's storeroom had been rooted in vanity and pride. He had renounced a difficult path of study, and vowed instead to redress the wrongs of a kingdom for his own personal glory. As though revolted by a foul taste, Lysaer sucked in a fast breath. He could hope his self-disgust was not exposed on his face, but Dakar regarded him strangely.

"*Do* you feel nothing?" The Mad Prophet slapped the straw from his cloak with sudden, biting sharpness. "I'd venture not. I'd say this place moves you as deeply as the rest of us."

Lysaer looked back, unflinching. However this spirit-cursed place afflicted others, his ingrained sense of fairness forced honesty. "My true heart stayed behind in Port Royal, I see, with my love, and my family, and my people. If that is a failing, it's at least no more than human. The problems that beset this land are not mine. Yet I will do my best to help right them."

The prince's conviction rang so far at odds with the future forecast by the strands that Dakar shied back, baffled. To cover his foreboding, he clambered back behind the dray's buckboard and sorted his tangled loops of rein. "Ath in his mercy, but I could use a flagon of dark beer and a fire," he groused to no one in particular.

"That makes two of us, friend." Lysaer remounted his chestnut gelding, unsure whether the lingering traces of Paravian tragedy or the unendingly dreary landscape caused him to hurt as if the chill cut his flesh to the marrow.

At Asandir's word, wagon and riders pressed onward through an afternoon that wept cold drizzle. Now the trail wound like tattered ribbon between Daon Ramon's vales and downs, intermittently flanked by stone markers capped with lichens and moss. No trees grew, but only bracken and tasseled grasses beaten down by wind and early storms. Dirtied ice lay scabbed in the hollows. Braced in his saddle against the cold, and resigned to yet another sleepless night on soaked ground, Lysaer did not realize their destination lay in sight until, rounding the crest of a hill, Arithon gasped and yanked his dun mare to a halt in the roadway.

She danced a piaffe at his roughness, her hooves clanging loudly on slate. Jostled in his saddle as his own mount bunched in reaction, Lysaer looked ahead.

Looming in eerie outline through the mantling mist rose Ithamon, city of legend, and seat of the high kings of Rathain.

The sight was one to stop the breath, even through the fog of Desh-thiere. No previous feature of landscape could prepare a traveler for the broad sweep of valley slashed across by a rock-strewn scar of dry riverbed. At one time, walls of rose gray stone had arisen from the banks, but what remained lay torn to wreckage.

Landslides left less ruin.

The greensward beyond was overrun with briar, what had been orchards, gardens, and tourney fields now choked by weed and bitter-root vine. A second wall had bounded the inner edge of the common. Embraced within gapped, half-gutted watchkeeps, the tumbled shells of town houses clung to the hillside's ever steepening pitch. Dismembered foundations marked off a tangle of narrow lanes and briar-ridden courtyards. As if a mighty army had once razed the buildings stone from stone with battering rams, the craftsmen's cottages, market stalls, and merchants' mansions all lay jumbled into chaos. Gabled roofs had caved inward, beams rotted away in the sunless damp of Desh-thiere. A scatter of fallen slates in what may have been a market court reflected the rain like coins thrown out for a beggar.

The devastation of the lower tiers was total, a memorial to unbridled violence. Yet as if moved by some powerful unseen force, the viewer found his sight drawn upward, where, slightly north of center, the native granite of the earth sheered up through soil and rock into a nearly vertical outcrop. The triangular summit on the cliff top was encased by embrasures of seamless, blue-black granite. Inside, an unkempt eyrie of broken walls and spires marked the site of the inner citadel, the castle where generations of Paravians and, after them, the s'Ffalenn high kings had held court.

There the eye hung captive, unable to draw away.

Amid that graveyard of ravaged splendor, of artistry spoiled by war into a cataclysmic expression of hatred, arose four single towers, each as different from the other as sculpture by separate masters. They speared upward through the mist, tall, straight, perfect; their existence held wonder that made sunlight seem murky, and beauty, a blindness to be endured. Somewhere between silence and sight, they exemplified the antithesis of cruelty. The very incongruity of their wholeness against the surrounding wreckage shaped a dichotomy fit to maim the soul. For their lines were harmony distilled into form, and strength beyond reach of time's attrition.

The rain still fell relentlessly into soggy earth; the wind keened and stung like a dulled skive in a cobbler's shop. No one noticed. Even the horses seemed strangely content to be stopped in their tracks in the roadway. The sordid, everyday miseries of winter and weather lost meaning, became less than the mumbles a half-wit might utter in solitude. Into that suspended silence Asandir began to speak.

"Ithamon was raised by Paravians in the First Age of Athera. The outer walls were leveled twice by Seardluin, hostile creatures native to this world that by the Second Age had been battled to extinction. The old races abandoned the city then, for its purpose as a fortress had been fulfilled. The lower tiers stayed in ruins until the dawn of the present age, when Men rebuilt the double walls upon the remains. The third tier wall left standing and the four surviving keeps were part of the original city. Built by the centaurs, refined by sunchildren, they were Name-bound and warded by the unicorns."

"Don't say anymore!" Arithon cut across, his bard's voice queerly strangled. "I beg you, don't!" Bloodlessly pale, his hands clenched and shaking on the rein, he sat his mare and regarded the site where his ancestors had ruled as if he were held chained and in thrall. "Please," he finished in a whisper.

But Asandir might as well not have heard. "The Paravian towers have withstood three ages of strife, eighteen thousand years of history. Mortal men have called them the Sun Towers, or Compass Points, for their alignment and their dizzying height, but the ancients who laid their stones had separate names for each. The white one with the alabaster combing is Alathwyr, and its strength is Wisdom. The east, the black one, is endurance, which represents the Paravian concept of Honor. The south, of rose quartz, is Grace, and the last, of green jasper symbolic of renewal, is Kieling, Compassion. When civilization has abandoned any of these qualities, its respective tower will fail, for the power that binds their structure is the force of each virtue, renewed. *Ithamon* means 'Five Spires' in the old tongue, and once this was so. Daelthain, the King's Tower, for Justice, originally crowned the highest knoll in the city. That one cracked on the day his royal grace, Marin Eliathe, was murdered in his hall by an assassin. The last of it crumbled during the rebellion. Now just the foundation remains."

Asandir's speech ended, leaving the moan of the lonely wind to fill the emptiness. Lysaer discovered he must have been gripping his saddle too hard for some time; both his arms ached to the elbows. He released his hands and shivered, moved by desire like ardor to wish the city's spoiled symmetry restored, to see the unearthly beauty of the Paravian towers returned into sunlight, and inhabited as they had been in past ages.

Arithon looked tortured to his very core. Shoved hard against the unwanted heritage of his ancestry, and struck blind and deaf by the chord of Paravian mystery first tuned to his awareness in Caith-al-Caen, he had wheeled his mare in the roadway. His wide green eyes were fixed upon Asandir. A betrayal too fresh to have sparked resentment tautened the planes of his face, and his voice was gravel as he said, "Ath's own mercy, *how am I to suffer this?*"

The Sorcerer sat his black stallion with the straight-backed formality of Daelion, Master of Fate. "I will answer when you ask out of care, Prince of Rathain."

Arithon recoiled in a high flush of fury. "No need to answer at all, Sorcerer. Everywhere I turn, it seems I get saddled with sand kingdoms. Well, pity has torn out my heart far and long before this. I bear the ache already, like a bad scar."

Explosively murderous, cocked on a hair-trigger edge of unconscionable violence, he drove his heels into the mare. Her nerves frayed into a white-rimmed roll of eyes and she reared. Arithon gave rein, kicked her again, and screamed what sounded like an obscenity ripped through by tears. His hands jabbed at the reins, and his mount clattered around in the roadway and shot blindly forward at a gallop.

Horse and rider thundered across the crumbling span that bridged the dry course of the Severnir at reckless speed and vanished into the ruin.

Dakar said something bitten under his breath, and the paint mare stamped. Shaken by his half-brother's savagery and pricked by cross-currents he lacked the background to grasp, Lysaer spun to confront the Sorcerer. "Why did you push him?"

His mildness shaped by grief, Asandir said, "This city has weathered seven major tragedies and three ages of history. So much dust to you perhaps, but to those of us who have borne witness, it means wisdom painfully gained, paid for by men who bled and died, and Paravians who weathered mortal failings time and again until the rifts in their world grew too wide to endure. Shall all that has been go wasted because Arithon dislikes responsibility? Athera's civilizations struggle on the brink of imbalance, with Desh-thiere's coming defeat. A restoration of just rule must follow. The reinstated prince who subdues Etarra *must* descend from the old kings if he is to close the rift between townsman and clan barbarian." The Sorcerer finished in bald-faced regret. "Put simply, Arithon's recalcitrance is a luxury the times can ill afford."

"You've made an enemy of him," Lysaer observed coldly.

"Merciful maker, I would that were all I had done!" Closer to giving way to anguish than any mortal man had ever seen him, Asandir shook out his reins. He pressed his black stallion ahead against the rain, and did not speak or look back the whole way through an afternoon of ascent through the ruins.

They found Arithon standing beside his horse within the broken circle that marked the old foundation of the King's Tower. His face was hard set, and his temper, brittle as iced-over current.

By now recovered from the outburst upon the riverbank, Asandir addressed him, whip-lash curt. "We shall camp in a tower. They are sound, comfortable, and dry. Which shall it be, my prince?"

"Kieling," Arithon said, determinedly blithe and uncaring. "Compassion."

Caithdein

The vast stone hall at the west outpost in Camris held only a solitary figure, but the fire had been built high in expectation of a momentous event. Wax candles burned in sconces and candelabra, and still, deep shadow darkened the corners. Winter had settled in. Winds moaned across the mountainside without, and drafts rippled the Cildorn tapestries, even the largest ones by the hearth. Slim and straight in her chair of state on the dais, and clad formally in Tysan's gold-bordered tabard over her traditional black, Maenalle s'Gannley, Steward of Tysan, fingered the gilt-tipped pen handed down through twenty generations to sign kingdom documents. The ornamental plume, though replaced at measured intervals, showed the ravages of last season's moths; yet the nib in its cloisonne barrel remained sharp and unworn. Since the fall of the last crowned sovereign, official word passed between clan chiefs by spoken courier, or not at all, for parchment could fall into the hands of townsmen if the messenger chanced to be captured.

Maenalle smoothed the feather's tattered fibers, her sharp-planed face taut with excitement. In the absence of written record, she wondered whether tonight was the first time since the desecration of the royal seat at Avenor that all of Tysan's clan lords would be gathered beneath one roof. She smiled fiercely, savoring the news she would deliver, that a true-born heir had returned through West Gate to claim the high king's throne.

Elder Tashan was giddy as a boy with anticipation, and young Maien, unable to contain nervous jitters for fear he might be clumsy and spill the wine—this after he had waited upon his prince without mishap. No scout from the west outpost had breathed a word of the royal arrival; Maenalle held cocky pride in them for that. Her announcement would completely surprise lords who had journeyed long, inconvenient distances through hostile country at her summons.

A sudden, preternatural stillness gripped the chamber, as if the insatiable mountain gales had forgotten to gust, or fire ceased for an instant to flicker.

Possessed of a scout's reflexes, Maenalle stiffened a heartbeat ahead of the logic that warned of something amiss. A second later, and without the fanfare of breezes carried in from far places affected by Kharadmon, the discorporate Sorcerer Luhaine flicked into existence. His image was robed austerely as a scholar, and posed with round face furrowed in concern as he gazed up at Maenalle in the high seat. "Lady, I bring tidings."

The Steward of Tysan felt her carefree mood evaporate. She regarded her visitor, aware never more than this moment that Fellowship Sorcerers did not pay visits for trivial reasons. Luhaine by preference was a recluse; his last appearance in Camris had been in her grandfather's time. "Tell me quickly," she said, afraid of the worst, and anxious most of all to recover her shattered solitude.

Luhaine returned a shake of his head. His heavy robes were not stirred by the drafts, and his eyes followed hers, aggrieved. "I cannot. Wards must be set first in precaution."

Maenalle shot to her feet. "Wards? *Here?*" Affronted that the vigilance of her scouts might be questioned, she gripped the heirloom pen with a fierceness that threatened to snap the quill. "Whatever for?"

A palm-downward gesture from the Sorcerer negated the implied insult. "Necessary, *Caithdein* of Tysan." His image flicked out, but a strange, weighted feel to the air evinced his continued presence and industry. Maenalle snatched the interval to recover herself and sit down. Since impatience only fueled her uneasiness, she laid the antique pen safely aside. But the wait turned out to be short. The flames in the sconces flared with sudden, hurtful brilliance, and ozone sharpened the smell of oiled wood and hot wax. Then Luhaine's image reappeared, round-shouldered and contrite, in the center of a subliminal corona of light that extended over himself and the shield-hung perimeter of the dais.

By then the steward had guessed why arcane protections might be called for. "Koriani," she surmised, her annoyance a shade less acid. "But why fear the enchantresses? This outpost is between power lanes, and their watchers see little in these mountains."

"Morriel has set a circle of seniors to scrying." Luhaine's image poised bird-like, as if on the edge of sudden flight. "Perhaps she searches once again for the lost Waystone." His frown deepened. "Worse and more likely, one of her seers caught wind of the future the Fellowship read in the strands."

Pricked by a ripple of chills, Maenalle tugged her tabard tighter around her shoulders. "What have you come here to tell me, Sorcerer?"

Luhaine's deep eyes turned frosty. "Dire portents, lady. After the Mistwraith's conquest will come war. Lysaer s'Ilessid will cast his lot with townsmen, to the detriment of the loyal clans."

Maenalle's hands recoiled into fists and fine linen crumpled, unheeded, as she shoved her weight forward in her chair. "Why?" Her voice came out a tortured whisper. "Our own prince will betray us?"

Never had the Sorcerer regretted his status as a disembodied spirit more than now; his mild face twisted in anguish akin to Maenalle's own, that he could not soften the impact of his words with the warmth of a comforting touch. "*Cathdein*," he murmured in compassion, "I cannot help. The Seven cast strands. We see the evil that will set s'Ilessid prince against s'Ffalenn will be prompted by the Mistwraith. But how such schism will come to pass is beyond our powers to know."

Thin-lipped, tight-jawed, and miserably fighting tears, Maenalle stared ahead without seeing. "I thought that was not possible."

"Yes, and paradoxically, no." Perpetually prepared with a lecture, Luhaine qualified. "Desh-thiere's nature is opaque to us. We have no insight into it as a cause, but only can read its effects since, from origins outside of Athera, it lacks Name to embody its essence. The Riathan Paravians quite wisely would not encompass its energies for interpretation. Traithe did, at need, when he sealed South Gate against the invasion. But the greater portion of his faculties withered in the process. Whatever enormity he discovered concerning the Mistwraith that besets this world, he is left unable to say."

Silent, saddened, Maenalle pondered this revelation. "Then our princes are your only recourse against Desh-thiere?"

Luhaine made as though to pace, stopped himself wasting effort for the sake of appearance, and equally sparely answered. "Events have forced us to choose between certain war and restoration of sunlight."

Blanched now as sun-whitened ivory, Maenalle stirred and sat back. "No choice at all," she allowed. Dwarfed by the grand chair of state, she laced fine-boned fingers on the table edge, restored to her usual dry irony.

Luhaine bowed to honor her courage. "My colleagues felt you should know at once that Lysaer shall not be sanctioned for inheritance. Yet you must not lose heart. There will be royal heirs, in time, that are not encumbered in Desh-thiere's moil of ills. Until then you must be more than the shadow behind the throne tradition dictates. Whatever comes, Tysan's heritage must continue to be preserved for those generations yet unborn."

Very straight and fragile, Maenalle inclined her head. "Rest assured, and tell your colleagues. The clans of Tysan shall endure."

"I never doubted." In better times Luhaine's image might have smiled. "Only handle this confidence with great care. The Koriani witches must not hear of this break in the succession beforetime. From the moment sunlight is restored to the continent, the balance of events becomes precarious. Every action, every word, will carry weight. The interval is most vulnerable to dangerous, even horrifying digressions."

Whatever the strands had foretold imprinted wary trepidation upon a Sorcerer renowned for staid propriety.

Unable to conceive of a blight worse than war and the loss of Tysan's prince to the cause of townsmen, Maenalle returned an assurance that rang shallow as banality to her ears. Cold to the heart, she watched unseeing as Luhaine's image dissolved away into air. For a long while afterward, she stared into the space his presence had occupied. She did not worry, at first, which words she would find to deliver ill tidings to the clan lords who would assemble within the hour; instead she agonized over what she would tell her young grandson, Maien.

For since the elegant, blond prince had left the outpost, the boy had spent his every waking minute in earnest emulation of the man's faultless manners and royal poise.

"Damn his s'Ilessid grace to the darkest torments of Sithaer!" Maenalle cried at last in an anguish that echoed and re-echoed off the tapestried walls. "More than the child's poor heart will be broken!"

Scryers

The chamber that had served the ladies of the old earl's court as solar smelled of dried lavender still, and of the birch logs that burned in the grate. Yet where the room in bygone years had been bright with light and laughter, now the shadows lay deepest in the lovers' nooks. Drapes of dense felt sealed out the drafts and also any daylight let in by ceiling-high arched windows. Curtains veiled the lion-head cornices, and the paintings of nymphs and dolphins, flaking now from damp and mildew. Only the rose, gold, and gray marble that patterned the floor in geometrics remained visible to remind of a gentler past, before the Koriani Prime Enchantress had chosen the site for her day quarters.

Morriel eschewed the comfort of carpets. Candles she counted a distraction from her meditation. Austere as new-forged steel, she straightened from the unupholstered alcove she preferred for contemplation, her head raised in expectation. A tap sounded at the door. The Prime gave a self-satisfied nod, the diamond pins netting her coiffure fire-points in the dimness as she commanded, "Allow the First Senior to enter."

The nearer of two pageboys hastened from the corner and unbarred the door.

Lirenda swept past as though the liveried child were furniture. She curtsied with a brisk swirl of silk, alert for the twitch of

Morriel's hand that allowed her permission to rise. Exhilaration flushed her cheeks as she shed her cloak with its ribbons of rank sewn in bands at hood and hem. As the remaining boy took her garment, she dared a direct glance at her superior. "It has begun."

"Show me." Spider still amid the arranged folds of her skirts, Morriel closed lightless black eyes. For a space the chamber held little sound and movement beyond the crackle of flames in the hearth. The page avoided clumsy noise as he set the latch on the armoire door and crept back to his place.

Lirenda cupped the crystal strung from a chain at her throat, dampened her thoughts, and dropped her inner barriers to permit her superior free access. Power flowed like current from mind to mind, focused to frame recall of two images gathered through lanewatch. . . .

Half a world away, across an expanse of ocean, sudden sunlight lances through a tear in streaming mist and shatters into sparkles against the wave crests. Ancient enough to have living memories of the natural world before Desh-thiere's conquest, Morriel did not gasp aloud. As if the vision were empty of wonder, she pressed on workmanlike, *to a later view of moonrise over an island fortress whose roofless keeps notch an indigo sky. . . .*

"Corith," Lirenda identified, breaking trance in the solar of the old earl's palace. "In the isles of Min Pierens to the west."

Morriel checked the interruption with a raised finger. "I see as much." On an edge of sharpness she said, "Our fifth-lane watcher has reported an increased concentration of the mist overhanging the site of Ithamon?"

"Exactly." The First Enchantress pressed eagerly to conclusion. "The Fellowship's royal protégés must have set Desh-thiere's hold under siege from there. Why else should its grip loosen elsewhere?"

Morriel disregarded the insolence. Three weeks had passed since the princes with Asandir had taken up residence in ruined Ithamon; here came first proof of their doings there. With the last attempted scryings on their activities an unmitigated failure, that the Mistwraith should now show signs of weakening offered exciting developments. But to rejoice over supposition would be blindness akin to folly. "I suggest our duty lies in knowing how the princes who are responsible come by their powers." Morriel's brow furrowed in speculation. "After all, they accomplish a feat their Fellowship benefactors cannot duplicate."

Lirenda's eyes brightened. "You suggest we try another scrying into Asandir's affairs at Ithamon?"

A cracked laugh issued from the alcove. "The idea suits you, does it?" For an interval Morriel stared into distance. "It pleases me to try." A snap of dry fingers called a page to attend her. "Fetch the chest that contains the focus jewel of Skyron. Be quick."

Unremarked by a glance from either enchantress, the boy bowed and let himself out. As his nervous footsteps dwindled down the corridor, Morriel stroked her chin with a fingernail. "I would tap the fifth lane and trace the eddies created by the events at Ithamon, yes. But subtlety is needful. Our efforts must blend with the pulse of the land itself, until chance affords us opening and Asandir leaves the princes' presence."

"But they work from one of the Compass Point Towers," Lirenda objected. "What source of ours can breach Paravian safeguards?"

The old Prime's look sparked daggers. "A defeatist attitude ill becomes your office."

Lirenda inclined her head. "I stand corrected before my better."

Morriel made a moue of disgust. "Don't be a hypocrite." In a shift of weight that eddied the scents of herbs and moth poison upon the air, she folded crabbed hands in her lap. "For all your diligence, your ambitions overstep your knowledge."

The chamber abruptly seemed chilly as a tomb. Disadvantaged by her posture of obeisance, Lirenda stifled irritation. The Prime was apt to be querulous on days when the weather ached her bones; and only the foolish bridled at truth in her presence. Lirenda held herself in submission until her senior at length relented.

"Were you not keen to replace me, you would be of worthless character. But if it is envy of the Fellowship's power that drives your desire to humble Asandir, beware. You will earn yourself the misstep such weakness deserves. You may rise." Rings flashed as Morriel motioned for her First Enchantress to be seated on the footstool by the hearth.

The chamber offered no other chair; the pages, as they waited, knelt on bare floor. But Lirenda suffered the inconvenience; wedded to supremacy the Prime might be, but her mind was quick and devious.

Across a quiet dense with the scent of lavender, the aged crone tartly qualified. "We shall defeat the Paravian wards by simplicity, First Enchantress. Our weapon shall be compassion."

Lirenda tautened to eagerness. "Arithon chose the tower Kieling," she mused unthinkingly aloud.

"Precisely." Rather than take umbrage at the lapse, Morriel said,

"The Teir's'Ffalenn unknowingly ceded us opening since initiate Elaira's escapade at Erdane. The enquiry we made concerning her misconduct in the Ravens' hayloft has left us a faultless imprint of innocent, unconditional love."

There lay the clue Lirenda had overlooked, and in honesty, would never have thought to examine. She cursed her shortsightedness as logic unfolded the method's diabolical symmetry. Asandir could not stand watch every hour that his princes fought the Mistwraith. Over-awed as Fellowship mages were wont to be over any and all things Paravian, he would expect Kieling's wards to shield out unwanted scryers in those intervals while he minded his other affairs. The richest innuendo of all was that his princes should have been un-touchably secure; and so they would be, except for anomaly.

"Kieling's defenses will detect no threat if our probe is masked be-hind our record of Elaira's care for Arithon. We will win through," Morriel concluded, her lips pursed, her eyes hooded, and her hands still as claws in her lap. "So long as we observe only and make no move to interfere."

All along Morriel had anticipated the advantage that Elaira's mis-placed feelings might provide. The admiration Lirenda gave her Prime was enraptured and pitiless as a predator stalking to kill, for the stakes of this hunt were as deadly. Envy could not color fact: that the Fellowship of Seven had held ascendency over affairs on the conti-nent for far and away too long.

"Yes," Morriel said in uncanny response to pure thought. "It suits me to try their authority. This time. When you're through acting dumbstruck, we may start."

A flush touched Lirenda's cheeks, for the pageboy had returned from his errand. He stood before her, fair-faced and formal as an icon, the iron-bound box that held the focus crystal of Skyron offered in trembling hands.

"Lead the probe" came Morriel's nettled instruction. "This is your test, if you think yourself fit to succeed me."

Excitement overrode Lirenda's distaste for the role she had been commanded to execute. She accepted the coffer, keyed the release of the wards, and lifted the crystal that lay like an ice shard inside. Tawny eyes fixed on the jewel, she stilled her inner consciousness until the room and its shadows fell away, swallowed by the stone's pellucid depths.

Her awareness settled. Poised into tranquility that allowed the creation all possibility and none, her selfhood encompassed paradox. Lirenda became both the spark to seed holocaust and the ice to quench all heat. She was light that could sear away sight, or darkness of a depth to crack rock; hers was the oblivion of the Veil between the void: perfect peace or ultimate stagnation. She was nothing, all things, every pitch and vibration that formed the warp and weft of Ath's Creation.

The Skyron focus framed her into a discipline that banished personal opinion. And yet, controlled as she was, demanding of excellence as her ambition required, she had to fight not to shudder as the Prime joined the link and connected her through the matrix to the crystal's reservoir of stored energies. Elaira's trial record was drawn forth, and a set of personal emotions overrode Lirenda's selfhood with an intimacy as stifling as suffocation.

Unable to speak or escape, she could only feel. The sensation forced upon her became a turbulence that transported—to a cheerless cellar in a fire-scarred inn where Elaira had lived through early childhood. In raw and cruel detail Lirenda experienced the misery of a hovel shared with beggars and scabby, disease-ridden prostitutes. . . .

Shivering in noxious rags and the sour, shedding leathers of spoiled furs, she remembered wakeful nights spent listening to the wet, tearing coughs of the old man who looked after her as he lay wasting of lung sickness. Friends were all the wealth a child of the streets might possess. Food, shelter, and belongings could be wrested away; as an orphan, disciple of thieves, Elaira well knew how easily. But love and good memories could outlast misfortune, even death.

Until the hour her fledgling talents had led her into straits with the town constable, who sold her into Morvain for rearing in Koriani fosterage, Elaira had made her life rich with caring.

Entangled in the Skyron link, Lirenda felt the mannered austerity she had cultivated as a rich man's daughter give way before simpler joys that lured her toward destruction like a siren's song. Wrenched awry by distaste, she forced her violated senses not to pull back and break trance. Her burning ambition to gain a prime's ultimate power and knowledge lent her strength. She embraced disillusion, accepted the forge fire of emotion that comprised Elaira's nature for her own, as Morriel and the demands of the scrying into Kieling Tower required.

Across a haze of distance, the matriarch's prompt reached her. "Nicely done. Be ready. I shall tie into the lane force now."

Morriel's praise reaffirmed concentration. Though prepared for a shift in perspective, the touch of the fifth lane's powers did not kindle as Lirenda expected. Trapped in Elaira's persona, she experienced, as the girl would have done, a sensation as wretchedly unpleasant as a drenching cloudburst. Fighting abhorrence and instinct, Lirenda endured this shocking, alien perspective of a spirit attuned to spell-craft through water, when she herself was all fire, unalterably opposed. She must not falter, or even flinch in disgust, even as self-identity became immolated by Elaira's unruly passions.

As trance discipline reduced the fifth lane's energies to a shimmering play of static, Lirenda drifted, embraced by the high, sweet vibration of earthforce. Since Morriel manipulated the scrying, her First Senior's altered consciousness could not track the flow of time. The next sensation Lirenda experienced was a view of translucent blue twilight over snow-clad hills.

The merlons of an embrasure jutted upward in silhouette; illuminated by what she first took for torchflame, three figures clustered in a semicircle. Two stood, while the other crouched with hands tucked under the elbows held pressed to his sides. By dint of clothing concocted from what looked like frayed layers of rags, Elaira's awareness identified the stout person of Dakar the Mad Prophet. The light proved not to be flame but a spark that seemed fueled by nothing beyond empty air.

Presented with a view of dark cloaks and hoods harried close by wind to hide the faces inside, Lirenda by herself could not differentiate between the royal half-brothers. Elaira's more exacting perception discerned at once that one figure was taller. A twist of blond hair flicked loose by a gust established and dismissed him as s'Ilessid. Fixed at once on the smaller man, the imprinted pattern that comprised Elaira's subjective reaction became swept by an ungodly thrill.

Framed by magelight and a backdrop of louring fog that imposed false dusk upon the scene, Arithon raised his head and looked around. Recognition suffused his glance, as if, impossibly, *he could sense the Koriani contact bridged through from Camris by crystal.*

As acting surrogate for Elaira, Lirenda felt scorched by that gaze. But the rapport that would have quickened her sister initiate to excitement only tantalized the First Enchantress as elusively as the receding edge of a dream. She shivered. As if touched to recoil by empathy, the s'Ffalenn prince on the parapet frowned. He tossed back his hood in sudden tension as a man might measure an opponent. Through a space while the winds whipped his dark locks into tangles, his hand flicked a gesture to Dakar. Captivated by the movement's instinctive grace, and spontaneously struck by stray recall, Lirenda shared a past memory—*of those very same fingers plucking straw from her hair with a tenderness impossible to forget.*

Morriel's voice jabbed through the diversion in a whiplash tone of command: "Do not get involved, First Enchantress!"

Lirenda struggled to bridle Elaira's fascination, as Arithon knelt before Dakar.

Whispered words passed between them. Then the Mad Prophet's face rearranged in pure deviltry. "You'd never dare."

A lift of Arithon's chin gave challenge as he rose back to his feet. "Ah, but I would." Beneath laughter, his voice held a dissonance like mallet-struck iron. Were Lirenda in control, she would immediately have severed contact, but Elaira's entrancement hampered judgment. The scrying enchantress dwelt a second too long, and Arithon s'Ffalenn seized his opening.

He called to Lysaer, who raised his hands. For a heartbeat the half-brothers centered a gathering vertex of pent-up power. Then light speared skyward, virulent as summer lightning. The hollow, booming report of heat-stressed air thundered outward over ruined Ithamon. Lirenda saw the Mistwraith boil clear with a howling clap of wind, to be razed aside by shadow that iced its vapors into a spindrift fall of new snow.

Then, impossibly, Koriani safe-wards crumpled, and the concatenation of reaction surged past shields and into the Skyron focus. Lirenda was tossed physically head over heels. She had no chance to feel bruises. A second surge erupted from Lysaer's clenched hands, followed by another and another, until her eyes were dazzled sightless and hearing became stunned by rolling waves of crescendoed sound. The link between the earl's court and Ithamon buckled into pinwheeling chaos as the lane connection surged into backlash.

Lirenda barely felt the jerk as the Skyron crystal was wrested from her grip. Her awareness of Kieling Tower shattered, and Elaira's persona ripped away, shocking body and mind beyond reach of coherent sensation. Lirenda never felt the cyclone of turbulence that scoured Morriel's chamber. Cushions exploded like confetti, and chests tumbled, and the rose and gray marble flooring erupted into a thousand eggshell cracks that showered sharpened fragments through the hangings. Daylight sliced in through rent felt, and Lirenda came back to herself. She lay unable to move, winded, befuddled, and half blind from the afterimage of multiple bolts of pure light.

"Ath, most merciful Ath," her own voice cried across confusion, the envy in her heart unmasked: "They hold command of elemental mastery, both of them."

Through drumrolls of fading thunder, and a headache that blossomed like a starburst, Lirenda heard Morriel's shrill outburst. "Imbecile! Fool!"

A dry palm cracked her cheek. The sting to her flesh and her dignity negated any lingering afterimage of Elaira's tender sympathies.

Limp as rags on the floor, the First Enchantress recovered her rightful sense of outrage. Her vision swam back into focus, marred by embarrassing tears. Through their blur, and the wan light that seeped through slashed drapes, she beheld a chamber that looked to have suffered the mangling brunt of an earthquake. Wreckage lay everywhere. The pageboys crouched beneath the tumbled-over splinters of the armoire, holding each other and shaking.

Lirenda could not have eased their terror even had she been of a mind to.

Morriel Prime towered over her, lividly displeased, the Skyron focus clutched in her claw-like grasp. "Were you blind and witless not to see? *The s'Ffalenn bastard's been trained to power!* However else could he and Dakar have collaborated to upset our scrying? Mischief and misery! What unconscionable recklessness prompted the Fellowship to loose this abomination upon our world?"

Lirenda propped herself upright, then pressed scratched and bleeding fingers to her pounding temples. She felt hollow as a drum and strangely reft; the banished intensity of Elaira's susceptibilities left her drab and spiritless in spaces she had never known existed. She distanced such discomfort in a show of self-righteous propriety. "Elaira may have known of the Fellowship's intent beforehand. That would account for her stubbornness throughout our probe into her escapade in Erdane."

But Morriel's priorities were wholly concerned with the future. "Recall the girl! Do it now! For pity us all, we're going to need analysis of both these princes' characters. If there's any hope of setting a counterbalance to the trouble they're bound to create, Elaira must find us an opening."

First Enchantress Lirenda arose, bowed stiffly to the Prime, then departed to fulfill her directive. Joylessly intent, she took no pleasure in the miracle revealed by the scrying: that the princes promised by prophecy did battle against Desh-thiere from the Kieling Tower.

In the remotest reaches of Athera, the Mistwraith no longer ruled the sky. Sunlight touched earth and ocean for the first time in five long centuries.

Triad

In Erdane, drowsing in her chair over knitting, the seer Enithen Tuer snaps awake with a cry, for dreams have shown her stars and moon against a backdrop of indigo darkness. . . .

Caught treed like a monkey in an orchard where she prunes dead growth, Elaira stiffens as Lirenda's arcane summons slices her awareness like a whip; that Morriel should demand her presence on the heels of last season's disgrace means trouble, she knows, and she curses in language that draws grins from the boy wards who gather her cuttings up for firewood. . . .

On a faraway isle, amid waters never charted, a unicorn stands sentinel as Desh-thiere's mists part; yet she does not dance for joy under the lucent sky—a horn-toss of inquiry displays her puzzlement as tree-filtered sunshine glances across a cave mouth and a weakened shimmer of ward-light fades back to quiescence without rousing the Sorcerer sealed under sleep spells within. . . .

XI. Desh-thiere

I n Daon Ramon's heartland, atop the battlements of Kieling Tower, the ongoing battle to reduce the Mistwraith suffered an unscheduled interruption as rapport between the royal half-brothers frayed away into nothing. Lysaer broke concentration with a quizzical expression. His hands fell slack, and the last surge of energy he held poised to send a light bolt skyward dissipated as a harmless dance of sparks. He snapped a tangle of hair from his eyes and said irritably, "Will one of you please share the fun?"

No one answered.

Dakar remained curled on his knees, doubled helplessly in a fit of laughter. Arithon seemed no more capable, close as he was to choking as he stifled an explosive whoop in the crumpled cloth of his cloak. Neither Shadow Master nor prophet recovered sobriety even when Asandir emerged at a run from the stairwell. His brows were drawn down at an angle that would have been forbidding had his eyes not held a glint of amused sympathy.

"I heard," he addressed without preamble. "*Sethvir* informed me from *Althain* that you two have upset the Koriani Prime and her First Senior. Tell me what prank you pulled, and quickly, since we may now anticipate a round of angry repercussions."

Although Arithon was quickest to rally, Dakar answered, through tears and outbursts of chuckles that he manfully strangled back to wheezes. "Damned witches tried meddling." He mopped streaming eyes, slapped his knees, and started over. "Morriel sought another scrying on the princes, through Lirenda and the Skyron focus. It was too obvious—" Here speech failed and the Mad Prophet relapsed into a paralyzing spasm of hiccups.

The Sorcerer shifted hopefully to Arithon. "So you hooked into the Koriani scrying, and allowed their matrix to absorb the energies you had gathered against Desh-thiere?"

Wiser to his limits than Dakar, the Master of Shadows simply nodded.

"Ath!" Lysaer interrupted, mortified by his half-brother's bald-faced confession. "You redirected our gifts *at the enchantresses*? You reckless fool! Somebody could have been killed!"

Arithon raised hands in denial, still grinning. "Not likely. The ladies had wards up. Nobody got hurt. Only curtains were shredded, and a lot of old stonework went flying to bits where their shields couldn't dampen the counterforce."

"Dakar!" cracked the Sorcerer across the schoolboyish mood of jubilation. "Tell me now! However did the Koriani Prime gain foothold to scry across Kieling's wards?"

The Mad Prophet shot straight as if smacked. "I haven't a clue. Ask your prince."

Arithon's exuberance vanished, his mien gone abruptly blank and implacable as a wall. The strained relations between himself and Asandir returned suddenly and in force, and knowing any query the Fellowship might pose would get rebuffed, the Sorcerer abandoned further questions.

His mage-sight offered means to find clear answers. Not even the murk of Desh-thiere could dim the abrupt unshielding of his will as he scrutinized the Master's taut stance. The effect was as merciless to the victim as a field surgery performed with cut glass. Out of stubborn, irate pride, Arithon neither flinched nor hid his face. This despite the shame that even to an uninvolved witness, the feelings bared to view were revealingly personal. Avidly watching, Dakar sweated outright; Lysaer found himself discomfited to the point where honor compelled him to avert his eyes rather than witness a violation of his half-brother's privacy.

But neither Sorcerer nor Master of Shadows had notice to spare for any onlookers, locked as they were in the absolute intimacy of their conflict.

"Compassion," the Sorcerer mused at length, his tone as apparently casual as a man counting facts on his fingers. "The Riathan Paravians set their wards in perfect surety. They never mistake false evidence, for theirs is the perception of Ath Creator. Kieling Tower may admit no force except unconditional love—" Asandir broke off, his face abruptly drained colorless. "The lady enchantress in the hayloft at the Ravens," he surmised, a spike to his tone that caused Lysaer to shiver where he stood.

Now Arithon did speak, his antagonism barely held in check. "The Prime used her. Elaira herself was absent, and had neither knowledge nor consent. Now say to me, and mean it, that her thieving pair of seniors didn't deserve the comeuppance they got."

Confused by a name he could not place, Lysaer watched Asandir weigh the comment, then allow its ferocity to pass. The look he trained upon Arithon held entreaty commingled with pity. "You must never, ever in your life allow Elaira to indulge in her feelings where you are concerned. Her care is real enough, and generous, but to acknowledge her in any way would lead her to ruin. The Koriani creed she is bound to obey is unnaturally opposed to human nature."

"And yours is not?" Arithon spun on his heel and braced his hands on Kieling's embrasure. The mist that streamed past strung droplets in his hair, but the rigidity of his shoulders had nothing to do with its chill. "If I'm to be made a crowned puppet to drag this wasteland out of darkness, I'd hardly entangle a lady along with me."

"See you don't," Asandir snapped back. "Where Elaira is concerned, I shall hold you to your word of honor, Prince of Rathain."

Arithon drew a slow breath, then spun back with the brightest of smiles. "You'll hold me to nothing against my will, Sorcerer. Elaira is secure from my attentions, most certainly, since I'd die before I'd give your Fellowship even one chance of getting an heir."

At this, Asandir released a bright laugh. "Five centuries is a very long abstinence, my prince. And if you want me to think that you hold the enchantress in light regard, you'll need better subterfuge than lying."

"Touché," Dakar murmured from the sidelines. His quip was ignored.

For an instant Arithon looked murderous. Then his green eyes went wide, and he spoke with a candor meant only for the Sorcerer. "What caused you to abandon the resolve you made to me after Maenalle's banquet in Camris?"

The promise of the free will that he was persistently being hounded to abandon stayed unspoken through the gust that raked the battlements.

Already pale, Asandir turned death white. For the first time Dakar could recall, the Sorcerer looked as if he wanted to retreat. He answered instead, though he suffered for it. "You shared for yourself the echo of the mystery that gentles the vales at Caith-al-Caen. Could you bear to see what originated that resonance fade forever from this world? If prescience revealed such a thing might happen, could you stand aside and take no action in prevention?"

"Oh, Ath! Not that!" Arithon gripped the parapet as if warded stonework might steady a universe that rocked under his feet. "Do you say that my kingship over Rathain is connected to recovery of the Paravians?"

"More and worse." Dakar could not resist his chance for vindication. "Refuse your crown, and you seal their final disappearance."

Asandir stayed silent, but the sorrow in his gaze denied nothing.

"Truth or lies!" Arithon exclaimed, suddenly savage. "The needs of this land are killing me, do you understand?"

The desperation to his stance caused Dakar regret for his outburst. Lysaer wished passionately to be any place else in Athera, but pity locked his limbs against movement.

Asandir stared down and appeared to ponder his boots, which were wet and caught with brown bits of gorse from his walk upon the hills of Daon Ramon. "Even so, Teir's'Ffalenn." His gentleness held an implacability that damned as he added, "I had to choose. Now so must you."

"Merciful maker, you call murder a choice?" Arithon's anguish rejected sympathy, enough that none dared to stay him as he spun away toward the stairwell.

Dakar shuffled his feet through the poisoned, abrasive stillness that remained. "I'm surprised you held him to that," he challenged, brash enough to fly in the face of the sorcerer's brittle mood.

But it was Lysaer this time who provoked. "Less than the truth would not bind him, is that it?"

Asandir stirred as if from contemplation of a topic that held ugliness personified. "Truth is like a gem with many facets—reflection and illusion from every outward angle." His damp hair blew in the wind, and his hands hung helplessly as he finished, "The one unsplintered view can only be found from within."

Against all natural inclination, the Sorcerer chose not to correct Lysaer's misapprehension. Truth by itself would not condemn the Paravians to extinction, as Arithon had so harshly presumed; but their exile might indeed become permanent, for by the uncompromising Law of the Major Balance, the old races were not any man's concern unless he embraced them for his own. Truth, Asandir reflected sadly, was the one principle in existence that could release the musician from blood ties to kingly heritage; but the barbs of the trap first closed in Caith-al-Caen had set full well and deeply.

No comfort could be gained that Arithon was physically absent throughout the struggle as his personal desires warred and lost to the burden of guilt-induced duty. Asandir sensed to the second when the Shadow Master's aspect became set. Brooding stillness claimed the Sorcerer as his mage-sight stung him with awareness: for he *saw* the thread of probability that held all of a gifted man's contentment fray away into nothing. The moment passed, and the chance died, that Arithon could become the bard the strands had promised at Althain, a musician cherished across the continent for his generosity and warmth of perception. The legacy of a beloved master singer, whose equal had not been seen since Elshian, for need had been cancelled out. In his place walked a prince whose competence would come to be feared, and whose gifts would be whetted by adversity to a cruelly focused edge.

Arithon would not now refuse the crown that waited at Etarra.

Consolation was nonexistent; through embittered years to come, the Fellowship must hope the man whose dream they had spoiled might become reconciled to the fate he had been coerced to undertake. Paravian survival might be bought with restoration of sunlight and war, but that the old races could be returned in joy to the continent, and the Fellowship be restored back to Seven, was by no means certain. The particulars of Dakar's Black Rose prophecy remained in question still.

Asandir shivered in an icy blast of wind. He tugged his cloak closer to his shoulders and discovered himself alone on the battlements of Kieling. Lysaer and Dakar had abandoned him to solitude, to the depthless mist that sheathed a glowering twilight sky. The Paravian towers seemed to brood through the gloom, lightlessly and empty and dark.

Elsewhere in Ithamon's ruins, Arithon perched on the curve of a fallen corbel, his lyranthe resting silent on his knee. He had chosen his vantage site at random. The littered courtyard before him in prosperous years had served the merchants who supplied broadcloth to the tailors. Those slates not scabbed over with grit and moss showed wheel scars from the drays that had carried imported velvets and brocades from weavers in Cildorn and Narms. But Arithon gave that past no thought where he sat, his hands clasped limp on his soundboard, and his eyes pinched closed in frustration.

His every nerve end was raw.

Music, which had always been his first solace, this day came to him soured. He could not play. Each time he set fingers to strings, the perception that inspired his art left him defenseless against the insatiable whirl of spirit life imbued within ruined Ithamon. Ancestors winnowed past his innermind, calling his name and imploring. Those whose ends had come untimely in the upheaval of the rebellion troubled him less than others born of an earlier era, when Paravians had inhabited the surrounding hills and diversion of the Severnir's waters had not rendered all the land barren. Spirits whose passage through time had left no regrets to sigh in descant between the winter winds; these had touched rock and soil and the weathered remains of fine carving with resounding vibrations of content. Their fragile, lost chord of celebration ached an uncrowned prince the most, for in the absence of heritage and inhabitants, their song cried out for restoration of the city that lay splintered in ruin.

Hounded to sadness by misfortune that he alone was empowered to redress, Arithon sighed. He should have chosen a sword to accompany his mood in this place, not the instrument he cradled in a silence that painfully accused. Stubbornness held him rooted. He would deaden his ear and strike notes that were feelingless, even false, before he opened himself to sorrows that had utterly reft his peace.

A fool he was, to have disdained Asandir's warning in Caith-al-Caen!

Mage-taught wisdom reproached him: any gift of power was two-edged. The awareness of Paravian beauty he had accepted in blithe carelessness now chafed him like a thousand raw sores. But to do without, to close off that channel of inner vision, was to render himself pitiful, to blind himself to hope, and what he now recognized for the shining, enduring truth that set the spirit outside time and mortal decay.

Sooner would he bind himself to the misery promised by the crown of Rathain. Ties of kingship, after all, were only temporary. Death would free him at the end.

Dusk blurred the pewter edges of broken stone. Light bled out of the mist, leaving murk as dense as musty felt. Arithon hunched against the chill, his arms crossed over Elshian's superlative lyranthe, unaware. If he heard the step that approached, he dismissed it along with the spirit forms that plucked incessantly at the conscience he held closed and barred against them—and others, more sinister, that reached as if to tear his living flesh.

"Blessed Ath, here's twice I mistook you for a statue," Lysaer called through the muffling layers of the scarf he had wound at his neck. The temperature had dropped since afternoon, and the air smelled of snow. "You must be freezing."

Arithon opened his eyes and saw that full night had fallen. He changed grip on his lyranthe, discovered his fingers were numb, and flipped down his cuffs to shelter his knuckles from the tireless bite of the wind. A musician's instincts died hard, to preserve the hands from the elements.

"Move over, will you?" Lysaer demanded of the half-brother who appeared to have forgotten him. "I'd like to sit down."

Arithon inclined his head in belated greeting. He shifted aside, his tunic snagging on edges of chipped fretwork. As he braced his shoulder against the broken door post at his back, a gust sang through the lyranthe's exposed strings.

Unsettled by the mournful ring of harmonics, and by the close-bound air of desolation, Lysaer crowded in and attempted without success to settle comfortably. "You pick the most miserable sites for your brooding. Is it perversity, or a masochistic effort to drive away unwanted company?"

Arithon faintly smiled. "Probably both." He did not ask what brought his half-brother out into a dismal winter night when Dakar had slaughtered the ewe bought from a migrant herder. A savory mutton stew was sure to be bubbling over the fire in Kieling's lower ward room, where, uncommon to stone buildings anyplace else, drafts did not chill a man's blood.

Unsurprised to be offered no opening, Lysaer picked at the lichen rooted deep in old carving and said, "I wanted to ask. Did you notice this place is haunted?"

Arithon loosed a bark of sharp laughter. "Did I *notice?*"

Lysaer stayed his impulse to draw away. He might not share his half-brother's inclinations to set music before the needs of kingdom and people, but he had sworn to try to understand. Since Asandir had done little by way of kindness to compensate for unwanted burdens, Arithon's pique was forgivable, if not entirely just.

His eyes on the grain of the marble revealed under his fretful touch, Lysaer tried a fresh approach. "I don't have a mage's sensitivity. Where you and Asandir see mysteries, I find only broken stone that fills me with an unmanly urge to weep." He gestured toward the interlace his hands had cleared of debris. "Except for the remains of their artistry, the Paravians to me are just a name, and the wistful feeling that's left of a dream after waking."

A sidelong glance showed Arithon's manner still inclined toward abstraction.

Reluctantly aware he must reveal himself to establish rapport, Lysaer pressed on. "I think of home and am not comforted. Somehow I sense that Amroth would disappoint me if I were to find my way back. As if this place holds a truth that taunts and eludes me."

Arithon turned his head. He was listening with no trace of his earlier, corrosive sarcasm.

Yet the captured quiet of the Master's attention became no more reassuring; a mage's mystery backed his calm, indefinably poised, and though it might not overtly threaten, it observed in ruthless detail. Lysaer put aside his fear of seeming foolish and forced himself to continue. "The haunting I speak of is not at all the same. I notice it when we are outside the protection of the tower. It seems to grow stronger, more suffocating, the longer we battle the Mistwraith. I wanted to know if you felt anything similar. Do you think the sensation could be connected? With Desh-thiere, that is, not Ithamon."

Now Arithon shivered once, violently, as though his prolonged exposure to the cold all at once caught up with him. His reply came dryly in the darkness. "Why not ask Asandir?"

Lysaer held to patience. "I did."

Arithon only closed his eyes.

The s'Ilessid prince had no choice but to sustain the conversation by himself. "Our Sorcerer contacted Sethvir immediately. The Fellowship sensed nothing amiss, and Dakar was too busy butchering sheep to have an opinion."

Somewhere downslope in the ruins a fox barked. A field mouse rustled through dry grass seeking seeds, and the mist coiled close, despite the wind. Arithon unfolded from his huddle, set his lyranthe carefully by his ankle, and rubbed his temples, disturbed.

Lysaer knew relief, that after Sethvir and Asandir had drawn blanks, the Master did not dismiss his concern as groundless fancy.

In fact, Arithon's disquiet was all personal. To open his mage's perception and sound for whatever uneasy presence had troubled Lysaer was to invite laceration from within. The very timing was a curse. The fullness of Ithamon's spirit legacy was too painful to be sorted so soon after Asandir's revelation concerning the old races' survival. Paravian wards did indeed dampen the sting from Ithamon's hauntings; yet since Kieling's protections were framed of compassion, and Arithon took hurt from his exposure, he had never thought to look deeper. Not once had he paused to question whether something else inherently harmful might have sourced the grace of the wards' surcease. Now that Lysaer had spoken, he berated himself for carelessness. Repeatedly the Rauven mages had stressed that assumptions were the weakness of the learned.

"Asandir and Sethvir found nothing, you say." The statement mused upon fact, and did not ask for answer.

Unsettled by the moist cling of Desh-thiere, Lysaer stopped worrying at the old carving. "You feel it, too," he accused.

Arithon shook his head, emphatic. "Just now I feel nothing. By choice, you understand. If I were to open myself, allow even a chink through my defenses, I'd be helpless and probably crying." He sighed, slapped his hands into his lap, and tilted his crown back into the stone that braced up his spine. "Did you by chance bring a handkerchief?"

"My valet always carried mine for me," Lysaer apologized. He shrugged in wry humor. "Will my shoulder do for a substitute?"

The offer was friendly and genuine—also painful as a slap to a man who wished no ties, at this moment, to anyone outside himself. Pressured to reflexive antagonism, Arithon curbed his angst. A threat that might stem from Desh-thiere was too dangerous a development to be sidelined for personal hurt; never mind that his half-brother lacked perception to understand that he did not care at any cost to drop his inner barriers to use mage-sight in this place.

When nothing moved beyond Arithon's clothing in the ceaseless sweep of the wind, Lysaer said, "You need not act on my word alone."

Arithon cut off protestations. "On the contrary. Given your nature, only a fool would ignore your worry. This begs to be seen to at once."

Now Lysaer shot up straight in dismay. "Here? This minute?" It was night and stingingly cold, never mind that the ruins themselves were unnerving in the extreme.

Clammy and chill, the mist had closed down like a shroud. Objects a half stride away were invisible, and the air smelled of damp decay.

The s'Ilessid prince tried humor to shake off a rising uneasiness. "I always supposed you were crazy. Should I be amazed that you want to freeze our balls to marbles in a ghost hunt?"

Arithon's hand shot out and clamped his half-brother's wrist. "Don't speak." He reached down and recovered his lyranthe with a haste that caused Lysaer alarm.

Amid the dark ruins, the wind had suddenly dropped. Their perch on the corbel abruptly and for no sane reason seemed precarious. Lysaer resisted a nearly overpowering urge to grab for the weapon he had stupidly left behind in the tower. He stifled his need to ask what was wrong, while his half-brother poised, stone still and apparently listening.

The mist held their surroundings pent in gloom. Hearing recorded only an eerie quiet that, under scrutiny, became suspect. No owls called. The mouse in the grass had frozen or fled in fear, and the very air seemed to have gone scentless, the frosty edge of snow and pending storm dissipated into cold that had no character.

Arithon's grip tightened on his half-brother. Just on the point of speaking, the tension that held him seemed to snap. He shot without words to his feet, dragging his half-brother after him. As if something he alone could perceive gave pursuit from the depths of the ruins, he pitched into a run. Lysaer was jerked headlong into flight across the courtyard and onward into a cross alley. Broken walls slapped back echoes of their footfalls and shadows closed over them like ink. A fallen oak barred their exit; Arithon bashed through like a hunted animal, unmindful of the scrape of bare branches as he turned his shoulder to spare his lyranthe. Unsure why they should be fleeing, and perversely suspicious that he might have been spooked by a prank, Lysaer asked to slow down before their dash through the ruins wound up ripping good clothes. But his breath came too fast for speech, and the hold on his wrist hauled him onward.

A moment later, he lost inclination to argue.

Though the breeze had utterly died, on their back trail, the limbs of the downed tree rustled: someone or something was following.

"If I made a mistake, I just compounded a second one," Arithon said, making Lysaer start. "I should have removed our conversation to one of the warded towers."

"What mistake?" Apprehension drove Lysaer to interpret past mage-trained obtuseness. "Our talk was noticed? Do you guess that some aspect of Desh-thiere is alive?"

"More than that." Arithon tugged him to the left, past the pit of a caved-in cellar. "This mist we've been given to subdue could be an intelligent entity, and hostile."

Alarmed, Lysaer said, "Asandir didn't know?"

They turned down a thoroughfare slippery with mossed-over stone, and laced with weeds and briar. Bits of what may have been pottery skittered and chinked underfoot. Perturbed, absorbed, and strangely, invisibly harried as they hacked through hammocks of ivy and tripped uphill toward Kieling Tower, Arithon gasped back, "Likely not." Given time, he might have qualified, but a clear and sudden jab of energy against defenses he had never let down urged him to cry out a warning. "Call light from your gift, now!"

For retreat was no longer an option.

Whatever invisible entity had attracted Lysaer's notice had flanked them and circled their position. Arithon slammed to a halt, jerking his half-brother to him. He spun in a half turn, his shoulder set to Lysaer's as he fought to dredge up wards laced of shadow and what magery he had learned from Rauven.

On faith, Lysaer matched his efforts. Brilliance speared outward, dissolving darkness in a magnesium glare of white heat. Crackled into turbulence by conflicting fields of shadow, close-bound coils of mist recoiled with a shriek of steam. Over the hiss the prince said, "What's happening? Are we under attack?"

"I fear so." Encumbered by his instrument, Arithon sidestepped, jostling Lysaer through a portal and into a weed-choked yard.

"Do you know from what?" Outside the thin blue ring that glimmered in manifestation of his half-brother's hastily wrought ward, Lysaer could see little beyond mist and cracked stone and darkness. He brightened his gift. Light picked out the ragged brick of a forge chimney and a quenching trough blackened with moss. Lysaer banged his hip as he scraped past. He tripped and recovered his footing in time not to stumble over the sharpening wheel that lay canted before a rust-flaked stockpile of scrap.

Arithon came back with a curse. "We face nothing friendly. Beyond that, I won't probe. It's spirit-formed, and unraveling my defenses as fast as I can maintain them. I'm not about to drop barriers to see what seeks to get in." He ripped off his cloak, tearing clasps, and wrapped up his precious lyranthe. Regret marked his face in the flash and dazzle of ward-light as he stooped and abandoned his instrument on the flagstone. "I'd hate to fall and see her break."

Distressed that his half-brother should abandon his most priceless possession, Lysaer asked, "Where are you taking us?"

"Here. The armorer's." Arithon veered toward a pitted anvil, visible in silhouette against the corona thrown off by his protections. "If Desh-thiere's aspects are an earthforce, iron may help turn them back."

But the explanation fell on deaf ears. Lysaer was beyond response. The scintillant hedge of light he had raised to drive back the mist snapped out at the next step. Darkness returned, impenetrable, and without a sound raised in warning, the s'Ilessid prince crumpled at the knees.

Iron did nothing to divert the advance of whatever bleak force moved against them.

Aware too late that his primary wards were ineffective, Arithon grabbed his half-brother's clothing to brake his fall. Through a fast-fading glimmer of failed spell-craft, he perceived a ghostly circle of faces. They closed in, leering with bloodthirsty ferocity. Sweat-drenched with fear, Arithon caught a fleeting impression: their image was wrought of seething mist and their strength was that of a multitude.

These were no part of Ithamon's troubled spirits, but something separate and wholly evil.

Unbalanced by Lysaer's sagging weight, and frightened to outcry by the suffocating sense of closing danger, Arithon let go his mage-formed barrier and lashed out in a fury of shadow.

Night became blackness distilled.

The ever narrowing band of hostile entities winnowed into a dusting of new snow, the mist that clothed their form pared away. Their essence of ferocity stayed untouched. A probe lanced Arithon's mind. He screamed, repulsed, his knuckles spasmed tightly in his half-brother's cloak. Lysaer was dead weight, unconscious, injured, or worse. Just how the attacking Mistwraith had pierced arcane protections to strike could not be figured. In moments Arithon saw his own reserves would crumple. He would be helpless as his half-brother.

Horrified and desperate that not even shadow brought protection, the Master found himself cornered without remedy against an aspect whose resources dwarfed his awareness.

In denial of acknowledged human frailty, he strove to fashion another barrier ward. Counter-forces ate at his efforts like a school of feeding sharks. His guard spells were chopped up piecemeal, his concentration too slow to recoup. Only freak luck had spared him, the protective inner block he had initially raised to distance the haunting of Ithamon's ruins. That shield of itself was under siege, then giving way before an onslaught as relentless as the tides.

Arithon gritted his teeth. He grasped after fraying concentration, panting in the throes of an effort that taxed him like physical pain. Still, the entity streamed past. It cut against his awareness with the pressure of a dull knife driven by the weight of all the world. As he tried and failed again to grapple the disembodied beings that pressed him, he at last knew the scope of the enemy.

The Mistwraith was more than just aware. It was intelligent and bent on retaliation against the princes who were its sure bane. But how it had hidden its multiply faceted nature, even from the Fellowship of Seven, Arithon lacked resource to determine. Battered to the bitter edge of consciousness by an assault his skills could never stem, he staggered.

Light flashed.

Harsh, searing glare rinsed away the dark. Running footsteps sounded over the wind-rush of foundering senses, and a shout echoed through Ithamon's ruins.

Beaten to his knees in wet moss, Arithon ripped out a reply. His cry brought help. A ward circle slashed into existence with a fountainhead of purple-white sparks. Hands caught his shoulders in support, and Asandir's voice said, "Let go. Dakar has hold of Lysaer."

Awash in dizziness, shocked off balance by the proximity of forces beyond imagining, Arithon loosed his grip. "Desh-thiere," he gasped out. "It's self-aware. More dangerous than any of us guessed."

"Let me turn my shields against it," said the Sorcerer. No longer leashed, his power radiated from him until the air in his presence blazed light, a flash and dazzle of force too piercing for fleshly endurance. Vibrations of palpable current caused inert rock to ring with shared resonance until the earth itself sang in answer. Arithon braced against shock from the contact as Asandir towed him to his feet.

But the Sorcerer's touch stayed surprisingly human and warm, until the moment sensation itself became cancelled by the annihilating surge of the wardfields. Asandir's protections unfurled around beleaguered flesh like a deluge of rays from a beacon. Arithon felt the invading pressure against his innermind relent with a soundless howl of rage.

Disparity remained, a sting in the mind that raised puzzlement.

For Desh-thiere was not repulsed. It did not join in conflict with Asandir's bared might, but with disorienting and baffling speed, seemed to fade beyond the pale of dimensional awareness.

The repercussions of this anomaly blurred as Arithon collapsed against the Sorcerer's shoulder.

There came no respite even then.

Harsh fingers seized his arm, spun him remorselessly around. He was aware of steel gray eyes and Asandir's implacable will boring into his consciousness with the directness of an awl piercing cloth. He had no reflex left to flinch. "I'm all right," he managed to convey, through the roaring cyclone of wardforce.

"We'll see," Asandir replied. To Dakar he added, "Drag Lysaer, or carry him. But we must get back to Kieling as quickly as we may."

"Lysaer?" Arithon asked weakly. He felt sick. The ground seemed to twist and buckle under his feet.

Asandir's response came back clipped. "Alive. Can you walk?"

The Master took a step and stumbled. Hands caught him up before he fell, cruel in their hurry to keep him moving. He managed to find his balance before the Sorcerer lost patience and lifted him, but he remembered little of the journey back through Ithamon's twisted lanes to the safety of the upper citadel.

Arithon's next impression was sight of the interlaced carving inside the double arches of Kieling Tower's lower entry. The runes seemed reversed and upside-down, an angle of view that disoriented him until he realized: Asandir had needed to carry him after all. He had a raging headache. The searing brilliance of magelight that had sourced the Sorcerer's protections had gone, rendered unnecessary by the ringing, subliminal vibration that marked the bounds of Paravian wards. A quietude as abiding as the heart rock of the earth enfolded around the party in Asandir's protection.

The calm brought surcease, but no ease of mind.

The nearly cataclysmic forces the Sorcerer had raised against attack remained stamped indelibly into memory.

Awe remained.

It was one thing to sense past shielded resonance to the potential of a Fellowship mage; quite another, to experience such potency unveiled in the close-pressed immediacy of action. Flame from the wall sconces showed Asandir's face etched to the planes of his bones by passage of the powers channeled through him. That a spirit of such vast resource should still be walking, clothed in humanity and flesh, defied comprehension. And yet the mage was himself. His expression reflected no grand depths, but only self-recrimination as he turned his head and saw Arithon had recovered awareness.

"My prince, I'm sorry." This admission played no part in the conflict that, only hours before, had sealed a prince to an unwanted destiny.

Disarmed, even shamed by the affection in Asandir's concern, Arithon evaded the personal. "How did you know Lysaer and I needed rescue?"

Driven off by banality, the poignancy of the moment fled. Asandir said, "I was given warning. The wards in your sword, Alithiel, went active and all but set fire to your clothes chest." The Sorcerer helped Arithon to a chair by the hearth, tossed him a blanket, then moved briskly to assist Dakar with Lysaer, who was unconscious still, and pale as a carving in wax.

Kieling Tower's wardroom no longer held the bleakness of an edifice standing whole amid a ruin. Its worn plank floor was made cheerful by a spread of Narms carpet, hauled from Althain Tower in the dray. Asandir's books lay piled near a wrought brass candle stand on an ebony inlaid table. Four chairs, without cushions, had been salvaged from a dusty upper chamber. In the pot over the flames, stew still bubbled as though all in the world were yet ordinary. Burrowed in blankets and handed a mug of bitter tea, Arithon lay settled and still, content to let the resonance of the Paravian defenses permeate his awareness. He drew in the smell of cedar from the delicate, patterned panels that adorned the wardroom walls. To mage-trained eyes the interlaced carvings of vines and animals sang with vibrant inner resonance. Whatever Paravian artisans had done the reliefs had instilled true vision in the work. To behold them was to share an echoed reflection of the great mystery that endowed the land with life. Slowly the chill that had invaded the inner tissues of Arithon's body flowed away into warmth. He released a last violent shudder. As if called by that movement from across the room, Asandir arose, leaving Dakar to watch the s'Ilessid prince, who was sleeping, perhaps under spell.

A second later, the Sorcerer knelt at Arithon's side in concern. "You look steadier. Can you tell me what happened?"

Haggard as though he had stepped intact out of a nightmare, Arithon considered the muddled impressions that remained. "You saved our lives and didn't see?"

The Sorcerer rested slack hands on his knees and stared aside into the fire. The play of bronze-gold light deepened the creases around his mouth and other finer lines that arrowed from the corners of his eyes. "I know you were assaulted by a manifestation of Desh-thiere. I'm not clear why, or how. Even Sethvir was fooled into belief the creature wasn't sentient." If the admission humbled him, it did not show; his gaze remained lucent as sun-flecked crystal beneath the jut of his frown.

Arithon closed his eyes, hands that had not stopped shaking clamped hard on his tea mug. "You were looking for an entity that had just one aspect?" he suggested, for the moment no prince but a mage sharing thoughts with a colleague.

Across a chamber whose unearthly symmetry was made squalid by the smell of mutton grease, Dakar stowed his bulk by the settle, surprised. "But there's no living spirit in existence that a Fellowship mage cannot track!"

Arithon fractionally shook his head. Desh-thiere had proven the exception: a thing wrought of who knew what malice, in the sealed-off worlds beyond South Gate.

Asandir maintained a charged stillness. As if perplexed by a twist in a puzzle, he only appeared detached as he said, "Whatever the Name of the Mistwraith, it maimed Traithe's continuity of function. Are you telling me the creature has spirit, and that it encompasses more than one being?"

"Try thousands," Arithon whispered. He opened his eyes. "Too many to number separately, and all of them bound captive in hatred. Our efforts with light and shadow here have been systematically reducing the mist and the area that confines them, nothing else."

"Ath's eternal mercy" was all the Sorcerer said. Yet as a shifting log in the fireplace fanned a spurt of flame, shadows shrank to show alarm on a face seldom given to uncertainty.

"But that can't be possible," Dakar interjected. "If it were, how could Desh-thiere's vapors cross Kieling's wards at will?"

"Easily," Arithon murmured, unnerved also but applying himself to the problem through habit and years of self-discipline. "The mist is no more than a boundary wrought of dampness. The entities I encountered move within it, self-contained. Paravian defenses bar them entrance, but not the fog that imprisons their essence."

Asandir did not contradict the Master's supposition. At some point his awareness had faded from the room, diffused outward into a net that expanded over the ruins.

Arithon was seer enough to catch impressions in resonance. Under his grandfather's tutelege at Rauven, he had studied the close-woven relationships that conjoined all worldly things. As he had traced the paths of his teacher's meditations into the nature of such interconnectedness, so he followed Asandir's scrying now. Yet where the Rauven mages had known how to feel out the paths of the air, to read in advance the wind-spun flight of dry leaves; how to sense warmth amid mist-chilled trees, and recognize a bird asleep with head tucked under wing; how to link with the weighty turn of the earth, the limning of frost crystals on grasses raked dry by the season; the perception of a Fellowship Sorcerer saw deeper.

Fully aware of Arithon's attentiveness, Asandir hid nothing. And like the unfolding of a painted fan, or a span of fine-spun tapestry shown whole to a blind man through miracle, Arithon saw familiar natural forms wreathed about with the silver-point etchings of their energy paths. The sheer depth of vision overwhelmed him.

Asandir did not see stone but the crystalline lattices that matrixed its substance, *and beyond that* to the delicate, ribbon-like glimmers that were the underpinnings of all being, that stabilized vibration into matter. More, as a man might know his most treasured possessions, the Sorcerer recognized everything he scried, not according to type but in Name, that unique understanding of every object's individuality. He held the signature of each plant, from the seed that had thrown up its first sprout, to the days of sunlight and storms that marked its growth, to the twigs and every turned leaf ever shed by the grown tree. One oak he would know from every other oak, living or decayed or unsown, on the basis of just one glance. Stresses, disease, or the robustness of perfect health were delineated plainly to his eye. He knew frost crystals, not as frozen water but as single and separate patterns in all of their myriad billions. Their Names were as visible to him as signatures. He knew the pebbles of the dry watercourse, each and every one by touch, and the tangles of bundled energies that signified each grain of sand. The detail, the sheer magnitude of caring such depth of perspective demanded, dwarfed the watching spirit.

Arithon found himself weeping. Not only for himself and the deadness of his senses, but for the beauty of common weeds and the unendurable complexity of the shed husk of a beetle's wing. He saw again, through finer eyes, the resonance of Paravian presence, and saw also that the coarseness in a clod of horse dung was held into balance by the same singing bands of pure energy. In Asandir's pass across the ruins of Ithamon, Arithon realized just how shallow was his own knowledge, and how inadequate. With punishing clarity he understood the scope of just what he had abandoned when he had left Rauven and yielded himself to another will, another fate, another calling; now, most bitterly, the loss would repeat and compound, as he assumed a second unwanted crown.

Then Asandir closed down his field of concentration. Released from that terrible mirror of truth which embodied a Fellowship mage's awareness, Arithon came back to himself and recalled the dangers that had prompted the search.

For all its awesome depth, the scrying disappointed. Tumbled stonework had harbored nothing untoward, only the mindless tenacity of lichens living dormant under the mantle of winter night. The Sorcerer had unreeled his probe past the city's edge, across untold miles of Daon Ramon's heartland, but no sign had he encountered anywhere of those aspects of Desh-thiere that had launched attack with such startling virulence.

No movement could be found but the flight of night-hunting owls; no death beyond the grass roots grazed by hares; no sound but the play of wind through dry brush. The Mistwraith's fog was just that—mist coiled cold in the hollows, lifelessly damp and inert.

Asandir snapped off the last of his vision in a curtness born of frustration. "I cannot find it." His voice held a scraped edge of pain, not for humiliation that his resource seemed short for the task, but for failure and heart-sore apology that the Fellowship's oversight had emperiled two princes whose safety was his charge to secure.

"But how can that be?" Dakar cried, his hands too cramped to pick up the spoon to stir the stew pot.

And Arithon wondered the same. The arts of grand conjury were wrought from the force that quickened the universe. Asandir's vision had but confirmed Rauven's teaching: that all things were formed of energy, arrangements of bundled light that were subject to natural law. The awareness of this truth, defined to absolute perfection, granted the mage-trained their influence. To know a thing, to encompass its full measure in respect was to hold its secrets in mastery. Life force was the basis of all power; as a confluence of collective entities, Desh-thiere's consciousness should have been vividly plain.

That its nature could in any way stay hidden seemed outside sane comprehension.

To anyone trained to the subtleties of power, it felt as if an evil of unknown proportions had sown chaos across the fabric of natural order.

His plaintiveness a mask for desperation, Dakar said, "What in Athera could escape the vigilance of the Seven?"

"Nothing of Athera." Arithon shifted gaze to the Sorcerer, his earlier antagonism set in abeyance. "I was blind to the Mistwraith's aspects also, until the moment they chose to attack."

Asandir stirred. "Neither strands nor seer can read Desh-thiere, only its effects. That this trait may also apply to the moment we know as the present is dangerous enough, but pursuit of the reason must wait. My first concern stems from need to build sound defenses, that our efforts don't call down some worse threat."

Dakar watched, afraid to move, as Fellowship mage and s'Ffalenn prince shared a deep understanding. Jolted to fey sight by the combined effects of exhaustion and fear and disillusion, for a split second Dakar perceived the scintillant brilliance of Asandir's being in mirror image, alike except in dimension to the pattern that was Arithon.

Then the trickster play of firelight and the fusty smell of drying wool overrode the spellbinder's fickle talent. The tableau shrank back to the unremarkable: a careworn, weatherbeaten old man in a rumpled mantle bent over a younger one left limp and tired.

To the Master so narrowly delivered from the malice of the Mistwraith he had pledged to subdue, Asandir said, "Sleep. Let the problem bide in my hands until morning."

A gentle edge of spell-craft laced the words. Calm to a depth that transcended pity, Asandir waited for the prince he had betrayed to sort his feelings. Although the offering of serene rest might have been rebuffed by a thought, Arithon capitulated with a gratitude that gave the Sorcerer startled pause. Despite the new depths of yearning unveiled through tonight's shared scrying, no grudge remained in this prince who had been shackled in guilt to a fate he had not wanted. The very s'Ffalenn compassion that sealed the trap in the end prevailed to bring absolution. The wounding begun in Caith-al-caen, that no effort at indifference might heal, would be carried into kingship in selfless silence.

Humbled by a forgiveness he had never expected to receive, Asandir stood stunned and still. Then he smiled as if touched by light, reached out with hands that could wring raw force from bedrock, and in a visible effort not to fumble, rearranged the blankets around the Master of Shadow. He tucked the musician's fingers with their contradictory scars and calluses into the warmth of dry wool, and set a binding of peace upon his handiwork.

When at length he straightened to address his apprentice, his face had assumed the bleakness of glacier-scarred granite. "We have a full night ahead. Lysaer had none of his half-brother's protections, and we must not presume him unharmed. Luhaine has been called to our aid. Kharadmon is already back at Althain, since Sethvir believes our princes' encounter could key insight into how Traithe came to be crippled. If we cannot unmask the nature of the enemy, we must determine what lets it slip at will through any but Paravian safe-wards. Otherwise, there can be no restored sun, for we'll have no means to contain the part of Desh-thiere that is spirit."

From his refuge on a bench by the settle, Dakar caught the poker from its peg. Clumsy in movement, his stocky calves dangling above the floor, he leaned to stir up the fire. The fact he had neglected to mind the supper pot this once in his life did not irk him. "If the thing is alive," he surmised in reference to the Mistwraith, "we cannot follow through and kill it, can we?"

"*If* it is alive," Asandir corrected, impatient as if drawn on wire. "If the life forces we witnessed were not born of illusion, if it is a being or beings embodied into mist, think, Dakar. We let our princes 'kill' it, reduce its confining vessel of fog, what then will be left?"

Hunched as a terrified child, the poker dangling from deadened hands, Dakar whispered. "Pure spirit. Ath's mercy, we'd actually be setting the thing *free*."

"So I fear, my prophet," Asandir allowed. "If, like our disembodied colleagues of the Fellowship, the creature as unfettered spirit could shift its vibration and continue to manifest in this world, so I most desperately fear." He followed with swift instructions that called for another trip out into the inclement night to set more wards of guard over the inner citadel.

Dakar glared at the stew pot, and the hot supper that must, of necessity, be eaten in savorless haste. With his chin cupped in his hands, and the ratty muffler he felt too chilled to shed trailing in twists about his ankles, he looked morose as a vagabond evicted from an alehouse. "Now, why couldn't I have chosen to be a tinker?" he demanded of the leaping fire. "Fixing holed pots would be better fun than banishment of invisible ghosts at night in a wind-plagued ruin."

"I agree," snapped Asandir. "Now get moving." Crisper than a whip crack, the Sorcerer stepped to where Lysaer lay under tidy heaps of blankets. "If we don't make certain this prince took no hurt from Desh-thiere, the leaky pots in this land aren't going to matter very much."

Backsearch

The blizzard whirled in off the bittern desert and eddied snow through the casement fanned a diamond dusting of ice across the carpet in Althain Tower's copy chamber. Sethvir's ink pots had frozen with their quills stuck fast where they stood, yet the Sorcerer appeared not to care. Clad in rumpled robes, his hair raked into tufts like some itinerant roadside fortune-teller's where he had savaged it with his knuckles, he glared at the dregs in his tea mug, cooled now to a mush of bitter leaves. As though the turnings of the world could indeed be read in the floating debris, he addressed a chamber that appeared to hold only books. "The damage, if that broad a term can apply to an attack of such focused proportion, has already been done."

Kharadmon's voice replied out of empty air, near a hearth heaped with ash that had not been raked since Asandir's departure. "But then the disturbance left by the Mistwraith's meddling should be obvious. To wit, a contradiction: Luhaine and Asandir found nothing amiss with Prince Lysaer."

"They checked in depth, I know," Sethvir said, brusque since the past night's report from Ithamon left him frustrated. Barring self-growth and maturation of character, Lysaer was, spirit and flesh, the same young man who had entered Athera through West Gate.

The Warden of Althain cocked his wrist, idly swirling his tea leaves as if the point in debate were not dire, demanding of his closest attention. To Kharadmon he admonished, "You're analyzing the nature of the universe, based on one view through a keyhole."

"Analogies again?" Cold air swirled snowflakes across the chamber; when embodied, Kharadmon had tended to pace, and as spirit, his restlessness was constant. "Which keyhole, then? Back your theory."

A rise of tufted eyebrows evinced Sethvir to be miffed. "Hunch," he corrected. He set the tea mug aside with contradictory care, as if soggy herbs could change nature at whim, and become brittle and subject to shatter. "My keyhole is present time, and Traithe's plight should bear out my conjecture." His ink-stained fingers cupped air. An image flickered to life as defined as a flame on a freshly lit candle. The reflected scene was not new. Time after weary time, in strands and in fire, the Fellowship Sorcerers had reviewed the moment of South Gate's closing, and the fate of the colleague who had single-handedly stemmed the disaster. . . .

The porphyry pillars of South Gate reared white-edged in the static flash of stressed energies. Weather forces skewed out of balance and a storm-charged sky raked the earth with lightning. Thunder slammed, and rain sheeted like a fall of slivered needles through the hellish play of light. Even after five centuries, the view could still inspire dread, as Desh-thiere erupted through the portal between worlds. It came on, gale-driven masses of fog like the boiled-over brew from a witch's cauldron. Toward the streaming influx at the gate, a lone figure plowed its way forward: Traithe, fighting a cyclone of disturbed air that twisted his robes and harried his progress to a standstill. . . .

There the image poised, with Traithe's face obscured behind the wind-flagged fabric of his sleeve. One hand raked out to fend off what seemed empty air, or perhaps a questing tendril of mist. Even locked against motion, the recalled moment from the past was confused by the violent extremes of the light.

"We interpreted the turbulence as wind shear," Sethvir murmured, "caused by the current through the gate. Now I think differently."

"An attack by Desh-thiere?" Kharadmon's stillness was telling. "The vortex centers upon Traithe, true enough, but its content is no more than mist. Sentient life force is nowhere in evidence."

"Apparently." Sethvir loosed his binding, and the vision continued forward once again. The sting of its following sequence hurt no less, for being a foregone conclusion. . . .

* * *

The revealing sleeve cracked away as Traithe raised his hands.
His expression no longer reflected the calm of a sorcerer in control of
his craft, but revealed a man in abject agony. Thunder reverberated,
cut through by his scream as storm and mist tightened down into a
whirlwind that battered him to his knees. He rallied in an extremity
of effort. Power answered. Raw, white, and wild as elemental light-
ning, it stabbed down at his call, wrapping like light-jagged wire
around his wrists and arms. It flowed untrammeled into his em-
brace, flowering into dazzling brilliance that slapped the eyes like a
nova, blinding, impenetrable, and wholly dedicated to ruin. The
Mistwraith recoiled, radiant with an afterglow of live charge. Its
coils rolled back and separated, to lay bare the pearlescent span of
South Gate. During the moment while its invading flow was inter-
rupted, a charred figure in spark-shot robes dragged itself up from
prostration. It raised hands seared with burns and traced a seal of
binding upon the air. Broken with agony, Traithe croaked out the
Names that composed the chant of ending. And like a sling cord re-
leased from great tension, spells sheared asunder; the webwork of
time bonds and energies that enabled South Gate as a grand portal
parted like singed silk and dissipated.

The Mistwraith's connection was severed, its vapors denied fur-
ther invasion. Rain lashed across the soil between the dead gate. It
pocked light-edged arrows in the puddles that interlaced into
streamlets of runoff. Traithe remained, a cramped silhouette that
could have passed for a pile of discarded rags, but for the fact that
he wept with the deep, shaking sobs a child might utter in pain and
terror.

Again the image paused, and like a file scraping rust from old
steel, Sethvir's commentary resumed.

"What if the backlash that maimed Traithe was not the mishan-
dling of grand conjury we first supposed? By intent, our colleague
may have caused his own binding to be grounded through his flesh.
The sacrifice makes sense, if in desperation he sought to burn out an
incursion of the enemy."

Cryptic as always, and now on the far side of the chamber,
Kharadmon said, "You suggest Desh-thiere's aspects besieged his
mind."

"Yes. Traithe opened himself to its essence, to find its Name, and
gain ascendency over it. He should not have been vulnerable, *unless*
the beings he sounded were out of phase from our time sense, re-
moved from our present a half step into the future."

Kharadmon seized the logical progression. "Traithe would naturally raise wards. But his countermeasure perforce would have been a fatal fraction too slow, perpetually behind the leading edge of Desh-thiere's attack."

"So I surmise." Sethvir stared at the space where the spirit of his colleague now rested. Neither of them spoke the painful truth, that to know a true Name in all of its individual ramifications was to hold power to unmake its being. Paradox, and at times cruelest irony, that mages who survived to gain such depths of wisdom were disbarred by understanding of the universe from use of the spells of Unbinding.

Sethvir fixed again on the image he had raised from five hundred years past, and resumed the dropped thread of conversation. "I postulate that Traithe seared away half of his awareness, truncated his own vision by blasting it out with raw power, that Desh-thiere could be stopped from enslaving him. He burned it out as a hill warrior might hack off a limb with a septic wound, by his own hand rendering himself crippled."

Traithe had lost memory in the process, and the greater vision that founded his faculties, and all trace of the Name of the being that had brought him to the brink of total ruin.

In a pass made savage by sorrow, Sethvir waved away his conjured image. "We are warned too late. Last night in Ithamon, Desh-thiere's aspects did not challenge Asandir's wards. Neither did they retreat; they simply passed elsewhen. Into another time. That implies their purpose was complete. My guess is our Teir's'Ilessid shows no sign of disparate change because the moment when tonight's damage shall manifest is still yet to come, and of a surety chosen most carefully."

"Arithon's coronation in Etarra," Kharadmon summed up grimly. "It will be there. Desh-thiere's intervention caused the strands to converge without digression."

Ferociously grim, all without words, Sethvir and Kharadmon shared their night's surmises: that if Desh-thiere's aspects were advanced enough to slip the constraints of time, the Fellowship as it stood could do little more than bind temporary wards against recurrence.

"A bit like closing the barn door after the cattle have been raided," Kharadmon raged, and snowflakes whirled like dust devils from one side of the carpet to the other.

"Restored back to Seven, we could resolve this." Sethvir sighed. As papers and parchments started to flap and whirl across the disarray of his writing table, he grabbed frozen ink pots and pressed them into service as paper weights. "Either still yourself, or stop the natural wind by closing the casement. My belongings cannot handle both at once." Sorrowfully mild, the Warden of Althain added, "We are as ants, scurrying in vain to stay a rock slide. You know that if we are ever to see an end to this threat, the coronation at Etarra must be permitted to run its disastrous course."

"I was aware, and wondering why rats and Dakar's prophecies were ever let into Ath's creation." The casement swung closed with a bang, and brass latches snicked into their settings. Left ringing across windless silence was Kharadmon's sardonic parting statement: "Like the raven in advance of the war, I go to call Traithe to the bloodletting."

Dispatch

The fenlands of southeast Tysan were a deserted and miserable wilderness to be caught in a snowfall on the shortened days past solstice. On foot in the mire, deep in a thicket of leafless willows and marsh maples, Elaira braced an arm on her mare's steaming shoulder. She scraped ice from a lock of hair that had escaped her hood, while flakes flecked with sleet whirled and rattled across frozen pools and the stalks of last season's cattails. Called away by Morriel's summons from the Koriani hostel by Hanshire, she had avoided the trade roads along the coast. The Prime Circle by this season would have resettled in winter quarters near Mainmere, where a ruined fortress deserted since the fall of the high kings of Havish overlooked the coast. The southern pass through Tornir Peaks offered the safest route, since the marshes and sink-pools that edged the high country were too sparsely settled to interest the headhunters who ranged through Korias and Taerlin seeking Caithwood's clansmen as trophies.

However more secure the boglands might be, amenities for travelers were nonexistent. The mare had cast a shoe in sucking mud, and if she was to escape going sore on the rockier ground in the highlands, Elaira was obliged to find a smith.

"As if any right-thinking craftsman would choose to keep shop in a swamp," she complained to the sedges that hooked her ankles and her only live companion, the horse. The bay nosed her hood, her breath a warm cloud in the damp.

"Why couldn't you rip off your shoe in the drifters' country?" The enchantress squelched over a hummock. "Better horsemen aren't born in Athera. Here we'll be lucky to find a trapper who knows how to work iron."

The mare stamped, and the skin of frozen water overtop of oozing mud chinked like shattered glazing over the knees of the oak roots.

"All right, we'll go on, then." Elaira picked her way to the next hummock without any thought to remount. Footing was chancy in the fens, where falling snow and fog could blend with Desh-thiere's mist and turn visibility to a wall of featureless white. A traveler could stray from the trail between one step and the next, and stay lost, to die of starvation or drowning. Sometimes old bones resurfaced in the sinkholes, clean-picked by scavenger fish.

Elaira slogged through a hollow, her boots already sodden from the iced-over, peat brown puddles that never quite managed to take her weight. The cold was so bitter, it hurt. To take her mind off discomfort, she noted the plants as she passed: the fibrous, half-rotted stems of marsh mallow, and sword-blade stands of cattails. Her mind catalogued them all, from the renwort, whose berries brewed poison, to the cailcallow and willow bark, valued to ease fevers. She saw through winter's sere mantle where watercress would flourish, and which hollows, clear of snow, held hot springs that might harbor green felscrine. Healing herbs were part and parcel of Koriani learning, and lately Elaira had devoted herself to memorizing tedious recipes for tisanes.

As if the annals of granny lore and crumbled texts passed down by generations of dead herbalists might help her to bury the memory of one inopportune encounter in a tavern hayloft.

So intense was her concentration, and accustomed as she had become to the startling, raucous calls of marsh pheasants and the whir of their wingbeats as they flew from her step, that she failed to notice the children until they were nearly upon her.

A motley band of seven, they were flying across the frozen streambeds on skates, clad in the same buff and browns as any other native creature of the fens. Yelling, screaming for pure pleasure, they raced and jostled through the stands of willow and mudbrake, until the mare shied back from their exuberance.

The snort of a horse where strangers seldom passed startled them. Heads turned, half seen through the stands of silver-barked, vine-choked maple; then a chickadee's trill cried warning. Their play ended in a scraping slide of bone runners as they whirled into hiding behind the thickets, hushing the youngest, who was frightened and starting to cry.

"It's all right!" Elaira's call raised no echo across what now seemed empty marsh. The pools lay pewter gray against peat black verges, and the snow, like salt rime on the hummocks; the sleet had let up to a whisper. Through streaming shreds of mist, even the sedges did not rustle. "I won't harm any of you. I don't even carry a weapon."

"Show us," shouted a boy whose voice had just finished changing. "Throw off your cloak."

Elaira swore under her breath. Wet as she was, the cold would cut through to her skin. She unhooked her ring broach and shed the heavy wool, in time to get a drenching as the ungrateful mare shook her mane.

The enchantress wore no belt beyond a sash of knotted wool. The only metals on her were three talisman buttons fashioned of copper coins, charms she still wore out of sentiment from her days as a street thief, for luck; and the hunting knife last used to strip branches for snares that most maddeningly had trapped nothing. Yesterday's supper pot had stayed empty.

"Turn around," said the boy.

Elaira held her arms outstretched and did so, though briars caught at her clothing. "I could use a dry place to sleep, and fresh supplies." Fighting a shiver that made her teeth chatter, she added, "I can pay."

Around her, the children had begun to creep from concealment. They ranged in age from ten years to late teens, the bloom on their cheeks the only bright color about them. Their clothing was fashioned of leather, small furs stitched together, and the woven fibers of fenland flax, all undyed. If most of them were dirty, their hair was brushed or braided, and each one carried little talismans of feathers, believed to be ward against drowning. Elaira threw on her cloak, which had fully had time to grow cold. She confronted a closing ring of wide, curious eyes, and said, "Of course, you do have a village?"

They led her off the trail, their shyness loosening into chatter. By their accent Elaira guessed them to be descendents of farmers displaced by the rebellion; survivors sometimes banded with exiles, outcast from the coastal settlements for some petty misdeed committed forgotten generations in the past. Refuge could be found in the fens, or the mountains, or the wilds too open or too barren to support the more numerous clanborn. Forage in such backlands was scarce, and the trust of the inhabitants, reserved; yet they understood the grace of hospitality more than rich families in the towns. By the time Elaira had reached the circle of huts built of mud brick and thatch, her mare carried two boys and a girl, all solemnly trying in their excitement not to spur the beast who bore them with the bone-bladed runners of their skates.

"Traveler!" shouted the oldest boy, and out of the huts came the fen folk.

Reed thin, gnarled as swamp roots, they looked unremittingly dour. Their generosity was not. Like their young ones, they made Elaira welcome once assured she was unarmed. Within an hour, her mare was settled in a pen of woven withies, and she, blessedly bathed and dry, sat before a peat fire sipping tea brewed from plants she had heretofore torn clothes on. The children stayed clustered around her, asking questions and staking buttons on the game of knucklebones she had taught them. Too young to be fascinated by gambling, the youngest squatted on the furs at her feet, picking up the unlaced ends of her bootlaces and trying to stuff them in his mouth.

"Come away." Elaira reached down through the press to raise the baby clear of temptation. "I don't think the mud will help the taste."

The thwarted child shrieked. His noise did nothing to obscure another, louder scream, this one issuing from outside.

Elaira was startled to her feet. The cry repeated, now identifiably the voice of the hut matron, gone out at dusk to haul in fresh water for the stew pot.

Elaira set the boy child aside on the stool, while the others ran like rabbits into the crannies between tied coils of basket reed. Trouble was no stranger to them, and even the little ones did not whimper. Grasping the crystal that hung at her neck, the enchantress leaped over the boys' abandoned knucklebones and burst out into icy winter air.

There she poised. Behind her, the hut door creaked closed on leather hinges. While the slush slowly numbed her dry toes, she struggled to fathom the source of the trouble. For off in the fens where the springs rose warm from the ground, the woman still screamed, wrenchingly, piercingly panic-stricken.

The sleet had stopped; the wind smelled oddly sharp. Elaira blinked. Her eyesight was all wrong.

The shadows, everywhere, lay crisp as knives and too blue. The diamond whiteness of the drifts hurt the eyes. Against them, reeds and winter-stripped thickets seemed to leap out, starkly honed as sword edges. Maples, swamp oaks, and willows showed their details in unnatural sharpness, their top branches delineated like entangled skeins, or blown ink. Elaira gulped a quickened breath. The mist had gone. Vanished. Around her, the night was fogless and bright. The spell crystal slipped forgotten from her fingers as she tipped her head, wondering, to view the sky.

There, between the black frames of bare branches, for the first time in life she saw stars: more beautiful than Morriel's diamonds, adrift in an indigo field that looked deep and vast as forever. Elaira was swept by a primal shiver of elation that transformed to a pealing shout of joy. "They've done it! Bless the blood royal of Athera, the West Gate prophecy is accomplished! Come out and look! Desh-thiere is beaten to retreat!"

But the door to every wattle and mud hut stayed fast shut. Elaira's wonderment was rudely knocked short as the howling, terror-struck fen wife clawed past in a headlong dash to reach safety.

Elaira picked herself out of the mud in resignation. The rank smell of swamp was an offense she would not be escaping for some while yet to come. Disenchantment still could not touch her. Euphoria and the undreamed-of beauty in the sky lent her boundless capacity to forgive. The soft, silvery light that limned the fens was a wonder, more miracle than magic, less substantive than breath. Elaira's honest nature could not shirk the truth: if not for Asandir's gift of trust, and without her privileged access to Koriani archives, she would have been as ignorant of the sky behind Desh-thiere as these fenlanders who cowered in abject terror.

For the rest of the evening, she tried to make amends. She rescued stew pots from burning to char over abandoned fires; she wore herself hoarse cajoling the fen folk out from under blankets, or barricades of upended furniture thrown hastily against doorways and root cellars. She used her crystal, set seals of peace and of calm until her fingers ached from making sigils in the air with the precision an enchanter's art required. Her success at such efforts was debatable. The settlement's headman found solace in a pottery jar of crude spirits, while one elderly grandmother continued to shriek and weep obscenities from under a mountain of bedclothes. Grateful to be spared from the wider-spread bedlam that must have afflicted the towns, Elaira finally yielded to weariness and answered her own need for quiet.

She threw on her cloak. Outside, in solitude, she stared at the miracle of unveiled stars in an amazement that renewed with each passing moment.

The deep-bound silence of the fenlands that always before had oppressed her now invited exploration of new mystery. Trees looked different, dappled in subliminal shadow and the fine-spun subtleties of starlight. Ice looked more silver than gray, and hollows, soft in their shadows as rich men's velvets. The amazing acuity of outdoor vision

she absorbed in sheer delight. Other avenues of thought she forbade
through brute force of will.

Discipline like iron let her look upon beauty and never once contemplate a desolate site in Daon Ramon, where a black-haired prince
labored with his half-brother to bring such a miracle to pass.
Morriel's warning was serious, and had in sober fear been taken to
heart. For whole days Elaira had succeeded in allowing no chink for
regret. She prided herself on unshaken performance through this supreme test, of bared skies and her first sight of stars.

She trembled, excited to imagine how untrammeled sunlight was
going to look. Envy did not sting her as she realized that those sister
initiates assigned the quieter duty of lane-watch most likely already
knew. Elaira wrapped her hands in her leathers. Contented despite
cold, and loneliness, and the desolation of the marsh by midnight,
she awaited the advent of dawn.

During that hard-won moment of balance, the message from the
First Senior reached her. It smote her through the pulse of the second-lane energies, and its directive shattered all peace:

*"To Elaira, revised orders from the Prime Enchantress: upon the
Mistwraith's defeat at Ithamon, the Fellowship of Seven has plans to
arrange the high king's coronation at Etarra. You are commanded to
journey there, to bring back for Koriani scrutiny your most intimate
insights into the royal princes' characters."*

Guard, Ward, and Bard

The gusts that sweep the broken outer walls of Ithamon join force with a second current, not natural, that twists the dead grasses and kicks up dry leaves in drifts; looking to the eye like a wind devil, the discorporate Sorcerer Luhaine lays wards against Desh-thiere that cut across time as well as worldly dimension.

When sunlight breaks finally over Havistock, the Sorcerer Traithe takes his leave of the craftsman who stands as foster parent to the growing heir to Havish: "Prince Eldir will assume his inheritance after Rathain's succession has been settled in Etarra. But let us be clear that until then, his studies continue. He is not to be excused from the dye vats."

North, in the town of Ward, under skies still grayed by Desh-thiere's mists, an elderly bard contains bitter disappointment as he rips down the message posted in bright hope the day before: "*Auditions for an apprenticeship to be held, beginning the following noon. Apply to Halliron at the tap in the Straw Cock Tavern.*"

XII. Conquest

The change in season brought buffeting winds to Daon Ramon Barrens, even as every spring had before the loss of sunlight to the mist. In past years, turbulent gusts mingled the fragrances of wildflowers and sweetgrass that mantled the backs of the greening hills. Unicorns had rejoiced with the quickening earth. But that had been before man's meddling had diverted the Severnir's waters from their natural course, Asandir reminisced as he stood vigil under the lichened span of Ithamon's wrecked southern gate. The valleys outside were robbed of their carpet of flowers. Saddened by the taint of mold and rot that Desh-thiere's hold had lent to the seasonal breezes, the Sorcerer trained his mage's perception upon the land until physical form became overlaid by the vision of his innermind. Before him all things stood revealed in primal patterns of light.

Beyond the imbalance marked upon the landscape by centuries of warped weather, he sensed something else: a more subtle wrongness, built of pent-up expectation and a near subliminal tingle, as if between air and the solidity of the earth, violence lay coiled in ambush. Asandir delved deeper. The anomaly faded before his probe, eluded him so thoroughly that for a moment he stood disoriented, unsure if he had chased some spectre of his own uncertain thoughts.

He released his focus, frustrated. His feet were clammy in dew that natural sunlight would long since have burnished dry. Asandir sucked in a deep breath. His fears loomed real enough, perhaps, to corrupt even true seeing. And yet he remained unconvinced that the sick things half sensed between the shimmer of life force were phantoms inferred by apprehension.

This day began the chain of events that must culminate in a s'Ffalenn king's coronation at Etarra. During the next hours, and spanning the course of several weeks to follow, Desh-thiere's meddling would skew the world's fate beyond reach of augury or strands to reflect any certain outcome. With luck and persistence, these hills could be restored to their former fairness. Yet although the moment had come to complete the Mistwraith's defeat, Asandir remained grim. Contrary to nature, his cloak hung in straight folds off his shoulders: winds that should have whipped in off the downs to strafe the ruined wall walks were this moment quelled by a barrier ward fashioned by his discorporate colleagues. When complete, the spell worked by Luhaine and Kharadmon would be a masterwork that twisted even time to subservience.

A cat's paw of air through the archway sent a dry leaf scratching. Aware the disturbance marked an arrival, Asandir drew breath and asked, "Ithamon is secure?"

Kharadmon replied from the mist-murky shadows, a sulky note to his tone. "Luhaine's not satisfied." A pause ensued. "There's clear sunlight not a dozen yards above the mists at the outer walls."

Asandir flicked back damp cuffs to chafe blood back into cool hands. "So Lysaer said. He sensed as much through his gift. That excited him to the point where he took himself off to practice sword forms. Dakar is still finishing the breakfast the others were too tense to eat."

Amid stillness, and a chill that gripped more than cracked stonework, Kharadmon's amusement whetted to anticipation. "You want your apprentice rousted from his comforts?"

"Not by your methods, ghost." In a lighter moment Asandir might have chuckled. "I've no patience today for soothing prophets with bruised dignity, particularly one griped by a bellyache brought on through overindulgence."

"And Arithon?" The discorporate Sorcerer's sarcasm blurred in reverberation through the gateway.

Asandir broke his pose of quietude and strode up the vine-tangled avenue that led to the inner citadel. Ahead of his step, leaves rustled in a burst of agitation as an iyat skulked out of his path. "Right now the Shadow Master's tuning his lyranthe with an intensity better suited to a man whetting steel for bloody vengeance. You're welcome to provoke that one by yourself."

Kharadmon barked a laugh and kept pace, an unseen flow of cold air. "A formidable weapon, Elshian's lyranthe."

"In Arithon's hands, not just yet," Asandir snapped. Then he sighed. "You've caught me as testy as Luhaine this morning." But the wards by themselves were enough to have done so without Kharadmon's provocation. Since the effectiveness of any arcane defense stemmed from Name, no spell could perfectly thwart what lay outside of the grasp of true seeing; to balk an essense wrought of mist and multifaceted sentience posed a nearly impossible task, like trying to fence darkness with sticks. Despite the combined efforts of four Sorcerers, Asandir could not shake a sense of helplessness. The strands had augered for failure. The strongest of conjured defenses might well prove inadequate to contain Desh-thiere's many entities. Its mist might be confined and Athera's weather restored only if nothing went wrong—only if the princes who centered the hope of two vital prophecies could be protected through the wraiths' final binding.

Not so preoccupied as he seemed as he picked steps over fragmented frieze work, Asandir pursued the topic sidelined earlier by his colleague. "Luhaine's not satisfied, you say."

Cold air became a snap of frigid wind near in vehemence to an oath as Kharadmon said, "Last I saw, Luhaine was upending rocks in the rivercourse and rousting up salamanders in droves."

"Would that were all," cracked a rejoiner from the entity Kharadmon's blithe tones just maligned. Arrived in time to defend himself, Luhaine said indignantly to Asandir, "We can't make a ward to plug every Ath-forsaken bolt hole in the earth!"

"Meaning?" Asandir frowned toward the matrix of energies that mage-sight picked out as the essence of the spirit he addressed.

If Luhaine intended answer, Kharadmon stole the initiative. "Even spread over three acres, Desh-thiere's concentration of malice is the most powerful threat we've ever handled. To pare it down further will add to its unpredictability. What happens when the princes cut it to a scrap, a shadow, small enough to scatter and hide?"

Asandir spoke the unpleasant thought outright. "Nameless, it cannot be traced." His mouth thinned. "Find another choice, I'd embrace it."

Kharadmon returned no glib comment. Luhaine lost his inclination to expound upon the nuance of every risk. Today, and until the upheaval augered for the time of Arithon's coronation, perils could not be avoided. All things, including lives, must be considered expendable, except one: the continuance of the great mystery imbued in earthly form, the survival of the Paravian races. The silence of

Asandir's discorporate colleagues stretched the more ominous in the absence of the seasonal winds.

The battlement atop Kieling Tower stayed wrapped in the same dire stillness when Asandir took stance alongside his discorporate colleagues. Voices echoed from the stairwell near his feet: Lysaer's, raised in some jocular quip, and Dakar's reply, hotly truculent.

"First, they don't *have* telir brandy in Etarra. Mention spirits distilled from fruits that the mist has turned sour for centuries, and the governors' minister of justice will howl, then see you staked through the arse. They're hysterically scared of hearing legends." Dakar paused to puff. The staircase was very long and steep. Still bitter, he added, "Sorcerers are regarded even worse. Admit you ever saw one, and they'll roast you whole without a hearing. I'm bored of this wasteland as you are, but damned if I'm eager to rush on to that stew of corruption and prejudice!"

"Well then," said Lysaer, stubbornly and spiritedly agreeable, "when Desh-thiere is vanquished, and we get there anyway, I'll buy the beer till you're passed out in your cups."

"You can *try*." Dakar's tousled brown head emerged into the mist, twisted aside for rejoinder down the stairwell. "First, when it comes to knocking back drink, I'll have you under the table, Prince. Next, Etarrans don't brew beer worth pissing. They like gin, from which half the populace gets headaches. You'll find their governors' council bad-tempered."

Lysaer trailed Dakar onto the battlement, saw his half-brother already poised between merlons with his knees tucked under folded arms. He called greeting. "Let's hurry and set the last of this fog under a cork."

Arithon absently nodded, then addressed what seemed like vacant air. "We're not going to finish this here, are we?"

Blocked by Lysaer's shoulder, Dakar craned his neck to follow this exchange until something unseen in between prompted a string of fervent curses.

Caught in the cross fire, and unconvinced that epithets which mingled blasphemies with the properties of fresh cow dung should be rightfully applied to his person, Lysaer said, "I seem to be missing some point." His good nature remained stiffly in place as he rounded to face his tormentor. "Could you stay the abuse until after you've explained?"

Dakar rolled his eyes, while behind Lysaer's back, the ghost-silent images of Luhaine and Kharadmon manifested upon the battlement. Each in their way looked inconvenienced: Luhaine's rotund figure and schoolmasterish frown at perpetual odds with Kharadmon's cadaverous slenderness.

Still puzzled, Lysaer turned around again, to find himself confronted by strange Sorcerers. Only royal poise curbed his startled recoil. Creditably courteous in rebound, he said, "We've not been introduced, I believe."

Kharadmon raised tapered fingers and flipped back his hood. Streaked piebald locks tumbled over his caped cloak as he swept through a courtier's bow. "My prince, we are colleagues of the Fellowship, members in spirit since the day that flesh suffered mishap." And he arose, confronting Lysaer with cat-pale eyes that studied in sardonic provocation.

Luhaine tucked his thumbs into a belt stout enough to halter a yearling bull. As flesh, he had always been careful to regale his portliness with restraint; as spirit, he forwent adornment as a frivolous waste of conjury. Against an appearance unrelentingly prim, his words seemed weighed like insult as he said, "The buffoon who speaks is Kharadmon, Your Grace of Tysan."

"Buffoon?" Kharadmon curled his lip. "Luhaine! Can your wit be that tired, to find you floundering for epithets?"

"After two ages suffering your lame taste, such failing would carry no shame." His eyes joylessly reticent, Luhaine measured the blond prince whose dignity made light of unpleasantness. Given Lysaer's staunchness of character, it seemed unnatural that the strands should unremittingly forecast war. Aggrieved that such beautifully trained poise might come to be channeled toward deceit, Luhaine turned sharp. "You think we should get on with defeating Desh-thiere?" He flicked a thick finger in reproach. "I say it's a fool who would rush to meet danger."

Taken aback, Lysaer flushed. Asandir set a hand on his shoulder and spared him from further embarrassment. "Kharadmon and Luhaine have worked nightlong to establish protections." He shot a pained look at both spirits. "Excuse their rudeness, please. Their labors have left them disagreeable."

Motionless up until now, Arithon abruptly stood. He did not speak, and Lysaer, unsmiling, found grit to ignore Kharadmon's challenging regard. "Since the last attack by Desh-thiere's aspects, I thought your Fellowship determined its hostilities couldn't be warded?"

Asandir said in honest discomfort, "We can't be sure."

Lysaer glanced at his half-brother. But Arithon stayed quiet as Luhaine shed his disapproval to explain.

"Permit me. What spirits the Mistwraith embodies cannot pass the tower safe-wards. Should your efforts with shadow and light drive its vapors to final extinction inside Paravian protections, the self-aware essence would become sundered from the bounds of the fog that enshrouds it. In brief, its wraiths would be winnowed separate, even as kernel from chaff." Warmed to his topic, Luhaine raised spread palms. "After that, our Fellowship cannot be sure whether natural death would banish such spirits. Should the entities have ways to evade Ath's law and continue existence as free wraiths, they might go on to possess our world's creatures with dire and damaging results."

"The *methuri* that plague Mirthlvain Swamp were created by a similar calamity," Asandir pointed out. "That might lend you perspective."

"Indeed, yes." Now set for a scholarly diatribe, Luhaine opened his mouth, then caught a glare from Kharadmon. Nettled, he said, "I must sum up."

Kharadmon hitched up an eyebrow. "Do go on." He tipped his palm in invitation as a courtier might, to defer to a lady in a doorway.

Luhaine stiffly turned his back and resumed with his speech to the half-brothers. "To counter the risk of loosing free wraiths, you must drive Desh-thiere to captivity outside of arcane protections. The wards set over Ithamon must serve as your bastion, and also as defense for the land in case of mishap."

"Brief, did you say?" accosted Kharadmon. Despite an image that stayed fixed in serenity as a painting, his impatience was plain as he said, "We waste time."

Unperturbed, Asandir gave the half-brothers his quiet reassurance. "The perils are not insurmountable. On faith, we have Dakar's prophecy, and the strands' further augury that the Mistwraith can be conquered. Yet there won't be satisfaction if we stall over details until sundown." He tipped his head at Lysaer. "Prince?"

Relieved to be excused from the friction between a ghost pair of Sorcerers who deeply unsettled him anyway, Lysaer called power through his gift. Light sheeted from his raised fist, a crackling, broad-banded flash that shocked through the murk overhead. Desh-thiere hissed in recoil. A backwash of steam fanned Kieling Tower, torn short as Arithon's shadow-wrought counter thrust sliced across the breach. Dark flicked the air and the temperature plunged. Snow flurried over the battlement, struck gold by filtered sunlight as the mist layer seared nearly through. The heavens moiled like dirtied water as Desh-thiere surged to choke the gap. Barriers of wrought shadow razed it short, and ice dusted the hollow before the crenels where the image forms of Luhaine and Kharadmon had vanished away, unremarked.

The half-brothers broke off the first-stage assault, breathing hard, and as always, the moment they snatched in recovery cost them.

The mist massed in upon itself. Purple-gray and sinister as thunderheads, Desh-thiere battened the winds in dank darkness and seethed over the patch of true sky. Lysaer's fair nature turned grim. Always the fog became thicker and more troublesome to manage after the initial attack. Charged to resentful revenge, grown adept at shaping his craft as a weapon, Lysaer hammered killing power into the gloom that oppressed the landscape.

The grease-thick miasma above the tower flared white, then burned to incandescence as the charge struck. Shadow ripped out in reply, and snow crystals scoured by the gusts slashed across the exposed stone parapet. The mists bulked denser, poisonously thick as poured oil. Lysaer's tunic dampened with sweat, and Arithon's hair whipped to tangles against dripping temples.

The half-brothers fought, while morning gave way to afternoon. Slowly, grudgingly, the Mistwraith's bounds were harried inward. Sunlight speared down and silvered the Ithamon's knoll with its interlocked stubble of foundations. Notched battlements and broken walls drowned the next minute under yet another counter surge of fog. Light and then shadow punched back. Again a ragged hole appeared. Sky appeared over Kieling Tower, besieged at once by rolling curtains of murk. Arithon cried out as the wraith-driven mists burst his barriers. Stonework shook to a thunderous report as Lysaer extended to heroic lengths to shock back the break in the attack line.

His light slashed into gloom that churned, congested as a blood-gorged bruise. Shadow answered him strongly. Snowfall snatched up into whirlwinds as stress-heated air snapped and shrieked through pocketed blizzards of ice.

And then a sudden and peculiar twist of change: interwoven through the violent play of energies, something tugged subtly out of balance. Across the concussive boom of backlash and a gale like a rising scream, Arithon shouted to Asandir. "We're in trouble!"

Less trained to nuance, Lysaer saw no cause to pinpoint. A third charge gathered in his hands, his sight congested by a darkness dense enough to suffocate, he groped to define his uneasiness. Aware of voices, but cut off from the others by the mist, he closed his fists.

And knew terror, for his gifted powers failed to dissipate.

Lysaer reached to recover control, but another will struggled against him, as if the mists had changed nature, without warning turned from a stubborn, resistant barrier that needed ever to be driven, into something repellently uncanny; a creature voracious and alive, which now fed off the very energies summoned to achieve its defeat. Lysaer felt the graze of unseen presences across his flesh. *Things* seemed to twist at his clothing and hair, while a heaviness dragged his thoughts.

Then a surge of overweening elation displaced all trace of alarm. They had triumphed! Desh-thiere now collapsed in a sucking rush toward annihilation.

A shout from Asandir ripped through that giddy unreality. Lysaer's mad urge to crack the sky with his powers became dashed as someone's hands snatched his wrists apart. Spell force slapped over his unshed light like soaked woolens thrown down to douse a wildfire.

No victory had been imminent on Kieling. Lysaer gasped in recovery. Murk wrapped him, dank as marsh vapors, and his body dripped sour sweat. "What happened?"

"Desh-thiere," cried Asandir above winds that keened like death angels whetting their armory of scythe blades. "It's hurled itself into the breach for a purpose!"

Magelight flashed and the air cleared, or seemed to. Only a circle closed off by some boundary of sorcery answered to Asandir's will. Beyond Kieling's walls pressed darkness, damp and impenetrable as shroud felt. Lysaer blinked streaming eyes. Brushed by settling snow, he noticed the winds no longer buffeted his body. Instead he felt crowded by noxious warmth the characterless temperature of shed blood. Pressured by nameless foreboding, Lysaer braced to continue, then flinched as Asandir cruelly tore his wrists apart again.

Affronted by the physical handling, Lysaer tensed to strike off restraint. Asandir met his glare, wordless, until reason displaced princely pride. Shaken to discover how near vanity had come to eclipse his good sense, Lysaer squared his shoulders to apologize.

Asandir forestalled him. "I'm not offended, and you were never rude. This Mistwraith has aspects that can turn the mind, and now you are warned. Stay guarded."

Upset and humiliated, Lysaer strove to pick sense out of chaos. "The mist flung itself on us like a suicide."

From across the battlement, Arithon said in a voice scraped and hoarse, "That last assault sheared out more vapor than we ever burned away through a half day. I presume the damage is done?"

"We'll see. Luhaine!" His hold still tight on Lysaer's wrists, Asandir cracked out. "How diminished is the radius of the fog?"

The discorporate mage forwent his tendency to patronize. "Only Kieling Tower remains enveloped, which leads me to suppose we have problems. If Desh-thiere's entities were subject to natural death, why should they rush their destruction?"

Kharadmon agreed. "It's too dangerous now to finish outside the tower. Whether our wards are found wanting or not, to cut the mist down on open ground is to beg a bid for escape. These ruins offer a thousand crannies. If the wraiths slip their bindings, they'll surely scatter and hide."

"That's Desh-Thiere's intention, no doubt," Luhaine snapped. "Or wouldn't it just lure us to take an outside stand, then make the two princes its target?"

"It could be attempting to do both." Asandir looked like a man faced with torture as his hands slackened, then at last released Lysaer. "We have a second choice of action."

"No!" cried Dakar in protest, half forgotten where he huddled on the sidelines. He strode to the center of the battlement. Nose running, eyes bloodshot, his hands bunched in fists before his chest, he bristled like a fat bantam rooster. "You wouldn't *dare* sully the wards of compassion on this tower! Merciful Ath, how could you think to disarrange the irreplaceable work of ages, and draw evil inside these protections?"

Asandir visibly hardened. "I would do so of sheer necessity." His look blazed back at his apprentice. "These wards are all that can dependably fence the Mistwraith. I will open them, and let Desh-thiere be driven inside, and see this land safe under sunlight. For the survival of the Riathan Paravians who sanctified this haven, you'll lend your strength to that cause."

Shocked, shaking, visibly afraid to hold his ground, nonetheless Dakar stayed stubbornly rooted.

"Desh-thiere has three times shown us guile," said Luhaine, his image indistinct through the turmoil of darkness and mist. "We could be the ones driven, and purposefully, to try just such a desperate action."

"The risk must be taken." Lysaer came forward. "Of us all, I'm the least fit to weigh risks. Yet I cannot set my life above the need to confine this monster. Kieling's protections will not fail the land. Though we all were to die here, sunlight for Athera would be secured." His hair like drowned gold in the gloom, he deferred to Asandir. "I prefer to trust you can protect us from the wraiths, as you did on the night my half-brother and I were attacked."

That mishap had occurred well before Desh-thiere's teeming entities had been crowded inside shrunken boundaries; yet Asandir kept dread to himself as he switched his most merciless regard back to the Teir's'Ilessid. "So be it, Lysaer. But let your heart not falter. When I call, you will act, and do so without question, to the utter dregs of your strength. Your gift of light will partner Arithon's shadows, and burn mist until all of Desh-thiere's entities are driven inside of ward boundaries."

The words and their depth of commitment struck Lysaer with strange force and finality, as if magic would be bound to his consent. Though warned he must forfeit any later change of will, he scraped up a ragged smile. "What resources I have are freely yours."

Wary though he remained, Asandir showed sincere respect. "Ath's blessing on you, s'Ilessid prince. You do seem to understand the stakes."

Ever the pessimist, Luhaine said, "Let Dakar leave the tower now, then. Should the worst befall, someone must stay outside to guard until Sethvir can set seals on this tower to permanently block chance of re-entry."

"I'll get my nose sunburned and blistered for nothing, waiting for you to come out!" Yet in his eagerness to quit the site of conflict, Dakar tripped over his feet in the stairwell. His peeved oaths faded with his hurried steps, first muffled by the close-pressed mists, and finally drowned by the moan of the eddying winds.

Desh-thiere swathed Kieling's battlements in unremitting gloom as the Sorcerers made preparations. Kharadmon appointed himself the task of safeguarding Lysaer. Luhaine's image dissolved also, but wearing an acerbic expression that cautioned Arithon to restraint. Whether moved by precocious knowledge or by edgy s'Ffalenn temperament, any attempt to broach Fellowship guardianship would be handled with flat intolerance.

Lysaer wiped sweating palms. Before he could imagine what arcane defenses might demand of him, a circle of blue-white force cracked around him. His eyes were flash-blinded, and his senses tipped spinning into vertigo. The wards set over his person by Kharadmon not only laced the surrounding air, they invaded and flared through his most private self with a persistence that raised primal rebellion. Lysaer felt every hair on his body stab erect. For a horrible, drawn-out moment his mind and flesh lay outside self-command, frozen in subjugation to another will. The unpleasant feeling soon faded. Magelight no longer etched his body to incandescence. Lysaer stretched in reaction. He flexed his hands, then his toes, relieved to find them not locked in paralysis. Then he tried a breath, and felt, like a spike hammered through the grain of growing wood, the ward's immutable presence.

He retained bodily control, but only as Kharadmon's protections allowed.

Moved to consternation by the scope of the strictures imposed by his open consent, Lysaer had no chance to wonder how Arithon reconciled such a pact. Above the moan of the wind, and through the ear-stinging pitch of ward resonance, Asandir delivered fast instructions.

"Once I've merged awareness with Kieling Tower's protections, I won't be able to respond. Should trouble arise, the discorporate Sorcerers who are linked with you will sense your needs and give help as the situation requires." Asandir paused.

His eyes, light, brilliant, piercing, studied the half-brothers, who for the cause of restored sunlight and Paravian survival were about to place body, mind, and spirit into jeopardy.

Pressed by unspoken anxieties, Asandir added, "I'll seek to key an opening in the wards and signal you when that's accomplished. Engage the Mistwraith then. With all of your strength and will, drive it inside the tower's protections. Once the last bit of fog is drawn in, I'll reseal the wards. After that, Luhaine and Kharadmon will strive with you to fend off Desh-thiere's hostile entities. If Paravian spell-craft can be plumbed for inspiration, and if forces of compassion that were created to be unconditional can be made to yield to necessity, I'll try to fashion a containment of wardspells. With luck we can imprison Desh-thiere and keep this tower unsullied." He hesitated, then finished off, "Hold to this through the worst: the auguries cast at Althain Tower did not forecast any deaths here."

But dying was hardly the worst fate to suffer, Lysaer reflected; possession was more to be dreaded. Kharadmon's apprehension thrummed as a deep, subliminal tingle through his flesh. This host of mist-bound wraiths that their party of five must incarcerate owned the malice that had disabled Traithe.

"I wish you all sure hands and good hunting." A figure of shadow against the charcoal roil of the fog, Asandir bent and slipped off his boots and hose. Barefoot in the cold, he scuffed through the crust of sleet and arranged his stance on freezing stone. Then he raised his hands. Rigidly still, his eyes a chill vista of emptiness, he held motionless for an interval that stretched Lysaer's nerves to the snapping point. To stave off morbid misgiving, the prince cupped his hands and fiercely concentrated to muster back will to use his gift.

A concussion of air smacked his face and a high-pitched ping like pressure cracks cold-shocked through a glacier ripped the sky. The tower seemed rinsed in white light. Lost in a dazzle that blinded, Asandir cried out in what could have been ecstacy or the absolute extremity of mortal pain. Then darkness opened in the brilliance, virulently black, and stonework that had stood firm through two ages shuddered under waves of vibration.

"Now!" screamed Asandir. The joined jasper of tower and battlement seemed to jar into brittleness with his cry.

Lysaer released light in a concatenation of sparks. Heated wind seared his cheeks. Black fell, velvet-dense, then a buffet of frigid air that he attributed to backwash from Arithon's counter thrust of shadow. Next a subliminal purple glow bathed Lysaer's skin, driving before it a sting like a thousand venomed needles. He struggled to breathe, to think, while Karadmon slapped a goad through his mind to gather his strayed wits and *fight*.

Lysaer struck at the encroaching mists in bursts of force like bright knives. He battled, though entities leered from the fog, gnashing fanged jaws and milling through darkness to reach and then claw him down. Savaged by the killing fields of energy demanded from his gift, Lysaer flung up latticed walls of lightning. Flash fire burned the wraiths back until his eyes were left stunned and sightless.

"Now! Again!" exhorted Kharadmon.

The battlements seemed wildly to tilt. Wrung out and disoriented, Lysaer could not tell if the stonework dissolved from beneath him, or whether natural law still held firm. Past the ongoing blaze of the wards, he sensed Luhaine and, teamed with him, Arithon, still slamming the Mistwraith with shadow spun frigid as the void before Ath's creation.

Lysaer choked on a breath that was half snow. Frost bit his lungs and kicked off an explosion of coughing. The air felt all strange, too thick and still to pass his nostrils. Gust-eddied ice raked his face. He ached with a sensation like suffocation, while Kharadmon pressed him to resume.

Driven to expend himself through his gift until he became as a living torch, Lysaer cried out. Charge after charge of pure light raked from him until his flesh felt mauled and reamed through, a bare conduit to channel his gift. The light torn out of his center slashed from him, a brilliance of chiseled force that the one mote of consciousness undrowned by the torrent recognized for the work of a stranger.

No more than a puppet impelled by a Sorcerer's whim, Lysaer felt stripped and crushed. The darkness and vertigo that assailed him were no longer solely the effects of spell-wards and Mistwraith. His body was starved for breath to the point where he barely stayed conscious.

And still the light ripped from him in crackling, searing white torrents.

His disorientation tripped off panic. While instinct screamed that he was being immolated, consumed by a scintillant spell-craft pressured outside of sane control, he clung in desperation to his willing consent to the Fellowship, and the honor that bound his given oath: to battle the Mistwraith for as long as he held to life.

Yet his endurance was only mortal.

Undercut by sharp anguish, that royal blood, and pride, and heart-felt integrity of purpose were not enough by themselves to sustain him, Lysaer lost grip on dignity and wept.

And then there was no thought at all, only gray-blackness more neutral than mist, more terrible than the dark door of death.

A harrowing interval passed. Sound reached Lysaer in a burst like tearing fabric. Then came voices, shouting above a roar like a mill-race in his ears.

Vague pain resolved into bruises on shoulder, knee, and cheek. Evidently he had collapsed on his side, for he lay facedown in thin snow. Too shaken yet to move, Lysaer shivered. Through air that pressed down like sulfurous smoke, voices whined and gibbered, moaning, mewling, and countless as Sithaer's damned. It hurt to breathe; tissues of his throat and lungs stung as if rasped by ground ice. Then hands were gripping him, tugging him urgently to rise.

"Get up," cracked Asandir.

Wasted and haggard, the Sorcerer was gratingly hoarse, as if he, too, had been screaming. Or else the powers he had engaged to reconfigure Kieling's protections had required focus through multiple incantations.

The winds had ominously stilled again.

Lysaer gained his knees. "The wards," he gasped. "Did you open them?" As dizziness slowly released him, he glanced about. "My half-brother. Is he all right?"

"Over there." Asandir pointed.

Arithon rested a short distance off, his back propped straight against the battlement. Had expenditure of shadow also drained him to a husk? Lysaer could not tell. Heavy mist blurred clear sight.

"Well done," the Sorcerer added, his tone a touch less rough. "We have the wraiths' collective presence contained inside Kieling, and the ward energies safely resealed. If the virtue that founds this tower's strength is not to be abandoned to desecration, we'll have to confine the creatures further."

On his feet now, and shaky as if wasted by a fever, Lysaer tried a light stab at humor. "I'm spent enough already that I wouldn't have the spark to charm a maid. The Mistwraith I hope needs less tact." At a sidewise glance from the Sorcerer, his foolery dissolved. "You'll have my best effort, in any case."

But even before Asandir looked away, the prince recalled: Kharadmon's presence was quiescent within him but not withdrawn. The Fellowship would have more than his best effort, though final cost became his life.

Mortified by doubts that the strain yet to come might break him, Lysaer snatched back the initiative. "What next?"

Asandir flung him a harried smile. "Let no one ever question that the strengths of s'Ilessid are not yours. The most difficult trial lies ahead." And he gestured toward a narrow stone flask that rested amid a dip in the stonework that floored Kieling's upper battlement.

Lysaer shoved back awareness that his courage had been frayed to undignified, whimpering shreds. Neither the container nor the declivity where it rested had existed previously. Its cylinder seemed wrought from the same grained jasper that framed Kieling's fortifications.

"Yes, the vessel to imprison Desh-thiere was cut from the rock of this tower," said Asandir in unprompted explanation. "Its wards were patterned from Paravian bindings, and there lies the heart of our challenge. The Mistwraith is self-aware enough to recognize its peril. We can expect a bitter fight to send it into final captivity."

Arithon offered no comment. Given his trained grasp of his gift, his quiet gave rise to trepidation. Lysaer hugged his arms across his chest. If he thought, if he hesitated, he could not in cold sanity continue. Dread sapped the dregs of his nerve. Raised to inflexible duty, he had learned at his father's knee that a king must always act selflessly. The needs of land and people must come first. If at heart he was human, and terrified, the justice that ruled the s'Ilessid royal line now prisoned his conscience like shackles. Lysaer raised hands that he wished were not trembling. From the core of him that was prince, and steadfast, he let go control and self-preservation, and surrendered himself wholly to his gift.

The raised light stung him in answer, as though his flesh balked at a talent that demanded too much. The eerie dark eclipsed time sense. It could be afternoon or well past sundown, or days beyond the pall of the world's end. The louring smoke-faces that comprised the Mistwraith veiled the tower, impenetrably dense with roused evil.

"Try now," urged Asandir. "You'll get no better chance. When your strength is gone, Desh-thiere will stay free inside Kieling. Ath help us all if that happens, for the flask and its wards of confinement cannot be locked into stability until we complete the final seal."

Touched to quick anger that yet another personal frailty jeopardized this dire expedient, Lysaer forced speech.

"Brother, are you ready?"

For reply, Arithon wrought shadow. It sprang from his hands like a net, laced, Lysaer could see, with fine-patterned rune chains and sigils. Together the Master and Luhaine entwined spell-craft to augment their assault against the mist.

Desh-thiere churned into recoil like steam dashed against black ice. Its wraiths lashed virulently back. Even as Lysaer kindled light, the demonic aspects embodied by the fog writhed and twisted, tearing and swirling around him. Their touch stung his skin as if corrosive, and each gust felt edged in slivered glass.

"Now!" Arithon shouted.

And Lysaer struck, his light a goad to impel the accursed fog down a gauntlet of shadow toward the flask. As glare scoured his sight, he sensed Kharadmon twining spell-craft into his effort. The fog burned, acid-rank, and the faces gnashed hideous teeth. Claws seemed to rake his person, and voices to whisper in his head. Lysaer shivered in a cold sweat.

"Again!" shouted Arithon in jagged stress.

Lysaer punished his body to response, though shadows and fog marred his vision and the churn of the wraiths obscured the flask. Guessing, he slashed out spears of lightning. Faces recoiled, hissing, and Arithon's warding shadows wavered like curtains in a draft.

Elusive as air, the Mistwraith surged to spiral clear. Lysaer blocked it, panting, his gut turned queasy from the spell-work contributed by Luhaine. He called light, and light again, white sheets that had no flaw for the sinuous wraiths to exploit. And still Deshthiere's entities danced free. Spell and shadow hammered what looked like nothing, but resisted like immovable granite. Through the gust-ripped air and the acrid, burning presences that hedged the neck of the flask, Asandir called encouragement.

"Keep driving! The endurance of the wraiths is not limitless. In time they must yield to fatigue."

Lysaer felt emptied, a brittle husk. The demands of the attack were insatiable. No oath could prepare for a harrowing such as this, that exhausted reserves and cut past, to the uttermost unraveling of spirit. The mists battled viciously back. The lessons of survival imposed by the Red Desert became as a mere inconvenience before the suffering required to fuel his gift.

"There," shouted Asandir. "It's retreating!"

A dull ache suffused Lysaer's inner being. The light that left his hands seemed force bought in blood, fueled at cruel cost to mortal flesh. Impersonal no longer, Kharadmon's presence hammered into him, viciously taking to keep the light coming in torrents.

But Desh-thiere was at last giving way.

Eyes stung by salt, or maybe tears, Lysaer discerned a brightening in the air about the tower. Arithon's barriers of shadow showed clearly now, skeined about with purple interlace that were spells lent his efforts by Asandir. Into a cone fashioned out of darkness and suspended over the mouth of the flask, Desh-thiere's coils were chased and burned and funneled onward by flailing tails of light.

Lysaer had no spark left for exultation that the Mistwraith verged on defeat. He could only heave air into lungs that felt scorched, and obey the rapacious demand of Kharadmon, who forced him past endurance to shape light.

The mist-wrought wisps whipped and darted in retreat past the spelled maw of shadow. Lysaer felt drained to his core. Wholly under duress, the summoned force sprang from his hands, screaming through air like rage given over to pure malice. A blinding flash sheared the murk, to lash the possessed mists inside the barriers.

Arithon's net of shadows wavered in recoil. The outlines blurred, softened, distended, as the trapped vapors inside thrashed to escape. The desperate strength of two mortal men and three Fellowship mages shrank to a pittance before the rage of thousands of meshed entities. Lysaer saw the ward shadows bulge, thin, and threaten at a stress point to crack.

One leak and Desh-thiere would burst loose all over again; only now mortal limitations had reached an irreversible crux. Lysaer understood that a second assault could not be mounted. Played out, undone by weariness, the defenders found themselves beleaguered as Desh-thiere's uncountable wraiths recoiled at bay and attacked.

To lose grip on the barriers above the flask was to die, and leave Kieling Tower forever defiled.

Arithon knew. Or perhaps the controlling essence of Luhaine compelled his hoarse shout to his half-brother to fire off another blast of light. Asandir had no encouragement to offer, besieged as he was within coil upon coil of defense seals. Though Lysaer desired with all his heart to respond, he found his spirit beaten listless by the overextended forces of his gift. Only Kharadmon's iron grip bore him upright and lent him the grace to respond.

Lysaer raised his hands and called light. The effort sheared through him as agony, leaving trembling that would not ease. His hands flared white, then dazzled. His palms stung to the rush of raw power as, ruled unequivocally by a Sorcerer, he bent to his knees before the flask.

In the moment he lifted his arms, he felt himself released to free choice. Gloved in fiery light, Lysaer fell back on a fiber he never knew he possessed. Driven by need to the sacrifice, he reached to smother the impending break in the shadow wards with the incandescent flesh of his hands.

He touched not a moment too soon. The barrier underneath unraveled and the wraiths ripped hungrily through.

Mist met light with a virulent shriek. Unwarded, the illumination his inadequate protection, Lysaer cupped his hands to cap the breach. A raging sting blistered his palms. Then the wraiths were on him, inside him, a legion of needles in his brain.

Light answered, a hedging dazzle of wards thrown up by Kharadmon. Trailing a half beat behind, the Sorcerer's protections failed to guard. Lysaer suffered jumbled impressions that overwhelmed the hurt to his hands. The tumult within him screeled to a whirlwind, scattering memories like debris. Through a ripped-up jumble of impressions he sensed Fellowship spell-craft flash lines of fire through past and future, hounding the Mistwraith's assault.

The chase re-echoed down every channel of Lysaer's being. Impressions surged and recoiled, his own mixed with others too alien for comprehension. Past moments snapped out of recall with edged clarity: the Lady of South Isle's lips on his, and her warm fingers twined in his hair . . . a night from early childhood when he had sat on the palace battlement with the chancellor's arm around his waist, as he recited the names of winter stars.

Then, in punishing detail, a later experience wrought of harsh sun and burning winds, and a thirst in his throat like torture.

Dissociated wholly from the present, cut off from joined conflict with the Mistwraith, Lysaer tumbled facedown once again in the scorching sand of the Red Desert. Arithon s'Ffalenn stood over him, blood-streaked features contorted with unforgotten antagonism.

"*Get up!*" the command a lash across a mind pinned by a vise grip of sorcery. Pain followed, lacerating the last bastion of conscious will.

"*Get up!*"

Then himself, a prince born royal, broken and screaming as personal dignity became trampled down and violated by the bastard half-brother *who was ever and always Amroth's enemy.*

Lysaer shuddered, racked once again by annihilating hatred for the s'Ffalenn born to mastery of shadows. Only now, in forced reliving, righteous s'Ilessid fury was shared and fanned hotter by a ravening horde of demon spirits.

The pain this time raged redoubled as sorcery flared and sparked in an effort to hack the wraiths away.

The psyche in torment turned to tricks. Spiraled down a tunnel like delirium, Lysaer glimpsed another place, a railed wooden gallery atop an outdoor staircase that overlooked a vast public square. The space between brick-faced halls and mansions was packed with a seething mob, and amid that multitude one face: *of a black-haired enemy who was wholly and unforgivably s'Ffalenn.*

The scene folded in on itself and vanished. Fire blistered Lysaer's hands. He screamed for a torment more terrible still, of sorcery scourging his inner mind. The invading hordes of wraiths shrieked and gibbered inside his skull. Their cries stormed together, tangled, then merged to a mindless blast of noise. Raw force answered their wail, and a barrage of sparks as thick as scalding rain. The spirits broke and threshed into spinning flight like singed leaves. Lysaer felt sucked under by tides of faintness and confusion.

Voices that were human turned distant, broken, then surged back clearly as a hand strongly steadied his elbow.

"Well done!" The tones, Asandir's; the touch, that of a Sorcerer enfleshed. Kharadmon's enslaving presence had withdrawn.

Lysaer leaned into the support, breathing hard and dizzied past reach of self-control. His mind felt scoured empty. Even his gifted sense of light seemed deadened, consumed as flaked ash in a smelter's pit. Fragments of nightmare flitted through his grasp and faded even as he grasped to recall them. A frustrated urgency remained, disrupted as Asandir spoke again.

"Lysaer? You've been party to a miracle. The Mistwraith's captivity is accomplished."

Belatedly aware he still breathed, that his palms stung with blisters that could heal, Lysaer at last managed speech. "It's bottled?"

For answer, Asandir drew him gently to his feet and forward two stumbling steps.

The narrow jasper cylinder still rested upright on the battlement. Ward light shimmered over its contours, which now showed no opening at all. The container was permanently sealed seamless, and the sky, cloaked in natural darkness, showed a terrifying tapestry of stars.

They were hard white, blue, and stinging violet, too bright by half to be mistaken for the heavens of Dascen Elur that Lysaer had known throughout childhood. None of the constellations matched any taught him by the chancellor.

The meaning took a long, sweaty moment to register.

"Desh-thiere," Lysaer croaked. "It's banished." And his handsome, weary face showed the grace of relief before he crumpled in exhaustion against Asandir.

For a moment the Sorcerer who supported him showed an expression of unalloyed sorrow.

Then, roused to purpose, he called a brisk command to the Shadow Master braced against the wall. "Help me get your brother down to shelter. After that, if you can manage the lower stair, call Dakar in. He's going to be needed to doctor burns."

Legacy

The evening after Asandir had ridden south with his discorporate colleagues to better secure the imprisoned Mistwraith, Lysaer sat with his back to the lee of a stone embrasure that once had been favored as a trysting place by generations of s'Ffalenn princesses. Between hands swathed in bandages and healing unguents rested a flask of telir brandy, left as a courtesy by the Sorcerer before his departure.

The contents were already half consumed.

Disappointed to have slept through the first day of restored sunlight, the s'Ilessid prince applied himself to belated celebration as he pondered Athera's savagely brilliant constellations, strewn in cloudless splendor overhead. "To our victory," he toasted, and offered the flask to his half-brother, who paced too quietly for his step to be heard through the ongoing sigh of the winds.

Arithon paused, a dark silhouette against a million points of light. "No," he said softly. "I'd drink instead to the crown that awaits you in Tysan. You've fully earned your right to royal privilege."

The expected note of bitterness was absent from his half-brother's manner. Taken aback that the Shadow Master's quirky nature should relentlessly continue to confound him, Lysaer smiled as Arithon accepted the brandy, took a token swig, and gently handed back the flask.

"You can't be looking forward to Etarra," Lysaer pressed. "There's more on your mind than you let on." He touched the bottle to his lips. The telir brandy went down with hardly a burn in the throat; the warmth came later, a glow like a bonfire in the belly. "You might feel better if you drank."

Arithon returned a quiet chuckle. "I don't feel bad. Just monstrously tired. Still."

"Still what?" The liquor was subtle; it undid barriers as a rake would seduce a prim virgin. When Arithon forbore to respond, Lysaer frowned in mildly euphoric irritation. "You'd think, after Deshthiere's defeat, the almighty Fellowship of Seven could reward you by finding a replacement hero to shoulder Rathain's throne in your place."

Arithon turned smoothly and set his hands on the wall. For a time he, too, seemed absorbed by the stars. "They won't because they can't, I suspect."

"What?" Lysaer elbowed up from his slouch, setting off a gurgle of sloshed spirits. "What do you mean by *that*? I hate to match sweeping leaps of logic while I'm tipsy."

A disturbance sounded from inside the roofless chamber that fronted the flagstone terrace. "Dakar," Arithon observed, though he had not turned to look. "Hot on the scent of the brandy, no doubt."

Sounds of a stumble and a muffled curse from the ruins affirmed his idle supposition.

Yet Lysaer on a binge could be bullishly stubborn; in judgment impaired further by fatigue, he resisted the interruption. "You're implying, friend, that our *Fellowship of Seven* might not have a choice as to whose head they crown at Etarra?"

Not exasperated but only lingeringly weary, Arithon said, "I think not. My best guess being that, with or without our ancestor's knowledge, somebody meddled with our family history." Silent, perhaps frowning, he tipped his head sideward in inquiry.

"Consent was given," affirmed Dakar from the depths of the archway that let to the terrace. "On behalf of your line, sealed in blood by Torbrand s'Ffalenn, on the day Rathain's charter was drawn by the Ciladis of the Fellowship."

"There you are," Arithon said in light irony to his half-brother. He accepted the brandy that s'Ilessid diplomacy offered out of instinct to console; after a deep swallow and a sigh, he relinquished the flask and ended, "I leave you all the joys of the night. I'm certainly too spent for witty company."

The Shadow Master vanished into the archway even as the Mad Prophet emerged, wearing an unlikely combination of ragged tunics layered one over another like sediment. These were topped by

Asandir's cloak, the silver-banded hem of which dragged on the flagstones around Dakar's stocky ankles.

Lysaer studied the Mad Prophet's choice of wardrobe with raised
eyebrows, while Dakar, vociferously defensive, slouched against the
wall that Arithon had lately vacated. "I'm getting a cold," he said in
excuse for the purloined cloak.

Since the timbre of Dakar's voice held no sign of a stuffy head,
Lysaer sensed a lecture coming on the effectiveness of telir brandy as
a medicine for pending coughs. He forestalled the diatribe by offering
the flask, and stuck like a terrier to his topic. "What did Arithon
mean, and what consent did his ancestor give at the writing of
Rathain's charter?"

Caught in mid-swallow, Dakar choked. He recovered himself, began afresh, and sucked at the flask until forced to stop and gasp for
air. Then he sniffed. "You don't know what you're asking."

"Obviously not." Too bone-tired for finesse, Lysaer hooked the
brandy bottle back. He regarded Dakar's spaniel eyes and said equably, "I need not inquire if that were true."

Dakar started to blot his dribbled chin with the cloak hem, then
recalled the garment's true owner in time to use his sleeve cuff for
the purpose. "Damn and damn," he said softly.

"Once for the brandy, which I won't share unless you speak,"
Lysaer surmised. "The other for the trouble you'll have earned when
Asandir discovers you've borrowed his best cloak without leave."

"All right." Dakar shrugged in resignation. "The royal bloodlines
are irreplaceable, as Arithon already guessed."

"Due to prophecy?" Lysaer swished the flask suggestively.

"No." Peevish, Dakar gazed fixedly on the brandy. "The Fellowship chose three men and two women to found Athera's royal lines.
They were selected, each one, for a dominant trait that would resist
corruption and other pressures that power brings to bear on human
nature. It is a grave thing, to alter, or to influence, unborn life. Yet
that is what the Sorcerers did, to ensure fair rule through generations
of dynastic succession. They set a geas ward that would fix those
chosen virtues in direct line of inheritance. Your ancestor gave them
consent, for all the good that does you." Here Dakar's own bitterness
showed for an apprenticeship that more times than not seemed the
result of manipulation.

Always smooth, Lysaer passed over the flask. Information desired
from Dakar on the nature of the Fellowship's workings was invaria-
bly touchy to extract. "What does that mean for Arithon?"

Brandy vanished down the Mad Prophet's gullet in prodigious
swallows, and this time Asandir's best cloak did not escape usage as

a napkin. "Ah, well," sighed Dakar. "It means that our arrogant Master of Shadows can never escape his nature."

This time Lysaer wrapped his arms around his knees, content to let the spirits work their magic. The breeze whispered softly over the terrace, and the terrible, alien constellations burned fiercely through the interval that followed.

In time Dakar took another pull from the flask. He peered mournfully into the dregs. "Torbrand s'Ffalenn was a man of natural empathy, a master statesman, because he could sense what motivated his enemies. He ruled as duke in Daon Ramon, and the compassion of the Riathan Paravians formed the guiding light of his policies. Which means, my friend, that Arithon will forgive the knife that kills him. He cannot do otherwise. To understand and to sympathize with the needs of every living thing is his inborn nature, the forced gift of the s'Ffalenn line as bequeathed by the Fellowship of Seven."

Lysaer took a moment to sort a cascade of revelations. This penchant for s'Ffalenn forgiveness explained many of the quirks of his half-brother's personality—behavior he had considered wayward until he was given the key to understanding. It explained why Arithon would be vicious in contention, up until the moment of defeat; how he could effortlessly shed any grudge for his balked desires, to embrace a crown he absolutely did not want without sign of bitterness or rancor. Lysaer stared at his hands, which were cold beneath their dressings. The blisters throbbed, but he had ceased to dwell on their discomfort. He badly wanted to beg back the flask of telir brandy, for in a heartbeat his cheerfulness had vanished. Yet courage in the end became his failing. He had to ask. "And s'Ilessid? What gift from my ancestor do I carry?"

Morose, Dakar said, "You will always seek justice, even where none can be found."

A moment later, Lysaer felt the flask pressed back into his poulticed hands. Careful not to fumble through his bandages, he swallowed brandy in gulps. Abruptly his euphoria over Desh-thiere's defeat had faded. Now he wanted to get drunk, to embrace the oblivion of forgetfulness before his busy mind could exhaust itself in perverse and futile review of past events. He could study a whole lifetime and probably never determine which actions were of his choosing and which others may have been influenced by those virtues bound by magecraft to his bloodline.

"Arithon was wise to seek his bed," the prince concluded. "I'm certainly too tired for this."

Generously leaving the last of the spirits for Dakar, he set the flask clumsily on the flagstones, rose to his feet, and took his leave.

Dakar remained in solitude. Night breezes worried his unkempt hair, while he picked in turn at the immaculate wool of Asandir's cloak. The Mad Prophet could wish until his heart burst that the flask by his elbow was still full, or that he knew a spell to conjure rotgut gin out of air. Any crude alcohol would have served to get him drunk enough to forget the nerve that had made him question the burns on Lysaer of Tysan's hands. Maybe then he could sleep with the knowledge Asandir had revealed in the hour before his departure.

Dakar shut his eyes before the stars his prophecy had seen restored could blur through a welling flow of tears. "Daelion Fatemaster take pity," he cried in sympathy for the departed prince of Tysan, "why, my friend, did you have to be the one used to block the Mistwraith's assault bare-handed?"

But Asandir on that point had been unequivocally clear: in the hour of final conflict, when Desh-thiere had threatened to break free, Lysaer had been Kharadmon's selection for the sacrifice. Dakar still agonized over Asandir's heartless assessment after the irrevocable event: "*Dharkaron, Ath's Angel of Vengeance, may damn us for the act, but Dakar, what else could be done? Of us all, Lysaer was least trained to the mysteries. If contact with the flesh allowed Desh-thiere's wraiths to access the mind, which of worse evil could we allow? To let such beings touch knowledge of true power might have led them to threaten all the universe. Sad as it is, tragic as the future must become, Lysaer's exposure offered the lesser risk. Weep with us all, the decision was never made unmourned.*"

"Unmourned, by Ath, that's not enough!" Alone on the wind-swept terrace, Dakar reached in sudden fury and hurled the flask and its priceless dregs away. It smashed against the wall, an explosion of flying shards that raked through air and settled to unsatisfying stillness. The events of the Mistwraith's confinement would never on a prayer end in bloodless quiet in Ithamon. Reproached by the sweetish smell of telir that evaporated away on the wind, Dakar buried his face in dark wool and wept until his chest ached. "You heartless, unprincipled *bastard*," he shouted finally, in a vicious hope that Sethvir would overhear and channel all his rage straight back to his Fellowship master.

For the seeds of evil had been sown, well and deeply. All the telir brandy in Athera could never soften the chaos still to be reaped at the ill-omened coronation in Etarra.

Insurrection

True sunlight blazed down upon the city of Etarra, whose squat red walls and square bastions had known only the gray dankness of mist since the day the first footings were raised.

The merchant guilds hailed the event as a catastrophe.

Trade stalled from the moment the lampblacks raced yelling to the watchkeeps with word that the east sky dawned red like running blood. Sentries reported the same from forsaken posts of duty on the walls. Terror-struck citizens huddled indoors waiting to die of Ath-knew-what sort of sickness as day brightened to a fearful white dazzle. The phenomenon had to be sorcery: the sky was *blue*, and the light burned harshly enough to make the eyes ache. Rumors ran rampant, and legends from the time before the uprising were whispered behind shuttered windows stuffed with blankets. By night, the city apothecaries opened their shops and fattened their purses on profits wrung from unguents to ward off blindness. When by the next day the herders holed up in their crofts failed to drive livestock to the butcher, city folk went hungry. Flour ran short. The rich resorted to bribes until the enterprising poor began to rifle guild warehouses.

Nobody died of exposure.

The meanest of beggars suffered no impairment of vision, though the burglaries were accomplished in streets ablaze under sunlight. Ministers whose guilds suffered losses howled for justice, while dispatching assassins on the sly; trade consortiums took advantage of the chaos to bash rivals, and given no lawful satisfaction, robbed merchants resorted to lynchings.

Already corrupt, Etarra grew dangerous in unrest.

Since the uncanny sky showed no sign of clouding back to normal, Morfett, Lord Supreme Governor, prepared with a martyr's stoicism to restore order and industry to his city. He dug out from under a massive heap of quilts, shed the clinging arms of his wife, and forced his trembling, weeping house steward to press his collar of state. When a morning spent sweating under the naked sun failed to inspire warring factions to resume commerce, he called Lord Commander Diegan to muster the city guard. At lance point the most recalcitrant citizen would be forced to accept the risk of roasting under the Sithaer-sent scourge of harsh sunlight.

For some days, awnings sold at a premium.

Still, bribes were needed to get the crofters and the caravan drovers to brave the open country. The tax coffers dunned for the headhunters' bounties by the end of that fracas stood empty. Lord Governor Morfett bolted comfits to ease his agitation. Pounds settled on his already ample girth and added pouches to his layers of sagging chins.

On the brink of restored equilbrium, worse happened.

A Fellowship Sorcerer appeared on the city's inner battlement.

No one had admitted him. He simply materialized, robed in maroon velvet, his eyes mild as pond water over a beard like frizzled fleece. The last thing he resembled was a power remanifested out of legend. The duty guard mistook him for somebody's misdirected grandfather until a kindly effort to offer an escort home earned him a list of outrageous amendments to be appended to the city's ruling charter.

Summoned in haste from his supper, Lord Governor Morfett stood thunderstruck in cold wind with his napkin still flapping in a tuck behind his collar ruffles.

"You will also air out the guest suite reserved for state visitors," Sethvir said with an aplomb that disallowed reality; the Lord Governor had already repeated that his first petition was preposterous.

"If it's lodging you want," Morfett protested, and stopped. The words he had intended to utter concerning dispensation of charity were forgotten as the napkin in his collar suddenly seemed to bind up his throat.

The Sorcerer said nothing, but only gave back a maddening, poetic smile that somehow looked slick as a cat's.

And though he insinuated himself into Morfett's private dining

hall for the duration of the Lord Governor's lunch, of a sudden everything went wrong. The crofters locked themselves indoors all over
again—naturally without offer to return the city's funds. The trade
guilds set up a yelping chorus of accusations and touched off repercussions like a fall of political dominoes. The poor in the streets
threatened riots. Morfett only belatedly discovered that two more
Sorcerers had joined the first. More guest rooms were aired in the
Lord Governor's private palace. His kitchens were cast into turmoil,
and upon inquiry his own house steward informed him that his cooks
were ransacking the larder in preparation for feasting royalty.

Livid could barely describe Morfett's reaction. He had eaten too
much for days, and now, under pressure, regretted it. His throat
swelled, his lungs filled, and his fat jiggled as he prepared to countermand everything. But rage rendered him incoherent a fatal second too
long.

Two more Sorcerers materialized at his elbows, one portly and
bearded and the other green-clad, elegant, in his eyes an unrighteous
gleam of amusement. Before Morfett could recover speech, he found
himself whisked without benefit of doors or stairs to his chambers.

There, Sethvir politely offered him cold tea, and with perfect diction, recited the list of Morfett's titles, a feat the city herald only
managed occasionally without mistakes. Morfett choked. There was
ice in his goblet, the crystal of which was finer than any piece in his
wife's dower cupboards. As three Sorcerers regarded him with the
piercing interest a bug netter might show a rare insect, he sketched
a sign against evil and collapsed in a faint upon the carpet.

"You'd think there'd need to be a backbone to support such a
grand weight of lard," Kharadmon said tartly.

He ignored the black look shot him by Luhaine, while Sethvir by
himself lifted a Lord Governor better than twice his size and weight,
and deposited his unconscious bulk upon an equally overstuffed sofa.

From his labors, the Warden of Althain raised eyes sparkling with
glee. "Be careful. When Morfett recovers his wits, he has a fast and
crafty knack for hiring assassins."

Kharadmon gave back a toothy grin. "Then, colleagues, we have
every sane excuse to keep him flustered." Devilish in speculation, he
said, "Do you think him a match for Arithon s'Ffalenn?"

Sethvir laughed. "We're going to find out all too quickly."

Upon his awakening, Morfett was told that he would be swearing
fealty to a s'Ffalenn king within a fortnight, and that governance of
Etarra would be made to conform to Rathain's original royal charter.

The Lord Governor's pouched eyes narrowed. "Over my dead body."

"If need be," Kharadmon said, unblinking.

Acute enough to differentiate a threat from a promise, Morfett gave unctuous agreement, then launched on a vicious course of subterfuge.

Two days of intrigue yielded no satisfaction. Bribes failed to budge even the greediest factions. Worse than implacable, the farmers had somehow become obsessed by the idea that guild overlords no longer owned land rights. They bandied legalities like barristers and backed their petition with threat of strikes. When hired assassins failed to silence their spokesman, Morfett discovered why. A soft-spoken stranger who wore a black hat had sown insurrection among the country folk with a tact that confounded. The city seneshal scribed a writ for the man's arrest, only to find that *he* was a Sorcerer also.

The incident left the Lord Governor indisposed.

He lay ill on silk sheets while, in disregard of politics or loyalty, his wife and daughters surrounded themselves with seamstresses who labored over sarcenets, brocades, and pearl fringework to create a whole wardrobe of new gowns.

"But this is the sensation of the season!" his wife hollered indignantly through the bedchamber doorway. "If we're going to be hosting blooded royalty, everybody important shall come calling. This prince might be welcomed as the devil, but your daughters would surely become laughingstocks were we all wearing last spring's fashions!"

Morfett clapped his hands over his ears and groaned. His city and his household had slipped his control. Held miserably supine by his churning stomach, he concluded that Etarra's citizens had been bewitched; only foul sorcery could corrupt them from five centuries of crownless rule. Storms, strikes, a plague of fiends, even the manifestation of Dharkaron's divine chariot, would have been kinder than this infestation of mages. The thought of kneeling before royalty caused Morfett to howl at his body servant to attend him at once with the chamberpot.

He got instead the imposing, blue-clad Sorcerer Asandir, who cured his upset stomach directly and sent every servant within earshot scurrying to fetch official clothing.

"Get up!" This mage evinced none of Sethvir's vague charm. "The council and trade ministers are convened in the oratory, and most of Etarra's populace crowds the trade square in hot anticipation of your speech."

The Lord Governor hauled his bulk upright and found himself

stuffed unpleasantly fast into an embroidered shirt with gold clasps. He might have feigned the return of his cramps had Asandir's steely manner not been impervious to falsehood.

Regaled in tasteful colors for the first time since his birth, Morfett, Defender of Trade, Protector of Justice, and Lord Governor Supreme of the Northern Reaches, lumbered like a disgruntled bear from his lair to initiate due process to re-establish monarchy in Rathain.

Overviews

In a hall of gilt and alabaster, Lirenda, First Koriani Enchantress, delivers her report to the Prime: "Desh-thiere's remains have been sealed under ward and imprisoned in the caves at Skelseng's Gate. This disposition is intended to be temporary. When royal rule is re-established at Etarra, the Fellowship will transfer the Mistwraith to a place of more permanent captivity. We might learn then why they faltered at the end and preserved the fell creature alive. . . ."

Under the Strakewood's evergreens in the northern reaches of Rathain, the clan gathering to celebrate new sunlight extends for a fortnight; bored with the feasting, too young yet to dance, a pair of barbarian boys break away from the festivities to play at raids on Etarra merchants. . . .

In a tavern yard shadowed by the snow-capped peaks of the Mathorns, Elaira waters her bay mare while the horse master offers well-meant advice: "If it's on to Etarra you're bound, let the cook fill your saddle bags. Provisions are scarce in the markets there. The post riders all say the same. Farmers won't sell to the townsmen, and talk of sorcerers and monarchy has the trade guilds lathered into an up-roar. . . ."

XIII. Etarra

The Lord Governor Supreme of Etarra was never a man to worry off weight in a crisis. On the morning the royal heir was to arrive, he found his carnelian-studded belt pinched his waist. His best boots were tight around the calves, and the bunions on his feet grown much worse. Small annoyances became major aggravations when one was forced to stand on display under sunlight too warm for brocades. Jostled by anxious city ministers who crowded the road and the verges before Etarra's southern gate, Morfett squeezed another sigh past the constriction of his pearl-studded collar. Today the Sorcerer riding herd upon his obligations was Sethvir. Offended that the Warden of Althain should flaunt his own demands concerning finery by wearing a robe as threadbare and ink-stained at the cuffs as the one he had first appeared in, Morfett silently fumed. His head ached, made worse by the nuisance that his gold-sewn scarlet clashed offensively with maroon.

At least the post was not filled by Asandir, who was altogether less forgiving over matters of personal sensitivity.

"Asandir will be escorting the prince," the Warden of Althain announced in uncanny response to private thought. He turned dreamy eyes upon the fidgeting person of the Lord Governor. "The ballads from times before the mists name him Kingmaker, because every royal head in the history of humankind has been crowned by his hand."

"How uselessly sentimental." Morfett tugged at his jacket, the buttons of which pinched his breath.

The outer gates of Etarra overlooked a steep slope, the city itself wedged across the gap between the Mathorns' eastern foothills and a west-jutting spur of the Skyshiels. Accessed by five roads, the approach from Daon Ramon was a switched-back conglomeration of mud bricks and shoring that broadened the original pack trail enough for the passage of wagons. What level ground remained before the gate turrets was already uncomfortably crowded, a forced stir through packed bodies indicating the arrival of still more city officials. The turnout commanded by the Sorcerers was thorough enough to impress. Beside guild ministers, trade officials, and council governors, many had brought along their perversely curious wives.

Still sore in the throat from the shouting required to keep his spouse and daughters properly at home, Morfett said, "The governors' council will never acknowledge your pretender's right to rule."

Sethvir gave back his most wayward and maddening smile. "Give them time."

Somebody coughed. Morfett twisted around and saw a lady in pearls and a gown edged in snow lynx raise a quick hand to her mouth. Her tissue-clad shoulders still shook, which betrayed her smothered laughter. At her side, cloaked in white ermine and official city scarlet, and bedecked with a dazzle of diamonds and gold chains, her brother Diegan, commander of the guard, looked stiffly furious. Oh no, concluded Morfett, neither time nor bloodshed would soften his city's stance. The prince Etarra's governors had been rousted out to greet was going to be driven from his grab to restore the monarchy with tucked tail like a mongrel cur.

The Sorcerer in his tawdry robe incongruously began to chuckle. "Dharkaron's chariot," he swore mildly. "I can't wait to see what happens when you meet your royal liege."

"A boy, just barely grown," Morfett sneered. "He'll be sorry to find that bribes won't buy him sovereignty."

At this, Sethvir seemed stunned speechless.

Lord Governor Morfett stroked his chins and fatuously gave himself the victory.

The prince's party must have rounded the last switchback then, for shouts arose from the countryfolk gathered along the lower roadway. Their cheers were boisterously joyful, after the Sorcerers' promise to pry croft rents away from the land guilds. Since the ministers whose authority had been bypassed had ratified no such relinquishment, of course, the blandishment was false. Morfett sweated in irritation. Though nothing could be seen yet from his vantage point before the gatehouse, the officials all began to elbow and press in their eagerness. Shorter than his peers by a head, Morfett had to crane his neck like any bumpkin to retain his view of the valley.

He anticipated a cavalcade, resplendent with jeweled trappings and trailing banners, and wagons with silk streamers and canopies. That was what one would expect of a prince, or so his wife had speculated in her gossip with cronies for a week. Since pomp in Etarra established status, a royal retinue would impress only if it was blindingly, ostentatiously lavish.

Morfett saw just four horsemen, unattended, on mounts that wore no caparisons. They carried no banners or streamers; neither did they prove to be outriders for another larger party. Asandir was the one astride the black; at least, the dark, silver-bordered cloak that billowed in the gusts was unmistakably his austere style. The fat man in russet on the paint looked too undignified for a prince; his companion, a fair man, owned the bearing, but though his velvets were cut from indigo deep enough to raise envy from the cloth guild, he wore no royal device.

That left the slight, straight figure on the dun with the irregular marking on her neck.

Morfett's narrowed eyes fastened upon that last rider with the keenness of a snake that measures its distance to strike.

A green cloak with the silver heraldic leopard of Rathain muffled the man and most of the horse. The hands that gripped the dun's reins were spare as any boy's, and skilled. The dun was inventively difficult. From a distance, the face of the rider looked fine-chiseled, and the black hair Morfett heard was distinctive of s'Ffalenn blew uncovered in the breeze.

The Lord Governor smiled in viperish glee. "A child," he exulted. His supposition to Sethvir fortuitously seemed confirmed: the pretender to Rathain's throne was a green youth, and Etarran politics would devour him.

Expansive, nearly happy, the Lord Governor bestowed a dimpled smile upon the Warden of Althain, who now looked distractedly deadpan. "Sorcerer," Morfett mocked, "here's my sanction. Let the affirmation ceremony for this prince's right of ancestry take place on Etarran soil. His Grace has my leave to chill his feet in our dirt, may he grub the worms' favor from the honor!"

Chuckles rippled through the ranks of Etarra's officials. Women tittered while, like the boom of a storm surge against the slope below the walls, cries of redoubled welcome arose from the riffraff of farmers.

"Come forward," Sethvir invited over the noise. "Your word as given, Lord Governor, we'll proceed to acknowledge Rathain's prince."

"Then I don't have to kiss his royal cheeks until he's barefoot?" Morfett roared with laughter; by Ath, he *would* retain the upper hand. "As you wish, Sorcerer! Let us go on to the courtyard of the fountains, and let your puppet prince forgo this sham of receiving my welcome at the gate!"

Flushed as he enjoyed his huge joke, Morfett parked his rump on the combing of a terra cotta retaining wall. The pruned-off stubble of rosebushes that hitched at his gold-stitched jacket scarcely merited attention, the charade to be enacted in the flowerbeds being far too rich to miss. In signal unconcern for their silks and their ribbons, high city officials and the pedigreed curious who were last to arrive jockeyed for position between rows of potted trees and greening topiary. The prince's party entered. Jeers blended with the trickle of the fountains, while Asandir caught the dun mare's reins to foil her spirited sidle. Her royal burden dismounted.

Up close, the green cloak more than ever overwhelmed the lightly knit frame of the prince.

"Do you suppose he's inbred to be so delicate?" muttered Diegan to a stifled explosion of hilarity. Somebody passed a flask of wine. Fanned by Morfett's bold sarcasm, the mood of Etarra's well-born displayed the viciousness gloved in gaiety that would have enlivened an out-of-season garden party. The courtyard's eight-foot-high mortised walls reflected the women's disparaging remarks with the clarity of an amphitheater.

The dun's reins were passed to an unseen attendant, while the fair-haired companion in his elegant velvets unclasped the green cloak and bared the royal shoulders.

Morfett moistened plump lips and lingeringly assessed his enemy.

To Etarran eyes, the prince who stood revealed was plainly clad to a point that invited ridicule. His tunic and shirt were cut of unadorned linen that anyone less lazy than a peasant at least would have bothered to bleach white. The natural fibers emphasized a complexion that looked tintless and porcelain pale. When Asandir faced the prince and took slender fingers into his own to escort his royal charge forward, Morfett could have crowed. The s'Ffalenn wore no jewelry. The only gemstones on him were the emerald in his sword hilt, which, though well cut, could not be called large, and an ordinary white gold signet ring that showed the battering of hard wear.

"Plain as a forest barbarian," jibed the minister of the weaver's guild.

Sethvir raised his eyebrows in reproof. "Every s'Ffalenn to be sanctioned for succession came to his ceremony unadorned."

But the spirit of exuberant contempt by now had infected the whole gathering.

The prince's poise showed stiffness as he removed his boots. He assumed his place in the flowerbed, ankle deep in black soil hoed up by the gardeners and awaiting the sprouting of spring lilies. Asandir kept hold on his hands and intoned a ritual in a softly sonorous voice. None of Etarra's elite cared to hold still enough to listen. Diegan's sister was loudly pointing out to the half-deaf seneschal of the treasury that the royal ankles had scars exactly like marks made by felon's shackles. The subject was snapped up in speculation by a junior clerk who gasped out improvised doggerel between whoops and snorts of stifled laughter. Morfett saw no need to offer reprimand.

The damned Fellowship mages had been duly warned how his council felt toward monarchy.

The prince knelt on cue. His Sorcerer chaperon bent with him and scooped a double handful of earth, which he lifted above wind-ruffled raven hair.

Morfett choked back a grin. Less restrained, Diegan murmured from behind, "Ath, did anybody check whether pig's dung and ditch waste had been spread in for fertilizer yet?"

The Sorcerer must have overheard. He cupped his burden nonetheless and his voice echoed back from sandstone walls, cutting through the busy buzz of satire. "Arithon, Teir's'Falenn, direct line descendant of Torbrand, first High King of Rathain, I affirm your right of succession. As this realm will be yours to guard, so are you bound to the land."

Diegan's chuckles choked off, replaced by blank rage. "Right of *succession!* Who sanctioned this?"

Caught weeping tears of suppressed mirth, Morfett rounded in a dawning explosion of anger. Without care for the dearth of privacy, he loudly upbraided Sethvir. "You said the royal bastard was only to be affirmed in his ancestry!"

But the Warden of Althain had all too conveniently vanished. While the Lord Governor wildly sought to find him, his peripheral vision caught a blurred flash of light. He whirled again to face the garden. There knelt the prince, and crowned, but not with soil or pig's dung. A circlet of shining silver crossed his brow that had been nowhere in evidence before. Asandir's hands fell away and then steadied him back on his feet.

"Ath!" someone shouted in shaky awe. "Did you see? That Sorcerer changed dirt into silver!"

Sethvir chose that moment to reappear. "It is done, the circlet of sanction wrought from the soil of Rathain, my Lord Governor. Time has come to congratulate your acknowledged prince."

"I gave no such consent! What has passed was done on false pretense!" Morfett dug in his toes, his chin out-thrust like a bulldog's. Yet no Sorcerer of the Fellowship forced him forward. Instead, Rathain's prince came to him.

All his adult life, Morfett had battled the misfortune that short stature forced him to peer up at even his lowliest scullion. The shock of meeting green eyes that were level with his own caused him an involuntary step back.

"You need not kneel," informed the silver-crowned personage whose face turned out not to be delicate, but as bloodless and defined as if chipped from white quartz. "I have not accepted your fealty."

"Nor will you!" Trembling with mortification for the fact he had been duped in public, Morfett curled his lip. "The governors' council, of which I am head, refuses to acknowledge your existence."

A breeze rattled the dry canes of the roses and flicked a twist of black hair from the circlet. Too late Morfett saw that this prince had the look of a sorcerer: eyes that were piercing and level and strikingly devoid of antagonism. Like those Fellowship colleagues whose nefarious machinations had produced him, he could answer a man's unspoken thoughts. "If you and your council rule justly, you need have no fear of me."

The officials surrounding Morfett were belatedly recognizing the legalities behind Asandir's late speech. From all sides, their ribald commentary was replaced by murmurs of incredulity and rage.

"You have not been given any right of sovereignty in this city!" Diegan, commander of the guard, interposed from behind his Lord Governor's shoulder.

"True." Arithon's gaze left Morfett to encompass the courtier who had spoken out of turn, and whose dandyish cloak was thrown back to reveal a hand clenched on a sword hilt. The weapon was flashily bejeweled; if the steel behind its gold-chased quillons was something more than ceremonial, Arithon dismissed the threat. His brows twitched up in flippant challenge. "But if this contest were a footrace, the outcome would hardly merit contest. Do you bet?"

"All that I have," Diegan answered thickly. "That should warn you."

"Oh, I was warned," said Arithon with poorly concealed impatience. "Too well, too late, and in rich and tedious detail. In some things I've had less choice than you have."

Too fast for verbal riposte, and in total disregard for the captain's aggressive posture, he whipped around to address Asandir. "You've had your display. Whether or not the person who took charge of my boots reappears with intent to return them, I would be pleased to retire."

The exchange ended so quickly that Morfett was left with his mouth open. The prince was whisked off amid his circle of Sorcerers, but the edged and dangerous antagonism he had sown among the townsmen remained, festering and unsatisfied. Diegan stared after the departed royal party with his jaw clenched. Amid widening circles of loud talk, guildsmen in brocades were shaking fists or banded together in disturbed groups. Etarra's three fraternities of assassins were going to profit, to judge by the speed with which curses transformed into whispering. As husbands bandied plots like vigilantes, wives and daughters were being unceremoniously bundled back home.

Livid and speechless, and left no target for his outrage, the Lord Governor leaned gratefully on the hand that answered his need for support. "The effrontery of the bastard!" he spluttered when he finally recovered his breath. "Footrace, indeed! Does he think us a pack of rank schoolboys?"

"He can be difficult," an impressive personage with pale gold hair volunteered in commiseration. "But I have never known him to be anything less than fair."

That instant Morfett realized that his benefactor was gently attempting to draw him apart from his councilmen. He yanked back, bristling fury. "Who are you?" Blue velvet clothing might fail to jog his memory, but the green heraldic cloak folded over the stranger's arm at once identified the prince's blond-haired companion. "Never mind," Morfett snapped. "You're one of the royal cronies, and assuredly no help to Etarra."

Still smiling, Lysaer said, "Quite the contrary. I'm the one royal crony who's not a sorcerer, and also, the only friend you have who understands the cross-grained nature of your prince."

The commander of the guard perked up instantly. "I know a tavern," he invited, and grumbling, Morfett allowed himself to be swept along into their wake.

The heavy door boomed closed. Tired to his bones, Arithon s'Ffalenn leaned back against uncomfortable, brass-studded panels. Muffled, the voice of the Lord Governor's wife nattered after him from the outside hallway. "Do make yourself comfortable, Your Grace. Of course, my house staff and servants will eagerly attend to your needs."

Arithon replied in tones of steel-clad politeness. "Your kindness is generous. I shall be content to sleep undisturbed." The decorative studs that gouged his back impelled him to straighten as he finished his survey of the guest chamber.

The glitter made his head ache. Glass beading riddled the paneled walls, and gilt casements with rose-tinted panes clashed unmercifully with a floor laid out in tiles. These also were patterned, a blaring assemblage of lozenges done in saffron, amber, and violet; the furnishings had raised knots in gold, every padded edge decked in silk twist and fringe. Even the carpets sported tassels.

A sortie from the bed to the privy would require lighted candles to forestall hooked toes and whacked shins.

Arithon shut his eyes and wished back the stark hills of Daon Ramon. The windswept ruins there at least kept the tatters of dignity.

"You haven't seen the fur quilts yet," Asandir invited in dry humor from the other side of the room. Against the chamber's blinding opulence, his preferred midnight blue and silver made him grim as an aspect of Dharkaron dispatched to punish mortal vanity.

"Excuse me." Arithon wished only to forget his first sight of Etarra; with copper-clad domes clustered thick as warts behind square bastions, the city resembled a fat toad squatted between weathered slate mountains. He sighed and reopened his eyes. "I presume Sethvir brought the records?"

"If you can make out lettering between the flourishes affected by Etarra's clerks," groused the Warden of Althain. Surrounded by leather-bound ledgers heaped in stacks in an alcove, he looked nothing less than beseiged. "I hate to pain you further." He waved a haphazard scroll case toward a pair of cherubs whose carved curls sprouted indigo candles. "But the lady of the house brought these when I asked for more light."

"Burn them, and the archives, too!" Arithon's laughter took on a baleful edge. "We'd save a lot of bother if we could level this atrocity and build a new city from the rubble."

Sethvir waggled a quill pen at him. "Don't imagine we haven't been tempted!" Then he blinked and looked vague and snapped his fingers: both cherub candles sprouted flame. The wax as it heated gave off a cloying perfume. A casement perforce was unlatched, and in the draft the new light wavered over features shaded toward concern. "A nasty night of reading for us both. You won't like it. Etarran guilds resolve their disputes on the blades of hired assassins."

Not too exhausted to field subtleties, Arithon hooked off his silver circlet. "How many wards of guard did you need to set over this room?"

Sethvir and Asandir exchanged a glance, but neither one gave him answer.

"Never mind." Arithon hurled the royal fillet into the nearest padded chair. "If the governors' council wants a knife in my back, by morning I'll make them a reason."

But reason had already been given, as the Sorcerers had cause to know. They did not discuss the three paid killers that had earlier been unobtrusively foiled. The viper's nest of factions that ruled the city stood united in their cause to see the s'Ffalenn royal line killed off. Vigilance over Arithon's safety could never for a moment be relaxed.

For the rest of the afternoon and well on into evening, the prince of Rathain and the Sorcerers remained in seclusion, poring over old records. Dakar came back. An exhaustive tour of the taverns had affirmed his opinion that Etarra brewed terrible ale. Dispatched, staggering, to the scullery, he fetched back a light meal, chilled wine, and candles from the servants' wing that thankfully did not merit any scent. His errands finished, he sprawled full-length on the fur quilts, the boots he had forgotten to remove sticking through the rods of the bedstead.

At midnight, Lysaer stepped in, lightly flushed, a satisfied smile on his face. He hooked Arithon's circlet off the chair, set it safely on a tortoiseshell side table, and sat. "Ath, this room is as overdecorated as the taproom I just came from." He sniffed and, grinning, added, "It reeks in here like a brothel madam's boudoir."

Arithon baited blandly, "You should have been here when the candles were fresh. They would've given you an erection. And anyway, I'm surprised you can tell."

At Lysaer's mystification, Sethvir said, "You smell like you bathed in cheap gin. By that, dare we presume you accomplished your assignment and lasted for the duration?"

Lysaer laughed. "When I retired, the elect of the guilds were banging their tankards on the table. The foppish-looking fellow who's commander of Etarra's guard was singing war songs off-key, and the barmaids were hoisting the Lord Governor into a brewer's wagon to be delivered to the arms of his wife. Gentlemen, what news I have is good. Tomorrow would have brought foul and secret machinations against our prince, except the messengers entrusted to spread word of the arrangements met with mishap. Kharadmon has an unsubtle touch, I must say, since one of them slipped in horse dung and apparently broke his elbow. His yelling disrupted half the prostitutes in the shanty district. The names he chose to curse at the top of his lungs were a frank embarrassment."

"That must have upset Commander Diegan's sensibilities," Sethvir ventured, his head disappeared behind the pages of yet another yellowed ledger.

"Oh, yes." Lysaer forgot his distaste for orange tassels and tipped his head back into the chair cushions. "The Lord Commander of the Guard rousted out his head captain—Gnudsog, is it? The squat fellow with the muscles and the scars. He silenced the uproar with a battle mace by breaking the messenger's jaw. The bone setters are still busy. To mend appearances, Etarra's council will convene tomorrow morning behind barred doors, to formalize reformed laws to ban the monarchy. The guild ministers already bicker like fishwives. Hung over as they're likely to become, they'll lock horns over the language until noon."

"Oh, dear." Sethvir forsook the accounts to jab fingers through a cock's comb of stray hair. "Are you saying you got them all in their cups?"

Dakar answered from the bed with his eyes still closed. "They were irked enough to dance on the tables, anyway. All Lysaer did was keep them filling their tankards."

"Who paid for the gin?" asked Asandir.

"That's the beauty of it," Lysaer said, infectiously lapsed into merriness. "The tavern was owned by the vintner's guild, and drinks were declared on the house."

Lord Governor Morfett set the massive gold seal of the city into puddled scarlet wax. Then, while the guild ministers added their own signatures and ribbons, he shoved his knuckles into a fringe of damp hair and cradled his splitting head. A servant had to touch his sleeve twice before he realized: the pounding came from the doorway, echoing the throb inside his skull.

"Let them in," he said through his palms. "The damned Sorcerers can raise a commotion all they like. Our edict is signed into law, and their prince will be in irons by afternoon."

A hag-ridden secretary scurried to unbar the door. He was all but knocked down as the panels burst inward and a flood of agitated barristers barged through.

The newcomers started shouting all at once.

From the governor's chair on the dais, Morfett screamed for order. By the time he made himself heard, his head was splitting. The councilmen around him were sweating, or vainly covering their ears to ease their hangovers. Not a few looked ready to be sick.

When the men could be made to speak in more orderly fashion, their complaints added up to disaster.

The Sorcerers and their prince had spent an industrious morning, beginning with a review of Etarra's condemned. By the tenets of Rathain's royal charter, it transpired that two-thirds of the city's prisoners were wrongfully tried and sentenced.

"Pardons and reprieves from execution!" Morfett howled.

"Worse," a clerk interrupted. "The prince has also vouched treasury funds for reimbursement of unfair fines."

"His effing royal grace can't do that!" Morfett jumped to his feet. "A Teir's'Ffalenn has no *right* to set his seal to any documents unless and until there's a coronation. The decrees are false! No such ceremony has been ratified!"

"No," corrected Etarra's seneschal sadly. He looked and sounded like a kicked hound. "But he could, and did, post documents that name the prisoners to be acquitted on the day he's invested as high king."

"Along with which laws will be repealed, which taxes eliminated, and how many public servants shall be relieved from their posts without pay!" This inveigling was worse than the feud ongoing between the iron mongers and the furniture joiners, who captured and tortured each other's apprentices to blackmail concessions for trade secrets. Morfett slammed his fists on the high table, spattering ink and official wax over mother-of-pearl inlay. "Is this what you've come here to tell me?"

Amid cringing rows of officials, not one met their Lord Governor's furious outburst.

"Dharkaron take you for a pack of piddling puppies!" Morfett stuck out his hand toward his commander of the guard. "Give me our new writ! Then go at once and tell Gnudsog to muster a squad of enforcers. I'll see that s'Ffalenn bastard in chains and flogged for fomenting insurrection. Fiends and Ath's fury, no meddling Fellowship Sorcerer's going to raise a hand to stop me!"

"No sorcerer will, but your people might," a voice volunteered from the entry. Sethvir stepped inside, bemused as a philosopher given new audience for his theories. "Have you been listening?" And he pushed the outer door panels open.

A wave of sound reverberated into the council hall. The mob in the streets beyond the antechamber was not outraged but cheering, and against any law of nature, Sethvir's mild tone carried clearly over the din. "Rumors spread that your ministers met to outlaw the royal charter. To keep an irate mob of farmers from storming your doors and tearing your councilmen limb from limb, the First City Alderman suggested the contrary: that the documents being drawn were in fact an abdication of the guilds from ruling power, and an affirmation

of s'Ffalenn right of sovereignty. Craftsmen and laborers have taken
to the streets in celebration. The north gate bell towers play carillons, and the shanty district whores are throwing posies. If you end
this session without a writ for a royal coronation, your people of
Etarra are going to riot."

"Let them!" Diegan's rebuttal rang like a whip crack over the
noise. "I'd rather find myself lynched than bend my knee to any high
king."

He made as if to push past, but the dignitaries beside him caught
his wrists. There were others of the council not so staunch. Should
the mobs turn lawless in the streets, the city guard could not stay
them. Looting would be followed by bloodshed, and the damage to
trade would be incalculable. Pressured to give in by a mournful flock
of peers, the Lord Governor of the city waved for Diegan to subside.
Then he sat down abruptly with his knuckles jammed against his
teeth. Today the Sorcerers' timing had them beaten. But the Fellowship could hardly shepherd the stew of Etarra's politics indefinitely.
Best to accept this defeat and save resources to upset s'Ffalenn rule
another day. On the floor, trodden under the milling feet of the pedigreed elect of Etarra, the morning's brave warrant to arrest the prince
came to an ignominious end.

Diegan tugged free of the dignitaries, unpacified. "It won't be that
easy," he lashed at Sethvir. "The rabble might love the idea of a high
king today. But when unrest drives them to turn, no blandishments
your prince can offer will appease them."

"Blandishments?" Sethvir looked thrilled as a madcap apothecary
prepared to make gold from plain clay. "I rather thought His Grace
would give them back their chartered freedom."

Diegan's lip curled in a snarl. Blithe as the Warden of Althain
could appear, as much as he seemed a doddering elder of a stripe to
knot strings around his wrists to nudge a senile memory, he was no
such vague old fool.

He had Etarra's council at bay, and he knew it.

But his position was dangerously precarious. Moment to moment,
any of a thousand missed details could erupt into bloody uprising as
upheaval gave rise to panic. The citizens outside the council hall
were far from tranquil, nowhere near under control. Only the poor
and the disaffected roamed the streets. Sensible citizens of stature
had barricaded their families inside their houses in dread. The Fellowship's straits were not invisible. They could not be everywhere.
Even as the governors' council drafted their formal abdication,
Diegan continued to collect reports.

Guilds were seizing the disruption as cover to wage less covert rivalries; five men of good families lay dead from unmarked knives. Asandir was busy protecting the moneylender who funded the treasury's bottomless capacity to dispense bribes from a stone-throwing mob, who protested paying taxes for usury. Traithe, at the south ward armory, barred Gnudsog's deputies from the spare weapons stores, while, impervious to attempts by all three fraternities of assassins, Arithon was being fitted for dress boots by Etarra's most fashionable cobbler.

The discorporate mages Kharadmon and Luhaine assuredly were behind the royal luck.

Before the wax on the writs that confirmed s'Ffalenn right of sovereignty grew cool, and despite the frustrated opposition of a governors' council hazed like smoke-driven wasps, His Grace emerged in princely splendor to read the Royal Charter of Rathain in the square before the guild halls. This time the ceremony was engineered with enough glitter to make even Etarran excess seem drab.

Afterward, the populace could speak of nothing else.

The only man in the city less pleased than the Lord Governor and Etarra's commander of the guard was Arithon s'Ffalenn himself. Set on display before the throng, he had managed his part as a musician might play to a rowdy taproom. Viewed as savior by the poor, unrelentingly hated by the trade guilds, he weathered the feast that followed less masterfully. Mantled in the green, black, and silver of the s'Ffalenn royal blazon, he mingled awkwardly with a merchant aristocracy of faddish extremes. The fine food and wines did not distract them from their newest pleasure, which primarily consisted of prince baiting. Intrigue poisoned the simplest word of courtesy, and while some wives and ladies battled for the chance to ingratiate, they had sharp, cunning minds that searched also for weaknesses to exploit.

This was a city where children were urged to select their playfellows according to their parents' rank and importance, and who were often as not sent out visiting with instructions to overhear all they could of the affairs of their schoolmates' fathers.

Arithon handled the pressure with the jumpy nerves of a cat caught unsheltered in a rain shower.

Amid an obstacle course of laden tables, heavy with gold appointments and pearl-stitched bunting, he needed his swordsman's footwork to escape becoming entangled. At his elbow, steady in support, was Lysaer, who deflected social ripostes with a wit that invited friendly laughter. Less skilled at diplomacy, Arithon buried distaste behind blandness. He escaped being targeted by insults by never for a minute staying still. He did not trust these people, in his presence or out of it. He most carefully followed conversations that took place

behind his back. Hounded as quarry set after by beaters, he saw openings. Even Diegan's hostility revealed ways to breach the arrogance,
the mistrust, even the depths of antagonism that fenced him round.
But the political complacencies such changes would demand of him
played false to his musician's ear.

Karthan, at least, had not been riddled with such viperish greed in
brocades; though piracy was no honest trade, its thievery had been
straightforwardly presented.

"You don't look well," murmured a female voice in his ear.

Rathain's prince turned to acknowledge the source: Diegan's
tawny-haired sister, who could drive a man silly with her looks, but
who was poised in her carriage as a snake.

Arithon inclined his circlet-crowned head. Physically graceful in
discomfort, he offered his hand. "Too much rich food. Your city's
cooks have outdone themselves. Shall we dance?"

She took his fingers, and her fine, arched brows sketched a frown
that swiftly erased. She had not expected his calluses. The tightening
around her eyes made plain that the discovery would be passed to her
brother: that despite the appearance of delicate build, this prince's
palms were no stranger to the sword. "I find conversation more interesting."

"How disappointing, for both of us. Too much talk has been driving me mad." Arithon returned a regret as impenetrable as chipped
quartz. "For clever conversation with a lady, I must defer to Lysaer's
charm." Gently, firmly, he deposited her on the arm of the blond
companion, who disengaged from discussion with two ministers with
a panache any statesman must envy. "Lord Commander Diegan's sister, Talith," Arithon introduced, and his grin came and went at his
half-brother's blank instant of appreciation.

The lady in her black-bordered, tawny brocades was enough to
disrupt conscious thought.

"My lady, Lysaer s'Ilessid."

"Commander Diegan mentioned you," said Talith in chilly politeness. She turned her head quickly, but Arithon was gone, melted into
the crowd neatly as a fugitive iyat. Her annoyance this time creased
her forehead. He had defeated her before she had quite understood
that her methods were under attack. Her stung pride would show if
she put aside dignity and chased him. No prince should have been
able to vanish that swiftly, burdened as he was in state clothing. The
gossips might be right to name him sorcerer.

"Allow me," Lysaer interrupted her thought. "Poor substitute
though I may be, in truth, his grace can be terrible company."

Talith turned back to find her pique met by a surprisingly earnest concern. Lysaer's elegant good looks did nothing to ease her thwarted fury. "He said he wanted to dance. I should have accepted."

Lysaer set her down on a chair and as if by magic, a servant appeared to pour wine. "Arithon anticipated your refusal." Smiling in the face of her crossness, he added, "Given his perverse nature, and his penchant for solitude, that's precisely the outcome he desired. He's much easier to collar when alone. Will you take red wine or white?"

"White, please." Talith accepted the offered goblet and raised it. "To his absence, then." She drank, surprised to discover herself mollified. Lysaer's sympathy held nothing of fawning. He appreciated her misjudgment and refrained from questioning her motives, suave behavior that was piquantly Etarran. Gauging the interested sparkle in his eyes, she smiled back. One missed opportunity could as easily be exchanged for another. From Lysaer she could glean as much, or perhaps more, to help the city's cause than from the irksome s'Ffalenn prince himself.

Not until very much later, when her brother the commander of the guard visited her chamber to ask what she had garnered, did she realize how thoroughly she had been beguiled.

Throughout the evening spent with Lysaer, she had done most of the talking.

"His charm is tough to resist," her brother grumbled. He loosened the amethyst buttons of his collar with fingers much softer than the prince's, and smoothly unmarred by scars. "Damned fair-haired conniver is a diplomat down to his shoes. Too bad he wasn't born townsman. We could've used one with his touch to restore our relations with the farmers."

At council the following morning, the acknowledged prince of Rathain was conspicuous by his absence. Worn by the tact needed to smooth down mutinous factions of councilmen, and strung up from picking apart intrigues that clung and interwove between the guilds like dirtied layers of old cobwebs, Lysaer decided he needed air. Of late he had been troubled by a succession of fierce headaches. Threatened by another recurrence, he begged leave of the proceedings when Sethvir called recess at noon.

Lysaer seemed the only one bothered enough to pursue his half-brother's irresponsibility.

A hurried check on the guest chambers at Lord Governor Morfett's mansion revealed Arithon nowhere in evidence. The bed with its orange tassels had not been slept in; the servants were quick to offer gossip. Laid out in atrociously warring colors over the divan by the escritoire were the gold-worked shirt and green tabard that should have attired the prince.

Alone with his annoyance in the vestibule, Lysaer cursed softly, then started as somebody answered out of the empty air.

"If you want your half-brother, he's not here."

"Kharadmon, I suppose," Lysaer snapped; the morning's dicey diplomacy had exhausted his tolerance for ghosts in dim corners who surprised him. "Why not be helpful by telling me where else he isn't?"

Equably the discorporate Sorcerer said, "I'll take you, unless you'd rather charge about swearing at empty rooms."

"It's unfair," Lysaer conceded, "but I'm not in the mood to apologize. Help find my pirate bastard of a half-brother, and that might improve my manners."

Kharadmon obliged by providing an address that turned out to be located in the most dismal section of the poor quarter.

"You don't seem concerned about assassins," Lysaer noted, his crossness now equally due to worry.

"Should I?" Kharadmon chuckled. "You may have a point, at that. It's Luhaine's turn for royal guard duty."

Etarra's back district alleys looped across themselves like a botched mesh of crochet. The paving was slimy and frost-heaved. Lysaer ruined his best pair of boots splashing through sewage and spotted on his doublet the dubious fluids that dripped from a brothel's rotted balconies. He lost his way twice. The street of the horse knackers where he arrived at last reeked unbearably of rancid tallow and of the waste from unwholesome carcasses.

He wanted to kick the next beggar who solicited him for coins; he had already given all he had, and against his promise to Kharadmon, his temper had done nothing but deteriorate.

Blackly annoyed for having volunteered responsibility for this errand, he stalked around the next corner.

Laughter lilted off the lichen-stained fronts of the warehouses, as incongruous in that dank, filthy alley as the chime of carillon bells.

The sound stopped Lysaer short. The joy he recognized for Arithon's, as joltingly out of character for the man as this unlikely, dreary setting.

Pique replaced by curiosity, Lysaer edged forward. Past the bend, under the gloom of close-set walls, he saw a band of raggedy waifs, his errant half-brother among them. The prince of Rathain had spurned fine clothes for what looked like a ragpicker's dress. The elegant presence of yesterday had been shed as if by a spell, leaving him noisome as his company, whose unwashed, cynical faces were enraptured by something that transpired on the ground.

Lysaer stepped cautiously around a maggot-crawling dump of gristle and tendons. His step disturbed older bones. Flies buzzed up in a cloud, and his eyes watered at the stink. He covered his nose with his sleeve just as a brigantine fashioned of shadows scudded out from between one child's bare legs. Of unknown sex under its rags and tangled hair, the creature screamed in delight, while the ship caught an imaginary gust in her sails and heeled, lee rail down, though a gutter of reeking brown runoff.

But the smell was forgotten totally as Lysaer also became entranced.

The little vessel cleared the shoals of a clogged culvert, rounded, and curtsied over imaginary waves. Banners flying, she executed a saucy jibe, and with the breeze now full astern, surged on a run straight for the mouth of the alley.

Lysaer's presence blocked her course. Caught by surprise, Arithon lost his grip on the complex assemblage of shadows that fashioned her planking and sails. His beautiful little vessel unraveled in a muddied smear of colors that dissolved half a second before impact.

Heartsick to have spoiled the illusion, Lysaer looked up.

To the children, his silks and fine velvets had already marked him for a figure of upper-crust authority. Huge eyes in gaunt faces glowered at him in accusation. Arithon showed a flat lack of expression. The moment's overheard laughter now seemed passing fancy, a dream put to rout by abrupt and unnecessary awakening. Had Lysaer not sensed the entreaty most desperately masked behind each hostile expression, he might have felt physically threatened.

One of the taller figures in a tatterdemalion blanket sidled away into shadow. A second later, running footsteps fled splashing through a side alley too narrow to be seen from Lysaer's vantage.

Trapped in the role of despoiler, he gave way to irritation. Although Arithon had not spoken to inquire what brought him, his opening came out acerbic. "Do you know I've been smoothing over your absence from the governors' council all morning? The guild ministers here are slippery as sharks, and just as quick to turn. The commander of the guard and his captain would wind your guts on a pole for mere sport. There cannot be a kingdom where now there is discord if you don't show them a prince!"

"Such affairs are your passion, not mine," Arithon said in desperate, forced neutrality. Several more children bolted despite his denouncement. "Why ever didn't you stay there?"

He had not denied his origins.

The accusing stares of his audience were quick to transfer to him. The girl nearest his side recoiled in betrayal, that the man who had thrilled with his marvels was other than the beggar he appeared. Arithon reached out and cupped her cheek. His attempt at reassurance was pure instinct, and remarkable for its tenderness, since every other sinew in his body was pitched taut in unwished-for challenge.

Rebuked by such care for the feelings of a vermin-infested urchin, Lysaer relented. "Arithon, these governors are your subjects, as difficult in their way to love as thieving children are to the wealthy whose pockets they pick. Show the councilmen even half the understanding you've lavished here, and you'll escape getting knifed by paid assassins."

Arithon abandoned his effort to hold his audience; their fragile trust had been broken and one by one they slipped off. Deserted in his squalid clothes amid a welter of stinking refuse, Arithon's reply came mild. "This bunch steals out of need."

"You feel the governors' lackeys don't? That's shallow! You're capable of truer perception." Lysaer shut his eyes, reaching deep for tact and patience. "Arithon, these merchants see in you an anathema made real. Records left from the uprising have been passed down grossly distorted. Etarrans are convinced the Fellowship Sorcerers mean to give them an eye for an eye, cast them from their homes, and expose their daughters to be forced by barbarians. They need so very badly to see the musician in you. Show them fairness they can trust. Give to them. They'll respond, I promise, and become as fine a backbone for this realm as any king could ask."

"Well, why come here and trouble me? You seem to understand everything perfectly!" Arithon visibly resisted an urge to hammer his fist against a shanty wall. "You've stated my fears to a fare-thee-well, that this city will ingratiate itself to become my indispensable right hand."

"What in Athera can be wrong with that?" Whipped on by Arithon's expert touch at provocation, Lysaer lost to exasperation.

"This!" Arithon gestured at the mildewed planks that enclosed the back of the knackers' shacks. "You socialize amid the glitter of the powerful, but how well do any of us know this city? Did Diegan's lovely sister tell you the guilds here steal children and lock them in warehouses for forced labor? Can I, *dare I*, stroke the Lord Governor and his cronies, while four-year-old girls and boys stir glue pots, and ten-year-olds gash their hands and die of gangrene while rendering half-rotten carcasses? Ath's infinite mercy, Lysaer! How can I live?" The fury driving Arithon's defense snapped at last to bare his nerve-jagged, impotent frustration. "The needs of this realm will swallow all that I am, and what will be left for the music?"

Lysaer stared down at the dirty rings that crawled up his gold-sewn boots. "Forgive me." He allowed his contrition to show, for after all, he had been presumptuous. "I didn't know."

Arithon's sorrow subsided to a gentleness surprisingly sincere. "You shouldn't want to know. Go back. I appreciate your help with the diplomacy, but this problem is mine. When I'm ready, never doubt, I'll give it my best effort."

Indiscretion

Dusk thickened the shadows over the forested roadway that led southward out of Ward. This stretch of highway, which snaked like a chalk scar over the frost-bleak hills toward Tal's Crossing, was the dread of every Etarra merchant. Caravans passed between the northern principalities of Rathain heavily armed, or they failed to reach their destinations. Yet a raid by marauding barbarians seemed not to concern the solitary old man who guided his pony cart over the cracked flagstones laid down by the decree of long-dead s'Ffalenn kings.

His conveyance was open, low-slung, and in sorry need of fresh paint; the beast between the shafts, a glossy buckskin with a tail like black wire and a feisty dislike of boy grooms. He carried his ears cocked back, as if listening for excuse to flatten them down in displeasure.

By contrast, the driver was ascetically thin. He sat atop his jolting board seat with a slouch that gave with the bumps; if his narrow face was creased by eight decades of life, the fingers laced through the reins were clean, supple, and sure. He whistled between widely spaced front teeth, and his jaunty melody carried over the creak of harness and cartwheel to a pair of barbarian children lying flat in the brush above the verge.

Twelve years of age and bold as coin brass, Jieret puffed a rust-colored tangle of hair from his lips. He frowned in stormy concentration. Bored of long feasting, impatient since the returned sunlight had disrupted the passage of caravans to raid, he elbowed his younger companion. "Ready, Idrien?"

The other boy shifted a sweaty grip on the stick he had sharpened for a javelin. Sneaking out of camp had been Jieret's idea. When their play at scouting had surprisingly turned up a victim, the excitement of plunder and ransom somehow lost their dashing appeal. A touch scared, Idrien wished himself back at the feast, tossing out nuts to the squirrels. "You know, his relatives might not be so rich."

Jieret grinned through another unruly red curl. "You saw the topaz brooch that fastens his cloak. Are you chickening on me?"

Wide-eyed, Idrien shook his head.

"Well, come on, then." Jieret wormed from the thicket, too brash to care if he snapped twigs.

Idrien followed, cautious in his uncertainty. Appearances could deceive; the man's jewel might only be glass. Yet already Jieret scrambled to his feet and charged full tilt down the hillside. Clan honor demanded that his companion not shirk him support.

Jieret slithered into the open roadway, hampered by a bouncing fall of stones. His jerkin had torn and slipped over one shoulder, and his javelin wavered despite his determination to threaten the elder in the cart. "Halt, as you value your life!" He shrugged up his deerskin to unburden his throwing arm, then fought for balance and decorum as Idrien plunged down the bank and crash-landed into his back.

The whistled melody ceased. Under threat of two sharpened sticks, capable hands tightened on the reins. The buckskin bared teeth and rolled eyes as it sidled and stopped between the shafts. Keeping tight hold on its mouth, the raid victim bent his light, startled gaze upon the dirty, briar-scraped pair of boys. His lips pulled crooked in a smile, and silver-tipped brows twitched up underneath his hood.

"Get out of the cart and disarm. Slowly!" Jieret elbowed Idrien to take the pony's bridle.

The old man hesitated. Then he released the reins and stepped carefully down, the gold silk lining of his cloak a fitful gleam in failing light. As if ready for Idrien's howl as the buckskin snaked its head down to nip, he shot out a fist and hammered the pony with an expert blow at the juncture of shoulder and neck. The creature grunted in curbed belligerence and sullenly shook out its mane. Its master, nonplussed, removed an ornamental dagger from his belt, turned the blade, and offered the handle to Jieret. He stood quietly while Idrien's grubby fingers rifled his rich clothing in a vain search for concealed weapons.

At length, threatened by his own knife as well as the brace of whittled sticks, he offered up ringless hands. "Whose captivity have I the honor of accepting?" His voice was pleasantly pitched, unmarred by the quaver that characterized the very old.

Jieret scowled. Hostages ought to show fear, not make genial greetings. Since the pony was demonstrably nasty-tempered, he settled for binding its owner's hands with the reins, then made him lead the miserable beast. He and Idrien clambered onto the buckboard and directed their mismatched draft team to haul the cart off the road.

The boys punched each other's sides, intoxicated by their success. A man taken for ransom—the clan lords would surely praise their prowess! The stranger might fetch the price of a sword, or better, a horse. Then, in consternation, the raiders recalled they had neglected to choose cover beforehand.

"Stupid," Jieret whispered, crestfallen at the lapse. "We can't drag a cart through the forest."

Idrien sucked his lower lip. "Drive to the dell and unhitch?"

"Maybe." Jieret nicked bark off his stick in serious thought. "Wind smells of rain. Our booty could get a good soaking."

At this point the captive good-naturedly interrupted. "A storm won't hurt. The tarps are new enough not to leak."

"Quiet!" Idrien glanced around in fresh worry. "Too much chatter will fetch the scouts."

Their captive considered this, his long, lean legs quick to compensate for the buckskin's short-strided trot. "Young raiders don't have their own scouts?" He might have been laughing; or not, dusk had deepened too much to tell.

Jieret skinned his knuckles in a belatedly frantic search, but found neither socket nor driving whip. He tried to hasten the pony's pace by flapping his arms. The buckskin snapped up its round quarters. Hooves banged vengefully against the buckboard. Smacked through the soles of his boots and stinging mightily, Idrien scowled.

Jieret clung grimly to propriety. "Our scouts are off to find other marks," he lied grandly. "If you hope to stay alive to be ransomed, keep silent."

For all their unplanned excitement, the boys guided the little cart swiftly through the darkness. In a natural declivity between chalk bluffs, they ordered the pony unhitched. Idrien held the old man at stick point, while Jieret piled brush to conceal their booty. Then, smothering back whoops of exhilaration, the boys chivvied their captive through the forest to the clan gathering they had forsaken to seek adventure.

Control broke on the camp perimeter. Jieret burst into shouting, while Idrien startled the dancers into an uproar by casting his toy javelin straight into the central fire. Sparks flew; the celebration unraveled in confusion as leather-clad scouts scrambled to grab weapons, and others on guard patrol converged from the wood with drawn steel.

Blinking against the shifting glare of torches, the captive stumbled to a halt. Jieret braved the buckskin's teeth to grasp a fistful of black and gold cloak and drag his catch a reluctant step closer to the fires.

"Here!" He waved to the tallest of the approaching men. "A sure ransom we've brought, Father, and a pony for Tashka."

Steiven, reigning regent of Rathain, was a hard man to miss, even in uncertain light amid his pack of leather-clad scouts. Lanky, dark-headed, he ran with the grace of a deer. His eyes, deep hazel, were wary as any forest creature's whose kind has been too long hunted. His hands were large and strongly made; his clean-shaven chin was square. The bones of his face hinted at a rough-cut, handsome beauty, an impression spoiled at first sight by a scar that grooved his cheekbone and jaw, to end in a ridged knot of flesh above his collarbone.

A wild boar's tusk might have ripped such disfigurement; in fact, Steiven's looks had been ruined by a harness buckle heated red-hot by a caravan master when, at ten years of age, he had chased the wagon that carried his brothers' scalps for credit as a bounty hunter's kill.

He had been fortunate to escape with his life.

The sight of his half-grown son gamboling into camp with a captive clad in town clothes gave Steiven a start that had much to do with memories that recurred in nightmares. Yet he was a man for listening before action; half a lifetime of chieftaincy had taught him to be exactingly fair. Though his heart beat too fast, and he wanted to strike his boy for this latest insanely foolish prank, he forced himself to think and to walk; and then the captive raised his head. Spaced front teeth flashed in a smile, and a snag of white hair escaped his hood.

Steiven stopped cold, the drift of Jieret's chatter disregarded. His fists uncurled. "Bare your head," he commanded.

For answer, the old man half turned.

The clan chief's ruddy complexion turned pale. "Dharkaron, forgive us."

At his tone, Jieret faltered into silence. Sweating, aware he had earned himself a hiding, he stared wide-eyed as his father drew his dagger and, with shocking diffidence toward a townborn, cut the ties from the captive's wrists.

The elder raised his freed hands and pushed back his hood. Black cloth lined in yellow silk fell away to expose a knife-blade nose and a spill of shoulder-length silver hair.

"Grant us pardon, master " Steiven said softly. Then he rounded in fury on his son. "You captured no merchant, foolish boy! Shame you've brought your clan, not ransom. You stand before the Masterbard himself."

"Him?" Jieret's insolence rang defensively loud as he gestured with his sharpened stick.

Steiven ripped the makeshift weapon out of his child's hands. "Didn't you find the lyranthe when you reviewed his possessions for arms?"

Jieret started to tremble.

"Ah," said Steiven. He caught the Masterbard's desperate attempt to hide amusement, and regained his own equilibrium. He affected a ferocious scowl anyway. "Not only did you raid the wrong man, you also kept slack discipline!"

Somebody giggled on the sidelines: Jieret's older sister Tashka. Humiliation would serve the boy better than a strapping in private. Steiven decided to pass off the affair as a stupidity beneath the notice of grown men. "Apologize at once, and offer Halliron your hospitality. Or else amend your insult by meeting his demand for honor-gift, and give him escort back to the road for the stupid bit of nuisance you've caused."

Jieret looked wildly around, but Idrien had seized his chance to vanish. Crestfallen but still brazenly unapologetic, he straightened before the tall minstrel.

"Don't speak," Halliron said with a wicked twinkle in his eyes. "Instead, I'll thank you to care for my pony, and fetch back my lyranthe from the cart." And he solemnly surrendered his buckskin's hacked-off reins into the hands of the miscreant.

At Jieret's first tug at the headstall, the pony snapped back black-tipped ears. A forehoof flashed up in a snake-fast strike, and the boy, yelling curses better suited to a caravan drover, jumped back to escape getting whacked.

"He can handle cross-grained horses, I trust?" said Halliron to the father, only to find the huge man sitting down without warning in wet leaves. Steiven's arms were clutched to his ribs as though he might tear a gut stifling laughter. "Fair punishment," the regent of Rathain snorted between wheezes. "A pony for Tashka, indeed! That creature would as likely rip his poor sister's hand off."

"Probably not." Halliron smiled, watching thoughtfully as bystanders scattered and the buckskin's striped rump bucked and sidled through the leaping ring of torchlight. "The little imp only hates boys. And, truth to tell, I'm not sorry. A storm rides the wind, can you smell it? Not even an initiate's hostel graces this stretch of forest. I expected to endure a nasty night."

When the weather finally broke, young Jieret was hours in bed, and Halliron, comfortably settled on cushions in the lodge tent of the regent of Rathain. Although no one had asked the Masterbard to perform, he had generously offered his talents to the clan chieftain's family until nature's fury defeated even his trained voice. The storm struck Strakewood from the south, battering with windy fists and rattling rain over oiled hide with such force that the crack and roll of thunder could barely be heard above the noise.

Steiven came in wet from helping the scouts secure the horse lines. "Strange," he mused as he peeled his sodden jerkin and swiped dripping hair from the unmarred side of his face. "We don't often get squalls from the south. Usually they spend themselves over the Mathorns and rattle the mansions in Etarra."

"Greater changes are afoot than mere weather since the return of true sunlight." Halliron hooked the final ties on the fleece-lined case that protected his lyranthe, and took wine from the hand of Steiven's lady. "You're too kind," he thanked her, and raised the flagon in tribute to clan hospitality.

Clad in rare finery, her magnificent, heavy russet hair braided with sequins worn for dancing, Dania shone with pleasure. "We're blessed. Your singing is a treasure unequaled."

Her warmth sparked sorrow from the bard, who seemed suddenly absorbed with savoring the taste of his wine.

"No successor yet," the lady sympathized with an insight that tended to disorient grown men. She shared a quick glance with her husband, who knelt and tugged a fresh shirt from a chest alongside the wall.

Halliron sighed. "Not for want of trying, lady. I've auditioned candidates by the thousands. Many had talent. Yet I was never satisfied. Something indefinable seemed lacking." He tried and failed to shrug off a bitterness at odds with a nature smoothed over by advanced years. "I've earned the reputation of an overbearing old crank. Perhaps justly."

But the bard's face by candlelight showed only heart-sore regret. Halliron's tragedy, Dania thought, that no apprentice had been found to inherit his title, perhaps the deepest regret of his long and gifted life.

"Dania," Steiven said gently. "Bring out the telir brandy and refill the Masterbard's cup."

The lady moved with the lightness of forest-bred caution to fetch the cut crystal flask, while the bard's attention strayed toward the shadows that dimmed the rear of the lodge. Lord and lady followed his gaze, to find Jieret slipped from his bedroll, the heavy curls that matched his mother's tousled still from sleep.

"Afraid of the lightning, are you?" Halliron said in gentle satire.

"Like Dharkaron he is." Steiven straightened up in annoyance. Muffled by a thick layer of linen as he belatedly donned his dry shirt, he said, "Jieret, haven't you stirred up trouble enough for one night?"

The boy licked his lips. As he took a hesitant step closer, the light fell full on him and revealed his alarming pallor. Shaking, he announced, "Father, I had a dream."

"Ath, it's the Sight," Dania exclaimed. Sequins sparkled like wind-harried droplets as she sprang across the carpets and swept her young son in her arms. "Steiven, he's cold. Find a blanket."

The bard was on his feet with a speed that belied his age. He flung the lady his own silk-lined cloak, then stood aside for Steiven, arrived in a flurry of untied laces. He lifted the boy from his wife and bundled him to the chin in rich black wool lined with silk.

Halliron helped the shaken mother to find a seat upon the scattered cushions. "The forevision runs in your line, my lady?"

Trembling now as violently as her son, a woman who was seasoned to disasters, and who had sword scars on her from past raids, gasped against the bard's shoulder. "Steiven's line. He has the gift also." She swallowed, her dark, fine eyes fixed worriedly on the crown of red hair that poked through the folds of the cloak. "The visions are too often bloody."

Halliron recovered his flagon, refilled it with brandy, and pressed Dania's icy fingers around the stem. "You need a blanket also." He fetched one, while the lodge poles rattled to a booming crash of thunder.

Throughout, the murmur of Steiven's voice never faltered. "What did you see? I know you're frightened, son, but tell me."

Jieret answered unsteadily that he had seen the king ride from Etarra.

"Blessed Ath." Steiven pressed his scarred cheek into his boy's crown to hide eyes that flashed with suspect brightness. After a moment, muffled by fox brush hair, he said, "And how did you know him for your king?"

"He wore a silver circlet, and a tabard with the leopard of s'Ffalenn." Ever an observant child, Jieret added, "His face matched the portrait of Torbrand that you keep in the cave with the sceptre."

Steiven swallowed. Fighting to keep his tone light, he said, "You're a scout reporting for a raid. I want the particulars, carefully and accurately."

"His grace was alone," Jieret said. "Armed with only a sword, and shorter of stature than Caolle. He rode in haste. His horse was winded almost to death, and by his handling of the reins, his right palm or wrist was likely injured. He was pursued." The boy stopped, wrung by a fresh bout of trembling.

"Who pursued?" pressed Steiven. He stroked the boy's back with a firm enough touch, but his eyes, when he raised them, were hard as rain-rinsed granite.

Doggedly, Jieret finished. "Twoscore lancers, Etarra city garrison."

"That has the ring of true vision." Steiven set the boy back on his feet. "Did you happen to recall if it was raining?"

Dania held her breath. Halliron reached out and patted her hand as the boy across the lodge tent frowned in tight concentration. At length Jieret raised eyes intent as his father's and said, "Funny, that. I saw snowfall. But the trees were green with new leaves." His chin raised, determinedly defiant. "I'm not lying. What I dreamed was real."

"Then dress yourself and fetch Caolle," Steiven instructed his son. In response to Dania's startled cry, he managed a bitter-edged smile. "Lady, would you have our king catch us sleeping? If snow is going to fall on spring leaves, and Etarra's guard fares out hunting, the future is going to bring trouble. Warning must be carried to Fallowmere, and the scouts assigned road watch must be doubled."

Introspections

Lysaer jerked awake in a tangle of sodden sheets. The nightmare that had ripped him from sleep still lingered, a sense of terror just beyond grasp of his consciousness. He slugged a heavy feather pillow out of his face in a choked-back fit of frustration. Guard spells set by the Fellowship might avert those threats that were tangible, but not the formless ills that harrowed his dreams. This was not the first night since Desh-thiere's defeat that he had awakened to a pounding heart and skin running with sweat.

Unsettled, caught shivering in the grip of reaction, he kicked free of his bedclothes. Though the casements showed no hint of brightening dawn, he arose and flung on yesterday's discarded clothing. He needed to move, to walk; even veiled in darkness, the close opulence of the bedchamber oppressed him. Having learned that one of the discorporate Sorcerers maintained a guarding presence over the room at all times, he announced, "I'm going out. Into the garden, probably."

Luhaine's reproving tone answered. "You'll want your cloak. There's heavy fog."

Lysaer raised his eyebrows in surprised question. "You'd allow dreary weather on the eve of Arithon's coronation?"

"There should have been rain," Luhaine admitted, a touch curt. Although he allowed for the need to avoid any sort of bad omen, he liked disturbing nature even less. "But Kharadmon diverted the storm northward. The ground mist will burn off before noon."

As Lysaer fumbled a course toward the wardrobe, he passed other beds in the chamber whose fur quilts lay undisturbed. Dakar would be out drinking. Despite his insistence that Etarrans brewed terrible hops, he was willing enough to remedy the lapse with gin; and if the prince of Rathain chose to spend his last night before lifetime commitment to a troubled kingdom in his cups, no friend would fault him for indulgence.

Still overheated, Lysaer tossed his cloak over one shoulder and quietly let himself out.

The high-walled garden that adjoined the guest chamber lay silvered and fringed with dew. Chilled to gooseflesh as dampness hit his wet skin, Lysaer sucked in a deep breath. The air brought no refreshment. The heavy oils burned in the street torches threw off dense smoke which stung his nose and throat. Mingled scents from the incenses used to mask the stench from the sewers also overwhelmed the natural fragrance of earth and unfurling spring lilacs. Two dogs snarled in the distance; a woman shouted shrill imprecations, while nearer at hand, running steps pattered ahead of a night sentry's tramp. Despite Lysaer's preference for cities, Etarra possessed an evasive, disturbing restlessness. The more determinedly he strove to grasp the deep currents of intrigue, to empathize with the needs of the guild ministers who held the reins of power, the greater his reflected unease. As little as he had liked Ithamon's desolation, he felt still less at home here.

He made his concession to the damp finally, and flicked his cloak over his back. Where he had been overheated, now his discomfort derived from chill. Certainly he held no envy for the kingship that Arithon was pledged to inherit.

Slowly, insidiously, Etarra's corruption had grown to haunt Lysaer in ways that undermined his beliefs.

Aching from too many sleepless nights, he parked his shoulder against a pedestal that supported the bust of a dignitary. Crickets cheeped in the flowerbeds; beyond them, the woman's shouting faded and finally ceased. The distant dogfight dwindled to yelps, and the sentry passed, grumbling, around the corner of the street-side wall. Lysaer absorbed the sounds of an unfamiliar world, and bitterly reflected upon how deeply the children in the street of the horse knackers had upset his priorities.

As prince on Dascen Elur, he had held his people's trust. Their needs had become one with his own, taken into his heart as fully as he had striven to embrace understanding of Etarra's governors' council. The high officials were responding; even Lord Commander Diegan had softened his stance to proffer an easy friendship. Confidence in his ability to mete out fair treatment had always before given Lysaer the focus to satisfy his inborn drive to seek justice.

Up until today, honor had seemed a tangible, changeless absolute that made each choice clear-edged.

The urge to pace, to storm across the dark garden to escape the entanglement of some unseen trap, became nearly too strong to deny. Lysaer forced himself to stillness. He sucked in the perfume of the lilacs and made himself examine why five minutes in the poor quarter should shatter his viewpoint's simplicity. The dilemma held multiple facets. One could not serve the guilds without destroying the children enslaved in the workhouses; the merchants' rights to safe trade could not be enforced without condoning headhunters and the butchery that visited bloodshed upon the woodland clansmen.

Whose cause took priority? In this world of divisive cultures and shattered loyalties, no single foundation of rightness existed.

The Fellowship Sorcerers withheld opinion. They would use their formidable powers to set a prince on a throne, and yet would enact no judgment; they did not guide or expect, but encouraged their chosen royal heir to rule by his gifts and his conscience.

That stock of responsibility became suffocating. Lysaer laid his head against the stonework that supported his shoulders and agonized over a justice no longer obvious. Principles were what a man made them. Sheltered since birth by the cares of a straightforward kingdom, he found himself painfully lost at formulating law for himself. Etarra tormented him by plowing up doubts and possibilities: his own lost realm of Tysan might bear equal measure of thorny, insoluble suffering. He had been taught his statesmanship there, and had perhaps never seen beyond the walls of his palace to notice.

"Daelion Fatemaster, what a muddle!" he exploded in tight frustration.

He believed himself to be alone. When a woman's voice answered from the gate trellis, he started and banged his shoulder against the scrolled beard of the statue.

Surprise caused her words to escape him. "What? Who's there?" He looked but saw no one in the foggy murk between the topiary.

"Not an enemy." Her voice was cool and pleasantly modulated, her crisp accent, other than Etarran. She moved, appeared out of the mists on the path as a silhouette muffled in cloaks—not elderly by her grace, but impossible to judge as to age.

"Who are you?" Vaguely familiar as she seemed, Lysaer could not push past recent memories of Talith to place where he may have encountered her.

"We've met, but so briefly you might not recall. In the house of Enithen Tuer." She had better night sight than he; at least, she sat without groping on a stone bench set invisibly in a cranny beside the hedge. A passing dray's lantern shot fuzzed diamonds of light through the latticed gate. Stray beams brushed copper glints in the hair that trailed loose from her hood.

"The enchantress," Lysaer said in recognition. He added, accusing, "but Arithon knew you better than I."

A nighttime visit to the hayloft in the Ravens' tavern hung unmentioned between them. Elaira tucked her hands beneath her cloak so that Lysaer might not see her nerves had been shaken. "You don't approve of your half-brother's midnight excursions."

Her guess was accurate—also, on the tail of his self-examination, hurtfully near the meat of his recent uncertainties. Unsure whether she toyed with him, Lysaer pushed away from the pedestal. He crossed the gravel path to gain a better view of her features. The layers of her hoods kept her veiled. He decided to risk honest answer. "I'm not sure. Arithon takes unconscionable risks, looking for pearls among beggars. I prefer the simpler reality, that the means to uplift the misfortunate are better controlled from the council chamber. A man can feed the hungry and clothe beggars all his life, and not change the conditions that make them wretched."

The lady considered a moment, then offered, "Your vision and Arithon's are very different. As a spirit schooled to power, his perception stems from one absolute. Universal harmony begins with recognition that the life in an ordinary pebble is as sacred as conscious selfhood. Both views are equally valid."

Lysaer responded in stifled antagonism. "And just what's your stake in all this?" He felt hag-ridden enough without her unasked-for exploration of his conscience.

She was stung; her sigh was drawn out and hinted at diffidence. Still, she did not shy back from the truth. "I was sent. Direct orders from my superiors: to seek out the princes given sanction to rule, and to interact enough to test their mettle."

He stepped back, felt the dripping lip of a second stone bench, and sank down facing her. Fiercely he said, "What have you found?"

"That Etarra offers entanglement enough to torture any man, and suffering very clearly bares the spirit. As a prince must, you place love and care for the masses before individual suffering." Her hood moved; perhaps she looked down in embarrassment for her snooping. Arithon trapped under such scrutiny would have cut off further inquiry through sarcasm; Lysaer more civilly chose silence. Drawn to shared sympathy by his tact, Elaira said, "I saw your half-brother earlier, when he made ships out of shadows in the knacker's alley."

Lysaer could not stem his curiosity, nor did he hide his concern for the strain on Rathain's prince that even the Sorcerers could not ease. "Arithon spoke to you, then?"

"No." She was sharp. "I dressed in disguise as a lad. He was never allowed to see my face. And please, I would mind very much if you told him."

The vehemence she could not quite curb sparked Lysaer to exclamation. "*You* were the lady he acted to defend when Koriani scryers tried to spy out our affairs in Ithamon!"

"I don't have a clue what you're talking about." She forestalled his impulse to explain, angry or intensely afraid. "Keep still. If it concerns the Koriani Senior Circle, I'm far better off left ignorant."

"Arithon cares for you," Lysaer said, his first impulse to soften her distress.

"He weeps for the grass that he treads on." Elaira stiffened, indignant at his solicitude. "You should know, as a scion of s'Ilessid, that the s'Ffalenn royal gift is forced empathy!" She stood in a reckless haste that showered dew from the bushes as her cloak caught. "I have to go."

"But your errand." Lysaer stood also. Effortlessly considerate, he bent and unhooked the snagged cloth without touching her. "Surely your purpose is incomplete?"

Elaira shook her head as he straightened. The dark had begun to lift with the earliest glimmer of dawn; the eyes that met his from under voluminous layers of clothing sparkled, filled with tears that only magnified their intensity. Yet when she spoke, her voice was hammered and level. "I have what I came to this garden for. You do not, if you left your bed to find calm."

Lysaer gently took her arm. "I'll see you to the gate," he said politely.

Relieved to discover he was gentleman enough not to pry, she smiled in piercing gratitude. In a sympathy tuned so closely to his inner dilemma that this time no sensibilities were offended, she said, "Speaking strictly for myself, I would spill blood to release those clan children from slavery in the knacker's yard. But then, female instinct drives me to condemn exploitation of the young. A man might arrange his priorities differently."

Lysaer steered her past the spears of the spring's sprouting lilies, his hand warm and sure on her arm. "It is not what you would do or what I would. Pity Arithon, for as he said, tomorrow Etarra becomes his problem. I only pray that the guildsmen don't murder him before he's had his chance to act at all."

They had reached the gate. Lysaer's touch dropped away as he raised the latch and opened the panel to let her through.

Elaira passed beneath the trellis. "What this realm will kill for certain is your half-brother's musical talent. Mourn that."

And then she was gone, a shadow vanished into foggy streets that no lantern could fully illuminate.

Preparations

As dawn silvers the cloud cover above the forested hills of Deshir, relays of barbarian couriers race at speed through thinning rains, bearing the call to arms for clan encampments to the north and east. . . .

Guarded from outside interference, sealed in a seamless stone flask, the uncounted entities that comprise the Mistwraith, Deshthiere, brood upon two half-brothers whose gifts have seen them doomed to oblivion. . . .

Gray seas heave off the north coast of Fallowmere, where a rainstorm spends the torrents that should have fallen upon lands far south; while skies brighten flawless aquamarine and citrine above the square bastions of Etarra, the Sorcerer responsible for nature's violation touches runes of well-binding upon plants, soil, and wild creatures, and begs their forgiveness for his act. . . .

XIV. Coronation Day

The hour past sunrise on the day appointed for Arithon's coronation, the door to Morfett's guest chamber banged open. Dakar
sallied in from the hallway, his head and torso eclipsed behind
a towering mound of state clothing. He tottered across the tile floor,
shed his armload across the nearest divan, and announced, "These
are yours. Asandir's orders." Gloating, insouciant, rumpled from a
night's hard drinking and the full-blown effects of a hangover, he
added, "I'm told to watch you dress to make sure that you leave
nothing out."

Curled in the window seat with his lyranthe lying silent across
his knees, Arithon regarded the spilled velvets and silks, shot
through each fold with costly metallic thread work. Dead sober, if a
touch haggard from lack of sleep, he made a study of Dakar and
grinned. "Silver to broom straws, your master's orders were directed
toward you as well. Anyway, you don't deck out in pearl buttons and
brocades by any choice I ever saw."

Dakar scowled, ashamed to discover that his offering also held
garments of brown broadcloth too generously cut for anybody's frame
except his own. "Get on with this." He folded his arms across his
chest. "Or by Dharkaron's vengeance, I swear, I'll call Morfett's va-
lets in to help!"

Arithon raised his cheek off the curve of his lyranthe and said,

"You couldn't get them. The entire household is too busy keeping the master from falling prostrate into his breakfast plate."

"Well, let's say your accession to Rathain's throne isn't a balm to anybody's temper!" Still distressed over Lysaer's endangerment at the time of the Mistwraith's confinement, Dakar vented his resentment upon the prince at hand. "Where were you last night?"

"Not drinking, or with a woman." Lightly, lovingly, Arithon dusted a finger across his strings. A haunting minor chord sighed forth; then, since even that slight sound galled like salt in an open sore, he laid his instrument aside. The eyes he turned upon Dakar were sharp and terrible for their emptiness. "Is there anything else?"

But the Mad Prophet refused to be baited. "If you were gallivanting again in the poor quarter, you'd better have taken a bath."

"What? The velvets aren't perfumed?" Arithon arose and stretched linked hands above his head. The linen he wore was plain, not dirty. He advanced through the flare of sunlight that fell through the amber lozenged windows, and Dakar saw in relief that the hair at his collar was in fact still damp.

Arithon stripped off his shirt. Marked yet by the physical scars from his past failed effort at sovereignty, he surveyed the array of kingly trappings in bright-eyed, self-mocking distaste. "Let's have this over with."

He dressed himself, while Dakar passed garments in roughly the appropriate order: silver-gray hose, white silk shirt, black tunic with leopard fur edging. Next, the ceremonial accessories that symbolized a sovereign's tie to the land: the belt of wooden discs inlaid with royal seals in abalone; the deer-hide boots studded with river stone and tied with feather-tipped thongs; the cabohon emerald set in silver that pinned above his heart. The fabrics held no scent beyond a hint of sweetgrass that lingered from the blessing ritual worked an hour earlier by the Fellowship. The fine-stitched tracery of interlace borders, the ribboned cuffs and hems, bespoke tailoring unmatched in Etarra. When and where such master work had been done, Arithon refused to ask.

Dakar volunteered, just to needle him. "Sethvir sews superbly, don't you think?"

"Ath," said Arithon in flat vehemence. "Not this, I hope." He raked through the garments still left and hooked out the ugly bit that jarred: a heavy, lacquer-worked sword sheath, hung from a baldric bossed with carbuncles.

Dakar looked sourly on. "Not that."

"The stones look heavy enough to sink a four-days bloated carcass." Arithon dangled the item aloft, his combativeness blunted by resignation. "This wasn't, by chance, a gift from the ladies of Etarra?"

"Bang-on right." Dakar stifled a chortle. "Asandir said wear it anyway."

Arithon glanced suspiciously back. He raised the jewel-encrusted leather to his nostrils and immediately laughed. "Damn you! It doesn't smell of sweetgrass. Is this your prank, to curse me with an ill wish in addition to this joy-forsaken realm?"

"Well," said Dakar, shrugging, "leave it out, and the ladies will be offended for sure. How could they know they'd made their contribution too late for the Fellowship's blessing? No ward I've heard of could make that thing look less hideous." Philosophically he added, "Bear up. You've got the tabard and sash yet to go before you need concern yourself with weapons."

"That thing is a fit weapon to strike a man blind at first sight." Arithon discarded the atrocity, and at Dakar's urging took the damask-lined velvet of the tabard.

The heraldic leopard sparkled as he pulled it over his head. Its weight of rich cloth seemed to burden his shoulders, while Dakar bound on the black sash with its silver wire wrapping. As if to delay the moment when he must gird on the tasteless scabbard, Arithon took up the circlet that Asandir's spell-craft had fashioned from Rathain's earth. Symbol of an unwanted succession, he gripped the cool metal with a tension that whitened his knuckles. Regret played across his expression. Then, firmly silent, he raised the fillet and pressed it over his black hair. It rested with deceptive lightness across his brow, as a crown yet to come never would.

Dakar chose that moment to look up. Imprinted against the amber casement, he saw Arithon's face crossed by the shining band that preceded Rathain's vested sovereignty. Chills roughened the Mad Prophet's flesh. One split second of vertigo was all the warning he received.

Then in a rush, his seer's talent claimed him wholly as instrument.

Trance shocked through him with such force that his mind became emptied. Dakar dropped to his knees.

A vision burned through: *of a square milling with people, among them Arithon, who drove in heedless, driven panic between tight packed factions of Etarra merchants.* The image formed fully and shattered, buried by a static blast of whiteness as a second shock slammed Dakar's innermind.

Vaguely aware that his voice shouted meaningless phrases, the Mad Prophet felt himself falling. His downward rush into darkness was suddenly and sickeningly arrested by a hand that caught and yanked him back.

He returned to himself with a wrench that left him disoriented. His face dripped sweat. Released to a welter of dizziness, he waited, panting, until orderless color resolved into the orange and purple tiles that floored the Lord Governor's guest chamber. Arithon had an arm around his shoulders. That support was all that held Dakar upright as he swayed, helplessly unbalanced.

"Ath," the Mad Prophet gasped as vertigo progressed into nausea. "Whoever named farsight a gift had the warped inclinations of a torturer."

"You should lie down." Arithon strove to lift him toward the divan.

Powerless to assist as his frame was shaken by spasms, Dakar doubled over. His breakfast stayed down, barely; the accomplishment seemed moot. He felt wretched. As Arithon helped him to straighten, he saw his morning's work wasted.

The royal tabard was rucked askew. Both of the prince's silk sleeves were blotched with perspiration. Whatever slight tolerance Arithon had attained toward kingship appeared on a moment to have fled. Against skin shocked to pallor, the hair dragged flat beneath the circlet crossed his forehead like pen strokes scribbled upon parchment. Wild-eyed as any cornered animal, the Shadow Master half forced, half propelled Dakar across the floor.

Too miserable to resist, the Mad Prophet collapsed across the divan. He had no strength to care for crushed velvets. That the scabbard with its carbuncles gouged his backside mattered less; the ugly gift from the dignitaries' wives now seemed some poor jest from a nightmare. "What happened?" he gasped; but the gut-sick aftermath of major prophecy was much too familiar to support pretense. "For Ath's sake, tell me what I said."

Arithon withdrew his hands, which were shaking. "You foretold an absolute disaster."

Terror hit Dakar in the pit of his unsettled stomach. He fought another twisting cramp as every formless uncertainty that had agonized his imagination since Ithamon replayed as a possible reality. "Lysaer. Desh-thiere has some hold on him, doesn't it?"

Mere supposition drove Arithon to an explosive step back. "Would that were all." He snatched up the sword, which rested unsheathed near the regalia he had not yet put on. "Where's the Sorcerer who should be here on guard?"

But a search of the dimmest alcoves where a discorporate mage was wont to lurk showed Luhaine nowhere in evidence. In dread that some dire facet of Dakar's prophecy had compelled the Fellowship guardian to abandon him, Arithon spun back toward the divan. "Where's Asandir!"

Dakar pressed his hands to his temples. Still trapped on the cusp of major prophecy, he cradled a skull on fire with headache. His thoughts dragged, too dim to keep pace with events, far less attach meaning to questions. Dully he repeated, "What in Daelion's province did I predict?"

Fast movement blurred his eyesight. The next second he was slapped by a blow that seemed to come out of nowhere. He crashed backward into the folds of the royal mantle. Over him towered Arithon, so consumed by dread he seemed possessed. The black and silver length of Alithiel pressed enpointe against the Mad Prophet's throat.

Shielded from bared steel by nothing beyond his shirt collar, Dakar shrank back. "Have you gone crazy?"

"Not yet." The words seemed lucid, but the insouciance Arithon usually flaunted in the face of trouble was swept away by his ragged fast breaths. "Where I can find Asandir! I have no moment to waste!"

Dakar measured the steel, then the terror that racked the man behind the sword grip. "Asandir's in the council hall. Keeping the city ministers from revolt before your processional."

The weight of the weapon lifted. Arithon spun on his heel, stopped; came back. The heraldic leopard worked into his tabard flashed as if tainted by unclean light as he jerked the plain cloak intended for Dakar from under its owner's supine bulk. He cast the garment over his finery as he bolted headlong for the doorway.

"Arithon!" Dakar shoved up on one elbow. "What did I see in that trance?"

For a split second it seemed Rathain's prince would not stem his frantic rush. But as the latch wrenched open under his hand, he threw back in anguished haste, "Dakar, as you love peace. If you care for my half-brother, *keep him from me!* For if we're brought face to face, the terms of your prophecy shall be met. The result will end in a bloodbath."

"What happened?" Dakar exploded off the couch. The black-lacquered scabbard hooked on his knuckles and fell in a clattering spin across the floor. He rushed forward, caught his toe on a carbuncle, and crashed shoulder down into an armchair. Too winded to curse, he pressed on, though the backlash and dizziness from prescience had yet to fully release him.

"It's not what's happened, but what *will*. Desperate steps must be taken." Arithon ducked out.

Dakar gained the entry just as the door panel slammed in his face.

"Fiends take you!" He hammered unyielding wood until his fists bruised before reason caught up with the obvious: that if Arithon had dispatched him to protect Lysaer, the outside latch would not be braced.

The next thought hit with more significance, that Luhaine had neither answered nor intervened to curb Arithon's distress.

Dakar kicked open the door and abruptly ran out of energy. Pinned by another wave of faintness, he thumped to rest against the door frame and sweated over implications he had no fit way to assess. His second spontaneous prophecy now entangled with the conditional forecast made earlier, the Black Rose prophecy that tied all the threads of future hope to the event of Arithon's accession. Luhaine's absence meant much more than the half-brothers' safety had been cast to the four winds and jeopardy.

The vaulted council hall of Etarra was no longer stuffy and cavernously curtained as it had been kept throughout Morfett's clandestine councils to thwart the return of Rathain's monarchy. Bedecked now for the coronation, the lofty chamber with its white marble frieze work and gilt pillars stood transformed. The faded, dusty trade guilds' banners stood jostled aside on their rods, overshadowed by the leopard blazon of s'Ffalenn. Lancet windows once darkened behind dagged scarlet drapes were flung open to the morning air. Light rinsed floors freshly sweetened with wax; sunbeams warmed the graining of maple parquet, and sparked reflections in the gems and tinseled silks donned for the occasion by the city's ranking ministers, who clustered whispering in their cadres and cast nervous glances to all sides.

But the Fellowship Sorcerer in attendance for once had no care for overhearing their seditious talk. Bleak as storm in dark velvets, Asandir presided over the aisle before the raised dais.

Morfett measured his stillness as he would have stalked an asp through his grape arbor. Let Arithon s'Ffalenn but once be caught unguarded, and the interfering Sorcerers who sheltered him would find a knife in his royal ribs.

"Where's Lord Diegan, anyway?" the minister of justice complained. "Odd that he should be late."

"Not at all." Morfett twitched at his cuffs, which were buttoned with pearls and too snug. Snappish with venom, he said, "Our commander of the guard invited that fair-haired flunky, Lysaer, for an after-breakfast social. His sister's infatuation with the man has delayed them both, no doubt."

Sourly the Lord Governor eyed the damask-draped chair set up to enthrone the coming prince. Such panoply would hardly matter, any more than a white-gold crown set with emeralds could shield against mortality. Today, tomorrow, or next year, the Teir's'Ffalenn would be overthrown. Etarra would never bow to royal rule. Never. Wishing ill on the day's proceedings, Morfett saw Asandir spin around. The Sorcerer gave no nod to smooth over the officials left gaping in offense at the abrupt presentation of his back.

Morfett smiled. Trouble, the Lord Governor wished fervently; upon the heads of the Fellowship, most ruinous, plan-befouling bad luck.

Asandir offered no apology, but turned on his heel again and pressed in visible agitation through the councilmen still clustered in shared outrage. His rush to reach the doorway left a moil of rankled dignitaries whose robes were raked askew by his passage.

Morfett sailed into the gap left opened in the Sorcerer's wake. He arrived in the foyer just after Asandir passed the outer door, caught the ring pulls as the panels swung closed, and shamelessly pressed an eye to the crack.

On the marble stair outside the entry, he saw Asandir flag down Traithe.

"Call your raven," the Sorcerer instructed his colleague. "The bird may be needed to relay messages."

The shorter mage in black and silver replied too low to overhear.

Asandir returned a slight nod. "Go inside. Smooth tempers, avert uneasiness, and above all, let nobody hear we have problems. Sethvir's just now sent warning: Lysaer's in serious trouble. The pattern that encompasses his Name has drifted. Worse: Luhaine reports that Dakar's been alarmed by premonition. Both events indicate that our s'Ilessid heir may harbor one of Desh-thiere's wraiths, picked up through the moment of confinement. If so, the crisis forecast by the strands is upon us. One mistimed judgment and we'll have no crowned king, or a restored Fellowship, just panic and bloodshed in the streets."

"Ath speed you." Denied by impaired faculties to share further details through magecraft, Traithe touched his colleague's shoulder before both went their separate ways.

Morfett straightened up from his eavesdropping and faced around. Prepared to announce the Fellowship's quandary to every official within earshot, his excitement overshadowed small descrepancies: that the doors at his back failed to latch, and that his rush of elation overwhelmed him to the point where his utterance choked in his throat. He hopped forward a step and filled his lungs to shout.

His effort emerged as a gargle, since Traithe slipped through the cracked door panel, clamped a gloved hand from behind, and gagged his mouth.

"Ah, but you won't," the mildest-mannered of the Sorcerers murmured into Morfett's left ear.

The Lord Governor moaned. His eyes bugged out and he ground out a smothered growl. He elbowed and kicked backward at his assailant, but managed to strike only air.

He bit down next on black glove leather, and got back a dig that shot paralyzing pain through his larynx.

Traithe called out cheerfully to those bystanders just turned to stare open-mouthed at the scuffle. "Could I beg your help?"

The stir widened; polite conversation faltered. Before Morfett's wheezes and moaned curses could impact the fast-spreading stillness, Traithe carried on in blithe chatter. "Your Lord Governor seems overcome. Is he prone to fits? Maybe he's prostrate from the heat. Anybody might faint under such fashionable layers of heavy velvet."

Pulled off balance, then downed by an ungentlemanly jab at the back of his knees, Morfett collapsed, mutely struggling, to the floor. A raven flapped down and lit on his chest. At least, that was the last thing his eyes recorded before he sank, dropped senseless by spells, upon carpets laid down for Arithon to tread in formal procession to the dais.

Invited for wine after breakfast in the richly appointed parlor of Etarra's commander of the guard, Lysaer suddenly flushed. A wave of heat swept through him, followed by bone-deep chill. Quickly he set down his goblet, before his unsteady hand sloshed the contents. Alarmed that he might have succumbed to sudden fever, Lysaer touched his forehead. A second wave of disorientation passed through him. He stiffened, transfixed by fear; for an instant he felt as if his mind spun to blankness, his self-awareness overturned by a will other than his own.

The sensation cleared a heartbeat later. Lysaer shivered in silly relief. He was just tired, not quite himself. Arithon's coronation presented no crisis; his momentary faintness surely had been due to nerves and imagination, a residual distress left by the nightmares that had plagued him off and on since Ithamon. As the patterned brocade chair that supported him swam clearly back into focus, Lysaer looked up.

Lady Talith's ringed hands had stilled in the curled fur of her terrier. She, her brother Diegan, and the beribboned lapdog all regarded him in polite and expectant silence.

What had he just said? Lysaer struggled to recapture the thread of conversation. A gap seemed torn from his memory. Inattention could not explain this. Embarrassed for a lapse that in hindsight seemed faintly ridiculous, he stumbled to fill in with banality.

Diegan interrupted and took up what had been a bristling argument. "But the children who work in the warehouses are not the get of the free poor, as your puppet prince led you to think." Etarra's commander of the guard set down the crystal goblet that for the past half hour he had toyed with. His wine sloshed untasted as he said, "These wretches that Arithon would champion are in fact the off-spring of condemned criminals, clan-blood barbarians who have harassed the trade routes with thievery and murder for generations."

Heat chased cold across Lysaer's skin. He resisted an urge to blot his brow, willed aside his unsettled condition, and studied the city's Lord Commander, whose finery and intellect made him more courtier than soldier, and whose words fanned up like dry cobwebs the clinging spectre of past doubts.

S'Ffalenn pirates on Dascen Elur had repeatedly manipulated political sore points to stir unrest and further their marauding feud against Amroth.

Lysaer snapped back to present circumstance with an inward lash of chastisement. This was Etarra, not Port Royal, and Arithon was not as his ancestors. More musician than buccaneer, he had been the sworn heir of a murderer in a past that no longer mattered. Fair-minded, Lysaer pushed off his uneasiness. "Do you suggest Rathain's prince would lie to discredit the city council?"

"I suggest he's in league with the Fellowship's intent, to see Etarra given over to barbarians." Diegan leaned forward. Diamond studs sparkled across his shoulders as he planted his elbows on his knees. "For that end, would he not act as the Sorcerers' purpose demanded?"

Never at ease with Arithon's mage-trained evasiveness, Lysaer re-examined matters from that angle. Only this morning Dakar had staggered in from his rounds of the taverns and attested in slurred certainty that Arithon had not spent last night drinking in any man's company. *"Wherever he was, only Daelion knows. His Grace himself's not saying."*

Lysaer blinked, pricked by association. This day's musician, who begged to be spared from royal position, was one and the same man as the chained sorcerer who had burned seven ships, then baited Amroth's council at trial with his own life offered as gambit.

"I can see you have reservations," Lady Talith observed. Her tight-laced taffeta rustled as she crossed her ankles; the terrier displaced by her movement whined and jumped plaintively down. "For our part, if this coronation is to be stopped, there's little time left to take action."

In fact, there remained but an hour before the noon ceremony. Lysaer snapped to, the odd bent of his thoughts cut off by his ingrained habit of fair play. "Don't think to suggest a conspiracy. I'll not be party to treason. The Fellowship's intentions toward your city are certainly not harmful, and Arithon's rights of inheritance are not in my province to deny."

"But you doubt him," Talith pressed.

There, most squarely, she scored. Honor demanded that the integrity of any ruler should be challenged over issues of social justice. Repelled as if brushed by something dank, Lysaer arose. Good manners concealed his private qualms as he gathered his velvet cloak and offered his hand to Talith. Her beauty might bedazzle his vision, but never his inborn integrity. He drew her suavely to her feet. "Lady, on behalf of your city, I'll question your prince. Arithon is secretive, crafty, and not always forthright about his motivations. But given direct confrontation, I've never known him to lie."

Diegan jangled the bell for the maid to collect the crystal and the wine tray. To Lysaer he added, "You'll tell us your findings before the coronation begins?"

Cold now, and unsure what should motivate him to undertake such a promise at inconveniently short notice, Lysaer found himself saying, "You have my formal word."

The room, the wine, and the company seemed suddenly too rich. Lysaer strove to recoup his composure. Sleepless nights and troubled dreams had sown his mind with unworthy confusion. For even if Arithon's sympathies were misguided, the thorns in seeing justice done remained: the laborers enslaved in guild service were still children, ill fed, inadequately clothed, and poorly housed. Although for simplicity's sake it would relieve a vicious quandary to fault them for the crimes of their ancestors, their plight deserved unbiased review. If Arithon would champion their cause, he must defend his decision to repudiate the city council's policies. Lysaer dodged the terrier that playfully circled his feet, and strode in firm purpose for the door.

"My lord, my lady," he said in parting.

A bang and a thump sounded in the passage outside.

The inbound commotion came accompanied by Dakar's voice, plaintively arguing with a servant. Protests were cut by Asandir, who demanded to know what was amiss.

Lysaer pressed his thumb on the door latch. The fastening seemed queerly to have jammed. A violent wrench failed to dislodge the obstruction.

Lord Diegan shoved the maid away from the wine tray in his haste to reach Lysaer's side. Their combined attempt to free the door caused the scrolled brass to spark white light. Heat followed, intense enough to raise blisters.

Lysaer noticed instantly that his skin took no mark from the encounter. No stranger to the effects of small sorceries, he cried out a reflexive warning. "Spell-craft!"

Diegan regarded him intently, while inexplicable heat and chills chased through his body once again.

This bout proved more fierce than the last. Lysaer swayed. For an instant the surrounding room seemed to flicker, in and then out of existence. His vision quickly steadied, but his ears were left buzzing with unnameable, untraceable sound. Rage touched him. The emotion came barbed with a thought so clearly delineated, it seemed more solid than the lintel he caught to brace his balance. Who but Arithon would have dared to interfere; the poisoned conclusion followed, that if the s'Ffalenn bastard was to blame, distrust of Etarra's council was emphatically misplaced.

Vindicated by Lysaer's dismay, Diegan said, "We're betrayed!" He matched a grim glance with his sister.

The servant in the outside corridor had fallen silent; the chambermaid cowered in a corner. Dakar's reply to Asandir breached the sealed parlor with damning, irrefutable clarity. "But of course I set wards to bind the door latch! Arithon begged me at all costs to keep him separate from Lysaer!"

"Where's the Prince of Rathain?" The Sorcerer must have glowered fearsomely, for Dakar's answer rose to a pitch very near to hysteria.

"He went out. Into the street, to look for you. If Luhaine's ghost still guards him, it's being obstinately close-mouthed. Didn't you see either one of them on your way over here?"

"No." Asandir's step approached the closed doorway. "Too late now to wish differently. Your prophecy bars us from action. You say Lysaer's inside?"

In mutinous self-defense Dakar said, "Diegan's servants insist he never left."

Lysaer felt a hand on his forearm, Talith's, pulling him quickly aside. A shock like a spark ripped through him; not for her beauty, which could stun any man, but for her unmannerly presumption. Before he had space to question his oddly irascible reaction, the feeling became swept aside and an urge he also could not trace prompted him to fast speech. "I promised I'd find Arithon and ask him for the truth. Can you get me out?"

Diegan grinned. "Every house in Etarra has a closet exit and hidden stairs to an outside alley. Talith will show you. I'll delay the Sorcerer."

"You'll try." Lysaer surrendered his hand to the lady, who breathlessly hurried him forward. "Be careful. No Fellowship Sorcerer has compunctions against prying into your private thoughts."

If the warning gave Diegan reservations, Lysaer was not to find out. Talith sank her nails into his wrist and bundled him through a doorway that had miraculously opened through the back wall. Thrust into a musty stone passageway, Lysaer heard only Talith, softly cursing the dust that grimed the gold hem of her dress before she dragged the panel closed and shut them in cobwebs and darkness.

In the parlor, the terrified maid began to sob. Balked from following its pretty mistress, the terrier's yapping changed pitch to barks and growls. The next instant the latch on the hallway door discharged a static shower of sparks. The dog bounded sideways, trailing mussed ribbons, while the panel explosively burst inward.

Asandir slammed into Lord Diegan's guest parlor, with Dakar hard on his heels. They were met by the commander of the guard, blandly seated, the decanter of wine he had been on the verge of pouring frozen in his hand in midair.

His typically Etarran urbanity made no impression upon the Sorcerer, whose gaze flicked to the other set of goblets that rested on the tray, their half-consumed contents abandoned. As the terrier subsided snarling under the nearest stuffed stool, Asandir studied Diegan with a chilling, unpleasant intensity. "Where has Lysaer gone?"

To the amazed admiration of Dakar, Diegan's nerve never faltered. He replaced the wine crystal on its tray with a faint, controlled clink. "Your man left to have words with his crony, the Teir's'Ffalenn. Should that disturb you?"

"We'll know shortly." Asandir stepped past the casement. His shadow swept over the commander of the guard, dimming the glitter of gemstones that studded his ceremonial pourpoint. Before Diegan's magnificence, the Sorcerer's dark robe hung sheenless as a pauper's cheap felt. "I want you to think, and answer carefully. While in your presence, did Lysaer show a loss of awareness? Did his attention seem to drift, even for a second?"

As Diegan made to brush off the question, the Sorcerer advanced again and forestalled him. "I said, answer carefully. For if you noticed such a lapse, your friend could be endangered. One of Desh-thiere's separate wraiths may have evaded captivity. If, unbeknownst to us, such a creature came to possess Lysaer, all of Etarra could be threatened."

Diegan gave the matter his dutiful consideration, then raised his goblet to curled lips and sipped. His eyes reflected black irony as he said, "When Lysaer left this chamber, he seemed in perfect self-command."

"And before then?" Asandir sounded worried.

"Never mind the commander of the guard," Dakar burst out. "He's got lying written all over him."

"Then keep him here under house arrest!" Asandir stalked across the carpet. "We don't need a call to arm the garrison to complicate disaster any further." He paused at the far wall, studied the bookshelf, and after a second's hesitation, reached out and thumbed the hidden catch. The false panel swung open, wafting telltale traces of Talith's lavender perfume. After an irritated glance toward Lord Diegan, Asandir departed in Lysaer's footsteps, through the bolt hole that led to the street.

"Fiends take you!" Dakar yelled after his master. He charged to the panel and wedged it before it could quite fall shut. Though the stone-walled gloom beyond by now held only drafts, he shouted anyway. "Will somebody bother to tell me what in Ath's creation I have prophesied?"

He received no answer, just a rip in his hose from the terrier, which in a belated fit of courage scuttled out from hiding and bit his ankle. Dakar's defensive kick cleanly missed. The door fell to with a thud. As the dog retreated to snarl over its pillaged shred of stocking, Diegan hefted his decanter toward the invader still left in his parlor. "Share a drink to soften misfortune?"

Dakar groaned. Already riled beyond sense by the effects of clairvoyance and a hangover, he pressed fat palms to his temples. "Wine won't help. The entire universe has gone crazy."

Diegan offered a chair and pressed a filled goblet upon the Mad Prophet. "Then let's forgo sanity also and both get rippingly drunk."

No sooner had the drapes been lowered over the windows of Etarra's great council hall than a hammering rattled the main entry. Despite the fact Traithe had sealed the doors with a minor arcane binding, one heavy panel cracked open. A raw streak of daylight slashed the foyer, raising a sparkle like a jewel vault across the agitated assemblage of officials in their wilting feathers, dyed furs, gold chains, and gem-studded sashes of rank.

Since none of Etarra's citizens held magecraft to challenge his warding, Traithe straightened hurriedly from the prostrate body of the Lord Governor. The raven on his shoulder kept balance to a flurry of wingbeats as he turned around to confront the disturbance.

Arithon's voice pealed out through the gloom. "Where's Asandir?"

Rapacious to recover their plundered advantages, every Etarran official not overawed by Morfett's collapse pressed forward, blinking against the sudden daylight. The few who were closest recognized the disheveled figure through the glare; the rest saw and identified the shining circlet that betokened Rathain's rights of royal sovereignty.

"Sorcery!" someone cried from the fore. Heads turned, hatted, bald, and formally beribboned and jeweled. "Here's the prince, burst through spells of protection. All the dread rumors are true!"

A surge crossed the gathering like a draft-caught ripple through a tapestry.

More muttering arose. "It's him. Teir's'Ffalenn. A sneaking sorcerer, after all. His Grace of Rathain."

The prince in the doorway called again. "In Ath's name, is there any Fellowship Sorcerer present?"

Traithe thrust through the press that jammed the foyer, his attention narrowed to include only Arithon's pale face. Though loath to create a public spectacle, he had no choice but bow to need. "Asandir's gone to find your half-brother. Sethvir's at the south gate armory. The streets are not at all safe."

Heartsick to realize he could not beg help, denied even privacy to speak plainly, Arithon called back. "I can't stay here."

Assuredly, he could not. The high council was keyed to animosity. If Traithe's presence momentarily stayed bloodshed, that abeyance would not long suffice. Every minister's layers of lace and brocades held hidden daggers and jeweled pins that could be turned in a moment to treachery; not a few would have in attendance paid assassins masquerading as secretaries.

Having interposed his own person between the threatened prince and the dignitaries in the chamber at large, Traithe sorted limited options. That Luhaine seemed nowhere in evidence was sure indication that the nexus of change forecast in the strands at Althain Tower had fully and finally been crossed. The wrong intervention now might displace the sequence of events that framed Dakar's Black Rose prophecy. Traithe raged at his impaired powers; unlike his colleagues, he could not gauge the broad import of this crisis at a glance. The best he could offer was a gesture. "My bird will lead the straightest course toward Sethvir."

The raven might have been a lifeline to salvation for the relief that touched Arithon's face. This the governing officials of Etarra observed. They began to press Traithe's back like wolves grown bold before weakness. Another moment, and the pack of them would turn as ungovernable as any mob in the streets.

"Go," Traithe called. The raven arose, flapping. Air hissed across splayed feathers as it shot through the gap in the door. Arithon shouldered the panel closed, just as the foremost ranks of the guild masters broke in a rush to tear him down.

Crippled Traithe was, but not powerless. As aggression crested around him, and elbows jostled him aside, he sensed to the second when the minds of the governors' council became aligned in mass will to wreak violence. Traithe seized his opening through their passion. He attached an entanglement of energies, and their intent to commit murder was bent aside and bridled as his warding snapped into the breach.

Shouts trailed off into quiet, cut by a sigh of rich cloth. The battering rush toward the doorway juddered to a slow fall forward, as every man who wished harm to his prince folded at the knees and collapsed. No townsman at the end was left standing. Nestled in their crumpled brocades, lying across flattened hats and fur-trimmed cloaks, every official in Etarra's high government settled where he lay, fast asleep.

Alone on his feet, one scarred, silver-haired mage regarded the rows of prostrate bodies, his heart aggrieved at too small a victory, won too late. The irony cut him, that but for Dakar's infernal predictions concerning the Fellowship's recovery, Arithon might now have returned here for sanctuary until the raven could summon Sethvir.

The downed councilmen snored on, oblivious.

"May every last one of you be harrowed by nightmares for your ignorance!" Traithe cursed in surly, sorrowful fervency. Then he straightened his wide-brimmed black hat and applied himself to the task of setting wards of guard over every door, every window, every closet and cranny in the chamber, that the ministers of Morfett's council should stay mewed up until the course of the tragedy forecast by the strands could guarantee what hope could be salvaged for the ill-starred Black Rose prophecy.

Lysaer closed his eyes as a third, fierce tingle played across his flesh. A still part of him analyzed this, and concluded that Fellowship Sorcerers must be seeking him through spell-craft. Heated elation followed. With uncanny certainty he realized he was no longer quite what he had been; the pattern sought out by the Sorcerers' probe had ceased to match his personality. Once he should have felt alarmed by an insight more appropriate to a mage-taught perspective. Obsessed now by compulsion to serve justice, he never questioned what caused the deviation, or his odd self-knowledge of its existence.

The paradox passed unregarded, that he lurked like a fugitive in an alley, all for a promise to call his half-brother to task. To Lysaer, this moment, the urge to uncover any latent breach of faith became overridingly important.

Every quandary that tormented his conscience and broke his night's rest with disturbed dreams had narrowed into sudden, lucent focus.

Lysaer gave a laugh in self-derision. He had fought so hard to give Arithon the benefit of the doubt that objectivity itself had become obstructive. He shivered and sweated, berating his idealistic foolishness. He had only to question, all along. For if Arithon was established as a liar, the ongoing weeks of heartsick recrimination might at one stroke become banished. Avar's bastard as a proven criminal presented Lysaer with moral duty to defend the merchants and townsmen.

A resolution in favor of complaints he understood would be a frank relief.

"I'll find you," he swore to the shadows, Arithon's name behind the vow. His tingling discomfort now replaced by fanatical resolve, he moved on.

Stray dogs that skulked across his path whined and shrank from his scent. When a braver bitch snarled and hounded his track, he dispatched a flick of light and stung her to yelping flight.

That cruelty to any animal that would have been beyond him just minutes before never once crossed Lysaer's mind. He picked his way over cracked paving and discarded bits of broken pottery and emerged from the alley into the brighter main thoroughfare.

People crowded the avenue, converging toward the square to attend the royal coronation. A sun-wrinkled farm wife stared at Lysaer's emergence, chewing toothless gums as she leaned on a strapping, dark-skinned grandson. Children darted past on both sides, tossing painted sticks in a throwing game that held careless regard for the neat clothing bestowed by their steadfast merchant parents. These, Arithon's intended victims, Lysaer greeted courteously. He smiled at a cake vendor, and paused to help her boy push her cart across the gutter.

The servant in attendance at Morfett's front doorway knew Lysaer by sight. Politely admitted inside, he asked, and was granted leave, to see himself to the guest suite on his own.

No Sorcerer guarded the back stairwell; Luhaine's wards were all faded. The room where Arithon quartered held only a still warmth of sunlight through latched, amber-tinged casements. Lysaer paused, breathing hard on the threshold. He surveyed the chamber more closely.

The callous character of its occupant stood revealed to casual inspection: in a king's cloak left crumpled into the cushions of a divan, and the gift of a carbuncle scabbard spurned and abandoned on the floor.

Lysaer scowled, that the sacred trust of royal heritage should suffer such careless usage. Only the lyranthe lovingly couched on the window seat gave testament to the heart of the man.

Urged by a pang so indistinct he could not fathom its origin, Lysaer crossed the echoing floor. By the time he reached the alcove, his feelings had fanned into rage. He shouted to the room's empty corners, "Are Rathain's people of less account than minstrelsy?"

Silence mocked him back. The silver strings sparkled sharp highlights, mute but all the same promising dalliance.

Rathain's prince would be reft from distractions; Etarra's needs *would* be served. Lysaer reached out and struck the instrument a flying blow with his forearm.

Parchment-thin wood, spell-spun silver, all of Elshain's irreplaceable craftwork sailed in an arc above the floor tiles. The belling dissonance of impact lost voice as the lyranthe's sound chamber smashed, and each scattered splinter whispered separately to rest in a swath of trammeled sunlight.

"You cannot hide, pirate's bastard," Lysaer vowed. Heat and chills racked his flesh as he spun, crunching over fragments, and burst back through the breached doorway.

The streets outside were packed by a crushing mob. Every tradesman and commoner turned out with their families now crowded toward the square before the council hall. Even a few white-hooded initiates pledged to Ath's service had left their hospices in the wilds to attend. Lysaer let the flow of traffic carry him. He felt no remorse for his destruction of Arithon's lyranthe; besieged by his drive to right injustice, he gave full rein to the ingrained gallantries of his upbringing. Lysaer touched shoulders, and patted the cheeks of children, and offered kind words to the plain-clad people in the streets. They stood aside for him, gave him way where the press was thickest, and smiled at his lordly grace.

Rathain's prince must be like him, they said; tall and fair-spoken and pledged to end the corruption in Etarra's trade guilds and council.

Lysaer did not disabuse the people of their hope. The whispered turbulence of his thinking bent wholly inward as the untroubled faith of Etarra's common folk caused him to measure his own failing. He too had allowed himself to be misled by the prince of Rathain; he, Amroth's former heir, who had lost blood kin to s'Ffalenn wiles, should at least have stayed forewarned.

A touch upon his arm caused Lysaer to start. He glanced in polite forbearance at the matron with the basket of wrinkled apples who gave him a diffident smile. "Did you lose track of your folk, sir?"

"Madam, no." Lysaer smiled. "I'm alone."

Abashed by his extreme good looks, the woman gave a little shrug. "Well, even by yourself, sir, you'd get a better view from the galleries." She raised a chapped hand from her knot-worked shawl and pointed.

Lysaer squinted against sunlight so pure it seemed to scour the air with its clarity. From his vantage at the edge of the square, the balconies of the guild ministers' mansions arose in tiers above street level. Their wood and wrought-iron railings striped shadow over a singing knot of cordwainers who boisterously shared a skin of spirits. As their least tone-deaf ringleader paused to take his swig, their ditty drifted cheerfully off key. "I have no invitation," Lysaer said above the noise. "And anyway, by now the best places are all spoken for."

"Well, that may be." Made bold by his friendliness, the matron gave him a swift appraisal. "But I've a cousin who has lodging at the front of the square. At my asking, a bit of space could be found."

Lysaer did not ask if the cousin perhaps had a marriageable daughter and fond hopes to attract a wealthy suitor. Neither did he accept on false grounds as he clasped the woman's wrist and kissed her palm. "You're most kind."

The dreams and the lives of just such honest folk were the first things Arithon's machinations would tear asunder.

Lysaer gently captured the matron's basket. "Let me. Any burden must hamper you terribly in this press."

"Not so much." But her fingers surrendered the wicker handle. Won to trust by his sincerity, the matron took his arm. "Come on. Hurry or we'll miss the procession."

Minutes later, squeezed between the granddaughters of a furniture maker and three strapping cousins who wore guild badges as vintners, Lysaer took the place he was offered.

From a third-story gallery accessed by an outdoor stairway, he gazed over the square's gathered thousands, which eddied below like currents pressed counter by fickle winds. The jeweled and feathered finery of the rich mixed uneasily with poorer fare, common laborers and beggars still clad in their jetsam of motley. Angry, outraged, curious, or joyful, the factions mingled uneasily. Etarra had turned out for Arithon's coronation in a welcome well leavened by enmity.

The atmosphere on the gallery where Lysaer came to roost was festive. The lads had been staked a cask by their master, and wine was freely passed around. The sharpness of red grapes mingled with the sweeter scent shed by apples doled out to the children.

Courteous but aloof, Lysaer smiled and offered compliments when the inevitable pretty daughter was presented. After that, though the girl in her neat paint and layered silk dresses shot him admiring glances filled with hope, he spared her little attention as he engaged in a predatory survey of the crowd.

Her little sister was more forthright.

She toddled forward and plucked at his rich sleeve. With her dimpled chin dribbled with apple juice, she demanded, "Who are you looking for?"

Behind her, older cousins were whispering, "It's him. The very one who's companion to the prince. Nobody else in Etarra wears indigo velvet like that."

The child with her fruit-sticky hands was pulled back to allow the exalted guest space.

Lysaer gave the family who hosted him scant notice as his gaze caught and fixed on an anomaly: above the sun-washed square with its heaving, raucous throng, a raven flapped, deep as shadow against the cloudless brilliance of the sky.

Heat and cold flashed through Lysaer, and a tremor coursed his flesh. Then the bird, sure harbinger of Traithe and the doings of the Fellowship, at the next heartbeat ceased utterly to matter.

Beneath the raven's flight path, a lone man shoved through the press.

Lysaer noted details in preternatural clarity. The fugitive had shirt cuffs worked in ribbons of green, silver, and black, and edged with bands of leopard fur. A plain cloak thrown on to conceal a heraldic tabard had been torn, and thread work glistened through the holes. The royal blazon might not show, but in his haste Arithon s'Ffalenn had neglected the circlet of inheritance that even still crossed his brow.

The face beneath was taut with a desperation that touched Lysaer to stark anger. "He's running away!" he murmured incredulously. "Breaking his commitment to the realm."

"Who's running away?" cried the vintner's drayman, full of red wine and brash fight.

Heat and cold and chills merged into scalding resentment. "Your prince," Lysaer snapped back. "The truth must be told. Your promised Teir's'Ffalenn is a criminal and a pirate's bastard, raised and corrupted by sorcerers."

The youngest children were staring, their half-gnawed apples in their hands. To Lysaer, the innocence in their faces reflected a whole city's deluded defenselessness.

Something inside of him snapped.

"Get the little ones inside, they're not safe here!" His command was instinctive, and charged with a regal prerogative that none on the balcony dared gainsay. A grandfather helped the house matron bundle her young through a side door.

The confused wails of the children, the scrape of a door bolt, the sudden cringing deference shown by family members still left on the gallery, made no impression upon Lysaer. From his unobstructed place at the rail, he drew himself up to full height. Delineated by a nimbus of sunlight, his hair gleamed bright gold, and his presence seemed charged with righteous wrath as any angel sent from Athlieria to scour the land of bleak evil.

Lysaer raised his hand and singled out the slight, disheveled fugitive that elbowed and shoved to escape the square, then lifted his voice in a thunderous shout.

"People of Etarra, behold the prince you would crown king and hear truth! Your lands have been restored to fair sunlight, yet one lives who can wield darkness more dire than any mist! Arithon Teir's'Ffalenn is full Master of Shadow, a sorcerer who would succor barbarians and waste your fine city to ashes!"

The roar of the multitude overwhelmed any further accusation, but the velvet-clad figure on the balcony drew notice. People thronging the great square stopped and tipped their faces up to stare. Lysaer's pointing finger and the circling flight of Traithe's raven drew notice to the other figure in that strange, partnered tableau.

Arrested in mid-flight by the grasp of two stolid merchants, Arithon cast a fraught glance at the bird.

To Lysaer, watching, the gesture affirmed s'Ffalenn guilt. A prince who was innocent of machinations would never count a dumb beast above his subjects or his own threatened fate. Jolted to savage antagonism, unaware he was the manipulated instrument of Desh-thiere's fugitive wraith, Lysaer raised rigid hands to call his gift. . . .

Buffeted by the crowd that streamed through a side street, an illusion cast over his person that lent him the semblance of somebody's benevolent grandfather, Asandir ceaselessly scanned the grand square. Then an odd flare of light drew his eye to the rail of a nondescript balcony. "There!" he whispered, his word too quiet to be overheard. His thoughts framed the image he saw: of Lysaer, poised in an unmistakable effort to summon light.

Although nowhere near the tumultuous scene by the council hall, Sethvir picked up the communication. He could do nothing, embroiled as he was in his own difficulties. His head cocked, one hand braced against the doors of the south gate wardroom, the Warden of Althain sent back acknowledgment. Under his palm stout planking shuddered and bounced, assaulted from without by a ramming squad under Diegan's acting captain. Ordered to disrupt the coronation, Gnudsog had pulled every sentry from the gatehouse with intent to breach the sealed armory. Busied with stayspells and bindings to withhold more weapons from the chaos in the street, Sethvir had no chance to express relief.

Quartering the city mobs for Lysaer had been worse than seeking a needle in a haystack. Where steel and straw could at least be winnowed separate by Name, the wraith that Desh-thiere had insinuated into the matrix of Lysaer's spirit posed a quandary. Without means to command its true essence, no stopgap spell of transfer could rescue the possessed victim from his stance of attack upon the balcony.

Sorrow and grief the strands foretold, were the Fellowship to stand restored to Seven, but with a second, unanticipated forecast entangled on top of the first, the validity of Dakar's Black Rose prophecy stood threatened. Caught in the critical crux, the Fellowship raged with tied hands. They dared use no power to divert, but could only inadequately observe the blow as, inevitably, it must fall.

"We can't even shift Arithon to safety," chimed in a sending from Luhaine, who yet tracked the s'Ffalenn prince's progress on the outside chance that the coronation might still be salvaged. *"Two interfering merchants have grabbed hold of him."*

From his stance on the street side, Asandir loosed one of Dakar's randiest oaths; an offended mother glared in his direction and scooped her toddler beyond earshot.

On the balcony above the crowd, Lysaer's hands bunched to fists. A crack split the air, and light flared raw brilliance across the sky.

"No!" Arithon's horrified cry tangled with Lysaer's scream of triumph. The Shadow Master, under attack, tore his forearm out of a man's grip, twisted, and thrust up his sword.

Silver-white light flared in a star burst that dazzled and blinded: Alithiel's Paravian-wrought protections sheared out a chord of pure heartbreak, sure proof the defending cause was just. Asandir saw and despaired.

The light bolt that speared from the balcony was wholly the work of Desh-thiere's vengeance, and the wraith that now fully possessed Lysaer.

Arcane energies collided in wrenching dissonance high over

Arithon's head. He thrashed, but despite a madman's contortions failed to evade the vigilantes who tackled him across shoulders and knees. His sword arm was seized and torn downward.

That he might have turned his blade and cut to kill never seemed to occur to him—as if the only peril that held meaning lay in Lysaer's unprovoked assault.

Asandir's hand was forced, the full might of his protections engaged to shield helpless bystanders from harm. He cursed fate, agonized that Dakar's new vision had upset the strands' forecast and precipitated crisis too soon. No coronation could take place now. On every side of the square, people were screaming, flash-blinded and whipped to stampede in raw terror that their city was being savaged by sorcery.

As light bolt and sword flash sheeted through the maze of his own conjury, Asandir mourned that Alithiel's bright magic would offer Arithon no shred of defense. The spells of Raithan Paravians were never wrought to take life, but only to dazzle an opponent and divert or deflect unjust attack.

Lysaer's was full command of light; his sight would be unimpaired by a ward that flashed just to blind.

The revenge engendered by Desh-thiere's possession arced on toward its targeted victim.

Isolate from the ward-light that shielded the chance-caught bystanders, Arithon yanked a wrist clear of encumbrance. He no longer held his sword. Only shadow cracked from his spread fingers: for defense of Traithe's raven, Asandir saw in split-second, grief-sharp perception.

Uncaring who noticed, the Sorcerer wept as Desh-thiere's offensive hammered down.

The bolt struck Arithon's raised palm and snaked in a half twist down his forearm. Scalded flesh recoiled in agony. Worse horror bloomed upon impact, as conjury well beyond Lysaer's means burst from his killing band of light.

Arithon screamed.

Red lightning jagged over his body. The merchants who struggled to bear him down were tossed away like ragdolls, leaving the Shadow Master a figure alone, strung through and threshed by patterns like tangled wire.

Asandir gasped in sick shock. The inconceivable had happened: *Desh-thiere's wraith had delivered a banespell against the half-brother beyond reach of possession.* Transferred by Lysaer's bolt of light, the evil mesh of its geas entangled in Arithon's aura.

Thunder pealed. For a heartbeat the packed square was rinsed scarlet, a tableau borrowed from nightmare. As Desh-thiere's curse claimed its foothold, Arithon's expression shifted from resistance and pain to a hatred that abjured all redemption. In purest, bloody-hearted passion, he howled and wrought shadow in answer to Lysaer's betrayal.

The air stung under a savage bite of frost, and darkness slammed over Etarra.

Night swallowed all without distinction, from Traithe's raven that yet flew unharmed on its faithful, straight course for Sethvir, to four vigilante merchants exposed to the backwash of murdering force shed from the Shadow Master's person. Cut down in sudden death, they lay twitching and seared amid smoldering brocades. Citizens scattered in fear from a carnage past grasp of sane experience.

Blackness dropped also like a curtain over the most ill-starred victim of them all, the s'Ilessid prince enslaved and ruined by the usage of Desh-thiere's loose wraith. Emptied by the powers that had driven him, Lysaer folded at the knees and collapsed against the gallery rail.

A last peal of thunder rattled the mansions that edged the square and boomed off the scarps of the Mathorns.

"Now," Sethvir sent in sorrow, "the cusp that rules the prophecy has passed. We can try to heal the smashed pieces."

Backlash

The armory that adjoined the south gate wardroom became the Fellowship's site to regroup after Desh-thiere's machinations struck the half-brothers. Sethvir by then had secured the stout doors to both chambers. Ongoing assault from the outer bailey by Gnudsog's squad of besiegers became reduced to muffled thunder by thick oak. Should the sheared-off lamp posts pressed into service as rams at length splinter down the braced panels, enchantments would remain that none but the mage-trained might cross.

Inside, ill lit by a single torch, oil and leather and the staleness of old sweat sullied the air with the leftover grimness of past wars. Dust from dry-rotted fletchings filmed the floors, smeared by tracks left from Sethvir's pacing and other marks scoured by the arbalists and pitch barrels he had dragged to clear space between the close-stacked stores.

After, his robe like old blood in the dimness, Sethvir stilled. As if, overcome by reverie, he had forgotten to move between steps. In contrary fact, his appearance masked a concentration so keen, nothing alive could escape him. Beyond distraction from the ram's thudding impacts, he unreeled his awareness beyond keep walls to measure the pulse of all Etarra.

Like individual currents in a cataract, he sensed the mobs that rampaged through streets battened black under shadow; restive city guardsmen who formed bands and drew steel to skewer any sorcerer they could search out and harry to final reckoning. Sethvir knew families mewed up in locked houses; he touched the spilled blood of the innocent, heard the cries of the raped, knew the rage and despair of the looted. Need left scant space for grief. He could set only small seals of peace.

The effects were infinitesimal: amid dusty cobwebs in a wine cellar, an infant hidden by its parents ceased its hysterical crying. Three huddled siblings quieted in relief, their terror of the dark given surcease; while in the air high above, Traithe's raven was rescued from blind circling and guided through black sky to safe roost. Yet of thousands of woes the Warden of Althain encountered, he eased but a very few. His greater reserves of necessity stayed poised as, stone patient, he scanned the welter of Etarra's disgruntled humanity, inset with the odd pool of calm that was Traithe's spell of ward upon the governing officials, asleep and barred inside their council hall.

Sethvir might have found humor in their predicament had the signal he awaited not chosen that moment to manifest.

"Reach," the Warden of Althain responded.

On a balcony in the darkened main square, Asandir acknowledged, then stepped into a net of forces held ready to receive him. His foot left the platform of a gallery redolent with spilled wineskins and bruised apples, passed through a nexus of spatial distortion, and came down in dust and steel filings on the floor of the south keep armory.

Sethvir stepped clear as the shadows cast by the weapon racks rearranged to embrace his colleague's tall form. In his arms Asandir cradled Lysaer s'Ilessid, unconscious. One jeweled, silk-clad wrist dangled down, and hair fanned gold strands across the shoulder of the Sorcerer's dark robe.

Clear-cut as a cameo, the prince's profile reflected the inborn nobility of his lineage; no shadow showed of the evil that had blighted life and honor. Unwitting pawn of ill circumstance, Lysaer had yet to waken and feel the change that disbarred him from royal inheritance.

Sethvir avoided Asandir's eyes, which were steel-bleak. The hands, too fierce in their grip, that crinkled fine lace and blue tinsel; his stance, forced and graceless from the sorrows unspoken between them: that after today's unconscionable sacrifice, the s'Ffalenn coronation had not happened.

The result did not bear mention, that the precarious Black Rose prophecy, which keyed Davien the Betrayer's repentance and the return of Ciladis the Lost, should be left unresolved and in jeopardy.

Desh-thiere had been allowed its ugly vengeance, yet the reunification of their Fellowship they had traded Athera's peace to guaran-

tee had escaped its conditional link to the future. The drum boom of
the siege ram disallowed space for regret, that every atrocity that
swept Etarra's streets might have been set loose in vain.

"Lay him there." The Warden of Althain indicated the weathered
canvas litter he had braced off chill flooring with upended casks of
catapult shot. Asandir shed his burden and knelt to rearrange blue
velvets before they became napped with grime and oil.

"You cannot blame yourself," Sethvir said quickly. He did not add
empty platitudes, that Arithon might one day rise beyond the day's
betrayals and change heart to embrace his inheritance; that Rathain's
mismanagements and hatreds, now vastly worsened, could somehow
be healed without scars.

Left bleak and empty-handed, Asandir slipped his dark cloak and
covered the fair-haired prince still left in their charge. Soft as a fall of
shadow, heavy wool veiled the glitter of rich thread work that proved
Lysaer still breathed. "We were remiss not to look for possession,"
Asandir said finally.

"Across *time?*" Sethvir closed his eyes, savaged by awareness that
continued to span the warp through weft weave of reactions that
marked a city's plunge into turmoil. The strain did not just leave him
vague; today he looked whitely haggard. "Had we Name for the one
wraith responsible, we might have unriddled its intent. But prevent?
The conflict etched by the strands has not altered. And Arithon is in
retreat, not dead."

Which was close as he could bear to come to pleading faith in a
major miracle.

In answer to unvoiced forebodings, the torch flame streamed in its
bracket, then extinguished as Luhaine's presence unfurled with untoward violence in the armory. "I've lost him," he announced in reference to Arithon. The ongoing thud of the rams clipped his words as
he added, "I managed to track him across the square, but his life pattern's drifted severely. I mislike the evidence, that Desh-thiere's
wraith wrought black sorcery whose taint has afflicted both half-
brothers."

"It's accomplished more than possession, we've confirmed."
Sethvir's admission came tired as he joined Asandir beside the litter
and cradled both hands under Lysaer's head.

"But not what," Luhaine fired back.

"Let Cal work, and he'll tell you." That Asandir used Sethvir's ancient and all but forgotten mortal name laid bare the depth of his distress.

Luhaine disregarded the lapse. "No one of us can afford to stand idle while you check!" He departed in a whip snap of wind more Kharadmon's style than his own.

Fibers of dry-rotted fletching spiraled away on the draft, faintly visible to mage-sight against a chiaroscuro of dark.

"It's bad," Asandir concluded softly. "How bad?"

"Ah, the unsuspected craftiness of the creature." Sethvir's voice seemed blurred to distraction as his awareness realigned with his flesh. "Desh-thiere's plot has been deviously thorough." He sighed and smoothed the rutched laces of Lysaer's formal collar. "It understood that its bane was comprised of paired strength. What better protection than to sunder our princes through hatred, and set their gifted talents against each other?"

"It cursed them to enmity, so." That implied long-range planning, a chilling fact. Asandir shared Sethvir's unsettled wariness, that the wraiths left under ward at Skelseng's Gate were far from secure as they stood.

But that complication must wait.

"What else?" Asandir prompted gently.

Abject in misery, Sethvir released his findings.

Not surprisingly, the Mistwraith's malice had begun that night when the half-brothers had been cornered outside of Paravian protections at Ithamon. Cognizant of them as its enemy, Desh-thiere had imprinted their personalities then. The Fellowship's nightlong search to uncover damages in the aftermath had been wasted effort: the wraiths had done no meddling, not then.

In shock and raw pain Asandir voiced the appalling conclusion. "Desh-thiere had already encompassed the scope of Arithon's training in that first split second of contact!"

Fenced by battered racks of weapons, the Warden of Althain propped his forehead on laced knuckles. "Worse." His words fell deadened against his sleeves. "The wraiths withheld from action, brooding upon what they had learned." And then when language failed him, he set his ugly findings into thought. Deep damage had not occurred until Lysaer's bare-handed, heroic exposure, in the throes of the last struggle to confine the entities at Ithamon. New knowledge reshaped the decision to shield Arithon's learning to a tragedy of broader proportions.

"Our protections were wrongly aligned," Asandir whispered, anguished. "We sought harm too soon, and protected craft teachings too late." Woe to Lysaer, his integrity left ruthlessly forfeit to an enemy that took him defenseless. The irony wounded, that Arithon's schooled protections might have deflected the attack, or at least sensed the presence of an invading wraith before it could move to possess. "Dharkaron damn us for fools, we threw the wrong prince into jeopardy."

Too late in hindsight to reverse a choice miscalled through crisis and desperation, Sethvir closed dry, chapped fingers over his colleague's wrist. "Without Desh-thiere's true Name, we were blinded. And still are." Gently, despondently, he clarified: that a stolen memory from Lysaer's trials in the Red Desert had offered foothold for Desh-thiere's revenge; when for the sake of survival, Arithon had once resorted to magecraft to break the recalcitrance of a half-brother whose hatred eclipsed hope of reason.

"The Mistwraith seized upon discord, then borrowed deeper knowledge from the bindings Kharadmon attached to Lysaer's consent on Kieling Tower," Sethvir said. "The spell curse just cast interlinks with the half-brothers' life-force. To dissolve or countermand its hold would separate spirit from flesh."

"Death," Asandir mused bitterly. His remorse did not lighten for past mistakes. While the Mistwraith's entities encompassed such grasp of the mysteries, the Fellowship and two princes from Dascen Elur had achieved no small feat to bind and confine all but one. There remained the unresolved menace of Lysaer's possession, and an entity that must of necessity be exorcised now.

"Are you ready?" Sethvir asked. Though the eyes of his colleague mirrored trepidation, the two Sorcerers took position across the makeshift pallet and placed hands upon the prince's brow and chest. Around them the gleam of a thousand weapons lay quenched in darkness, kept keen for blooding mortal flesh. Yet against a phantom entity, steel offered only brute ending: the sharp, final agony of the mercy stroke that exchanged live suffering for the grave.

Cruel comfort. Asandir snatched a shaky breath. "You know, if we fail, we'll have to kill him."

Sethvir chose not to answer. At some point the shivering boom of the ram had stopped. Deep quiet spread over the armory until a sorcerer's profound concentration could pick out the sigh of each settling dust mote. Aimless air stroked the blades in their racks, and rang from them tone that sang of death. Distanced from such distractions, Sethvir stilled into trance. His awareness merged into Lysaer's to ferret out the elusive energies which made up the enemy wraith.

No simple exorcism, this delicate unraveling of spirits, since the entity they sought to extricate stayed unnamed.

To Asandir fell the task of safeguard. Submersed in Sethvir's labors, he paced a hunt through the complex, interlocking auras that composed Lysaer's spirit. Like inventory, each strand and loop and whorl of light became mapped; those that belonged to s'Ilessid were set under ward by Asandir. Any that felt alien Sethvir marked aside. The nuances of identity were perilous, slight—in some cases outside logic or intuition. A wrong choice would cause a fragment of the victim to splinter off, an amputation of the soul more permanent than the most devastating bodily mutilation. Yet without Name to compel the invasive spirit out of its entrenched possession, the Fellowship had no other recourse. The risk of error widened with the taint of the spell-curse that bound the half-brothers into enmity. At first hand Asandir was forced to share the anguish of Sethvir's prior assessment. For the hatred instilled into Lysaer for his half-brother was so thoroughly intermeshed with his life force that it defeated outside help to unravel. The geas to take down Arithon both was, and was not, a part of the s'Ilessid prince's essence. To miscall just one twist of its bindings would be to condemn Lysaer to death.

Sweating, frustrated, intermeshed in life threads complex enough to fray reason to the bittermost edge of bewilderment, Asandir grasped why Sethvir had met his last statement in silence.

More likely their attempted exorcism would go awry and kill the victim than any aspect of an unnamed wraith be left at large to require an execution.

Time lost meaning. The paired Sorcerers submerged in the immensity of their task made countless, agonized choices. Near the end, in ragged exhausion, they examined their respective progress.

The patterns that contained the known wraith were layered too thinly to be credible.

"That can't be all of it," Sethvir sent in ringing despair. "Where in Ath's name can it be hiding?"

They began afresh, untangled Lysaer's memories strand for strand. Some rang false—far too few. The wraith's entirety yet escaped them. Sick with trepidation, Asandir said, "We had better reexamine what was artificial at the outset."

Sethvir's grief came back barbed with white anger. That Deshthiere's aspect might attach its possession to the given gift of the s'Ilessid royal line was unthinkable. And yet there it was: the rest of its meddling essence enmeshed so subtly with Fellowship sorcery that their own review had missed it out.

"Dharkaron, Angel of Vengeance!" Sethvir all but wept. "No wonder the ill creature had him! It gained entry through the one avenue of conscience he was spell-charged never to question." The fault and the weakness were never Lysaer's, but the Fellowship's own, for sorrowful lack of foresight.

That moment a key rattled in the outside lock to the wardroom.

Gnudsog's bass shout cut off on somebody's testy command, this followed by a mortal yelp of pain.

Dakar said, his diction slurred and quarrelsome, "Well, I warned you there'd be wards. Let me."

Sethvir sighed. "Company. We had better finish this quickly."

The rush sat poorly with Asandir. But if the panic-driven bloodshed in Etarra's streets was to be curbed, Lysaer's talents would be needed to dissolve Arithon's barrier of shadows. Crisis allowed no time to triple-check steps that at best were uncertain business anyway. Asandir steadied the defenses set to shelter Lysaer's spirit. Then, braced as if for a cataclysm, he said, "Go."

Sethvir unleashed counter-bindings like a trap over the parasitic wraith. Light crackled over Lysaer's body. A convoluted mesh traced like fire upon the air, reflected in sword steel and pole arms. Asandir felt a burn of force tear against his wards as the wraith interlaced through its victim's being thrashed to maintain its hold. The pull increased, terrible as the tug of a rip tide or the wrench of barbed grapples from seasoned oak. Asandir resisted. To lose grasp on even one strand of the pattern was to cede a bit of Lysaer with the wraith.

Sethvir's draw spells sharpened. Stress points flared cold blue, and the lines over Lysaer's body blurred and spiked where they dragged one against another, like entangled wires pried to separation.

The wraith clung, obdurate.

Sorcery peaked to compensate. On the litter, Lysaer spasmed taut. The pain of the forced unbinding cut even through unconsciousness, and a harrowing wail tore from him.

The cry as well had been Asandir's, for the prince's torment became shared. No resource could be spared for small healing, absorbed as the Sorcerer was in holding spirit united with flesh. Even as powers twisted and flashed at his directive, he could not shed the feeling that this exorcism was going too hard. As if the wraith had sunk fangs into some part of Lysaer, it seemed intent upon ripping him asunder rather than relinquish its possession.

And then on the heels of that uncertainty, the wraith came unraveled from Lysaer's being so abruptly that recoil hit like a slap. Spellcraft sheared the last connections and pinned the creature down in midair. For good or ill, the deed was done. The trapped wraith froze, burning in malice like a marsh candle; the freed man lay dazed senseless on the litter. The Sorcerers braced at his side regarded each other, beaten and drained from their labors. Between them passed understanding: that cost had been set upon this unbinding. The s'Ilessid gift of true justice, bent to ill usage by the wraith, had suffered untold further damage.

Asandir ventured hoarsely, "The curse that sets Lysaer against Arithon had sullied the s'Ilessid gift in any case."

Hunched with his chin on clasped knuckles, Sethvir sighed. They dared correct nothing now. Not without risk of disturbing Desh-thiere's binding and chancing the s'Ilessid prince's life. "There's always the next generation," he said sadly. "The wraith, at least, is defeated."

The barest hitch to Sethvir's statement snapped Asandir to keen scrutiny. The Warden of Althain avoided contact, his mind held shuttered and dark. His eyes stayed stubbornly averted. Asandir said, "There's more. You've got Name for the ill-starred being, don't you?"

Now Sethvir did look up, bleak as ice on spring blossoms in the sickly glimmer shed by the wraith. "Once the creature was human."

Stunned by cascading implications, scraped raw by a forced reassessment of the countless doomed spirits imprisoned under wards at Skelseng's Gate, Asandir lost speech. Dread burdened him as each wraith's disfigured humanity set his Fellowship too bleak a quandary. A Sorcerer's judgment was not Ath's authority, to trap unconsenting spirits in a limbo of indefinite imprisonment. Neither could the riddle of Desh-thiere's nature be unwound to free those damned thousands until the Fellowship stood at full strength, their number restored back to Seven.

All and more swung in pivot upon one chancy cipher: the life of the last s'Ffalenn prince.

As Sethvir and Asandir shared this final, most vivid disclosure compounded of miscalculated risks and urgency, immediate troubles returned to roost.

The bar on the armory door clanged up. A stayspell flared dead and steel hinges wailed open as, bemoaning a headache in a carping counterpoint, Dakar pitched sideways into the breach. The shoulder that hit against the lintel became the only scrap of luck that kept him upright.

"It's dark!" Diegan's complaint shivered the still air with echoes. "Dharkaron take your drunken whimsy, I heard no screams. Nobody's in here."

"Oh, yes." Dakar launched off and rocked two tipsy steps across the threshold. "They're here. Trust me. Sethvir just forgets to light candles."

Suspicious, still bristling from the force required to stand down Gnudsog and his squad at the ram, Diegan sniffed. An acridity like cinders yet lingered, as if a torch had gone out not long since.

"There." Dakar swayed on braced feet, forgetful that darkness masked the area where he pointed.

The space proved not to be empty. Clipped and grainily hoarse, Asandir said in ghostly rebuke, "You call *this* keeping Etarra's captain of the guard under house arrest?"

Diegan started nearly out of his jeweled doublet.

Dakar lost his balance and sat. "The wine," he admitted on the tail of a soulful grunt. "We drank both flagons, and Diegan pleaded. Where's Lysaer?" Then, as muddled wits or his eyesight recovered, he noticed the nearly subliminal glow fixed under ward before Sethvir. Dakar squinted, identified the configurations for a seal of imprisonment, and inside, a whirling, twisted light that made his stomach heave. Not the aftereffect of indulgence, this sickness, or the clench of impending prophecy; his nausea stemmed instead from reaction to something warped outside of nature.

Dakar's stupor cleared. "You knew!" he accused.

Asandir's correction was instant. "Suspected. Without command of Name, we had no means to foresee how Desh-thiere's harm would choose to manifest. And with your second bout of prophecy made in conflict with the first, we had no clear path to choose."

"I don't even *know* my second prophecy." Deflected by personal injury, Dakar looked down as if to make sure of the floor. That led him to cast about for something solid to lean on, until sight of Lysaer on the pallet refueled his disrupted train of inquiry. "So you did nothing," he berated his Fellowship masters, and rage bled away into a sorry, drunken grizzle. "Ah, Ath, like us all, Lysaer trusted you."

Through the cracked-open panels of two siege doors beat the roar of an enraged populace, cut across by Gnudsog's bellowed orders. Words carried faintly, reviling mages and royalty. The rabble had begun to chant.

Against that backdrop of ugliness, Diegan confronted two Sorcerers. "So, will you also do nothing now?"

Sethvir arose. At his wave, flames burst afresh from the torch stub. Hot light flooded across the armory, snagged to sparks on the metal filings scattered in swaths from the sharpening wheel; on the racked gleam of blades that soon would run dull with new blood; and on the amethysts and diamonds sewn on Diegan's doublet, which jerked to his passionate breaths.

Mild as sun-faded velvet before the whetted weapons that ringed him round, the Warden of Althain blinked. "Do you wish our help?"

"I wish Dharkaron's curse upon you all, never more fervently than now!" Diegan shoved briskly forward; bullion fringes snapped at his boot cuffs as he stopped and stared down at Lysaer. "What have you done to him? Killed him? Because he spoke out against your prince?"

"They wouldn't harm him," Dakar interrupted. "Lysaer's gift of light will be needed to lift off Arithon's blight of shadows."

"So, it's true!" Diegan's black eyes flicked from Sethvir to Asandir. "The king you tried to foist on us is one of you, a sorcerer born and trained. You forced our governors to stand down, on threat of riots. Well, we have them now regardless. Guild houses are afire. The minister's palace and governors' hall are being stormed this moment by the rabble."

To every appearance unruffled by Diegan's accusations, Sethvir fingered his beard. Of Lysaer he said to his colleague, "I do regret to release him before we know Arithon's fate."

"We don't have any choice." Asandir set his hands to the blond head of the prince on the litter and engaged a gentle call to awaken. Sethvir's appalling disclosure of one wraith's botched humanity had overturned every priority. The disposition of Desh-thiere to safer captivity at Rockfell perforce must take precedence, and Etarra survive its own course. The Lord Governor's standing had been undermined past the point where his authority could be salvaged. Lysaer alone could burn off Arithon's stranglehold of shadows and stop the spread of panic and misdirected bloodshed, even if, afterward, Desh-thiere's curse would drive him to turn the city garrison as a weapon against his half-brother.

The strands, after all, had converged in this forecast of war.

"You shall have what you asked for." Asandir met Diegan's rancor with a calm made terrible by perception. "Battle, misunderstanding, and a cause to perpetuate bitter hatred." Under his ministrations Lysaer stirred and moaned.

Diegan quickly knelt and shook the s'Ilessid prince's arm. "Are you all right? Friend, did they hurt you?"

Lysaer opened his eyes. He looked lost for a moment. Then he turned his head, frowned, and focused clearly upon Asandir. "Ath forgive me," he whispered. "I had a nightmare. Or is it true, that I smashed Elshian's lyranthe?"

Asandir all but flinched; his glance of inquiry hardened to misery as, from the sidelines, Sethvir gave sad affirmation.

Pity roughened his words as he said, "Whatever you recall was no dream. Etarra has been driven to riot. Since your actions have discredited Rathain's prince, your talents are needed immediately to restore the city to order."

The grinding noise of the mob only then reached Lysaer's notice. He sat up, saw Diegan, then flushed as other memories flooded back. "Arithon. Whatever I said, he's caused mayhem, set shadows and terror in the streets." Then, his inflection so changed that it jarred, he added, *"Where is he?"*

"You speak of your half-brother," Sethvir rebuked, hoping against chance to shock back some buried spark of conscience.

But Desh-thiere's curse had imbedded irrevocably deep, and old malice resurfaced in force. "He's bastard born, and no relation of mine."

"Ill feeling cannot alter fact, Teir's'Ilessid," Asandir cracked back. "You go to spill a kinsman's blood."

Lysaer was unmoved. "I go to redress an injustice. Mark this. When I find your lying get of a s'Ffalenn pirate, I'll see him dead and thrown in pieces to the headhunter's pack of tracking dogs!"

"Then we have no more to say." Asandir arose, cold to his core. He stepped over Dakar, who drowsed in an inebriated heap.

Lord Diegan, commander of Etarra's garrison, was first to move toward the door the Sorcerer swung open. Tight-lipped in vindication, he said to Lysaer. "I admire your ambition. But first, my friend, we have to hunt down this prince of shadows."

"He's prince of nothing! And finding him should be simple." Lysaer matched step beside the elegant Lord Commander. Urgently speaking, he departed without a backward glance.

From the wardroom, Lord Diegan's shout cast back echoes. "Gnudsog! Forget about the spare arms. Assemble a patrol double quick! Dispatch them to the warehouse district to scour the alleys. If fortune favors, the Master of Shadows will be there. Hustle, and we'll take him in the act of freeing convicts!"

The wardroom doors boomed closed. Shut off from the din in the streets, a contrary draft eddied between bowstaves and halberds and showered red sparks from the torch flame. Left amid crawling shadows and the slowly falling dust of the armory, Asandir sat on a shot cask. The glance he cast after the vagrant breeze was balefully focused and grim. "Arithon's been and gone from the warehouse quarter, I trust."

Luhaine's staid tones answered. "I couldn't be sure. The child convicts were released within the hour. The locksmith and the wagoners hired to free them were paid off with gold gotten from the pawn of a crown emerald. The gem took some trouble to recover."

"The children?" Sethvir cut in. For a fast check into the district had revealed the same wagons overturned by the fury of the mob.

"Disbursed. They'll hide like rabbits, then bolt for open country as they can." Luhaine resumed his report. "Arithon's horse is gone from the stables. A half canister of the narcotic herb tienelle was taken from Sethvir's saddle packs."

The Warden of Althain brightened. "Let Arithon keep it. He's not unschooled in its use, and against Etarra's armed garrison he's going to need every advantage."

"So I thought also." Luhaine paused. "I contacted Kharadmon."

"To reverse the storm?" Sethvir sucked in his cheeks to stifle a harried, madcap smile. "But that's brilliant! If Diegan's going to roust out the garrison, let his search parties rust their gear to a fare-thee-well in a cold, northeasterly downpour." Next moment, his expression distanced into self-satisfied relief. "Bless Ath, he's shown sense."

"Arithon?" Asandir cut in. "You found him?"

No small bit irked, Luhaine said, "How? Where?"

Long used to untwisting the myriad affairs of five kingdoms, the Warden of Althain tugged out a tangle he found in his beard. "There's but one dun mare in this region with a white splash marked on her neck." Then, in delight undimmed by the reproof of expectant colleagues, he answered the original question. "She's past the main gate, and driving at speed down the north road. Which means Arithon eventually must ride into the patrols of Steiven, Regent of Rathain."

"That's no good news," Dakar grumbled from his pose of flat-out prostration.

Luhaine was swift in agreement. "Steiven has just one ambition, and that's to collect every Etarran guild master's severed head."

Sethvir threw up his hands. "Bloody war's a fine sight better than the s'Ffalenn royal line cut dead by a sword in an alley!" He subsided in belated recollection that Luhaine was yet uninformed; the revised priorities forced on them by the Mistwraith's warped ties to humanity had yet to realign his opinion.

While Asandir in tart chastisement jabbed a toe in the ribs of his apprentice, who seemed inclined to drop off snoring. "Arithon dead, don't forget, would doom your Black Rose prophecy to failure."

"You *want* Davien back?" The Mad Prophet opened drink-glazed eyes in martyred affront. "That's fool rotten logic, when his betrayals were what dethroned your high kings in the first place!"

Muster

Shadow lay thick over Etarra's streets, the torches in their rusted brackets smothered to halos of murky orange. The strife, the cries, the clash of steel weaponry, and Gnudsog's gruff oaths sounded eerily muffled, as if the unnatural darkness lent the heavy air a texture like wet batting. Kept insulated from the jostle of the mobs, embedded like fine treasure amid the fast-striding tramp of armed escort, Diegan regarded the ally but lately forsworn from the Fellowship Sorcerers' grand cause.

Lysaer looked angry pale: white skin, gold hair, bloodless lips. His expression remained remote as they passed some rich man's door page being bullied by ruffians from the shanties. The curve of Lysaer's nostrils did not flare at the stench of spilled sewage that slimed the cobbles. His wide, light brows never rose at the measures the guard escort used to clear a rampaging gang of masons who had smashed a butcher's door to steal cleavers. Torches and halberds cut reflections on those eyes; but their gem-stone hardness stayed untouched.

From a side alley too squalid for lanterns, a woman cried entreaties. A man's bellowed curses quit with the sound of a smack against flesh, and a cur with raised hackles raced into the vanguard ranks, caught a boot in the flank, and tumbled yelping. The advance guard turned another corner in their progress toward the town hall, and Lysaer stepped over the crippled dog with barely a flicker of a glance.

Diegan fastened his braided cloak ties against a shiver of discomfort. "Is it true?" he asked softly.

That splintered sapphire gaze disconcertingly turned on him. "What?" Lysaer blinked, and seemed partially to come back to himself. "Is what true?"

Cold eyes, warm voice; Diegan steeled himself. No coward despite his dandy looks, he forced the necessary inquiry. "Your lineage. Are you royal? Does that sorcerer's upstart really share your blood as half-brother?"

Lysaer's look went straight through him. "Would you claim kinship with a byblow forced upon a queen by abduction and rape?" The little falsehood came easily, that his mother's flight to embrace her s'Ffalenn paramour had never extended through a year of willing dalliance. A frown marred Lysaer's features as he wondered upon the memory that once he would have spoken differently; that he had in some other time challenged his royal father to intercede for the pirate bastard's comfort.

That event seemed distant, as cut off as a stranger's memory. Brave, Lysaer had seen himself then; honorable and just. Now his past pity seemed the puling naivete of a fool, to have invited his own downfall, and thrown away heirship in Amroth for adherence to one painful truth. A lie cost so little in comparison; and by today's outcome, his losses being permanent, and Arithon having shown his true nature, the fib to Diegan as well had been the plain truth. Feeling giddy and light, as if the burden of heaven's arch had been unyoked from his shoulders, Lysaer almost laughed.

"You're royal as he, then," Diegan murmured in dark conclusion. He caught Lysaer's fierce flare of mirth and reassessed: both hysteria and the queer lack of emotion were quite likely the effects of profound shock. Moved to sympathy, the Lord Commander softened his accusation. "That's difficult. Most awkward."

"Not at all." The next lie came easily to Lysaer's tongue. "I may be a king's son, and legitimate, but not on Athera's soil. What inheritance I could claim by birthright lies beyond the span of a worldgate, unreachable, reft from me by the doings of s'Ffalenn."

"A prince in exile, then?" pressed Diegan.

Lysaer's smile was sudden as thaw in spring snow. "No prince at all, friend. I was formally disinherited, a victim of sorcerer's wiles, as you are. Etarra's people shall have my help for their own sake. Rest content. I find just vengeance sufficient."

They passed the juncture of another alley; Diegan scanned the cross street out of ingrained habit, since such sites were prime places

for high-bred officials to be ambushed. "Then your mother was not
s'Ffalenn?"

"No, can't you guess?" Lysaer grimaced on an edge of pain deep
buried from childhood. "My mother, may Dharkaron Ath's Avenger
visit judgment on the seed of her shame, was the sadly ravished
queen."

Ahead loomed the market square, its arched entry ghost-lit by the
lamps. In the strange and strangled light, the luck shrines tucked
under carven gables were grotesquely clotted in wax from the candles
left lit by ambitious merchants. The little tin talismans that should
have jangled to warn of iyats hung silent, gripped fast in the windless
dark.

The mob pressed thicker, where farmers won over to the cause of
restored monarchy hurled insults and loose bricks at guild tradesmen.
Now and again the cross fire of debris would clang off the face of a
targe. More soldiers had bolstered Diegan's escort. These newcomers
brought the fire-caught glint of gilt trappings, and the weapons they
brandished to clear headway were still streamered in ceremonial colors. Drawn from the squads originally posted to keep order through
the coronation processional, their splendid appointments lent
Gnudsog with his scars and nicked field gear the hard-bitten look of
a felon.

Disturbance ruffled the ranked columns. A messenger in governor's livery burst through, breathing hard, his cheek disfigured by a
bruise. He cried above the din for Lord Diegan.

"Here's news!" bellowed Gnudsog to his commander. "You can't
want it now, lord. Better to hear inside sanctuary after we reach the
council hall."

"No!" The courier's voice cracked in terror. "Not there! The hall's
been locked fast by fell sorcery."

"Traithe," Lysaer said tersely. At Diegan's taut-jawed flare of outrage, he raised a placating hand. "The ministers inside won't be
harmed."

Amethysts and diamonds spat glints through murk as the commander of the guard spun around. "Send the man through. I'll hear
him now."

Soldiers gave way to admit the courier. His shirt was torn at the
shoulder, and the knuckles of one hand were skinned raw. "I'm lucky
to have reached you at all, lord. Looters have kicked down the lamp
posts for quarterstaves, with three city aldermen battered dead."

"You have news?" Diegan yanked the man up by his collar.
Just then aware of who attended his Lord Commander's right

hand, the messenger gasped and flung away. "But, my lord! That blond man is lackey for the sorcerers!"

High-tempered, about to hail Gnudsog to end the fool's dithering by blows, Diegan started at a touch upon his arm. He swung, restrained by the steady gaze of Lysaer.

The prince who had abjured all rights to royal rank said gently, "No. After Arithon's betrayal, any man's enmity is fair. Let me prove myself worthy of trust, his, yours, and Etarra's." The prince in his tinsel velvets showed a proud, unpracticed majesty, and the result of unprepossessing humbleness clothed in grace and shining wealth combined to powerful effect.

The messenger was moved to stand down. "Your pardon, great lord." He bent to touch his forelock and stopped, aghast at his dripping knuckles.

Lysaer startled him from embarrassment with a kindly clap on the shoulder. "Forget titles. Against the Master of Shadows, we are equal in station, you and I." Then, as if screaming, rampaging mobs were not being thumped by Gnudsog's soldiers, as if no darkness choked sight, he probed with gentle questions for information.

Diegan watched, awed, as the messenger stopped quaking and answered. Very quickly they learned that Traithe's spells disbarred the council lords from action. Surly as an old, scarred tiger, Gnudsog allowed that while his squads could batter down door panels well enough, wards of sorcery were another matter.

"Then we won't use force," Lysaer said equably. To the courier he added, "You've crossed the main square by the council hall. What's become of the grand dais built for the s'Ffalenn pretender's speeches?"

The courier rolled his eyes. "Rioters been having at it, sure enough. A pack o' guild apprentices came with pry bars and staves to tear it down, but there's farmers with drays blocked it off, flying leopard banners and swearing they'll enforce the crown charter for their land rights."

"Extremists from both factions?" Lysaer grinned. "That's perfect." He laughed and turned shining, exultant eyes toward Diegan, who remained mystified, and Gnudsog, who kneaded the scars on his sword arm in fixed and unholy irritation. "Since your councilmen cannot act to calm their city, here is how we'll do it for them."

They marched briskly and gained the square. Gnudsog formed his men into a flying wedge and bashed through the rioting apprentices from the rear. Swords and steel-shod halberd butts made short work of wooden staves; the dray with its spilled crates of melons and string-tied half-trampled chickens afforded only minimal delay. Gnudsog's men used pole arms for levers and had the vehicle set upright in a trice. By then combatants on both sides screamed curses, united in common cause against the soldiers.

While the fighting shifted focus, Lysaer mounted the unguarded stairs, littered with torn-down snarls of bunting and leopard banners that beleaguered torchlight re-rendered from s'Ffalenn green and silver to funereal black. Fired by righteous purpose, he paused to comfort a farm lad who knelt with his gashed cheek compressed with the wadded-up tail of a streamer. A word, a touch, a light joke, and the boy was induced to smile. Today's ripped face would leave a scar that would win him no endearments from the tavern maids. Another bit of ruin to swell an already vicious score. Unmindful that a curse drove his enmity, Lysaer reached the upper platform, where a s'Ffalenn turned traitor to his birthright should have pledged Etarra his protection.

The Fellowship had chosen a site of favorable visibility and acoustics. Lysaer paused between the stripped and splintered awning poles, given vantage to every corner of the square.

Before him spread the city's tragic turmoil. Picked out in pallid lantern light, small episodes stood out: the screaming craftsmen who brandished tools and uprooted stakes from the awning ties; the drunken laughter and gyrating celebration of a raggedy band of looters; a woman clutching a torn dress. And an elderly burgher beset in extremity, his cane struck away, the rim of a broken flower pot his last weapon to fend off his attackers.

Misgiving for their plights dispelled the disorientation that lingered since Lysaer's reawakening. Desh-thiere's realignment of his loyalties was irrevocably complete.

His hour under the wraith's possession he now blamed on spells laid to daze and confuse him; that the Fellowship would act to abet Arithon's escape was foregone conclusion, since they had persistently refused to lend credence to any of his past crimes of piracy. That fallacy must no longer be allowed to hinder mercy. Neither could widespread riots be stopped through hard-edged action. Restored to compassionate perception, Lysaer saw he had been callous to presume he could loose the full might of his gift and crack the pall of shadow from the sky.

A populace driven by mass panic might well mistake a violent counter strike for an attack by enemy sorcery; no act, however well intentioned, must lend further impetus to panic. A subtle approach would encourage reason; light must flow gently as a balm over a city whose loyalties were ripped open like bleeding wounds.

Lysaer raised his hands.

His gift had become more malleable to his will through the months of battle against Desh-thiere; further, the hours spent working in partnership with Arithon lent Lysaer every confidence that he could plumb any weaving of shadow.

The shouts, the screams, the crack of wood against steel as roisterers harried Gnudsog's line of soldiers, faded before deep concentration as Lysaer sent a subliminal tracer glow aloft. Quietly, subtly he tested the bindings of darkness the Shadow Master had set over the city.

The probe became utterly swallowed. A dark inexhaustible as ocean, as seamlessly wrapped as a death caul, seemed to make mockery of his effort. Lysaer clamped down on fresh anger. No shadow pall could be infinite. Not even the Fellowship commanded limitless power. Lysaer turned reason and objectivity against the heat of his enmity and reassessed more carefully. His next probe picked up the thread of magecraft cleverly intermeshed with the shadows. Not only had the illusion tricked him to assume the night had no boundaries, Lysaer exposed a second error of presumption, that Arithon must be inside city walls.

Stayspells anchored these shadows. A sorcerer's training allowed the Master's spun darkness to abide outside of his presence.

Very likely the daylight had been banished to cover a bolt to escape. Lysaer found no cause to forgive, that the attack had not been turned in direct malice against Etarra's citizens. Riots had arisen from the upset. By royal duty, the man who should have been first to keep peace had without scruple seized the most damaging means at hand to duck his responsibility.

Justice would be served, Lysaer vowed. For each life lost, for each hurt caused by negligence, Arithon s'Ffalenn would be brought to account.

The dark-ward must be lifted straightaway. Lysaer extended his arms. A glow bloomed upward. Golden as late day sunlight fallen over an autumn meadow, the halo he cast from his person could never be mistaken for torchlight.

Across the rush and tumult in the square, through the barricade of raised pole arms wielded by Gnudsog's guard, eyes turned toward that source of indefinable illumination. Etarra's traumatized citizens saw one man who flung brave challenge against the dark.

Someone shouted. Hands raised in the press, pointing toward the glow that spread from the lone blond figure on the dais. The fighting nearest Gnudsog's embattled lines faltered. Farmers stared, the bricks and the cart axles torn out for bludgeons dangling forgotten in their hands as belligerence gave way to wonder. Rough men who prowled to steal and pillage spun from doorways suddenly rinsed clean of shadow. Stripped of their cover, they dodged away into side streets to avoid arrest by the watch. Guild bands of more directed hatreds paused on their way to disadvantage rival factions. Least brazen, the craftsmen and the shop keepers clustered in their fearful, worried bands cried out at the rebirth of the light that would spare their property and livelihood. "We are saved!"

Lord Diegan answered from the dais stairs. "By the grace of Lysaer of the Light, our city shall recover prosperity!"

"Lysaer of the Light!" hailed a mason with roughened hands. His chant was taken up until the central square of Etarra rang to a thousand raised voices.

The golden circle widened, waxed brighter. Lysaer's hands seemed bathed in a fountainhead of gilt sparks. Light burnished his hair like fine metal, and glanced off the tinsel stitching that banded his lace cuffs and pourpoint. The face held tipped upward under that swath of illumination showed no change at the clamor of the crowd. Fine-chiseled in concentration, the lord from the west who wrought miracles seemed an angel sent down into squalor from the exalted hosts of Athlieria.

Even Gnudsog was inspired from dourness. "He has the look on him, like a prince." Eyes dark as swamp peat swiveled and fixed on Lord Diegan. "Don't let your ninnies in the council be handing him a crown in silly gratitude."

Not entirely mollified as the chanting swelled to rattle the farthest windows of the square, Etarra's Lord Commander gave back a grim grin. "What Lysaer wants for his service is the head of the prince of Rathain."

"Good." Gnudsog smiled. On his grizzled features the expression made no improvement; the scars and chipped teeth from past scraps made him baleful enough to inspire prayers of deliverance from a headhunter. "For that, on my sword, he'll have my help."

The subject of Etarra's adulation alone remained oblivious; Lysaer's engagement with Arithon's sorceries required total concentration. Even under barrage by pure light, the shadows proved stubborn to shift. Like an ink stain set in pale felt, they resisted with a fierceness that at times made them seem to push back. Again, Lysaer stepped up his counter measure. Time passed. As the light poured steadily from him, he tracked only the retreat of the dark. Blind to all else, deaf to Diegan's encouragement, he missed the exultant moment when Etarra lay lit from wall to wall by the fiery glow of his gift. Lamps and torches brightened even the dimmest back alleys where Gnudsog sent patrols to quell any unreformed rioters.

By afternoon, the merchants unlocked their mansions. Drawn by wild rumors and by the burning, continuous flow of light, people from all quarters of the city re-emerged to pack the main square. The chanting subsided and later died into an awestruck silence.

Locked in his private crusade against the dark, Lysaer did not stir when the city governors reawakened to discover their council hall doors were fastened closed by nothing beyond everyday bolts and latches.

At some point, unseen, the Sorcerer Traithe had departed.

Humbled as they heard of the s'Ilessid prince who had shouldered their cause against monarchy, Etarra's high officials gathered on the dais. Amid splintered laths and ripped silk they stood vigil at Lysaer's side.

Lost to their presence, bathed in a blinding dazzle, Lysaer wrestled the frustration that Arithon's greater training had defeated him. Determination held him steadfast. Etarra's plight would be spoken for until his last strength became spent. The shadows by now were beaten back outside the walls. Beyond hearing that the bloodshed had ended, driven past the point of caring by the curse-born obsession to obliterate the works of his half-brother, Lysaer hammered out light in single-minded ferocity.

Diegan was closest when the widespread arms began to shudder. The light-rinsed hands finally spasmed to fists in the extremity of advanced exhaustion, and a tremor racked Lysaer's body. He swayed on his feet, and there at his side was Etarra's Lord Commander to lend him support as he crumpled.

Lysaer's eyes flicked open then, agonized in abject defeat.

Moved to compassion, Lord Diegan said, "Lysaer, it's all right. The riots are ended. You've done well enough to stop the bloodshed, and the shadows are cleared past the gates."

"All is not right!" His next line a whisper of unrequited fury, Lysaer collapsed in Diegan's arms. "Nothing is ended. Neither dark nor the prince of darkness shall rule in Rathain while I live."

Spoken from the dais where a crowned king should have sworn oath to uphold the royal charter, the acoustics arranged by the Fellowship picked up the softest words. The passion in Lysaer's promise carried clearly to the edges of the square.

Silence reigned for perhaps a dozen heartbeats. Then the air itself seemed to shatter as the gathered mass of Etarra's thousands released its pent-up breath and cheered in full-throated approval. The roar of the accolade shook the earth. Yet the prince who had won their re-

prieve from pure terror heard no sound at all, having fainted in
Diegan's embrace.

The shadows set over Etarra by Arithon s'Ffalenn cleared shortly
after midnight of their own accord. By then the populace had become
enamored of the hero in their midst; rumor attributed deliverance to
the blond-haired prince from the west. The last band of looters lan-
guished in irons. Too taciturn to show satisfaction for a long day's
work well done, Gnudsog sat enthroned in the window seat alcove of
Lord Governor Morfett's best guest suite.

He looked out of place as a botched carving amid violet and gold
tassels and amber cushions. Stripped of his field gear, clad still in the
sweaty fleece gambeson he preferred to wear under chain mail, he
slugged wine from a huge brass tankard. His peat-bog eyes watched,
brooding, as the city's governing elect crowded the rest of the room's
furnishings and argued in overheated elegance over disposition of his
troops.

Their wilted ribbons and sadly creased sarcenets lent the chamber
the feel of a second-rate bordello. Couched in their midst, resplendent
as any in his velvets and the frost-point fire of his sapphires, Lysaer
s'Ilessid lay unconscious or dead asleep in the aftermath of exhaustion. The healer who had examined him said to let him rest, then left
without daring a prognosis.

Apt to be ambivalent over fine points, Gnudsog drank. He cracked
his knuckles in rank impatience. The cant of the councilmen irked
him. Repeated searches had established beyond doubt that every Fellowship Sorcerer appeared spontaneously to have vanished; squads
had turned the warehouse district inside out to no avail. The meat
knacker's conscripts had scarpered. Little could be done to further
justice until one shadow-bending criminal could be traced in his
flight and eventually arraigned for execution. To which end Gnudsog
ran the house steward's pages breathless, sending dispatches to his
lieutenants and to his far-flung network of scouts.

When the long-sought news came back to him, along with incon-
trovertible proof that Arithon's trail had been picked up, no one heard
him through the din of raised voices.

Gnudsog lost his temper.

He cracked his tankard down with such force that wine geysered
over the brim. Silence fell. The governing elect of Etarra turned
heads, balding, curled, and hatted with felts pearled and feathered, to
glare down superior noses at the author of untimely poor manners.

Sublimely untroubled by protocol, Gnudsog wiped his stubbled
chin on the back of one hirsute wrist. "As I said, he is found. Your

shadow-meddling little sorcerer has fled down the north road. By now he has five hours' lead, on straight course for the clans of Deshir."

The pronouncement launched the room into uproar. The minister of the dyers and spinners guild fired off into maundering monologue, while the mayor of the south quarter flailed his chair arm with his bonnet in a vain attempt to recall order. His thumps were overwhelmed by an excited jabber of speculation, shrilly over-cut by the governor of trade's expostulation. "Ath preserve us! We are lost! Against sorcery and shadows, our best troops will be cut to bleeding dog meat. What use are good swords unless the Prince of Light can be convinced or coerced to give us aid?"

The heads swiveled back, belatedly covetous of the jeweled asset ensconced in their midst. Only now the blue eyes were opened. Lysaer had wakened to their bickering.

Gnudsog chuckled at the speed with which Etarra's high officials rearranged themselves in solicitude. The most prideful and disdainful of pedigreed high-bloods bent to their knees at the side of their intended savior.

Amused a bit by their pandering, Lysaer sat up. Thoughtful, frowning through disheveled gold hair, he said seriously, "My support was never in question." Declaiming voices stilled to listen. "You have my help as long and as much as you need it. But Etarra must act without hesitation. There will be war if Arithon survives to win allies. With the northern clans behind him, he could escape justice altogether."

"The barbarians may be troublesome, but they can't mount a serious threat," interjected Pesquil, sallow and lean in the sable sash that denoted top rank in the northern league of headhunters. "Our city garrison could wipe out the clans. That much was never at issue. For years we've mapped the campaign. We know the barbarians' campsites, their bolt holes, even the location of their caches. What was ever and always the deterrent was allocation of funds to send troops."

Lord Governor Morfett blotted streaming temples on the bedraggled lace of his cuffs. "After today's display of sorcery and shadows, I much doubt the treasury will stint."

As the minister of city finances cleared his throat to argue, Lysaer s'Ilessid arose. "Ath spare us the war, why wait?" He caught Diegan's nod of approval and added, "Strike now with a mounted division, and we might need nothing more than a block and a scaffold for execution."

"Twenty lancers already ride." Across the chamber, Gnudsog was smiling as the officials again heeded his presence. "They left the north gate half an hour ago."

Lysaer regarded the grizzled captain with engaging concern and respect. "Your city could be indebted for your foresight, but lancers might not be enough. Arithon s'Ffalenn is as wily and ruthless as the pirate who fathered him. The more time he gains, the more dangerous he becomes. If we are not to be taken unaware, we must assume now that he will evade your patrol and reach the northern barbarians. Gentlemen, for all your safety, I urge your city to muster immediately for war."

"We have a quorum," Diegan cracked out from his perch of cat comfort amid the fur quilts. "Shall we take the issue to vote?"

Hands were raised, a count taken, and Gnudsog's smile became voracious. He redirected the outgoing stream of pages to scare up scribes and ink. The city seals were sent for as an afterthought. Within the hour, Morfett's ornamental tables were pressed into service as desks, and Gnudsog's horny fists became weighted with requisitions for provisions, arms, and draft teams. Throughout, Lysaer paced the chamber, consumed by restless passion, haranguing reticent officials and cajoling the minister of finance to yield up the keys to the treasury. "Strike thoroughly and at once," he stressed. "Or I can promise, you'll have trouble on a scale your histories have never seen."

In all of Athera, he was the sole man qualified to measure the damages that s'Ffalenn wiles could inflict. His greatest fear was in making the Etarrans understand just how perilous an enemy they had against them.

Just past dawn, Gnudsog's troop of light cavalry clattered into the citadel's north bailey. Tired riders dismounted amid the noisy, uprooted industry of a city arming for war. By then the governors' council looked toward one savior for guidance. The patrol's weary officer was sent apace to Lysaer with news that his riders had failed in their mission to capture Arithon.

Presented across a table littered with crumb-scattered plates and charts spread helter-skelter with the inked-over marks of evolving strategy, the young lancer finished his report. "We could not overtake him, my lords. The Shadow Master had a wide lead already, even without Sithaer's own darkness and a cold that dropped snow to hide his tracks. When we learned he'd snatched a remount from a caravan, we had no choice but turn back. To continue was useless, with our horses winded near to foundering."

Sunlight slanted across creased layers of parchments that crackled as Diegan leaned on them; that sound, and the rasp as Lord Governor Morfett scratched his fleshy, stubbled jaws, filled an interval of still-ness. None of the men had refreshed themselves, or slept, throughout a night spent planning.

The lance captain shifted from foot to foot, justly nervous.

"Why didn't you commandeer fresh horses from the caravan's road master?" Diegan demanded at length.

"My Lord Commander, the merchant who owned the pack train wasn't under Etarran jurisdiction." Still bitter, the captain added, "Even so, we might have had help, had we been able to bribe his road master a tenth as generously as the renegade."

Lysaer frowned. Beaten pale by fatigue, long past finesse or polite-ness, he said, "But you claimed that Arithon stole the horse."

"He did." The captain clamped his teeth against frustration. "Your Shadow Master dared not attempt a fair offer as his speech, like yours, begging pardon, my lord, is very like the barbarians'. Rather than risk being skewered the instant he opened his mouth, he fired a supply tent for diversion, brought his shadows down, and made off with a cart horse. Asked no man's leave, mind, but left a cloak pin fixed to the picket line set with emerald big enough to choke on. The road master was sick drunk on beer by the time my lancers had the story. The hired troop guarding the caravan were Sithaer bent on having a holiday, and in no mood for chasing any fugitive."

Lysaer slammed both hands into the clutter. Crumbs bounced, and an ink flask tottered to the chime of a disarranged butter knife. "How like the bastard, Dharkaron Avenger take s'Ffalenn cunning."

At the prince's expostulation, Lord Diegan showed the fashionable bland interest, while Governor Morfett started from the act of dab-bing smeared butter from his chin. "I beg your pardon, my lord?"

Lysaer's glance flashed anger. "Arithon is quick, innovative as a fiend, and aware of our weaknesses to a fine point. I've seen his fam-ily's work before. Given any chance, he will play us one against an-other until we are driven to spoil our own cause for the havoc. But this time will be different. Arithon's twisted strategies will be turned back against him. When that happens, Daelion grant that I be on the field to break him."

Roused from obsession by the lance captain, who cringed in his dust-streaked cloak and sweaty boots, Lysaer softened to sympathy. "I see you're tired. Rest assured, your competence in this matter was never for an instant in question." As naturally as if loyalty were his due to praise, he finished, "Should all of Etarra arise against the prince of shadows with service as willing as yours, his death will be swiftly accomplished."

Sojourns

Lane-watch report reaches Prime Enchantress Morriel, that Etarra musters for war; her summons to her First Senior is immediate, and her orders, stingingly curt: "The Fellowship Sorcerers have misplayed the s'Ffalenn succession. Arithon is in flight as a fugitive, and your guess was apt: if Elaira was forewarned of this development, her escapade at Erdane held more than infatuation. Recall her westward to Narms, and pack for travel. We shall meet her there with all speed."

Bearing the last wraith exorcised at Etarra across the deepest wilds of Daon Ramon, Asandir and the Mad Prophet press on toward Skelseng's Gate with intent to remove Desh-thiere to a place of better security; while across the sky at their shoulder, sunset burns angry scarlet on a snarl of storm clouds that Kharadmon has unleashed, to close over lands to the north. . . .

While on the plain of Araithe, pounding at a gallop away from the city of Etarra, a fugitive mounted on a stolen draft horse rides hunched against the falling slash of rain. . . .

XV. Strakewood

T he last of the equinox storms that Kharadmon released to pass southward encountered the fierce dark of Arithon's shadows some leagues to the north of Etarra. The result warped nature. For a time, snow fell like a madman's tangle of lacework and patterned lands barely clothed by green spring.

Covered by darkness, given a clear road by the biting, unnatural cold, Arithon spread spells of illusion and concealment over the hillsides he traveled, until his reserves burned dry within him. His protections lifted finally because fury and strength were spent to lassitude.

The snowfall thawed to sleet, and then to rain that slashed in blinding torrents; soaked soil heaved porous by frost churned up to a froth of mud and puddles. The deep footing made his horse labor. All gaits past a walk became a rolling, sliding misery that begged for torn tendons and lameness. Out of pity for the dun mare, Arithon turned her loose to wander the sedge-grown downs before she stone-bruised or crippled herself.

Her markings made her far too conspicuous to keep anyway; for all the good sense in his decision, her relinquishment stung him, which surprised. Since Ithamon and Etarra, he had not expected he had any place left in him for sentiment.

The cart horse he stole to replace his spent mare fared worse. Ill

shod and less sure-footed, it stumbled and careened until Arithon at
last dropped the reins and let it go forward as it could. He had abandoned his saddle, the dun's girth being too short to accommodate a
draft breed. Rain soaked both mount and rider to the skin, the only
warm patch shared between them the place where human seat and
thigh made contact with steaming wet horse.

Contrary to belief in Etarra, Arithon had not chosen the north
road by design. He had gone that way because he had been driven,
and because south there lay only Ithamon.

Three days and two nights of blind flight had left him so wrung
by exhaustion that when the scouts sent by Steiven to intercept him
closed in a ring to bar his way, he had neither strength nor inclination to wheel his head-hanging mount and try even token resistance.

They brought him under escort to a camp in a copse between the
hills which channeled a river that wound its course north toward the
sea. Dawn had broken, the storm by then slackened to drizzle. A silvery patter of droplets off leaves and budding twigs interlaced with
bright notes of birdsong. Except for small sounds, the chink of bits,
and soft snorts from an inbound scout's mount, sign of human habitation remained scant. No smoke trailed from any fire pits, and no
dogs whined or barked.

Confirmed in his suspicion of an encampment in enemy territory,
Arithon dismounted. The wet ends of his cloak dragged streaks
through the muddied lather caked to the gelding's heaving sides. Barbarian hands steadied him as he swayed on his feet. The draft horse
was led away, while a scout pointed toward a hide tent pitched a
short distance off through the trees.

"Lord Steiven awaits you within, Your Grace," she said.

Arithon followed her direction, too weary to disclaim the royal title. To move at all required daunting concentration. His hips felt on
fire, and extended hours astride had left him a jelly-legged mess of
hurting muscles. He stumbled into the lodge tent, bringing the scents
of skinned grass and fusty wet wool into an atmosphere of warmth,
tinted in autumn colors by fine-patterned carpets and candlelight. As
the tent flap slapped shut on his heels, he stood blinking, vaguely
aware that a cluster of people regarded him expectantly. A rustle of
motion shifted their ranks.

Belatedly he understood that they had not simply sat down at the
low table scattered across with quill nibs, tin flagons, and battered
rolls of parchment. Instead they were kneeling behind the clutter, all
four: one young man, one middle-aged female, and two elders. The
fifth, a dramatically imposing man who wore a russet leather brigan-

dine, said in deep-voiced command, "Honor and welcome to s'Ffalenn, Your Grace."

Arithon flinched. A right-handed gesture of denial spattered droplets from pleated cuffs and laces sadly ingrained with dirt. His left arm held something bulky cradled amid the spoiled and wadded wool of his cloak, while, touched to hard highlights in the candle glow, the circlet of Rathain gleamed forgotten through a rain-plastered swath of black hair. He spoke finally, in a rasp that sounded dredged from his boot soles. "I ask guest welcome as a supplicant and a stranger. None here owes me any fealty."

His eyes were adjusting to the dimness, but the dazzle of candles defeated what clarity of sight he regained. The speaker arose, smiling in welcome, and in a nerve-stressed flash of intuition Arithon beheld his aura as a mage would. This man with his scarred face and arresting dignity had a seer's gift. Forevision had revealed this moment to him, and his manner held no fear for compromise as he said, "You are Teir's'Ffalenn, and sanctioned for succession by the hand of Asandir. I am sworn to serve your line, as my forefathers before me were appointed regents of the realm until return of Rathain's true high king."

"*Caithdein,*" Arithon whispered, white-lipped.

A stir swept the others at his use of the old tongue, but the phrase for "shadow behind the throne" merely caused the large warrior's smile to broaden. "I've preserved Rathain's heritage and fighting strength only in the absence of a royal heir. Claim your inheritance, my prince. My regency is ended."

Arithon clamped his teeth against anger. "Tell your clansmen to stand up." He was too tired for this. The light hurt his eyes, and his head spun, and the burden wrapped up in his cloak could not be put off for much longer. "I'm a bastard son," he added desperately. "I lay claim to no man's loyalty."

"Your Grace, that does not matter." The aristocratic elder at the clan chieftain's shoulder was silver-haired, and attired as if for court in a black tunic elegantly slashed and lined in gleaming saffron silk. Sure in stride and bearing, he left his place and crossed the piled carpets to bow in quiet style before the prince. As he rose, wing-tip eyebrows turned up. A mouth seamed deep by gentle humor revealed a flash of spaced front teeth. "Birth cannot negate your birthright. Illigitimacy has never before deterred the line of s'Ffalenn succession. Back to Torbrand's time, direct descent has always ranked above the claims of cousins or siblings by marriage. I can name a dozen ballads as quick example."

Arithon stared at the straight-backed, spare-voiced old man, and weariness spread across his steep features. "Who are you?" he whispered.

The gentleman ignored his question and instead raised a voice too flawless to be mistaken for anything less than a singer's. "You are of s'Ffalenn blood, and the Fellowship of Seven themselves have marked you heir."

"Who are you?" Arithon repeated, strain setting edges to a tone already rough.

"I'm called Halliron and I, too, have claimed guest welcome of the clans of the north."

Color drained from Arithon's features. The irony hit him like pain: before him stood the Masterbard, the single individual in Athera's five realms who could grant his heart's first desire, had an unwanted throne not spoiled opportunity.

A candle burned on a staked brass stand not a foot from Arithon's elbow. He reached out and pinched the wick, a half second too late; light had already betrayed his naked longing to every stranger present.

He seized his only diversion and unfurled the wadding of his cloak. "Take her," he said as veiling cloth fell away from the blue-tinged corpse of the child he had carried in his arms since Etarra. Perhaps five years old, she was stunted and drawn by starvation. The bony arm curled and stiff across her breast showed the ravages of a wound gone septic, and the hand half hidden by its stained shreds of bandage reeked overpoweringly of corrupted flesh.

Those clan councilmen not already standing shot to their feet in distress.

"She died in the night," Arithon said. "She was one of yours, conscripted to serve Etarra's horse knackers. Others enslaved with her were freed to make their way home as they could. This one was too sick to walk."

Someone spoke an oath in the old tongue. Someone else hurried forward to relieve him of the dead child's weight. This last was a woman clad in the leathers of a scout, and in more ways than her hardness reminiscent of Maenalle of Tysan. "It's Tanlie's girl, can't be doubt. No other had that mole on her earlobe."

Caught aback by the sudden change in his balance, and the loosening of an arm bound by cramps, Arithon fought a battering wave of sorrow. "Please, then, offer Tanlie my sympathy. Her girl died bravely, none better." He slipped the sodden velvets of his tabard and offered Rathain's leopard blazon for her shroud.

The woman accepted with tears in her eyes. Before the shock

could pass, Arithon rounded on the others, who advanced as a body to surround him. "I bring you no legacy but strife!"

His cry halted nothing. Quite the contrary; their tall, scar-faced chieftain said firmly, "Tanlie's girl is no grief we've not seen, and many times, in the generations since Ithamon was torn to ruins."

"No. Not this grief." Arithon broke through hoarseness to achieve a tone that finally, mercifully, checked them cold. "I've been bound and spell-cursed by Desh-thiere to fight my half-brother, Lysaer s'Ilessid. There is no sanity in the hatred that drives us both, only unbridled lust to kill. Lysaer has raised Etarra against me, and their garrison will march within days. Would you spend your lives for a stranger not even born in this world?"

Concern rather than force shaded the clan chieftain's rebuke. "Townsmen have held our lives cheaply since centuries before your birth, and for less cause than butchering horseflesh. Tanlie's girl lived for naught if she failed to teach you that." His glance toward the snuffed candle betrayed his suspicion that his liege's inveigling tactics hid infirmity. "By right of Rathain's charter, the northlands clans have cause to stand in your defense."

"Will you listen?" Arithon lost grip on his temper. "Oppose Lysaer, and you'll call down certain ruin on your loved ones. Rights are not at issue. Causes are fallacy. We are speaking of geas-driven obsession, a madness that holds to no limits. Against my half-brother I have no shred of conscience. For that most basic fact I refuse the responsibility. Your clans would become no defense for me, but just another weapon to be squandered."

A stir rippled through the gathered clan lords, while a sough of breeze spattered raindrops across the tent roof. The storm outside might be ending; the one brewing inside threatened to break into open contention. The fugitive arrived among the clans was unquestionably of s'Ffalenn blood, but he spoke with the forevision of a sorcerer, reminding uncomfortably that his were the powers of the West Gate prophecy that had banished Desh-thiere from the sky. He might wear Torbrand's image, yet he was a stranger, unknown and unnamed, promising disaster and pleading release from his birthright. Hotly awaited though his arrival had been, lives hung in the balance. The council would be wise to listen.

Blunt-faced, his hair grayed as worn steel by years of ambush and skirmish, Caolle urged his chieftain to stay wary. The rest marked his words in respect, for the toughened veteran presented opinions few others cared to voice.

Steiven was moved, but not to caution. He left his place by the council table and took stance beside Halliron. His rangy frame dwarfed the Masterbard, who was not short, and his hazel eyes shone bitter as he admitted, "I have Sight. For years I have lived with fore-knowledge of the moment and manner of my death. There is no op-tion, Your Grace of Rathain, elders. Etarra will march upon the northlands whether or not a Teir's'Ffalenn is given sanctuary among us." He half turned to face down Arithon, his large hands hooked in the lacing that clasped his belt with its row of black-hafted throwing knives. "My liege, our destiny is to defend you. The city garrison will campaign against us, and we must stand to fight. Your choice is sim-ple. Shall we die for an empty title or a living, breathing sovereign?"

Arithon measured the taller man. His stillness bespoke distaste, for the claim upon his conscience was shameless—also double-binding as Sithaer's traps for the damned, since the plea gave proof of the clan chief's supreme dedication. Only the tap of the rain across canvas, and the whispered hiss of hot wax as draft fanned the candle flames, lent sound to the tense atmosphere.

Arithon's response, when it came, was pitched for the chieftain's ears alone. "My lord. Ath and Daelion Fatemaster have conspired. They should have sent me a regent I could hate, a man drunk on power and tied to petty interests. Where the unlucky accident of my birth would never bind me, your courage leaves me humbled and tied. As the sovereign cause of your death, what is left? It's a shabby, spiritless gesture to beg in advance your forgiveness."

"That you have," said the clan chieftain of Deshir, neither speech-less nor subdued. "But in exchange I ask your friendship, Arithon of Rathain."

The prince managed to curb his recoil at the unexpected knowl-edge of his name. "Did your dreams spoil all of my secrets?" And then strain and sleeplessness undid him. He had to cover his face with both hands to mask his unbidden emotion. "What are you called?" he said through his fingers.

"Steiven s'Valerient, Earl of Deshir."

A shudder jarred the prince. The oddly singed silk of his shirtsleeve slithered back to reveal a seared weal that snaked the length of his right forearm, to vanish under cloth at the elbow. Arithon ignored the murmurs that broke out among the clan lords as, through blistered, shaking hands, he swore guest oath.

"To this house, its lord, and his sworn companions, I pledge friendship. Ath's blessing upon family and kin, strength to the heir, and honor to the name of s'Valerient. Beneath this roof and before Ath, count me brother, my service as true as blood kin. Dharkaron witness."

Arithon's fingers fell away to uncover features as hollowed as stripped bone. "You've seen this before," he accused.

Steiven laughed. From his towering height he embraced his royal liege like a son. "I've lived for it."

Then, aware that Arithon's extreme exhaustion threatened collapse, he shouldered the prince's weight as he had done for his own spent scouts, and in peremptory command sent his clan elders packing to fetch bath water, hot food, and dry blankets.

The war council resumed upon the moment Arithon's needs had been attended. Etarra was capable of mounting an invasion force ten thousand strong, and with an understanding shaded to grimness by five long centuries of hatred, Steiven dared not assume that the army sent after Arithon would be one man less than full muster.

Etarran lives would be counted cheaply for the ruin of the s'Ffalenn royal line.

"I'll need another message run through the relay," said the gaunt old earl of Fallowmere, his single, unclouded eye fixed like a gimlet on his regent. "By tomorrow every scout I have of fighting age will march to support your Deshans."

"Well, they'll get here too damned late!" Caolle drove his poniard into the rough-split wood that planked the table. "You know that fey princeling is right. If we stand, we're going to have a massacre."

"If we don't stand, we'll be slaughtered on the run, or else die of rot and fever in the boglands of Anglefen by summer." Quietly, Steiven added, "We'll fight. But the field must be chosen to our advantage."

"Biggest, blood-spilling raid we'll ever stage," said the last Earl of Fallowmere. "For myself, I wouldn't miss it."

Caolle glared.

And in a warmth of brotherly bickering, the strategies were argued, discarded, and reworked, chart after chart unrolled and shoved aside until parchments layered the carpets like quilting. A site was finally chosen, in a range of valleys along the Tal Quorin, where the current ran wide and shallow between a grassy verge of low banks.

"All right, then." Steiven raised his corded arms, the dull studs on his brigandine winking in sequence as he stretched. "Roust last night's patrol. All our camps must relocate east to the river site. The first arrivals will need to start cutting timber to build the traps."

"And the prince?" Caolle demanded. His chapped lips thinned at the softening he saw on his chieftain's scarred face. "Ah, no, my lord, you're not thinking to wait out His Grace's infirmity. This is unsafe territory, and we need to break camp before nightfall."

There followed a moment where clan lord and war captain clashed glances across the candle tops. In Deshir the custom was unbending: any scout unfit for travel was given a mercy stroke and abandoned where he lay by the trail. In lands ranged by Etarra's headhunters, litters for the wounded and the lame endangered those men still hale; and no man, however minor his injury, was ever left at risk of captivity.

"You wake him," Steiven invited with a fierce flash of teeth. "I warrant he'll walk just to spite you. It's the gray he rode in on we'll likely be leaving for crow bait."

Arithon came half awake as a warm weight settled over his knees. Something else, perhaps soft fingers, tugged at his hair, and another touch trailed across the knuckles of the hand not bandaged, that lay outside of the blankets.

He drew breath and stirred, and the stiffness of his body caught him up in an ache that made him gasp.

"You woke him up," a child's voice piped anxiously.

"Didn't," said another, fast as echo, from the other side of the pallet.

Arithon opened his eyes.

"Did too, see?" said a brunette perhaps six years old, with tea-colored eyes and dimples, who lounged against the ticking by his shoulder. "He might get mad."

Exactly what he chose to do next became the focus of four pairs of eyes, from the auburn-haired angel astride his knees to the tallest, regarding him with preteen dignity from the bedstead, to the least of them, as dark-haired as the father she resembled, sucking on two fingers and staring shyly from behind her eldest sister.

Arithon elbowed himself halfway upright, and froze as the slide of the blankets warned he was naked underneath. His sluggish thoughts scrambled to reorient and to integrate hide walls and the patchworked fur coverlets of a sleeping cubicle with his last waking memory, of an inadvertent nap in the saddle that had ended in a fall from a moving horse.

"You aren't mad, are you?" said the sable-haired ten-year-old with another bounce against his knee.

He hurt everywhere. He was too tired still by half, and if he wanted to be annoyed, he lacked the will. Outnumbered, and pinned beneath the coverlets by a weight of small admirers, he adjusted his tactics to accommodate.

A short interval later, Steiven's wife, Dania, peeked into the alcove. She carried a bowl of bread dough braced against her hip, and was fumingly prepared to dress down daughters warned all morning to leave their guest in peace.

The miscreants had found a length of rawhide. Five heads bent together over a puzzle that, with the help of tiny hands and much patient instruction from the prince, was forming into an intricate lace of knotwork.

Dania's reprimand died unspoken. Quietly, carefully, she moved to slip the privacy flap closed. But he had heard her, involved as he was, even through the giggles of the girls.

"It's all right. Tashka has told me the camp is to move this afternoon. I should have been wakened soon in any case?" Green eyes turned in question toward the doorway, made the more vivid by close proximity of the oldest child's fiery hair. "You have beautiful daughters, lady. They are yours, I see, and Lord Steiven's? The resemblance is too striking to overlook."

The bread bowl suddenly seemed an encumbrance. Aware that as her sovereign he deserved a semblance of courtesy, Dania froze with the intuition that if she curtsied, she was going to see him angry.

Her youngest displaced one awkwardness by creation of another.

"Mama, look!" Edal called, and pulled her hands too fast from the hide lacing. Oblivious to her sisters' cries of dismay as the pattern collapsed into tangles, she seized Arithon's wrist in chubby hands and said loudly, "Look, the prince has scars."

"Everybody who escapes from Etarra has scars, Edal," Dania scolded in gentle exasperation. "But it's never polite to speak of them." She raised the bread bowl as if it were a shield before her breast, and delivered a succession of orders that set pretty daughters to flight like butterflies. As the last one vanished through the privacy flap, she discovered the prince still regarding her. He did have scars, she knew from attending him the night before, ones not in keeping with his station, and except for the queer burn on his arm, too old to have happened in Etarra.

The awkwardness remained. Unused to strangers, far less ones born royal, Dania wished her curiosity could be deflected as easily as her daughters', by a ploy with a scrap of hide string.

He found words that had equal effect. "I should like to help with the packing."

Gracefully turned to practicalities, Dania said, "Your clothing is still wet from being washed. There are leggings and a tunic that should fit you in the chest by the wall. When you're dressed, we'll see about food."

"The Masterbard," asked Arithon in the same light tone of conversation. "Is he still with the clans?"

"Yes." Despite her diffidence Dania smiled. The expression lifted cares from her face and softened the seams of hard living and weather. "Halliron groused too much to refuse. Danger, he said, went hand in hand with history. At his age, he claimed he'd expire from impatience before he'd hear news at second hand."

Something retreated behind Arithon's expression, though his eyes like shadowed emerald never shifted in their framework of gaunt flesh. It stung her not to know why the Masterbard's presence should cause upset; aside from prodigious talent as a musician, Halliron was the very soul of kindness. When Arithon graciously dismissed her with his thanks, Lady Dania was relieved to escape to undertake the much tidier frustration of punching bread dough.

Arithon arose and stiffly dressed in the black-dyed leathers offered for his use from the chest. These were sewn of deerhide, beaten soft, and adorned with pale thread work at collar, shoulder, and hem. The silk needlework was finely embroidered, and the thought occurred that silver lacing had not been used for a purpose. In Deshir's forest, one did not wear garments that might inadvertently flash or catch light. Dania's mention of damp clothing was likely an excuse to wean away the coronation finery that was utterly ill suited for the trail.

Arithon emerged from the alcove to find, embarrassed, that the only clan lodge tent still standing had been the one under which he sheltered. Every other hide dwelling sat on the beaten earth in a pine clearing, furled tight as puffballs just sprouted after a rainfall. A team of children appeared immediately to begin striking the s'Valerient tents. Dania's daughters were everywhere under the feet of the boys who yanked stakes and unreeled spun cordage to coax collapsing hide to fall in folds. They all carried knives, though the eldest among them looked not a day past fourteen.

Nowhere did Arithon encounter signs of grief or burial of the dead child he had borne from Etarra. At first impression, these clanfolk seemed more hardened even than Maenalle's, more scarred, more grim, more ingrained by desperate necessity. By overhearing stray comments, Arithon gathered the men had marched ahead of the camp to the site on the southeast edge of Deshir forest, where pitched battle would be fought with Etarra's army.

Found at her baking over an open-air trestle, Dania pushed a fallen coil of hair from her cheek with the back of one floury wrist. "We'll need journey cakes for the trail. These are hard and savorless, so I've made sweet bread that's soft. Edal's gone to the ovens so you can have yours hot." She turned her head, prepared to call, when a tardy daughter reappeared with steaming bread in a linen napkin. "Eat,"

Dania urged, still absorbed with the batter that clung to the bowl. "You must be famished."

He was. Three days and four nights with too little food had left him faint to the edge of sickness. Arithon took the linen and lifted the bread, forced despite his hunger to pick at it slowly. Even bland sustenance sat uneasily in his painfully empty innards. To hide that discomfort, he addressed the other, inescapable recognition that he was being treated as an invalid. "Last night." His voice was very soft. "What happened?"

Dania banged her hands down so hard the wooden bowl close to cracked. "Ath, you would ask." Although her back was turned, motherly instinct pinpointed little Edal's eager regard. Dania reflexively packed her daughter off to fetch back a bucket of clean water. "You were too tired to ride. Any fool could have seen. But the men, they've lived with troubles for so long that I sometimes think we've come to value all the wrong sort of things."

"I didn't ask for excuses," Arithon interrupted mildly. "What happened?"

She was blunt. "You fell off your horse. My Lord Steiven took you up across his saddle bow."

That jogged his recall. Fragments came back to him of Caolle's sarcastic comment that he should be left in the mud by the trail, that the clans had outgrown any need for royal sovereignty; of somebody else in drier tones suggesting he should be lashed to a packhorse like deadwood, that the scars chafed on his wrists were enough indication that this sort of happenstance might not be new.

Dania began to stack up dirtied spoons and bowls to allow him the chance to let down his odd barrier of silence, maybe broach what had hounded him out of Etarra in the first place with only clothes fit for feasting on his back.

When his stillness became prolonged, she risked a peek and found him gone, the napkin filled with crumbs abandoned in neat folds upon the rock where he had been sitting.

The clouds and the rain had passed and left the air redolent with evergreen, underlaid by the mustier wet of shed needles. Arithon strolled the hard-beaten paths of what had once been a long-term campsite. He should have been unobtrusive in his soft black leathers, under sun-striped shadows beneath the trees; the fact he was one man in a company of older women, bearing mothers, and young children made him not. Busy enough with securing leather bundles, or sealing wrapped belongings in oaken casks, they seldom gave more than a glance at his approach. Behind his back, they were all wont to stare.

He allowed them, of a mind to make observations himself. Small birds with gold-banded wings foraged, pecking at the dirt where the lodge tents had set. They took off in fan-shaped flocks, wove and wheeled, to alight again just ahead. A small girl told him they were pine sparrows. Arithon thanked her and moved on.

Like the last, this camp kept no dogs. Infants rode on their mothers' backs; toddlers too young for chores laughed at their play, but did not stray into the pine woods. Half clad, or wearing leather patched with motley, they tussled at sticks and ball between mounds of household goods left stranded by the furled lodges. The casks, the chests lashed in protective layers of oiled leather, the thick-woven carpets with their bright colors hidden in rolls, all were tied and stacked in piles, to be carried off to a warren of hidden root cellars dug into the woodland floor. The bitter conclusion was inescapable. The site the clans were leaving was a home of sorts, familiar and often revisited. The place they were going on account of their prince was bare and temporary, and necessities would be carried on their backs.

Arithon fingered the little tin canister purloined from Sethvir's saddlebags. He had not hesitated to take the tienelle in the heat of his escape from Etarra; still less did he regret the theft now. Against Lord Diegan's army, the defenders of Strakewood Forest would be outnumbered nine to one. That quandary added weight to the ache of total weariness. Should he shy from using his talents, directed by every scrap of augury he could draw from the herb's narcotic visions, the people who sheltered him must rely upon chance for survival. But to smoke the leaves to sound the future, he required absolute privacy.

In that he was already thwarted.

Even had there been a refuge among the bustle where no one would disturb or remark on him, the packers were hurrying to complete their tasks by afternoon. Aware that two boys had sneaked up on him, to dog his steps in exaggerated imitation of his carriage, Arithon regarded the rain-matted detritus of pine needles that his boots passed across without track. A thought and a chill ran through him; he might escape by becoming too visible. At once, with some savagery, he scuffled his heels to foster false impression of his ignorance, that these folk needed less than a secretive caution necessary to survival in the wild.

The contempt the boys copied from their elders, that Rathain's royal scion was weak, or maybe helpless, was a trait that might suit him to foster, Arithon thought. The frustration he had leashed behind forced and mild courtesy perhaps was a perverse sort of kindness. Nights and days in the saddle had worn his body; in spirit, the wrenching realignment that had taken place in the course of Desh-thiere's curse lay compounded by reckless overuse of spell-craft. Resisting the creeping and insidious urge to turn back to Etarra and attack Lysaer claimed further toll upon his strength. His depleted grip on self-command made mastery of the herb's ill effects too risky to try until he rested; in the throes of the poison's withdrawal symptoms, Arithon knew he would be lucky to be able to walk.

Better for his future if these clansmen believed him overbred to the point of uselessness. Once they had repulsed Etarra's invasion, his shadows and his aid would not be needed. Their disdain might drive them finally to release him from the blood bonds of Rathain's sovereignty.

Finished with pacing, charged with perverse and bitter humor, Arithon left the canister's deadly contents for later. He retrod his course through wheeling pine sparrows to Lady Dania, where, seemingly overcome by her distressed protestations, he allowed himself to be talked out of his earlier insistence that he help with a share of the packing.

In the course of the next four days, Arithon let slip the stern barriers imposed by a lifetime of mage training. For his puzzles and his oddments of sleight-of-hand illusion, he won the undying adulation of Dania's daughters, who had never known a grown man to play games with them. The clan boys stayed aloof, until he captivated the smallest with a whistle carved of beechwood and given voice with shaved shims of river reed. After that, Arithon spent every waking hour the domestic camp was not moving on the trail seated by someone's fireside, whittling.

For a morning, their going was made raucous by the young, hooting on their new toys and laughing at their daring, to be making noises unnatural to the wakened wood.

The whistles were confiscated, and Arithon, chastised by a weatherbeaten woman who would have born arms alongside the fighting men had she not been near term with a pregnancy. "You'll have headhunters on us with your addle-headed, frivolous ways. Our boys are needing no such silly influence!"

Arithon regarded her hardness with green-eyed, languid resignation, and murmured soft apology. The woman left in disgust.

"Royal he may be, but what use have the clans for a dreamer!" he heard her exhorting some others in a rest stop farther down the trail.

He let the comment pass, though heads turned to see whether he had overheard and what would be his reaction. He gave them back his closed eyes, and crossed hands behind his head, to all appearance asleep with his back against a tree so rough, the bark had turned silver with dried moss.

The whistles had drawn no headhunters, because he had set arcane defenses against any outside seeker who should chance to track their company. The entrapments were subtle, a fooling of the eye to make sight linger on the flick of a leaf in the breeze, or deflect thought into futile reflection to read meaning in some willow's gnarled roots.

Dania had to shake him out of trance when the time came to move on.

Nights by the fireside, with one or another of Dania's daughters fallen asleep across his lap, Arithon immersed himself in Halliron's music. The Masterbard had an exquisite, expressive style upon the strings, and he did not shy from imparting passionate emotion into his playing. The lyranthe he carried was ancient and ornate in a sparely elegant way. Her voice was so like the one that Arithon had been forced to abandon at Etarra that she, too, might have been crafted by a Paravian maker. Arithon dared not touch her fretboard to look for Elshian's rune. The feel of polished wood, of responsive, silver-toned strings, would have overcome his defenses like drugged wine. The hope could hurt too much, that the chance of reprieve from kingship seemed a scant step closer.

Those evenings by the fireside, Halliron's ballads wove their mystery as though just for him. He chuckled at their merriness and let the tears track unabashed down his face. The whispers this created suited his purpose. By daylight, while he walked abandoned to reverie down the trail, he replayed in his mind Halliron's exquisitely polished arpeggios, his trills of ornamentation, his clean, meticulous cadences whose simplicity itself shaped naked force. Such times, when the stares of Deshir clanswomen turned aside in disgust, he would draw the eyes of the bard.

Halliron had depths of sublety well disguised by his congenial nature. Since the oddity intrigued him, that the prince so taken with his music had never sought closer acquaintance, he took pains to hide his interest.

The domestic camp moved by night and rested only after full daybreak. On the morn they were to reach their destination, the mantling mists of early dawn ripped and dispersed into tatters, cut by slanted shafts of white sunlight. The birds were loud at their nesting calls. Like strands of silvered silk wound through its green forest tapestry, the river Tal Quorin re-emerged in a bend, to flow once again beside the trail. The thin, acid soil of the heights gave up its black mantle of pines. The fertile trough of the watershed here lay broken into long, irregular valleys. Winding through hollows and glens, the river current lisped over glacial deposits of smoothed granite, and skeined eddies around willow roots like the nobbled knees of old men. The demise of Desh-thiere had bought change. Little plants pressed up through moss and pine needles, and opened colored petals for the first time in five centuries untrammeled by the sooty prints of fungal spores.

Steiven's daughters clung to Arithon like shadows as, together, they enjoyed discovery of each new bud and petal; where the wild-flowers matched those he remembered from Rauven's deep woodland glens, he gave their names. Where they did not, he knelt, the sun mantling warmth across his back, and shared wonders otherworldly and strange in drifts of dew-drenched leaf mold.

His absorption was not so complete that he overlooked the faint, sour ring of steel that threaded through the trilled cries and fast-beating wings of disturbed marsh flickers. Halliron's fascination had not quit at appearances, for all that the camp women had already dismissed their prince as a fanciful dreamer. Only the bard remained observant enough to spot the brief frisson that shocked through the prince's bearing.

Puzzled, Halliron tossed damp hair from his temples, the better to watch as Arithon straightened up from contemplation. Swift words from him, and the children ranged eagerly ahead to scout their next find on their own. Arithon hung behind, a shadow in dark leathers under the light-flecked boughs of a hazel thicket.

From the crest of an unseen hillside, the axe blows reached a ragged crescendo. The tree bole under punishment gave a juddering crack and fell to earth in a whipping tangle of greenery that hissed like a rip through warm air. Arithon recoiled. He turned as if jabbed by sharp pain, and his eyes passed unseeing across the bard standing not twenty feet behind, with the forest shade hatching his elegant court velvets that stood out too plainly to be missed.

Another tree cracked and fell. Exposed full face to an observation he would have avoided, Arithon paled in the grip of some deep, introspective discomfort.

And Halliron caught his breath in comprehension. Acquainted with the Warden of Althain, befriended by Asandir, he saw into this prince and recognized like a watermark in fine paper, the stamp of a mage-trained awareness.

Arithon's interest in trailside wildflowers had been a ruse to mask an attention linked to the deeper mysteries of the forest. Caught as he was in partial trance, the axe-cut, dying trees sent a scream of pain across his nerves. Shaken to his core, an unprepared part of him *was* bark and leaves and running spring sap, slashed untimely from its taproot by blows from sharpened steel. The shock momentarily upset his mastery. He struggled, stumbling slightly, to tear his stung consciousness free.

Pushed by reflex before thought, Halliron hastened forward and caught the prince by an elbow to support his unsteady step.

The touch caused Arithon to snap stiff. His head came up, around, and in green eyes the Masterbard caught a flare that looked like smothered anger. The impression was false. Halliron saw past hostility to what perhaps was an envy sprung from offense; indisputably the resentment was directed fully and personally toward him.

Halliron's startlement caused him to let go, simultaneous with Arithon's instinctive jerk backward, with the result that sensitive musician's fingers recorded an instant impression. The forearm under its covering of water-spoiled silk was wiry and fit, not at all the constitution of the fine-drawn dandy the prince purported to affect.

Arithon spun away to hide an expression Halliron would have bribed in gold to have read. Between the two men lay a silence heavy with secrets, and as if their burden were at once too much, the prince abruptly sat down. He fingered the edge of a rock hoarded like some hoary, moss-crusted jewel between the miserly grip of old roots. "I'm sorry." His apology was too quick and cold. "I believed I was alone."

Halliron absorbed this display with narrowed, tawny eyes. He observed on intuition, "You had wards set, and not just to hide the notes of whistles."

"If so, that's no business of yours." Arithon let his knuckles fall loose in dry grass, left wind-broken from winter's snowfall like the bundled small bones of dead birds. He had regained control. At least, he no longer shivered as the axe falls rang. Only the earth seemed to shudder in vibration as each quick trunk slammed the ground.

After a moment the bard said, "If you want Deshir's clans to disown you, desert them."

That touched a nerve. Arithon's smile at the barb was full-lipped and brimmingly, off-puttingly merry. "Desert me, instead. Your perceptions feel like a tinker's spilled needles: a punishing trap for false steps."

Halliron was not easily irritated. Years of settling vain, even senile patrons and short-tempered, envious peers had taught him to treat with human nature sparely, to unwind misunderstanding like a snarl in fine-spun wool. Intrigued by Arithon's reticence, he gave no ground, even as the man pressed to escape and regain untrammeled access to the trail.

There was no gap to squeeze past. Halliron had him boxed between a stand of dense brush and the seamed, ungiving face of another rock.

Spoiled as his behavior suggested, the Teir's'Ffalenn did not have the nerve or the anger in him to shoulder an old man aside to have his way.

"I could ask," Halliron said in the Shandian drawl that seeped back occasionally from his boyhood. "Why, when you first met me, did you react as if I were a threat to you?"

"Because," Arithon began, and on impulse, switched liquidly to the Paravian, *"cuel ean i murdain ei dath-tol na soaren,"* which translated, "you are the enemy I never expected to meet." His accent was flawless. And the coiled hardness in him this time would not be denied. Halliron moved aside before he was indeed shoved physically.

Undeceived by the show for a moment, the Masterbard watched the scion of Rathain's murdered high kings stride away. The man was not angry. However desperately he wished to foster that impression, to a bard's ear for nuance, it was obvious that Arithon was unbearably distressed.

Halliron resumed his walk in pensive thought. For some pernicious reason he felt guilty for even this slight an intrusion into the Teir's'Ffalenn's altogether raptly guarded privacy. If anything left the bard irked, it was his suspicion that Steiven's daughters were entrusted with an honesty nobody else in the camp seemed to merit.

The clans of Deshir were altering the landscape in the valleys to either side of the Tal Quorin's watercourse. The woods rang with the noise of their feverish haste, of axes and falling timber and the grinding over stones of makeshift sledges. A party of raiders had stolen draft teams. The chink of chain and harness fittings blended with drovers' calls. Even Halliron's pony was pressed into service, hauling hampers of cut brush.

Upon arrival, the women left tents and belongings still furled in their packs in a clearing. Every free hand was set to work, while the children and the elderly were sent out to forage or dress the game sent in by the hunting parties who ranged the glades farther afield. The racket had scattered the deer, the birds, and even the beavers were driven into hiding by rafts of cut logs sent downstream.

Lord Steiven was south, below the white-water rapids where the river fanned into sheets of open water between grassy green swards of marsh. There he oversaw the remaking of innocent landscape into traps to mire Etarra's army. Arithon did not join him. Neither did he lend his strength to the shifting of logs and stones. Conspicuous for his idleness, for even the Masterbard had volunteered to help the cooks, Arithon Teir's'Ffalenn sat in the shade through the morning, apparently taking a nap. Nobody saw him move, or as much as open an eye.

When the work crews returned to eat at midday, he was still there and had to be wakened for the meal.

And yet he had to have stirred. A scout who passed through the armory lodge found the tactical maps disturbed. Penned in the margins of a supply draft in fussy, over-ornamented script were concisely drawn summaries of the weapon and training profile of Etarra's garrison troops, along with names, numbers, and insightful characteristics of most of its ranking officers.

Since the prince neither mentioned nor arose to claim credit for this contribution, the matter became overshadowed. The contempt of the clan's womenfolk became all the deeper entrenched by Arithon's current absorption, of drawing puzzles in the dirt with the toddlers. His laughter tangled with the talk of the men at the boards and the scrape of knives as they sawed and hammered the dry waybread into chunks to soften in hot gravy. Veiled looks of incredulity were cast at the prince between bites. The younger scouts began to sound bitter, while the most campaign-scarred grew silent. Steiven was not present to stem the quietly acid speculation, which Arithon joyously ignored. His mood stayed isolate, as thoroughly unshakable as if he were deaf or a half-wit.

Afternoon saw the Teir's'Ffalenn kneeling amid the patchwork shadows of a beech grove to receive oath of fealty from the fighting scouts of the clans. The timing of the ceremony had been at Steiven's orders; men grumbled in dour, closed knots, that the roster might have been changed if their earl had come back from the lower valley in time to hear gossip from his wife.

But delayed until the last minute, Steiven arrived still winded from his hurry to reach the glen. That Strakewood's clansmen had gathered in his absence, half stripped and muddy, or sweating in leathers still grimed from their labors on the defense works, was in tribute to the loyalty given their chieftain rather than respect for the prince about to become their liege lord.

Steiven assumed position a half step to one side of the s'Ffalenn prince. Except for recovery of Asandir's circlet that was proof of his sanction for succession, Arithon still wore the black suede tunic and leggings that had once belonged to Lady Dania's younger brother. As at the earlier ceremony in Etarra, Arithon carried no ornament beyond his father's signet. The smoke-dark blade forged by Paravian mastery was struck upright into the earth at his elbow, the emerald in the pommel a hard green sparkle underlying the reflections of the foliage. Already in place, on one knee in the crumbled detritus of last season's fall of copper leaves, he met no one's interested glance. His attention seemed absorbed more by the cheep of nesting wrens in the branches than in the greeting murmured by his regent.

For a moment Lord Steiven knew regret, that occasion as momentous as this should be held at short notice in the greenwood. The last such ceremony would have taken place in Ithamon, under beautiful vaulted ceilings rich with jeweled hangings and banners. Customarily held on a prince's twentieth birthday, past events had been preceded and followed by grand celebration and feasting.

Saddened by the somberness of this gathering, and moved to a crush of emotion that would barely allow speech, that he had lived for this day, that he, of all his exiled ancestors, should be the one to stand witness to the returned s'Ffalenn scion, Steiven drew breath to renew a ritual many thousands of years old.

"I, Teir's'Valerient, appointed Regent of the Realm and Warden of Ithamon, through my father, and his fathers, back to the last crowned sovereign, bring before you Arithon, son of Avar, sanctioned heir and direct descendant of Torbrand s'Ffalenn, founder of the line appointed by the Fellowship of Seven to rule the principalities of Rathain. Let any man who questions the validity of this prince's claim now stand forth."

Feet shifted, deadened from sound by damp earth. The shrill cry of a hawk hung loud upon silence.

Steiven resumed. "Arithon, Teir's'Ffalenn, turn your back. A prince who would accept oath of fealty must trust those he would lead and defend. If any among this gathering have earned your ill will, state their names for all to hear, that they may be excluded."

Seeming delicate as porcelain before his regent's scarred height, Arithon tipped up his face. "I bear no man grudge." The words were clear, for all that his eyes were barriered. As if he fought back panic, his fingers shook as he gripped and pulled Alithiel's blade from the earth. "I appoint you my guardian against treachery." His raised knee shifted; he pivoted and neatly, still kneeling, turned his back.

According to time-worn ritual, Steiven positioned himself at Arithon's shoulder, facing the waiting company. "Let those who would be feal companions of Arithon, son of Avar, step forward and present a weapon in pledge of service and defense."

The clan chieftain then drew his own sword and ran it point to into the ground. One by one, his scouts and his fighting men, his hunters, and his women who had no family representative to swear for them, filed forward. They passed with bent neck beneath the unsheathed threat of Alithiel guarding the royal back, and left knives, daggers, poniards, or heirloom swords in token of their trust. When the last of them had returned to their place, Arithon was permitted to turn around.

But not, even yet, to arise. On his knees, white now as any mayor's bleached linen, he bowed his head before that hedge of steel and crossed hands that looked fragile over the hilt of the nearest sword.

Thin and weary as a fox run to earth, he drew breath to renounce personal claim to the life he had found in Athera. "I pledge myself, body, mind, and heart to serve Rathain, to guard, to hold unified, and to deliver justice according to Ath's law. If the land knows peace, I preserve her; war, I defend. Through hardship, famine, or plague, I suffer no less than my sworn companions. In war, peace, and strife, I bind myself to the charter of the land, as given by the Fellowship of Seven. Strike me dead should I fail to uphold for all people the rights stated therein. Dharkaron witness."

"Arise, Arithon, Teir's'Ffalenn and Crown Prince this moment of Rathain." Steiven stepped back, smiling, as his liege at last gained his feet. "Ath grant you long life and sound heirs."

Arithon laid hand on the chieftain's huge bastard sword and drew its weight from the earth. He offered the weapon back to Steiven with his royal blessing. And one by one, for what seemed like an hour, other weapons were returned in like fashion, binding their owners to loyal service. The steel was their oath; the burden of their lives and safety, now and forever, Arithon's, as he was now theirs until death.

The muttering over his weaknesses cut off sharply as Steiven's barked orders sent each team back to felling trees and digging pitfalls for the incomplete defense works.

As the clearing rapidly emptied, Arithon met his Lord Regent's regard. His green eyes not quite yet rinsed to bleakness, he said, "My first act will be the rending of that oath."

Steiven's easy humor vanished as he proffered Alithiel to his prince. "I've heard. The talk doesn't fool me. And you dwell on the matter, Your Grace, like one blind to the lay of the weather. Etarra's hatreds smolder hot enough that it takes no spark at all to set them burning."

Arithon accepted back the icy weight of Alithiel. The haste with which he had fled his coronation had kept the blade without a sheath; he was obliged to slide her bared length through a belt that was nicked and sliced from such usage, and the force as he rammed the weapon home roused an angry ring from the steel. "Lysaer is not fit to be judged by rational men. He has been cursed, as I have, and feuds or justice have no bearing on his actions. I would not see your clansmen become the tool that Etarra's garrison has."

He brushed past before Steiven could answer. Without further word to anyone, Arithon left the clearing in the opposite direction of the camp.

Steiven started after him, but a hand on his forearm caught him back.

"Let him go," murmured Halliron in that musical gentleness that could and had stopped killing fights. "My heart tells me this prince knows all too clearly what he's about. You cannot shoulder what troubles him." A smile revealed the sly gap in front teeth. "Besides, if he's touchy as the ballads name his forebears, he'll tolerate no man's interference."

Steiven swore explosively. "I know that. You know that. But likeness to his ancestors isn't going to satisfy my clansmen. If this womanish brooding continues, my war captain has vowed he'll strip the royal person to his short hairs to find out if they hide a castration. By Ath!" the former regent ended with rare and exasperated fierceness, "if Caolle tries, it's on my mind I'm going to let him!"

Attraction

Etarra prepared for war. The clangor of the armorers' mallets rang from the smithies day and night, counterpointed by the whack and slap of practice staves as last year's recruits were drilled to professional polish. Almost overnight it seemed that every young man of fighting age appeared in the streets wearing half armor.

Not all would be leaving for battle. The highborn elite, those whose pedigrees traced back without taint to the original burghers who had overthrown the old monarchy, found themselves sidelined in the bustle created by the renegade prince. Their exploits, their mischief, and their profligate debts born of gambling were no longer the talk of the ladies' parlors. Arithon's name had supplanted them, and out of fear of his shadows, mistresses and favored courtesans turned fickle in sudden preference for strapping big fellows with less refined manners and swords.

The parties of the rich and young grew the more frenzied to compensate. From Diegan, Lady Talith heard details: of how the bluest-blooded and brashest had drunk claret until they staggered, and then staged a race up the alarm tower to see who could be first to swing from the bass bell's clapper. The winner had emerged miraculously unscathed. Those less lucky, judged by the nature of their scars, became heroes, or the butt of scathing jokes, which was the fashionable way to test their charm. One gallant had twisted an ankle. Another had fallen through a railing and suffered two broken wrists. He appeared in splints at the soirees and bragged that the ladies could kiss him on both cheeks at once, as he lacked a sound hand to fend them off.

Once Lady Talith would have sat front and center, to egg on admirers and dare foolish feats to gain her favor. She would have laughed at the cleverest wit and gleaned all the gossip, to unravel the fierce tapestry of intrigue that underlay the glitter of Etarran society.

But this night found her separate from the festivities, breathing in the outdoor airs that perfumes inside the ballroom behind her were selected with care to overpower. There was nothing attractive by night in damp stone; starlight, to her, was too uncomfortably new to feel safe. The laughter, the dancing, and the delicate sparkle of light through the pierced porcelain of a thousand candle shades should have drawn her back like a moth to flame. Her gown of costly damask was new and her jewels simple but dazzling.

But the parties now seemed silly shamming. She resisted the creeping ennui to no avail and just as fiercely fought to deny its cause, to avoid setting name to the day, no, the moment, when the wild antics of the men had become reduced to just games, and empty ones at that.

Diegan had experienced a similar change. Though brother and sister had not compared thoughts, his humor had been flat for days. Where once he would have battled jealously to retain his circle of admirers, now they were deserting his side like ebb tide, with himself the one least dismayed. It felt, Talith decided, as if somebody had entered her childhood home and maliciously rearranged all the furniture.

She could not flee the recognition that her life seemed dreary since Lysaer s'Ilessid had stepped into it.

Talith leaned over the balustrade. Never before then had she known admiration that did not arise from flamboyance; humor that did not belittle; power not bought through brutish intrigues or bribes.

The man's direct nature had cut through Etarra's convoluted greed and excesses like a sharpened knife through moldy rinds.

A breeze whispered through the garden and loosed a small blizzard of petals that almost masked the footfalls approaching from across the terrace. She was annoyed. She had fended off four dandies on her way to the doorway.

"Go away." Cold, disastrously discourteous, she refused to look aside and so much as acknowledge the identity of the man she dismissed.

The footsteps stopped.

Warm hands reached out and gently gathered the twist of hair that trailed down the nape of her neck. She stiffened, dismayed to realize she could not spin and deal a slap for the impertinence. His fingers had tightened too firmly; like a boat, she was effectively moored.

"They insisted inside that you had grown tired of the party," Lysaer s'Ilessid said in greeting.

She shivered. Then blushed; and would have slapped him then for his boldness, that had wrung from her such a reaction. She was unaccustomed to being played like a fish.

He let her go. Cool air ruffled through the strands his fingers had parted. Mulberry blossoms showered in a swirl of white, and eddied in the lee of the railing.

Talith stepped around, prepared to use her pretty woman's scorn to drive him off balance. He deserved as much for his confidence, that everywhere he went he would be welcomed.

Wonder stopped her cold. Strung in his hands was a chain of lights, delicate as flame hung on bead wire.

Lysaer smiled. His eyes sparkled with reflections; his face, struck out in shadow and soft light, held a beauty to madden a sculptor to fits of missed inspiration. The pale, fine hair that just brushed his collar was his sole ornament.

The effect stopped Talith's breath.

"Do you want me to leave?" Lysaer teased.

Pique snapped her out of entrancement. "You haven't been invited to stay." But her glance betrayed her as she marveled at the shining string that quivered and danced between his hands.

His smile deepened at the corners. "No jewel can compare."

He looked down at the bauble, made it gleam and spit sparks like stirred embers. "This cannot compare. It's a poor, flashy phantom. A worthless illusion sprung from light. But if you insist on hiding in the darkness, at least if you wear it, you'll be gilded." He reached up, stepped closer, and with a gesture that brushed the bared skin of her collarbones, settled his spell around her neck.

The lights were neither warm nor cold; in fact, their presence against her flesh raised no tactile sensation at all. That for an oddity made her ache. As if, like a gem or a pearl, she should feel something tangible from his gift.

"Gold suits you," Lysaer murmured. He watched in quiet pleasure as she experimented with his handiwork, let it spill like captive fireflies through her fingers.

And then, too suddenly, he gave the reason for his coming. "The army marches out on the morrow."

She looked up, her head tipped provocatively sideways; the necklace of lights brightened her chin to fine angles. "Should that trouble me?"

Lysaer paused, thoughtful. He seemed not offended or set back. "I don't think anyone in this city understands the threat in the man we leave to cut down."

"Arithon?" Talith tossed back her mane of hair, about to say, disparagingly, that even allied to barbarians the deposed prince could hardly challenge a fortified city.

Lysaer stepped to her suddenly and caught her arms below her bared shoulders. He did not shake her. Neither did he raise his voice to chastise. His touch stayed soft and the eyes that stared down into hers were wide open, very blue, and anguished only with himself. "Lady, I fear for your city, for your safety, for your happiness. And about Arithon s'Ffalenn, I can make nobody comprehend."

"What else is there to know?" She looked back at him, graceful as some tawny cat assured of its power to captivate.

Lysaer slid his palms down her arms lightly as a breath. He backed away, set his hands on the balustrade, and stared out over the darkened garden. He was troubled, deeply, and she realized with a snap of vexation that her allure had not even touched him. He gave her no chance to retaliate, but said quickly, "I grew up in a land that was terrorized by the predations of the s'Ffalenn. We in Amroth had wealth, good ships, skilled men with quality weapons to defend us. We should have triumphed easily, for the Isle of Karthan the pirate kings ruled was little more than a sandspit. The people were poor, with few resources, fewer men. But what they had, they used with the cleverness of demons."

He stilled for a moment. Talith saw that his hands had balled into fists. Unsure whether his tension might be troublesome to cross, she waited, patient because his lordly display of dedication was novel enough to intrigue her.

Presently, Lysaer spoke again. "The killing and the grief went back for generations, through my great grandfather's time. Both of my uncles were lured into traps and sent back to us pickled for burial. Grief left my father unreasonable, even mad. He lost a wife before my mother. Two daughters died with her, who would have been my half-sisters had I known them. No one told me they existed until I was twelve, when I forced my father's seneschal to say why the royal crypt held an unmarked vault."

Lysaer took a breath. "All my life, I remember the campaigns, the fleets, and the generals sent out to eradicate the s'Ffalenn. We accomplished little for great efforts. We managed to burn villages, poor shanties whose loss seemed scarcely to hurt. Karthish lookouts would spot the inbound fleets and warn the people to escape. Men sent ashore to track refugees would scour the desert to no avail. Sea engagements went as badly. Our ships were lured into exhaustive chases, wrecked in shoal waters because the artisans who drew our charts had once been fed false information. Our captains and crews died fighting against lee shores in gales. They died of thirst, hunger, mutiny, and fire, because the weapon of the s'Ffalenn was ingenuity that seemed inexhaustible as the tides. The pirate princes reveled in feuding. Their trickery never repeated itself, and they sailed to no predictable pattern."

Remembered anguish drove Lysaer to straighten from the balustrade. "These past captains were only men, clever and hungry for bloodshed. The last of their line, the s'Ffalenn heir bequeathed to Athera, is far more. He was born to an enchantress, raised to the ways of power. A sorcerer, a shadow master, his tricks will come barbed in spells."

His eyes at last turned and met Talith's, dreadfully deep and revealing. "Arithon fooled even me, lady. He drew me to believe he was harmless, then cozened true friendship from me. If not for your brother's apt questions, if not for the doubts he reawakened, no one might have acted in time. Arithon might never have stood before Etarra and revealed his true nature in the square."

Lysaer ended in harsh and personal discomfort. "That is what I cannot teach your people to know and fear."

Caught up in fascination exotic enough to make her shiver, Talith said, "But you are lord over powers of light. You can defend against witchery."

"I'm a man," Lysaer amended. "Men fail."

Uncertainty flawed Talith's entrancement. She had been affected inside, and surprised by that recognition, she wanted his hands on her. "You'll come back. Diegan's army will win that black sorcerer's head."

Breeze stirred a drift of mulberry petals between them. They dusted Talith's cheeks and caught in her hair and on the abalone tips of lacquered pins. With a gentle hand he brushed them away. "We can try. We can hope." He cupped her face, bent and kissed her with maddening lightness.

She reached to pull him closer, but the slithering drag of her caped sleeves warned him in time to draw back. From a safe half pace away he smiled at her. "No. Not now. You'll wait for me, lovely lady. When Arithon s'Ffalenn is vanquished and your city is safe, I'll return. If your desire for my presence still endures, we shall build something great between us then."

She swallowed back her annoyance, the more amazed because he did not mock her frustrated passion as Etarran men might have done. "What if you don't come back?"

His lightness vanished. "Then you'll be left to find out why Etarra's army lost. In my memory, you'll use such knowledge to warn your people so that Arithon's predations don't catch them unprepared when the time comes to fight him again."

"You can't believe you'll be defeated!" Talith cried, forgetting in distress to be artful.

"I can't be so cocky as to think for a second I might not." He gave a stiff shrug in apology. "S'Ffalenn pirates in the past have ruined better men than me."

"You're all we have." Talith corrected herself with passionate sharpness. "All I have."

Inside the ballroom the musicians struck up a merry tune. Past the opened double doors dancers gathered, formed lines, and began to tread the first measures. Their movements seemed meaningless. Mute in her appeal, Talith saw with a relief that made her tremble that Lysaer would not, after all, depart without thought for her happiness.

"One dance." The s'Ilessid prince laughed gently and gathered her, silk, pearls, and ruffled, layered skirts as delicately as if she were a blown bit of thistledown captured in the circle of his arms.

Deduction

Under a breeze from the east, the soured mud of bare tide flats and the dye works of Narms swept a reeking pall over the town, which consisted of box-fronted wooden mansions, one-story warehouse sheds, and a harbor. A craft center from first to last, the place recognized no elegance beyond the bustling purpose of commerce.

Up coast, where the beautiful yarns spun and dyed in these wind-raked, ramshackle shops were woven into famed rugs and tapestries, Cildorn's stone buildings held the deeper mystery of more ancient sites; a resonance that lingered from Paravian inhabitance still drew the earth's forces to flow very near to the surface. For the advantage such powers lent to spell-craft, the Koriani Prime would have preferred to conduct her errand there. But since the Fellowship's gross misjudgment over Arithon's failed coronation, Elaira could make Narms with better speed.

The building let for Morriel's use was owned by the widow of a former Koriani boy ward. Since his death, hard times and slatternly management had caused his dye works to fail. Long abandoned to the whims of stray iyats, the yard stood cluttered with cracked buckets silted wrist deep in dead leaves. The shop, crudely shuttered, lay sandwiched between a brewery and the mudflats. Storms in winter sometimes flooded the warehouse. The building smelled now of moldered rags and worm-rotted planking, underlaid by the taint of hops and fish.

One lingering fiend had to be chased from the rafters. Then the sole vat not cursed with slow leaks was dragged inside by Morriel's servant, wedged level on packed sand flooring, and filled now for scrying. A yarn rack propped up and sumptuously padded with quilts had been prepared; but the Koriani matriarch disdained the seat. Hunched under shawls like a crow draggled down by wet plumage, she waited in the flickering light of the resin torches with a patience her First Senior could not match.

Sustained by voracious ambition, Lirenda reveled to be the only one chosen for active duty. Though the time was well past midnight and her fellow Seniors had long since retired, for pride she would not show weariness and sit in the presence of her Prime.

Sharing attendance upon Morriel's needs was the huge half-wit who stood as her door guard. Witness to more secrets than any living Koriani Senior, the man sat cross-legged in a corner, drooping in his effort to stay awake. The streets outside were mostly quiet. Sometimes a late worker from the brewery strode whistling by. The stillness in between magnified the hiss of burning resin and the distant beat of combers off Instrell Bay. A sudden clatter of iron as a horse arrived outside caused the half-wit to startle from his doze and hasten to unbar the door.

Elaira's voice carried in on the gust that swept the threshold as she dismissed the livery groom who would return her mount to the stable. She entered a moment later. Hair blown loose from her braid was screwed into wisps by the seaside humidity, and her skin was like chalk with exhaustion.

She had ridden a hundred leagues in under three days. Chafed raw at the knees from leathers stiffened with horse sweat, her ragged state showed as she made obeisance to the Koriani matriarch. The formal words of greeting came courageously steady from her lips.

Lirenda watched, avid, as Morriel beckoned Elaira closer. Under browless hoods of bone, the Prime's deep-set eyes did not merely study, but raked the rider who stepped forward on command.

Exposed full figure in flame light, Elaira withstood the inspection. Awareness left her flushed, that the sisterhood's arts of observation would take in all, from the scuffs on her boots left by pebbles kicked in impatience at post stables too slow to tack her remounts, to the stains on her cloak where a drunk in a wayside tavern had upset the broth she could not stay to have replenished.

The Prime observed, "Your journey was trying, I see."

Eased by the unexpected kindness, Elaira straightened sore shoulders. "Not so bad." In wry humor that Lirenda found particularly grating she added, "If the inns had lice in the bedclothes, at least I escaped finding out."

Morriel's lips twitched, perhaps in the ghost of a smile. "Your spirits are intact, I can see. When did you last eat?"

Elaira paused for thought, which gave answer enough in itself. The crone gestured to her half-wit. "Quen, go next door to the brewers and buy some bread and sausage." To Elaira, in disarming solicitude, she added, "Do you wish beer?"

Not so tired she failed to sense a trap, Elaira shook her head. "On the heels of an emergency summons, I think not, thank you. Unless I have leave to go to bed?"

"You have not." But the Prime's approval was apparent, that the girl had kept sharp wits. "Though you deserve the rest, surely. I'm not unaware that you had to bid against the trade guilds' couriers, jammed as the livery stables have been with bearers carrying ill news."

Inordinate numbers of state messengers had crowded the roads as well, but Elaira had been too pressed to hear gossip. "Worse happened since I left Etarra?"

"A great deal." Fog curled through the door as Quen slipped back in with a steaming parcel. As the torches hissed and spat in the damp, Morriel motioned toward the vat. "Bring your meal while you study the water. I would see you brought current with events, that you understand the importance of the demands you've been called to attend."

To thank Quen for any service was to invite an embarrassment of obsequious gratitude. Elaira patted his rough hand and took the food, half braced in pity in case his fawning should displease the Prime. But Quen only ducked his head in pathetic ecstacy for her kindness, then retired back to his corner.

Elaira unwrapped greasy coils of sausage and trailed after her mistress toward the vat.

Lirenda knew bitterness, that the order's most incorrigible junior initiate should be casually stuffing her mouth, while beside her, Morriel Prime prepared to admit her to the highest level of Koriani affairs, and for no better cause than a disobedient escapade with a man.

With no thought spared for Lirenda's disaffection, Morriel hitched up one hip and with a drag of thick woolens, perched on the rim of the vat. Graced by a balance at odds with her years, she unhooked the crystal that hung on fine chains at her neck and informed Elaira, "The images you will observe reflect events that occurred today."

Morriel dangled her jewel above the ruffled water, then completed a pass that engaged spell-craft. Elaira leaned over a surface bound into mirror smoothness, while the vision induced by the Prime's clairvoyance overlaid the madder-stained depths. . . .

* * *

Morning sun tinted the square brick turrets of Etarra's watch keeps and struck shafts through the dust billowed up by the garrison that tramped outbound from the northwestern gate. Its columns were narrowed by the flanks of the Mathorn pass, and rank after rank of raised pikes and lances gridded the pale, hazed sky. Windowed in water, men marched like toy figurines given life, the gold and red banners of the City Guard cracking in the breeze like snipped cloth.

"Fatemaster's mercy," Elaira murmured, her sausage cooling in fingers that felt sapped of nerves. "There's to be war, then?"

For reply, Morriel shifted vantage to display Etarra's host in its entirety.

Ten thousand strong, spearheaded by caparisoned rows of mounted lancers and trailed by the light cavalry under the standard of the headhunters' league, the army advanced down switched-back roads like a serpent roused hungry from its lair. Crowds packed the city ramparts to cheer, foremost among them a tawny-haired woman in a glitter of gold-netted silk. Heralds raised trumpets emblazoned with tassels, and silent fanfare sounded for the smiling, bejeweled figure of Lysaer s'Ilessid, mounted on his chestnut horse, flanked by Lord Diegan and Etarra's field general, the grim-faced, leonine Gnudsog.

Shocked beyond thought for protocol, Elaira accosted her supreme superior. "*Lysaer* has raised Etarra? Daelion forfend, whatever for?"

A gust hissed through the gapped warehouse, sour with the reek of dried seaweed. Where Lirenda braced in expectation of immediate displeasure from the Prime, Morriel simply sighed and tugged with thin hands to rearrange the burden of her shawls. The image in the dye vat erased. In dry conversation, the crone said, "I believe this next image should tell you."

She effected a second pass.

The water's glassine surface now showed the mild haze of a midspring afternoon. Shadows pocked the stubble of a stripped hillside. Brown and unobtrusive against mats of hacked bark and wilted greenery, a band of barbarian scouts left the timber they had cut and packed in six-foot lengths onto sledges. They gathered presently in a clearing, where the only man among them not dirtied from labor waited on his knees before the blade of his own drawn sword. A start in her nerves from recognition, Elaira beheld Arithon s'Ffalenn. Beside him, stiff-backed and vexed, stood the rangy frame of the most powerful barbarian in the north: Steiven s'Valerient, *Caithdein* of Ithamon and high chieftain of the clans of Deshir.

"But this makes no sense." Elaira abandoned her half-eaten meal in its folds of steam-soggy paper. Just one breath away from a thunderous headache, she raised hands to rub her temples. "The clans in Strakewood are no match for the might of Etarra."

"They believe otherwise." Morriel removed her jewel. The spell that fueled her clairvoyance snapped, and woodlands vanished away, leaving waters that flashed and puckered over a blood-dark silt of old dyes. "Three valleys along Tal Quorin's banks have been riddled with deadfalls to that end. War is in the offing. The princes so fondly received by the Fellowship are themselves at the root and cause."

"No." Elaira raised her chin in sick protest. "The Seven wouldn't—" She stopped, fought down dread for a slip that could betray her past trust with Asandir. "The Sorcerers must surely intervene if their princes are caught at the heart of this."

"Ah," said Morriel, her flash of discovery well hidden, though across the warehouse, Lirenda looked vindicated. "But the Sorcerers have all fled Etarra. Like rats off a foundering ship, they abandoned their post of responsibility on the instant Desh-thiere's curse claimed the half-brothers."

Morriel paused. Acute, colorless eyes flicked aside to encompass Elaira's strained face. "Your friend Asandir made a misstep."

The implication of collaborative association with a Fellowship Sorcerer went unnoticed before the disclaimer that stormed Elaira's thoughts: that the power she had encountered in the loft of Enithen Tuer's was no likely candidate for mistakes. If the Fellowship of Seven had withdrawn, they must surely have done so deliberately.

Morriel's eyes held her gaze like a snake's. Exposed to the Prime's sharp dispassion, that would see past nuance and draw out frightful truths, Elaira's fought down raw nerves and dread. Too late, with both hands locked in fear to the cold stone edge of the dye vat, she waited to be denounced for far worse offense than a silly romantic entanglement.

"Oh, yes, the truth behind your illicit visit to the Four Ravens' tavern last autumn is known to us." The Prime tucked her focus stone in her lap with a clicking of hooked yellow fingernails. "However, we deem your visit to Asandir too petty for pursuit in light of the present crisis. Since the actions of s'Ffalenn and s'Ilessid have brought Rathain's factions to arms, a character scan must be made of both princes. Our sisterhood must know how five centuries of exile have altered the Fellowship's royal lines."

The blow so long suspected fell at last as Morriel gathered her skirts and stood erect. "You have been summoned here, Elaira, as the only initiate we have who has been in close enough contact with the royal heirs to undertake the attempt."

Stunned as if her guts had come unhinged, Elaira thrust off from the dye vat. The Koriani order owned her, flesh and mind, but this demand threatened to annihilate her. Perfect, unbiased recall, down to the smallest detail of the princes' features, dress, and bearing, was required of her or Morriel's scrying would be useless, her delicate chains of deductions ridden through with dead ends and errors. Though every Koriani initiate had been exactingly trained for clear recall, reproducing images for character scan was a task given only to the most time-proven, gifted Seniors. The perils involved were no secret. The ritual unleashed emotion, could and had linked participants to depths of insight that a bond of sympathy with the subject under study became nearly impossible to deny. As if poised on the rim of a pit that beckoned her spirit to damnation, Elaira fought black despair. If this was the Prime Circle's test to determine whether she had excised her attraction for Arithon s'Ffalenn, it was too much, far too cruelly soon.

Wind wailed through the boarded windows; over the white noise of breakers, a gull flew calling through the dark. Elaira shuddered, unnerved by Morriel's regard still pinned on her.

To protest a direct order from the Prime was to beg instantaneous destruction. Hollow with dread, hounded by Lirenda's antagonistic wish to see her crumble, Elaira bowed to Morriel Prime. "Your will."

The matriarch of the sisterhood said no more as she raised her crystal spinning on its chains and rehooked the clasp at her neck. She snapped bird-boned fingers for Quen, who hastened forward and offered Elaira a small stone pipe and a sealed tin that held tobacco steeped in water mildly infused with a tienelle extract. Less potent than the uncut, dried leaves, the mixture used by junior initiates was still toxic enough to cause multiple unpleasant side effects.

Elaira exchanged the items for her mangled chunk of sausage, and this time found no thanks for the half-wit.

Morriel said, not unkindly, "Make yourself ready as you can. Do not rush. When you have achieved a trance heightened by the drug, we shall begin."

Minutes later, as the lighted fumes from the pipe curled through the mildew-dank warehouse, Quen slept curled like a dog by the doorway. Equally oblivious, though deadly pale, Elaira sat cross-legged, her eyes closed and her back propped straight against the dye vat. Her strength of self-discipline could not be faulted as she laid the pipe aside and drew the slow, measured breaths that indicated full surrender to the broadening, glass-sharp awareness induced by the poisons in the herb smoke.

Across a gloom deepened by the embered stubs of the torches, Lirenda stirred. "You were easy on her."

Morriel sighed. Fragile under crushing layers of shawls, she crossed the floor and sank into the quilts her servant had prepared for her. "You think so?" The voice so precisely edged but a moment before now sounded querulous and tired.

Belatedly, Lirenda stirred to attend her Prime's comfort.

Yet as she reached to assist with the blankets, Morriel fended her away. "You pay no mind to your heart, First Senior. That is a most wasteful fault."

Taken aback to be criticized, Lirenda was forced to reconsider. "Then Elaira is to think she's forgiven for falling prey to distractions of the flesh, not to mention the further possibility she has abetted the despoiler Asandir?"

Morriel clasped skeletal fingers. Her eyes as she looked up were empty, like fog or featureless rain. "Elaira pulled a girl's prank that placed her most woefully in a bad place at the wrong time. She is intelligent, and gifted with an insight that runs rare and true. Which strengths caused her to see the s'Ffalenn heir through to his depths and let him touch her. I venture to suggest that her reasons for attraction are real, and dauntingly powerful to any mind-born female. That is why you alone were called to witness the scrying that shall take place tonight. I would shield our other Seniors from exposure to fearful temptation. There is warning for you in this. Heed the risk."

"You do feel sorry for Elaira," Lirenda observed, thrilled by discovery that Morriel had any softness left for sentiment.

The Prime denied nothing. "I pity the fact I have ruined her."

Lirenda would not believe this. Planks creaked as she crossed a fallen trestle to brighten a fresh set of torches. "Nobody asked Elaira to create that scene in the taproom, or to seek Asandir out beforehand. The silly girl ruined herself."

"No. She would have recovered from the mistake. Had done so quite admirably, in fact, until I sent her afterward to Etarra." Hard to her core now, and misliking the strengthened light which inked shadows in every seam of her face, Morriel drew a short breath. "You will learn from this, First Senior, if you covet the position as my successor. Elaira is a valuable tool, a window into Arithon's character we're going to need sorely if we wish to track the conflict the Fellowship has set loose upon the continent. We must tenderly encourage that girl to keep discipline. She is dedicated. With judicious handling, her botched bit of insight will prove useful for a very long time before she breaks. For as you guessed, if our order's training had held, she should have rejected the curiosity that prompted her foray into Erdane. Elaira is a flawed instrument. But she will serve as no other can, until the day comes when she is driven to forsake her vows. Let her own shortfalls, and not your vindictive perfectionism, be the quality that throws her to destruction."

The Prime closed her eyes to snatch an interval to meditate, stiff enough indication that she had spent her reserves on talk. Lirenda as ever was wily enough to respect the line that was drawn—too wily, the aged Prime sometimes thought. Like many another former matriarch, she wished the last trial of initiation for the Koriani seat of prime power was not fatal to almost every aspirant.

Lirenda was the forty-third hopeful selected to attempt the succession. Morriel battled to separate her consciousness from the ache of her brittle bones. She feared afresh to become the first to break the chain of command: to become the Prime that death would overtake before an heir survived to finish training.

Old she was, and bitterly tired. Morriel snatched what solace she could from the disciplines of her office. What Lirenda did through the minutes that passed held no concern. Years since, the Prime had ceased to invest interest in the particulars of any one candidate. The woman who succeeded—that one only she could love. Since the death of the first, the rest had been nothing but ciphers.

Informed at length by the scent of charred herbs that the pipe had been fully smoked, Morriel stirred. On the moment the narcotic peaked Elaira's powers of recall, she shed piled blankets and arose. Lirenda had already stationed herself over the dye vat, her rapt expression clear enough indication that an image already lay in view. Careful of joints over-worn from centuries of unnatural lifespan, the Prime Enchantress crossed the warehouse to share what the waters would show.

"A throwback," Lirenda murmured as the matriarch drew abreast. "He could almost be Torbrand's double."

Humbled by Elaira's courage, which had dared display Arithon first, Morriel said nothing. Then she looked, and her heart would not allow speech past the stunningly expressive detail instilled in the image in the vat.

The chosen moment was one that Elaira had stolen: when the man had foolishly supposed no observer with higher interests would be present, he had crouched in a filthy alley, attended by those who least cared for power, and sorceries, and bloody contentions between factions. Surrounded by a tattered pack of children, Arithon bent in the act of setting a brigantine fashioned of shadows to capture the breeze in full sails.

Elaira had caught him glancing up to see his illusion under way. His face held untrammeled peace. A laugh of delight and satisfaction lightened the corners of his mouth. His eyes were unshadowed, and the sharp-angled features of s'Ffalenn inheritance had fleetingly softened to expose, in vivid clarity, the depths of generosity and caring that buttressed his musician's sensitivity.

The effect was spirit stripped naked. The accuracy of Elaira's recreation gave the lie to every sharp edge, every cutting word, every difficult and cross-grained reaction that Arithon had ever employed to defend this, his vulnerable inner heart.

"Daelion Fatemaster," Morriel gasped. "The girl's unmasked him for us, wholly. I never believed it could be done."

Totally absorbed by the image, Lirenda never noticed that her nails had broken under force of her tightened grip on scaled stone. "He can be brought down, though. The killing will unman him finally, for s'Ffalenn conscience must force him over time to back down."

Morriel gave the image long study, her head cocked in unlooked-for, grandmotherly fascination. "Look again," she urged. "War will not be what stops this prince." When Lirenda made no response, she added, "My point is subtle. But plain to be read if you study his hands before his eyes."

Obedient, Lirenda regarded Arithon's fingers, which were slim and quick and, in this frozen moment of Elaira's recall, graceful in completion of a difficult spell. The green eyes were deep, not dangerous. "I fail to find further conclusion," the First Senior said with reluctance.

Morriel's cackling laugh echoed through the ramshackle warehouse. "But he is not clever! Not when he's truly honest. That means the deceit Arithon so readily displays when provoked is not rooted in venal ingenuity. No. Sadly not. What drives this prince's wit is not craftiness, but the gift of true farsight imbued in the s'Ahelas royal line."

Lirenda considered this, while outside, something that crashed in an alley disturbed a cat with a yowl from a cranny. Roused back to herself by distraction, Morriel reached out and tapped Elaira's hand. "Show us the half-brother now."

The image of Arithon swept away, replaced momentarily by another. Now the s'Ilessid prince stood in the fog of a pre-dawn garden, half lit by a shaft of lamp light that escaped through the gate from the street. He leaned against the pedestal of a statue, his lashes and cloak beaded with damp that sparkled as he breathed like fine diamonds. The water was the only jewel on him; for once his clothing held no artifice. Even his hair lay unbrushed. Although in public Lysaer maintained the flawless manners of diplomacy, here, alone, his lordly fine looks lay hagridden by doubt as he wrestled some inward dilemma his conscience could not resolve. The pain on his face, in the bearing of his shoulders and the lamp-gilded knuckles of clenched hands, was unanswerably intense. Elaira's observance had peeled back all poise to expose him in a moment of soul-rending self-distaste.

"Oh, Elaira, well done!" murmured Morriel.

At her side, whetted to heightened sensitivity by the fumes that trailed from the pipe bowl, Lirenda felt her being struck and jangled by that chord of conflicted emotions. She not only saw but felt how s'Ilessid justice warred with the s'Ahelas farsight inherited from the distaff side of Lysaer's pedigree.

His mouth in this captured instant held none of the tenderness that adoring women back in Amroth had experienced while plying him for kisses. Unyielding as tempered wire lay calculation threaded through by royal upbringing, and the machinations of Desh-thiere's latent wraith. The result charged the nerves to disquiet, as if for one heartbeat pity were absent, and mercy an omitted entry.

"We have seen what we must," the Prime announced in jarring abruptness. To Elaira she added, "You're permitted to relax from your trance."

As the image dissolved, Lirenda looked up, sparked by unsated excitement. "Misfortunate luck. Both princes have inherited the gifts of two royal houses."

Discomfited at last by trepidation, Morriel tucked her arms beneath her shawls. "Unlucky and perilous. Arithon's is an incompatible legacy. His mind is fatally flawed. The Fellowship should never have sanctioned his right of succession, for suffering shall dog his path as surely as seasons must turn."

Elaira shuddered in transition back to consciousness, opened her eyes, and whitely fought the first twinge of tienelle withdrawal. "My Prime, you mistake him," she said shakily.

Amazed she should dare contradiction, Lirenda shot a swift glance at the Prime.

Only Morriel showed no offense for the impertinence.

Given this tacit liberty, Elaira insisted, "Lysaer's the one who bears watching. Ath's mercy, I've met him. He's a living inspiration, the flesh-and-blood example of human kindness. The masses must flock to his standard, for his cause shall be presented in passionate and upright idealism. Then indeed shall the towns upheave and suffering result, since bias toward noble principles offers a weapon already fashioned for a ruler of his trained talents. All Prince Lysaer need do is pose in that mold, and set by Desh-thiere's curse to turn his gifts toward bloodshed, he has no other course."

"That's a predictable cycle," Lirenda interjected, annoyed beyond restraint by the Prime's unfathomable license. "We know where Lysaer will turn and what will be the result. What can be anticipated can also be controlled or prevented. Arithon owns no such stability."

Frustrated by narcotically enhanced perceptions, Elaira cried protest. "But Arithon is a man devoted to harmony, a musician with a seer's perception. He's conscious of his actions as Lysaer can never be!"

"Which is precisely what makes him dangerous, Elaira," Morriel corrected sadly. "For Lysaer's sense of justice and farsight will answer to logic, and therefore be reconciled by compromise. But since when can compassion ever be made to condone pain? S'Ahelas blood gives Arithon full grasp of cause and effect; mage training compounds this with awareness of the forward reactions of power. These traits aligned against the s'Ffalenn gift of sympathetic empathy cancels the mind's self-defenses. The shelter of petty hatred becomes untenable. Arithon is a visionary placed at a nexus of responsibility. Desh-thiere's curse will embroil him in violence he can neither escape nor master. Stress will prove his undoing, for the sensitivities of poets have ever been frail, and the broadened span of his thinking shall but inflame and haunt him to madness."

"You're mistaken," Elaira insisted, recalling the whiplash resilience the living man had possessed. "Ath be my witness, the conclusion you've drawn from this is wrong."

"Time will tell." Morriel motioned dismissal. "You are excused to rest. The widow will have a bed waiting and a basin to wash. Remember to drink enough water lest you take harm from the tienelle poisons."

The traditional response all but caught in Elaira's throat. "Your will." She dragged herself to her feet, managed a graceless curtsy, and before the cramping that marked the aftermath of tienelle usage tore her composure to shreds, contrived to walk out of the warehouse.

Outside, wrapped in darkness with the dank winds cooling her sweated face, and her back to the mildewed sill of a craft shanty, the tears came.

Elaira could not cast off the ripping, unhappy remorse, that in keeping loyalty to her order, she had effected a betrayal much deeper. Her every intent had just misfired, to expose a man's private self, that his hidden pregnabilities should win him the protection of Koriani sympathy. Yet understanding had turned awry in her hands. Elaira ached with recognition that she had only succeeded in granting a weapon to an enemy.

Daybreak

In a widow's attic bedchamber, First Senior Lirenda wakens once again, restlessly entangled in her bedclothes, and the dream that spoils her sleep is the same, of a man's green eyes imbued with a compassion deep enough to leave her weeping and desolate in the icy chill before dawn. . . .

As fog curls silver through the marshes flanking Tal Quorin, Deshir's clansmen break fast on dry journey biscuit and take up their shovels and axes; although they speak little on the fact their crown prince has been absent since his oath-taking ceremony the previous afternoon, Steiven's son Jieret overhears enough to become intrigued over Arithon's whereabouts. . . .

In the chimney-warmed garret of a north kingdom hostel, a caravan master nurses a flagon of spirits; in between gulps and recriminations, he cannot fathom what possessed him to give over the horse thief's jeweled pin to that dreamy-eyed graybeard in maroon who had met him in the alley and simply asked for the gift, as if acorn-sized emeralds were proper to claim as charity from an absolute stranger. . . .

XVI. Augury

In a place of his own choosing, well removed from the activities of the clans, Arithon disengaged mage-trained senses from the webs of subliminal energy that delineated the surrounding forest. Gently the awareness bled from him, of living leaves and dappling sunlight; of roots rejuvenated by the Mistwraith's defeat groping warmed soil in new growth; and of birds that flicked in bursts through the branches as they gathered small twigs for their nesting. His touch upon the land's pulse had been thorough but light; even the secretive night lynx had not been disturbed where she slept denned up with her young. Arithon opened his eyes at last to the fluting calls of thrushes and the light-shafted haze of midmorning.

Absent since his oath taking the previous afternoon, Rathain's new crown prince laced his fingers and stretched kinks from his shoulders and back. Worry he would have masked before others sat all too plain on his face.

Deep trance had absorbed him for twelve unbroken hours, a necessary interval to ensure that this small, stream-side glen would stay isolated enough for the arduous scrying that lay ahead of him. Game deer within his proximity browsed untroubled by hunters, the paths they tracked never trodden by clan children sent out to forage for herbs and firewood.

Muscles released from the demand of perfect stillness cramped as

Arithon arose. The gimp in his movement dismayed him, forced a reckoning for a self-discipline sadly slackened since his apprenticeship at Rauven. No small bit wrung by trepidation, he knelt. Alone beside one of the Tal Quorin basin's many streamlets that bent in dark courses through towering oaks and tangled thickets of witch hazel, he dipped his hands and drank.

Icy water hit his empty stomach and shot a quiver through him. While he rested on his heels for an interval to allow his body to settle, a half smile tugged at his mouth. His unexplained night in the open had hopefully confirmed the feckless character he had fostered among Deshir's clansmen. Let them think he went off to mope. Unless he shied clear of Lady Dania's sharp perception, and Halliron Masterbard's meddlesome curiosity, he could never have fasted to purge his system without becoming embroiled in a Sithaer-bent mess of unwanted inquiries. No frivolous excuse could mask the unbending requirements of spell-craft. Let the clans suspect he was mage-trained, and every deception he had played to win his freedom would be irremediably spoiled. Concealed in place and purpose, Arithon engaged his mastery and methodically centered his will.

If the clans of the north were determined to war against Etarra's army, his oath to Rathain bound him to make sure that no man's life be needlessly endangered. Given means to tap prescient scrying through Rauven's teaching and the tienelle filched from Sethvir, Arithon took out the stolen canister. Fearfully aware of risk to himself, he unwrapped the stone pipe inside and packed the bowl with silvery, notched leaves that sheared the forest air with their pungency.

Narcotically expanded senses might sound whether Caolle's battle strategies would deflect Lysaer's assault, but the perils could not be ignored. Until the drug's influence faded, the scryer's awareness would be hyper-sensitized, every nerve left unshielded before the risk of chance-met interference. This was not Rauven or Althain Tower, ringed around with defenses and intricate wardspells that would protect the unshuttered mind. And Arithon had cast away the second safeguard instilled by his grandfather's tutelage: that trance under influence of tienelle never be attempted while alone. If he lost his iron self-command, if his concentration became shaken by the maze of drug-induced visions, no one stood by to realign his frayed concentration.

Arithon smoothed a last leaflet into the pipe and rammed it firm. More than his personal hope of happiness held him adamant. Events may have cornered him against an inborn compassion he could not shed, but the deeper danger still stalked him. He could not evade the certainty that his oath to Deshir was a fragile thing before the curse Desh-thiere's wraith had left embedded and coiled through his being. The endangerment to Rathain's feal vassals must be shouldered, while every minute the temptation to take and twist clan trust into a weapon to bring down Lysaer ate like a darkness at his heart. Only a mage's sensitivity allowed Arithon to separate that poisoned urge from active will, and the passage of days wore him down with the draining, constant effort such distinction took to maintain. Until he won free of royal obligation and could dissociate himself from any claim to sovereignty, the double-edged burden would continue to chafe at his control.

No cause must jeopardize the image of weakness so painstakingly fostered among the clans. Though Halliron had breached that pretense, the Masterbard was one that Rathain's new crown prince least wished to admit into confidence. The wild need to seize upon false escape, to accept companionship and release through musical indulgence, could too easily lure him into misstep.

Finished preparing the pipe, Arithon arose. He braced his back against a massive old oak and took a full breath, clean scented with growing greenery and the sharper pungence of evergreens. He invited the peace of the forest to calm him. Absorbed by the lisp of current over moss-capped rocks and calls of chipmunks in a fallen log, he stilled his clamor of self-doubt and drew on his mastery to create a spark.

The herb in the pipe bowl ignited. Silver-blue smoke trailed and twined like ghost spells on the breeze. Touched to a frisson of apprehension by the sting of acrid fumes, Arithon collected his will. He set the pipe stem to his lips and drew poisoned smoke deep into his lungs.

Vertigo upended his physical senses. Well prepared, he pressed against the tree and let live wood reaffirm his balance. The kick as the drug fired his nerves was harder by far to absorb and master. He gasped in near pain at the explosive unreeling of his innermind as sights, smells, and sensations launched him through a spiraling hyperbole.

He was immediately grateful he had seen through the precaution of fasting. The plants Sethvir had dried at Althain were fiercely potent and pure.

The trickle of the stream by Arithon's feet became an avalanche of sound in his ears, the squall of a jay a torment that flicked his hearing like a whip. Battered to the verge of bewilderment, he clenched his right hand, let the dig of his nails in half-healed burns anchor his scattered concentration. The instant he had firm control, he cast his mind ahead into the many-branching avenues of possible happenstance.

Reeling holocaust met him. Fire and smoke swallowed all, while the higher-pitched vibration of dying trees screamed across his lacerated senses. Arithon cried out in forced empathy. Through a wilderness of chaotic sensation he groped, and finally separated the cause: Lysaer's army, waiting until the tinder-dry days of midsummer, then firing Strakewood, that the wind-caught blaze drive the clans out of cover to be rounded up and slaughtered. Vistas followed of razed timber and dead men, blackened with ash and feeding flies. Clan children marched in ragged coffles, then died one by one in a public display that packed Etarra's square with vicious, screaming onlookers. Arithon's stomach wrenched at the smell of the executioner's excitement, charged and whelmed to a sickness of ecstasy by rivers of new-spilled blood.

The Master of Shadows bit back horror and physical distress, and in forced effort as difficult as anything he had undertaken throughout training, transmuted revulsion to the icy detachment necessary to re-impose control. The hideous sequence was arrested, only to slip his grasp again as sensitized perceptions careened off on a tangent.

He saw a hillside strewn with corpses; banners fallen and snarled by the trampling passage of horses; and beyond these a clearing that held townsmen who were also Rathain's subjects, hideously disemboweled and hung by their ankles from game hooks.

"No!" Arithon ground the heels of his hands in his eye sockets, then ripped in a shuddering, clean breath of air. Whirled by a firestorm of prescience, he grappled to recover mental balance, to reach past the reeling crush of nightmare for the single thread dictated by Caolle's prudently laid strategy.

Control escaped him.

Harrowed by atrocities that deluged his mind in shock waves, Arithon bent double in dry heaves. Gagged by the taste of bile, he sucked in another fast breath. Sweat poured off him in runnels. His sensitized flesh recorded the slide and fall of each salty drop. Another breath, this one deeper; his mind cleared fractionally. He managed to pry his consciousness away from the herb-induced barrage of farsight. He had been right to fear! One wrong choice, one misplaced scout or mistimed attack, and all he had envisioned might result.

Arithon tightened his hold on concentration, then locked onto the sequence he desired. His hand trembled as he shallowly drew on the pipe. Prepared this time for raw carnage, he traced through the spinning nexus of possibilities that deluged his innermind to follow the single one that mattered.

Caolle planned to lure Etarra's thousands up the Tal Quorin's creek bed. Upstream, where the river shoaled and fanned out into reed beds and swamp, the tight phalanxes of townsmen would be compelled to split their ranks. The terrain as they progressed would divide them farther, until two rising, parallel ridges parted the garrison three ways. As battle became joined with the clan scouts, Arithon reviewed the unfolding engagement with deliberate slowness, while tienelle-inflamed awareness touched off in branching visions the thousands of alternate outcomes each action in due course might take. Natural and man-made barriers would successfully disadvantage two of Etarra's split divisions. Archers placed in earth-bank embrasures Caolle hoped would disable the third.

Arithon paused to steady himself. The bowmen would not be enough, he saw, as prescience swooped and spun to frame a grim chain of disasters. Etarra's guardsmen slaughtered clan scouts like meat behind overrun embankments until the screams of dying men gave way to the croak of sated crows, all because the left flank of Etarra's army would be commanded by a man whose lifetime obsession had been the study of barbarian tactics.

The butcher had grizzled gray hair and hands that were narrow and expressive. The face with its pocking of scars and out-thrust jaw was that of Pesquil, Mayor of Etarra's League of Headhunters. His were the orders that sent city officers upslope like terriers to secure the ridge tops. Etarra's west division of pikemen would split two ways, then weaken the cohesion of barbarian resistance by storming both ends of the ridge. Then the light horse cohort dispatched single file through a ravine to the east would circle back and eventually bottle the valley from the north. They would crush the barbarian right flank and rejoin Gnudsog's troops in time to effect rescue of the main columns bogged in the Tal Quorin marshes.

Faint and sick, Arithon watched the Deshans left alive at that juncture become herded into slaughter to a man.

Attempts to forestall their fate by assassinating Pesquil saw three scouts dead under torture. Whether fated by luck or by Daelion, the man would remain in command on the morning that battle commenced.

Sad recognition followed, that even the gravest misuse of shadow mastery and sorcery could not clinch a fourth effort. Pesquil's Etarran paranoia made him carry a talisman, an artifact passed down since the rebellion that would ward against mischance by magic.

Arithon wept then for sure knowledge: that his hope and his preferred future were forfeit. Left to their own resource, the clans were destined for ruin. Whether he left them outright or played through his charade of weak prince and carried his sword at Steiven's shoulder made no difference. Did he fight as a man and not a sorcerer, his own corpse would be part of the carnage.

He yanked himself clear to escape a second reliving of the aftermath and the children's executions in Etarra.

Shivering, wrung by a storm of guilt and grief, Arithon rallied wits enough to realize his pipe bowl held only ashes. Though his body ached for reprieve, he could not let go yet.

The sweat on his lips mingled with a dampness salty enough to be tears as he forced unsteady hands to move and function. He pried the lid off the canister, repacked the pipe, then sucked in a redoubled dose of the herb to use trance to sound an alternative.

Back to the initial deployment, he reran the sequence of Caolle's battle plan. Only this time, before Pesquil's cat-cunning strategies could unravel clan defenses, Arithon added pertinent contributions of his own. Inspired to terrible invention by the breadth of tienelle awareness, he gave his whole mind, bent the talents his grandfather had nurtured to full-scale killing. Wrought of magecraft, and shadow mastery, and devious cunning, he tested strategies that brooked no conscience. He toyed with the visions, slanted and skewed them to tens and thousands of variations. He weighed and recombined results, counted the dead and the wounded with a will locked hard against any acknowledgment of suffering. To feel, to think at all, was to lose the mind to sorrow. Dogged, driven half mad by his oath-taken weight of responsibility, he inhaled more tienelle and threshed through each chain of happenstance in exhaustive review for blind errors.

By the end, spent to a weariness that soaked in dull pain to his bones, he had garnered a handful of tactics that might yield the lowest toll of lives. His work would hold only if no unforeseen circumstance arose to upset his tested effect patterns, if against odds he had managed to circumvent all possible avenues of probability.

He was not Sethvir, to be tracking a scope of events as wide as the chance interaction that could happen between eleven hundred human lives. He could only try his best and leave his frailties to hope.

The tienelle was finished off in any case.

Arithon blew his lungs clear of the last, spent smoke. He sank on his heels and let the empty canister drop between his feet. At the edge of mauled senses, he sensed the quick, running tremors of withdrawal that must be damped and subdued before they built and racked through his body. He held motionless. Unlike the drug that had nearly ruined him in Amroth, tienelle's toxins were not addictive. Once he had regained inner stillness, he could use mastery to annul the poisons. The torment would pass without craving. Arithon bent the lingering influence of the drug's sensual enhancement toward steadying himself until his awareness could stabilize and let time reassume natural proportions.

The liquid call of a lark trilled through the glen. Eyes closed, Arithon savored the sorrowful melody. He had done well, he knew. Amid odds so bleakly tipped toward defeat, he had plowed an alternate path. Bitterness squeezed his heart for what felt like a tragic failure. To the farthest-flung limit of his abilities, a scant third of Steiven's clansmen could be kept alive. How could a prince, mage or otherwise, brook the scale of such sacrifice? Etarra would suffer greater losses, but the cost would be cruel for a stalemate, particularly when mishap could yet play a hand and snatch back the chance of even that.

No trick of magecraft could fully anticipate bad luck. All guarantees had been forfeit since the day Etarra's garrison marched upon the north.

Arithon rapped the ashes from the pipe bowl. The slightest attempt at motion now shot lancing pains through his skull. Warned to pay heed to common sense, he took swift stock of his condition.

His clothing lay wrung with damp sweat and his flesh was drawn from dehydration. Since tienelle could kill if its lesser poisons were not rinsed from the body, he bent at once and tried a swallow from the stream.

The water hit his stomach and set off a rolling bout of nausea. He clamped his hands to his mouth, unsettled by the fight he underwent to keep the precious moisture down. Worn through a brutal and difficult scrying, he recognized his judgment had blurred. Had he considered with his full wits about him, he should never have dared try this much tienelle in one session, far less in total seclusion. He needed herbal tea, and a bed, and the presence of another mage to ward the thought paths that yet lay vulnerably open. Lacking such comforts, he had no choice left but to wait. The herb must be allowed time to fade. Only when his senses released from its burning scope of vision would he be able to transmute the residual poisons the water could not flush through. Until then he could tolerate no human company.

Twilight fell. Birdsong stilled, and the boughs overhead became sprays of black lace against a sky pricked by pale stars. Engaged in private struggle against the fevers of withdrawal, Arithon sat with his head tilted back against an oak bole that kindly performed its appointed function and kept his body propped upright. The dark tunic lent by Lady Dania melted his form into shadow, while stray spurts of drug-born intuition stung him with unwanted revelation: that the clothing on his back had belonged to the lady's younger brother, fallen wounded in a raid at fifteen. Caolle's hand had delivered the mercy stroke that gave the boy clean death. Arithon ground his knuckles in his eyes to drive off the scents of a forest clearing and blood fallen hot on green ferns. Too beaten to avert the bounding starts of truesight that flickered like delirium through his consciousness, he schooled his thoughts to rough order by labored, exhaustive reviews of long-winded ballads.

Engrossed in Dakar's favorite drinking song, which was long and lewd and only funny if both singer and listeners were flat drunk, Arithon groped through the first stanzas. He might be stretched thin, but he did not lack the fiber to master himself. Yet when between the fifth and sixth chorus his whispered recitation went ragged, he stumbled to shivering silence and realized. Someone had invaded his retreat.

Arithon felt his ears whine and his sinews draw tight under the eddying, electrical pull of another mind. Unlike the nearly mystical calm radiated by birds or wild animals, this presence was unmistakably human. Its excitements, uncertainties, and randomly chaotic energies tugged, burned, and rebounded through the channels still defenselessly opened by the herb.

"Come around where I can see you," he managed in a tone dragged husky by discomfort. Grateful that the falling darkness would conceal the worst of his weakness, he waited.

Sticks cracked. A stand of hazels shivered, parted, and disgorged Jieret, who emerged looking sheepish from the depths of a nearby thicket.

"How did you know I was there?" Peevish to find himself discovered, Steiven's son approached, bent down, and with a curiosity that brazenly challenged, hooked up the empty tienelle canister from the verge of the stream bank. He sniffed the pungent odor that lingered inside, curled his lip, and darted a sidelong glance toward Arithon.

The boy expected a reprimand, Arithon knew; also he repressed the curious urge to ask if his prince was some sort of addict. His liege obliged him by saying nothing. Politeness triumphed. Jieret shrugged and set down the container, then fixed the man with an accusation quite spoiled for the fact that his tunic was plastered with damp leaves. "I made no noise."

Arithon concealed a shudder of dry heaves behind a chuckle and lied outright. "The mosquitoes told me."

"But I didn't swat even one!" Jieret objected.

"Next time, don't scratch," the Master of Shadows advised. A flinch escaped his restraint at the boy's explosion of laughter.

"You don't miss much, Your Grace." The implication remained unspoken, that drugs or drink should deaden the senses.

"You will use no title when you address me," said Arithon. "Your blade was not one I swore oath over yesterday afternoon. You owe me no homage at all."

"But I was too young!" Jieret dropped to his knees. "Here." He groped at his belt and proffered the knife he kept for whittling. "Take my steel now. I'll be of age next season."

Arithon forced a smile over a discomfort that riled him to dizziness. The razor-edged perception of herb prescience kept him humble, presented him bluntly with recognition that Jieret's impetuous offer held no hero worship. A piercingly observant child, his knife was a boy's way of testing the mettle of a prince his clan elders but pretended not to scorn.

Tenderly as his condition would allow, Arithon chose his answer. "Lad, you've a good ten years to grow yet before you can cross your father's will. If Steiven forbade you to swear vassalage, I cannot dishonor his judgment. We can share friendship if you wish, but nothing more weighty than that."

Jieret recoiled in affront and sheathed his knife. "I'll be twenty in just eight more years." His presence a blur amid thickening gloom, he added, "Tashka says I'm large for my age. But she's my sister, and what do girls know?" His chin tipped up at a cocky angle his mother would have viewed with trepidation. "I'll fight with the men at your side, Prince, when Etarra's army invades our forest."

The visions, soaked in blood, still threatened. Arithon dragged back wandering attention. "I forbid you."

"But it's custom!" Jieret rebounded to his feet. "Friends always fight together. And Halliron bet Elwedd you're even better with a sword than Caolle is."

"The bard will lose his silver, then," Arithon snapped, and at once regretted his outburst. Unbalanced by his pounding head, he labored to restore his pose of harmless indecision. "You can serve me best by staying aside to protect your little sisters."

Jieret sneered. "Caolle's right, you think like a townborn. Clan girls don't need protection, a chief's daughters least of any. Except for Edal and Meara, my sisters will be in battle, too, disarming the fallen and catching the enemy's loose horses."

Arithon gasped. Hurled into an explosion of prescience like a bloodbath, he reeled, caught back from toppling only by the tree at his back. His mind, his heart, the very breath in his throat, all but stopped as involuntary foresight seared through him: of women and girls lying gutted in pitiful death. The peace of forest night became cancelled by the din of future screaming. Shocked to hot tears and futile fury, Arithon struggled to recover, while the moss dug up by his spasmed fingers seeped warm red with the blood to be reaped by the vengeance of Etarra's steel.

Consciousness dwindled despite his best effort. He fought in a breath that became a choked-off cry as his mind was wrenched and then jarred back to focus by Jieret's grip tugging his arm.

"My prince." The boy regarded at him anxiously. "Are you ill?"

"No." Arithon shuddered, his pain reinforced and compounded by Jieret's unwitting solicitude. While nightmare futures sawed through him, he had only enough constraint to be gentle as he disengaged from the child's touch. "If I'm boring, that's because I'm worried. Take me back to your father, boy. I have news of grave importance he needs to hear."

Dubious and critical as any scout on reconnaissance, Jieret looked on as Arithon bent by the spring and swallowed water in sucking gulps. The prince looked sick—was in fact shaking and running with sweat that smelled of fear. But Jieret had not lost sight of the fact that he trespassed; by nature too canny to contradict, he accepted the conclusion that Halliron's wagered coin would end up in Elwedd's purse.

The water and the walk seemed to help. Arithon breathed more freely as movement and increased circulation eased the worst of his withdrawal. Through the hour's hike back to camp, he regained at least the semblance of his accustomed equilibrium.

Which was well, because the mother of a boy who has lit off into open forest with no word of explanation was bound not to wait with complaisance. Lady Dania intercepted her miscreants at the flap of Steiven's lodge. She had shed her daytime leathers for a tight-sleeved dress of lilac blue. Russet hair that Arithon had never seen unbraided trailed like undone crochet down her back. The effect of softened femininity hit him like a blow, and he stopped, struck briefly speechless.

But his momentary awkwardness escaped notice as Dania latched onto her errant son. "Jieret! What possessed you? It shames me to see a boy of twelve behaving with less care than a toddler!"

Recessed in the shadow beyond the entry, Arithon interrupted. "The boy was with me, and quite safe."

Lady Dania shot him a scorching glance.

Awed by the briskness with which she abandoned her scolding and ordered him off to bed, Jieret saw that, prince or not, Arithon was going to suffer all of his mother's thwarted temper. Wary of his fate should he linger, the boy beat an escape through the curtain that separated the nook he shared with his sisters.

Dania cracked back the tent flap, cross to her core from the license of intemperate royalty. She bent a severe gaze upon the culprit, who escaped her by standing stone still in the darkness. Reminded afresh that Arithon could be disquieting and difficult, and that Caolle had warned earlier he might have remedied his nerves since the oath taking with drink or some other indulgence, Dania too said nothing, but busied herself lighting candles.

While new flame fired the delicately embroidered patterns that bordered her bodice and hem line, and sparked a brighter warmth of color in her hair, she barbed her subtlety in a smile of sweetened welcome.

"Steiven will be back shortly," she offered. When Arithon's reticence remained, she dared him to try sheer bad manners. "Come in. Sit. Be comfortable while we wait for him."

Appreciative of her heroic effort not to nag, and piquantly aware she would rifle what deductions she could from his appearance, Arithon slipped through the door flap. Her mind matched his measure far too often to make him comfortable. He half smiled to see that her rearguard attack had defeated him; not a cushion in the lodge remained in dimness enough for concealment. He countered her candles by an absolute refusal to settle. While Dania ducked past the privacy flap to make sure of young Jieret and tuck him with canny firmness into bed, Arithon gave rein to restlessness and paced.

This lodge was not as fine as the one left in storage at the last camp. Bereft of tapestries, fine carpets, and permanent furnishings, the dwelling still displayed evidence of civilized inhabitance. One corner was flaked with wood chips and bark where Jieret had whittled toys for his sisters. An opened book rested on a woven reed mat, a half-spent candle close by. The text in the surfeit of lighting flashed as he stepped, with bright colors and gilt illumination. The wall behind had been painted over with an elaborate scene of a stag hunt. In the corner, cushioned on a pallet stuffed with evergreen, Halliron's lyranthe lay abandoned.

Silver strings strung reflections like beads, numerous and scintillant as the candle flames. Arithon set his teeth, but could not quite manage to turn aside. Topaz settings and small emeralds beckoned for his attention amid the carved and inlaid bands that laced from the scrolled base to the peg head with its rows of ebony tuners.

Before thought could stop him, he had seated himself. He extended a finger and tentatively, lightly brushed the strings.

The timbre that answered wrung his heart, so perfectly did it match the voice of the instrument left and lost in Etarra. The maker's rune stamped in pearl inlay on the back of the soundboard was not visible, but tone was all the signature Arithon required to identify Elshian's handiwork.

The temptation became too much.

Framed against a painted backdrop of deer hounds frozen in full cry, he lifted the lyranthe, set his hand to silver frets, and began very softly to play.

The burns where Lysaer's light bolt had seared his right palm and wrist had barely started to heal. Tripped up as the pull of the wound marred his timing, Arithon struck out a rough and moody line of notes. Lost to his irritation, half unmoored by light-headedness, he had space in him only for song. He flexed his stiff hand, cursed mildly as the scab cracked, and launched off in a run that seemed to banish hide walls and let in space like cloud-blown sky.

Notes trilled and spattered across quiet in a statement that through unsullied expression of beauty negated his uncertainty and pain.

Newly returned from Jieret's bedside, Lady Dania was arrested by the sound. Unwitting party to something not meant to be shared, she poised stock still with the fringed end of the privacy curtain forgotten between her clenched hands.

A soaring arpeggio introduced a change in key like an epiphany. Major chord to minor, the lyranthe rang through a boldly personal statement that flashed with a grace like edged swordplay. Stirred through the stuffy, airless heat trapped inside hide walls, Dania shivered in delight. This prince could bind spells with his playing. Entranced beyond fear of impropriety, she smiled her appreciation and advanced.

The privacy flap smacked shut like a slap, but her attempt at warning passed unnoticed. The notes built and blended and sprang separate while Arithon laid his cheek against the curve of resonating wood. His eyes were closed, his whole being intertwined with the notes that danced under his hands.

A slipped finger shattered the spell. There came a pause while his wrist lifted. Then his hands dipped again through a jarring, heavily plucked statement that skirted the edge of discord.

Arithon silenced the strings with an impatient caress, then turned his hand to find his cut split and a bead of blood welling through.

Dania discovered herself half dizzied from some reasonless urge to hold her breath. She moved another step just as the prince looked up.

The emotion in his eyes struck her with the force of a storm front alive with the beat of summer thunder.

She gave way and sat across from him. "I didn't intend to eavesdrop. But I have to admit you have a gift even Halliron must envy."

Mention of the Masterbard pricked Arithon to an irritable glance down. Had the instrument in his hands not awed him, he might have answered his first impulse and flung it away as though his skin hurt. "Lady, your praise is far too generous."

He did not blot the burst burn on his tunic. A tiny start unsettled her as she wondered if somehow he *knew:* the garment had been her deceased brother's. His eyes were on her again. He saw, and she realized too well, that her intuition set keen challenge against his intentions.

Dania absorbed the awkward moment by rearranging the skirt over her knees. Blue cloth settled a ring of twilight over a tawny landscape of flax hassocks, and her hands, like paired birds, nestled together in her lap. Arithon ducked quickly forward and hoped his fallen hair would shade his face. His breathing was harder to temper; Steiven's wife had a vivid, magnetic beauty beneath the wear of hard living and the fullness lent by childbearing. The fact she tracked his mind without effort evoked an intimacy that played havoc with drug-heightened senses and provoked him to shameless response.

Preternaturally conscious of her quick, timid glance toward his face, he turned his head.

"Something troubles you," she said. "Is that why you seek my husband?"

Her voice had that velvety timbre associated with wind through high grass. A fine-grained tremor shook him, and he shut his eyes fast as the dregs of the tienelle fanned a bursting flare of heat through his veins.

"Some things are best to let lie." He stamped down the flicker of vision too late. Prescience arose, full-bodied and ugly enough to choke him, of Lady Dania sprawled in black leaf mold, the leathers she wore for workaday ripped down to expose muddied thighs, and her throat slashed open by a sword stroke.

Dimly he realized she was speaking. "If it were up to me, I would drop every weapon in Etarra into the bogs of Anglefen, and hire you as bard of Deshir."

Arithon opened his eyes, flashed her a glance hot and molten as brass tailings stirred in a crucible. He said no word, but hooked back the lyranthe with an urgency concealed behind languidness.

Dania was not deceived. Neither could she deny the compulsion that drove him, rooted as it was in the gentleness that tonight for some reason he could not mask. The music he loosed with his hands held a spirit that gave easy surcease from talk.

He took the release she allowed him with gratitude that sang through E major, then plunged, in sliding falls, to tread deeper measures that rang lyrically placid and dark. He tempered his impatience in the mathematical progression of schooled notes. Pinched between physical discomfort and the horrific pageant of images inflicted at random upon his innermind, Arithon longed for Steiven to come, that he could finish this business and be alone. He wanted the forest, with the calls of whippoorwills and running water to smooth his abraded nerves. He needed delicate, exacting concentration to unbind the residual taint within his body. Yet the urgency of the final revelation which had shown him clan girls and wives lying slaughtered disbarred the solitude he required.

Arithon channeled himself into music as a substitute for thought until steps at the door flap spoiled his cadence.

"Must you deal behind my back?" Halliron's demand shattered the spell before the last note had quite faded.

Dania started and jerked her scented skirts aside to allow the bard space to take a seat. "How long have you been here?"

Arithon damped the dwindling ring of silver strings and proffered Elshian's lyranthe to her master.

Halliron took back his instrument, derisively abrupt. "I heard it all. The fragment preceding as well." Pale, hard eyes touched the prince in a look as inimical as a knife thrust. "I know the voice of my lyranthe better than that of my own child. She would call me, you should have known. Did you lack the guts not to speak to me beforehand?"

"I'm sorry." Arithon's hands balled up. He forgot his torn scab, and tension rimmed one fingernail brightly scarlet. "I was thoughtlessly selfish. Here's my promise not to meddle after this."

"Meddle!" Dania had never heard the bard's voice so charged with fury. "You arrogant, manipulative young fool! Don't insult my intelligence by playing your falsehoods on me. It's an Ath-given talent you've been hiding. I say it here, you've no right to see that strangled."

Arithon sat backward sharply, discomfort plain upon his face. The bard had managed to shock him as nobody else ever had, and his recovery lacked courtesy or grace. "That was not my intent." For once too upset to try pretense, he hitched his shoulders in dismissal. "Of course, I'm touched by your regard. But I saw no reason to inflict my inadequate fingering upon you." The sarcasm used in desperation bloomed now to drive back tearing anguish. "My sword, you'll recall, is now wedded to the cause of a kingdom."

Halliron shrugged off the protestation. "The mechanics of your playing can be improved upon, definitely." He cradled the lyranthe against his shoulder, set fingers to strings, and repeated several bars of Arithon's work. Beneath his skill, melody emerged refocused into a rendition to make the heart leap for pure pain.

The effect left Dania with her fingers pressed to her lips, and the prince of Rathain dead white.

Halliron damped the strings with a slap the exquisite soundboard magnified like a shout. "With work you shall surpass me. Study, apply yourself to life training, and no one alive could match your style." The Masterbard pressed his instrument back into Arithon's lap.

"If, if, if!" Arithon spurned the invitation in a recoil that dragged air in a whine across strings as he thrust the instrument aside. "Where is Steiven?"

"Stop evading." Incensed, Halliron held to his subject. "I've searched all my life and never heard the equal of your natural ability."

Arithon whipped taut with a speed that belied the indolence he had perpetrated since his arrival. The weave of moving shadows as he thrust to his feet plunged the painted stag into darkness, leaving hounds with bared muzzles exposed to the merciless candlelight. To Dania he said crisply, "If Caolle is available, I'll speak to him instead."

Dismayed, the lady instinctively forestalled him. "You haven't eaten, Your Grace. Let me bring wine and fresh bread."

Arithon abruptly shook his head.

He was a man who never used gestures when a verbal backlash would serve better. Alarmed, Dania surveyed his face. "You're unwell."

"Which is not your concern, dear lady." Arithon caught her hands and kissed her knuckles, inspired to ruthless certainty that his clammy sweat and fine trembling would set her off balance enough to quiet her. "Caolle or your husband, it doesn't matter which. But I must speak with one of them immediately."

Silence followed his demand, a rugged war of wills that Halliron finally broke because he disliked risking Deshir's lady to the edged temper the s'Ffalenn heir was wont to vent when his depths of vulnerability became encroached upon. "Steiven and Caolle are closeted in the tent that serves as armory. They're taking inventory and probably won't mind the interruption."

Arithon gave the bard a smile of astonishing gratitude. Then he kissed the lady's hands again. "My respect, and my thanks for your hospitality." Need before gentleness commanded him as he released his touch and departed.

The lodge flap sighed closed on his heels, and infused the close tent with the night scent of dew-soaked evergreen. Lady Dania stared blindly across an emptiness left brilliant with candles, her arms hugged forlornly across her chest. "He tries hard to make us think he takes us lightly."

Wordless in sympathy, Halliron caught her shoulders. He turned her, sat her down, and fetched her wine. This once in his life unwilling to seek music to quiet an uneasy mind, he poured a second goblet for himself. "It's fate that's his enemy, not ourselves." He drank deeply, to dull a grief he could not bear, that his search for a successor had found its match in a man who had no use at all for an apprenticeship.

Underlit by the glow of a single candle, the war captain of Deshir's clans crouched, counting unfletched arrows in their bins while Steiven marked numbers on a talley. Caolle was first to look up at the disturbance when the tent flap stirred and admitted a drift of night air. A smile broke through his weathered scowl. "Well, well. Look who's come."

Arithon stepped through the entry. Burdened with a rolled set of parchments, and in no mood to be subtle under needling, he had done nothing to ease his withdrawal symptoms beyond a pause to drink at the river. The water had not settled well. By that, he knew he had very little time to make his point before weakness forced him to retire. Driven to fast movement to conceal a resurgence of cramps, he chose a table arrayed with swords set aside for the armorer's attention in the morning. These he swept aside with a belling clangor that made Steiven jump to his feet.

"Your Grace?" The clan chieftain left his captain, the tally slate abandoned in his haste.

Caolle tossed aside an arrow, lifted the candle, and followed. His distaste intensified as Arithon shed a cascade of scrolled documents and whipped them flat across the tabletop.

The parchments so callously handled were the tactical maps that culminated painstaking labor and days of vociferous debate.

Annoyed enough that his gorge rose, Caolle's steps became deliberate. "If you're finished with moping for the day, perhaps you'd care to tell us the name of the man presently in command of Etarra's reserve corps of archers?"

Braced against the table to steady a nasty rush of dizziness, Arithon tried to answer. His throat was already bone dry. The drink at the river had not been sufficient to satisfy the demands of withdrawal. Warned that his neglect had now set him on dangerous ground, that the effects of herb poisons would have him unconscious if he pushed without care, he looked but saw no place to sit down.

"Or have the sulks clouded your memory," Caolle goaded. "You need not trouble. Our plans have already been set."

Arithon returned an impatient lift of his head. "The commander's name is Hadig. And you're going to have to change tactics."

Caolle gave a gruff, low laugh and at once confronted his clan chief. "This womanish daydreamer suggests that our councils have been wasted. Do we leave our arrows uncounted just to let him show us better?"

Arithon neither acknowledged the insult nor allowed Steiven's puzzled regard any interval to unravel his personal state. He reached with a hand forced to steadiness and swept across an inked arc of symbols that his fickle mind twisted into bodies, bent and broken and bathed in congealed blood. "Here," he half gasped. "And here. I'll suffer no man's mother or child in the path of Etarra's armies."

Lip curled in contempt, Caolle said, "You think us gutless as townsmen."

"I took an oath!" Arithon locked eyes with him. "I speak out of concern."

Caolle set down the candle and leaned on bunched hands across the charts. "You'd make a prime town governor."

"You'll listen," Arithon returned, a jab of command in his tone. "Would you ruin your people for sheer pride? My objection has no grounds in sentiment."

"Sentiment? Fiends, are you blind?" Caolle's scarred fists crashed onto the tabletop, jarring sword blades in ringing counterpoint while the candle guttered and spattered hot wax across the maps. "There are nine hundred sixty of us of age to wield weapons. That includes every man of the northeast forest clans who will not, cannot, even with Ath's help, get here in time to make a difference. Ten to one odds, had you counted. Dharkaron Avenger couldn't balance such stakes. And you've the puking gall to fly in my face with objections?"

"Caolle! Recall you address your sovereign lord." Steiven reappeared out of shadow with camp stools salvaged from a field kit. He distributed the seats around the table and said as sharply, "Your Grace, if you wish changes, speak your reason. Argument serves no purpose here."

The clan lord sat down then, and in iron-clad example directed his attention to the maps. If a night of communion with nature had jolted Arithon out of apathy, he would never ridicule the change. This prince's hand had helped to banish Desh-thiere; if the powers used then could help now, he must be encouraged to offer them. Yet, confronted by Arithon's unsteady bearing as he pulled up the stool and sank onto it, Steiven wondered silently if Caolle's supposition had been right, and his liege had retired from the oath taking to get himself royally drunk.

Arithon rested his chin on folded fingers. "I've had warning," he opened without preamble. "The lives of every clan woman and child will be lost if they are sent out to stand against Lysaer. Butchery best describes the method. I could sound no alternative sequence."

Caolle for a mercy stayed silent, while Steiven adjusted to this implied application of mage-schooled prescience with a care he might have used when taking aim on a half-startled buck. "Can you be more specific?"

"Unfortunately not." Arithon resumed a tone beaten level by an unpleasant ringing in his ears. "Your son disrupted my scrying. Small talk of his sisters provoked a precognition. His presence masked further development. I suggest, and not lightly, that you take full heed and arrange safeguards."

Steiven regarded his prince and desperately suppressed the thought that rose inside him like a scream: that his own life already had been pledged. It seemed most cruelly unjust that loyalty to this Teir's'Ffalenn might claim his wife and five young ones as well. He said only, "You wish me to remove the women and younger children from the lines?"

"At the very least." Arithon sounded strained.

"Suicide," Caolle interrupted. He stuck broad thumbs in his belt and licked his teeth. "We cannot act in fear of who will die. If we hold back any one resource, where do we stop? We'll have no need at all for fussy strategy if our lines get overrun and all of our fighting strength falls jack dead on the field!"

"There are alternatives," Arithon interjected. At his word, the candle flicked out, though no hand had moved to pinch the flame.

When Caolle leaned out to test the wick, Steiven stopped him on instinct. "Don't. Snuffed candles usually smoke. I smell none, which must mean the light is still burning."

"The sun can be blackened as easily," Arithon's voice resumed out of dark. "Mine is full command of shadow. Though I am loath to kill by trickery, the night can be a formidable weapon."

He released the captive candle as abruptly, and in a steady, undisturbed spill, flamelight glinted in multiple reflection on the helms and scale brigandines of a dozen men at arms, conjured from nowhere and arrayed behind the prince's chair.

Caolle broke his chief's hold. He surged erect. His hands in frenzied urgency sorted through the weapons that weighted the map ends for just one blade with a serviceable edge.

Until Arithon's grating laughter stopped him cold. "Illusion only," the prince admonished. His magery disbursed into thin air, with Caolle left blinking and foolish, his fists interlocked behind the cross guard of an ill-balanced antique broadsword.

The prince said with stinging coolness, "I'm hardly the green boy you imagined. By the grace of my grandfather's upbringing, I hold the sole alternative. Listen and live. Or I'll step back, reject my oath, your feal defense, and every last trace of your memory."

As if taunting the temper that, in one move, could finish a swing up to gut him, the Shadow Master held the clan captain's gaze in tight-lipped, bristling antagonism. Until, suspicious that the prince might not be drunk but rather driving for the opening to provoke, Steiven intervened. "Caolle, put down that blade. Whether or not you've been mocked, I can tolerate no violence against a guest who's sworn at my hearth."

Caolle settled, hunched as a mastiff forced to give ground. He watched with hot eyes as Arithon applied a stick of charcoal to the map and reformed the deployment of Deshir's forces. As the fine, unsteady hands revitalized the plans with new strategy, the irascible veteran became forced to revise his impression of the s'Ffalenn heir. The prince was impressively clever, if weak. His hands trembled, and the green eyes burned beneath slack lids, as though driven to fever by high-strung nerves. Battle experience might toughen him enough to make him a passable sovereign, Caolle thought, but he kept his opinion to himself.

Near the end, they suffered interruption. Framed suddenly against the torchless blackness of the doorway, a scout in weapons and leathers made a hasty entrance. "Your Grace. Lord, Caolle. The lady Dania requires the presence of her husband. Young Jieret has had another nightmare, and is out of his senses with grief."

"Forgive me," Steiven blurted, on his feet and gone in a bound that riffled stacked maps in his wake.

Relieved to be quit of his message, the scout came fully inside and settled on the stool his chief had vacated. He gave Caolle an apologetic shrug. "Ath ease his suffering, poor young one." For Arithon's benefit he explained, "Jieret has Sight, as his father does."

"Jieret has natural prescience?" Hunched over crossed arms on the tabletop, Arithon snapped straight in wild-eyed, sweating attention. "Ath's mercy, why did nobody think to tell me?"

Cynical before this unlooked-for burst of concern, Caolle drummed his knuckles on his sword belt and watched, while the scout, less dour, let out a sigh. "No kind gift for a boy, to be sure. Whatever he's dreamed broke his heart."

"I'll tell you what he saw." Arithon shot a vicious glance toward Caolle. "The slaughter of every living relative. If I'd known that child had Sight, I'd never have allowed him to stay near me. I was still half tranced from a tienelle scrying, and my defenses at the time were wide open. If he's gifted, he'll have picked up the sequence from me. Mine's the blame if he's taken any harm."

Magecraft and jargon left no impression upon Caolle, who disdained outbursts of any sort. He pulled his skinning knife from his boot sheath, and in the extreme and failing candlelight expertly shaved off a hangnail. "You worry for nothing," he said to Arithon. "Deshir's young are hardly fragile. Any such weakness in clan bloodlines, town headhunters have long since stamped out."

The reassurance appeared to settle Arithon's mind, for by the time the captain looked up to sheath his blade, the prince had apparently fallen asleep. His black hair feathered a pillowing wrist, with the other hand outflung across the map, as if he had started to surge to his feet, then surrendered the inclination.

If arcane scrying had exhausted the prince to the same degree as his recent flight from Etarra, the man was a fool who tried to roust him. The scout said as much, his long face gloomy in disgust.

For his part, Caolle gave grudging credit for Arithon's contribution to the defense strategy; he did not curse his liege lord's failing out loud, but in tones of mulish reserve, requested help to shift Arithon back to Steiven's lodge tent.

"That's twice in a week our chief's left us to haul deadweight like deer dressers," the scout grumbled. The candle fluttered at his movement as he kicked back Steiven's stool, leaned over, and hooked his forearms under Arithon's shoulders. "Phew. What's he got on his clothes? Smells like burnt spice or something."

Caolle shrugged. The finicky habits of mages being outside his province to fathom, he hefted the royal legs without comment.

As both men maneuvered their prince around the chart-strewn table, the scout gave a breathless, short laugh. "Well, he's small enough, Ath be thanked. Easy to sling as a puppy. If I have to strain a sword hand for my liege, I'm glad to know I'll do it killing townsmen."

"Ye'll do it standing extra turns at duty!" Caolle snapped, moved at last to vent the spleen he had too long bent aside to please his chieftain. "Get back to your post where you belong, and leave yon princeling's nursing to me." The mettlesome captain of the Deshans shouldered the unconscious prince like a game carcass and huffed on alone to Steiven's lodge tent.

Dania's extravagant expenditure of candles by this hour had burned low; those few wicks that still struggled alight fed on drafts, half drowned in puddled wax. Other candles snuffed to conserve resources stood tall white in a gloomy play of shadows. As conscious of their cost as of the life in the burden he carried, Caolle took care not to knock against them as he bore Arithon toward the cushions in the corner where Halliron's lyranthe lay propped, unshrouded still, if not forgotten.

Caolle shucked his load, tugged straight a twist in his tunic, and considered his duty to his sovereign completed. He raised a forearm to blot his brow, caught a whiff of his leather bracers, and nearly spat. The exotic reek from whatever rite of magery the prince had trifled with had transferred itself to his person. Moved to seek fresher air outside, Caolle spun to depart but checked halfway to the door flap as Steiven re-emerged from the alcove set aside for his children.

To forestall answering for the prince, Caolle asked, "Is Jieret settled?"

Steiven sighed, strolled crunching through scrolls of dry birch bark, and uncorked the wine flagon his wife had left out for the Masterbard. "He's coherent. Halliron's telling him a story. If we're lucky, he'll choose something boring that will ease the boy back to sleep."

"The nightmare was truesight, then?" Ruled by habit, Caolle braced broad shoulders against the king post and regarded the master he had first raised and now served without question. Neither man could have named the day when duty had deepened to respect; the nuance of who was master had never mattered between them. "Did Jieret say what he dreamed?"

Caught in mid-swallow, Steiven parked the flagon on his forearm. He shook his head. "Dania says he told nothing beyond the name of Fethgurn's daughter. Though what Teynie has to do with an ugly precognition, Daelion Fatemaster knows. My boy cannot tell us. Whatever Jieret dreamed, it's too much for him to bear. His mind has closed to recall, as mine did once." And he stopped, knowing Caolle would remember; it had been the captain's gruff hands that had soothed him the night before his father found his death.

A shiver swept over Steiven. His regard upon his captain lay heavy with understanding that, too soon, Etarra's troops would invade these valleys.

Wordless, Caolle extended his hand for the flagon. Steiven watched while his first captain drank, his eyes as deep with worry as his oldest confidant had ever seen them. "We must withdraw the girls and women as Arithon wishes. Seer or not, his objections and Jieret's nightmare are too close to be a coincidence."

"The boys over ten years of age will have to disarm the fallen then," Caolle insisted, his eyes beneath the crag of his brow line deepened to pits as the candle by his elbow fluttered out. "Those few absolutely can't be spared."

Steiven nodded, took back the wine, and paused with the neck of the flagon half raised. As if he expected a rejoinder, he glanced around and across the darkened tent. "Where's the prince?"

Caolle jerked his chin past his shoulder. "There. Fell asleep on the tactical maps, so I brought him." Deshir's war captain folded thick arms in expectation of Dania's scolding as she and Halliron emerged from soothing Jieret into bed.

"Ah, well." Steiven sighed, aware how little reprimand would accomplish with his war captain planted like a bull. Finally, softly, he set the flask aside. "Our Teir's'Ffalenn's entitled to his comforts, I would guess, if he spent last night smacking midges in the open."

A rustle of skirts and more flickering from spent candles, and Lady Dania reached her husband's side. "Arithon ought to sleep," she said tartly. "When he left here, he was unwell."

Caolle smiled. While the Masterbard crossed the lodge to fetch his instrument, the captain stole the moment to bait her by hooking back the flagon. "A man can be unwell and not be the least bit sick." He drank, his eyes on hers.

Dania gave no ground. The captain's blistering insolence she suspected held a hint of jealousy; at least, Caolle had never subjected her to teasing before the day she had wed. Her lord shied well clear, since better than anybody else, his lady could keep the war captain in his place.

Dania's mouth tautened in conclusion that Caolle's antagonism toward Arithon was the same: that he would treat even a dog with contempt if it dared to claim Steiven's affection. As though the grizzled captain were an overbearing brother, she reached out and slapped the flagon from his mouth. "Now what would his grace be drunk on, stream water?"

Caolle choked to kill an untimely burst of laughter. "He has a weak head, our royal heir, or maybe just a weak stomach?"

The discussion just then was cut short as Halliron cried out from the corner. "Ath Creator, *how long has he been like this?*"

Steiven spun around on reflex; Caolle, with considering deliberation. Half lost in the maze of deepened shadows, the Masterbard bent over Arithon, one hand clasped over the royal wrist and feeling in concern for a pulse.

"Sithaer's fires, man." Caolle rubbed his eyes, which were stinging tired from too much stress. "You act as if he's dying. He only dropped off to sleep."

"He could be dying," Halliron said, his performer's voice bladed to satire. "Did none of you notice the smell on him?"

"Is something wrong?" Steiven released the hand that cupped his wife's waist as Dania moved to light candles.

Halliron made a sound of exasperation. When Caolle looked brazenly blank and Steiven's expression failed to clear, the Masterbard raised Arithon's other wrist and hauled him into a half-reclining posture that needed several pillows to support. As his fingers untied the prince's shirt cuffs, he said, "Have you ever read anything on herb lore? In particular on the leaves of the mountain flower called tienelle?"

"Seersweed?" Shocked to quick action, Steiven yanked the flagon from Caolle's grasp and crossed the tent. "Ath preserve us. Not the narcotic used by mages . . ." He knelt, touched the prince's clammy flesh, and bits of remembered trivia fell together with an alarming, unpleasant feel of truth. The prince had spoken of scrying. If tienelle had been part of his method, it would indeed induce visions, followed by illness from toxins that had no listed antidote. Enraged at the prince's reticence and then by his own slow perception, Steiven ripped out a word he had never used under his own roof pole, or in the presence of his wife.

"He told us he was trained!" Caolle protested.

"And so he must be. I much doubt he would leave us by suicide." Steiven withheld his sympathy, while Caolle started to pace.

Halliron continued his ministrations, aggrieved to a depth that none but Lady Dania understood. Her hands trembled on the striker as for the second time that night she lit wick after wick in succession. The Masterbard resumed condemnation. "How long did you delay him, badgering and questioning his manhood?"

"Never mind that," cut in Steiven. "Just tell us what's to be done."

The Masterbard's smile was white-lipped and merciless, and directed to stop Caolle between strides. "Wake him up and ask," he invited. "I'm no mage at all. My tunes and your prowess at war in this case are no foil for fatal poison."

"Well, His Grace volunteered for the sacrifice," Caolle snapped. "Don't make me slap him back to consciousness. I'd be too much tempted to break his neck."

Nobody answered that outburst. Dania stood with the striker wrung between her fingers. Halliron steadied the prince's head, while Steiven raised the flask and began forcing wine down the flaccid royal throat.

Arithon roused, bent in half by a cough that immediately progressed to nausea. Between spasms, he gasped for water. A basin was proffered. He drank and was sick. He drank again, his hands locked one on another in a torment that left Dania silently, desperately weeping.

This time the liquid stayed down. When the Master of Shadows raised green eyes rinsed blank by the force of will he needed to command his reflexes, no one present could escape recognition of the mettle he had masked behind laziness.

Arithon knew as much. Even through pain, his manner suggested the chagrin of a joke undone as his gaze locked level with Caolle's.

Caught on his knees by the sick bed, the captain of Deshir's defense said no word, but gripped the basin as if blunt metal might sprout legs and kick him in the stomach.

The deep s'Ffalenn eyes never flickered, but the mouth twitched in a pinched-off, flippant smile. "I'll try you at foils on the morrow," Arithon challenged, prepared to take bruises for his falsehood.

Grudgingly forced to revise his assessment of the s'Ffalenn prince yet again, Caolle snarled, "Save your steel for the heart blood of Etarra's city guard."

Work on the defenses continued without relenting as Arithon rested from his debilitating bout with the tienelle. He did not rise to cross foils with the clan captain, but on Steiven's enforced orders kept to his bed. He heard in thin-lipped silence the ultimatum, that the participation of boys in the battle was a matter beyond his royal right to question.

If his initial reaction was too quiet, his response came typically obstinate. He waited until Dania's back was turned, called young Jieret to his bedside, and with the blade of a boy's knife for carving, nicked his left wrist. There and then he swore a blood pact of friendship with his *caithdein*'s only son.

Confronted minutes later by the father's anger, Arithon gazed up from his pillows, peaceful with grieved affection. "That is the best I can do for you, whom I love as my brother. I can see your heir survives this war to continue your line and title."

Struck speechless by emotion, Steiven whirled and left the prince's presence. With his own death already a sealed fate, the Earl of the North could have asked no better parting from this life, save the chance to better know the spirit of the man who had graced him.

"Ath lighten your burden, my prince," he murmured. And he stumbled on blindly across the lodge tent into the arms of his wife.

Dania exclaimed in dismay at his kiss. She tasted salt tears on Steiven's lips. Drowned in silent, close embrace, she pulled half loose and caught his hand, and guided him to slip the laces on her bodice.

Steiven accepted her invitation. In the sun-warmed air of their sleeping nook, he allowed her quiet touch and hot flesh to absorb his bitter brew of sorrow. But the pleasure of release was saddened by the knowledge that this moment was to be among the last.

Incarceration

Dakar the Mad Prophet stopped cold in his tracks, wiped his streaming forehead, and glared askance down a sheer rock drop toward a valley spread like quilting between a dizzying array of black peaks. Fresh
sweat rolled off his temples. Left faint and sick from the effects of exertion and extreme altitude, he complained to a point of empty air.
"You call this a trail? I say it's a death trap. And I hope you have defense wards set. If a fiend chances by and possesses a loose stone, it's
sure to make mischief and trip me."

Made the more mutinous as his outburst drew no response, Dakar
plucked at the straps of his knapsack, which bulged from his back
like the shell of some malformed turtle. "And anyway, I'd think you
Sorcerers wouldn't chance my taking a fall, not lugging *this*, anyway.
And I don't see why I was appointed to act as the Fellowship's pack
mule in the first place!"

A breeze flicked through a fan of alpine flowers adjacent to
Dakar's feet, perhaps provoked by Kharadmon's invisible presence.

"Oh, come on!" Dakar griped. "A miser in a poorhouse has more
to say than you! Why not admit you know why Asandir has stuck me
with packing his Ath-forsaken Mistwraith to the summit of Rockfell
Peak."

"You need the exercise?" Kharadmon quipped. A daisy fell out of
nowhere and brushed past Dakar's left ear.

The flower might as well have been a fly the way the Mad Prophet swiped it away. He scraped forward, his shoulder pressed to the mountain, until the narrow ribbon of trail reached a switchback half blocked by boulders. There he seized the opportunity to plump himself down. The perch he chose was moss-grown. Seepage from a glacial spring made him grimace and huff like a walrus, yet laziness triumphed. A soaked rump notwithstanding, he bent at the waist and shucked off the knapsack. Inside, girdled in tingling spells of guard, lay the flask that bottled Desh-thiere. "I should heave this off the nearest precipice, and see you all juggle spells to catch it back," the Mad Prophet suggested nastily.

"Try," Kharadmon invited.

Dakar's glower deepened. "A damned iyat has more sense of fun than you."

"I should hope so." Below their vantage, the slowly falling speck that was the daisy winked out. A second later, Kharadmon's image unfurled, extravagantly poised in midair. "Else I'd throw you off the cliff, and see how far and long you'd bounce."

"Do that." Dakar sighed. "Break my back. I'd like to lie down and rest for six months or maybe a year."

A stickler for exhibition, Kharadmon stroked the spade black beard that thrust from his chin. Piebald hair streamed on the winds that whipped off the snow fields higher up, and his green eyes glinted, shrewd. "You're thinking your master has misused you?"

"Not me," Dakar snapped. "I said so before, Prince Lysaer." Cautious not to try Kharadmon's impatience, he heaved to his feet, and with a martyred roll of his eyes, resettled his pack on sore shoulders. "Sithaer take your Fellowship's grand plans, you used a good man and then broke him."

"Ah." Kharadmon flicked away into nothing. A cold draft at odds with nature, he flowed upslope against the wind.

Dakar resumed inching up a track better suited for small goats. "You don't agree," he said sourly.

The discorporate mage surprised with an answer. "You've seen Asandir take deer for the supper pot."

"He never hunts anything I ever saw." The Mad Prophet bent, clawed out a pebble that had worked its way into his boot top, then sidestepped through a hairpin bend, his buttocks pressed to sheer rock while his beer gut jutted over sky. "Asandir just goes out and sits in a thicket somewhere. Eventually a buck happens along, lies down, and dies for him."

"He projects his need and asks," Kharadmon corrected, a tart sting to his tone. "The deer chooses freely, and its fate and man's hunger end in balance."

"You're not saying Lysaer *volunteered*," Dakar protested.

The trail doubled back, its frost-split stone scoured lifeless except for mustard and black flecks of lichen. From ahead, Kharadmon sent back, "No. Your prince answered circumstance according to his innate character. The Fellowship imposed nothing outside his natural will and intentions."

Dakar viewed the next span with trepidation, and ended scrabbling forward on hands and knees. Gravel loosened by his passage slid and bounced, and rocketed finally into the abyss that was Rockfell Vale. Between stertorous panting he gasped, "You can't claim . . . Desh-thiere's wraith . . . submits to any Law of the Major Balance."

"Where opening did not already exist, the creature could not have gained foothold," said Kharadmon.

Squatted now on his hams and blowing harder, Dakar squirmed to shift the bite of the pack straps. Already blistered on his heels, his temper had abraded to match. "But Sethvir as much as admitted the s'Ilessid inborn gift was at fault. Had Lysaer not been driven to seek perfect justice, the wraith would have found nothing to exploit."

Frostily unmoved, Kharadmon said, "If so, our Fellowship has a reckoning to answer for."

Dakar took a second to recognize capitulation. "Well, then," he cried, and closed for the kill, "why in Ath's name did you surrender Lysaer knowing he'd have no defense?"

The flicks and slaps of breeze that expressed Kharadmon's displeasure died into ominous stillness. Even the winds off the ridges dared not cross the imposed circle of his silence. "Because," his reply cracked back at length, "Ath Creator himself did not insist that his works spring perfectly formed from the void. We are permitted our mistakes, for which, my fat prophet, you should kiss the earth daily and be grateful."

Dakar refused to be humbled. Hunkered like a bear on damp haunches, he prepared to argue further. But a second voice admonished from below: "Best give less thought to Lysaer's business and more to your own, which is jeopardized. The outcrop where you've chosen to pontificate is not terribly well anchored to the scarp."

The Mad Prophet ejected a filthy word. Sweating over more than bad footing, he scooted forward and cautiously peered downward.

Soundless, graceful, in a stroll that disallowed fourteen thousand feet of vertical drop, Asandir ascended the switchback just below. Gray hair, gray cloak, with both wrists adorned by talisman bracelets runed in white metal, he was silver from head to foot.

"Where did you disappear to this morning?" Dakar shot back. "I cooked some breakfast and found you gone, and never a word of instruction as to what you wished me to do."

Asandir stopped. His brows lifted. The mouth underneath never moved. He looked at Dakar and said acidly, "That's no reason to threaten to pitch Desh-thiere off any handy vertical precipice."

"Ah, fiends," moaned Dakar. "A man can't say one word without you hearing it." He resignedly hugged the cliff face and hauled himself back upright.

"Sethvir heard you, too." By then Asandir had hooked the loops of the knapsack. As the Mad Prophet obligingly shucked straps, the Sorcerer reappropriated custody of Desh-thiere's flask.

Lightened enough to try boldness, Dakar stole a glance slant-wise at his master. "What were you doing, anyway?"

Asandir attended the pack straps, in need of commodious readjustment to fit his slimmer anatomy. "What did you use here, spider's knots?" He abandoned the tangle and more efficiently called a spell to clear the ties.

"I'm no sailor, to be handy with strings or a sewing awl." It served any sorcerer properly, Dakar thought, to have left him in charge of such matters. He watched, envious, as the rawhide slithered free of itself with a sinuous ease of living snakes. "How did you do that?"

Silver-gray eyes now flicked up, keenly bright in their scrutiny. "Which question did you actually want answered?"

Hopeful, Dakar said, "Both."

But Asandir's mood since Etarra had not been the least bit forgiving. "When a peak such as this has served through two ages as a prison, prudence would dictate a check to be sure the rock is still willing to absorb the antagonism of the entity we wish to confine."

"And how does one bribe old stone into becoming a sewer for human refuse?" Dakar smirked in thick sarcasm.

Asandir looked back at him, serious. "Rocks outlast all our doings. Longevity gives them great respect for politeness, a tendency you would benefit from copying."

"You can have your stones and your trees, and your communion with both for permissions," Dakar retorted. "I'll save my appreciation for a paid woman, if we don't break our necks on this peak."

A warning shift in Asandir's regard prompted Dakar to spin around and resume clambering up the trail. As stones gouged his knees, he avowed under his breath that henceforth he would restrict his inquiries to spells that could untie string. Then the next time he attracted a pack of mischief-bent iyats, he need not cut his laces to pry his boots off.

The ledge faded out at the snow line. Confronted by a rock face cracked into vertical ladders and packed under scabs of blue ice, Dakar swallowed. "We're not going up that."

Nobody answered. He blinked, rubbing sweat from his eyes. "Well, I'm not going up that."

"You could spend the night here," Asandir agreed. "You might even be comfortable, before the storm."

"What storm?" Dakar studied the sky, which deepened now toward clear aquamarine. Sunset was nigh, but the air smelled of glacier, not snow. "There aren't any clouds! I could spit and hit the moon."

Asandir kept climbing. The Mad Prophet fidgeted from foot to foot while arcanely frigid air eddied upward as Kharadmon also passed him by.

Dakar scrubbed his face on his tunic sleeve, then reviewed his position. The pitch they had already climbed was frightful, Rockfell's southeastern exposure a needle to split the wind. The nethermost spine of the Skyshiels nipped the horizon all around, while below, hulking as somnolent dragons, two ridges hoarded the valley between. Farthest down, dark tarnish in a gloom of cut-off sunlight, river Avast's ice-fed streamlets wound through forested ravines napped and ledged like rumpled velvet.

Just looking made Dakar's head spin. He could wait, but if he nodded off to sleep for one second, he would tumble off the cranny that marked the trail head. Above, sharp rocks as bleak as nightmare swooped up, lost in clouds gilt-hemmed by failing daylight. Asandir had already disappeared.

Beaten at last to resignation, Dakar stuffed his fat hands in a cleft and inched upward toward fog that was powdered with whirling snow. He inhaled the flakes repeatedly as he climbed. Eyes squeezed shut, he spoke through teeth clamped against a sneeze, and hoped to Sithaer that Asandir would take pity on him. "How much farther?" His muscles felt wrapped in hot wire.

Kharadmon's chuckle answered. "Not far at all. Unless you prefer to keep scrabbling along by your fingernails?"

Suspicious of some prank, Dakar risked a look.

Then he, too, laughed aloud. Not half a pace to his left, some capricious carver had fitted a staircase into the rock face. Elegant to the point of absurdity, the risers were black marble adorned at edge and corner with leering, haughty gargoyles. An extravagance of scrolled newel posts had once supported railings, until weather had scoured the brass away. Now only fastening holes remained.

"Damn me," exclaimed Dakar. "What fool engineered that?"

"Davien." As if bemused by the quirks of his mountebank colleague, Kharadmon qualified. "Fifteen centuries back, when he fashioned the pit into Rockfell, Davien insisted the stone of the mountain might decide one day to shrug him off. He was right to assume that anyone who braves the ascent this far does a mage's business here anyway."

Crabbing sideways across the face, Dakar was ill inclined to argue with the Betrayer's skewed sense of logic. He caught a post, swung onto the stair, then bit back his relief as the inimical gazes of gargoyles seemed hungrily to follow his progress. He tested the risers in suspicion. Everything else Davien had built was untrustworthy and clever with traps; if this stairway was either harmless or safe, it should be the glaring exception. Almost, Dakar wished he was clinging like a bug to wild rock.

Dewed with clammy fog, the Mad Prophet broke through the cloud layer. Ahead, the last sunshine glared off Rockfell's knife-point summit. Suspended between that pinnacle which supported heaven and a netherworld floored in combed cotton and shaded rose and purple by the encroaching twilight, Dakar sucked in a nervous breath. Dire cold froze the hair in his nose. He coughed, which caused Asandir to beckon impatiently from the ledge where Davien's stairway ended.

The pack by then rested at Asandir's feet, a lump of weatherstained canvas that Dakar gave a wide berth upon his arrival. The thing might appear as innocuous as somebody's bundled picnic, but even an apprentice's awareness could sense the hedging sting of guard wards from two paces away.

Asandir poised before a vertical slab of black rock, his ear pressed to its mirror-smooth polish and his palms rested flat on either side. He seemed prepared to spend motionless hours that way, while his apprentice shivered, abandoned to boredom.

A whining snap split the air.

"Kharadmon," Asandir commanded, and suddenly, sharply, stepped back.

Dakar smelled ozone, then all but fell over as a bolt stark as lightning seared across the blank stone. A mapwork of convoluted spellcraft flared across the face, chiseled with charged lines of runes. Lit blue by a chained might that dazzled and dwarfed him, Asandir stood unmoved, while from below, the fog moiled up in disturbed billows to hedge Rockfell around with anvil formations like thunderheads.

Though only nature responded in reaction to the proximity of energized coils of power, the likeness to the moving mists of Deshthiere left Dakar hollow with dread. The sun had dipped low. What sky remained visible glowed aquamarine, the moon a burning disk as fey in its light as the dagger-edged fire of raw spells. But these rang in high, subliminal vibration, haloed by silver-blue veilings of disturbed fog. Then, abruptly as the power had been raised, it flickered, flared violet, and faded.

Where rock had been lay a door.

Dakar gaped. "How did you do that?"

Asandir muttered words about physical rearrangement and briskly hooked up his pack. A second later he vanished into the square black vault that formed the unsealed entrance to Rockfell.

Flash-blind and blinking, Dakar advanced more cautiously. Swallowed at once by the dark, he felt oppressed to the point of suffocation. But the air came and went from his lungs, unrestricted. The innards of the mountain were dry, and bone cold, and smelled like metal filings and dust. The doorway at his back seemed a cube rinsed with light, as dangerously transient as a tienelle vision. "You didn't happen to bring candles?" Dakar asked wistfully.

Out of pity, Kharadmon made a light. His glow punched through gloom to reveal a bare chamber carved on floor and walls in complex patterns and runes of guard. At the center rested a slab, set askew to reveal a pit that contained a bottomless well of blind dark. The cobwebbed rungs of a ladder poked through, its origin swallowed in shadow.

Asandir hefted the sack with the flask and started down. Before he had gone three steps, dry wood gave way beneath his boot. Slivers whispered falling through air, and long seconds elapsed before their impact echoed back, proving the shaft had a bottom.

The well was dreadfully deep.

Unfazed at being poised on rotten footing over what amounted to an abyss, the Sorcerer said, "Kharadmon? You'll need to strengthen the ladder or Dakar will surely break his neck."

"I'm not going down there!" The Mad Prophet folded his arms across his chest and obstinately planted his toes.

"If you don't, you're quite likely to freeze." Pragmatic, Asandir waited while the rungs under his hands flared red under Kharadmon's binding. He moved on, his hair stirred by air currents that funneled down into the pit.

Dakar steeled himself and swung onto the ladder that dropped away into the unknown. His hands left sweat marks on wood still warmed from enchantment. He forced himself to start down, while Kharadmon's light traveled with him until he moved encircled by stone walls. The descent seemed to go on forever. His calves quivered as overstressed muscles bore his weight. The Mad Prophet could not shake the impression that the well had been cut deeper than the roots of Rockfell Mountain itself.

The jar as his foot struck bottom about startled him out of his skin. He looked about. The shaft ended in a five-sided cell, scrawled with entangled sigils and spiraling lattices of power that made the eyes burn and the head swim in vicious, twisty dizziness.

"Don't stare," Asandir cautioned. "The patterns here both dazzle and bind. You could lose your mind in this maze of wards to the point where even I can't call you back."

Such were the safeguards upon the chamber that the Sorcerer's warning fell dead against the air. Even the echoes were trapped. Dakar ripped his gaze away, then knuckled his eyes until they teared. "What was the last thing confined here?"

Kharadmon snorted in contempt. "You might better ask what last escaped. Everything ever shut in here eventually worked its way out."

"Not the iyats," Asandir contradicted. He ran his fingers over the walls. His touch raised uneasy vibrations in the air that riled the skin but made no sound. Green sparks danced from the contact that caused Dakar to grit his teeth. Unfazed, the Sorcerer added, "Those were released, you'll remember, to add havoc to Davien's rebellion."

"We're not going to sleep here," Dakar interrupted. He felt claustrophobic, and strongly inclined to throw up.

Asandir glanced abstractedly over one shoulder. "I advise you to try. You'll feel less ill with your eyes closed, and rechecking the symmetry of these wards will likely take most of the night."

"You didn't need me," Dakar retorted. "Why insist that I come?"

"But Kharadmon told you already." Impatient, Asandir abandoned the intricacies of his spellwork. He turned fully around and gave Dakar a regard that was testy enough to peel skin. "Your body needed the exercise."

Which point incensed Dakar to black rage. He filled his lungs to shout imprecations.

No word emerged. His jaw opened, shut, and opened again like a fish's. His eyes bulged. Then, in some odd fit of difficulty that had no visible cause, his features crumpled in frustration and his knees buckled. His Fellowship master caught him before he collapsed.

Laughing, Asandir lowered the Mad Prophet's bulk the rest of the way to the floor. "How timely."

Kharadmon's ripe chuckle answered. "Quite." His image unfurled, posed in satisfaction over Dakar. "He'll sleep through the night. Good. That should leave us some peace in which to work."

* * *

The next thing Dakar knew, Asandir was shaking him awake.

"Get up," the Sorcerer insisted. "You're lying across space we need for the final defense ward."

Dakar grumbled and finally yielded to the prodding that urged him back to his feet. His bones ached from hours spent on hard and chilly stone, and his eyes felt bored through by a blast of unbearable light. He determined after a moment that the glare emanated from the centermost area of the pit. He blinked, squinted through hurting vision, and at the heart of the dazzle, barely made out the shadowy outline of the flask that contained the Mistwraith.

About then he noticed that his skin tingled as if drenched by a tonic, and all of his body hair had lifted. Throughout his service with Asandir, he had never witnessed such a presence of raw force. For once in his life awed to silence, he gaped.

From behind him, Asandir's voice rose and fell in incantation. The words, Dakar noticed uneasily, were not in any language ever spoken upon the soil of Athera; and the halo of light that netted Deshthiere's flask was not solid, but seemed as he stared to be composed of flecked light that shuttled in convoluted, interlocking spirals that ached the eye's attempt to follow.

Then a grip closed on his wrist and tugged him back. "Cover your face. At once," Asandir commanded. "Else the energy flare as Kharadmon sets the ward will leave you blind."

Dakar began to comply, then paused. "Wait," he said on impulse. "Let me help."

"You can't." Asandir's curtness stemmed from weariness. He worked to soften his delivery as he added, "I can't. The energies involved would vaporize flesh. The final binding must be sealed by Kharadmon alone."

Eyes shielded, Dakar heard Asandir give his colleague word. A violent crack cut the air. Heat flashed across the pit, stinging exposed skin, and accompanied by spitting rains of sparks that left behind an acrid scent of brimstone.

"It's safe to look," Asandir said presently.

Dakar lowered his hands, to find the flask at the center of the pit encircled by a cold blue halo. If the light was subliminally faint, its effects upon the mind were not; just standing within the ward's proximity caused a bone-deep, aching discomfort. Whatever arcane unpleasantness the Fellowship Sorcerers used to fashion their prisons, Dakar refused to know.

Asandir also seemed reluctant to endure the ward's resonance, since he started immediately up the ladder. Dakar hastened after, glad to be quit of Rockfell with its dread overtones of magic and the supremely dangerous entity left there in incarceration.

Morning sunlight washed through the opening to the outside by the time Dakar crawled off the ladder. Never so pleased to breathe in cold air in his life, he did not even mind the prickle against his skin as the icier draft that was Kharadmon flowed from the well on his heels.

"Are you entirely clear?" Asandir asked his discorporate colleague.

Kharadmon shot off a phrase in the old tongue that surprised Dakar to incredulity. Before the Mad Prophet could take stock and appreciate the discorporate mage's use of expletives, Asandir said, "Help me drag the cover back over the well." He indicated the massive round slab that rested ajar across the opening.

Dakar glared at the offending rock. "Don't be saying I need the exercise," he griped before Kharadmon could bait him further.

"You know," Kharadmon observed in blithe enthusiasm, as Dakar grunted and heaved and the stone grated, and slowly gave way to brute force. "Be careful how you place that. I much doubt you can see around that beer gut of yours to tell if you're going to crush your toes."

Caught with every muscle straining and the veins in his neck about to burst, Dakar could do naught but grind his teeth. When at length the pit was covered over, he was too breathless to effect a rejoinder. His pique lasted all the way through the setting of the secondary wards. Hours passed. By the time the Fellowship mages finished raising spells and guard circles to assure permanence, the chamber floor showed no flaw to indicate the existence of any pit.

Outside, Dakar expected, fully exposed to the weather, the pair would repeat the exhaustive process until the cliff face was impenetrable. "By Ath," he commented sourly. "You've taken precautions enough to repel Dharkaron himself. One would hope after this, that Rockfell pit would prove more secure than ever it has in the past."

Asandir cast a jaundiced eye at his apprentice. "It might, you know, if we tried dark practice and chained a slain spirit to stand as sentinel."

"Oh, no." Dakar backed up a step and crashed heavily into spelled stone. "You'd hardly drag me up mountains for exercise if you'd wanted to make me a sacrifice." Nonetheless, he moved his fat bulk with alacrity through the portal onto the outside ledge. While the Fellowship Sorcerers resumed painstaking labor, and set their final seal over the rock at the head of Davien's stair, he remained inordinately quiet.

By noon, Rockfell Peak was secured. The trio of visitors departed, leaving behind them the Betrayer's watching gargoyles and serried banks of clouds that drifted to the play of frigid winds. Confined the Mistwraith might be, but its toll of damages upon their world remained yet to be measured. For down in a lightless pit of rock, sealed behind fearful rings of wards, Desh-thiere's wraiths brooded in confinement, awaiting the vengeance curse laid on two half-brothers to burgeon into bloodshed and war.

Warning

Unsettled through the days since the scrying in the dye-yard warehouse, Elaira walked the tide flats of Narms. Around her, twilight cast gray veiling over wind-ripped clouds and fine drizzle. Here the rush of incoming waves dampened the bay-front clamor, of barking dogs and the hurried curses of wagoners who threaded low-slung fish carts back from market. A stiff breeze off the water carried away the endless bickering of children and singsong cries of wood venders and the boys who sold buckets of steamed crabs layered in straw to keep them hot. Ahead, a meandering shadow against gloom, a beggar scavenged the tidemark for cork floats or broken slats from fish crates that could be salvaged for firewood.

Elaira heard only the waves and the crying gulls who dipped and whirled, scant minutes away from night roosting. Troubled already in spirit, she was wearied from playing at pretense. She would not return to a meal with Morriel's entourage at the hostel, to pick at food when she had no appetite. She refused to retire, to huddle frustrated under blankets touched dank by the salt-laden fogs that smothered Narms after dark. This one night she would resist the demands of sleep, would not close her eyes and dream again of fine-chiseled s'Ffalenn features that reproached her in aggrieved accusation.

What could not be forgiven, she had done. The repercussions could not be reversed. The Prime Circle had sealed their final decision; formal verdict would be sent out at midnight, when the lane tides ran least disturbed by static thrown off by the sun. The Prime's decree concerning the latent danger Arithon presented to society allowed for no mitigating circumstance: his moves were to be exhaustively tracked. Wherever his intent could be hampered and dogged, Koriani would act to disadvantage him.

Elaira sidestepped a patch of seaweed thrown up in tangles on pale sand. Ahead, the beggar paused to rest on a rock, the rags that tied his hooded head flapping in the wind. She passed him by without greeting, which was unlike her, since his kind had replaced her family through early childhood.

She rounded a jumble of boulders, then picked her way over the breakwater that protected Narms harbor from the sea. Sheltered there, fishing smacks and trader galleys loomed at anchorage, or sat low on their marks, made fast to the bollards at the wharf. Deck lanterns threw greasy orange streaks across waters pocked with light rain. At the taffrail of the nearest vessel, a woman crooned a melody, her knees tucked up under a fishing tarp as she peeled vegetables for her supper. Down the docks a bent grandfather trundled a wheelbarrow of cod toward the street, while a boy and his brother mended nets. The reek of fish offal and the squabble of the gulls that dipped and dived through dank pilings checked Elaira as if she had run against a wall.

She deliberated, aware that to go forward was to tread the safer path. What she wanted more was seclusion—and a salt pool left behind by the tide that she could use to attempt forbidden scrying.

Under her damp cloak she shivered. The intention that lurked at the edge of her thoughts was dangerous, foolish. Still, she turned back toward the beach.

She found herself alone with temptation. The beggar had gone, the rocks where he had perched glistening with barnacles burnished like carbuncles in the torchlight off the street. The bayside surf was overlaid by deeper thunder as two stout brewers' boys rolled tuns from an ale dray parked outside a tavern. Sailors caroused in the side alley, laughing, while the shrieks of a bawdy woman taunted them to sport their prowess in her bed. The din of workaday humanity seemed remote and far off, without any overtones of comfort. Made aware that her months in the fenlands of Korias studying herb lore had retuned her nature to prefer silence, Elaira sighed. Change had overtaken her too fast since her unlucky foray to meet with Asandir. She picked a spot where the breeze blew clean off the water, and sat, her head propped in her hands. She watched the incoming surf, but tonight no

iyats rode the waves to refuel their energies on the forces of winds
and tides.

Night fell gloomy and damp. At her feet, ruffled over in pewter-
edged ripples, lay the tide pool she longed for. Torn by indecision, she
wondered which of her loyalties she should suffer for: the one, to
Arithon, already breached; or the other, now cruelly strained, which
tied her to Koriani service through sworn bond to a spell crystal that
Morriel would certainly use to break her.

Eyes closed, her hearing awash with the seethe of salt foam, Elaira
reviewed the unalterable absolutes that imprisoned her in misery.
Where once she could have lightened her mood with flippant behavior and sarcasm, now the frustrated, circling grief of knowing a man
with indelible intimacy ate at her, night and day. The surcease of
physical release was denied her. That one act of spirited curiosity had
caused her to be culled, and now used, as Morriel's personal instrument to map Arithon's motivations could neither be escaped nor
avoided.

But interlinked with this were other trusts acquired in her visit to
Enithen Tuer's Erdane garret.

"Girl, you're shaking, and not at all from the cold," said a kindly
voice from the shadows.

Elaira started, then exclaimed aloud as a hand lightly grasped her
shoulder.

The beggar had not left her but stood, guarded from prying eyes
and wind by an overhang of sea-beaten rock. His earlier appearance
had deceived. Clad all in black, he wore no ornament. None of his
clothing lay in tatters. What had first been mistaken for a frayed head
cloth was revealed now as a raven, hunched and damp on its master's
shoulder, regarding her with eyes too wise for a bird's.

"Who are you?" Elaira blurted. But before he gave answer, she
knew. His eyes upon her were too still and deep to encompass any
less than the vision of a Fellowship Sorcerer.

A wave that was larger than most hurled and broke against the
shore. Fingers of foam clawed up the rocks, then splashed back in silver lace foam. His voice as he addressed her held the same ageless
timbre as the sea. "I am Traithe, sent by Sethvir to give you a message from the Fellowship."

As Elaira moved to speak, he restrained her. Though his step was
careful and lame, his hands could grip hard enough to bruise. "No.
Say nothing. You're aware, the wrong words could set your vows to
your order into jeopardy."

She stilled, shocked by his bluntness.

Traithe said, "Understand, and clearly, that my purpose here is to shield you from any such breach in your loyalty."

Stung still by guilt-ridden thoughts, Elaira's sensibilities fled. She wrenched off Traithe's hold and stepped back. "My Prime might command my obedience. She does not own me in spirit!"

"Well spoken." Traithe sat, which irritated the raven to a testy flapping of wings. He raised a scarred knuckle to soothe its breast feathers, then peered slant-wise at her, chagrined as a grandfather caught in a bout of boy's mischief. "Hold on to that truth, brave lady."

Yet his affirmation of natural order could not undo vows sealed to flesh through a Koriani focus stone. A piece of herself had been given over into Morriel's control that Elaira was powerless to call back. Her ambivalence toward the traps that Traithe most carefully never mentioned gave rise to an outraged admission. "Ath's mercy, I was six years old when the Prime Circle swore me to service. They claim, always, that power must not be given without limits. But lately I suspect my Seniors prefer their trainees young, the better to keep their talent biddable."

Traithe reached out and touched her, a bare brush of fingers against her hand. Yet warmth flowed from the contact, and a calmness that lent her surcease to think.

Unsure his kindness did not mask warning like a glove, Elaira chose a rock and sat also. "Courage saved nothing two days ago." She laced unsteady hands around her knees, self-conscious in the Sorcerer's frank regard.

"If you speak of Arithon, he doesn't need any man's saving." Petulant and ready to roost, the raven sidled and clipped its master a peck on the ear. Traithe called it a rude word, which prompted Elaira to smile.

"Better." The Sorcerer had a crinkle to his eyes that bespoke a readiness to laugh. "The occasion wasn't meant to be solemn." He pushed his bird from his shoulder, then watched with what seemed his whole attention as it croaked in indignation and finally settled in a nook and tucked its head under one wing. "Let me say what I was sent for, and see if your heart doesn't lighten." As Asandir had done once before to ease her nerves, Traithe bent down and made a small fire. The kindling he used was a beggar's gleaning of broken cork floats and bits of jetsam. Flame caught with a hiss in the dampness, and shed fine-grained halos in the drizzle.

Oddly content to be still, Elaira wondered whether some spellward of quietude had been set along with the flames.

Traithe answered as though she had spoken. "What peace you feel

is your own, but it may perhaps be helped by the ward of concealment placed over this space between the rocks." He grinned in glee-
ful conspiracy. "To your sisterhood this fire doesn't exist."

Elaira said, "Then you know about—"

He sealed her lips fast with a finger. "Let me say what we know.
Otherwise," he stopped, let his hand fall. Inscrutable as a stone in a
millpond, he studied her a moment with his head cocked, then
yielded before her straight strength to his impulse. "Otherwise,
Sethvir was most plain, the misery of remorse will later drive you to
use this tide pool. In salt water that will fail to protect you from discovery, you will attempt to send warning of your sisterhood's doings
to the one of my colleagues who might listen."

On her feet before she could react rationally, Elaira backed at bay
against the rocks. Even her lips were white.

As if she had not budged, Traithe continued. "Which act would be
treason against your Prime Senior's directive." He tipped up his face,
sharply and brutally blunt. "Unnecessary treason, brave lady, *which
is why you will sit back down.* Morriel may not own you in spirit,
but she does command your absolute obedience. The Fellowship can
shield from her what happens by our actions, but not what you undertake in free will."

The rush of waves through sand and stone seemed to consume all
the air for the moment while Elaira poised, half on the edge of panicked flight. In the end, she sat because her legs gave out; and because
Fellowship Sorcerers would hardly stand back and allow the half-
brothers to commit a whole kingdom to war without some emphatically sound reason that Koriani intervention of any kind might
shortsightedly come to disrupt. In a croak more like the raven's than
human speech, Elaira capitulated. "Say your piece."

"Well," said Traithe. Less solemn in his ways than Asandir, he
was smiling. "For one thing, you need not warn us of an event that
Sethvir already knows. Morriel doesn't breathe these days without
some sort of surveillance from Luhaine."

"You shouldn't confide in me," Elaira said in a gasp of smothered
surprise.

As if she had piqued him with a riddle, Traithe's brows rose.
"Morriel's aware of the fact. It's a sore point she won't tell Lirenda,
so I much doubt she'll challenge you to make it public." He went
on, his manner as piquant as any matron sharing gossip at a well.
"Furthermore, if your Prime has chosen to meddle with Arithon
s'Ffalenn . . ." The gleam in his eyes hot with mischief, the Sorcerer
shrugged ruefully. "Let's by all means stay plain. I'm not saying she's

resolved on such an action. But if she should, her pack of conniving Seniors will be richly entitled to the consequences."

"You imply that Arithon is defended?" Intrigued despite her better judgment, Elaira edged closer to the fire.

Traithe tucked back a flap of her cloak that the breeze pushed dangerously near the sparks. "I'm saying the Teir's'Ffalenn himself is well able to guard his own interests." When Elaira looked dubious, he gave back a look that happily embraced shared conspiracy. "Fatemaster's judgment, lady, the Fellowship itself had a tough time trying to shepherd that spirit! Let me tell you what happened once when Morriel tried a scrying on Arithon."

His hands stuck out to warm near the fire like any innocuous old man's, the Sorcerer went on to describe in satirical detail exactly what transpired the day the wards over Kieling Tower had been breached during conflict with the Mistwraith.

Traithe gave the telling no embellishment, but used humor and bluntness like scalpels to bare a rotten truth. He spared nothing. Not Lirenda's furious humility or Morriel's' arrogant overconfidence. Least of all did he avoid Arithon's vicious reaction to the fact that Elaira's private feelings had been used as a tool for unscrupulous prying.

Choking and spluttering through a mirth just shy of a seizure, Elaira tried and failed to picture Lirenda upended in her own tangled skirts. "A worthy prank." She caught her breath finally, stung from her laughter by real grief. "I'm a game piece." She, who most questioned Koriani tenets and practices, had unwittingly become their most indispensable cipher in the course of the coming conflict.

"Arithon knows that," Traithe said, equally serious and plain. "He doesn't like it. Should Morriel cross him again on those grounds, he's going to hit her back with far more than a harmless warning. Have you access to the histories of the high kings?"

As she nodded, he said, "Good. Read them and see what happens when past scions of s'Ffalenn were pressed to embrace open enmity. Make no mistake when I tell you, Arithon has inherited all of his line's rugged loyalty. He's got Torbrand's temper, too, intact as I've ever seen it."

The scanty bits of fuel had burned now to a scarlet nest of embers. Across a rising puff of smoke, Elaira looked at the Sorcerer whose forthcoming nature came and went like broken clouds across sunlight. Traithe had turned reticent again. Though his eyes never shied from her regard, and his kindly air of listener remained intact, his stillness invited her to question him on her own. "You're asking me to trust Arithon's judgment?"

"I ask nothing," Traithe amended gently. "I offer only the observation that Arithon is qualified to defend himself from any Koriani
interference that originates through you. And he will do so, never
asking your preference on the matter."

Hands clasped hard beneath her cloak, Elaira chuckled. "I see. He
breaks none of my vows in the process, and therefore I won't get
hurt. Very neat. I shall allow him to act as my protector, and en-
deavor to be the dutiful initiate." She gathered her skirts to rise, a
lump in her throat brought by surety: this time the Fellowship's intervention had diverted her from breaking Koriani mores. But in fact,
the measure was a stopgap. Traithe's concerns had the more firmly
grounded her self-knowledge, that the vows of her order were as unsuited to her nature as crown and kingdom were to the music that
fate had forced Arithon to stifle.

Which of the pair of them would be first to break? she wondered
as she watched Traithe douse the sparks of their fire with effortless
spell-craft. The incoming tide would sweep off the ashes and leave
sands smoothed clean of footprints.

Traithe stood and roused his raven, which croaked like a drunk
with a hangover and hopped sullenly to its master's wrist. Never so
absorbed by his bird as he appeared, the Sorcerer said suddenly,
"You're not alone, brave lady. Nor are you entirely Morriel's play-
thing. Not since the day you chose to seek out Asandir in Erdane."

"Ath," said Elaira in a futile effort to bury her anguish behind
toughness. "Now didn't I think that one escapade touched off my
troubles in the first place?"

The Sorcerer returned a look that drilled her through and gave no
quarter. "Never sell yourself so short!"

"Take care of him," she blurted in heartfelt reference to the
s'Ffalenn prince.

Poised to leave, unobtrusive as the beggar she first had mistaken
him for, Traithe reached out and stroked her cheek, as the father she
had never known might have done to reassure a cherished daughter.
As his hand fell away, she cupped the place he had caressed, and now
the tears fell and blinded her.

"Lady, great heart." He sighed gently. "The love within you is no
shame. And since you fear to ask, I'll tell you: there is no secret to
be kept. The Fellowship stepped back at Etarra because the grace of
spirit we know as life lay in danger of permanent imbalance. Asandir
urged but never forced your beloved. Arithon chose his kingdom
ahead of music by his own free will."

"What?" Elaira stared back in ice-hard fury and disbelief. "Why
would he?"

Suddenly bleak as the clearest winter star field, Traithe said, "Because he would not be the one man to stand in the path of the Paravians' return to this continent."

"Well," said Elaira wretchedly. "For his sake, I hope the creatures prove worth it!"

"That you must judge for yourself." A wistfulness haunted Traithe's manner. "I can tell you as fact that the Riathan Paravians are the only unsullied connection we have to Ath Creator, and that their return is the cornerstone for the future harmony of this world. But words impart meaning without wisdom. To understand, you and Arithon must both survive to experience a unicorn's living presence." A wave broke. Driven on by rising tide, salt spray showered down, mixed in coarser drops with the drizzle that never for an instant ceased to fall. "I must leave you now, brave lady. The fire is out, and the wards on this place will soon dissipate."

Elaira blotted a dripping nose and tried through resentment to recover courtesy. "I owe you thanks."

Seamed features lost beneath cloth that the raven sidled under to take shelter, Traithe shook his head. "Take instead my blessing. You need the consolation, I suspect. I was sent to you because an augury showed the Warden of Althain that, for good or ill, you're the one spirit alive in this world who will come to know Arithon best. Should your Master of Shadows fail you, or you fail him, the outcome will call down disaster."

Elaira resisted an ugly, burning urge to stop her ears. "And if neither of us fails?"

Traithe soothed his bird with his fingers, that being the only comfort he could offer to any breathing creature at this juncture. "Ah, lady, we've been entrusted with this world and free will, which certainly cancels guarantees." He touched her hand in aggrieved farewell. "Never doubt. At the Ravens', your action was right and fitting."

He turned and departed, while wind and thin rain reduced him to a fast-striding shadow against smothering fog and white sea. Elaira stayed on alone until the waves that surged with flood tide encroached on the rocks and soaked her feet. Dragging wet skirts above her ankles, she felt ready to return to her colleagues. The depression that had weighed on her earlier had lifted, replaced by milder sadness shot through by the bold and heady challenge of exhilaration.

Morriel might command her to Koriani loyalty and obedience, but where Elaira chose to give her heart was a choice reclaimed for her own.

Eventide

His hook-nosed profile hard-lined in shadows and torchlight, Gnudsog of the Etarran guard brings word from the war council held at the border of Strakewood Forest: "Diegan and Lysaer are reconciled," he informs his captains who wait in the meadow. "We take the sure route tomorrow, poison the river and the springs to kill the game, then methodically starve out each campsite. Pesquil's plan is best. Children are the future of the clans, and without women the wretched breed will die. . . ."

Deep under the eaves of the forest, in a valley riddled with traps, clansmen under Steiven s'Valerient sharpen their swords and their knives, and for the last time, wax their bowstrings; while on a lyranthe the last of its kind, Halliron Masterbard plays ballads and bright songs from better days, to inspire their hearts to a valor he grieves will be futile. . . .

Returned to his post at Althain Tower, Sethvir bends his regard toward Rockfell Peak to check the wards which bind the Mistwraith; he finds no flaws, and a small ease of mind, for though Arithon could build on his training and possibly unravel those securities, having suffered to subdue such an evil, Rathain's prince was least likely to meddle in foolishness. . . .

XVII. March upon Strakewood Forest

D ressed out in clean tunics edged in city colors of scarlet and
gold, gleaming under polished helms and smart trappings, and
bearing on their backs and in their scabbards the newly
wrought arms and chain mail purchased by the merchant's treasury
at cost of eight hundred thousand coin-weight, fine gold, the men of
Etarra's garrison formed up and marched just past dawn. Set like a
sapphire in their midst, Lysaer sat his bridleless chestnut. Lord Commander Diegan and Captain Gnudsog were positioned at either flank,
while the banner bearers of the greater trade houses and message riders on their lean-flanked mounts clustered in formation just behind.
Four companies of standing army and reserves paraded after, in
disciplined units twenty-four hundred strong.

Lysaer made no conversation. Groomed as befitted his past stature, every inch the princely image of restrained pride, he was disinclined to trivialize his first foray against the s'Ffalenn who had
demolished a fleet on Dascen Elur. Fighting was ugly business. No
pennons, no style, and no fanfares could mask that these men in their
brilliance and finery marched, some to die in blood and suffering.
Still, a heart not made of stone must thrill to the muffled thunder of

war destriers. Each tight square of troops boasted ninety mounted lancers, four hundred crossbowmen and archers, and a perimeter of pikemen numbering nearly two thousand. Deep within their protection rolled the supply wagons and support troops, and rearward, the additional thousand light cavalry under the black kite standard of the northern league of headhunters.

Weather was also in their favor. The last spring rains had finally lifted; the rivers ran placid and shallow.

Sunlight pricked the horizon, edged to the east by the black trees that rimmed Strakewood Forest. For a time as the air warmed, the companies marched knee deep through mists that swathed the meadows in blue-gray. These disbursed last from the hollows to bare rolling hills and the dew-spangled grass of early summer, bespattered and dappled with patches of red brush bloom and weathered rock. A craggier landscape than Daon Ramon, the plain of Araithe wore the season like a cloak of rippling new silk, lush and sweet with flowers, overwhelming the senses in living green.

Lysaer gazed across the vista, untrampled yet by the advancing mass of his army. In his birthland of Amroth, such rich forage would have been grazed short by sheep. He promised himself that if barbarian predation were to blame for the lack of shepherds, his campaign against Arithon would amend this. Then, in belated reassessment he realized that had these hills been used once as pastures, they should be crisscrossed by remains of stone fences and sheepfolds.

There were none, or any foundations of ruined cottages.

These acres had possibly stayed untouched by man's industry through the ages since Ath's first creation. Why such obviously prime pastureland should go wasted puzzled Lysaer, until his thought was broken off by the hoofbeats of an outrider returning at a gallop.

The scout wheeled his mud-splashed mount and reined into step beside Gnudsog. "Lord," he saluted to Diegan, and then his commanding field officer, "Captain." But he looked at Lysaer as he delivered his report, which was startling enough to call a halt to the advance.

Six barbarian children had been spotted, practicing javelin casts in a glen just upriver of the ford across the Tal Quorin.

"A stroke of luck, Your Grace," Diegan said. To avoid embarrassment, he allowed Lysaer the titular courtesy due his birthright. Since no honorific at all implied a laborer's stature, and thus demeaned both parties in conversation only socially acceptable between equals, other Etarran officials had followed suit. "To find barbarians so easily, and they, overtaken unaware."

Stolid on his horse as a figurehead, Gnudsog scowled his annoyance. "Clan scouts are never so careless!"

"Elders, surely," Lysaer agreed. His clear gaze swung toward the scout. "But children? What would you guess were their ages?"

The answer held no hesitation: the largest had looked no more than twelve.

"Rat's get all, and bad cess to them." Gnudsog slapped a fly that landed but had no chance to bite his horse. "They'll know every inch of this country, Deshir's scouts. Likely as not, they're part of a camp that's laid in an ambush farther on."

"Against an army?" Diegan grinned, the gilt scroll work on his helmet and the plumes on his bridle and harness the fashion of the daredevil gallant. "The odds would hardly be sporting."

"Barbarian's don't play at odds" came a querulous interruption from the sidelines. "In these parts, they prefer pits lined with sharpened stakes, and spring traps that rip out a man's guts or tear the axles off wagons." Smart in a black and white surcoat over chain mail dulled with grease and years of polishing, Pesquil rode up to determine the cause of the delay. At the head of the column, he jerked short his brush-scarred gelding that he liked best for its toughness. "So you chase those children thinking to find an encampment of scouts you can surprise, eh? Well, try that. Then find yourselves bloody."

Lysaer regarded the dip of the hills that unfolded in curves toward the ford. Chilly in courtesy he said, "Would you send your ten-year-old son out as gambit before the weapons of a war host?"

"Perhaps. If the stakes were arranged in my favor." Sallow, pock-scarred, and quick with nervous energy, Pesquil shrugged. "For sure, I've known clanborn chits who'd dangle out their newborns if they thought any gain could be wrung from it. The slow plan we follow is safest."

But Diegan was ill-pleased to spend a summer swatting insects and enduring rough camp in the open when a bolder victory might be possible. "Send in a small troop of light riders," he ordered Gnudsog. "See where the children flee, and let the army follow if it's safe."

Pesquil reined around so hard his mount grunted in pain from the bit. "Fools," he muttered. "Idiots." And he spurred to a canter back through the lines to his headhunters.

Gnudsog watched him go, his huge hands crossed at his saddle pommel. Then his eyes, black as rivets, swung to Lysaer. "What do you think, Prince?" From his lips, the title implied insult.

Lysaer raised his head in genteel challenge. "Send in your riders," he suggested. "If a trap exists, then spring it with fewest losses."

"You don't think it's a trap." Diegan soothed his restive destrier. Then, his regard in speculation upon Lysaer, he raised a gauntlet chased in glittering gold to signal the columns to rest at ease. "Why?"

"Because I saw Arithon in a back alley with a band of knackers' conscripts once, when he didn't think he was being watched." Fair-skinned as an ice figure in the early sunlight, the prince stroked the black-handled sword newly forged for his use in the field. Rumor held that the blade had been engraved with Arithon's name in reverse runes, which may have been the armorer's insistence for shaping a blade to kill a sorcerer. Lysaer did not look superstitious or afraid, but only pragmatic as he said, "The Shadow Master has few scruples. But I know him well enough to hedge that he'd sanction no ambush that involved any use of small children."

At this, even Gnudsog reconsidered. "You could be right." Supporting evidence lay with the arrangements for the escape of the knackers' brats. Arithon's bribes had been lavish enough that hard measures had been needed to pry loose the names of which parties had treated with him. Etarra's field captain scraped an itch underneath his right bracer. "Let's prove Pesquil a sissy."

Forty riders were dispatched to track the children. From the rear of the column, Pesquil watched them go, his narrow lips clamped in disdain. "Those lordly fops Gnudsog has to nursemaid didn't listen. We'll keep our distance, then."

The mounted lieutenant at his elbow stopped fingering the scalp locks that fringed his saddle, and widened seamed eyes at his commander. "They're going in with the army, you think? And you'd send our league riding after?"

"Any trap laid by Deshans is bound to be placed deep in Strakewood." Head cocked in consideration, Pesquil picked his teeth with a fingernail. "We'll go in, yes." He clipped out a breathy laugh. "With two whole divisions of garrison troops ahead, and another pair blundering on each flank, whatever surprise the barbarians fixed'll be sprung before we try the trail. Even Steiven's dirty tactics can't murder ten thousand troops without exposure. We'll win our bounties in the mop-up."

"I hope your score's well squared with Daelion Fatemaster." The lieutenant adjusted studded reins in laconic resignation. "They say we fight a sorcerer who weaves darkness. For myself, Sithaer, I'd always planned I'd die rich."

As Etarra's two score light riders crested the rise above the ford, six young boys snatched up javelins and bolted like hares for the forest. Whether they had defied their parents to play in the open or been posted in plain view for bait became moot as the riders drove their mounts and charged after them. They were quarry, and fear for their lives spurred their flight. Flat out across dew-tracked greensward, enemies with drawn blades swept down at their heels. The boys made straight course for shelter, vaulting the switched-back curves of marshy streamlets on the butts of their toy wooden weapons.

They were small and light, and shod in deerhide that made little mark on the hammocks, while the steel-rimmed hooves of the horses bit deep through the soft turf and sank. The riders were forced to take a zigzagging course over firm ground or tear their mounts' tendons in the bog. They shouted and whipped on their horses and brandished sabers in a show of bloodthirsty frustration, their orders plain. The clan boys were to be routed, not killed. Pursuit must hound them into Strakewood until they tired, then slack off and appear to give up. Trackers would take over from there. The youngsters would be followed in stealth back to their parents' encampment: a sensible plan, which pleased the garrison's light horsemen, carefully chosen as fathers who might condone the slayings of headhunters, but who had little inclination themselves for the horror of skewering youngsters.

Hard-bitten to bitterness by the atrocities of his profession, Gnudsog was not given to foolish chances.

His forty light riders crashed into the hazels and saplings that edged the forest just seconds behind the last straggler. Thickly tangled summer scrub swiftly isolated children from hunters. Crows startled up from feeding on blackberries flapped away with raucous calls of warning. Squirrels scattered chattering in alarm. Raked by briars and low branches, the horsemen determinedly pressed onward. Their mud-flecked mounts gouged through dead sticks and moss, the odd hoof fall a dissonant chink of steel against buried scarps of granite.

Ahead, all but invisible in their deerhides, the barbarian children raced in fierce silence, the one towhead among them picked out in the gloom by the chance-caught flicker of filtered sunlight.

Intent on keeping him in sight, the lead rider never saw the wooden javelin left braced at an angle in his path. His mount gathered stride and cleared a rotten log, then crashed, shoulder down, impaled. Its scream of mortal agony harrowed the dawn-damp wood, while the rider, thrown headlong, struck a bough at an angle and broke his neck.

First casualty of the Deshir barbarians, he died with his eyes still open and the taste of blood on his tongue.

Attracted to the site by the thrashing convulsions of dying horseflesh, the survivors gathered and pulled up. With spur and rein they stayed their mounts' panic, while the first man in called the verdict.

"He's stopped breathing."

A still, stunned moment progressed to passionate contention over whether to stop now and call the army, or to ride down verminous whelps whose parents had trained them for murder.

"Dharkaron's Spear!" raged one rider. "I'd say there's no clever trap waiting! Or the Sithaer-begotten brats would just draw us on and not bother stopping to kill!"

That outcry was silenced, and grimly, by an officer given his authority through Etarra's pedigreed elite. "We stick with orders and track. One man will go back as spokesman. Lord Diegan's no coin-grubbing headhunter. He may roust up the garrison. Else risk finding himself laughingstock as craven."

Which recast the affair as rank insult, for a boy's prank with a wooden spear to have killed a man before the armed might of Etarra.

Shouts of agreement endorsed this plan, while the dismounted volunteer asked for help. Willing hands lifted the slain man and tied him over the saddle for transport back to the main troop.

Fled in swift silence up the marshy course of Tal Quorin, the children were long since lost to sight. But in the beds of green moss, under the sills of the sedge clumps, water pooled in a flurried progression of footprints. These the iron-clad hooves of the destriers milled under as the main strength of Etarra's garrison plowed past. The ground was left harrowed to brown mud that sucked and spattered, causing the horses to stumble and the riders to curse as their tassels and trappings became begrimed. Lances hooked in the greenbriar, and the foot troops slogged silently to the rear.

The supply wagons perforce had stayed behind. If Gnudsog had opposed the decision to turn the main army up the riverbed, he knew better than to belabor the mistake. His mouth a grim slash in his hardened leather face, he brought his lancers forward with professional determination.

Noon passed. No ambush seemed in evidence. The fall of the floodplain sloped more steeply, and the ground firmed, though the soil beneath its canopy of deep wood still reeked strongly of bog. Swarming gnats remained in force. The heavier shade at least curbed the growth of brambles, and as the footing improved, so did spirits and eagerness. Aware for some time that the hemming effect of the hillsides was crowding his troops along the bank, Gnudsog consulted with Lord Diegan and received permission to regroup.

"I mislike the feel of this entirely," he grumbled, his eyes on his men as their ranks wheeled and reformed to order despite the unsuitable terrain. The garrison split and regrouped, two companies to divide and cross the ridges on either side. These would advance up adjacent valleys and flank the main force along the river. Gnudsog kept ruminating in monologue. "Too easy."

At his side, stripped of his helm to adjust a crest plume disarranged by low branches, Diegan raised his eyebrows. "Does everything have to be difficult?"

"Here? Against Steiven's clans?" Gnudsog curled his lip and spat. "Yes."

"But the clan chief might not be in command," Lysaer pointed out, his regard, chilly blue, on the veteran captain, and his hands, lightly crossed, on his sword.

"Well." Gnudsog cleared his throat. "Yon thieving little stoat of a sorcerer's clever enough, if your cant to our council held truth." Unfazed before lordly affront, he grinned through his yellow, broken teeth. "You and my Lord Commander will ride behind with the second division. And if we go back proving you hazed the city ministers like the ninnies they are, so much the better. I like my killing quick, with the advantage of superior numbers. Should things fail to get grim, you can always strip me of rank. It's my pension I'm risking, not your necks."

His helm half raised, his reins looped over one forearm, Lord Diegan stiffened in the costly glitter of his accoutrements.

Aware the Lord Commander would protest, and quick to see Gnudsog was earnest in a concern he lacked any polish to express, Lysaer diplomatically intervened. "No one loses pensions for good sense." He stroked his horse's neck, smiled, and said to Diegan, "Since I spoke truth to your council, we'll ride behind. Whether or not this clan encampment is taken by surprise, should Arithon s'Ffalenn be with them, we must expect counter thrust by sorcery. Our presence may well become needed to bolster the middle ranks."

"My sister will call you fainthearted," Diegan warned.

"She may." Lysaer's smile never faltered. "Better that than have her weep for me dead." He nudged his horse around and made his way to the river's verge to find a place when the second column passed. Diegan jammed on his helm, disgruntled, and hastily rearranged his streamered reins. When the Lord Commander of Etarra's guard had trotted his horse beyond earshot, Gnudsog spat again, this time in rare admiration.

"Dresses like a daisy, like they all do who sport pedigree," he confided to the sergeant who awaited the order to march. "But yon royal puppy is canny at handling men. He might be a priss at his sword-play, still, I don't think I'd want him for my enemy."

Unable to find an appropriate reply to criticism involving his betters, the sergeant complained instead about the gnats.

"Well," cracked Gnudsog, out of patience. "Sound the horn for the advance! Clansmen are waiting, I know it, so we might as well call them to the bloodbath."

In moving waves of pennons and lances that juddered and cracked through the greenwood, the army surged on upriver. Half lost in the creak of armor and the jingle of stirrup and bit, a jay squalled in raucous complaint.

Up the valley, a second jay answered. Striped in shadow behind a paling of saplings, charcoal smeared in patterns across his face, Caolle hustled six breathless children past him and on upslope toward safety. To the runner crouched at his elbow, he whispered a hasty "All clear."

Soundless in his boots of beaten deerhide, the messenger departed. Branches slithered back into place across the thicket, and through slits between trembling leaves, Caolle measured the advance of Etarra's thousands as they crashed up the riverbed below his vantage. The last cohort passed and, carefully counted, the last rank.

Two divisions, in line with every hope and plan. The other pair had parted ways from the main troop to quarter the valleys to either side. Caolle smiled.

A third jay called from the marshes.

"Now," Caolle mouthed. The hand he held raised for the signal dipped and raised, and then fell.

The command was seen and relayed upriver by a dozen scouts in concealment, until it reached the head of a dried streambed that sliced like a scar across the hill.

"Hie!" yipped a barbarian teamster. His whip fell with a crack like the snap of a quick-broken twig, and four horses slammed weight against their collars. Ropes whipped taut through oiled blocks. As the strain transferred, mechanically redoubled, the huge logs which braced a timber dam sucked and shifted in mud settings. Again the clansman urged his draft team. Veins bulged in the necks of the horses, and their hooves bit deep as they strained.

A brace gave; others canted, and the dam bowed, its log joints streaked black with the first jetting trickles of leaked water. While the structure creaked and gave outward, the clansman slashed his team free and drove them to a canter up the bank.

The dam burst apart on their heels. Timbers flew like splinters, driven by the loosed force of waters held in check through the last weeks of northland spring rains. The torrent reclaimed its balked course with a roar, fanged in its froth by a burden of sharpened stakes. The clansman soothed his draft team to a halt just barely out of reach. While the torrent swept by like a demon, tearing up mats of elder and birch, his pulse leaped in excitement. The thunder of racing waters was answered from five other sites throughout the valley, where other holding ponds in Tal Quorin's watershed were simultaneously released to rampage through rock-stepped courses by the weight of held gallons and gravity. The plain alongside the riverbank in moments became a gouged maelstrom of boulders and white flood.

On the banks of the river Tal Quorin, the birds in the marshes fled. A herd of deer took bounding flight over mallow and cattails, then veered in fresh panic as they caught wind of the oncoming army. About then the lead horses began to snort and sidle and shy, while men cursed, and spurs dug, and Gnudsog raised his chin listening.

Too late he heard what animals sensed ahead of him: the booming growl of thunder, with no cloud visible overhead. The sound was deep, and oncoming, and weighty in voice to shake the earth. His fist on his destrier's reins like iron, even as the forward scout outriders crashed shouting and gesticulating through the brush, Gnudsog spun his horse on its haunches and slammed sideways into the lighter mount of his message bearer.

"Ride!" he screamed. "Find Lord Diegan and the prince, and tell them to seek cover on high ground." Next, he barked orders for the troops to wheel, though ranks were disordered and broken, and half the war horses were mindless with fear, jammed one on another in herd instinct to bolt.

Locked against motion by the weight of their own vast numbers, the lead ranks saw the flood coming.

It rampaged over a snake-twist curve in the river, a towering, tumbling brown wall jagged with logs, uprooted trees, and slashed greenery. The vanguard of Etarra's proud army was allowed a split second of terror but no escape.

The water hit.

Men, mounts, and bright pennons crumpled as if struck by the log-mailed fist of doom. Horses screamed, upended, their cries as one with their riders, who were crushed, and scythed under, and drowned. The foaming jaws that crested over Tal Quorin's banks thrashed on in a welter of chaos to cut down everything standing, to smash living flesh without quarter, and to turn the snapped shafts of the lances against those maimed, to impale, and gut, and club unconscious with a force more furious than man's.

The passage of the flood was cataclysmicly swift, and it dragged on its course the mangled destriers, the rent and sodden banners, and the dismembered, drowned, and dying men of all but the extreme flanks of Etarra's first division.

Given warning by the dispatch of Gnudsog's staff messenger, Lord Diegan did not turn tail and abandon his second company in a bolt for higher ground. In a rapid-fire string of orders, he commanded four reliable men to escort Lysaer out of danger, then called to muster the ranks behind for a speedy retreat from the riverbank.

The ground was soggy. The suck and splash of many horses and men drawn to a halt in one place foiled the most effective shout; and Diegan lacked Gnudsog's bull bellow. So that when the soldiers he had dispatched to attend the prince closed instead around his own horse and insistently grasped the bridle, he thought his first orders had been mistaken.

"The prince!" he cracked out in white anger. "I said, you escort His Grace, Lysaer."

The men continued to seem deaf.

Lord Diegan spun in his saddle, suspicion in his eyes as bright as the glint on his jewels.

And Lysaer met him, harder still. "Go! This was my error. My fight. Let me save what I can. For I fear the worst still awaits us."

Enraged and far from willing to desert his post of command, Lord Diegan hauled to wheel his horse. Between his hands the reins recoiled into slack; his own men had cut the leather at the bit ring, and were traitorously goading his mount to trot away from the river and his troops.

"Damn your royal effrontery to Sithaer!" cried Lord Diegan.

Lysaer gave him back an insouciant wave, while he directed cracking strings of directions that effected a miracle of smooth deployment among the troops. As Lord Diegan was dragged up the rise toward the forest, his last, venomous thought was that no man alive should be blessed all at once with looks, and toughness, and such surpassing talent for leadership; grudging resignation followed that perhaps this was why the Fellowship had insisted on restoring royal rule to start with.

Three-quarters of the men were clear of the river course when the spate gushed from the narrower channel of the upper valley and raced to claim the marshy stretch of flatland. Tal Quorin's fury was less spent than engorged on its burden of disemboweled horses and wracked men. Laced in dirty foam, encumbered by stripped caparisons and bodies both thrashing and lifeless, the flood bore down upon the second division of Etarra's city garrison.

Lysaer heard the hiss and splash, felt the thunderous shake of the pummeled earth translate from the ground through his horse. He did not turn. Although every nerve in his body was keyed to the disaster about to overtake him, he continued in his clear, even voice to issue concise instructions to convey the next cohort of pikemen to safe ground.

The men who dragged Diegan by force up the rise from the marshlands watched helpless as the waters closed, threshing down. They saw the fear scribed on the faces of their front-rank companions, impossibly trapped; they saw and could do nothing to stem the disordered burst of panic and the tragic unraveling of an order that against odds had held until now. And they saw, some of them weeping, the prince on his magnificently trained chestnut struggle with spur and seat to hold his ground.

The Lord Commander they had spared from destruction ceased in that moment to fight them, but drove his fist again and again in balked fury against the mailed flesh of his thigh. No man could do aught now but watch. The gelding was schooled to the sternest standards by the best-gifted horsemen in the continent. But as the waters crashed hungrily down, bridleless, it reverted to instinct. The Lord Commander and his escort in the wood saw it rear and then bolt like an arrow through straw, straight into the pressed ranks behind. The army seethed in a mass stampede of berserk flight. Footmen were trampled, and companions shoved and even stabbed as soldiers clawed to reach the high ground. Then the flood closed over all with a slap that diminished the screams, the shouts, and every other futile mortal protest.

Because the pair, mount and rider, were moving with the flow, the crest did not at once immolate them. Heads surfaced, upflung in struggle, noble chestnut with an eye rolling white, the other sleeked wet and shining blond. Lysaer had discarded his helm, but could do nothing to shed the chain mail that could drown him. Then the unseen thrust of a log, or maybe a submerged corpse entangled in shed loops of harness, battered and encumbered the swimmers. The horse rolled and went under in the sucking rush of current. Of the rider they saw no more sign.

Lord Diegan's fury went cold. "You and you!" he said through clenched teeth to the men who still held his horse's bridle. "Knot my reins to the bit!" He snapped the severed leather in their faces without caring if he took out an eye. Then he spurred down the bank and reclaimed his post with a shout that carried even over the gush of Tal Quorin's black torrent. "Etarrans! To me! Reform ranks."

Somewhere upstream lurked the clansmen who had arranged this disaster. They would die very messily, Diegan swore as he reviewed for losses and discovered still wider calamity. Of the first and second companies of Etarra's guard, scarcely a quarter remained standing. These waded, dripping, toward the bank. They towed the maimed and the dying; still, these were the luckier ones, since horror did not end with the flood. For the troops Lysaer's considered logic had sent clear in advance of the waters, the hillsides now offered poor haven. Where the riverbanks appeared most solidly inviting, the footing lay undermined in a maze of deadfalls and traps. The ground give way beneath the lancers' destriers. Their screams rent the air as they fell twisting into pits lined with sharpened stakes.

"Stay in the shallows!" Diegan cried. He muscled his mount by main force off dry ground, then plowed girth-deep through rushing waters to rally his straggle of survivors. The horse cloths wicked up water, dragging his mount at each step. He cut them away. Since they bore his house blazon and badges of rank, a grazed and bleeding lieutenant lashed them up crudely to a pike pole. Around that dripping, swamp-sodden standard the second company struggled to reform denuded ranks. They gathered, hauling in their moaning wounded, and killing in deft mercy those horses unable to rise. The flood torrent crested and passed to leave a foam-laced train of muddy rapids, pocked into rills and potholes that were not caused by rocks but by the flesh, bone, and sinew of Etarra's brave fighting force, with its eighteen hundred lancers, its silk pennons, its handpicked recruits, and its chain mail and arms, bought new from the merchants' levy.

As the diamond lines of stiff current eased into slack ripples, the river receded to yield up its toll of carnage and dead. Of the body of a drifter-bred chestnut gelding there was no sign, nor had any man of Diegan's company seen trace of its royal rider.

Of Lysaer no one spoke, but his absence weighed on the calm that fell as the roar of Tal Quorin diminished. On the bank, a band of archers fussed with spoiled fletching and stretched bowstrings. Knee-deep in muck and flattened sedges, pikemen drew daggers and slashed the drenched pennons that unbalanced their pole arms in desperate, grim-faced need to seek out clan enemies and kill. Hardly a man was not bleeding. Scarcely a horse was not lame.

The only outcry to be heard was the cross scream of jay.

Something whipcracked through the foliage. A standing man staggered and collapsed and around him, others started shouting.

The clanborn were firing off arrows.

Another man buckled against Diegan's horse. He fought the beast's sideward shy; felt a whisper of wind flick his cheek. The flights came not in volleys but singly, shot at leisure from a point of heavy cover up the slope. The shafts snicked and cracked through pale birches. They whined through windless air to smack with the malevolent skill of scout marksmen into the stranded ranks in the marshes.

Diegan cried orders for the sensible counter move, to retreat and duck shoulder-deep in water, to seek bulwarks behind hammocks and the brush-caught mounds of dead horses. As he used the flat of his sword to belt his bucketing mount into the reed beds, only a seasoned few followed.

Unmoored by a lust for blood and vengeance, the hotter-blooded men and fresh recruits charged at the origin of the cross fire.

The deadfalls, the spring traps, and the slip nooses set in waiting all claimed their inevitable toll of lives. Steiven's scouts owned a gristly ingenuity, and their toil's harvest laced the greenwood yet again with the agonized screams of townsmen who died, slaughtered, without one blow struck in defense.

Four hundred yards downstream, creeping silent and unmounted through marshes flash-flooded under waters rinsed opaque with yellow clay, Captain Mayor Pesquil's advance scouts found Lysaer s'Ilessid. Stranded on a sandbar with swift waters sheeting past on either side, he stood skin-wet and shivering, one forearm bathed in blood. His face was grazed, his clothing ripped. His sword also was scarlet, though the right hand gripped white to the pommel showed no wound.

Half unmoored from thread settings, sapphires hung like clots from his surcoat, each sparking cold fire at the ripping jerk of each breath. At the prince's feet, mud-caked as his boots, sprawled the corpse of a fine chestnut gelding with a log staked through its lean barrel. Its throat had been cut. Questing flies already sucked its filmed eyes.

Knee-deep in a current still treacherous with debris, the scout who encountered the pair discreetly queried, his voice a bare breath above a whisper, "Your Grace?"

Lysaer whipped around. He had a black bruise on his chin. The rest of his face was white to the bone, and his eyes, bright and empty as his jewels. Clumsily stanched with a knotted rag, his arm seeped from a nasty gash. Faced forward, the reason for his unsteady breathing was disclosed by the plum-colored swelling pressed against the burst rings of his mail.

No stranger to injuries, the scout added, "You appear to have broken your collarbone."

He received no answer. A nearly imperceptible tremor swept the man before him from head to foot.

"It is shock. You must sit." The scout stepped forward fast, prepared for the chance his charge might faint.

"Not here." As if the drowned and disemboweled corpses wadded like rags in the sullied waters did not exist, Lysaer shifted his regard back to the horse at his feet. "Never here." Beyond him, a clot of logs and brush rolled in the current. Sunlight silvered the crescent bill of a pike, its sodden streamers fanned across the cheek of a corpse left in open-mouthed surprise: his jaw had been fully torn away. Lysaer dropped his sword, raised his hand, and masked the side of his face between the arch of his forefinger and thumb.

Since he looked on the edge of collapse, the scout presumed and gripped the royal elbow in support.

A shudder jarred the prince in recoil. Lysaer's head snapped up. He wrenched free, and the scout saw in dawning horror that His Grace suffered no confusion at all but a self-revulsion so deep it shocked the watching spirit to behold.

"I was wrong," Lysaer said with the same, self-damning clarity. "Daelion's pity upon me, every man who has died in this place has been ruined for a misplaced belief and my idealistic folly."

Pesquil's scout stumbled to find a banal reply. "Clan tactics are ever without honor, Your Grace."

But it was not the barbarians' touch at warfare that had splintered Lysaer's heart into rage; it was the knowledge, delivered on two companies' ruthlessly massacred bodies, that he had been masterfully deceived.

Arithon was a trickster to make his s'Ffalenn forebears in Karthan seem as mere simpletons in comparison. For this trap to have been baited with children meant the scene over the shadow brigantine in Etarra's back alleys *had all been a sham, most carefully engineered, most exactingly executed.* Here, over the corpse of a horse, amid a riverbed swollen still in carnage, Lysaer understood that the joy, the compassion, the agonized self-sacrifice Arithon had shown toward the brats conscripted to the knackers' yards had been nothing, *nothing at all.* Just another ruse, another play of diabolical sleight of hand and seamless guile.

This man, this bastard of shadows, had no scruple, but only an unholy passion for lies of a stripe that could cajole human sympathy and then turn and without conscience rend all decency.

Quite aside from Desh-thiere's curse, Lysaer rededicated himself to moral purpose. His half-brother, so gifted in magecraft and so superior in unprincipled cunning, was a blight and a threat to society.

With a continent riddled with encampments of barbarians, each one a ready weapon for his hands, no bound existed to the havoc Arithon might choose to create.

Lysaer stirred. Seared to numbness by the enormity of his mistake, he bent, closed his hand, and retrieved his sword. The blade he cleaned on his surcoat, and the scout's banality he ignored. "My horse is dead," he said crisply. "I shall need another."

"No man goes mounted with my headhunters," interjected a severe voice from the side. Unseen, unnoticed, Captain Mayor Pesquil waded the last strides toward the sandspit, several scouts arrayed at his heels. The interruption in his patrol had been noticed, and reported with a zeal that suggested his underlings knew what their posts were worth.

Lysaer disregarded the impertinence. Wide and unflinching in candor, his eyes transferred to the commander of Etarra's league of headhunters. "This was my mistake. Since my ignorance has led to disaster, I'm ready to listen. But in one thing I will not be swayed. Arithon s'Ffalenn will be stopped. And killed. And if you deem it necessary to slay children to keep a weapon such as Steiven's clansmen from his hands, I shall no longer obstruct you."

Pock-scarred and twitchy with a flame of nervous energy, Pesquil's black eyebrows arched. If he was startled, his mocking inquisitiveness stayed unblunted. "Did my Lord Diegan survive?"

"I hope so. I sent him to cover on the bank with all of the men I had time to send out of danger." Tartly polite, Lysaer added, "Is the interrogation finished?"

Now Pesquil was astonished, and not quite glib enough to hide it.

Urbanely defensive, Lysaer said, "If my judgment was lacking, my first duty was to see the men didn't lose their commander by it."

The lanky, curled braid that Pesquil wore for battle slapped his cheek as he jerked his head. "To Sithaer with your honor. I would ask, rather, how you got any pedigreed scion of Etarra to agree to take orders from anybody."

Now Lysaer's expression turned arch. "Simply put, there are certain advantages to being born and raised a king's heir." A heartbeat later, he smiled. "The nasty-minded sort of arrogance that stops a man being gainsaid is one of them."

"Hah!" Pesquil slapped his thigh in contempt, but around him, the men who knew him best hid grins. Lysaer saw as much, and understood they had reached an agreement. And so he kept his humor when Pesquil added, "Well, then, Prince. There won't be much advantage if you choose to keep up bleeding and wind up keeled over on that horse."

Stiffly, for his dignity balked at public handling, Lysaer extended his badly wrapped arm that by now dripped messily scarlet. The man Pesquil signaled stepped forward, and with a deft expertise took charge. The binding and slit bracer beneath were pulled away, the gash examined and bandaged.

Of the men, only Pesquil dared comment. "You're lucky. The cut is deep, but it runs with the line of the muscle. You'll scar, but have no loss of function."

Neither grateful nor relieved, Lysaer half turned his face as his collarbone also was examined, the arm he did not need for a sword slung and strapped immobile. Beneath the hauberk at his neck as they had cut away the padding to probe the bone, his pulse could be seen, heavy and rapid with anger. He said in a tone almost level, "How many do you think survived this?"

"None." Pesquil squinted across muddied waters, while snarls of brush drifted by and a corpse trailed, moored by a wrack of ripped trappings. "There would have been deadfalls, of course. Pits and spring traps that rip to disembowel. These are Steiven's clans you have marched on."

When Lysaer endured this, still steady in silence, Pesquil's lips quirked in a sneer. "Ah, Gnudsog, you are thinking. Why not say so? The veteran who saw fit not to question, despite his years and experience . . ." The officer who had led Etarra's headhunters through a career of blazing obsession studied Lysaer with pity. "You should know about Gnudsog that his brother and young son died at the hands of barbarians. They fell with a merchant's train on their way to East Ward to attend a cousin's wedding. Etarra's great captain got his start hunting heads, as anyone would readily tell you. He stopped because he loved it too much. Dearer than his own life, he once told me." Irked now, and bristling because this prince was listening sincerely, as no scion of fine pedigree would deign to do, Pesquil curled his lip. "If he thought he could kill a few barbarians, old Gnudsog would've thrown every soldier he had to Daelion and the pits of Sithaer."

"I was the one who did that," Lysaer corrected with quick acerbity; the scout finished with his dressings and withdrew, embarrassed as the discussion went on as if both men were private. "I thought I was waiting for you to say what was left to be done. We still have the companies on our flanks."

Pesquil laughed, but softly. "Do we?"

And across from him, Lysaer's gaze wavered as cold remembrance touched him: that bad as the river had been, they had yet to encounter any shadows. He collected himself in a breath. "Are you afraid to find out?"

"No." Come to his decision, Pesquil disbursed his scouts on a hand signal. As they fanned out, efficiently soundless, and vanished in pursuit of lapsed duty, their leader backstepped into the shoaling waters of Tal Quorin. "Come, then, Your Grace," he invited. "But this time we hunt Deshans *my* way."

In stealth they worked upriver; past the sprawled dead with their eyes and their mouths clogged with mud; past scarlet-rinsed puddles and broken swords and destriers, the curve of their bellies like whales on a beach, but for the straps of breastplate and saddle girth or the brush-jammed arch of a stirrup. Lysaer did not flinch from the carnage. When Pesquil demanded that he rip the jewels from his surcoat to kill their chance sparkle in the sunlight, he obeyed, for clansmen were stationed in these woods. Upstream, less faintly as they progressed, they could hear sounds of shouting and the high, shrill screams of dying horseflesh.

The barbarians were still at their slaughter.

From pale, Lysaer had gone sick white. It took every shred of self-control and a humility more demanding than courage to keep still, to stay with Pesquil, moving silent from a thicket of reeds to the shadowy pool beneath a deadfall, keeping each step shallow, so their boots did not break water and cause a splash.

They stopped again. Lysaer clenched his teeth against the pain of his cuts and contusions, and the flaring stabs that resulted when his side or his collarbone was jostled. Movement came, ever so soft, in the fronds of a willow by the riverside. A scout returned. Head bent, Pesquil received the report.

Lysaer could not hear the words, though in the forest, no birds called. The rush and tumble of high waters had receded also, and the gnats were swarming, bloodthirsty. They bounced off his nose and his ears in maddening circles, and inhaling, he had to struggle not to sneeze.

From upstream also came silence.

Ankle-deep in flat water, Lysaer gripped himself hard to keep from shivering in a paroxysm that had nothing to do with cold or shock. Several moments passed before he became aware that Pesquil stared at him from under half-closed lids.

Under that piercing scrutiny, court training alone enabled him to speak with no reflection of urgency. "You have news?"

Pesquil's upper lip twitched, then relaxed in a one-sided smile that held no shred of joy. "Shadows," he said clearly. "Shadows and traps, to the west of us. More traps and archers, over the ridge to the east.

The flanking divisions have not passed unscathed. But unlike those drowned by Tal Quorin, there are numbers enough to stand, fighting."

Arithon *was* here. Confirmation triggered in Lysaer a tumultuous anticipation.

In a vise of self-control tighter than anything he had needed previously, the prince stayed his sword hand from ripping blade from scabbard in a curse-driven lust to rend and kill. Etarra's troops were still dying of his mistakes. Their needs claimed his first responsibility. "Up this valley there were living men left just a bit ago."

"I know." Pesquil surged ahead, lightly mocking to hide admiration. "We'll pass upstream first, never worry."

The sun beat down, and the flow of falling water subsided. Here and there, marsh reeds pricked out of beds slicked into herringbone patterns, dulled with a velvet of drying silt. The air hung thick and quiet. Lysaer chafed at their progress, which stayed slow since Pesquil insisted their advance remain cautious and covert. Tossed across the sheen of bared flats like wads from a ragpicker's pack lay the limp dead of Etarra's garrison, conspicuously lacking both wounded and living horses. Not all had perished of drowning; not all bore macerating wounds. Lysaer paused in the act of stepping over the body of a petty officer, and the jolt of what eyesight recorded transferred like a blow to his belly.

The man's throat had been cut.

Choked by an explosion of nausea, Lysaer felt a hand chop the small of his back and propel him forcibly onward. "Such surprise," Pesquil said sourly. "You didn't really think, did you, that the river could've done for them all?"

The heat, the swimming reflections off wet mud, the fall of drops from draggled cattails, all conspired to turn Lysaer's head. He fought back the dizziness, enraged at how long he needed to recapture the semblance of self-command. "Whoever did this could not have murdered two divisions without suffering a single loss."

"Damn near," murmured Pesquil, paused to receive yet another report from a scout. "Lord Diegan is alive, at least. He's downriver, safe but unable to fight. My surgeon is just now picking an arrowhead and sundry bits of chain mail out of the gristle of his flank."

But the news that Etarra's Lord Commander had survived brought Lysaer little reprieve. "I've seen no barbarian dead."

"I have." The scout had silently vanished. Pesquil now scanned the wood ahead intently. "But precious few, my prince. No clansman will fight when he can ambush. He will not leave cover until his killing is accomplished, and even then he'll do so warily. To catch him and engage him, you must creep close and never let him sight you. And then you must lie in wait with the patience of almighty Ath." Pesquil suddenly froze and caught Lysaer back by the shoulder. "Don't answer," he breathed sharply; and as the prince stiffened to his touch, "Don't move."

His attention was trained into the shadows, away from the lit expanse of flats. Lysaer too watched the forest. Past the sun-flecked dances of gnats, under the silvered boughs of beeches that upheld their vaultings of copper leaves, he saw gaping holes torn in the ground, and the slashed earth that marked where horses had struggled as the footing gave under their forelegs. He saw the white gleam of a fallen sword, the gilt fringes torn off a caparison; he saw too the bundled dead, with arms outflung or hands slackly curled over the shafts of the arrows that had killed them. Through the raw beat of pulse through his veins, and a fury too bitter for expression, Lysaer forced himself to exhaustive search, and to read, beyond omission, in ripped brush and scarlet-tipped stakes and desecrated flesh, the fates of the men who had fled the river.

Steiven's clansmen had been nothing if not thorough.

A man whimpered, unseen in the gloom. Lysaer tensed to rise, prepared to succor survivors. Pesquil snatched him back with a grasp that jarred the broken ends of his collarbone, and also the cracked ribs in his left side that the scout who strapped him had not found. Next, Pesquil's horny palm closed over his face, stifling even the hissed air that was all his expression of pain.

On a breath scented in garlic, Pesquil mouthed in his ear, "Keep silent. The wrong move, the slightest noise, and you kill us all." He maintained his suffocating grip while, in cruel vindication of his warning, the unseen soldier's suffering became cut off in mid-cry.

There followed a bubbling sigh whose cause could not be mistaken. Somewhere very close by, barbarians were yet about their business of slitting the fallen men's throats.

Slowly, deliberately, the headhunter captain released his restraint. Lysaer blotted his cheek where the studs of Pesquil's bracer had gouged a scab, the look he returned a blast of stifled frustration.

Snake silent, the commander of Etarra's headhunters dispatched a series of hand signals to the hidden ranks of his scouts. Then he touched Lysaer's wrist and crept deeper into the forest.

Progress was more cautious than before. Since deadfalls and traps might lurk unsprung between the trees with their matted mantles of creepers, Lysaer learned a headhunter's way of probing the soil with a weapon before inching forward, and to stalk head down, careful to leave undisturbed any brush or vine or loose root that might hide the trigger for a spring trap. The scents of burgeoning summer foliage hung unsettled with the reek of recent death, and often the tufted mosses squelched under hand or knee with the wet heat of fresh-spilled blood. The gloom deepened. Ahead, his attention trained forward, Pesquil poised. With fingers pinched to steel to damp stray sound, he slowly, silently drew his blade.

Lysaer crept abreast and followed his guide's line of sight.

Through a lattice of birches and black firs, a light-footed squad of boys busied themselves among Etarra's fallen. Clad in deerskin, furtive in movement as wild creatures, they were there to pilfer weapons, Lysaer presumed—until his eye was arrested by a telltale glimmer of steel. Horrified incredulity shook him. The shaded depths of the thickets no longer masked the fact the boys' hands were bathed scarlet to the wrists. Small fingers and sharp daggers ensured that town-bred wounded never rose. Before his stunned eyes he saw a son of Deshir's clans end a man pleading for mercy with a practiced slash across the windpipe. Other victims who sprawled unconscious or moaned facedown in their agony died as fast, of a well-placed stab in the neck. The butchery was done in speed and silence, and ruthless efficiency without parallel.

"The little fiends!" Lysaer gasped softly.

"Vengeance," Pesquil whispered. "This time we have them. There won't be another trap waiting."

Etarra's league of headhunters deployed with oiled care, and at length the little rise lay triply ringed with poised men. When Pesquil signaled the attack, only the inner rank charged. They cut directly for the kill and did not mind if a child or two slipped past. The outer lines would mop up any fugitives.

At the forefront of the strike force, Lysaer thrust his sword inside the guard of youngsters' daggers with no more hesitation than a man might feel who stabbed rats. This was not war but execution, the lives he destroyed of tainted stock. Royal requisites inured a man to cruel decisions; if they sickened him, it must not show, and if they softened him, he was no fit vessel to rule.

If Arithon s'Ffalenn used children for his battles, the scar upon the conscience must be his.

First Quarry

On a thicketed knoll amid the valley adjacent to Tal Quorin, the half-brother that Lysaer had sworn to kill sat in a brush brake alongside five of Steiven's archers. Young Jieret knelt restlessly at his shoulder, wielding a bow with a nervous prowess the equal of any grown man's. Arithon himself bore no weapon. Empty-handed, he perched with his legs drawn up, his wrists dangled lax on his knees. Head bent and eyes half lidded, he appeared on the lazy edge of sleep.

In fact, he kept his immediate senses detached out of bleakest necessity.

Clan runners had earlier confirmed that the s'Ilessid prince had marched with the doomed divisions that advanced up Tal Quorin's banks. His fine chestnut horse had been seen to go down, but that its rider survived both flood and deadfalls was never for an instant in doubt.

The burning urge of Desh-thiere's curse continued insidiously to gnaw at Arithon's inner will. He felt it always, a tireless pressure against reason, an ache that pried between every thought and desire. The knowledge of Lysaer's presence played on his nerves like a craving, volatile as a spark fanned dangerously close to dry tinder.

The nightmare was too substantial, that he could not encounter his half-brother alive and retain his grip on self-will. Had Deshir's clans not relied upon his gifts for survival, he should have been far from this place.

"Here, Jieret," one of the scouts chided as the boy retested the tension of his bow and at full draw pretended to take aim. "Don't be wasting your shots, boy. Use up those arrows that suit you for length, and we've not got spit for replacements."

"I know that." Jieret glowered, his fingers running up and down, up and down the new gut string of his recurve. He wore his hair tied back in a thong like the men, and tried brazenly hard to hide dread. Ever since the prescient dream that slipped his recall, he had been moody and difficult to manage.

A word from Arithon might have eased him. But the Master of Shadows this moment had no shred of perception to spare anyone. No mage would willingly broadcast his finer vision across a field of war. The wrench as quickened spirits were torn from life in the bursting pain of mortal wounds could and had unhinged reason. Barriered as tightly as he had ever been through his nerve-haunted stay at Ithamon, Arithon engaged his talents with the delicate precision of a clock maker winding the coil for a mainspring.

Throughout the previous night, he had walked the valley barefoot, crossing and recrossing familiar ground as he laid in spell and counterspell and anchored them in fragile tension to the subliminal pull of the compass points. This oak, and that stone, and eastward to west, a sentinel line of brush and saplings and old trees; a thousand points of landscape became his markers. Now he played his awareness across the fine-spun net of his night's labor; he tuned his wards, or moved them, or cajoled them from strength to dormancy, the results all balanced to a hairbreadth to spin a maze-work of shadows across the vale. To this, the strategy painstakingly wrought from the fruits of his tienelle scrying, he layered energies to warp air and deflect the natural acoustics.

If he did not engage his talents in direct intervention to take life, the distinction was narrowly made.

By his hand, the neat ranks of Etarra's right flanking division blundered abruptly into darkness. The rocks, the mires, the twisted stands of runt maples, broke their advance into chaos. Calls of inquiry rebounded between distressed soldiers, while the orders of officers to rally split to untrustworthy echoes and sent whole cohorts stumbling awry through rock-sided ravines and marshy dells.

The shadows themselves defied nature. A townsman who spun around to backtrack would see his path open to clear sunshine. If he yielded to fright and instinct and fled that way in retreat, he encountered no further hindrance. But any Etarran soldiers high-hearted enough to use that reprieve to recover their bearings at next step became swallowed by darkness. Blinded and lost to direction, they thrashed through branches and bogs, twisted ankles and bruised shins on an unkindness of rocks and crooked roots. The terrain funneled them north, where they floundered, battered and disoriented, into a dazzling brilliance of sudden sunlight.

Arrows met them in whispered, even flights loosed off by hidden clan marksmen. Soldiers screamed, and crumpled, and died; others warned of ambush by the cries of their fallen ducked back toward the cover of the shadows, to be cut down in turn by companions too rattled to distinguish town colors from the deerskins of enemies.

Bewildered shouts and groans of agony, all rebounded into echoes, recaptured by webs of complex conjury. Arithon sensed like ebb tide the continuous draw on his resources. Like a killing frost out of season, the spell-craft taught by his grandfather mixed uneasily with murder. The line was most critical where magecraft subsided, and dying men spasmed like seines of dredged fish, gasping their final breaths. As though he wound silk past raw flame, Arithon worked to a perilous paradox: attuned to the outermost demands of sensitivity, while sealed still and deaf within self-imposed strictures of silence. He heard but did not answer the quips between the archers as they sorted fresh arrows, or passed around waterskin and dipper. Pressed by doubt, and by knife-edge awareness that townborn enemies must be allowed to break through only in manageable numbers, Arithon beat back the weariness that pressed aches to the core of his flesh. Should he slip, lose track and grip on just one lancer or foot cohort, Steiven's clansmen could be swiftly overrun. Engrossed in concentration that must target exactly which victims to release, he sensed nothing momentous as, by the river course over the east ridge, the lifeblood of Deshir's young sons soaked on the banks of Tal Quorin.

But young Jieret, who had Sight, cried aloud. "Ath, Ath, it's Teynie!" He threw down his bow and tugged Arithon's shoulder in dawning, agonized horror. "Hurry! She's going to betray them all."

Dazed and burdened with his interleaved mesh of maze-woven shadows and defense wards, Arithon neither heard the words nor felt the boy's urgent touch. He roused anyway. The oath lately sworn with Steiven's son had been a blood ritual, and for the mage-trained such things became binding beyond a mere promise; his life and the boy's were subtly twined. Like a man slapped out of a coma, he mustered back full awareness and moved, but not in time.

Lost to panic and raw grief, Jieret shoved past the archers and vaulted the paling that served as cover.

No chance existed for second remedy. Arithon dropped hold on the spells, let them collapse in a tangling cascade of frayed energies. The shadow barriers being easiest to stabilize, he locked a lightless pall across the valley that would partially hamper Etarra's troops. "You're on your own," he informed in clipped apology to the archers. "Stand or retreat as you will, but at least send a runner to warn your fellows."

Then he was over the breastworks and after Jieret with his sword sliding clear in midair.

Of the scouts posted with him, half remained. The rest grabbed up weapons and bows and jumped after, hailing companions as they went. "Jieret's run off, the prince after him. Divide your numbers and come, they'll need support."

Dodging through elders and thin brush, Arithon spared no thought for regret. Had Jieret's spurious talent recaptured the vision that led to the slaughter of Deshir's innocents, any futures traced through his tienelle scrying would now carry unknown outcomes.

If Deshir's clans were beyond saving, he had vowed that Steiven's son be spared.

He poured all his heart into running, slammed through a last stand of birch, and at last overtook the fleeing boy. Once abreast, he made no effort to stop, but matched stride and gently guided, bending the child's flight toward the thicker stands of forest on high ground. "Easy. Up here. That's better. Fewer pikemen, and don't forget the swamp."

Jieret choked back a sob and plunged through a gully in a furious rush that tripped him up.

Arithon caught him as he stumbled, steadied him through the moss-slicked rocks up the bank. Between heaving breaths he kept talking. "Explain. What about Teynie? We're blood-sworn. It's my oath to help."

"The tents!" Jieret pushed through a stand of witch hazel, whose downy spines powdered his jerkin. "She's going to lead headhunters to the tents!"

Slammed by a wave of foreboding, fending off branches that raked his face, Arithon squeezed the boy's hand. "Don't talk," he gasped. "Just think in your mind what you dreamed and imagine that I can see it, too."

But panic had already impelled the vision to the forefront of Jieret's awareness. The instant Arithon opened a channel to test the boy's distress, the ties of the blood pact took over. Jieret's terror became his own. The prescient vision that tienelle scrying had snatched back in fragments unfolded now in entirety. The scrub-grown hillside seamed with weather-stripped gullies blurred out of vision as mage-sight unveiled another place. . . .

. . . of torn earthworks and slaughtered bodies, where Pesquil's advance troop of headhunters tracked prints across blood-rinsed earth. In swift, efficient silence they exchanged swords for daggers and cut scalps to claim bounty for their kills.

The corpses raised by the hair for the knife cut were small, the faces smudged in leaf mold and gore unlined by life and years. . . .

Boys, Arithon realized with a choke that all but stopped his heart. He tripped hard on a stone, felt the tug of Jieret's grip save his balance. Present awareness slapped back, along with anguished recognition of total helplessness. The deed was done, the sons of Deshir dead. All hacked and disfigured were the little ones Caolle had insisted be sent to dispatch the enemy wounded because men for that task could ill be spared—amid whose company Jieret would have been, if not for a blood pact of friendship.

"Jieret, they're gone," Arithon gasped out in defeat. "We're too late."

But Jieret's mute and furious head shake forced back unwanted recollection that the appalling scene by the riverside had failed to include the fated girl. At what point does the strong mind falter? Arithon wondered in a cascade of renewed despair. The feud between Karthan and Amroth had inspired atrocities enough to wring from him all tolerance for suffering. Between townborn and clan, the hatred ran more poisonous still.

Ground creepers tore at his footfalls as he fought toward the crest of the ridge. At his side, Jieret was laboring, his eyes stretched sightless and wide, as if he viewed vistas of horrors but lacked any breath to cry protest.

At what point should the strong heart shy off and preserve itself from wanton self-destruction? To go on was to risk every shred of integrity to the mad drives of Desh-thiere's curse. Arithon swore in fierce anguish. He tightened grip on his sword, braced tired nerves, and cast off the protective barriers that confined his sight to Jieret's dream. Every prudent precaution he had taken was tossed away as he reached out directly with his mage-sight.

Disciplined, efficient, too well versed in the ways of forest clansmen to suffer delay or needless noise, Pesquil rattled off orders. His men crammed dripping trophies in their game bags. Nearby, wiping a sword whose blade bore chased patterns of reversed runes, a strong, straight man in a ruined surcoat clenched his jaw against the hurt of cracked bones.

Framed in that place, over the bodies of slain children, *that man's* lone figure imprinted stark as flame against a scorch mark, and wakened the pattern of Desh-thiere's curse. Backlit by a slanted shaft of sunlight, the soft, feathered greenery of pine boughs knit a backdrop for disordered blond hair and a regal profile grazed and scratched, but unmarred in expression by any furrow of remorse. . . .

Arithon gasped as if hit. His stride faltered despite Jieret's efforts, shouting and tugging, to urge him on. He heard nothing, felt nothing beyond nerves pitched and twisted to a geas-driven impulse to attack.

Vision and reflex merged. Alithiel's blade sang through air. The sour, belling whine as sword steel sheared through sticks and green bracken jolted turned senses back to reason.

Arithon stood, breathing hard, the sweat drenched over him in runnels. He caught one breath, two, the hand gripped white to his sword hilt trembling in waves of reaction. Fingers could be relaxed into stillness. The mind could be forced to shake off madness. Eyes closed, quivering as if racked by a fever, Arithon called every shred of his training to repress the screaming urge to fling aside Jieret and bolt, not to rescue but to kill. Through and through him ran the sick recognition that he had tasted worse than his fears. He had fatally near underestimated the havoc that even indirect scrying on his half-brother could unleash through the core of his being.

Half undone by despair, for there existed no escape from this quandary, he gathered self-command and looked up.

Attending him in staunch readiness were Jieret and eleven clansmen who had without questions left their defense works to support him. Enmeshed as he was in sorry fears and the unmistakable throes of wrecked dignity, their kindness offered temptations a curse-marked spirit could ill afford.

Enraged as a scalded cat by the flaw that twisted through his character, Arithon's first impulse was to let fly with words and send them packing, away from his reach lest he wantonly compromise their safety. Humility stayed him, and grief. If Deshir's wives and daughters were still threatened, these men owned their right to defend them, and he must find courage to see how.

Wordless, he turned his grip on Alithiel and pressed the hilt into Jieret's startled hands. Then he stripped off his sword belt and thrust it toward the nearest of the scouts. "Take this. Bind my ankles. Somebody else, unbend a bowstring and lash my wrists tight behind my back."

The clansman regarded him, stupefied.

"Do it!" Arithon snapped. Salt sweat burned his eyes, or maybe tears. "Dharkaron take you, it's necessary."

The belt buckle swung from his fingers, flaring in bursts of caught sunlight. No one made a move to take its burden.

"Mercy of Ath, tie my hands!" cried their prince, his voice split and baleful with anguish. "I've a scrying to try that's very dangerous, and I can't say what might happen if I'm free." He waited no longer but spun toward Jieret. "I beg you, do as I ask."

"Don't put such a task on a boy!" A blunt, scar-faced man shoved to the fore, prepared in hot outrage to intervene.

Arithon bit back a retort that worse things had been asked and done already. "Loop it tight," he insisted as the man bent and tentatively began to lash his ankles.

"You've gone mad," someone murmured from the sidelines.

Arithon, eyes blazing, said, "Yes."

He had no time to explain. To Jieret, standing braced with the black blade cradled flat across his forearm, the Master said emphatically and calmly, "You're oath-sworn. Now listen to me. I'm going to try sorcery to find out what's amiss on the riverbank. You must keep my sword and hold it ready. If my body is taken by a fit, call my name. If that fails to rouse me, or if any of these restraints breaks away, you must cut me deep enough to bleed."

"But why?" a man pealed in protest.

Arithon's attention never shifted from the child.

Under that sharpened scrutiny, Jieret s'Valerient did not waver. The steel rings sewn to his boy's brigandine flashed in time to rapid breaths, and his eyes, gray hazel, never turned. Of them all, only he and Arithon yet knew of the butchery that drenched the moss by Tal Quorin. Between blood-pacted prince and young protégé an understanding passed, that word of the atrocity must be kept from the men. The small, square chin, so like Steiven's, and the dark red hair that was Dania's caused Arithon a spasm of grief.

"Will you trust me?" he asked. Man to boy, he made no effort to hide his misgiving. "For your family's sake, can you do this?"

Jieret answered him, faintly. "I'll try."

For a second the severely steep planes of the s'Ffalenn face eased; straight lips bent almost to a smile. Then Arithon crossed his wrists behind his back and waited in stiff impatience while a clan archer diffidently tied him. "For your very lives," he finished in soft threat. "Don't any of you change my instructions."

The bowstring was knotted tight and tested. Far off, a wood thrush trilled a liquid cascade of arpeggios. The breeze fanned trembling through fern and birch and pale elder, and the smell of pine mulch and soil filled the senses like a mother's embrace. Torn by the pull of such comforts, Arithon squeezed his eyes closed. He let go into trance in skittish haste, lest nerves and strength both forsake him. The men close-gathered around him ceased to matter, nor did he feel the touch and slide of light-patterned leaves that raked his body as his knees loosened and gave way. He slipped unceremoniously to the ground, conscious only of another place. . . .

Buried from sight behind a thicket of fir, someone gave a retching cough. Bent over the corpse of a boy with talisman thongs braided at his neck, Pesquil jerked erect and froze listening. Around him, spattered like reivers in a stockyard, his jubilant headhunters did likewise. The sound did not repeat itself. Never patient with waiting, and apprehensive of being spotted by an unseen patrol of Steiven's scouts, Pesquil deployed his lieutenants to secure the area and beat the brush.

Before the ring closed, a child bolted into the open, running hard. This one carried no dagger. In place of a leather jacket sewn with rings or bone discs, this youngster wore a tunic smutched with river mud and briars. Barely seven years of age, he ran in gasping panic away from the headhunters with their terrible crimsoned swords. A man-sized fox cap offered a fleeting glimpse of cinnamon as it bobbed from mottled light to forest gloom.

"Give chase," Pesquil clipped out. His teeth flashed in a smile that became a low whistle as the new quarry ducked a trailing vine.

The fur hat was snatched off to free a rippling banner of dark hair.

"Daelion's Wheel," exclaimed Lysaer. "That's a girl!"

"Obviously." Pesquil hefted his sword. "Come on. A scalp isn't valued by sex, and if I'm right, we're about to find the camp Gnudsog died for."

"She shouldn't be here, then?" Lysaer braced his bandaged forearm against his side in readiness to run. "Not even as some sort of lookout?"

"She probably tagged after her brother." Fired to haste, an unholy spark behind his humor, Pesquil gave the prince a pock-flecked leer. "Are you going to just talk or join the fun?"

Lysaer clamped his jaw against the ache of ribs and collarbone and grimly matched pace with the headhunters.

The scrying shattered.

A scream of crazed frustration ripped from Arithon's throat. Pain lanced his shoulder, followed by a coruscation of white light. A ringing, pure chord of harmony exploded bleak insanity with a shock that sieved through his bones. He fell back, weeping and panting, unprepared for tearing heartbreak as the thundering brilliance of Paravian spell-craft ebbed away, leaving him hollow and desolate.

The earth felt fragile underneath him as he opened his eyes to the fast-fading glimmer of the star-spell inlaid in the blade of his own weapon. Alithiel was poised above him like a bar of smoked glass, edged in his own bright blood. Jieret held the grip in shaking fingers, tears tracked in streaks across his cheeks.

"It's all right." Aghast to find his larynx torn raw, Arithon need not meet the scouts' embarrassed faces to derive that he had howled like an animal. He could tell by the burn of fresh abrasions that he had flipped and wrenched against his bonds. And nothing was right, nothing at all. The wasted lives by Tal Quorin were only the prelude to disaster. In this, his second encounter with Lysaer by scrying, only his sword's arcane defenses had arrested his reaction to Desh-thiere's curse. For the moment he commanded his wits. As long as he kept his distance and strictly eschewed the use of mage-sense, he could hold against the urge that coursed through him, driving, needling, hounding him to rise and to run—to find his half-brother and call challenge and fight until one or both of them lay dead.

Jieret had quieted. Silent, straight, he regarded his sovereign prince in haunted trust, while a contrite scout knelt to lend assistance. The movement as Arithon was helped to sit pulled at his shoulder, but the scratch was neat and shallow, a credit to the boy's determination.

"The bonds can be loosened," Arithon said gently. He added instructions to be sent at speed to Caolle, and tried not to let them see it mattered, that nobody cared to meet his eyes.

"Your hands, they're ripped bloody," said the man who attended his wrists. "At least, these scars." He faltered, then burst out, "You've done scryings like this one before?"

The note of awed epiphany in his voice incensed Arithon to revulsion. "Ath, no!" He did not qualify, but kicked the loosened belt from his ankles, surged to his feet, and took back the burden of his sword.

"Run," he snapped, and then did so, fighting off acid futility. They were too far from the grotto where Deshir's girls and women were hidden, too hopelessly distant to bring reprieve. But knowing Pesquil's headhunters were hot in pursuit of Fethgurn's daughter, he had to make the attempt; for when Deshir's clansmen discovered the extent of their losses, the grief of husbands, kin, and fathers would for a surety touch off another bloodbath.

Last Quarry

The girl flushed by Pesquil's headhunters led them on an arduous chase upstream. Above the initial site of the ambush, the valley narrowed. Tal Quorin's bed sliced Strakewood in a steep-walled ravine, while springs that fed white-water currents splashed in plumed falls from high gullies. Here the late afternoon shadows slanted through serried banks of broken, sunlit rock.

Pesquil disliked any country where the least chance noise would reverberate to a dance of wild echoes. Crannies between buttressed cliffs devolved into narrow, crooked grottos, any of which might contain a hidden camp. To search each one with a strike party would be fool's play.

"Noise and numbers would wreck all our chance of surprise," he complained in dry annoyance to Lysaer. "Clansfolk holed up in this place won't be waiting about cowering like mice."

While Pesquil debated over a dozen nooks where clan sentries could be posted, Lysaer fought drifting concentration. He felt faint. His bruises had settled into stiffness that cased the steady ache of cracked bones. The strapping on his wrist showed a damp patch of red, and he wondered how much blood he had lost. The ferocity had not blunted from his anger, quite the contrary; but his reserves were worn away and temper by itself was no longer enough to sustain him.

Resolved on his course of precautions, Pesquil prepared for the moment when the fleeing girl crossed back into open ground and brought his best man with a crossbow to the fore.

"Shoot clean," he whispered softly. "I want her to seem like she tripped."

The marksman set his quarrel with a steadiness Lysaer could only envy, aimed his weapon, and lovingly squeezed the trigger.

The click and hiss of the bow's release blended with the susuration of tumbling water.

Upslope, the running child missed stride.

"Perfect shot!" Pesquil said.

The bolt had struck her lower back in the soft flesh between ribs and hip. Her outcry rang and rebounded, multiplied from rock to rock as she folded to her knees. A dragged escort of small stones marked her fall in flat arcs and dust, swept off in the leaping rush of rapids. But the girl snagged on an outcrop at the water's edge and hung there, one limp arm swinging.

From the vantage in the thickets, her dark hair could be discerned, fanned back from her face with the trailed ends sleeked by the spray.

"Damn!" Pesquil wiped sweat from his cheeks, then rubbed his palms on his leathers. "Bad luck. If she'd hit the river, they might not suspect an assassin."

Lysaer s'Ilessid stifled any flicker of revulsion. As strategy, Pesquil's move was unassailable; nor had his effort been wasted. High in the rocks, a leather-clad woman left cover to rescue what looked from above to be the wounded victim of a misstep.

Poised in tense stillness the more explosive for the fact he dared not fidget, Pesquil spent a moment in furious thought. He waited until the clan scout negotiated the most precarious segment of her descent, then touched his marksman on the wrist. "Again," he whispered. "Messier this time. Have this one die hollering."

The bowman muffled the ratchet of his weapon under a borrowed surcoat and wound it cocked. Smooth-faced and taciturn in concentration, he selected and slicked the feathers of another bolt. Weapon raised, he nervelessly fired again.

The clan woman windmilled into space, gut-struck and screaming in agony.

"Move!" Pesquil signaled his men. "Hurry, fan out, and keep close watch on the rocks." Beside him, the young marksman readied another quarrel, his instruction to dispatch the woman fast if her howls showed any sign of coherency.

Sweated and chafed under the quilted gambeson rucked in wet wads beneath his mail, Lysaer gritted his teeth and refrained from comment. Revulsion did not excuse responsibility. Toward his sworn purpose of destroying Arithon s'Ffalenn, he had sanctioned Pesquil's foray against the clansfolk. No matter how unpleasant, duty demanded that he see the action through.

Again the crossbowman loosed his trigger. Quiet restored, the hiss and splash of the river once more swirled over sinkholes and rocks. Pesquil picked a green stick while reports from his scouts were relayed in.

Movement had been sighted three different places along the rocks. Crouched beneath an undercut bank whose tree trunks angled drunken reflections on broken waters, and chewing a scraping of sour bark, Pesquil sent stalkers to reconnoiter. Based on their findings, he used his stripped twig to sketch a crude map between his knees. "Here's how we'll deploy." The instructions he gave his lieutenants erased the last doubt he may have earned his command through any nicety of Etarran politics.

At a speed Lysaer found inconceivable, headhunter parties were called up from downriver and dispatched in wide, covert patterns that lined the canyon rims with crossbowmen. Pesquil's design unfolded like well-oiled clockworks: the frontal attack designed to distract; the word at first engagement that the grottos held only female defenders and small children; then Pesquil's smirking comment to Lysaer before they crossed the river on strung ropes. "Man, don't expect an easy victory. Clan bitches fight like she-devils."

On the far bank, the men split into teams to scale the rocks. In deference to Lysaer's strapped arm, Pesquil dispatched scouts to find him an easier route. Pain and exhaustion by now had outstripped the first numb shock of injury. Lysaer moved with gritted jaw, his skin gray. He would not let the men ease the pace. Slipping, sliding, grunting, he labored upslope, past stunted cherry trees with their wild fruits green on the stem; over weather-split granite and twisted brush, and washed-out gulches where the gravel turned under his boots and the jar of every wrong step made his breath jerk and spasm in gasps. The headhunters who accompanied him as escort might have disdained their assignment at first, but when at last they reached the ridge top and rejoined their commander, Lysaer's determination had earned their guarded respect.

By then, action in the steep-sided glen was nearly wrapped up, the initial attack supported from behind by the stationed crossbowmen, who now cast about for the last living targets trapped against the walls of the canyon. Down through the fronds of ferns and cross-laced trailers of hanging ivy, Lysaer saw the sprawled bodies, bloody and hacked beyond anything recognizably female, or else nearly unmarked except for feathered bolts that left flowering stains on the backs of deerskin jerkins. Half sick from his hurts, too spent for strong emotion, the prince felt wretched and maudlin. For the first time in his life he understood his royal father, who also had been provoked to require annihilating attacks on villages allied to the s'Ffalenn. That such forays had mostly come to nothing drove his sire to lifelong frustration. Lysaer, who in distant lands and exile had not failed, looked upon his dead with flat eyes and tried not to fret whether any of the corpses had been pregnant.

A headhunter lieutenant touched his shoulder. "Come. The able-bodied fighters are beaten down and our scouts say the tents are surrounded."

They would fire the hides, Lysaer gathered. He braced his sore side and stiffly moved on. Of the hike up the canyon rim he remembered little. The lowering sun hurt his eyes and patchy bouts of dizziness made progress difficult.

Pesquil seemed in rare high spirits. He spat his wad of bark and playfully tossed his bone-hilted dagger with its peculiar blade, curved and sharp on both edges. Since the need had passed for surprise and silence, he grew expansive, calling boisterous jokes to his lieutenants.

The men, too, seemed ebullient. Too drained to attend to their talk, Lysaer gave cursory study to the high ground where they stopped. The sun's angle had lowered, throwing the ravine into premature twilight. Under shaded rim walls and deeper cover of palings and thickets clustered the painted hide walls of the clan tents. Faintly, from the inside, came the wailing cry of an infant, swiftly muffled.

Lysaer found a broad old maple and rested against the trunk while the men whistled and laughed and kindled fires. Too battered to join the activity, he stayed, while the arrows were wrapped, and the bows strung, and the wool tips set soaking in oil.

"All right." Hands on hips, his lantern jaw out-thrust in broken profile against the shimmers of black smoke on the wind, Pesquil delivered his order. "Fire them out."

Lots were drawn. The losers, grumbling, chose bows. Fighting an insidious detachment that felt like the onset of delirium, Lysaer hardly noticed the arrows crack down until the reek of burning hide wafted out of the ravine. The tents were well aflame. Heat beat in waves from the fissure. Orange light played across the rocks, and above the grotto, green leaves began to shrivel and wilt. Lysaer closed his eyes against the glare, vaguely aware of screaming. The archers now fired to kill infants, and the cries of bereaved mothers beat and shrilled against his ears.

Pesquil's tart sarcasm punched through. "You seem just a touch overcome."

Lysaer pushed straight and forced his eyes back to clear focus. In fact, there was a lot of screaming, in pitch and timbre quite different than hand-to-hand battle had caused earlier; neither were these the uncomprehending cries of newborns. Sickness fled before anger.

"You aren't killing them cleanly," Lysaer accused. He shoved hard away from the tree.

"Killing them?" Pesquil grinned, startled to savage delight. "That wasn't quite the idea. Not for the pretty women, anyway. My men accomplished what Etarra's garrison couldn't. Do you think they haven't earned their bit of sport?"

Lysaer pushed past toward the rim rocks. The sound of a slap ricocheted up from the canyon. A man guffawed while a woman's voice wept obscenities.

"Better gag her," someone advised in cheerful encouragement. "She'd gnaw your face off for sheer spite."

A glance was enough. Lysaer wheeled back, white to the lips, and possessed by a frightening control. Coldly, clearly, he said, "Call them off."

Pesquil stood and stroked his crescent knife. "In due time, Prince. Not to worry. My men aren't picked for sentiment. They can kill well enough when their pleasure's met. We won't be bringing home any doxies."

More laughter erupted, and sobbing cries that seemed barely more than a child's. Lysaer never flicked a muscle. "Call your men back." He took a fast breath. "Or I will."

"Such scruple!" Pesquil crooned. Then, as Lysaer broke from stillness, the captain's mockery fled and his manner abruptly went stony. "Man, man, you're serious." He reached out in swift purpose and snatched back the shoulder tightly strapped under wrappings the exact instant Lysaer called out.

Bone grated under his fingers. Lysaer doubled with a gasp, his eyes wide black with pain and fury.

"My men wouldn't take your command," Pesquil warned. The crescent knife remained in his right fist, its angle now openly threatening. "Prince."

Lysaer chopped with his good arm and broke the headhunter captain's hold. The blade at his midriff as well had been air for all the attention he spared it. *"Call them off!"*

"Ath, you soft fool." As if he reasoned with an idiot, Pesquil said, "You want the barbarian clans dead, do you not? And the neck of one black-handed sorcerer? Well, leave my men to their business! If they don't force the girls and make plenty of noise, how *else* d'you think we're going to draw their eight hundred odd fathers and brothers out of cover and into reach of our weapons?"

"You've done this before," Lysaer gritted, wrenched by the spasm of abused muscles.

"Oh, many times. Though I admit, never in quite such choice quantity." The sneer was back. Touched with sweat, Pesquil's pockmarks glistened orange. On the floor of the ravine, the tents threw up shimmering curtains of flame. Nothing alive remained inside their cover. Beyond the fires fringing the guy ropes, outside a circle of red-soaked and motionless bundles, men whooped and tore buckskins with abandon. Pesquil's gaze lowered to his knife, still pointed at the prince. "It's a time-proven tactic, *Your Grace.*"

Lysaer straightened, breathing hard. Sunlight through the tree crowns played over his gold head, and a breeze-flickered mote touched his grazed cheek to gilt. The mauling he had taken had spoiled his elegance. Nothing distinguished remained about his ripped surcoat and mud-crusted mail, or the bruises glazed with sweat that darkened neck and chin and temple. Yet a forceful sense of majesty clothed him all the same, that made even Pesquil reassess.

The s'Ilessid prince laid no hand on his sword in dispute. He weighed his case and made judgment in the solitary arrogance of a king. Then he turned his back on the silver crescent blade and called upon his birth-born gift of light.

His bolt sheared the grotto like bladed lightning and slammed in bursting brilliance through the charred and blackened leather of the tents. Flash fire exploded. Sparks flew and a barrage of deep-throated thunder smote the air. Where hides had flamed, nothing burned any longer. If no one had been harmed by the blast, still the ground showed a black, seared circle, while toppled king posts flaked with ash trailed sullen smoke over the previously broken bodies of little children.

From the grotto, the screaming had ended. Men in the act of lust felt engorged flesh shrivel from the heat of ravished girls, while in stunned terror they scrambled back and took stock of wisped hair and blisters and outer clothing lightly singed upon their bodies.

Into stupefied stillness, across someone's low whimpers of fear, Lysaer delivered crisp orders. "Townsmen! Cover your nakedness and stand aside. Let any who are clad form a shield ring and herd every girl and woman inside. Let none of your company handle them except as necessary. For peril of your lives, do as I say."

"You can't let them go," Pesquil protested. A tremor threaded his voice, and all his sour mockery had vanished.

Lysaer looked at him. "No." As devoid of contempt as Dharkaron Avenger, he added, "But I will end them cleanly."

"To what purpose, Your Grace?" Stubborn in recovery, Pesquil flung his knife hilt deep into the dirt. "We've clan menfolk still left to deal with."

"They'll come." Lysaer's dispassionate regard flicked back to the grotto and stayed there as the half-stripped girls and women were shoved tightly into one group. "I'll draw in Steiven's barbarians. When I do, be sure of this, the s'Ffalenn bastard with his shadows will be unable not to come with them."

Three Valleys

Streaming sweat from an arduous sprint, the runner sent from the west valley arrives at the breastworks where Caolle and the bulk of Deshir's clansmen fight unassisted by sorceries or flooded rivers against Etarra's right-flanking division, who outnumber them three to one. "Tell Lord Steiven," he cries, gasping, "I've come from our liege. Arithon said you would know what he meant, that the disaster he foresaw has not been stopped. . . ."

Plunging through woods toward the grotto where the women and young hide for safety, Arithon, Jieret, and eleven clansmen hear screams and male shouting cut off as a burst of light shears through the trees; lost in a ground-shaking report of fell thunder is Arithon's abject denial, *"Lysaer, oh Ath, Lysaer, no!"*

In the vale to the west of Tal Quorin, a shadow-wrought barrier ward shatters and lifts, which leaves half a company of Etarra's beleaguered garrison fighting mad and unimpeded to regroup and engage the handful of clan enemies who no longer can shelter behind sorceries to inflict damages and death with impunity. . . .

XVIII. Culmination

Thunder cracked the air to whirlwinds as light bolts ripped the grotto in sheets that immolated trees to flayed skeletons. On protected ground some distance from the rim rocks, checked by flares etched like lightning through gaps in forest greenery, Arithon caught the back of Jieret's brigandine. In a despair too horror-struck for expression, he yanked the boy cold from his run and bundled him into an embrace. Around their locked forms the coruscation flared and died. Gusts spent themselves to a fall of unmoored leaves, while echoes raged on in vibrations that slapped and slammed through Tal Quorin's chain of ravines. Arithon pressed his cheek to red hair, while under his tight hands the orphan he had sworn blood pact to protect convulsed into sobs against his shoulder.

As clansmen they had outstripped in their rush caught back up, nothing could be done except end their hope quickly. "It's over. We're too late. Stay here."

The reverberations from the blast rumbled and faded into quiet. Arithon stared unseeing as three older men caught back a teenager whose berserk rage impelled him to plunge ahead toward the grotto regardless.

Held arm-locked and struggling, the young scout pealed in wild protest to his prince. "They can't all be killed, some were sword-trained."

Arithon, icy, cut him off. "They are dead, *every one*. You can't help them."

No one could; the brutality of Jieret's vision had been graphic, of bodies tossed and charred, flash-burned in an instant to flaked carbon and bones crisped beyond all recognition. To the scout still driven to argue, Arithon said baldly, "It's your clansmen we'll have to save now."

Against him, Jieret moved impatiently. "Our liege speaks truth." Though muffled by the cloth of his prince's sleeve, the boy's dull pronouncement was still clear enough to be heard. "I had Sight. None in the grotto survived."

The scout subsided to stunned quiet, and guarded companions let him go. In response to Jieret's push, Arithon also loosened his arms. He cupped the boy's chin in the hand not burdened by Alithiel and gave him a searching study.

Jieret *had* seen, in merciless, involuntary prescience; three sisters burned, and one forced, and a mother lying bloody in dead leaves. The dream's memory stamped his child's face with a hardness that might not, now, ever leave him.

"I would have spared you if I could," Arithon said in a voice so racked not a man in the company overheard him.

Jieret looked up into green eyes that held no barriers against him. Offered depths and mysteries whose difficulties were beyond him, he could answer just one shared pain. "My liege lord, behold, you have done so."

Arithon's touch jerked away. "Ath," he said on a strangled note of pure rage. "Just don't let me close with my half-brother."

To the scouts who saw only rebuff, uncomprehending in scope and viciousness just how far Desh-thiere's curse might turn him, the Master of Shadows said plainly, "Run. Back downstream and find Caolle. Keep the men out of the canyons."

"I'll go." The younger scout pushed forward, desperate to distance grief with action. "On the way I can recall the boys."

Jieret made a sound of protest; pressed past tact, Arithon shook his head. "Forget them. Just go straight to your captain."

"*Forget them!*" Raw with emotion, the scout rushed him. "What are you saying?"

"That they're beyond help." Not a quiver of reflex changed Arithon's stance. Weariness tautened his face, and he seemed not to care whether or not he was assaulted. He said, "I'm sorry. Just go now and stop thinking."

The scout drew up short of striking him because Jieret interposed himself between. Shamed by the boy's stiff loyalty, and by the disbelief that paralyzed his fellows, he regarded his prince, who had drawn, as he warned, the might of Etarra to the clans. "Sorry! Sorry isn't enough." He spun away and blindly sprinted.

"Don't mind him." White-haired and scarred to stoic toughness, the scout Madreigh offered brusque sympathy. "That boy's not bad-hearted, only sore. Next month he was to marry." The others were content to leave him as spokesman as he tactfully fingered his sword edge. "We should send another runner after Steiven?"

Arithon moved not at all, but only closed tortured eyes.

"Ath!" said Madreigh. "Forget I ever asked." Then, in a queer catch of breath, he caught Arithon's wrist and clamped down. "Trouble's here."

A metallic click cut the quiet. The scout just sent off reached a distance of fifty paces, then pitched in a spinning fall, a crossbow bolt through his neck.

Arithon broke free and flung Jieret violently behind him. "Boy, stay out of this. As your sovereign, I command you." His sword whistled up to guard point while he backed behind the thickest tree to hand, an old beech raked rough where bucks had shed their summer velvet. He pinned Steiven's heir with his body as shield, while the clan scouts fell in around him to enclose the boy.

Their rush to reach the beleaguered women could have drawn them to spring the perfect trap. Hidden troops could lie anywhere in ambush. The crossbows were their greatest liability, shadows their surest defense. But Arithon dared not try his gift openly lest he pinpoint his presence to Lysaer, and invite an uncontrolled confrontation with the compulsions of Desh-thiere's curse.

Three clansmen still armed with recurves and full quivers began to climb the tree to snipe for the crossbowman. Arithon gave the shortest one a boost. Fast and furiously thinking, he said, "They have quarrels, why wait? Why don't they drop us where we stand?"

"They're bounty men." Madreigh showed a grim flash of teeth. "Arrow kills make fights over scalp claims."

Quite probably the headhunters' best marksmen would still be stationed on the rim rocks, or deep in the chasms of the grotto, where orders would shortly recall them.

"The bolt had red fletching," Jieret added.

"It's Pesquil's league that's against us," another scout picked up in explanation. "We'll be surrounded already. They'll attack us with numbers, hand to hand." He jerked his stubbled chin toward the exquisite weapon held steady in his liege lord's grip. "I hope you're good with that."

"We'll know in a moment." Arithon withheld encouragement that his sorceries might offer them salvation. Any ward against combined assailants required time and concentration to arrange. No moment was given for response. From the glen that led toward the rim rocks, shadows flitted, and occasional chance gleams of metal. These fits and starts of movement resolved into a wave of charging foes. The instant before they closed, Arithon noticed worse: shouts, then the distant clash of steel as a skirmish broke out in the river gully farther downstream.

"Caolle's men?" Alarmed, Madreigh added, "Ath, what could press them to strike openly? Etarra's garrison's still behind them. They'll be engaged on two fronts and torn apart."

Inarguable fact, as Arithon knew. But even Caolle's blunt savvy could hardly stay fathers just come from discovery of the scalped and slaughtered bodies of their sons; clansmen who tracked the reivers upstream to find headhunters awaiting them in force, and who attacked without the knowledge that their families in the grotto were past saving.

"If you pray, beg Steiven's division won't be with them," Arithon said.

Then the enemy was upon them. A rough face, a sword, and a fouled set of gauntlets absorbed all of Arithon's attention. Alithiel whined once, twice, in flurried parries. His opponent was large and heavy-handed. Arithon lunged, then blocked another thrust. His riposte was controlled, an understated springboard for the feint which followed. A disengage on the next thrust finished the attacker. Arithon yanked Alithiel clear, sidestepped the headhunter's dying thrash, and in speed that blurred, caught the next man behind in a stop thrust.

Hard-pressed himself, the adjacent clansman turned his shoulder to cover Arithon's extended body through the moment of recovery. "Elwedd's wasted a wager, I see. How'd the Masterbard know you were gifted at blade work?"

"Escape this, and we'll ask him," Arithon said.

Though joyless, the scout's grin gave endorsement that his liege was capable enough to be entrusted with full share of Jieret's defense.

Which fine point would shortly mean nothing, with the headhunters too thick to beat off and more of them coming by the second. Arithon saw this. Braced against the tree, forced to close quarters, his style was cramped. Crushed moss and roots hampered footwork, and fallen enemies were adding to the hazard. The archers up the tree were less encumbered, but one of them already dangled, head down and dead in the branches. The headhunter crossbowman was still busy. Arithon could not see past the heave of the fighting to approximate his location. Another bolt whapped through green leaves and torn shreds of foliage spiraled down.

Inevitably more crossbowmen must arrive, and Caolle's men could hardly drive a foray through to rescue Steiven's heir since they could not know he was pinned down. Arithon beat aside a blade that thrust at him and fought a slipping stance in wet leaves. A friendly arrow from above dispatched the brute in the conical helm who shoved in to grapple, and Arithon escaped with a bruise and a graze. Behind him, Jieret had out his dagger, determined to enter the fray.

"Not now," said Arithon. "Jieret, this isn't your fight."

Three swords came at him. He ducked one, felt the flat of a second jar his cut shoulder, and met the third in a screaming bind. Locked steel to steel with an enemy, exposed on his left side to fate, he saw his choices reduced to the one that, in Karthan, had undone him.

He must use magecraft to kill, or allow Jieret and Steiven's grief-crazed clansmen to die as victims of Desh-thiere's curse.

Arithon turned the wrist above Alithiel's guard, felt his steel catch his opponent's cross guard.

The headhunter anticipated the wrench that would leave him disarmed. A burly man and well trained, he gave with the pressure, then grunted in surprise as Arithon's right-footed kick added force to his counter move and staggered him sideways. He crashed across other headhunters who thrust through an opening no longer opportune. Slashed and half skewered through the side, he went down, two men's steel mired in his fall and a third man bashed off balance into the tight-pressed advance of his fellows.

While the knot in the fighting swirled momentarily backward, Arithon dropped his blade, leaped, and caught a tree branch, then swung hard. His boot lashed another attacker and upended him over the foeman who engaged Madreigh. "Guard Jieret," ordered Arithon. "What needs to be done, I can't accomplish from here."

"You've got spells for a miracle?" grunted the clan scout, his blade busy. He sidestepped into his prince's vacated position, feinted low, and cut. Blood pattered down, filming the leaves, the tree trunk, and Jieret, buffeted and jostled by his defenders as he watched his liege lord hoist himself after the archers who were now, all three, dead of crossbow bolts.

Another quarrel snicked bark by Arithon's head. He ignored it, gave a quick smile downward to Jieret which held more worry than reassurance. A sailor's move and a slither saw him up and then prone on a tree branch.

Below him, Madreigh fought half blind from a gash that trickled blood off his brow and right eye. Arithon drew his belt knife, threw, and took down an opportunist who bent for a low stab at Jieret.

Madreigh finished the action by stomping the fallen man's face. He said, blade harried, "If you know something that'll save us, just do it!"

Already two more clansmen lay dying, with another one wounded about to follow. Torn that such bravery should go wasted, Arithon stilled his nerves and focused his mind to cold purpose. The crossbowman perforce must come first.

He cast about the wood, but could not pinpoint the man's cover. That was bitterest setback, since his purpose must be accomplished without broad-scale use of shadows or any wide sweep of illusion that might terrify an army into rout. Unless he maintained his anonymity among the clans, everything that mattered would go for naught.

Amid a battle that assaulted concentration, Arithon distanced his senses, walled off awareness of everything outside a discrete sphere of air that immediately surrounded his person. The ward snare he shaped was risky and difficult, an amalgamation of illicit magelore and inspiration he would on no account have attempted to save himself; nor had he to spare his own father.

But to Deshir's clansmen, he was oath-bound. Steiven's people would never have faced annihilation if not for his tie to Rathain.

The forces he tapped were forbidden by any right-thinking mage. The tiniest miscalculation, just one slipped step, and the vortex he fashioned could rend himself, the tree, and the last of Jieret's defenders. Arithon pitched the far fringes of his knowledge against dependency that with his person offered as target, the town bowman would shoot to kill. The attention must be poised like strung wire; he must not feel his cut shoulder, must not rouse at the choke of dying men, or even spare thought to question whether his clansmen might already lie slain. Ringed in perilous energies, Arithon touched the air, *became* the air, as one with its currents and small breezes that skeined through uncounted spaded leaves.

Air did not feel death; it registered screams only as rhythms, intricately concentric as ring ripples spread through a pool. There was peace, and the terrible beauty of Ath's order, until a tip of turbulence bored through, swift and barbed for death as only man-made ingenuity could contrive.

Arithon closed the net of a ward just finished but not yet tested for weaknesses. Too fast for care, too late for regrets, too utterly final to abort, the headhunter's quarrel whistled in.

A small thing, the dart, composed of a hand span of wood and steel, wound string, glue, and dyed feathers; but a shaft notched and barbed that sped with a force to pierce mail. Each particle of its substance had Name, each grain of its mass an energy signature for which Arithon had subverted Ath's order and patterned a banespell.

By nature, any snare of unbinding held a lawless compulsion to annihilate. Counter to the Major Balance and in parallel with chaos, frail strictures bent to harness the ungovernable were wont to spin dangerously awry.

In raw fact, Arithon's effort was only plausible though a tangle of tricks and paradox, a loophole in the world's knit that hinged on a theoretical blend of fine points: that the object to be overmastered was itself made for death, and that its uninterrupted natural action must set forfeit the conjurer's life.

Everything, *everything*, depended upon the headhunter crossbow-man having scored a lethal hit.

And if the man was such a marksman, and his aim did not drift, and the baneward successfully intercepted his bolt before the instant it broached living flesh, the result offered perilous instability. The safeguards contrived to limit the unbinding's ill effects were by no means infallibly sure.

Doubts were all Arithon had, and stark fear, when the quarrel hissed into his defenses.

To unmake any particle of Ath's Creation came at hideous cost. Arithon shuddered, then blocked a scream with his knuckles as the mote he had captured exploded in a battering burst. Tied to his conjury, his body convulsed in a spasm that seemed to crush out his marrow as law and matter unraveled in a whistling rush of wild energies. Arithon felt the nexus of his uncreation graze his protections, burning for entry to twist, tear, and unravel his whole flesh as well as any other thing that lay within range of its reach. Inflamed as though he noosed magma, he flung out the shielding second stage of his counterspell.

He deflected his ugly package of wrecked order through air, back along the disturbed eddies traced by the quarrel's first flight path, then trailed with a stop ward set to the resonance of wrought steel.

A hiss arced through space above the skirmishers that partnered no physical projectile. Arithon opened his eyes, running sweat and winded as if he had been whip-struck. With every nerve screaming, he waited.

Until, behind a thin screen of alder, the crossbow exploded in the hands of its wielder.

Splinters and wound wire and metal burst like shrapnel and flayed the headhunter's face. He dropped, choking, holes torn through his chest and his abdomen, and blood spattered like thrown ink across the bleached trees. The only bit of his weapon not fragmented was the trigger latch, the first steel to contact the spell and engage it limited safe-ward.

That stricture at least had worked and cancelled the unholy destruction. Arithon shivered in relief. Let there be no more archers among the enemy, he hoped, gasping as he clung to the tree branch. If there were, then Deshir's clans were finished. He lacked stomach to repeat those defenses. Torn by nerve-sick reaction, he regretted the victim, whose death was not needed but who could not in the pinch of the moment be distanced from the means that destroyed his weapon.

Below the beech tree, fighting still raged. Casualties mounted ferociously. Only five clansmen remained standing. Madreigh battled on one knee, his right arm useless and his blade in his left hand, parrying. Jieret had taken up Alithiel in braced readiness for the moment when his last adult defenders should be cut down.

Again, Arithon stamped back the temptation to grasp at the easiest expedient. Whoever he might spare by using shadow, he could later kill without compunction in the grip of Desh-thiere's curse. No risk was worth the chance he might draw Lysaer. Hedged by untenable choices, Arithon recouped a concentration that felt as if sloshed through a sieve. Need drove him again to abjure safe limits and to further violations of integrity that were going to cost bitterly later.

He must not think of that. Now all that mattered was the preservation of Jieret's life, and after him, any other clansman who could be saved.

Clammy with chills, hollowed by weakness that sapped like the aftermath of fever, Arithon rested his cheek on the tree limb. He closed his eyes, inhaled the peppery scent of damp bark, and let that fuse with his being. He quieted. His clasped hands settled and sensitized to the languorous flow of sap. His thoughts became the whisper of leaves, the sun-lit flight of pollinating bees, the unfurling of green shoots that thickened with each season's turn into stately crown and mighty wood branches. His consciousness spiraled down to encompass the thick black depths of earth, the firm anchored network of taproots.

Through the irreproachable pith of the living tree, Arithon twined his spell. Like the buds, the leaves, the branches, all groping outward for new growth, he spun the fine tendrils of his wards away from the trunk, that any defender who used its bulk to shield his back would be spared. But any attacker facing inward would find his eyes drawn and subtly captured, while his thoughts slowed to syrup, then to the languid drip of sap.

A human mind ensnared in the consciousness of a tree will sleep, immersed in slow dreams that measure time in stately rhythms, of clean sun and silvered snow and seasons that slide one into another like the rain-kissed drift of autumn leaves.

Which meant, Arithon knew, that any Deshan still standing' would slaughter his victims in the half second their reflexes dragged and the hand on driving blade faltered. Unlike the Etarrans entrapped by the shadow maze in the adjacent valley, these townsmen were given no reprieve. Mastery of their fate was reft from them, with no offered moment of free will in which they could choose to turn aside.

Against a powerful temptation to shelter with them in sun-washed oblivion, Arithon disentwined his consciousness from the tree's green awareness. He opened his eyes too soon. The part of him still paired to heart sap and earth peace ripped away into noise and the blood reek of animal carnage. Below him, the beech roots were mulched over with dead men, their wide-open eyes still dreaming, imprinted with sky-caught reflections of bark and boughs and leaves.

Arithon retched, then forced a tight grip on raw nerves. He clasped the branch in sweated hands and through guilt and revulsion, took charge of the fruits of his conjury.

Madreigh was down and wounded, Jieret at his shoulder with Alithiel bloodied in his hand. Two clansmen, both injured, were still on their feet, while outside the canopy of the beech tree, enemies crumpled to their knees, lost to mind and awareness. Beyond these, more headhunters checked in fear of the bane that had invisibly struck down their fellows. Outrage would soon overcome their apprehension and drive them to vigorous retaliation.

"Don't face inward, don't look at the tree," Arithon instructed the surviving clansmen. He then asked numb limbs to move, and proved shaking hands could still grip. Somehow he swung to the ground. Hands tried to steady him as he swayed. He pushed them impatiently away. "Don't trust what you're going to see. The reinforcements will all be mine." He caught his sticky blade from Jieret's grasp. "Just run, and don't for any reason turn back." To the boy's alarmed look, he added quickly, "I'll be with you. Go."

He punctuated his instruction with a light slap on Jieret's shoulder. Then, leaning on Alithiel to keep balanced, he knelt, bent his head, and spun illusion.

Even depleted as he was, his inborn gift would always answer. Now he was alone and the risks were to himself, he dared risk shadow in limited counter measure. Darkness flowed freely to his use as water might beat from a cataract. And as he had done another night in Steiven's supply tent, he bent conjury into the shape and form of warriors.

They emerged from brush and thicket with weapons gleaming and bows nocked with broadheads in their hands. If their faces lacked character, if their step was inhumanly silent, discrepancy was covered by the scream and clash of fighting that echoed from the grottoes by Tal Quorin. Since the appearance of reinforcing clansmen befitted a strategy to cover the flight of three fugitives, any headhunters not turned by the sleep snare were scarcely minded to pause in analytical study. Caught inside arrow range when Arithon's shadow men knelt and pulled recurves, most wisely Pesquil's men who still had wits and footing broke and dived under cover.

Their panicked haste might have amused had the arrows when they arced not been made up of fancy and desperation.

Arithon stirred, looked up, and tried to muster resource to rise and continue after Jieret. He managed neither. His miscalculation was not surprising after the strictures he had broken. Before the foot and the knee that failed his will lay Madreigh, a tear in his chest that welled scarlet over his buckskins at each gasp.

"Ath," Arithon said. He sat. Stupid with weakness, he met the eyes of the man, which stayed lucid through a suffering that should have eclipsed recognition.

"My liege." Madreigh drew a scraping breath. "Go on. After the boy. You're oath-bound."

A scathing truth, one Arithon understood he had to answer for. Except he was drained to his dregs from misused expenditure of magecraft. Since he could not immediately master himself, he did as he wished and snatched up Madreigh's wrist. In a whisper that seemed the utterance of a ghost he said, "I also took oath for Rathain, and see, you die for it."

Beyond speech, Madreigh looked at him.

Arithon spread the clansman's limp fingers and pressed them, already chilled, against the bole of the beech tree. He closed his own hands overtop. Then in a gesture that lanced blackness and sparks through his mind, he wrenched back the fast-fading glimmer of his spell-craft and let it flow like a mercy stroke over the clansman's consciousness.

Sleep took Madreigh's tortured frame. His face under its grit and gray hair gentled, all sorrows eased into the sun-drenched serenity of ancient trees.

Empty with remorse, Arithon opened his fingers. Half tranced from exhaustion, he regarded his circle of quiet dead, clad in leather and blood, or wearing city broadcloth and chain mail pinched with weed stalks and dirt. The only censure for the mage-trained, he sadly found, was adherence to truth and self-discipline. No mind with vision was exempt; creation and destruction were one thread. One

could not weave with Ath's energies without holding in equal measure the means to unstring and unravel.

The blood had left his head. He understood if he tried to move, he
would only spectacularly fall down. Oblivious to the shouting and
the battering scream of killing steel, he cupped his chin and surrendered to the shudders that racked him. He had acted outside of greed
or self-interest, had to the letter of obligation fulfilled his bound oath
to the Deshans. Duty did not cleanly excuse which lives should be
abandoned to loss or which should be taken to spare others: Steiven's
clansmen, last survivors of savage persecution, or Pesquil's headhunters, still heated from their spree of unlicensed rapine and slaughter.
No answer satisfied. No law insisted that justice stay partnered by
mercy.

The day's transgressions abraded against s'Ffalenn conscience like
the endless pound of sea waves tearing bleak granite into sand.
Through a fog that forgot to track time, Arithon noticed the rhythmic well of fluid from Madreigh's chest had slowed or stopped.
Whether this was death's doing or the endurance of sap laid deep for
long winter, he had no strength to examine.

He managed to recover his sword, and after that, his footing, before the disorientation that distanced him bled away and snapped his
bemused chain of thought. His senses reclaimed the immediate. The
belling clang of battle had now overtaken and surrounded him, and
arrows sleeted past in flat arcs that gouged up trails of rotted leaves.

Not shadows this time. The beech tree was solid at his hip. None
too steady, Arithon backed against it. Though reawakened to his
needs and obligations, his mind stayed bewildered and unruly. Dis-
jointed details skittered across his awareness: that the sun had lowered; that copper leaves in red light trembled as if dipped in blood;
that the brawling and the noise were distracting because they were
caused by fighters, not shadows dressed up as illusion. Clansman and
headhunter and disheveled knots of city garrison were engaged in annihilation as ferocious as a scrap between mastiffs.

Caolle had not sent reinforcements. The clansmen Arithon recognized were Steiven's division, and they battled to a purpose that was
anything else but haphazard. For their wives, their children, for their
sons sadly slaughtered by the riverside, they were vengeance-bent on
killing headhunters.

Though it cost them their last breathing clansmen, Pesquil's
league would not live to leave Strakewood to cash in their loved
ones' scalps for bounties.

Waste upon waste, Arithon thought, brought to sharp focus by anger. As Rathain's sworn sovereign, he would stop them, separate them, ensure that Jieret had a legacy left to grow for.

Careful only not to tread on fallen bodies, Arithon launched himself into the skirmish that ringed the trees, knotting and twisting through undergrowth and hammock, the lightning flicker of sword stroke and mail like thrown silver against falling gloom. He engaged the first headhunter to rush him, inspired beyond weariness by necessity. He fought, parried, killed in rhythmic reflex, all the while searching the melee for sight of just one of Steiven's officers. Given assistance, he held half-formed plans of using magecraft to stage some diversion, that locked combatants might be separated. He would control the berserk clansmen, bully them, or fell them wholesale with sleep spells if he must. Though as his stressed muscles stung with the force of a parry, he recognized the last was pure folly. His earlier unbinding had left damage, and he was lucky to stay on his feet.

"Arithon! My liege!"

The call came from his right, toward the downslope that devolved toward the grottos. The Master of Shadow beat off an attacker and spun. The patter and hiss of sporadic bowfire creased the air and snatched through veilings of low foliage. Through a drift of cut leaves and air dusky with steep shafts of sunlight, Arithon searched but never found who had shouted.

His gaze caught instead on a clustered squad of headhunters led by a pock-scarred man in muddy mail; then another, tall, straight, of elegant carriage in a ripped blue surcoat, gold-blazoned and bright as his hair.

Lysaer.

They saw each other the same instant.

Arithon felt the breath leave his chest as if impelled by a blow. Then Desh-thiere's curse eclipsed reason. He was running, the air at his neck prickling his raised hair like the charge of an incoming storm. Sword upheld, lips peeled back in atavistic hatred, he closed to take his half-brother without heed for what lay between.

A baleful flash brightened the trees. Lysaer, as curse-bound as he, had called on his given gift of light.

Arithon expelled a ragged laugh. They were matched. No bolt, no fire, no conflagration, lay past reach of his shadows to curb. Strakewood could burn or be frozen sere as barren waste, and supporters and armies would be winnowed like chaff in the holocaust. The end would pair Lysaer and himself across the bared length of steel blades, with no living man to intervene.

Lysaer raised his right hand and the headhunters around him fanned out.

Savoring eagerness, Arithon slowed. He felt someone grasp his shoulder, heard shouting like noise in his ears. Owned by the curse, he shook off restraint, then backhanded whoever had interfered.

When the light bolt cracked from Lysaer's fist, he let it come, a snapping whip of lightning that parted the wood like a scream. Through its glare Arithon saw the men around Lysaer kneel and raise white-limned weapons to their shoulders. Crossbows, he realized in undimmed exultation.

Arithon toyed with them, used mage-schooled finesse to twist shadow with a subtlety his enemy could never match. The headhunters who aimed were struck blind to a degree that negated they had ever walked sighted.

Some screamed and threw down their weapons. The rest fired a barrage of wild shots. Quarrels whined through a rising bloom of incandescence.

Arithon laughed and let the fire of Lysaer's own making char the bolts to oblivion. Then he cancelled the force ranged against him with a veil of neat shadow, even as he once had deflected the fires of a Khadrim's fell attack. He barely cared that he trembled in a backlash of overstressed nerves, but reveled in his powers to smother all light to oblivion.

The earth shook to a thunderous report. Throughout, straight-shouldered and animated by the geas that enslaved him, Arithon withheld any counter measure. His quickest satisfaction lay with steel, and holding Alithiel poised, he waited untouched at the apex of a singed swath of carbon.

"Will you fight," he called to Lysaer, derisive. "Or will you stand out of reach and play at fireworks just to waste time and show off?"

"Defiler!" Lysaer screamed back. His handsome face twisted. Cuts and bruises made his expression seem deranged. "Weaver of darkness and despoiler of children, your crimes have renounced claim to honor."

Unsmiling, Arithon took a step. As the distance narrowed and panicked headhunters scrambled from his path, he noted that Lysaer looked peaked. The left arm beneath its muddied velvets was bandaged and strapped as though injured. A wolfish thrill shot through him, that the enemy before him was disadvantaged. Arithon said, "That's your blade? Did you really think reverse runes could charm my death?" He flourished Alithiel, inviting, "Find out. Come fight."

"Why cross blades with a bastard?" Contempt in his bearing, a mirrored obsession in his eyes, Lysaer shot his hand aloft again.

Sensitized to air that flowed over his skin, Arithon felt the ingathering of force Lysaer drew to call light. This effort would be more than a killing bolt, as devastating as any formerly pitched to carve the Mistwraith into submission. Shadow could still shield him, but the broad trees of Strakeforest would burn. Clansmen and game would crisp in a burst of wildfire, and earth itself would char to slag.

Mage-taught instincts clamored in warning and alarm, but against the overpowering ascendance of Desh-thiere's curse any stir of uneasiness lost voice. Arithon advanced. His whole being resonated hatred, his oath to Rathain just meaningless words, the rasp of dry wind and dead intent. As long as Lysaer was before him, he had eyes only for his enemy. Like a puppet pulled on wires he would close with the blond nemesis leagued against him. Over parched ground or quick, their swords would cross until one of them died, and whatever impediments were swept aside beforehand became simple sacrifice to ensure this.

The air seemed to sing in its stillness. The chasing on Alithiel's dark blade appeared bodilessly inscribed on the gloom. Since the sword was now pointed with the grain of ill geas and enmity, its Paravian starspell stayed mute. More nerve-worn than the curse would permit him to acknowledge, Arithon slipped without volition into mage-sight. His vision recorded the interlocked litanies of leaves, of branches, of men partnered in useless struggle on the fringes, embodied even while killing in the light dance that founded all life. The soil beneath his step shimmered with the mysteries of rebirth, and even these lost their power to redeem him.

The drive of Desh-thiere's curse whelmed all.

At the palm of Lysaer's raised hand, light burned and then glared, and then erupted to a core of hot brilliance. The nexus swelled, fountained, raged into coruscation that ravaged the forest with back drafts. Lysaer by now stood isolated, his headhunter allies driven back by the gathering fury of his assault.

Opposite him, a wind-whipped silhouette with a hand lightly gripped to a sword's hilt, Arithon faced him in challenge. Unarmored, clad in the same spattered deerhides as any of Steiven's scouts, he seemed a figure diminished; until, half seen through lashed tangles of black hair, an expression bent his lips that held no regret but only derisive impatience.

The flaring brilliance lit the s'Ffalenn features to inescapable clarity. The detached assurance, the sheer nerveless arrogance on that face, slapped back remembrance of the manipulation that had undone Amroth's king and councilmen. Swept by a counter surge of antipathy, Lysaer shrieked his ultimatum. "By Ath, you unprincipled bastard, your wiles shall cause no more damage. This time, not counting for cost, the justice of my people will be served!"

If such rationale was wholly subverted by the workings of Desh-thiere's curse, Lysaer endorsed usage with consent. He screamed and surrendered to his passion, and something inside of him snapped. That instant he hurled his bolt.

Arithon surged to meet the attack. Gripped by queer exultation, still wakened to mage-sight, he perceived with a lucidity that damned that the curse had overmastered his half-brother. Lysaer's offensive had erased the bounds of sanity and self-preservation. As at Mearth, when a crossing through a worldgate had been snatched beyond grasp by adversity, the s'Ilessid prince now channeled the whole of his being through the destructive aspects of his gift.

The light of his own making would martyr him. Strakewood with its armies and its clansmen would be immolated at a stroke. Whether Arithon could shield himself in shadow became a point most gloriously moot. Desh-thiere's purpose would be served.

At least one of the half-brothers that comprised its bane would be expunged from the face of Athera.

Arithon howled at the irony. Swept to madness by the wraiths' savage triumph, he flung wide his arms, taunting the light to come take him, to lock with his shadows, and let his enemy be destroyed in one fiery burst of self-sacrifice.

In that moment of consumed self-control, that ecstatic certainty of victory, Arithon felt his sword arm caught and his hip blunder into something moving. Enraged, shoved off balance, he squinted through a blooming flare of incandescence. Whoever had meddled would die for it.

"Your Grace of Rathain, we are oath-sworn," cried a boy in shrill-voiced terror. "I came back as you asked, to keep you apart from your half-brother."

A blood oath bound and sworn by a mage set its ties to the living spirit.

"Sithaer, *Jieret!*" Arithon shouted, his cry split from him as the exultation of Desh-thiere's vengeance became flawed by his pact with Steiven's son. The unholy pleasures of the instant transformed to torment, as enslaved consciousness and true will became torn between opposite masters. Then the irony, of crippling proportion: that any shadow spun to save the boy must also spare the s'Ilessid prince from the forge fires of the curse's conniving.

Anguished between personal care and the lure of the curse's directive, tainted by the seductive truth that to forswear s'Ffalenn conscience and leave Jieret betrayed would buy Lysaer's death and final freedom, Arithon wrenched his will into alignment against Desh-thiere's geas.

For ill or for folly, the paradox would be permitted to renew itself; Lysaer had no training to understand or control how Desh-thiere's meddling had twisted him. Assured of his righteousness, avowed to bring justice, he would use his survival to labor until this day's atrocities became repeated. That colossal futility made a mockery of will, that perhaps reprieve came too late. One victim's lamed effort at compassion might buy only failure at the end.

A split second shy of annihilation, Arithon jerked Jieret inside the arc of a sword blade dropped sideward to guard.

The ache of exhaustion, the sucking drain against resources long overstrained, seemed to founder his mind and his reflexes. Obdurate, Arithon fought. He called, commanded, and savaged from his gift demands that edged the impossible. The curse pulled and hampered him. He wrestled its treacherous crosscurrents, while his shadows flared and snapped. Darkness arose like a howling gale, unleashed to run rampant across torrents of unchained light. The air itself seemed to scream in white agony as the gifts of two half-brothers collided.

Men at arms wailed and fell prone, their weapons discarded as they locked shaking arms to shield their hands. Trees tossed and rattled, wrenched into splinters by snaking trails of wildfire. Still trapped in mage-sight, Arithon heard the shriek of natural energies battered and tortured out of true. He felt the frosts of his own conjury flash-freeze living greens to glassine hardness that shattered in the pound of the winds. Intermixed were cries that were human. He groaned, wept, plundered intuition and training to force his reserves without mercy for the power he required to compensate. With his fists pressed to Jieret's back, his eyes blind and his senses spinning, Arithon widened his defenses.

And as he had once done at Etarra, his conjury cloaked Strakewood in darkness.

He could not see to know fate's joke was actualized; that Lysaer had collapsed from blood loss and stress, and that Pesquil and a dedicated lieutenant now labored to draw him clear of the conflict. Arithon could not breathe the air for the smells of dead earth and burning. He could barely stand upright for the voracious demands of weaving shadow.

Jieret said something. The words faded in and out unintelligibly. Then hands caught Arithon's arms and shoulders, lifting, cajoling, supporting his legs that would not any longer bear weight.

A touch that had to be Jieret's peeled his fingers away from his sword, then clasped his hand in steady warmth.

"Ath," said a scout, appalled. "You sure he isn't hurt?"

"Leave him be," snapped another, maybe Caolle. "If he loses his hold on these shadows, every clansmen in these woods will be doomed."

Arithon held on. He clung to consciousness and craft with a determination that bled and then racked him. Spinning impressions whirled through him, of burning trees and falls of water, and bodies blacked and crisped on sere ground. That made him cry out.

Such visions must be lent him by mage-sight; he prayed and he begged this was so. When he could sort out no distinction, he punished drowned senses for reassurance that a dark deep as felt, starless, lightless, battened Strakewood in defenses that could smother any outburst of reiving flames.

An indeterminate time later, he shivered and snatched a breath of air. "Are they safe yet?"

"Soon," answered Jieret, or maybe Caolle. The word flurried without echo through the walls of eight thousand dead.

At some point after that, the last shred of awareness slid away from Arithon's control. The dark and the shadows he conjured seeped through his frayed concentration, and then he knew nothing more.

Arithon reawakened on his back, to stars set like jewels between a black lattice of oak leaves. A soft cry burst from him as nightmare and reason collided, and he thought at first that he looked upon a dead landscape, formed of carbon and char.

Then his nostrils filled with the sweet scent of sap, the resins of pine not far off. At his side, someone said kindly, "Strakewood is green still. Your shadows preserved. There are clanborn survivors."

Arithon lacked voice for his bitterness, that what lives had been saved must be few, with none of them a woman or a child. For a long time he could do nothing except shut his eyes and silently, fiercely weep.

The tears cleared his mind; no mercy. Raw as he was, and helplessly unable to barrier himself in detachment, he was forced to take full stock.

"Jieret?" he asked first, the word a bare rasp of breath.

"At your side," came the answer, reassuring. "He sleeps. Except for singed hair, he's unharmed."

Arithon released a pent-up sigh. "Steiven fell. Where?"

"Does that matter?" The voice held an edge now, and a movement in darkness marked out the form of a clan scout, seated cross-legged a short distance off.

Stubborn and silent, Arithon waited.

"All right," the scout relented. "Caolle said make you rest, but if you're going to be difficult, I'll tell you."

A skeptical quirk turned Arithon's lips. "Caolle said nothing of the sort."

The stillness grew expansive with surprise. "All right." The scout sighed. "Caolle cursed you. Jieret insisted you needed rest."

The boy, now Earl of Deshir, *caithdein* of a kingdom, thrust into inheritance of Rathain's stewardship an orphan scarcely twelve years of age. The facts were given quickly after that, starting with Steiven's response to Arithon's first warning of disaster, orders that his war captain had begged on his knees to be released from: to gather and withdraw from the fighting by force if need be three hundred hand-picked young men. Steiven s'Valerient had then led the rest into ill-fated vengeance at the grottos.

"He was among the first to fall," the scout said, his tone flat and tired, his hands wrung with tension around his knees. "A crossbow quarrel caught him before we cleared the marshes, which was well. He never saw the scars of the burning, or what happened to his lady in the dell."

"I know how she died," Arithon grated. "Caolle broke orders, didn't he?"

Snapped past the memory of the brutalities beside the Tal Quorin, the scout shrugged a shoulder and resumed. "The three hundred circled wide and approached the melee from upstream. As well they did. Jieret and two wounded scouts could hardly have pulled you out alone."

Quiet, Arithon absorbed this. If he had done nothing else, his final intervention with shadows had spared most of those clansmen Steiven had selected to survive. After an interval, he prodded, "And now?"

"The headhunters' league are mostly destroyed and Lysaer's Etarrans in retreat. Outside of Strakewood, we expect they'll regroup. The ones not nerve-broken or wounded will probably stay on and poison springs to destroy the game and starve us out." A breeze wafted through the trees, edged with the acrid tang of ash. The scout drew a dagger and tested the edge with a thumb, over and over seeking flaws. "Caolle won't give them satisfaction. His plan is to abandon Strakewood and join up with Earl Marl's band in Fallowmere."

Somewhere a wakeful mockingbird loosed a melodic spill of notes. A hunting owl cried mournfully. Jieret stirred in the depths of some dream, and the scout cut a stick in thick silence and nicked off a rattling fall of chips.

Arithon lay still and noticed other things: that his body was clothed still in blood-tainted leathers, though somebody thoughtful had bound his cuts. In fits and starts of mage-sight, he recognized the neat work for Caolle's. By the odd flares of light that scoured the edge of his vision, and by his current inability to keep focused on the physical aspects of reality, he knew he still suffered the effects of overplayed nerves. His twisted misuse of spell-craft had caused damage beyond distress to the body. His thoughts had an odd start and hitch to them, as if pulled to the border of delirium. The curse itself had left ravages. His opposition by shadows had plundered also, when he had wrenched that thundering torrent of enslavement aside to reclaim his free will.

He dared not guess how much time must elapse before he could sleep without nightmares. A nagging ache in his bones warned how greatly his resources were depleted. Pain and plain restlessness drove him finally to stop circling thoughts by getting up.

The scout abruptly stopped whittling. Knife poised, chin raised in query, he said, "Where in Sithaer are you off to?"

Over his shoulder as he departed, Arithon flipped back an insouciant quote from a ballad. " 'To free the dazed dead, and reclothe cold flesh in fair flowers.' " Whether his line was delivered in Paravian words did not matter; his mood was too shattered to translate.

As if nature held light as anathema, no moon shone over Strakewood in the aftermath of Etarra's assault. Traced by faint starlight or by the fluttering, uncertain flame of small torches, Caolle and Deshir's clan survivors moved through the fields of the dead. They went armed. The body that groaned in extremity might not be a kinsman's, but an enemy's; the hand that stirred in trampled mud might not reach in acceptance of succor, but instead hold a dagger thrust to maim. Scouts too tired for sound judgment searched logs that looked like fallen clansmen and gullies that conspired to conceal them. Through swamp and on hillside, there came decisions no repetition could ease; of whether to send for a healer or to deal a mercy stroke and finish an untenable suffering.

Each call for the knife underscored the sorrow that clan numbers had been close to decimated.

Quiet as any man born to the wood could cover deep brush, warily as he tried to guard his back, he sometimes flushed living enemies, who for hours had blundered through ravine and thorn thicket, lost and frightened and alone. Townsmen caught out of their element who were jumpy and keyed to seize retribution for their plight.

With one valley quartered, the acres still left to patrol seemed a punishment reserved for the damned.

Sticky clothes, and dulled blades, and hands that twinged from pulled tendons did nothing for Caolle's foul mood. His years numbered more than fifty, and this had been a battle to break the stamina of the resilient young. As he crouched over yet another corpse, a young boy in chain mail so new it looked silver, he cursed the caprice of fate, that he should be alive instead of Steiven. The losses had yet to be tallied, of friends that had passed beneath the Wheel. Nobody wanted to number the kinsmen their own knives had needfully dispatched.

Ahead, jumbled and jagged against a sky like tinseled silk, the rock cliffs in their seams and webbed shadows narrowed toward the mouth of the grottos. No wounded waited in the charred glen beyond, only dead that rustled in the winds like dry paper. To Halliron, who walked at his shoulder, Caolle said "You might just want to turn back."

As begrimed as any clansman, though his shirt was embroidered and cuffed in fine silk, and his lyranthe stayed strapped on his shoulder, the Masterbard calmly gave answer. "I'll not leave." He pushed on through a stand of low maples. "Don't punish yourself over hindsight."

Caolle sucked an offended breath. "I should have listened. We could've scattered and separated the women."

"The men would still be as dead. The divided families could not survive." Halliron finished in quiet certainty. "Your children would have died in Etarra. Arithon told me. He saw their executions in the course of his tienelle scrying."

Loath to be reminded, Caolle pushed past. "Ath. If you have to tag after me, the least you can do is quit talking." But the bard's tenacity impressed him. Though no fighter, Halliron tended to show up where he was useful. If in this fire-seared abattoir his touch with the wounded and dying was unlikely to offer any benefit, his unstinting service had earned him the right to go on.

The pair moved ahead, oddly matched: the stocky, grizzled warrior in simmering, skeptical bitterness and the lean musician whose flared boots and court clothing were unsuited for rugged terrain, but whose grace stayed unmarred by the setting.

They came across a slain Etarran pikeman. The man did not lie as he had fallen. Someone had laid his fouled weapon aside, removed his helm, and turned his young face to the sky. Eyes closed, he now rested straight with his hands gently crossed on his breast.

"Odd." Caolle coughed out the stench of ash. "One of ours wouldn't bother. Fellow must've had a companion."

Halliron said nothing, but raised his head and peered into the murk of the grotto.

"You know something," Caolle accused.

"Maybe." Halliron pressed on.

After the fifth such corpse, this one a clansman's, the discrepancy

became irksome. Caolle stopped square in the moss where a dead
scout had been as tenderly arranged.

"You never heard the ballad of Falmuir?" Halliron asked softly. "I
think we are seeing its like."

"Ballad?" Caolle straightened. He scrubbed his face with his
knuckles, as if tiredness could be scraped from his flesh. "You pick a
damned odd time to speak of singing."

Halliron stood also. A warm glint of challenge lit his eyes. "And
you don't out of reflex view every man you meet and measure his potential as a fighter?"

"That's different." Caolle sighed. "Maybe not." He rechecked the
hang of his sword and his knives, and stalked from the riverbed into
shadow. "Then what should I know about Falmuir?"

"That two cities took arms over marriage rights to an heiress."
Halliron slowed to negotiate a wash of dry river pebbles, where a misstep could easily turn an ankle. "The girl," he resumed, "had a seer's
gift. She begged her guardian to allow her to wed an uninvolved
suitor as compromise, and to forfeit her rights of inheritance. For
greed and for power, her wishes were refused. A war resulted, with
losses very like this one."

Caolle led deeper into the defile, his disgust rendered bodiless in
full gloom. "These Etarrans had only to mind their manners and stay
home. Their city was never assaulted."

Which truth could be argued, from the viewpoint of townsmen
terrorized by shadows they could hardly be expected to know were
harmless. Cut off ahead of his conclusion, Halliron pondered the clan
captain's impatience. "You suspect another treachery lies ahead?"

"What else?" The defile narrowed. Sturdy, as silent in motion as
a predator, Caolle drew his knife. With the river fallen behind, the
thrash of white waters diminished. In darkness now humid with dew,
the casualties lay thick on the earth. Clansman and foe alike were arrayed in still rows, head to feet aligned north to south, and weapons
pulled clear of folded hands.

Caolle checked each one anyway to ascertain no body still
breathed.

Above the soft scrape of his boot soles, Halliron said, "You won't
find what you think."

"So we'll see." Nettled as a wolf over a disturbed cache, Caolle
adhered to his wariness.

Cautioned by the angle of the captain's shoulders, Halliron let ballads and conversation both lapse. The ravine they trod held an unsettled feel. Where deer should have bounded from their watering, the

song of the crickets rang unpartnered. Here only bats flitted and swooped erratic circles between the scarred walls of the rim rocks.

And then between steps the mosses that cushioned the trail bed were seared to papery dryness. Trees became fire-stripped skeletons, while ahead, the grotto lay ravaged and razed to split stone filmed over with carbon.

The air hung poisoned with taint.

Inside the ruin where the tents had stood, limned like a ghost in soft starlight, knelt a man.

Breath hissed through Caolle's clenched teeth. His knife hand lifted, caught back from a throw by Halliron.

His urgency queerly muffled, the bard said, "Don't. That's no enemy."

"His Grace of Rathain. I can see." Tension did not leave Caolle's arm. "By Ath, I could thrash him! Why in Sithaer should he bother with corpses while our wounded lie unfound and suffering!"

"You misunderstand him, you always have." The Masterbard released his restraint, and jumped back at the speed with which the clan captain turned on him.

"And you don't?" Caolle enforced incredulity with a whistling gesture of his knife.

Recovered, Halliron stood his ground. The night breeze stirred his white hair, and his face, deeply shadowed, stayed serene. "This moment, no. I think it best you don't disturb your liege." Then, his tone changed to awe, he added, "It is like Falmuir. *To free the dazed dead, and reclothe cold flesh in fair flowers.*' " At Caolle's look of baffled anger, the Masterbard said, "Prince Arithon's mage-trained. You don't know what that means?"

"I'd be hardly likely to, should I?" Caolle presented his shoulder, his profile like a hatchet cut against the soot-stained dark of the grotto. "Killing's my trade, not fey tricks with poisons and shadows."

And behind the captain's harshness, in a knife blade demarked by a trembling thread of reflection, Halliron perceived the grief of crushing losses: a clan lord gone, and Dania, and four daughters cherished as if they had been Caolle's own. The present was robbed, and the future stretched friendlessly bleak. A difficult task must for love be repeated all over again; another young boy to be raised for the burden of leading the northland clans: first Steiven and now, when a man was aging and wearied of adversity, Steiven's orphaned son.

That Caolle's sullen nature would greet such desertion in anger, Halliron well understood. What could not for tragedy be permitted was that blame for Deshir's ills stay fastened on the Teir's'Ffalenn. Time had come for the bard to ply the service he was trained for.

There and then in the darkness, amid the charred ground where the dead lay, he unwrapped the cover from his instrument.

Caolle snapped, "Ath, we'll have ballads again?" He made to surge forward and stopped, caught aback by the bard's grip on his wrist. Court manners or not, Halliron could move nimbly when need warranted.

"You'll not touch him," the bard said in reference to the man, still kneeling, who had neither looked up nor shown other sign he had heard them. The schooled timbre of a masterbard's voice could fashion an outright command. "Sit, Caolle. Hear the tale of Falmuir. After that, do exactly as you please."

Disarmed as much by exhaustion, Caolle gave way. If he chose not to sit, he had little choice but to listen, as any man must when a singer of Halliron's stature plied his craft. For a masterbard, the edges of mage-sight and music lay twined to a single wrapped thread. The lyranthe had been fashioned by Paravian spell-craft, and under supremely skilled fingers she evoked an allure not to be denied.

From the opening chords, Caolle looked aside. By the close of the first verse his stiffness was all pride and pretense. As his knife hand relinquished its tension and his face eased from antipathy, he heard of the siege of Falmuir, where a princess had walked out alone on a battlefield where defenders and abductors lay slain. Lent refined vision by the spelled weave of words and bright notes, Caolle was shown in humility the legend of the ballad reenacted here, in the grotto of Deshir's slain.

His gaze at some point drifted back to Arithon. Even as a princess had once done in grief and total loss, the Shadow Master poised amid the burned remains of clan kindred. His fine-boned hands were filmed with black ash for each of the corpses he had settled. His hollowed cheeks glittered with the tracings left scoured by tears. He was speaking. Each syllable rang with compassion, and each word he spun formed a name. He summoned in love, and they came to him, the shades of tiny babes and silent women, of girls and grandmothers and daughters and wives, sundered from life in such violence that their spirits were homeless and dazed. They formed around him a webwork of subliminal light, not burned but whole; no more aggrieved but joyous as he added words in lyric Paravian that distanced the violence that had claimed them.

Arithon gave back their deaths, redeemed from the horror of murder. One by one he cherished their memories. In an unconditional mercy that disallowed grief, they were fully and finally freed to the peace of Ath's deepest mystery.

In time, no more forms shone in soft light, but only a man alone, who rose unsteadily to his feet, while the sad cadence of Halliron's voice delivered the princess of Falmuir's final lines: *'She went not to wed, or to comfort or rest, but to free the dazed dead, and to reclothe cold flesh in fair flowers.'*

But in this cleft of sere earth and split rock, there were neither bodies to bury nor blossoms to seed over grave sites. Caolle blotted his cheeks with the knuckles still clenched to his skinning knife. His gesture encompassed his prince as gruffly he said, "The man was sent to bed once. If he faints on his feet, he's like to whack his head on a rock."

"Let him be." Halliron stroked the ring of fading strings into silence. "What he does brings solace we cannot."

"It's healing he needs," Caolle groused. "Though by Daelion, I don't like the post of royal nursemaid."

Attuned to the change in the captain's railing, the Masterbard tied up his instrument. Too grave to be accused of amusement, he waited while a shame-faced Caolle noticed and then sheathed his knife. Then, unspeaking, they trailed Arithon's progress up the grotto; they sorted out and administered to the living, Rathain's prince to his uncounted dead.

Night passed. The bard's face showed every sleepless hour, and Caolle wore an expression like boiled leather. While gray dawn crept in and the forest rang with birdsong undisturbed by mankind's sad strivings, they reached a dell scattered with the shafts of fallen arrows and, beyond a broad beech, ringed with casualties so closely fallen that one lay entangled upon the next like tidewrack stranded by storm.

Roused from the half trance that had sustained his passage through the grotto, Arithon reached out sharp and suddenly, and touched Halliron on the wrist. "Let me work alone, here. There won't be any wounded among these fallen."

To kill a man untimely with a blade was not the same as using magics to twist his destiny, to overrule his fate by ill usage of the forces that endow life. To release those spirits cut down in Jieret's defense was a costly, exhaustive undertaking more taxing than anything accomplished previously.

For these dead did not welcome intervention, but shrank from Arithon in stark fear. He was more than their killer; he was a master who had betrayed them on levels they had no conscious means to guard. To bind them long enough to free them, he had to expose to them all that he was. He had to lower his defenses and let them shriek curses to his face. He had to endure their pain, let them hurt him in turn, until his passivity left them mollified and quiet.

And when the blessing of the Paravian release let them go, the peace they took with them was not shared. Arithon looked desolate and haunted, and remorse had stolen even tears.

Long before the end, Halliron found he could not watch.

Caolle, who had no gift to know the scope of what was happening, saw only that Arithon suffered. "Why should he do this? Why?"

But the answer the bard gave was inadequate, that this prince was both musician and king. Caolle understood only that the heart of the mystery lay beyond him.

When the captain who thought he knew all there was to sample of human grief could no longer abide the awful silence, he spoke the greatest accolade he could offer. "Arithon is greater than Steiven."

"You see that," said the Masterbard. "You are privileged. Many won't, and most will be friends."

By then the town dead had been numbered and most of the clansmen. There remained now only Madreigh, open-eyed, his loose hands empty and outflung and a gaping hole in his chest. Aching in body, riven in spirit, Arithon paused in a moment of stopped breath. He looked upon the face of one scarred old campaigner not twisted in rigor, but content with the peace of the seasons.

This, the man who had defended his back while, for Jieret, he had shaped baneful conjury. A cry wrung from Arithon's throat before sluggish thought could restrain it. "Dharkaron Avenger witness, you should have had better than this!"

Shaking in visible spasms, he brushed back gray hair and cupped Madreigh's face between his palms. Blind to daylight, deaf in grief, he closed his eyes and spoke Name; and met not blankness or confusion, but the abiding fall of spring rains, and snow, and warm sunlight. He encountered the peace of the trees.

The awareness shocked him. The spell that ensnared more than fifty to spare one had inadvertently preserved another life.

Rathain's prince tilted back his head. Halliron and Caolle loomed above him. His balance tipped toward dizziness, and what seemed the yawning dark of Dharkaron's censure opened before his wide eyes. "This one, also, I saved," he said as if pleading forgiveness. "Tend him well. I would beg that he lives."

"My liege," said Caolle. He knelt quickly, and when nerve and consciousness faltered, he was there to catch Arithon in his arms.

First Resolution

When the tors on the plain of Araithe were raked at sunrise by the winds, the mists still clung like combed cotton in the valleys as they had the dawn before. Only now the tick and splash of droplets off dew-soaked rock mingled with the moans of wounded soldiers. Wrapped in the tatters of his surcoat, his camp blanket long since given up to alleviate the shortage of bandaging, Prince Lysaer s'Ilessid knelt to hold the hand of yet another lancer who shivered and thrashed in mindless suffering.

"Delirium this time," the healer diagnosed; this victim raved from wound fever, not as some of the others in a madness brought on by terrors of sorcery and shadows. His raw hands helpless and empty, the healer straightened up from his patient. He had abandoned his satchel, there being no more medicines to dispense. Needles could not suture without thread, and last night's case load of fatal injuries had burned him stark out of platitudes.

Not in a lifetime of service had he seen a war cause such damage as this one. To the prince still determined to lend comfort, he added, "I doubt this lad knows why you're there. The wagons are loaded. Did you want to see Lord Diegan on his way?"

"I'll go in a moment." His head bent, the damp ends of his hair flicked in coils over his arm sling, Lysaer let the healer study him in a mix of exasperation and approval before, fed up and weary, he finally gave in and stalked off. One dying garrison soldier might well be past solace. But the prince responsible for the strike into Strakewood needed the interval to think.

Lysaer buried his face in the hand not strapped up in bandaging. Far off, the pop of a carter's whip sounded over someone's hoarse shouting: another officer striving to curb the paranoia that had men drawing steel at plain shadows.

No one who had tangled with Arithon's sorceries in Strakewood would ever again view darkness as friendly.

Grooms hauling buckets to the picket lines observed Lysaer's pose of despair. They murmured in sympathy for his exhaustion, for all the camp knew he had not rested. The prince had labored with Pesquil to compile losses too massive to list. Commanding despite his discomfort, he had been on the riverbank to encourage each wave of tired soldiers who emerged alive from the forest. He had walked beside litters, talking, reassuring. Cracked bones had not stopped him from breaking up disputes or throwing steady light with his gift to quell massive, hysterical fear. Throughout a long and terrible night he had chafed frightened squires and bloodied his hands beside the surgeon to clean and stanch open wounds. However a man might deplore royalty, this prince had accepted no cosseting.

To find his ragged magnificence still among them in the cheerless gray of the morning made men break their hearts to meet his wishes. That Etarra's concerns were foremost in his mind, no town survivor ever questioned. Without Lysaer's light to stay the shadows, many more would have died by the grottos, or been abandoned to the mindless distress induced by Arithon's maze wards that had ensorcelled the troops in the west valley.

If not for Prince Lysaer, Lord Commander Diegan himself would not have left Tal Quorin's banks alive.

In nervous speculation and vehement rage, Etarra's garrison made clear whom they blamed for the carnage. Men hailed the prince, then brandished weapons and cursed the shifter of shadows their campaign had failed to take down.

Unsettled by his reflections, Lysaer stirred. At his knees the soldier tossed and groaned, an arrow that had not quite killed lodged keep inside his lower gut. His suffering would be prolonged and painful, and a peppery barmaid who wore his trinkets would be widowed with no parting kiss to cold lips. Without enough wagons for the wounded, the dead must be interred where they lay, amid the flinty soil of the tors with only piled stones for their markers.

"I'll see you avenged," the prince vowed in a spiking rush of sincerity. He touched the man's shoulder and arose.

While darkness had lasted, the cries and the noise of arriving stragglers had filled the camp, queerly amplified by the fog. The scope of disaster had loomed through the night, still possible to deny. But now as day brightened and the mists shredded away, the damages became appallingly apparent. In a campaign planned for easy victory, two-thirds of a war host of ten thousand had been decimated in a single engagement. Lysaer walked as the impact of sight rocked the campsite, men's voices tangled in anger and shrill disbelief. The worn band of officers struggled yet again to rechannel shock and grief into tasks, while others exhorted crushed and silent men to gather for biscuit and beef around the cookfires.

Raised to rule, well hardened for the trials of leadership, Lysaer shared the burden where he could. He spoke, and touched shoulders, and once faced down a man who had wildly drawn a dagger and raved to anyone who would listen that he intended to lead a foray to go reiving back into Strakewood. Sympathetic to the men but possessed of a cool self-containment, the s'Ilessid prince reviewed the wreck of Etarra's garrison with no incapacitating pang of conscience.

Where he passed, his unassailable assurance touched the men and left them silent with awe. His equilibrium could encompass seven thousand casualties. He could feel haunted and sad that Arithon had engaged in unscrupulous use of little children, but not have lasting regrets that the wholesale elimination of barbarian women and young had been necessary to guard town security. No city could recoup from a defeat as terrible as this were they left with belief such casualties could recur again.

"Your Grace, have you eaten?" A fat cook tagged his shoulder, diffident and anxious to please.

Lysaer inclined his head in courtesy. "I've hardly noticed I was hungry." He let himself be led to a fire, politely tasted the soup that was handed to him.

Haunted by association as his gaze became tranced by the flame, he found himself reliving the moment when *he had actually endorsed self-destruction to buy the Shadow Master's death.*

Although no cost could be counted too great to eradicate the s'Ffalenn bastard before more innocent lives could fall prey to his wiles, in daylight and cold reason, hindsight recast self-sacrifice as an impulse of hotheaded idiocy. Lysaer shivered, set his soup bowl with a clink on the board the cook used to stack utensils. No guarantee insisted that Arithon should have died in that strike. He was clever enough to escape, perhaps; Rauven's teaching lent him tricks.

The stalking uncertainty lingered, that the inspiration to risk martyrdom for the cause might not have been Lysaer's own.

Once in *Briane*'s sail hold, and another day in the Red Desert, Arithon had used magecraft to turn his half-brother's mind. Plagued by doubts, Lysaer wondered. Had the bastard plotted the same way in Strakewood? For if mockery and goading had been paired with sorceries to eliminate the only man with powers over light that might threaten him, the evil inherent in such design upheld a frightening conclusion.

How better for Arithon to win license to toy with this world as he pleased than to dedicate his enemy to self-destruction? Lysaer burned inside with recrimination. If faintness from blood loss had not disrupted his attack, worse horrors could have visited Athera than seven thousand dead Etarran soldiers.

"Your Grace?" interrupted a staff messenger.

Lysaer glanced up and identified livery with the black and white blazon of the headhunters' league. Immediately contrite, since the boy could have stood several minutes awaiting acknowledgment, he said, "Pesquil sent you?"

"The wagons are ready to leave, Your Grace." Embarrassed by the intensity of Lysaer's attention, the boy regarded the grass, in this place trampled and muddied by the grinding passage of men seeking comfort to ease their misery. "My lord Pesquil said Lord Commander Diegan is awake and asking after you."

Lysaer dredged up energy to give a quick smile of reassurance. "Would you lead me to him?"

The boy brightened. "At once, Your Grace."

Together they crossed the camp. The mist was thinning quickly now. Grooms stood in for tired messengers, since sorrowfully decimated horse lines left them short of duties. Some of the watch fires were doused. Between the leaning scaffolds of weapon racks and the comings and goings from the officers' pavilions, patrols prepared to ride out. The nearer circuits would be quartered on foot, sound mounts being precious and few.

Lysaer assessed all with the sure eye of a ruler, and where he made suggestions he was given deference and respect. He took care to acknowledge every greeting with a nod, a smile, or with names, if he knew the speaker; Pesquil's young staff runner was overwhelmingly impressed.

In subdued little groups, conversation underscored by the screeling hiss of busy grindstones, the veteran pikemen mended gear. A few commiserated over losses. Most others slept sprawled on wet ground, their blankets reapportioned first for litters and then used for pallets and rough bandaging. Past the phalanx of the supply stores, unloaded in haste from the wagon beds and lashed under tarps by the carters, the racket and confusion of the night was subsiding. In sunlight, the green recruits who had seen their companions half butchered or drowned were less driven to seek blind relief in scraps and hysterical boasting. Shrieks from the camp followers' tents raised in dissonance over the sobs of refugees from the west valley still deranged by terror of the dark.

The core of the army remained, Lysaer assessed. Carefully handled, these men could be reforged into a troop of formidable strength. All he lacked was excuse to stay; already his authority was not questioned.

The wagon train bound for Etarra formed up, its escort of fifty lancers in twitchy lines as men made last-minute adjustments to tack and gear. One of the few banners not lost in the river flood flapped erect at the column's head. Pesquil gave instructions with rapid-fire gesticulations to the dispatch rider who would report to Lord Governor Morfett. A mule strained at its lead rein to graze, bearing a lashed bundle in city colors: Captain Gnudsog's remains, to be interred in the mausoleum gardens reserved for the city's most revered.

The rest of the wagons bore wounded, ones with privilege and pedigree foremost. The little space remaining had been alotted to men with irreplaceable skills or standing, and then grudgingly to the staff and supplies needful for a slow journey home.

The cart draped in the Lord Commander's horse cloths was easy to spot. Lysaer dismissed his young guide with a word of praise that left him blushing. Then he crossed the open ground, threaded past an ongoing, heated dispute, and dismissed a hovering servant.

Lord Diegan lay under blankets, dark, untidy hair emphasizing a drawn face and eyes that wandered unfocused from soporifics not fully worn off. He murmured in question as Lysaer's shadow fell over him, then settled as his sight recorded a sun-caught head of gold hair.

The prince said gently, "I am here."

"Your Grace?" Diegan struggled with a fuzzy smile that dissolved into discomfort. He struggled painfully to concentrate.

"Don't trouble," Lysaer said. "I shall speak for both of us."

"We lost Gnudsog." The Lord Commander plucked at his blankets. "You knew that?"

Lysaer captured the wandering fingers and caged them in gentle stillness. Clearly, firmly, he said, "Pesquil has charge of the garrison. He's got twenty good men left who will instruct on barbarian tactics. Enough men remain to finish our original intent. If you still want to destroy the Deshans, Strakewood's springs will be poisoned, and the game by the river shall be hazed and killed. With nothing to hunt, the few clan survivors will be starved out of the forest. The north will be cleared of such pests. No disaster such as happened by Tal Quorin shall visit these northlands again."

Color flushed Diegan's cheeks in patches. "They say you're staying with the troops."

Lysaer smoothed the Lord Commander's hand and let go. "I must. If I cannot bear arms, I will use my gift of light to safeguard our forays against sorcery."

Weakly, Diegan cursed. "He survived, then."

The name of the Shadow Master hung unspoken between them as an answering grimness touched Lysaer. "We haven't lost. The Deshir clans are finished, there will be no next generation. And your city now knows the measure of its enemy."

Lord Commander Diegan shut his eyes. A frown pulled at his brows, and shadows of stress and fatigue seemed etched in the hollows of his bones. "This pirate's bastard. You know we can't take him alone. Without your gift of light, any army we send to the field would be ensorcelled and ruinously slaughtered."

Lysaer weighed the wisdom of pursuing this subject with a heart-sick man who was also drugged and gravely ill. Heavy between them lay the unspoken accusation: that Lysaer had sent Diegan into safety on Tal Quorin's banks, and by risking himself to the river, had exposed them all to unconscionable peril. Aware that Lord Diegan had rallied himself and was watching in fragile-edged fury, Lysaer smiled. "I've had all night to ponder regrets. Here's my promise. No more exposure on the front ranks for me. The next campaign you launch should be planned and executed to make use of every advantage. Years will be needed to prepare. I could suggest you have the head-hunters' league train the garrisons, then sharpen their field skills in small forays to eradicate barbarians. And when the army is readied and equipped to perfection, send out heralds to recruit allies. The burden should not fall to Etarra alone."

Diegan shifted in distress. "You say nothing of yourself."

"I am royal," Lyasaer said, his eyes clear blue and direct. "Once, you thought that a liability."

Lord Commander Diegan swore explosively, then curled on his side in a spasm of wrenched muscles and bitter pain. "If I get Lord Governor Morfett to issue an invitation under the official city seal, would you stay?"

Lysaer smiled. "Do that, and I shall labor with you to mobilize cities the breadth of Rathain. Then we shall march upon Arithon s'Ffalenn, and we shall take him with numbers no sorceries can overwhelm."

Lord Commander Diegan relaxed in his blankets, his eyes veiled in drug-hazed speculation. "I like your plan. Pesquil agrees?"

Lysaer laughed. "Pesquil made your scribes miserable jotting letters to headhunters' leagues the breadth of the continent before our casualties were tallied." For Pesquil, the near total loss of his troop had been a sore point, alleviated by moody bursts of elation that after feuding years and too little funding from the city council, the Earl Steiven's dominion over Strakewood had been decisively broken.

"I shall have to buy manuscripts on strategy," Diegan said in mixed recrimination and distaste. "They're long-winded and boring, I presume. Hardly entertainment for the parties." But fall season would be dreary as it was, with so many ladies forced to mourning. Diegan drifted for some minutes near sleep, while the prince, who knew far more about armies and the art of command than he, attended him in tactful respect. Finally, eyes closed, Lord Diegan murmured, "Come back to us safely in the autumn. My sister Lady Talith will be waiting."

"Tell her . . ." Lysaer paused, gravely pleased, while the captain at the head of the column shouted orders, and whips snapped in the hands of cursing drovers, and carts began, groaning, to roll forward. Striding alongside Diegan's wagon, the sun in his hair like sheen on the wares of a silk spinner, Lysaer spoke from his heart. "I'll return to pay court to the lady. No Master of Shadows with his darkness shall be permitted to keep us apart."

Last Resolution

The deadfalls, stripped of stakes, became grave pits to bury the fallen. Deshir's clansmen accomplished the work in whirlwind expedience, laying loved ones atop of dead horses, or the bodies of enemies still clad in plumed helms and mail shirts. Plunder entered nobody's mind. On a field holding slain by the thousands, there were more abandoned weapons than living men to wield them; and by long and bitter custom, Deshir's clans gave no time in respect for their fallen that might endanger the living.

Of Strakewood's complement of nine hundred sixty, scarcely two hundred men lived, half that number wounded; fourteen boys of Jieret's generation were all that survived Etarra's campaign against Arithon. The Tal Quorin's waters rolled muddied and stinking, and swaths of ancient greenwood lay razed and fire-scarred and smoking.

Unless the hunters ranged far into the mazed back glens of the river basin, game for the stew pots was thin and scarce.

As hungry and tired as the men who had lost their families and their lifestyle to defend their rights of territory, Arithon s'Ffalenn raised a stone still clotted with mud and moss and placed it against the cairn that marked the burial of Steiven, Earl of the North, *caithdein* and Warden of Ithamon. Interred at his side rested his beloved lady Dania, whose piercing wit and intuition would provoke and delight no man further. Silenced by remembrance, the Master of

Shadows scuffed dirt from split fingers on the leathers her kindness had provided him. Then he bundled an arm about the shoulders of the boy who stood motionless at his side.

"Your parents were fine people, Jieret. Ones I was proud to know. Forgive me if I can't always match up to your memory of their example." Under his hands the boy quivered.

Arithon tactfully let him go.

Jieret pushed back his sleeve cuffs and pulled out the whittling knife he had used to carve toys for his sisters. He turned it over and over like a talisman, while, careful not to watch the boy's tears, Rathain's prince knelt on earth still thrashed and torn from the passage of heavy destriers. "Here," he said, and gently removed the dagger from the boy's hands. With a care that appeared to consume his attention, he began to scratch runes of blessing and guard on the river slate that crowned the cairn.

The patterns used in the ritual configuration of magic held a certain stark beauty; each traced line captured thought in severe simplicity which offered its own consolation. As Arithon sketched the intricate angles, the circular curves and interlocked ciphers, he spoke. "A kingdom and its prince are only as strong as their warden. *Caithdein*, when you come of age, I'll be honored to swear oath on your blade. I can already say you've served this land's prince. If not for your courage, Rathain's royal line would be ended, and your father's fine work gone for nothing."

Jieret dashed his cheek with the back of one dirt-grained wrist. Red hair sprang like wire between the folds of a bandage, cut from the silk shirt sewn by Sethvir for the ceremony of Arithon's coronation. The peculiar sharp attentiveness he had taken from his mother stayed trained in unswerving contemplation of the grave stones. In words not those of a child, he said, "Your Grace, my father's life was never wasted in your service. He made me understand as much when he told me he knew he was going to die. One day, perhaps before I come of age, you will need me again."

Oddly caught out in embarrassment, Arithon paused. "Well. On that, Ath forfend, I hope you're wrong." The figure under his hands was complete. He lifted the blade and studied the balanced geometrics of patterns learned when his fingers were barely old enough to grip a chalk stick. But unlike his childhood scrawlings on slate in his grandfather's study, he sensed no subliminal surge of energy. Whether this mark in Strakewood held power to ward, or whether its lines were just pretty scratchings copied over by rote from memory, he had no means in him to tell. The odd, static flashes of mage-sight that had plagued him since shaping the banespell had diminished, until finally, he could summon no vision at all.

The self-discipline learned at Rauven remained, but to the craft he had mastered, his senses had gone dumb and dead. Arithon sought the essence of the trees and the air, but perceived only as other men saw.

Grief remained, of a depth he could share with no one. Not for the first time since his choice to pursue his s'Ffalenn inheritance, he missed the counsel of the cantankerous s'Ahelas grandfather who perhaps still lived in Rauven's master tower. Dascen Elur with its wide oceans lay behind, forever lost. Here spread a land whose sky, hills, and rivers held secrets only partially studied. Cut short in the midst of discovery, Arithon felt deprived of an arm, or a leg; or as an artist suddenly blinded to color in a hall filled with masterworks.

Across the glen, through the sun-dappled pillars of lichened trunks, the layered harmonics of a lyranthe being tested for pitch threaded the forest. As personal as written signature, Halliron's favorite tuning phrase spattered fifths like a running spill of coins. Each note pierced Arithon's perception, separate as the impact of small darts. As if in counterbalance to reft senses, his awareness of sound had grown acute. Birdsong never rang so pure in his ears, and the clang of pickaxe and steel as graves were covered over never clashed so wincingly dissonant.

Still on his knees, Arithon stabbed Jieret's knife into dirt. He bowed his head. As he had the past night laid hands to cold flesh, today he touched his palms to old stone and stilled his inner awareness. He had personally accomplished the ritual to free the sundered spirits of these, his lost friends. Something of residual peace should emanate from the bones now embraced in quiet earth.

Nothing; he felt nothing at all.

Arithon sighed, a tightness to his shoulders the only sign of the ambivalence that wrenched him. Even the cairn stones were mute. Where the least fleck of sand from the creek bed should ring in its essence with the grand energies that defined all existence, these disparate rocks gave back the scrape of rough edges against the uncallused burn barely scarred over since Etarra. Left only memory, Arithon touched nothing of the true reality known to mages at all, but saw only the flat spectrum of visible light. The ghostly resonance left on this land by Paravian inhabitance, that Asandir had attuned to his being in the hills of Caith-al-Caen, would neither thrill nor harrow him now. If he wished he could walk Ithamon's ruins and not be haunted.

Mastery of his shadows remained, but no knowledge to suggest whether time would heal his other gifts.

"They're starting." Jieret touched his prince's wrist to rouse him. The shadows had moved. An interval had passed that Arithon found difficult to measure. Deshir's survivors at some point had set aside tools to gather into a circle for the rite to honor their dead.

Arithon recovered Jieret's knife from the earth and straightened up. "I'll listen from here." He began to return the small blade to the boy, then impulsively hesitated. "Let me keep this," he asked. "As the steel we used to swear blood pact, I'd like to have it. To use. To have you know that I think of you often."

"You're leaving us." A statement: Jieret did not sound surprised. Not yet a man, more than a boy, he had too much pride to ask why. In a manner that reminded painfully of Steiven, he said, "You forget, I think, that I offered you that same blade already."

Arithon tossed it, absorbed by the flash of the river pearl handle as it turned and landed with a slap in his palm. "When I'd finished the tienelle scrying. I remember."

"That's a good knife for carving willow whistles," Jieret said. "I shan't be needing it any longer." And he gestured toward its replacement, a narrow, quilloned main gauche he wore strapped to his belt. "Ath go with you, my prince."

Arithon tucked the little knife into the tight-laced leather that cuffed his shirt. Then he pulled Jieret to him and exchanged a fierce embrace that he broke with a quick push to send the boy off toward his people.

Within the latticed sear of strong sun that striped through branches singed of foliage, Deshir's clansmen in their war-stained, ragged leathers joined hands. Their circle parted to include Jieret, then unraveled a second time as a stocky figure in studded belts and black bracers broke away. Caolle, Arithon identified by the vehement thrust of the man's stride. The clan captain had keen intuition, but in the absence of Dania's sisterly intolerance, he retained all the style of a thrown brick.

At the center of the circle, incongruous in the slashed elegance of black silk and gold, Halliron stood in the restored splendor of his court clothing, his lyranthe tuned in his hands. He called.

But with Steiven dead and himself left trustee of the clans, Caolle deferred to no one. He stamped across the churned ground with his boot cuffs slapping and his shoulders hunched up, and his whiskered chin jutted for argument.

At his back, somebody said something commiserating, and the clansmen quietly closed the gap.

Craggy from strain and sleeplessness, grazed by brush burns, and patched red from accumulated midge bites, Caolle looked ready to murder. "You're leaving us," he accused.

Suppressing a wince as his tone grated against an almost painful sensitivity, Arithon felt no answering anger. "I must." He looked back in forceful directness that forestalled Caolle's bluster. Across the thicket the soft, sad notes of Halliron's lyranthe gentled the quiet: the opening phrases of the ritual to sing Deshir's dead into memory. This was the first open sentiment any clansman had shown, and would firmly and finally be the last.

The flight to take refuge in Fallowmere would begin immediately following the ceremony.

Caolle waited, fumingly impatient. Then as the poignance of Halliron's playing touched even his bearish mood, he hooked large-knuckled thumbs in his sword belt. "You can tell us why."

Unflinching, Arithon continued to regarded him. "I think you know. Where I go, Lysaer's armies will follow." He drew a breath.

As though daring insults or evasions, Caolle clamped his hands under taut forearms. He was a man who liked his clothing loose and his belts tight; the blades that were visible on his person drew all the quicker, while the invisible ones stayed unobvious. He regarded his silent liege lord, his black eyes inimical as shield studs.

The prince of Rathain gave no ground. Sincere where before he had been secretive, he said, "I can neither repay nor restore your losses. Nor would I cheat you with promises I'm powerless to uphold. You gave me life, and offer a kingdom. Your lord shared a friendship more precious. In return, I give my word as Teir's'Ffalenn that I won't squander these gifts."

That softness covered a will like steel wire, as Caolle had cause to respect. Touched by an uncharacteristic patience, he recalled the ballad of Falmuir and the uncanny tableau up the grotto. Forbearance allowed him not to rise to the hurt, that even after Etarra's armies, this prince seemed too reticent to place his full trust in the clans.

In the clearing, at the center of the circle, Halliron raised voice in cadenced expression of pure sorrow. Laid bare by the music, Arithon lost all composure. His throat closed, and he half spun away, ashamed of the tears he could not curb. The music broke his will, and his feelings for these stern, unbending people undid him. He felt Caolle's hand close on his shoulder, as it had many times to comfort Jieret.

"You could be my bastion," Arithon admitted, rarely vulnerable. "Except for Lysaer. Any who shelter me will become target for his armies. I would not see your great-hearted clans exterminated for my sake. And so I ask your leave to depart, unsupported and alone, until such time as I can return and fulfill your cherished hope, to rebuild a city in peace on the foundations of old Ithamon."

"I've misjudged you." Caolle withdrew his gruff touch, and for a long minute the rise and fall of Halliron's beautiful voice resounded through wood and clearing. Both men listened, each haunted by different regrets. Then Caolle raked back his scruffy, iron gray hair. "I'll do so no more. But in return, I ask your sanction to raise the clans of Fallowmere, and after them, clansmen the breadth of the continent."

"I'm against it." Arithon spun around. If his eyes blazed through a sparkle of unshed tears, the force in him was that of a sword unsheathed. "I wish no more killing in my name."

Caolle's stiff stance rendered the short silence eloquent.

And Arithon gave a sigh that seemed wrung from his very depths. "My wife and children weren't just murdered by headhunters." Gentled in a way Caolle would once have disparaged, the prince of Rathain traced the rune on the clan chieftain's marker with fingers too fine for the sword, but that could, and had, killed in battle. "My losses are as nothing to yours. I say that raising an army begs a repeat of this tragedy. But I'm not cold-hearted enough, or maybe I'm no true king at all. I haven't the nastiness to refuse you. My blessing is yours, if not my approval. Go in grace, Captain. Care for Jieret, whom I love as my brother."

In token of friendship, Caolle offered his palms and accepted the prince's double handshake. Across their clasped grip, while the song of lamentation spiraled and dipped through the greenwood, he gave his liege a voracious appraisal. The small build and fine bones, the green eyes with their depths and veiled secrets: both harbored deceptive strengths. Nearly too late Caolle had discovered an integrity that admitted no compromise. He would never in words be forced to admit that this scion of Rathain was both perfectly suited and tragically paired with a fate that must waste his real talents. "One day you'll be grateful for our support, Your Grace. We lend ourselves gladly. One could say it's not meet for Maenalle s'Gannley in Tysan to swear fealty to s'Ilessid unwarned." He released Arithon's hands and stepped back. "Ath keep you safe from all harm."

"And you." Arithon's mouth bent, a softening just short of warmth. "We've been adversaries. I'm not sorry. If I had my choice, your sword would go rusty for want of use. Hate me for that all you wish."

Caolle's chin puckered. For the sake of the mourning song still in progress, he coughed back a raw burst of laughter. "My sword," he said firmly, "will only get rusted when I'm dead. Dharkaron break me for idiocy, how did I come to swear fealty to a dreaming fool?"

"You were duped." Arithon grinned. "Lord Steiven did that to both of us." He turned and with quiet lack of ceremony, strode away from the riverbank.

Caolle watched him go, narrow-eyed, tightness like a fist at his throat. As Halliron struck chords for the lamentation's final stanza, the war captain of Deshir's clansmen whispered, "Go in grace, my prince."

The song dipped and mellowed, softened through its closing bars to a brushed note that quavered and trailed away into the rustle of flame-seared leaves. By then the Teir's'Ffalenn in his tattered black tunic had vanished from sight. Whether trees had hidden him, or some trick of shadow, Caolle found impossible to tell.

Dusk settled over Strakewood. In clear silver light, under trees like cut felt against cobalt, Arithon sat on a beech log. His tucked-up knees cradled folded arms. His cuff laces dangled over hands without tension as he listened to the first, uneven chorus of frogs in the marshes. He savored the quiet as day ebbed and softly surrendered to nightfall. The first star appeared, a scintillating pinprick between the pines; he looked on its solitary beauty without mage-sight to unlock its mystery.

Later was soon enough to decide where to go. This moment content to hang his thoughts on the sweet descending triplets of a wood thrush, he closed his eyes and lost himself in the abiding whisper of pine tassels stroked by the breeze.

He had no one to answer to. Nothing burdened him but a scorched conscience and a sword he would have given sight to have exchanged for the lyranthe left in Etarra.

Absorbed and relaxed, Arithon suspected nothing until a stick snapped loudly behind his shoulder.

He shot spinning to his feet and came face to face with a figure picked out in sparkles of gold chain and jewels.

Halliron Masterbard stood still decked out in his topaz studs, sure sign he had ended his stay with the clans. The fine buttons that fastened his cloak and hung his beautifully cut cape sleeves swung and glittered even in failing light.

Serene, his veined hands folded on the strap that slung his lyranthe, the Masterbard said, "It's a poor time for solitude, Your Grace."

Arithon bridled. "It's a worse hour for companionship with close to eight thousand lives done and wasted." Since the bard had presumed he was brooding, he would foster that impression to be rid of him. "I didn't ask for sympathy. I thought I made my wishes clear to Caolle?"

Halliron clicked his tongue behind spaced front teeth. "No need to raise your temper." Unwilling to accept such short shrift, he seated himself on the log the Master of Shadows had just vacated. Against his dark doublet his pale hair spread over his shoulders like watered silk. "I thought it wouldn't hurt to ask whether you'd join me on the road. Fallowmere holds little to attract me. I've lingered overlong in the north."

Nettled now deeper than artifice, Arithon recoiled backward. "Ah, no." He sounded as if somebody had hit him, or as if he shied off from hidden fear. "I'll be no man's company after this. You of all men should best understand my motive."

"You're not the first prince to take your oath through times of strife." Gold chains shivered in reflection as the bard shrugged. "Daelion knows you won't be the last. And you won't, though you try, put me off through a show of self-pity."

Arithon stiffened. "I think you've said enough." The words were a warning, which Halliron ignored by remaining in unbroken tranquility on the log. In the forest, the wood thrush had silenced. More stars burned through the branches, and the frogs sang their rasping bass chorus. The balance had fled; twilight had ebbed unnoticed, and the gloom now swallowed even the brittle spark of the topaz studs.

The veneer of peace so thinly established shattered suddenly beyond recovery. Into a silence that reproached, Arithon said in breaking anguish, "Ath help me, I *had* to stay. Without conjury or shadow, do you think any clansman would have survived to hear your lament for Deshir's dead?"

"Well, that's now behind you," Halliron said placidly. "Guilt is no use to anybody. The only thing a man gains from his past is the power to ensure his future. You can see the same circumstances are not permitted to happen again."

"I was doing just that, I thought." Arithon's anger intensified to a level that admitted only pain. The moment still haunted and cut him, that Lysaer's death and an end to Desh-thiere's geas had been balanced by Jieret's life. His voice skinned and raw, the Master added, "Will you leave? I'm quite likely to survive without counsel."

"Well, that may be. Except that *I* was the one come begging." The Masterbard folded his supple hands and maddeningly, solemnly regarded the ground between his boots. "If you'd unstop your ears and still your infernal s'Ffalenn conscience, you'd see that I'm an old man. I need a strong shoulder on the wheel when my pony cart mires in these bogs, and somebody ought to partner my rambling on the nights when cold rains drown my fire." A mischievous tilt to his lips, he looked up. "Never mind that your talents need schooling. If those fingers of yours are ever to shape more than promise, I'm offering the lowly station of minstrel's apprentice, Your Royal Grace. Will you accept?"

Arithon stared at him, his rigid bearing abandoned, repudiation stupid on his face. He sat down on the deadfall, banged his elbow on a branch, and tangled his calf in the sword scabbard he had forgotten he still wore. Faintly breathless, he cursed.

Mildly amused, and also queerly tense and vulnerable, Halliron chuckled. "The choice is that awful? You can't pretend to be surprised."

"No." A choke or a strangled phrase of laughter twisted in Arithon's throat. "Does the minstrel Felirin have prescience?"

"*What!*" The Masterbard lost his composure. His heart in his eyes, and his knuckles clamped together in white knots, he radiated panicked trepidation.

Arithon looked back at him and grinned. "Well, it's simple. Felirin forced me to promise once, should you ever come to offer me apprenticeship."

"And?" Halliron sounded smothered. He had raised both hands to his throat as if he needed help to keep breathing. "And?"

"I shall have to accept," Arithon said. "I've been party to all else but oath breaking, these days. My score with the Fatemaster's bad enough."

"You devil!" Halliron shot to his feet with a force that jostled a thrum of bass protest from his soundboard. "You let me think you'd turn me down!"

"Well, you let me think you'd come to lecture." Arithon laughed now with a bursting joy that dissolved the last of his antagonism. "Fiends take me, I wanted to kill you for that."

"Well, you lost your chance. You carry the greatest blade in Athera, and never once thought enough to use it." Halliron started walking decisively. "My pony and cart are hidden in a brush brake somewhere up the Tal Quorin. Once we find them, I'm fixing a strong pot of tea."

Then he stopped with a suddenness that caused Arithon to narrowly miss crashing into him.

"No," said Halliron, his expressive voice queerly jangled. "No. I'm needing no tea. The truth is that's not what I'm wanting at all." There and then in the darkness, he unstrapped his bundle and tugged off oiled leather coverings. "Play me that tune I once asked for." Not waiting for answer, he thrust his beautiful instrument into the arms of his apprentice.

Arithon caressed the scrolled soundboard, drew a breath that smelled of wax and resins and fine wood. He could not speak. He feared to move lest he disturb the frailty of his happiness. Halliron Masterbard had laid a lyranthe between his hands and offered his heart's whole desire.

Unseen in the fragrant summer gloom, the shy wood thrush ventured a last, lyric arpeggio. Crickets rasped undisturbed by any approaching footstep. After a moment of fractured suspension Arithon laid to rest his final fear. He accepted that no one would burst from the wood in appeal for a cause he could not for conscience fail to shoulder.

For this night and others he was free. He could sit, set his hands to silver strings, and at long last bend sorrow into music.

Reflections

In Mirthlvain Swamp, Asandir and Dakar join Verrain's patrol of black pools to check for resurgence of meth-snakes before the seasonal fall spawning; Traithe and Kharadmon arrive in Shand; and while the Fellowship's hope for the south centers on one last prince raised in hiding, the Warden of Althain tracks two cursed royal heirs who survive, and awaits against hope any sign that the Black Rose prophecy might still hold valid. . . .

In Korias the hour after sunrise, First Enchantress Lirenda presents report from the lane-watch to her mistress, Morriel Prime; and the news is unhappily received, that the initiates entrusted with scrying through fifth-lane vibrations have lost track of the Master of Shadows. . . .

In the lightless shaft of Rockfell, sealed behind triple rings of wards, the Mistwraith that once blocked sunlight from Athera languishes in confinement; and if it knows that its grand curse to destroy two half-brothers has once been tested and thwarted, it endures in unquiet hatred. . . .

Glossary

ADON—statue of centaur king, one of the twins who founded the Ilitharis Paravian royal line in the First Age. The carving forms one side of the arch of Standing Gate on the road leading east into the Pass of Orlan, Camris, Tysan.

    pronounced: a-don, rhymes with "hay don"

    root meaning: *daon*—gold

ALATHWYR TOWER—one of five towers built by Paravians in the middle of the First Age at Ithamon, principality of Daon Ramon, Rathain. Its stonework of white alabaster is warded by the virtue, Wisdom. It stands North, of the four towers that remain standing in the Third Age; hence the common name used by men, being Compass Point Towers, or Sun Towers.

    pronounced: ah-lath-weer (a's to rhyme with as) emphasis on middle
        syllable

    root meaning: wisdom: *alath*—to know; *wyr*—all, sum

ALITHIEL—one of twelve Blades of Isaer, forged by centaur Ffereton s'Darian in the First Age from metal taken from a meteorite. Passed through Paravian possession, acquired the secondary name Dael-Farenn, or Kingmaker, since its owners tended to succeed the end of a royal line. Eventually was awarded to Kamridian s'Ffalenn for his valor in defense of the princess Taliennse, early Second Age.

    pronounced: ah-lith-ee-el

    root meaning: *alith*—star; *iel*—light/ray

ALTHAIN TOWER—spire built at the edge of the Bittern Desert, beginning of the Second Age, to house records of Paravian histories. Third Age, became respository for the archives of all five royal houses of men after rebellion, overseen by Sethvir, Warden of Althain and Fellowship Sorcerer.

 pronounced: al like "all," thain to rhyme with "main"

 root meaning: *alt*—last; *thein*—tower, sanctuary

 original Paravian pronunciation: alt-thein (thein as in "the end")

AMROTH—kingdom on West Gate splinter world, Dascen Elur, ruled by s'Ilessid descendants of the prince exiled through the Worldsend Gate at the time of the rebellion, Third Age just after the Mistwraith's conquest.

 pronounced: am-roth (rhymes with "sloth")

 root meaning: *am*—state of being; *roth*—brother "brotherhood"

ANGLEFEN—swampland located in Deshir, Rathain. Town of same name at the river mouth with port to Stormwell Gulf. One of the six port towns that link sea trade-routes with Etarra.

 pronounced: angle-fen

 root meaning is not Paravian

ARAETHURA—grass plains in southwest Rathain; principality of the same name in that location. Largely inhabited by Riathan Paravians in the Second Age. Third Age, used as pastureland by widely scattered nomadic shepherds.

 pronounced: ar-eye-thoo-rah

 root meaning: *araeth*—grass; *era*—place, land

ARAITHE—plain to the north of the trade city of Etarra, principality of Fallowmere, Rathain. First Age, among the sites used by the Paravians to renew the mysteries and channel fifth lane energies. The standing stones erected are linked to the power focus at Ithamon and Meth Isle keep.

 pronounced: araithe, rhymes with "a wraith"

 root meaning: *araithe*—to disperse, to send; refers to the properties of the standing stones with relationship to the fifth lane forces

ARITHON—son of Avar, Prince of Rathain, 1,504th Teir's'Ffalenn after founder of the line, Torbrand in Third Age Year One. Also Master of Shadow, and the Bane of Desh-thiere.

 pronounced: ar-i-thon—almost rhymes with "marathon"

 root meaning: *arithon*—fate-forger; one who is visionary

ASANDIR—Fellowship Sorcerer. Secondary name, Kingmaker, since his hand crowned every High King of Men to rule in the Age of Men (Third Age). After the Mistwraith's conquest, he acted as field agent for the Fellowship's doings across the continent. Also called Fiend-quencher, for his reputation for quelling iyats; Storm-breaker, and Change-bringer for past actions in late Second Age, when Men first arrived upon Athera.

 pronounced: ah-san-deer

 root meaning: *asan*—heart; *dir*—stone "heartrock"

ATAINIA—northeastern principality of Tysan.
  pronounced: ah-tay-nee-ah
  root meaning: *itain*—the third; *ia* suffix for "third domain" original
    Paravian, *itainia*
ATH CREATOR—prime vibration, force behind all life.
  pronounced: ath to rhyme with "math"
  root meaning: *ath*—prime, first (as opposed to *an*, one)
ATHERA—name for the continent which holds the Five High Kingdoms;
one of two major landmasses on the planet.
  pronounced: ath-air-ah
  root meaning: *ath*—prime force; *era*—place "Ath's world"
ATHLIEN PARAVIANS—sunchildren. Small race of semimortals, pixie-
like, but possessed of great wisdom/keepers of the grand mystery.
  pronounced: ath-lee-en
  root meaning: *ath*—prime force; *lien*—to love "Ath-beloved"
ATHLIERIA—equivalent of heaven/actually a dimension removed from
physical life, inhabited by spirit after death
  pronounced: ath-lee-air-ee-ah
  root meaning: *ath*—prime force; *li'era*—exalted place, or land in har-
    mony; *li*—exalted in harmony
AVAR s'FFALENN—Pirate King of Karthan, isle on splinter world
Dascen Elur, through West Gate. Father of Arithon; also Teir's'Ffalenn
1,503rd in descent from Torbrand who founded the s'Ffalenn royal line in
Third Age Year One.
  pronounced: ah-var, to rhyme with "far"
  root meaning: *avar*—past thought/memory

BRIANE—name of the warship that was crippled in the engagement
against the brigantine in command of Avar of Karthan; the vessel later
took Arithon s'Ffalenn captive and bore him to South Isle, and thence to
Port Royal on the splinter world of Dascen Elur.
  pronounced: bry-anna to rhyme with "fry anna"
  root meaning: *brianne*—gull
BWIN EVOC s'LORNMEIN—founder of the line that became High Kings
of Havish since Third Age Year One. The attribute he passed on by
means of the Fellowship's geas was temperance.
  pronounced: bwin to rhyme with "twin," ee-vahk as in "evocative,"
    lorn as in English equivalent, mein rhymes with "main"
  root meaning: *bwin*—firm; *evoc*—choice

CAILCALLOW—herb that grows in marshes, used to ease fevers.
  pronounced: rhymes with "kale-tallow"
  root meaning: *cail*—leaf; *calliew*—balm
CAITH-AL-CAEN—vale where Riathan Paravians (unicorns) celebrated
equinox and solstice to renew the *athael*, or life-destiny of the world.

Also the place where the Ilitharis Paravians first Named the winter stars—or encompassed their vibrational essence into language. Corrupted by the end of the Third Age to Castlecain.

    pronounced: cay-ith-al-cay-en, musical lilt, emphasis on second and last syllables; rising note on first two, falling note on last two.

    root meaning: *caith*—shadow; *al*—over; *caen*—vale "vale of shadow"

CAITHDEIN—Paravian name for a high king's first counselor; also, the one who would stand as regent, or steward, in the absence of the crowned ruler.

    pronounced: kay-ith-day-in

    root meaning: *caith*—shadow; *d'ein*—behind the chair "shadow behind the throne"

CAITHWOOD—forest located in Taerlin, southeast principality of Tysan.

    pronounced: kay-ith-wood

    root meaning: *caith*—shadow "shadowed wood"

CASTLECAIN—corrupted name for Caith-al-Caen, Vale of Shadows, see entry above.

    pronounced: castle-cane

CASTLE POINT—port city at the western terminus of the Great West Road, located in the principality of Atainia, Tysan.

CAL—mortal name held by Sethvir before he swore pact with the Fellowship of Seven.

    pronounced: kal

    root meaning is not Paravian. (From English, Calum)

CAMRIS—north-central principality of Tysan. Original ruling seat was city of Erdane.

    pronounced: kam-ris, the "i" as in "chris"

    root meaning: *caim*—cross; *ris*—way "crossroad"

CAOLLE—war captain of the clans of Deshir, Rathain. First raised, and then served under Lord Steiven, Earl of the North and *caithdein* of Rathain.

    pronounced: kay-all-e, with the "e" nearly subliminal

    root meaning: *caille*—stubborn

CIANOR SUNLORD—born at Caith-al-Caen, First Age 615. Survived both the massacre of Leorne (caused by methuri, or hate-wraiths out of Mirthlvain Swamp) in year 815, and led the Battle of Retaliation on Bordirion Plain (which by the start of the Second Age had been enveloped by the swamp). In 826 Cianor's forces were defeated at Erdane by Khadrim; Cianor retired to Araethura, gravely wounded. Crippled but alive, he was on hand at the arrival of the Fellowship of Seven, when Crater Lake was formed in First Age 827. Healed by Fellowship Sorcerers. Appointed Keeper of the Records in 902; stabilized the realm after the murder of High King Marin Eliathe in Second Age 1542. Crowned High

King of Athera in Second Age 2545 until his death when a rise of Khadrim called him to war in Second Age 3651.

pronounced: key-ah-nor

root meaning: *cianor*—to shine

CIERL-ANKESHED—venom of certain strains of meth-snakes, which causes dissolution of nerve tissue. Paralysis is almost instant, with death following days later. Without a known antidote, the poison is caustic and can be absorbed through the skin.

pronounced: key-earl-an-kesh-id

root meaning: *cierl*—nerve; *ankeshed*—pain/agony

CILADIS THE LOST—Fellowship Sorcerer who left the continent in Third Age 3462 in search of the Paravian races after their disappearance after the rebellion.

pronounced: kill-ah-dis

root meaning: *cael*—leaf; *adeis*—whisper, compound; *cael'adeis,* colloquialism for "gentleness that abides"

CILDORN—city famed for carpets and weaving, located in Deshir, Rathain. Originally a Paravian holdfast, situated on a node of the third lane.

pronounced: kill-dorn

root meaning: *cieal*—thread; *dorn*—net "tapestry"

CORITH—island west of Havish coast, in Westland Sea. First site to see sunlight upon Desh-thiere's defeat.

pronounced: kor-ith

root meaning: *cori*—ships, vessels; *itha*—five for the five harbors which the old city overlooked

DAELION FATEMASTER—"entity" formed by set of mortal beliefs, which determine the fate of the spirit after death. If Ath is the prime vibration, or life force, Daelion is what governs the manifestation of free will.

pronounced: day-el-ee-on

root meaning: *dael*—king, or lord; *i'on*—of fate

DAEL-FARENN—Kingmaker, name for sword Alithiel; also, one of many Paravian names for the Fellowship Sorcerer, Asandir.

pronounced: day-el-far-an

root meaning: *dael*—king; *feron*—maker

DAELTHAIN—fifth Compass Point, or Sun Tower, built by Paravians at citadel of Ithamon. This was the King's Tower, whose warded virtue was Justice. The structure fell on the eve of Marin Eliathe's murder, and crumbled further through the course of the rebellion. By the time of the Mistwraith's conquest all that remained was the foundation.

pronounced: day-el-they-in

root meaning: *dael*—king or lord; *thein*—tower, sanctuary

DAELTIRI—sword carried by s'Ilessid High Kings. Forged in Second Age

1240 by Paravian artisans to commemorate friendship on the occasion of Jaest s'Ilessid's ascension to the crown at Avenor.

pronounced: day-el-tee-ree

root meaning: *dael*—king, lord; *tieri*—steel

DAENFAL—city located on the northern lake shore that bounds the southern edge of Daon Ramon Barrens in Rathain.

pronounced: dye-en-fall

root meaning: *daen*—clay; *fal*—red

DAKAR THE MAD PROPHET—apprentice to Fellowship Sorcerer, Asandir, during the Third Age following the Conquest of the Mistwraith. Given to spurious prophesies, it was Dakar who forecast the fall of the Kings of Havish in time for the Fellowship to save the heir. He made the Prophecy of West Gate which forecast the Mistwraith's bane, and also, the Black Rose prophesy, which called for reunification of the Fellowship.

pronounced: dah-kar

root meaning: *dakiar*—clumsy

DANIA—wife of Rathain's Regent, Steiven s'Valerient.

pronounced: dan-ee-ah

root meaning: *deinia*—sparrow

DAON RAMON BARRENS—central principality of Rathain. Site where Riathan Paravians (unicorns) bred and raised their young. Barrens was not appended to the name until the years following the Mistwraith's conquest, when the river Severnir was diverted at the source by a task force under Etarran jurisdiction.

pronounced: day-on-rah-mon

root meaning: *daon*—gold; *ramon*—hills/downs

DARI s'AHELAS—Princess of Shand who fled through the western Worldsend Gate at the time of the Mistwraith's conquest, to escape the rebellion engineered by Davien. Sethvir trained her in the foundational arts of power to increase her line's chances of survival. Her descendants ruled Rauven in the splinter world of Dascen Elur.

pronounced: dar-ee

root meaning: *daer*—to cut

DAVIEN THE BETRAYER—Fellowship Sorcerer responsible for provoking the great uprising that resulted in the fall of the high kings after Desh-thiere's conquest. Rendered discorporate by the Fellowship's judgment in Second Age 5129. Exiled since, by personal choice. Davien's works included the Five Centuries Fountain near Mearth, on the splinter world of the Red Desert, through West Gate; Rockfell shaft, used by the Sorcerers to imprison harmful entities; The Stair on Rockfell Peak; and also, Kewar Tunnel in the Mathorn Mountains.

pronounced: dah-vee-en

root meaning: *dahvi*—fool, mistake; *an*—one "mistaken one"

DASCEN ELUR—splinter world off West Gate; primarily ocean with isolated archipelagos. Includes kingdoms of Rauven, Amroth, and Karthan. Where three exiled high kings' heirs took refuge in the years following the great uprising.

pronounced: das-en el-ur

root meaning: *dascen*—ocean; *e'lier*—small land

DESH-THIERE—Mistwraith that invaded Athera from the splinter worlds through South Gate in Third Age Year 4993. Access cut off by Fellowship Sorcerer, Traithe. Battled and contained in West Shand for twenty-five years, until the rebellion splintered the peace, and the high kings were forced to withdraw from the defense lines to attend their disrupted kingdoms.

pronounced: desh-thee-air-e (last "e" mostly subliminal)

root meaning: *desh*—mist; *thiere*—ghost or wraith

DESHANS—barbarian clans who inhabit Strakewood Forest, principality of Deshir, Rathian.

pronounced: desh-ee-ans

root meaning: *deshir*—misty

DESHIR—northwestern principality of Rathain.

pronounced: desh-eer

root meaning: *deshir*—misty

DHARKARON AVENGER—called Ath's Avenging Angel in legend. Drives a chariot drawn by five horses to convey the guilty to Sithaer. Dharkaron as defined by Ath's adepts is that dark thread mortal men weave with Ath, the prime vibration, that creates self-punishment, or the root of guilt.

pronounced: dark-air-on

root meaning: *dhar*—evil; *khiaron*—one who stands in judgment

DIEGAN—Lord Commander of Etarra's garrison. Titular commander of the war host sent against the Deshans to defeat the Master of Shadows.

pronounced: dee-gan

root meaning: *diegan*—trinket a dandy might wear/ornament

DURMAENIR—centaur, son of the armorer who forged the twelve Blades of Isaer. Sword Alithiel was fashioned for Durmaenir, who died in battle against Khadrim in the First Age.

pronounced: dur-may-e-neer

root meaning: *dir*—stone; *maenien*—fallen

EAST WARD—city in Fallowmere, Rathain, renowned as a port that served the trade-route to Etarra from the Cildein Ocean.

pronounced: ward

no Paravian root meaning as this city was man's creation

EDAL—next to youngest daughter of Steiven and Dania s'Valerient.

pronounced: ee-doll

root meaning: *e'* prefix, diminutive for small; *dal*—fair

ELAIRA—initiate enchantress of the Koriathain. Originally a street child, bought up in Morvain for Koriani rearing.
> pronounced: ee-layer-ah
> root meaning: *e'* prefix, diminutive for small; *laere*—grace

ELDIR s'LORNMEIN—prince of Havish and last surviving scion of s'Lornmein royal line. Raised as a wool-dyer until the Fellowship Sorcerers trained him for kingship following the defeat of the Mistwraith.
> pronounced: el-deer
> root meaning: *eldir*—to ponder, to consider, to weigh

ELSHIAN—Athlien Paravian bard and instrument maker. Crafted the lyranthe that is held in trust by Athera's Masterbard.
> pronounced: el-shee-an
> root meaning: *e'alshian*—small wonder, or miracle

ELTAIR BAY—large bay off Cildein Ocean and east coast of Rathain; where River Severnir was diverted following the Mistwraith's conquest.
> pronounced: el-tay-er
> root meaning: *al'tieri*—of steel/a shortening of original Paravian name; *dascen al'tieri*—which meant "ocean of steel" which referred to the color of the waves.

ELWEDD—clansman under Steiven's rule. Wagered Halliron Masterbard that Arithon s'Ffalenn had poor swordsmanship.
> pronounced: el-wet
> root meaning: *el*—short; *weth*—sight

ENASTIR—sunchild, Paravian High King. Son and heir of Lithorn. Ruled in the early First Age until his death on the talons of Great Gethorn.
> pronounced: ee-nas-teer
> root meaning: *e'* prefix for small; *nastir*—warrior

ENITHEN TUER—seeress in residence, city of Erdane. Where Asandir stays while passing through Camris, Tysan.
> pronounced: en-ith-en too-er
> root meaning: *en'wethen*—farsighted; *tuer*—crone

ERDANE—old Paravian city, later taken over by Men. Seat of Earls of Camris until Desh-thiere's conquest and rebellion.
> pronounced: er-day-na with the last syllable almost subliminal
> root meaning: *er'deinia*—long walls

ETARRA—trade city built across the Mathorn Pass by townsfolk after the revolt that cast down Ithamon and the High Kings of Rathain. Nest of corruption and intrigue, and policy maker for the North.
> pronounced: ee-tar-ah
> root meaning: *e'* prefix for small; *taria*—knots

FALLOWMERE—northeastern principality of Rathain.
> pronounced: fal-oh-meer
> root meaning: *fal-ei-miere*—literally, tree self-reflection, colloquialism for "place of perfect trees"

FALMUIR—city, once in Kingdom of Melhalla, ruined during a war of succession/never rebuilt. Princess of Falmuir subject of a ballad that Halliron uses to illustrate a point to Caolle after the battle of Strakewood.

   pronounced: fal-mu-ear

   root meaning: *ffael*—dark; *muir*—cause

FELIRIN—minstrel who joins Asandir's party enroute to Erdane.

   pronounced: fell-eer-in

   root meaning: *fel*—red; *lyron*—singer

FELLOWSHIP OF SEVEN—sorcerers sworn to uphold the Laws of the Major Balance, and to foster enlightened thought in Athera

FFERETON s'DARIAN—centaur armorer who forged the twelve Blades of Isaer, among them, Alithiel.

   pronounced: fair-et-on

   root meaning: *ffereton*—craftsman/master-maker

GHENT—mountainous principality in Kingdom of Havish; where Prince Eldir was raised in hiding.

   pronounced: gent, hard "g"

   root meaning: *ghent*—harsh

GNUDSOG—Etarra's field-captain of the garrison under Lord Commander Diegan; acting first officer in the battle of Strakewood Forest

   pronounced: nud-sug to rhyme with "wood log"

   root meaning: *gianud*—tough; *sog*—ugly

GRITHEN—last descendent, earls of Erdane. Leader of the raid on Asandir's party in the Pass of Orlan.

   pronounced: gri-then, rhymes with "with hen"

   root meaning: *kierth*—mistake; *an*—one

HADIG—commander of archers, Etarra City Garrison

   pronounced: hay-dig

   root meaning not from Paravian

HALDUIN s'ILESSID—founder of the line that became High Kings of Tysan since Third Age Year One. The attribute he passed on, by means of the Fellowship's geas, was Justice.

   pronounced: hal-dwin

   root meaning: *hal*—white; *duinne*—hand

HALLIRON MASTERBARD—Masterbard of Athera during the Third Age; inherited the accolade from his teacher Murchiel in the year 5597.

   pronounced: hal-eer-on

   root meaning: *hal*—white; *lyron*—singer

HALMEIN—statue of centaur king, one of the twins who founded the Ilitharis Paravian royal line in the First Age. The carving forms the left side of the arch of Standing Gate on the road leading east into the Pass of Orlan, principality of Camris, Tysan.

pronounced: hal-may-in

root meaning: *hal*—white; *mein*—haired

HANSHIRE—port city on Westland Sea, coast of Korias, Tysan. Where enchantress Elaira is stationed following her escapade at the Ravens Inn.

pronounced: han-sheer

root meaning: *hansh*—sand; *era*—place

HAVISH—one of the Five High Kingdoms of Athera, as defined by the charters of the Fellowship of Seven. Ruled by the s'Lornmein royal line. Sigil: gold hawk on red field

pronounced: hav-ish

root meaning: *havieshe*—hawk

HAVISTOCK—southeast principality of Kingdom of Havish.

pronounced: hav-i-stock

root meaning: *haviesha*—hawk; *tiok*—roost

IDRIEN—Jieret's companion on the raid in which they take Halliron Masterbard captive on the road south from Ward.

pronounced: i-dree-en

root meaning: *e'*—prefix for small; *drien*—partner

ILITHARIS PARAVIANS—centaurs, one of three semimortal old races; disappeared at the time of the Mistwraith's conquest.

pronounced: i-li-thar-is

root meaning: *i'lith'earis*—the keeper/preserver of mystery

IMARN ADAER—enclave of Paravian gem-cutters in the city of Mearth, who dispersed in the times of the Curse which destroyed the inhabitants. The secrets of their trade were lost with them. Surviving works include the crown jewels of the Five High Kingdoms of Athera, cut as focus-stones which attune to the heir of the royal lines.

pronounced: i-marn-a-day-er

root meaning: *imarn*—crystal; *e'daer*—to cut smaller

INSTRELL BAY—body of water off the Gulf of Stormwell, that separates principality of Atainia, Tysan, from Deshir, Rathain.

pronounced: in-strell

root meaning: *arin'streal*—strong-wind

ISAER—power focus, built during the First Age, in Atainia, Tysan, to source the defense-works at the Paravian keep of the same name.

pronounced: i-say-er

root meaning: *i'saer*—the circle

ITHAMON—city built on a fifth lane power-node in Daon Ramon Barrens, Rathain. Originally a Paravian keep; site of the Compass Point Towers, or Sun Towers. Became the seat of the High Kings of Rathain during the Third Age and in year 5638 was the site where Princes Lysaer s'Ilessid and Arithon s'Ffalenn battled the Mistwraith to confinement.

pronounced: ith-a-mon

root meaning: *itha*—five; *mon*—needle, spire

IYAT—energy sprite native to Athera, not visible to the eye, manifests in a poltergeist fashion by taking temporary possession of objects. Feeds upon natural energy sources: fire, breaking waves, lightning.
    pronounced: ee-at
    root meaning: *iyat*—to break

JIERET s'VALERIENT—son and heir of Lord Steiven, clan chief of Deshir, Earl of the North and *caithdein* of Rathain. Bloodpacted to Arithon Teir's'Ffalenn prior to battle of Strakewood Forest.
    pronounced: jeer-et
    root meaning: *jieret*—thorn

KARFAEL—trader town on the coast of the Westland Sea, in Tysan. Built by townsmen as a trade port after the fall of the High Kings of Tysan. Prior to Desh-thiere's conquest, the site was kept clear of buildings to allow the second lane forces to flow untrammeled across the focus site at Avenor.
    pronounced: kar-fay-el
    root meaning: *kar'i'ffael*—literal translation "twist the dark"/
        colloquialism for "intrigue"
KARMAK—plain located in the northern portion of the principality of Camris, Tysan. Site of numerous First Age battles where Paravian forces opposed Khadrim packs that bred in volcanic sites in the northern Tornir Peaks.
    pronounced: kar-mack
    root meaning: *karmak*—wolf
KARTHAN—kingdom in splinter world Dascen Elur, through West Gate, ruled by the Pirate Kings, s'Ffalenn descendants of the prince sent into exile at the time of the Mistwraith's conquest.
    pronounced: karth-an
    root meaning: *kar'eth'an*—one who raids/pirate
KARTHISH—from Karthan, term denoting nationality.
    pronounced: karth-ish
    root meaning: *kar'eth'an*—pirate
KELSING—town immediately south of Erdane, located in Camris, Tysan. Nearest inhabited site to the old earl's court, which served as summer quarters for the Koriani Prime and her Senior Circle at the time of Lysaer and Arithon's arrival through West Gate.
    pronounced: kel-sing
    root meaning: *kel*—hidden; *seng*—cave
KHADRIM—flying, fire-breathing reptiles that were the scourge of the Second Age. By the Third Age, they had been driven back and confined in a warded preserve in the volcanic peaks in north Tysan.
    pronounced: kaa-drim
    root meaning: *khadrim*—dragon

KHARADMON—Sorcerer of the Fellowship of Seven; discorporate since rise of Khadrim and Seardluin leveled Paravian city at Ithamon in First Age 3651. It was by Kharadmon's intervention that the survivors of the attack were sent to safety by means of transfer from the fifth lane power focus.

    pronounced: kah-rad-mun

    root meaning: *kar'riad en mon*—phrase translates to mean "twisted
                thread on the needle" or colloquialism for "a knot in
                the works"

KIELING TOWER—one of the four Compass Points or Sun Towers standing at Ithamon, Daon Ramon Barrens, Rathain. The warding virtue that binds its stones is Compassion.

    pronounced: kee-el-ing

    root meaning: *kiel'ien*—root for pity, with suffix added translates to
                "compassion"

KORIANI—possessive form of the word "Koriathain;" see entry.

    pronounced: kor-ee-ah-nee

KORIAS—southwestern principality of Tysan.

    pronounced: kor-ee-as

    root meaning: *cor*—ship, vessel; *i'esh*—nest, haven

KORIATHAIN—order of enchantresses ruled by a circle of eight Seniors, under the power of one Prime Enchantress. They draw their talent from the orphaned children they raise, or from daughters dedicated to service by their parents. Initiation rite involves a vow of consent that ties the spirit to a power channel keyed to the Prime's control.

    pronounced: kor-ee-ah-thain (thain rhymes with "main")

    root meaning: *koriath*—order; *ain*—belonging to

LANSHIRE—northwestern principality of Havish. Name taken from wastes at Scarpdale, site of First Age battles with Seardluin that seared the soil to a slag waste.

    pronounced: lahn-sheer-e (last "e" is nearly subliminal)

    root meaning: *lan'hansh'era*—place of hot sands

LIRENDA—First Senior Enchantress to the Prime, Koriani order; Morriel's intended successor.

    pronounced: leer-end-ah

    root meaning: *lyron*—singer; *di-ia*—a dissonance (the hyphen denotes
                a glottal stop)

LUHAINE—Sorcerer of the Fellowship of Seven—discorporate since the fall of Telmandir. Luhaine's body was pulled down by the mob while he was in ward trance, covering the escape of the royal heir to Havish.

    pronounced: loo-hay-ne

    root meaning: *luirhainon*—defender

LYRANTHE—instrument played by the bards of Athera. Strung with fourteen strings, tuned to seven tones (doubled). Two courses are "drone strings" set to octaves. Five are melody strings, the lower three courses being octaves, the upper two, in unison.

    pronounced: leer-anth-e (last "e" being nearly subliminal)

    root meaning: *lyr*—song; *anthe*—box

LYSAER s'ILESSID—prince of Tysan, 1497th in succession after Halduin, founder of the line in Third Age Year One. Gifted at birth with control of Light, and Bane of Desh-thiere

    pronounced: lie-say-er

    root meaning: *lia*—blond, yellow, or light; *saer*—circle

MADREIGH—senior scout, Deshir clans. One of the eleven who stood to Jieret's defense in the battle of Strakewood Forest.

    pronounced: mah-dree-ah ("ah" is near subliminal)

    root meaning: *madrien*—staunch

MAENALLE s'GANNLEY—steward and *caithdein* of Tysan.

    pronounced: may-nahl-e (last "e" is near subliminal)

    root meaning: *maeni*—to fall, disrupt; *alli*—to save or preserve/
            colloquial translation: "to patch together"

MAIEN—nickname for Maenalle's grandson, Maenol.

    pronounced: my-en

    root meaning: *maien*—mouse

MAENOL—heir, after Maenalle s'Gannley, Steward and *caithdein* of Tysan.

    pronounced: may-nahl

    root meaning: *maeni'alli*—"to patch together"

MAINMERE—town at the head of the Valenford River, located in the principality of Taerlin, Tysan. Built by townsmen on a site originally kept clear to free the second lane focus in the ruins farther south.

    pronounced: main-meer-e ("e" is subliminal)

    root meaning: *maeni*—to fall, interrupt; *miere*—reflection; colloquial
            translation: "disrupt continuity"

MARIN ELIATHE—Paravian High King murdered in his own hall by an assassin in Second Age 1542.

    pronounced: mahr-in el-ee-ath

    root meaning: *marin*—happening; *e'li*—in harmony with; *ath*—prime
            force behind all life

MARL—Earl of Fallowmere and clan chieftain at the time of the battle of Strakewood Forest.

    pronounced: marl

    root meaning: *marle*—quartz rock

MATHORN MOUNTAINS—range that bisects the Kingdom of Rathain, east to west.

    pronounced: math-orn

    root meaning: *mathien*—massive

MATHORN ROAD—way passing to the south of the Mathorn Mountains, leading to the trade city of Etarra from the west.
    pronounced: math-orn
    root meaning: *mathien*—massive

MEARA—daughter of Steiven, Earl of the North, and Dania; older sister of Jieret.
    pronounced: mere-ah
    root meaning: *meara*—willow

MEARTH—city through the West Gate in the Red Desert. Inhabitants all fell victim to the Shadows of Mearth, which were created by the Fellowship Sorcerer Davien to protect the Five Centuries Fountain. The Shadows are a light-fueled geas that bind the mind to memory of an individual's most painful experience.
    pronounced: me-arth
    root meaning: *mearth*—empty

MELOR RIVER—located in the principality of Korias, Tysan. Its mouth forms the harbor for the port town of West End.
    pronounced: mel-or
    root meaning: *maeliur*—fish

METH ISLE KEEP—old Paravian fortress located on the isle in Methlas Lake in southern Melhalla. Kept by Verrain, Guardian of Mirthlvain. Contains a fifth lane power focus and dungeons where methuri were held temporarily captive before transfer to Rockfell.
    pronounced: meth isle
    root meaning: *meth*—hate

METHLAS LAKE—large body of fresh water located in the principality of Radmoor, Melhalla.
    pronounced: meth-las
    root meaning: *meth'ilass'an*—the drowned, or sunken ones.

METH-SNAKES—crossbred genetic mutations left over from a First Age creature called a methuri (hate-wraith). Related to iyats, these creatures possessed live hosts, which they infested and induced to produce mutated offspring to create weakened lines of stock to widen their choice of potential host animals.
    pronounced: meth to rhyme with "death"
    root meaning: *meth*—hate

METHURI—iyat-related parasite that infested live host animals. By the Third Age, they are extinct, but their mutated host stock continues to breed in Mirthlvain Swamp.
    pronounced: meth-yoor-ee
    root meaning: *meth*—hate; *thiere*—wraith, or spirit

MIN PIERENS—archipelago to the west of Kingdom of West Shand, in the Westland Sea.
    pronounced: min (rhymes with "pin") pierre-ins
    root meaning: *min*—purple; *pierens*—shoreline

MIRTHLVAIN SWAMP—boglands filled with dangerous crossbreeds, located south of the Tiriac Mountains in principality of Midhalla, Melhalla. Never left unwatched. Since conquest of the Mistwraith, the appointed guardian was the spellbinder, Verrain.

pronounced: mirth-el-vain

root meaning: *myrthl*—noxious; *vain*—bog/mud

MORFETT—Lord Governor Supreme of Etarra at the time the Fellowship seeks to restore Rathain's monarchy following the captivity of the Mistwraith.

pronounced: more-fet

no root meaning from the Paravian

MORRIEL—Prime Enchantress of the Koriathain since the Third Age Year 4212.

pronounced: more-real

root meaning: *moar*—greed; *riel*—silver

MORVAIN—city located in the principality of Araethura, Rathain, on the coast of Instrell Bay. Elaira's birthplace.

pronounced: more-vain

root meaning: *morvain*—swindler's market

NARMS—city on the coast of Instrell Bay, built as a craft center by men in the early Third Age. Best known for dyeworks.

pronounced: narms to rhyme with "charms"

root meaning: *narms*—color

ORLAN—pass through the Thaldein Mountains, also location of the Camris clans' west outpost, in Camris, Tysan. Where Asandir's party is waylaid by Grithen enroute to Althain Tower.

pronounced: or-lan

root meaning: *irlan*—ledge

ORVANDIR—principality located in northeastern Shand.

pronounced: or-van-deer

root meaning: *orvein*—crumbled; *dir*—stone

PARAVIAN—name for the three old races that inhabited Athera before Men. Including the centaurs, the sunchildren, and the unicorns, these races never die unless mishap befalls them; they are the world's channel, or direct connection to Ath Creator.

pronounced: par-ai-vee-ans

root meaning: *para*—great; *i'on*—fate or "great mystery"

PESQUIL—Mayor of the Northern League of Headhunters, at the time of the battle of Strakewood Forest. His strategies cause the Deshir clans the most punishing losses.

pronounced: pes-quil to rhyme with "pest quill"

root meaning not from the Paravian

QUEN—halfwit who serves as door guard and servant to the Prime Enchantress of the Koriathain, Morriel.
  pronounced: cue-en
  root meaning: *quenient*—witless

RATHAIN—High Kingdom of Athera ruled by descendants of Torbrand
s'Ffalenn since Third Age Year One. Sigil: black and silver leopard on
green field.
  pronounced: rath-ayn
  root meaning: *roth*—brother; *thein*—tower, sanctuary
RAUVEN TOWER—home of the s'Ahelas mages who brought up
Arithon s'Ffalenn and trained him to the ways of power. Located on the
splinter world, Dascen Elur, through West Gate.
  pronounced: raw-ven
  root meaning: *rauven*—invocation
RENWORT—plant native to Athera. A poisonous mash can be brewed
from the berries.
  pronounced: ren-wart
  root meaning: *renwarin*—poison
RIATHAN PARAVIANS—unicorns, the purest and most direct connection to Ath Creator; the prime vibration channels directly through the
horn.
  pronounced: ree-ah-than
  root meaning: *ria*—to touch; *ath*—prime life force; *ri'athon*—one who
              touches divinity
ROCKFELL—deep shaft cut into Rockfell Peak, used to imprison harmful entities throughout all three ages. Located in the principality of West
Halla, Melhalla; became the warded prison for Desh-thiere.
  pronounced: rock-fell
  root meaning not from the Paravian
ROCKFELL VALE—valley below Rockfell Peak, located in principality of
West Halla, Melhalla.
  pronounced: rockfell vale
  root meaning not from the Paravian

SAERIAT—name of the brigantine captained by Avar of Karthan, defeated
and burned in engagement against seventeen warships of Amroth.
  pronounced: say-ree-at
  root meaning: *saer*—water; *iyat*—to break
s'AHELAS—family name for the royal line appointed by the Fellowship
Sorcerers in Third Age Year One to rule the High Kingdom of Shand.
Gifted geas: farsight.
  pronounced: s'ah-hell-as
  root meaning: *ahelas*—mage-gifted
s'DARIAN—family name for a line of centaurs who were master armor-

ers in the First and Second Ages. Most renowned was Ffereton who forged the twelve Blades of Isaer, Alithiel being for his natural son Durmaenir.

    pronounced: dar-ee-an

    root meaning: *daer'an*—one that cuts

s'FFALENN—family name for the royal line appointed by the Fellowship Sorcerers in Third Age Year One to rule the High Kingdom of Rathain. Gifted geas: compassion/empathy.

    pronounced: fal-en

    root meaning: *ffael*—dark; *an*—one

s'GANNLEY—family name for the line of Earls of the West, who stood as *caithdein* and stewards for the Kings of Tysan.

    pronounced: gan-lee

    root meaning: *gaen*—to guide; *li*—exalted, or in harmony

s'ILESSID—family name for the royal line appointed by the Fellowship Sorcerers in Third Age Year One to rule the High Kingdom of Tysan. Gifted geas: justice.

    pronounced: s-ill-ess-id

    root meaning: *liessiad*—balance

s'LORNMEIN—family name for the royal line appointed by the Fellowship Sorcerers in Third Age Year One to rule the High Kingdom of Havish. Gifted geas: temperance

s'PERHEDRAL—line of sunchildren whose issue succeeded Athera's High Kingship after Enastir, who died heirless.

    pronounced: per-heed-rall

    root meaning: *para*—great; *hedreal*—oak

s'VALERIENT—family name for the Earls of the North, regents and *caithdein* for the High Kings of Rathain.

    pronounced: val-er-ee-ent

    root meaning: *val*—straight; *erient*—spear

SEARDLUIN—vicious, intelligent cat-formed creatures that roved in packs whose hierarchy was arranged for ruthless and efficient slaughter of other living things. By the middle of the Second Age, they had been battled to extinction.

    pronounced: seerd-lwin

    root meaning: *seard*—bearded; *luin*—feline

SETHVIR—Sorcerer of the Fellowship of Seven, served as Warden of Althain since the disappearance of the Paravians in the Third Age after the Mistwraith's conquest.

    pronounced: seth-veer

    root meaning: *seth*—fact; *vaer*—keep

SEVERNIR—river that once ran across the central part of Daon Ramon Barrens, Rathain. Diverted at the source after the Mistwraith's conquest, to run east into Eltair Bay.

    pronounced: se-ver-neer

root meaning: *sevaer*—to travel; *nir*—south
SHAND—one of the Five High Kingdoms of Athera, cut by South Strait, the portion on the western shore being West Shand.
    pronounced: shand
    root meaning: *shand*—two
SHANDIAN—refers to nationality, being of the Kingdom of Shand.
    pronounced: shand-ee-an
    root meaning: *shand*—two
SITHAER—mythological equivalent of hell, halls of Dharkaron Avenger's judgment; according to Ath's adepts, that state of being where the prime vibration is not recognized.
    pronounced: sith-air
    root meaning: *sid*—lost; *thiere*—wraith/spirit
SKELSENG'S GATE—chain of cliff caves in the foothills of the Skyshiel Mountains, abutting Daon Ramon Barrens in Rathain. Became a temporary holding place for the Mistwraith just after captivity.
    pronounced: skel-seng rhymes with "tell bring"
    root meaning: *skel*—many; *seng*—cave
SKYRON FOCUS—large aquamarine focus-stone, used by the Koriani Senior Circle for their major magic after the loss of the Great Waystone during the rebellion.
    pronounced: sky-run
    root meaning: *skyron*—colloquialism for shackle; *s'kyr'i'on*—literally
        "sorrowful fate"
SKYSHIEL—mountain range that runs north to south along the eastern coast of Rathain.
    pronounced: sky-shee-el
    root meaning: *skyshia*—to pierce through; *iel*—light/ray
STEIVEN—Earl of the North, *caithdein* and regent to the Kingdom of Rathain at the time of Arithon Teir's'Ffalenn's return. Chieftain of the Deshans at the battle of Strakewood Forest.
    pronounced: stay-vin
    root meaning: *steiven*—stag
STRAKEWOOD—forest in the principality of Deshir, Rathain; site of the battle of Strakewood Forest.
    pronounced: strayk-wood to rhyme with "stray wood"
    root meaning: *streik*—to quicken, to seed

TAERLIN—southwestern principality of Kingdom of Tysan.
    pronounced: tay-er-lin
    root meaning: *taer*—calm; *lien*—to love
TAL QUORIN—river formed by the confluence of watershed on the southern side of Strakewood, principality of Deshir, Rathain, where traps were laid for Etarra's army in the battle of Strakewood Forest.
    pronounced: tal quar-in

root meaning: *tal*—branch; *quorin*—canyons

TALERA s'AHELAS—princess wed to the king of Amroth on the splinter world of Dascen Elur. Mother of Lysaer s'Ilessid, by her husband; mother of Arithon, through her adulterous liaison with the Pirate King of Karthan, Avar s'Ffalenn.

    pronounced: tal-er-a

    root meaning: *talera*—branch or fork in a path

TALIENNSE—Paravian princess rescued from Khadrim attack by Kamridian s'Ffalenn, for which the Isaervian sword Alithiel was awarded to the s'Ffalenn royal line.

    pronounced: tal-ee-en-se

    root meaning: *talien*—precious; *esia*—feather

TAL'S CROSSING—town at the branch in the trade road that leads to Etarra and south, and northeastward to North Ward.

    pronounced: tal to rhyme with "pal"

    root meaning: *tal*—branch

TANE—father of Grithen, heir to the earldom of Erdane.

    pronounced: tain to rhyme with "main"

    root meaning: *tane*—sire, father

TANLIE—mother of the dead child that Arithon brought in from the horse knacker's yards in Etarra.

    pronounced: tan-lee

    root meaning: *tun*—brown; *lie*—note struck in harmony

TASHAN—Elder on Maenalle's clan council, present at the west outpost at the time of Grithen's raid on the Pass of Orlan.

    pronounced: tash-an

    root meaning: *tash*—swift, quick; *an*—one

TASHKA—daughter of Lady Dania and Steiven s'Valerient, Earl of the North and *caithdein* of Rathain.

    pronounced: tash-ka

    root meaning: *tash*—quick/swift; *ka*—girl

TEIR—title fixed to a name denoting heirship.

    pronounced: tay-er

    root meaning: *teir's*—"successor to power"

TELIR—a sweet fruit somewhat like a cherry grown by the Paravians, from which they made telir brandy. Telir trees did not bear fruit after the Mistwraith's conquest and no new seedlings sprouted in the absence of sunlight.

    pronounced: tel-ear

    root meaning: *telir*—sweet

TELMANDIR—ruined city that once was the seat of the High Kings of Havish. Located in the principality of Lithmere, Havish.

    pronounced: tell-man-deer

    root meaning: *telman'en*—leaning; *dir*—rock

TENIA—young girl from Rauven in Dascen Elur, the splinter world through West Gate. Deeply attracted to Arithon s'Ffalenn, though her fear of his Shadow Mastery prevented any serious ties.

　　pronounced: ten-ee'—ah

　　root meaning: *itenia*—uncertain

THALDEIN—mountain range that borders the principality of Camris, Tysan, to the east. Site of the Camris clans' west outpost. Site of the raid at the Pass of Orlan.

　　pronounced: thall-dayn

　　root meaning: *thal*—head; *dein*—bird

TIENELLE—high altitude herb valued by mages for its mind-expanding properties. Highly toxic. No antidote. The leaves, dried and smoked, are most potent. To weaken its potency and allow safer access to its vision, Koriani enchantresses boil the flowers then soak tobacco leaves with the brew.

　　pronounced: tee-an-ell-e ("e" mostly subliminal)

　　root meaning: *tien*—dream; *iel*—light/ray

TIRIACS—mountain range to the north of Mirthlvain Swamp, located in the principality of Midhalla, Kingdom of Melhalla.

　　pronounced: tie-ree-axe

　　root meaning: *tieriach*—alloy of metals

TISHEALDI—name given to Arithon's dun mare for the irregular white marking on her neck.

　　pronounced: tish-ee-al-dee

　　root meaning: *tishealdi*—splash

TORBRAND s'FFALENN—founder of the s'Ffalenn line appointed by the Fellowship of Seven to rule the High Kingdom of Rathain in Third Age Year One.

　　pronounced: tor-brand

　　root meaning: *tor*—sharp, keen; *brand*—temper

TORNIR PEAKS—mountain range on western border of the principality of Camris, Tysan. Northern half is actively volcanic, and there the last surviving packs of Khadrim are kept under ward.

　　pronounced: tor-neer.

　　root meaning: *tor*—sharp, keen; *nier*—tooth

TRAITHE—Sorcerer of the Fellowship of Seven. Solely responsible for the closing of South Gate to deny further entry to the Mistwraith. Traithe lost most of his faculties in the process, and was left with a limp. Since it is not known whether he can make the transfer into discorporate existence with his powers impaired, he has retained his physical body.

　　pronounced: tray-the

　　root meaning: *traithe*—gentleness

TYSAN—one of the Five High Kingdoms of Athera, as defined by the charters of the Fellowship of Seven. Ruled by the s'Ilessid royal line. Sigil: gold star on blue field.

pronounced: tie-san
root meaning: *tiasen*—rich

VALENDALE—river arising in the Pass of Orlan in the Thaldein Mountains, in the principality of Atainia, Tysan.
    pronounced: val-en-dale
    root meaning: *valen*—braided; *dale*—foam
VASTMARK—principality located in southwestern Shand. Highly mountainous and not served by trade roads. Its coasts are renowned for shipwrecks. Inhabited by nomadic shepherds and wyverns, non-firebreathing, smaller relatives of Khadrim.
    pronounced: vast-mark
    root meaning: *vhast*—bare; *mheark*—valley
VERRAIN—spellbinder, trained by Luhaine; stood as guardian of Mirthlvain when the Fellowship of Seven was left shorthanded after the conquest of the Mistwraith.
    pronounced: ver-rain
    root meaning: *ver*—keep; *ria*—touch; *an*—one original Paravian:
            verria'an

WARD—a guarding spell.
    pronounced: as in English
    root meaning: not from the Paravian